'There are moments of real emotional force . . . which brought real salt tears to my eye' *Evening Standard*

'Constructed like the Labyrinth at Knossos, this massive, addictive novel revisits English society over the last forty years. A mighty strong narrative thread leads the reader past the just-recognisable shades of wicked men and celebs into the light of the new century' *Harpers & Queen*

'With a wickedly deft touch, the author coherently portrays the aimlessness of a generation adrift between entitlement and irrelevance. Coleridge . . . paints a hilariously grim picture of an island muddling through change but somehow managing to remain exactly the same' *Vanity Fair*

'So riveting it'll have you phoning in sick. Coleridge's big, bold brick of a blockbuster is the perfect antidote to the current sombre mood and your passport outta here'

Glamour

Nicholas Coleridge is Managing Director of the British Condé Nast magazines. He lives in Oxfordshire and London with his wife, Georgia, and children Alexander, Frederick, Sophie and Tommy. He has seven godchildren of his own.

By Nicholas Coleridge

Godchildren

NICHOLAS COLERIDGE

ORION

An Orion paperback

First published in Great Britain in 2002
by Orion
This paperback edition published in 2002
by Orion Books Ltd,
Orion House, 5 Upper St Martin's Lane,
London WC2H 9EA

A CIP catalogue record for this book is available
from the British Library.

ISBN 0 75284 841 0

Typeset at The Spartan Press Ltd,
Lymington, Hants

Printed and bound in Great Britain by
Clays Ltd, St Ives plc

To my own godchildren

– Helena Allan, Edie Campbell, Cara Delevingne,
Ned Dahl Donovan, Ione Hunter Gordon,
Willa Montagu Petty and Ewan Wotherspoon –

who luckily in no way resemble
the godchildren in this story.

Acknowledgements

Several friends helped with the writing of this novel: Cristina Monet Zilkha, Tessa Dahl, Sarah Standing, Pandora Delevingne, Julia Dixon and Victoria Mather, all of whom made penetrating observations on characterisation and plot. I would also like to thank Nick Allan who, as with previous novels, has been my special advisor on Asia, rock music and the financial markets, though he cannot be held responsible for errors where I have only partially followed his expert advice. I am grateful, too, to Georgina and William Petty and Monty Risenhoover of Moab, Utah, the late John Morgan, Vassi Chamberlain, Kathryn Greig, Kate Ancell, Sandy Swinton, Rupert Rucker, Julian Allason, Mary Iliff and James Alexander Sinclair, who respectively put me right on Midwest cattle ranches, classical music and pinstripes, social life in Lyford Cay, the internal routine of the Sotheby's Client Relations department in New York, New Jersey suburbs, fund management in Moscow, Down's Syndrome, secretarial employment agencies and landscape gardening. Harriet Robertson, Lucy Callingham, Bean McCall, Lisa Murray and Annabelle Hood kindly typed different stretches of the manuscript.

The brilliant editor, Rosie de Courcy, commissioned the novel in the first place and subsequently made suggestions which improved it beyond measure. My omnipresent agent, the great Ed Victor, was involved every step of the way. Anthony Cheetham acted as godfather to the book, and Kirsty Fowkes was godmother. Lynn Curtis copyedited the manuscript.

As ever, I am hugely indebted to my wife, Georgia, who reads and edits early drafts of each chapter and cheerfully consents to discuss the various characters and their motivation *ad nauseam*.

Prologue: 4 January 2000

The great tycoon Marcus Brand, who was one telephone call away from bankruptcy, gave instructions that, when the call came, it should be patched through to the *casita* by the swimming pool. He would be practising yoga as usual, but could be interrupted.

Bartholomew, who had worked for Mr Brand for twenty-eight years, recognised the gravity of the situation, but continued to give instructions to the two Balinese houseboys laying the table for dinner on the terrace. Gilded wooden finger bowls and night-lights were put in front of each place setting, and the tablecloth strewn with frangipani blossoms. For the eighth consecutive evening, they would be twelve sitting down to eat. All of Marcus Brand's godchildren were staying for the New Year holiday, most of their husbands and wives, and several small children.

From somewhere out in the bay came the chug-chug of an outboard and delighted screeches as the inflatable banana bounced across the tops of the waves. The Crieff children were enjoying themselves for once. Bartholomew privately regarded the three Crieff offspring as the most obnoxious and spoilt of Marcus's godchildren's children.

From the top terrace of the Nusa Dua beach house, with its teak and coconut-wood pavilion, you could see the whole compound and the ocean beyond with its pattern of small, wooded islands.

Saffron and her mother were sunbathing at opposite ends of the deck. After last night, everyone was feeling shifty and anxious to avoid their host. Bartholomew had noticed that Saffron had been tense ever since she'd arrived. The whole holiday, he reckoned, had not gone well, though why exactly he couldn't say. Perhaps it had something to do with Mr Brand's financial problems, though it was hard to believe these wouldn't be resolved. According to *Forbes*,

Marcus Brand was the twenty-seventh richest man in the world.

Down by the infinity pool, Stuart and Abigail were tapping away on their laptops. Bartholomew shrugged. They were supposed to be on vacation, but all over the property people were working. Ever since the financial markets had reopened after the long Millennium shutdown, Stuart had been hunched over his computer – trading stocks over the Internet, he said.

Bartholomew had first met Marcus's godchildren as teenagers when they had come to stay at the old plantation house at Lyford Cay in the Bahamas. Looking at Stuart now, he couldn't believe how much he had changed. Abigail too; she used to be so fat, but now look at her. All the godchildren had altered, not always for the better. Extraordinary to think they were in their forties now with families of their own, some of them.

Mary arrived on the terrace. The bedrooms at Nusa Dua were dotted throughout the grounds in cottages, each equipped with an electric golf cart for guests to drive themselves up to the main house for meals.

'Hi, Bartholomew. Where is everyone?'

'Mr Brand is doing his yoga. Some people's down by the pool, some's having a siesta. The children's out on the banana boat. Jamie and Charlie are riding the jetskis.'

Mary was relieved Charlie Crieff wasn't around. She tried to spend as little time as possible alone in his company. It must be twenty years now, but she still hadn't forgiven him. Ever since they'd arrived in Bali, he had been insufferable, drinking too much and shouting at the children. There was no Miranda, of course, and the nanny he'd brought along in place of his ex-wife was worse than useless.

'You like me to mix you a drink?' asked Bartholomew. 'Some fresh fruit punch is very nice.'

Of all the godchildren, Mary was the one he liked the best. She wasn't beautiful like Saffron, but she was pretty and considerate, which couldn't be said for all of them.

'I'm fine, thanks,' Mary replied. 'Bartholomew, I ought to

ring my poor old mother. She's still not terribly well. Is anyone using the communications room?'

'Mr Mathias is in there. He's been shut inside all day, talking with banks, I don't know exactly.' The butler looked troubled.

Stuart, poolside, looked at his watch. New York would be opening in ninety minutes. The Brand Corporation stock price had already dropped by six dollars, or 17 per cent, in London. He couldn't predict what would happen once Abigail's explosive piece of news leaked out.

In the communications room – as Marcus's office had come to be known, with its high-speed telephone and satellite links which circumvented the unreliable Balinese grid – Dick Mathias, his American attorney, was hooked up to the Otsuka Bank in Tokyo, attempting to persuade them to roll over the debt. Until recently, neither he nor Marcus had realised that his principal lenders had resold parcels of debt so widely. The Brand Corporation now had 123 different creditors all over the world. For three months, they had been shuttling between financial centres, attempting to charm and cajole officials at Credit Suisse, Banque Nationale de Paris, Bank of America, and dozens of smaller institutions in London, Israel, Zurich and around the Pacific Rim.

Nobody could charm a lender like Marcus. But now, the Otsuka Bank of Tokyo refused to be seduced. A small bank with a minute loan – a fifteen-million-dollar share of a larger facility – the Otsuka was refusing to roll over.

Dick was trying to persuade the bank's chairman to talk to Marcus directly, but kept being referred to the chief loan officer. He didn't want to put anyone as lowly as a loan officer through to Marcus, whose face had twice appeared on the cover of *Fortune* and who had been the subject of a special two-hour segment with Charlie Rose, but finally there was no alternative.

Mary drove in the golf buggy back to her bungalow where she'd left Clara sleeping. Even now Clara was sixteen, Mary still worried about leaving her daughter alone in the room, in case she woke up disorientated and did herself an injury.

3

It had been a mistake bringing Clara to Bali, she thought. Seeing her with Marcus reawakened memories she'd tried to bury.

Jamie and Charlie were accelerating back across the bay on the jetskis. Jamie was playing the fool, cutting across Charlie's wake, trying to nudge into him and causing him to swerve. His laughter echoed across the sea to the beach house, and even Charlie looked relaxed for once. Watching them from the swimming pool, Stuart thought Jamie still looked absurdly young for his age. He must be forty-three but, at this distance, could have passed for a student. Closer up, he looked more like his real age, of course, which was hardly surprising. Charlie, on the other hand, had aged noticeably in the last eighteen months under the strain of the divorce and all the rest of it.

The boatboys were waiting in the shallows to drag the jet-skis up on to the sand. Without bothering to acknowledge them, Charlie lumbered out of the sea. Looking around him, he could see no visible evidence of things falling apart: quite the reverse. They had flown out to Bali on a Brand Corporation jet as usual, there were hot and cold running servants and the sun was beating down on his back. The rumours, he was sure, were grossly exaggerated, put about by Marcus's competitors. He certainly hoped so. As the favourite godson, he couldn't afford for anything to go wrong.

Marcus's astounding speech at dinner last night had all been totally unnecessary, of course, and had come straight out of left field. But Charlie reckoned it was a typical Marcus joke to wind them all up.

Dick Mathias put through the call to the *casita*. He heard it ring a couple of times, then Marcus picked up. 'I've got Mr Choshoku, the Jap from Otsuka Bank. He still hasn't committed to the package. It's over to you now.'

Abigail tilted her laptop away from the sun's glare. The e-mail she'd just typed out was up on the screen. For a moment she let it sit there, unsent, half dreading and half exhilarated by what she was about to do. The message was addressed to a colleague in the Sotheby's Client Relations department on York Avenue, but the Chief Executive, and probably the Chairman too, would be involved in taking the final decision. For something this sensitive, it would go all the way to the top.

She gazed out across the ocean, feeling treacherous. Why did she ever agree to come here, with all this going on? The timing was hideous.

Mary swung Clara up by her shoulders so she was upright on the edge of the bed and helped her on with her shirt. At least it took less time to get her dressed out here. In London, getting ready for a winter walk, it could take half an hour to struggle, limb by limb, into jackets, coats, scarves, gloves and shoes. Mary glanced at her watch. Dinner was not for another hour, but Marcus liked everyone to be up on the terrace in good time for drinks. These luxurious holidays were all very well, she thought, but they were hard work. Marcus expected everyone to be dressed up to the nines for dinner, relaxed and bathed and primed for intelligent conversation. Mary shook her head. It had been exactly the same for thirty-four years, except now she had a nearly-adult Clara to worry about too. And, after last night, she was dreading dinner in any case. How could they possibly face Marcus again after all that?

As usual, the first person to arrive on the terrace before dinner was Marcus's wife. She checked that the champagne was the marque her husband had requested earlier in the day, and that the canapés prepared by the French chef were properly presented. Night-lights were already flickering prettily on the table, and joss-sticks had been placed before the Shiva in the *gedong* shrine.

Charlie strode on to the terrace wearing a blue blazer and white chinos, and ordered a large whisky on the rocks. He had had a couple already, from the mini-bar in his bungalow, and was consequently feeling more on his old form. His two elder children were occupied playing table football in the games room on the lower terrace, and Kosova the nanny could put them to bed on her own. She seemed to think Bali was meant to be a holiday for her too, which it damn' well wasn't considering what he was paying her to work over the Millennium.

5

Finding their hostess on the terrace, Charlie gave her a kiss on the cheek. He remained profoundly suspicious of her, but felt he had to keep in with her now, considering her change of status. He blamed this whole ridiculous New Age phase Marcus was going through – the yoga and obsession with ecology – on his godfather's new wife. It was more than ridiculous actually, it was a positively sinister development.

Abigail and her husband appeared arm in arm, as they had done every evening since they'd arrived in Bali. Charlie had to admit Abby looked great these days. Whether it was the money, the job or the new love interest, or a combination of all three, he couldn't work out. With her bobbed black hair, Donna Karan shift dress and pearl pashmina, she looked every inch the Manhattan executive. If you could only forget what a great fat lump she'd been at sixteen, she was almost fanciable. But she looked strained this evening, which was hardly surprising after last night.

Mary arrived with poor Clara, who Charlie strongly hoped he wouldn't be placed next to again at dinner. Frankly, he didn't see why Clara had to eat with them at all. He could tell Marcus was irritated by it too. Perhaps he should say something.

The Balinese houseboys were circulating with trays of Thai canapés. Charlie took a deep-fried prawn and dunked it in the bowl of soy. Looking round at the rest of the party, he wasn't sure who he wanted to be put next to. Almost everybody, in their different ways, annoyed or depressed him, Stuart most of all.

There was still no sign of Marcus. Charlie saw Mrs Brand walk over to the pergola and press a number on the house telephone. Getting no reply, she told one of the houseboys to delay dinner for another fifteen minutes. Dick Mathias, cradling a martini, said something to her, and she shrugged.

Stuart, having bitten the bullet, felt unnaturally calm. Events would now run their course. He had no doubt his decision had been the right one, it would have been irresponsible to have done anything else. He kept expecting Marcus to appear on the terrace. Stuart hadn't seen him all day, not since last night's great confrontation. He must know by now, he guessed, about everything. Marcus had always been the best informed. It was one of his unique strengths as a businessman.

'I think we had better sit down and eat,' Mrs Brand said. 'I can't think what's happened to Marcus. He must be tied up on a call.' She seemed uptight, Stuart noticed, which figured. He couldn't tell whether she was mad at Marcus for being late or still resentful of his remarks last night.

All the godchildren, looking back on that fateful dinner, remembered it in the same way: the vacant wooden throne at the head of the table, the huge array of wine glasses and water glasses that were always a feature of dining at any of Marcus's houses, the sense of expectation and dread that hung over them like a cloud of mustard gas. The prospect of his imminent arrival inhibited conversation. Jamie later described it as, 'One of the most fucking tedious dinners of all time. I'm not remotely surprised Marcus decided to take a rain check.'

The plates were being cleared for the Thai green curry when they became aware of a commotion down below on the beach. The armed security guards who patrolled the compound at night were jabbering to each other in high, excitable voices. A few minutes later, two of them appeared on the terrace followed by Bartholomew, already apologising for the intrusion.

One of the jetskis, they reported, had disappeared from the beach. There were tracks where it had been dragged across the sand into the sea. For the briefest of moments, Abby caught Stuart's eye before looking hurriedly away.

'Probably a thief came in round the point,' he suggested. 'Maybe some of us should take a look round.'

'Someone should tell Marcus, too,' said Mary.

Part One

1: July, 1966

'You are not going to believe what's turned up in this morning's post,' said Lady Crieff to her husband in the breakfast room at Ardnessaig House. 'I must say, I do call it a nerve.'

Alistair Crieff, who was known throughout Angus for the elegance of his calves in canary-yellow shooting stockings, was frowning over an item in the *Dundee Courier*. The new socialist Prime Minister, Harold Wilson, was threatening to introduce a wealth tax, which would oblige the Crieffs to estimate the value of their pair of Landseers and the small Lely in their bedroom, and pay a proportion of their value every year to the Exchequer.

'An invitation for Charlie to stay in the South of France,' said Verena sharply. 'When I tell you who it's from, you're going to be horrified . . . Marcus Brand.'

'Marcus? Good heavens, we haven't heard a squeak out of him for five years.'

'Longer. Not since Charlie's christening. That was the last time he was up. Of course nobody realised what he'd been up to then, or we'd never have asked him at all.'

'And he's asked Charlie to stay in France? Why the devil has he done that?'

'I'll read you what he says,' said Verena. 'The letter's written on his office writing paper, which is typical. A not very nice address in Broad Street. ' "My dear Verena, I haven't seen you for far too long" – I should think not – "nor, I'm sorry to say, have I seen Charles since his christening eight years ago and I feel it's time I started to get to know my godson" – well, I call that presumptuous, considering what happened – "so I have decided to invite my six godchildren to the South of France for the third week in August, where I have recently bought a villa on Cap Ferrat." Oh, yes, with poor Lucy's money, no doubt! "I have

11

engaged a couple of maids to help look after them all, so I can assure you the children will be well cared for. If you feel able to part with Charles for that week, I will send his aeroplane ticket for Nice which I will, of course, provide." '

Verena Crieff emitted a sharp little cough of disapproval. 'The sheer cheek of the man astonishes one. Wait until I tell the Macphersons . . . Hector told me that if he ever set eyes on Marcus again, he couldn't be held accountable for his actions. They've never got over it – Lucy was always the favourite – though they have to accept some of the blame themselves. They never should have allowed her to marry someone like Marcus. I mean, nobody knew the first thing about him. Such a frightful fellow, as I said right from the beginning. Didn't I say so?'

'You never were quite sure about him,' agreed Lord Crieff, as he invariably did agree with any statement made by his forceful, dogmatic wife. 'But we did ask him to be one of Charlie's godfathers, so we must have liked him at the time.'

'Nonsense! We merely asked him to stand in for Lucy. It was Lucy we wanted, not Marcus. Lucy we all loved. The christening was only a week after that ghastly motor accident. Marcus was still up here, and after all, nobody had the slightest idea then about his awful fiddles.'

'I wonder what Marcus is up to now? He always was a clever fellow.'

'Too clever by half, that was his trouble. Imagine using Lucy's money for his business deals. Macpherson family money! It would be like you using Arbroath money.' Verena Crieff invariably invoked her own side of the family when she wished to imply great wealth and grandeur. 'Hector got to the bottom of it all eventually, but he could never retrieve the missing money. How could Lucy have left it all to Marcus? I thought that's what trusts were for, to prevent capital from leaving the family.'

Nothing aroused greater outrage in Lady Crieff, as the elder daughter of the youngest sister of the 13th Earl of Arbroath, than the thought of inherited money passing into the hands of outsiders.

'Do we know whether Marcus ever remarried?' asked Alistair.

'I wouldn't put it past him. I was never convinced he was all that faithful to Lucy while she was alive, if you really want to know. Now he's got his hands on her money, he's probably shacked up with some brassy little piece of work. The Macphersons couldn't bear him. He used to give Lucy the most awful common jewellery, which he bought somewhere in London.'

'What will you do about the invitation?' asked Alistair.

'I shall refuse it, of course. It would be highly unsuitable. We're never going to see Marcus Brand again, nobody is, so there's no point encouraging him.'

There was the sound of subdued voices on the staircase, and the despotic figure of Nanny Arbroath appeared at the dining-room door trailed by Charlie and his elder sisters, Mary Jane and Annabel.

'Good morning, Nanny,' said Alistair. 'All had your breakfast already upstairs, have you?'

'Yes, thank you, Lord Crieff,' replied Nanny Arbroath in her severe Peebleshire accent. 'I'm taking the children for a walk up to the end of the drive to see if the men have made any progress with that gate. Come along now, Charlie, don't put your hands on that table, I've told you I don't know how many times. And you can wipe that smile off your face too, Annabel. If there's anything to smile about, I'd be the one to know about it – not you.'

At the age of forty-four, Nanny Arbroath, who was always known by the surname of the grandest of three families whose offspring she had systematically terrorised, was at the height of her intimidatory powers. Physically rather a small woman – her height augmented by the two-inch lifts in her black walking shoes – with close-cropped black hair, she had an ability to inspire obedience in her employers and charges alike. Never known to take a day off in the twenty-eight years since she'd entered service as a nursery maid, she admitted to no family of her own. Too conscious of her status in the hierarchy of life to fraternise with the other servants, she spent her evenings alone in the day nursery surreptitiously tippling sweet liqueurs. As she endlessly reminded the Crieff children, she had accepted the position at Ardnessaig House with considerable misgivings, finding it a comedown after Arbroath Castle. Alistair Crieff did his best never to be trapped in the same room as Nanny Arbroath from one month to the next, with the consequence that he scarcely saw his children. Even Verena Crieff had to remind herself of her own well-mapped lineage before broaching any subject liable to inconvenience her children's keeper.

Charlie Crieff, gangly and curly haired, slunk across to the mahogany sideboard. There, under the guise of inspecting the stuffed stag trophies which punctuated the walls of the dining room, he dug his fingers into a jar of marmalade and thrust them into his mouth.

Nanny Arbroath was reminding Lord Crieff that when she'd been at Arbroath Castle she'd had not one but two nursery maids working under her. 'And neither one of them ever took a single day off, that was something I was always most particular about.'

Charlie's hand edged towards a cut-crystal pot of honey. It stood, along with the marmalade and jams, on a round silver tray, covered by a linen napkin. A horn spoon, its handle engraved with the Crieff crest, had all but submerged itself in the honey.

He glanced round to see if he was being observed, and sunk his fingers into the pot.

'Charlie's stealing honey!' Mary Jane's tell-tale voice sang out. 'Look, everyone, his fingers are in the honey.'

Nanny Arbroath, darting with the quickness of a cobra, caught Charlie a sharp slap across the back of his legs.

Jumping back to avoid her, and trailing honey across the mahogany surface from his fingertips, Charlie knocked over a large silver-plated capercaillie which stood, tail feathers displayed, on the sideboard. The hideous table-centre toppled forwards, its silver beak gouging into the polished wood while its clawed feet left skidmarks an inch long.

'Charles, you will go straight up to your bedroom and stay there,' snapped Verena Crieff. 'And you will not come out again until breakfast time tomorrow morning.'

Charlie shot out of the dining room before anything worse should happen, leaving Mary Jane smirking sanctimoniously behind him – he *hated* Mary Jane – and Nanny Arbroath huffing and puffing and declaring that she'd never come across a more troublesome child in all her born days. Only his father, who dared say nothing, and Annabel, who loved her little brother dearly, had any sympathy for Charlie.

After the fuss had died down, and the girls set off on their walk up the drive, Verena Crieff said, 'I really don't know how we're going to get through these summer holidays with Charlie behaving as he is.'

'Oh, he's all right,' Alistair replied. 'He's no worse than any other boy of his age.'

'It wouldn't surprise me if Nanny handed in her notice. She's at the end of her tether.'

'Why not send him to France then? That'd give us all a break.'

'To Marcus Brand?'

'Seems a God-given opportunity. Get him out of our hair for a week.'

'But Marcus is such a ghastly man. I couldn't bear to be beholden to him.'

'We wouldn't be. We need never see him at all.'

Verena considered the matter. 'It would free up Charlie's bedroom. We've asked far too many people to shoot that week. I've been having sleepless nights worrying where we're going to put them all.'

'That's settled then. Fire off a letter to Marcus and tell him his godson can't wait. It'll be a nasty shock for Marcus once Charlie gets there, but that's his look-out.'

'Just so long as the Macphersons never find out,' said Verena. 'We mustn't breathe a word. They'd see it as treachery.'

Saffron Weaver crept downstairs to the kitchen of her mother's house in World's End and opened the Electrolux fridge. Inside she found a saucer of lemon slices, a bottle of Polish vodka, an open bottle of white wine, a mug half-full of black olives and a bottle of milk. Carefully removing the milk without spilling any, she carried it over to the table. Her bare feet felt cold on the kitchen lino. Then she fetched the cornflakes from the cupboard, tipped some into her bowl and poured the milk on top. She did everything as quietly as possible – hardly daring to place the milk bottle down on the table – so as not to disturb Amaryllis and Trev who were asleep upstairs.

It had never occurred to Saffron that she shouldn't get her own breakfast. No one else had ever offered; no one had ever been around. In her eight-and-a-quarter years, she had seldom seen a grown-up before lunchtime. At weekends, Amaryllis – which was what Saffron called her mother – never got out of bed until three or four o'clock. Even when her dad was still around, nobody had surfaced before lunchtime.

When she'd finished her cereal she carried the bowl over to the sink and went upstairs to get dressed. One of the best things about Saturday mornings was deciding what clothes to wear. Saffron liked trying things on. With her pale blonde hair and enormous blue eyes, she resembled the heroine of a Grimms' fairy story, Gretel or a neglected Goldilocks. Sometimes, in the hours and hours before anyone else got up, she liked to see what she looked like with Amaryllis's scarves wound round her head or her waist; and sometimes she tested out her mother's lipstick and kohl-stick too.

Another thing she did on Saturday mornings was colouring. She liked to do pictures for Amaryllis to put up in the kitchen. Today Saffron drew a picture of her mother and Trev asleep in bed, Trev with a hairy face and all his cameras over the floor. When she did her best colouring she screwed up her face and clenched her tongue between her teeth, she was concentrating so hard. Trev always said, 'Take care, angel, or you'll bite it right off one day.'

At nine o'clock the postman delivered some letters, and a few hours after that Trev came down to look for his cigarettes.

'Seen my fags anywhere, doll? It's no good all this, you know, I'm gasping.' Amaryllis and Trev had been together since Christmas, and if they got married Saffron was going to be a bridesmaid.

Around two o'clock Amaryllis appeared in the kitchen in her black transparent kaftan. Saffron thought her mother was beautiful, just as pretty as Twiggy who got all the best work. Amaryllis had already been in *Nova* and been called in for a look-see by *Queen*. Trev was helping her get together a portfolio.

'Be a kind girl and fetch me a black coffee, won't you?' croaked Amaryllis, sitting down at the kitchen table. 'I don't know what time it was we got in last night . . .'

Saffron made a coffee and carried it to her mother, along with the picture she'd drawn.

'Is that meant to be me and Trev? There we are, look, Trev and his scratchy face and me looking like death warmed up. That's really nice, Saffron. Did you do it all by yourself?'

They could hear Trev moving about upstairs, searching for his clothes amidst the debris of the bedroom. To find anything in that house you had to act like a rag picker, sifting through the shallow mounds of old frocks, scarves and kaftans.

'You will be all right on your own if Trev and I go out for a couple of hours?' said Amaryllis. 'He wants me to meet this creative director of an ad agency.'

Although Amaryllis loved her daughter, she was conscious that eight-year-old Saffron was a bit of a giveaway about her own age. She had lopped several years off when she'd told Trev she was twenty, and fortunately he hadn't puzzled it out yet. But having Saffron around her neck could be a drag at times.

Amaryllis gathered up the post and idly examined the envelopes. She was half expecting one from her ex-husband in Limerick, with money inside for Saffron's maintenance, but – no surprise – it hadn't come. Billy was hopeless.

The bills she didn't bother with, but there was one interesting-looking letter with writing she dimly recognised.

'Saffron, come and look at this,' she said when she'd opened it. 'You remember your godfather Marcus?'

Saffron shook her head.

'You haven't seen him since your christening, so I suppose you wouldn't. Anyhow, he's invited you down to the South of France.'

For Saffron, whose horizons had hitherto extended no further than Edith Grove in Chelsea, the words 'South of France' conjured up almost nothing. But for Amaryllis, they encapsulated everything glamorous and desirable. 'What a jammy invite,' she said. 'You'll probably get to visit St Tropez.'

It was strange seeing Marcus's handwriting. He'd been more of a friend of Billy's originally, that was how they'd first met. And, for a while, he'd been a big thing in their lives. Amaryllis wondered how he was getting on. Judging by his notepaper, he was doing very nicely, thank you. Not that there had ever been much doubt about that where Marcus was concerned.

Trev appeared in the kitchen in tight black hipsters, holding a motorcycle helmet. 'We ought to hit the road, angel. I told Davey we'd meet at the Goat in Boots.'

'Saffron's going to the South of France,' said Amaryllis. 'Her godfather Marcus has asked her down to his pad in August.'

'That's great, baby. We can get away somewhere ourselves without the kid, just you and me together.'

Belinda Merrett heard the post drop on to the doormat at Fircones while she was preparing nine o'clock breakfast for her husband and their daughter Mary. On weekdays, Belinda liked to provide Derek with a proper cooked breakfast before he ventured off to the railway station; then she'd go back to bed for fifteen glorious minutes with a cup of tea and the newspaper, before getting Mary dressed and ready for school. But on Saturdays they all enjoyed a bit of a lie-in, and breakfast wasn't until nine o'clock. This gave them just enough time to get organised before running Mary up to Miss Green's livery stables for her Saturday morning riding lesson.

The moment Belinda read the letter, standing in the

kitchen waiting for the kettle to boil, she ran upstairs to tell Derek. He was wet-shaving in front of the bathroom mirror, which he still preferred to the new electric jobs that were coming on to the market.

'Derek, you'll never guess! Mary's been invited to the South of France by Marcus Brand. He's asking all his godchildren to stay.'

'Good Lord. Well, I never. How absolutely wonderful.' Derek felt, at that moment, an extraordinary surge of pride. His daughter had been asked to stay by Marcus Brand. He rinsed the shaving cream off his chin and quickly read the letter. Then he read it a second time, taking in every detail. Marcus's company writing paper was considerably thicker than his own, he noticed, despite their working for the same firm. Chairman's privilege.

'I wasn't even aware Marcus owned a place in France,' he admitted to his wife. 'Knowing him, I bet it's one hell of a set-up.'

The more Derek thought about it, the happier he became. It really was the most unexpected, incredibly generous thing for Marcus to suggest. And, in a way, it vindicated their choice of him as a godfather. Recently, the Merretts had felt almost uncomfortable about having Derek's boss in that role, but, as they reminded themselves, they had selected him long before he'd become so success-ful. At the time when Mary was born Marcus and Derek had actually shared the same office, with four desks in it, and the whole firm hadn't employed more than twenty people altogether. When you told people that today, they didn't believe you.

As the company diversified, Derek had seen much less of his old friend. Months would pass and their paths hardly crossed. Marcus and the directors were on a whole separate floor and, from what you heard, were up to all kinds of tricks. Shipping and property were only a small part now, apparently.

But this invitation to Mary proved that old friendships still counted for something. If truth be told, Marcus hadn't always been the most attentive godfather, from the point of view of sending Christmas and birthday presents, which was hardly surprising when you considered how busy he was. But he'd more than made up for that now. A week in the South of France!

'Do you think we should allow her to go?' asked Belinda. 'She is really rather young to go off on her own.'

Derek frowned. In his elation at the invitation, he'd never considered the possibility of refusing. And, of course, Belinda had a point, Mary *was* very young. Had it been anybody else inviting his daughter to go abroad with them, Derek would have said no. Only a few weeks ago, Mary had been asked to sleep over with her best friend Sarah and, having given the matter a lot of thought, the Merretts had decided it would be best to wait until after her tenth birthday.

'Marcus does say he'll have people to look after them all.'

'It's not the same,' said Belinda. 'Mary's never spent a single night away from home. And remember how shy she is with people she doesn't know.'

'It could be good for her, mixing with youngsters her own age.'

'I'm sure she'll have other opportunities. Eight isn't very grown-up, it worries me.'

But Derek had set his heart on Mary going. He wanted her to go for her own sake, because she ought to know her godfather. And he wanted her to go for his sake too. Lately he had felt the distance between himself and his boss. It now seemed barely credible that, only eight years ago, they'd sometimes enjoyed a glass of beer together at the end of the working day, at the Ship's Compass in Minster Lane. He'd like to have a channel to Marcus again.

During the course of this conversation, Mary arrived at the breakfast table, dressed in jodhpurs and a tweed hacking jacket, where she unobtrusively ate a boiled egg. Her clean black hair was pushed back from her forehead by a navy blue hairband. It did not occur to either of her parents to elicit Mary's own wishes on the subject of the invitation to Cap Ferrat, because the decision would naturally be taken by themselves. At this time, in a town like Dorking in the heart of the commuter belt, few happy families would have reacted differently.

After breakfast, Derek drove his daughter up to the old Godalming Road where the livery stables were situated. For every little girl within a radius of five miles, a Saturday morning hack with Miss Green was an institution, and – it must be admitted – a mark of status for their parents. Already a small crowd of fathers was congregating in the concrete yard, watching the girl grooms saddle up the ponies and adjust the girths and shorten or lengthen the stirrups, while their daughters in jodhpurs with elastic beneath the heels patted the sleepy old nags.

Taking Mary by the hand, Derek loped over to the stables. A tall man in a navy blue blazer with brass buttons, he already walked with a slight stoop and wore a permanent expression of anxious self-effacement.

'Morning, Dudley,' he eagerly greeted his train friend from the 7.53 to Waterloo. 'Everything all right?'

As they leaned together against the iron fence, Derek found himself telling Dudley Mount-Jones about Mary's invitation from Marcus Brand, and how Belinda and he were in two minds about letting her go.

'I say, we are moving in rarefied circles these days,' said Dudley. 'Marcus Brand's villa in the South of France, no less.'

'He's a very old friend,' explained Derek. 'We used to share an office together. So one doesn't think of him as anything very special.'

'Well, he's certainly making a name for himself. They say he's buying Pettifer & Drew next.'

Derek, who had heard nothing of any scheme to take over that well-established firm of stockbrokers, made a non-committal blowing sound, meant to imply that he couldn't possibly comment.

Belinda Merrett, meanwhile, had nipped down to the shops to buy an Arctic Roll for pudding. While queuing up to pay in the Post Office and General Stores, she bumped into Mary's school friend Sarah and her mother, Ann Whitley. She soon found herself confiding in Ann about

Mary's exciting invitation and asking her honest opinion on whether or not they should allow Mary to go.

Ann Whitley, remembering how strict the Merretts had been when they'd suggested the sleep over, said that she reckoned Mary was still on the young side for unaccompanied foreign travel.

'Well, Marcus did say there'd be proper help to take care of them all,' said Belinda, almost beseechingly. 'They would be supervised.'

'I suppose it partly depends on how well Mary knows her godfather,' said Mrs Whitley.

'He is rather a special person,' replied Belinda. 'He's the chairman of Derek's company, you know, and a very long-standing family friend. He's a charming man and doing awfully well for the firm. He's really got it going, Derek says.'

Belinda found that, in the course of discussing the invitation with her neighbours, she became less opposed to the idea herself. In fact she was inclined to interpret any objections they might put forward as signs of jealousy. She was certain that Sarah Whitley's godparents included no one half so prominent as Marcus Brand, with a villa in Cap Ferrat. Outside the bakery, she told Meryl Dunn she felt sure Mary would derive benefit from a trip to France, and that it would be an education for her to experience foreign food. 'One could become awfully insular if one never left Surrey.' She said much the same to Jennifer Jones, when she found her collecting for the lifeboats on the corner of Market Street, and to Mrs Dodd-Harvey whose husband Gerald was a governor of Mary's school.

Over lunch, when the Merretts talked of little else, Belinda began to feel that her original misgivings had been unjustified. And by the time Derek returned home from his regular Saturday afternoon golf game, the matter was decided.

When the invitation had arrived that same morning at the Boltons' flat in a Smethwick terrace, it was conspicuous as the only item of post. Jean Bolton was making her son Stuart his proper Saturday morning fry-up, which was something he looked forward to; on weekdays there was never an opportunity because of Jean's job.

'Now whoever can this be, writing to us from London?' she asked. Rhetorical questions played a large part in Jean Bolton's conversation. She felt it was good for Stuart to be enveloped by chatter. As an only child without a father, she didn't want him to grow up in a silent home.

'Goodness me! I can't believe it.' After eight years, she thought she had come to terms with everything that had happened, but the letter still made her uncomfortable. Even the way Marcus Brand put things, the phrases he used, his almost illegible, impatient signature, brought it all back.

'Who's it from, Mum?' asked Stuart. 'We haven't won the Premium Bonds, have we?'

'No, love. It's from your dad's old boss, Mr Brand. The man he used to drive for.'

'Aw, that's unfair! I hoped we'd won a million pounds or something. Then we could buy a television.'

'Eat up your breakfast, love. I'm reading.'

Jean found the invitation a bolt from the blue. It was the last thing she'd ever have expected. She regarded that period of her life as utterly closed; associated it only with tragedy. She could never forgive Marcus Brand, though she accepted he'd been generous financially. But every decision she'd made since Ron's death – the move to Birmingham to be near to good schools, her part-time jobs at the solicitor's and with the cleaning contractors – had been taken to draw a line under the episode.

She had almost forgotten that Mr Brand had insisted on becoming Stuart's godparent. It had been his idea and, in the aftermath of the terrible crash, with Ron dead and Mrs Brand first in intensive care and later dying herself, Marcus had taken over.

'You have my word, I'll always see Stuart's all right,' Marcus had declared when he came round to the cottage that afternoon with his lawyer, Mr Mathias. 'Your husband demonstrated personal loyalty to me, and I always reciprocate.' Then he had appointed himself Stuart's godfather, though she never did get round to having him baptised.

For eight years they'd heard nothing, though the money had arrived at the bank like clockwork. And now this.

'You've been reading that letter for hours,' Stuart said. 'What's so interesting?'

Jean looked at her son. Sometimes she thought he seemed much younger than eight – Stuart was the smallest lad in his class, though he ate like a horse. His short brown hair was cut in a lopsided pudding-bowl fringe and his new wire-framed glasses gave him a bug-eyed, studious air.

'As a matter of fact, it's to do with you.' A part of Jean was reluctant to tell Stuart about the invitation, but it didn't seem right to keep it from him, so she read out the letter, explaining as she went along. 'The South of France is very, very hot in August, and everyone has a sleep in the afternoon called a siesta because you can't go outside.' She had no intention of allowing him to go, but to suppress Marcus's letter would have gone against the truthfulness she promoted in her small family.

When she'd finished, Stuart said, 'Wow, *great*! Flying in an aeroplane. When am I going, Mum?'

Jean hadn't expected this reaction at all. Normally Stuart's shyness would have made him instantly apprehensive. It took all her ingenuity to coax him to kick a football around with the other boys in the park.

'I'm sure you wouldn't want to go to France all by yourself.'

'Please, Mum. *Please*. I really do want to. I haven't even been in an aeroplane one time. I could see the cockpit. They have machine guns and everything, and you shoot down enemy aircraft when they attack.'

'Remember how much you hate going to swimming club,' said his mother doubtfully.

'That's only because of Mr Tandy. He ducks people underwater.'

'And it would be far too expensive going to France.'

'No, it wouldn't. My godfather's going to pay for it. It says in the letter you get sent your ticket for the aeroplane. You've got to let me go, Mum, you've *got to*. You know

24

Danny at school – Mick's brother Danny? He's been in an aeroplane. His dad took him to an airshow.'

On Sunday evening, with a heavy heart because she felt that no good could come of it, Jean Bolton picked up her fountain pen and wrote a letter to the man she privately knew had caused her husband's death.

At the Belgrave Row end of South Eaton Place there is a tall stucco mansion with an extra storey. The houses in the rest of the street all have five floors with basement included but this particular building has a penthouse plonked on to the roof, with incongruous plate-glass patio windows. Anybody noticing it today invariably comments, 'Unbelievable. I wonder how they ever got that past the planners.'

The eyesore was, in fact, the sixties brainchild of the commercial property developer Michael Temple, and was subsequently the focus of an internal inquiry within Westminster planning department. Nothing conclusive was ever proved, though at least two officials were quietly transferred to other duties. Michael Temple continued to occupy the house until the late seventies, and many of his most notorious development schemes, including the rebuilding of large tracts of Holborn, Kingsway and central Birmingham, were first conceived in his ornately corniced study in Belgravia.

At the time in question, Michael was still married to his first wife, Margaret, and South Eaton Place was home to their eight-year-old son Jamie and his three-year-old sister Lucinda. That morning, as he studied Marcus's letter over the breakfast table, Michael wanted to know just one thing: why?

'Why would Marcus Brand want to invite a bunch of screaming kids down to the Côte d'Azur?' he demanded of his wife. 'I don't get it. He's absolutely loaded, beautiful women crawling all over him. Come on, Margaret, what's he up to? What's his motive?'

Margaret Temple was peeling an apple and trying to remember what time Peter Jones opened on Saturday mornings. If it was nine o'clock, she'd have time to nip into the electrical department on her way to Hermès on the corner of Cadogan Street, before taking a taxi down to Casa Pupo to look at lamps.

'Who are his other godchildren anyway?' Michael said. 'It could be he's trying to get to the parents through the kids.'

'I couldn't tell you, Michael. I haven't the faintest idea who they are.' Sometimes her husband's conspiracy theories got on her nerves. Because he was involved in so many scams himself, he automatically suspected everyone else of having a similar agenda.

'Think about it,' Michael was saying. 'In ten years that company's grown out of all recognition. They say he cleared half a million from the Montpelier Mansions development alone. And he picked up those leases in Bayswater for a song. He must have several hundred people working for him now, all told. So, I ask myself, what's his game with these godchildren?'

'Perhaps he simply wants to get to know them, like he says in his letter,' suggested Margaret.

Michael Temple snorted with ironic laughter. He was an enormous man, handsome in a thickset way, with a full head of black hair of which he was very proud, and which he had trimmed and friction-rubbed once a fortnight by George at Trufit & Hill. For his shirts, which were made by Turnbull & Asser, he favoured stripes as wide and bold as a zebra's. His collar and sleeve measurements were known the length and breadth of Jermyn Street.

'Marcus Brand – wanting to get to know a bunch of children! Last time I saw him, which was three weeks ago in the Members' enclosure at Royal Ascot, he was escorting a young lady who looked suspiciously like a Playboy bunny. I don't see children as his *milieu* at all.'

'Why not ask him?' said Margaret. 'He's probably just being kind – but ask him if you're that interested.'

'I couldn't do that, he'd think I was checking up on him.' Michael coated another slice of toast with lime marmalade. 'One thing though,' he said, 'it's a bit off colour, Marcus inviting Jamie down to France without us. I've heard this new place of his is a serious set-up. Used to belong to some

French count. Marcus paid an arm and a leg, he's bought all the original furniture, the whole bang-shooting match.'

'Perhaps he'll ask us another time,' said Margaret vaguely. She was thinking: Should I buy the scarf with the stirrups and bridles all over it, or the nautical print with the flags and anchors?

'It's a bit rich, when you think about it. We're the ones who are meant to be Marcus's great friends, not Jamie. We're the ones who invited him to be our son's godfather. And now he goes and buys this ruddy great property on Cap Ferrat and doesn't even ask us down to see it.'

'I'm sure Jamie will have a lovely time.'

'I'm quite sure Jamie will. It's not Jamie I'm worried about. I've a good mind to fly down to Nice myself, just to see what Marcus is up to.'

It took a further week for Abigail's invitation to cross the Atlantic and arrive at the Schwartzman residence in Franklin Lakes, New Jersey. Zubin Schwartzman had set off for Manhattan long before the post was delivered, so it wasn't until that evening that he and his wife Harriet had a chance to consider it.

It was the Schwartzmans' habit, on the evenings when Zubin didn't have to stay over in the city for one business engagement or another, or when Harriet wasn't driven in to join him at some function involving wives, to sit together in the den overlooking the lawn and discuss the events of the day. There, surrounded by their collection of decorative French furniture, and with the Fragonard of the young woman with a porcelain complexion prominently displayed above the fireplace, they liked to have their daughter brought down to them to say goodnight. Carmelita Hernandez, the Dominican maid who acted as Abigail's nanny, would dress the little girl up in one of her best party frocks, fasten the clasp of the little diamond-encrusted necklace around her neck, tie the gold moiré bows into her hair, take her downstairs to the door of the study and usher her across the threshold with a Hispanic word of encouragement and a gentle push.

'Hey, if it isn't my little princess,' exclaimed Zubin that evening, as he exclaimed every evening when Abigail was brought to him. 'Come over here, Princess, and give your daddy a big hug. He's missed you.'

Abigail hovered in the doorway, suddenly overwhelmed by the sight of her powerful father with his arms outstretched, a tumbler of bourbon in one hand.

'Go on, Abigail. Greet your father like he's told you to.' Harriet Schwartzman, with her remorseless impetus for self-improvement, had no tolerance for shyness or self-consciousness.

'There, that's better,' said Zubin, enveloping his daughter in a bear-hug. 'Now, you tell your daddy everything you've been doing today, while he was working in his office.'

Abigail glanced over at her mother, as if to ask 'Should I tell him?'

Mrs Schwartzman nodded. She was a tiny creature, a birdlike size six, perched on the velour chaise in one of the little black cocktail dresses she had made for her in Paris. Her feet, encased in their gold court shoes, resembled doll's feet, they were so small and neat. But nobody who knew the Schwartzmans were in any doubt that, while it was Zubin who directed his businesses with a ruthlessness and eye for the main chance that matched that of any other commercial landlord in New York City, it was with Harriet that power resided at home. It was her taste that was expressed in the ornately framed paintings, in the over-fidelity to the Rococo in the style of their furniture, and the elaborate manner in which they set their table. Next to Harriet, Zubin was a pushover.

Abigail opened her mouth to tell her father the news, but the words wouldn't come out and Harriet, exasperated, answered for her.

'What Abigail's trying to say, Zubin, is that she's been invited to stay in France. A letter came this morning from Marcus Brand. He's asking all his godchildren in August.'

'Ridiculous. Why would Abigail be his godchild anyway? Jewish children don't have godparents.'

'It was you who asked Marcus yourself,' Harriet reminded him.

'I asked Marcus?'

'That evening you brought him round to Mount Sinai, the day after Abigail was born. I don't know why you did that without telephoning the hospital first. I wasn't even wearing a bed jacket.'

'Oh, come on, Harriet. Marcus and I had just finished dinner together at the Rainbow Room, celebrating a big deal. And Abigail's birth too, of course. I thought he might get a kick out of coming to see my new baby girl.'

'Well, that's when you invited him to be her godfather. I reckon you'd been drinking. There was a strong smell of liquor on your breath, that I do remember, I was hoping the nurse wouldn't notice.'

'You quite sure about this godfather bit? I'd kind of forgotten about it.'

'What you mean, Zubin, is you don't want to remember. You're still mad at Marcus because of that deal falling apart.'

Zubin pulled a face. 'That double-crossing scumball! The whole thing was in place – the finance, everything – we'd shaken on it. And then he goes and screws me. You know something? That bum wouldn't even *be* in this city if it wasn't for me introducing him to the right people. I don't want to talk about it. No way is any child of mine going to be his houseguest in France. Far as I'm concerned, he doesn't exist.'

'He sends her gifts. Every birthday without fail.'

'That annoys me too. It's damned intrusive.'

'I think it's very thoughtful,' said his wife. 'He gave her a beautiful diamond pin last time, shaped like some kind of bug.'

Zubin shrugged. If Abigail wanted jewellery, he'd buy her jewellery. He didn't need Marcus Brand in on the act.

'And Abigail should go to France,' urged Harriet. 'It would be good for her. She should start learning to appreciate Europe. All the best things come from there.'

'You think so? Barman at the Hotel Meurice can't even mix a decent martini.'

'Don't pretend to be a philistine, Zubin. I'm referring to culture. I for one would like Abigail to grow up appreciating it.'

The minute the invitation from Marcus had arrived, Harriet had seen in it an opportunity for herself too. 'I've been giving this serious consideration,' she told her husband sternly, 'and I want Abigail to go. It's important for her cultural development.'

'Let me get this straight. You want my seven-year-old princess to fly all the way to Europe on her own? And you think *that* will be good for her cultural development?'

'I can go with her on the aeroplane, and fly back with her afterwards,' his wife replied. 'I'll spend the week in Paris. There are new couturiers I need to see.'

2: August, 1966

Stuart showed his passport to the man, who bashed it with an inky stamp, and then came out into the arrivals hall where someone would be waiting to collect him. He had been told to look out for a board with his name written on it.

The flight to Nice had been brilliant – they'd even handed out boiled sweets when they were taking off – and he'd kept the miniature pepper and salt pots that had come on the dinner tray. Stuart was excited, but also apprehensive. As he'd stepped off the plane he'd been hit by a blast of hot Riviera air. It even smelt different in France, like diesel and flowers mixed up.

There were about a hundred people standing behind a barrier and his eyes scanned the boards for one saying Bolton or Stuart. He couldn't spot either, and the crowd began to thin out. If nobody turned up, he didn't know what he was meant to do.

'*Vous êtes* Monsieur Bolton?'

A man wearing a light grey suit picked up his suitcase. He was holding a sign that said 'Brand'. Stuart followed him out through the doors of the terminal and across a road to a car park. He wondered whether this man was his godfather.

The man opened the back passenger door of a large black Mercedes for him to get in. The inside of the car was the biggest Stuart had ever seen, with white sun blinds on the rear windscreen. Outside, it was still light. The plane had been scheduled to land at eight o'clock English time, which was nine o'clock French time. 'You'll be worn out when you arrive,' his mother had warned him.

Stuart rechecked the pocket of his shorts for the French money Jean had given him for the holiday. They'd specially ordered it at the local bank in Smethwick, where everyone had been very impressed he was going in an aeroplane all by himself.

The man began driving through the centre of a big town full of tall yellow apartment buildings with balconies. Before he'd turned the engine on, he had put on a pair of black leather driving gloves with a cut-out pattern through which you could see sections of his fingers. He didn't talk to Stuart, who began to feel shy in the back of the car. He decided the man probably wasn't his godfather.

It was stuffy inside the Mercedes and he wondered if it would be all right to open a window. He turned the handle an inch and warm air rushed in against his face.

The driver glanced over his shoulder and said '*Non!*', gesticulating at him to close it again; then, sighing crossly, he drew a lever on the dashboard and hot air circulated around the interior with a whoosh.

The road now ran parallel to the sea, which was flat as a mirror and dotted with sailing boats. It wiggled around the coast, past cliffs covered with wire netting and tall pine trees. The evening sun glinted golden on the tips of the small waves and, close to the shore, Stuart could see people water-skiing. Everywhere smelt hot.

The car turned off the road on to a smaller road, past pink villas set in groves of umbrella pines, and eventually stopped at iron gates within a high wall. The driver parped the horn and a man in a white jacket came out and opened the gates and they drew up in the flagged courtyard of the Villa des Sapins. There was a flight of steps up to a massive wooden door. Inside, a maid wearing a white apron over a finely striped pale blue dress was waiting for him.

'Stuart Bolton? *Bon. Venez avec moi, s'il vous plaît.*'

He trailed her up two flights of stone stairs and the woman paused outside a door and listened. Then, holding her finger up to her lips, she beckoned him to follow her inside. The room was in darkness, but from the light in the passage Stuart could see three beds, two already occupied by sleeping figures covered with sheets.

Someone carried in his suitcase and placed it at the foot of his bed, and then the woman returned with a glass of hot milk on a saucer with an almond biscuit, and stood over him while he changed into his pyjamas. After she'd gone, as he lay in bed in this strange room, in this house where he knew nobody, Stuart could hear the hum of cicadas and, more than once, the sound of laughter from outside in the garden.

When he woke in the morning, the other beds were already empty. He wondered what time it was. Sunshine was leaking into the bedroom through a gap beneath the shutters. The beds all had wooden headboards painted with flowers, and the ceiling was vaulted like a castle's. He padded over to the shutters and peeped out through the gap. All he could see was brilliant blue sea stretching to the horizon, and a wooden swimming-raft bobbing in a bay.

He looked round for the clothes he'd arrived in, but they'd disappeared, as had his suitcase. There was a chest of drawers between the windows, painted with violets and poppies, and he pulled open one of the drawers. It was full of boys' clothes, but they weren't his. Then, in the bottom drawer, he recognised his own stuff; it took up less space than the other boy's.

He put on his long grey school trousers, snake belt and a white school shirt and went downstairs. Nobody was about and, suddenly shy, he wondered whether he should go back to his room and wait until someone came to find him. Somewhere in the distance he could hear the drone of a vacuum cleaner.

When he reached the hall where he'd arrived last night, he saw there were doors leading into other rooms. There was a drawing room with tapestries and old-fashioned gold chairs with turquoise seats arranged around the wall. French windows opened on to a paved terrace full of geraniums in pots, a swing seat and a hedge of lavender. In the opposite direction, he found a kitchen.

A table was laid for breakfast for six people, though the other places had already been used. There were croissants and rolls wrapped up in a linen napkin in a silver filigree basket, and jugs of fresh orange and grapefruit juice, and thermoses of coffee and hot milk. Just then, a cook appeared and addressed him in French until, realising he didn't understand, she shrugged and returned to her work.

Stuart gulped some orange juice and ate half of a hard

roll, then slipped back outside on to the terrace. A maid was laying a table for lunch under a bougainvillaea-covered pergola. Already the temperature was rising; his legs were sweating inside his flannel trousers, and the steel bridge of his glasses was hot to the touch. There was a flight of paved steps down to a swimming pool, which a gardener was cleaning with a net and a long brush. Stuart, feeling very alone, sat apart on grass strewn with needles from the tall pines.

He heard children's voices from the sea below, shouting and yelping, and the deep throttle of a motor boat. A sleek mahogany Riva was circling in the bay. Inside, Stuart saw five children of his own age. A tall man in maroon bathing trunks and dark glasses was standing up very straight in the boat, while two boatmen in white trousers and t-shirts steered it towards a stone jetty.

'Now, who's swimming back to the jetty?' the man was asking. 'Charlie? Jamie?'

Two boys jumped over the side, holding their noses. The waves, as they came close to the jetty, were choppy and the boys found it difficult to grab hold of the iron ladder. They kept being pushed back by the swell. Stuart hoped he wouldn't have to swim in the sea.

'Give me your hand, Saffron,' the man said. 'When I say "Now" I want you to jump. *Now*.'

A small blonde girl in a violet swimsuit and espadrilles skipped neatly on to dry land.

A boatman hoisted the other two girls on to the jetty, and then the children followed the tall man up the steps from the beach.

'Enjoy that, any of you? Want to go out in my boat another time?'

'Yes, *please*,' everyone replied, with the boys' voices loudest of all. 'That was so great,' said the one with curly fair hair. 'I love it when we go really, really fast, and the boat keeps banging on the waves.'

'When *can* we go out again?' asked the other boy, whose mischievous face was tanned a rich conker brown. 'Can we go again this afternoon, *please*?'

34

'What about you, Saffron? Fancy another trip round the bay?'

'I *think* so, Godfather Marcus,' she replied in a reedy little voice. 'But not too fast.'

'Aw, no,' groaned the curly-haired boy. 'That's so unfair. What's the point of a speedboat if you have to go *slow*? That's why it's called a *speed*boat, dum-dum. The girls needn't come if they don't like it.'

'That's enough, Charlie,' said Marcus Brand. 'It'll be me, not you, who decides who goes out again and who doesn't.'

Reaching the swimming-pool terrace, he spotted Stuart hanging back behind a lavender hedge, suddenly too shy to make himself known.

'Stuart!' Marcus bounded across the lawn, like a panther closing in on its prey. 'Stuart, my dear godson!' He radiated an extraordinary, intense delight at seeing Stuart, who, being unaccustomed to it, felt intimidated. 'My God, it's good to see you. You are the exact spitting image of your father.' To Stuart, his godfather seemed terrifyingly big and broad-shouldered with very brown muscular legs, dark hair smoothly brushed back from a wide forehead, white teeth flashing from his deeply tanned face.

Marcus addressed the other godchildren standing about on the lawn in their swimsuits.

'This is Stuart Bolton. His father and I worked together for many, many years. I want you all to know that Stuart's father was a complete and utter *hero*. Stuart, you must meet my other godchildren – my *God*, it's fantastic having all of you here together.' There was an intensity to his enthusiasm that was almost scary. 'Now, where shall I start? This is Saffron – Saffron Weaver.' The little girl with blonde hair and the violet swimsuit was knotting a towel around her waist. 'And these two scoundrels are Charlie Crieff and Jamie Temple. You boys are all sharing the dormitory at the top of the house, and I don't expect to hear a lot of ragging, be warned. And this is Mary Merrett.' Mary smiled sheepishly at Stuart. She was skinny in a blue bathing suit covered with school swimming badges. 'And over there is Abigail Schwartzman. Abigail is the best-dressed of my goddaughters, coming from the city of New York.' A plump girl in a skirted red swimsuit, covered by tiny silver bows, adjusted her hair slide.

'Now,' declared Marcus, 'lunch! On the terrace in ten minutes. Anyone who wants to change into dry clothes, powder their noses, whatever, do so now, because one thing I will not tolerate is small children jumping up and down from the lunch table. Meanwhile, if any of you are thirsty, there should be bottles of Coca-Cola in the ice box. Help yourselves.'

There was a whoop from the godchildren who bounded up the hot steps to the terrace.

'Charlie, Jamie, please *do not* elbow my goddaughters out of the way. There are plenty of drinks for everybody. Oh, and Stuart, I recommend you put on something cooler for lunch or you'll melt in this heat.'

Stuart, changed into PE shorts, found everyone already sitting down under the pergola. Marcus sat at the head of the table wearing a wide-brimmed straw hat, with Saffron next to him on one side and Charlie on the other. The table was formed of a huge single slab of marble with bevelled edges. There was a place left for Stuart between Mary and Abigail. Looking at the other godchildren, Stuart thought he liked the look of Jamie best, and maybe Saffron. For some reason, he felt wary of Charlie.

Two maids came out from the kitchen carrying dishes of a fat white vegetable. Stuart had never seen anything like this before and, judging by the dubious looks on their faces, nor had any of the other godchildren.

'Now, who knows what these are?' asked Marcus.

There was a silence.

'White slugs?' suggested Jamie, and everyone laughed.

'No, not slugs. Any other ideas?'

'Old men's willies?' said Jamie and this time the laughter was louder, especially from Charlie and Saffron. Stuart sniggered, Mary looked embarrassed and Abigail probably didn't get the joke.

'That's enough of that,' said Marcus. 'It's asparagus. Best food in the world. Fresh today from the market in Beaulieu.

French believe it acts as an aphrodisiac, but you can discover that for yourselves when you're older. Far as eating it is concerned, use your fingers, never those frightful tongs they try and give you in restaurants, and never, ever a knife and fork. Dip the tips in the hot butter, get them nice and juicy – that's right, Saffron, it's got to be oozing with butter – then straight into your mouth. More the butter dribbles down your chin, better you're doing. What do you think of that, Abigail?'

She frowned. 'It doesn't sound like very nice manners.'

'Well, with asparagus it *is* nice manners. So you've learnt something today. When you get back to America, you'll have to tell them that. Say "Marcus Brand taught me", if anyone disbelieves you.'

The asparagus was cleared away and the maids returned with two covered silver tureens.

'Now, what do you think we've got in here? Anybody prepared to guess?' Marcus's eyes scanned the table. 'Come on, come on, the implements should be a clue. What does one do with these lethal-looking instruments?' He picked up a pair of silver crackers and a button hook.

'Pull out teeth?' suggested Jamie.

'Good try, but they're not intended for dentistry.' He lifted the lid off the dish. '*Lobster*. Who's eaten this before? Nobody? Charlie, surely they give you lobster at Ardnessaig, or is it just grouse every day?'

'We do eat grouse a lot,' replied Charlie. 'My father owns a grouse moor, you see.'

'I've shot with your parents,' said Marcus. 'Now, what about you, Mary? Catch many lobster down in Surrey, do they?'

Mary blushed red. She had been hoping she wouldn't be picked on. 'Usually we just have chicken at home,' she heard herself saying.

'Lobster's very like chicken,' said Marcus. 'Sea chicken. Only a more interesting texture and, of course, considerably more expensive.'

'My father loves lobster,' said Jamie. 'It's one of his favourite things.'

37

'Your father would love lobster,' Marcus replied dryly. 'He probably loves it precisely because it's expensive.'

He demonstrated to his godchildren how to break the claws – 'exactly like cracking walnuts, same technique' – and extract the flesh with the button hook. 'Now, who's going to be brave and try it? Charlie?'

Charlie, with wrinkled nose, took a tiny bite. 'It's quite nice actually. It tastes a bit like venison.'

'Jamie?'

'It's really chewy. Like eating potty putty.'

'Mary, how about you? Good as Surrey chicken, is it?'

Mary, who had forced herself to swallow a tiny morsel of pink claw, and desperately wanted to throw up, merely nodded politely.

'Stuart? Ever seen a lobster before in Birmingham?'

He shook his head. 'But I don't mind it that much, it's not too bad.'

'Abigail? You haven't touched yours.'

She looked stricken. 'It's shellfish.'

'Oh, come on, Abigail. They caught these this morning out in the bay. Boatboys brought them in.'

'But it's forbidden.'

'God spare us the chosen race! Ann-Marie,' he summoned one of the maids, 'fetch Miss Schwartzman an *omelette naturelle*, quick as you can. You can eat eggs all right, can't you, Abigail? Nothing in the Torah about omelettes, far as I know.'

Towards the end of lunch, another guest made an astonishing appearance on the terrace. She was topless, with golden-brown skin and big pouty lips, and was carrying a cup of black coffee. She looks a bit like Brigitte Bardot, Saffron thought.

'Morning, Clemence,' said Marcus. 'Sleep well?'

The girl made a face. 'I was trying to sleep,' she replied. 'But with all the noises from the terrace . . .' Judging by her accent, she must be foreign, Stuart reckoned.

Mary, who had never seen bare bosoms in real life before, and programmed by her mother to disapprove of topless sunbathing, didn't know where to look.

Clemence swayed over to the table with her coffee and perched herself on Marcus's lap, draping one long, brown arm around his shoulders. 'So, how do you enjoy yourself, Marcus, as the father of so many childrens?'

Saffron thought: One day, when I'm grown up, I'd like to look like her. Jamie kicked Charlie under the table to make sure he'd clocked Clemence's voluptuous breasts.

Years into the future, reflecting on this holiday in the South of France, Stuart worked out that Marcus must have been no older than thirty-four, and the girlfriend, Clemence, about twenty-two. But, at the time, they seemed impossibly grown-up and sophisticated. Clemence arranged herself on a sun-lounger, at some distance from the children, occasionally shifting position on to her back or her side.

At the end of lunch, Marcus announced he had business to attend to.

'I don't expect to hear a squeak from any of you for an hour, not a squeak, otherwise you won't go out again in the boat. Is that understood?' When he addressed his god-children there was something in Marcus's voice that made them want to do as he said. Then he withdrew to a distant part of the terrace where three men in dark suits were waiting with open attaché cases. They sat in an arc of cane chairs reviewing documents, while Marcus picked at a bowl of olives.

Under the pergola, Charlie whispered, 'If anybody fools around so we're not allowed in the boat, I'm going to beat them up, OK?'

'I don't want to go back on the ocean,' said Abigail. 'It made me seasick.'

'Only because you're a scaredy-cat American,' said Charlie.

'That's being mean,' said Saffron. 'Anyway, my mother's boyfriend's been to America.'

'So what?' said Charlie. 'My cousins own a castle. And we own a grouse moor.'

'What is a grouse moor anyway?' asked Stuart.

'A moor. Don't you even know what a moor is?'

'No.' Stuart already wished he hadn't asked. Mary, who didn't know either, stared down at her plate.

'Doesn't your father shoot?' asked Charlie.

'He was killed.'

'Wow!' said Jamie. 'That's so cool. Was he fighting Germans?'

'He died in a car crash, I think. I don't know that much about it.'

'So who looks after you?' asked Jamie.

'My mum, except when she's out at work.'

'Your mother works?' said Charlie. 'What's she do?'

'She works in an office, and sometimes she cleans offices too, before the people get in.'

'You mean, she's a *cleaner*? Did you hear that, Jamie? Stuart's mother's a charlady.'

Marcus's meeting broke up and he returned to the children's end of the terrace, the dealmakers following in his wake. 'These are the hooligans I was telling you about,' he said, as they reached the pergola. 'My six godchildren. What do you reckon, Dick? Think the house will be standing by the end of the week?'

'They look like well-behaved kids to me, Marcus,' said Dick Mathias, whose eyes resembled martinis with clouded viscous membranes and irises the colour of green olives. At that time he bore the title Legal Director of the Brand Group. Later, as the business and personal affairs of Marcus Brand grew in size and complexity, he was to become a constant presence, involved in any acquisition, tax matter, house purchase, litigation, termination or dirty work that came along.

'Didn't you mention that a daughter of Derek Merrett's is staying here with you?' he asked.

'The girl in the blue swimsuit. Mary – I'd like you to meet Dick Mathias.'

She stood up and awkwardly shook hands. 'I know your father,' Dick said.

'He's very well,' replied Mary, not knowing what else to say.

'Remember me to him,' growled the lawyer.

'Everybody ready to go back out again?' said Marcus, suddenly restless. 'The boat should be waiting at the jetty. I've asked the boatboys to organise something special for us this afternoon.'

The godchildren, led by Charlie and Jamie, charged down the steps to the beach. Stuart hurried to keep up, torn between his eagerness to see the speed boat and apprehension about swimming in the sea. He prayed they wouldn't have to. He hated his head going underwater. In the school pool, he could do three widths without arm bands, but big expanses of water scared him.

The Riva was ticking over alongside the jetty, and the boatboys in their whites and dark glasses lifted the children down on to the long white cushions beneath the canopy. In the stern were six large tractor tyres lashed together with rope.

'What are those for?' asked Jamie, as Marcus vaulted down from the steps.

'Wait and see.'

They accelerated into the bay, smacking across the tops of the waves. The sun was still high in the sky and the sea a vibrant comic-book blue. Marcus stood erect in the prow, perfectly balanced, staring into the distance in his straw hat, maroon trunks and a duckegg blue shirt. Looking back at Cap Ferrat, Stuart watched the villa recede into the tall pines that sprouted from the promontory; already, the jetty and strip of private beach had melded into the rocks. Across the bay, the godchildren could see the public beach with its rows of coloured umbrellas and pedalos ploughing their course around the roped swimming area.

'Stop here, will you, please?' Marcus said and the driver cut the engine. 'Now, if you could lob those tyres over the side.'

The boatmen hoisted the tyres one at a time and heaved them into the sea with a splash. For a brief moment they disappeared beneath the waves, then resurfaced, glistening with salt water as they bobbed out from the side of the boat.

When all six tyres were overboard, Marcus said, 'Now, all

of you, jump in, and swim to the nearest tyre. Then I want you to *sit* on top of your tyre, with your backside inside the hole.'

'I get it,' said Jamie excitedly. 'We're going to be dragged behind the boat on ropes. *Fantastic*!'

Stuart felt sick. The prospect of getting into this huge blue sea, half a mile from the beach, terrified him.

Jamie and Charlie jumped over the side, followed by Saffron and Mary. Stuart watched them swim over to their tyres and scramble on.

Abigail said, 'Marcus, I don't think I'd really like this. I'd rather stay in the boat.'

'Nonsense,' he said. 'You'll love it. Greatest thrill in the world, promise you. You help her, Stuart. In you get, both of you. Stuart will swim with you to your tyre, Abigail.'

One of the boatmen hung steps over the side. Shivering in the bright sun, first Stuart then Abigail clambered over the edge and into the sea.

'Stuart, swim behind Abigail and help her on to the first tyre. Then take the back tyre for yourself.'

He concentrated on his swimming and tried not to think about how far out they were. Five metres ahead, he could see the soles of Abigail's feet kicking out behind her and the silver bows of her swimsuit as her shoulders moved through the water. How deep was the sea anyway? A mile? Ten miles? If he drowned, would his body just go down and down to the bottom?

'Get a move on, you two,' Jamie shouted. 'Some people are waiting for their rides, you know.'

Abigail reached her tyre and clutched it gratefully with her plump arms.

'That's right, Stuart,' shouted Marcus. 'Give her a leg-up. Tread water and grab hold of her leg – or her arse.'

Jamie sniggered – 'That won't be difficult' – and Charlie laughed.

Stuart grabbed on to the rim of the tyre with one hand while trying to push Abigail from below. Her legs thrashed wildly as she clambered on to the ridged rubber and edged into position.

'Good work, Stuart,' shouted Marcus. 'Now, quickly, swim over to your own tyre and we'll get started.'

The exertion of helping Abigail had left Stuart breathless. He could see the vacant tyre forty metres ahead, bobbing in and out of view on the swell. To reach it, he would have to swim past the whole line of tyres on which Saffron, Mary, Jamie and Charlie were already installed. His own tyre looked so far away, he wasn't sure he could make it; it would be like swimming three lengths of the school pool.

He reached the first tyre and Saffron smiled at him. She looked like an astronaut in her Michelin capsule, her head resting on the hard rim and her legs pulled into her chest.

'Please God, let me reach the tyre,' Stuart kept repeating to himself. 'Please let me get there.' He closed his eyes and swam and swam, his arms and legs growing weaker with each stroke.

The waves seemed to become choppier as he swam further from the boat. When he reached Mary's tyre he clung on to it, panting.

'Keep going,' shouted Marcus. 'We need to get moving.'

He heard the driver start the engine and the ropes went taut as the boat inched forwards. He saw his own tyre jerk like a marlin on the end of its line as it was towed closer towards him.

Charlie's tyre passed him in the sea, and Charlie said, 'Buck up, slowcoach. I hope your mother isn't so slow when she's doing her cleaning.'

The Riva circled and Stuart's tyre bobbed into reach. He grabbed the rim and tried to heave himself up. But his arms were too weak and he kept falling back.

Distantly, he heard the engine rev up and the line of tyres began moving through the sea. The driver couldn't have noticed that he hadn't got on yet.

'Hey, wait!' Stuart's voice was drowned out by the motor.

'Yes, yes – this is *great*.' Jamie was waving his arms about and cheering. 'Faster! Go faster!'

Charlie, if truth be told, felt they were going fast enough already, but he joined in the chant: 'Faster! Yeah, faster!'

Stuart clung on to the tyre as he felt the boat gather speed.

Water was rushing into his face as he was dragged forwards. The rim of the tyre began cutting into his hands and he struggled to keep hold. If he let go, the boat would keep going and they wouldn't even know where he was, he'd be left in the middle of the sea.

He was dimly conscious of the other tyres bouncing across the waves ahead of him, but nobody looked round. The Riva was speeding up, now lifting his whole body out of the water and skimming it across the surface in its wake. The friction against his chest singed the skin like razor burn. His shoulders felt like they'd be ripped out of their sockets. Spluttering, he tried to call out, but the sky was suddenly obliterated by a great wall of water. It crashed over him and he felt himself drawn under, then dragged back upwards into sunlight.

The speedboat began to circle. They had to see him now. Again he opened his mouth to shout for help, and his lungs filled with salt water. He was coughing and retching but still he hung on.

He heard his godfather's voice shouting, 'Man overboard, Jean-Luc. Stuart's in the drink.' And then he must have blacked out because the next thing he knew he was being hauled up into the boat and laid flat on his stomach on the white cushions, with Jean-Luc pummelling his back.

Afterwards, he was treated as something of a hero. When it came out that Stuart had never got on to the tyre at all, and the boat had started before he was ready, Marcus said, 'You must be jolly tenacious. We dragged you half a mile round the bay.'

Jamie said, 'I wouldn't mind trying that one day. Water-skiing without skis.'

Mary said to Stuart, 'I'm awfully sorry we didn't notice you. You were on the back tyre.'

Only Charlie seemed unhappy at the turn of events. Later, he said to Jamie, 'If he'd swum a bit quicker in the first place, he'd have got on.'

For the rest of the week, Marcus referred to Stuart as 'Charles Atlas' when he spoke to the godchildren at all. After his initial enthusiasm, his interest in them noticeably diminished. Much of his time was occupied with meetings with Dick Mathias and the procession of men in business suits who arrived and departed on the same day. Sometimes they were brought over to the children's end of the terrace and introduced; other times they returned to the airport as soon as their meeting was finished. Clemence, during these days of intense negotiations, filled an ambivalent role, alternating between the business end of the terrace and the godchildren's end, where she spectated on games of draughts and chess, not bothering to disguise her boredom. She seldom, in any case, made an appearance before lunchtime.

For Stuart, the days crept by in a state of anxiety while nights became a time of fear. Unsupervised in the bedroom at the top of the villa, Charlie missed no opportunity to taunt and bully him.

'Come here, Stuart,' he would say, dropping his shorts and socks in a heap on the floor. 'You pick those up. If your mother's a charlady, you should do it.'

Or else he would steal Stuart's snake belt from his trousers and wave it round his head like a whip, so the silver buckle cut through the air, narrowly missing Stuart's face.

One night, long after they'd gone to bed and the only light was from the floodlights on the terrace leaking beneath the shutters, Charlie crept over to the window, threw open one shutter and hurled Stuart's shirt outside.

'Who the hell did that?' Marcus's voice boomed up from below. 'What the devil's going on up there?'

Nobody spoke. Then Charlie called out, 'Stuart threw his shirt out of the window for no reason.'

'Well, he'd better come down here and collect it then, hadn't he?'

Stuart, terrified, went down to the garden in his pyjamas. Marcus, Clemence and Dick Mathias, and several other grown-ups he hadn't seen before, were having dinner at a table beneath the pines. The garden at night smelt overpoweringly of oleander. Candles flickered on the table inside storm lamps. His school shirt was lying where it had landed on the stone terrace.

'What the hell are you up to, playing the fool?' demanded Marcus.

'I'm sorry,' said Stuart, trembling as he retrieved the shirt. 'It must have blown out of the window by accident.'

Then Marcus erupted with laughter. 'Blew out of the window! A likely story. If you ask me, one of those scoundrels upstairs helped it on its way.' Then he said, 'Do you like brie? Take a piece up to bed with you. Go on – and some bread. If I were you, I wouldn't share it with the others either. Teach them a lesson.'

On the last evening in France, after the businessmen had all departed by taxi for Nice, Marcus – exhilarated – strode over to the pergola and announced, 'Well, it's a done deal. Your godfather has just made a fortune. We need to *celebrate*.' He was pacing the terrace, restless with surplus energy.

And then maids were dispatched to fetch champagne and eight golden goblets, and everyone including the children was given a glass, and Marcus made a toast: 'To the future. And to my six incredible godchildren.' And then, realising he had made no reference to his girlfriend, he added, 'And to the beautiful Clemence, of course.'

Then Saffron asked, 'Godfather Marcus, have you really made a fortune like you said?'

'A small one anyway.' He laughed. 'I've just bought a factory, Saffron. I don't think the people I've bought it from have any idea what it is they've sold, or its potential.'

'How much is a fortune anyway? Is that more than one hundred pounds?' asked Saffron.

Abigail said, 'More like a million bucks is a fortune. Though my dad says even a million bucks isn't what it was.'

'That's the great conundrum of wealth,' said Marcus. 'That's what makes it so endlessly fascinating. You can't define what a fortune is, it means different things to different people.'

'If I had a fortune,' Jamie said, 'I'd buy that speedboat and drive it all the way to Australia or somewhere.'

'What about you, Charles Atlas?' said Marcus. 'I don't suppose you particularly covet a Riva after your nasty experience?'

Stuart thought. 'What I'd really like is my own table football, like they have in the youth club, with those players that spin round on bars and you spin them really fast to shoot goals.'

'Mary?'

'Definitely a pony. Daddy says he might buy me one for my birthday if he can save up enough money.'

'What about you, Charlie? What would you do with a fortune?'

'Buy an Aston Martin or a pair of shotguns or something.'

Saffron asked, 'What are you going to get, Godfather Marcus?'

'Me? Haven't given it a moment's thought, too much else going on. Anyway, I haven't made a sou yet from this deal. Quite the reverse – I've just agreed to pay a lot out.'

'But there must be something you want,' said Abigail. 'If it was my mom, she'd take an aeroplane to Paris and buy a hundred couture dresses.'

'Good idea. Maybe I'll do that, Abigail. One of my ambitions in life is to be as well turned out as your mother.' Jamie Temple found this reply so hilarious, he laughed until his ribs hurt.

'One thing's for sure,' said Marcus, 'you can't take your money with you. Minute you die, whatever you've made, whatever you own – houses, speedboats – it's all codswallop. Government swipes half of it, or tries to, children squabble over what's left.'

'But you haven't got any children, Godfather Marcus,' said Saffron.

'Observant girl, full marks. I don't have any children. In which case I suppose I'd just have to leave this villa and the boat to my godchildren to play with. You'd look after it for me, wouldn't you, all of you?'

All the godchildren affirmed that they would, with Charlie answering quickest and loudest.

'Well, don't get too excited,' said Marcus. 'I'm not intending to die quite yet. And, you never know, I might even discover how to make children myself.'

Then he laughed, and led Clemence upstairs by the hand.

47

3: September, 1968

Owing to the paucity of good preparatory schools in Scotland at the time, it became the tradition for Scottish boys to be sent south at the age of eight-and-a-half to attend one of the many fashionable boarding schools in England. It is not known for sure what it was that prompted the Crieffs to choose Broadley Court for their son Charlie, as opposed to Cothill, Summer Fields, Temple Grove, Ludgrove, Scaitcliffe, Sunningdale, Horris Hill or any of the dozen other establishments that they might as easily have gone for; but undoubtedly the fact that their kinsman the Earl of Arbroath had sent his son Jock to Broadley was a factor in the decision. In the case of the Temples, however, their choice of Broadley Court for Jamie was easily explained. Its convenient location between Ascot and Wentworth, barely six miles from the third exit of the M4, meant that they could reach the school from South Eaton Place in under forty minutes on a clear day and, furthermore, the French Horn at Sonning, the Bell at Aston Clinton and the Compleat Angler at Marlow were, as Michael Temple put it, 'Just three of the top-notch watering holes within striking distance of the school gates.'

Charlie and Jamie had arrived at the school on the same day, less than a month after their holiday with their godfather at Cap Ferrat. With the advantage of knowing each other already, and finding that they were both in the same dormitory, they had rapidly become close friends. Over the next two years, as they moved up the school and into more senior dormitories – Gibraltar, Tristan da Cunha, Basutoland, Honduras (all the dormitories at Broadley Court were named after British Colonies) – they became inseparable.

Physically, the two boys could not have been less alike. Fifteen generations of Scottish inbreeding in cold bedrooms had given Charlie a natural air of chilly superiority. He had a way of staring down his nose that antagonised his teachers; more than one of his school reports spoke of his 'haughtiness' and expressed the view that 'Crieff might learn rather more if he didn't always give the impression that knowledge was somehow beneath him'. The only subject for which he showed any aptitude was history; to general amazement, he won the Broadley Court Junior History Medal for his essay on James IV's invasion of Northumberland with thirty of Scotland's oldest and most gallant aristocratic families, including the Crieffs and the Arbroaths, which ended with the massacre at Flodden Field. In all other subjects, Charlie got by. Partly because of his sallow skin, he appeared permanently off-colour. Aside from his one week in the South of France, he had spent the first eleven years of his life under the brooding skies of Angus. His hair, which grew from a high forehead in tight curls like coils of barbed wire, he washed twice a term with a bar of green medicated soap that was kept on a high ledge in the communal shower room.

In contrast to the tall and curly-haired Charlie Crieff, Jamie Temple was small and beguiling, with straight brown hair, shiny as a conker, and mischievous green eyes. Although he caused infinitely more trouble than Charlie did, there probably wasn't a teacher in the school who wouldn't rather have had Temple in his class than Crieff. He had one of those smiles that made everyone in his orbit want to smile too. When he got into trouble, which was frequently, he could talk his way out of it with such charm and sincerity, that the masters were inclined to let the whole matter drop, even when they didn't believe one word he was saying. Even in winter, he was sun-tanned. For the Temples, it was a matter of principle that they should have a week's skiing in Courchevel at Easter and a fortnight in the Caribbean over Christmas.

In other respects, too, their lives were noticeably different. For the Crieffs, living so far north, the effort and expense of travelling down from Ardnessaig to Broadley Court meant they only made the journey once or twice a year. Charlie was consequently left without a visitor on most

Sunday exeats, and the Temples were generous about scooping him up and taking him with them on their expensive jaunts to riverside restaurants.

On these occasions, when the boys had piled into the back seat of the dark blue Jensen that Michael Temple was driving at the time, and they were heading off down the school drive past the clumps of dripping rhododendrons, Jamie's father would invariably ask Charlie, 'Heard anything from your godfather Marcus lately?'

To which Charlie would reply, 'He sent me five pounds for my birthday, but nothing else.'

'He's involved in some rather interesting deals at the moment,' Michael would say, as much to himself as to the children. 'Some quite risky, so jolly good luck to him. But if you haven't heard anything . . .'

The friendship between Crieff and Temple was surprising to many people; it surprised them that Jamie had so much time for Charlie. Jamie had numerous friends of all ages throughout the school. He made friends instantly and effortlessly. To sit next to Jamie in a class or to play on the same team was to become his friend. If you asked every boy at Broadley Court to write down their ten best friends in a straw poll, Temple's name would have come up again and again, whereas Crieff's would barely have registered. It wasn't exactly that Charlie was unpopular, but there was an aloofness about him that made people wary. For Jamie, this had never been an issue; he had a way of snapping Charlie Crieff out of his cocoon of grandeur. 'Don't be snotty, Charlie,' he'd say. 'You're acting like Clemence in the South of France.'

They talked frequently about the holiday in Cap Ferrat. Jamie liked to impersonate Clemence, Marcus's French girlfriend, with his dressing gown wound round his loins like a skirt, rolled socks pressed to his chest as tits, and a comic French accent: 'So, 'ow do you enjoy yourself, Marcus, you sexy man, as ze fathere of so many childrens?' Stuart Bolton was remembered, at least by Charlie, as a fraud. 'I bet he never did get dragged all that way by the speed boat. It's impossible. He just said it to swank.' Abigail

– poor, nervous, fat, American Abigail – was remorselessly mimicked: 'I don't want to go back out on the ocean. It made me seasick.' Mary was scarcely mentioned. Only Saffron was recalled with much affection, by Jamie anyway.

'Saffron was quite sexy. I like blondes.'

'Yuk!' said Charlie. 'You don't really like girls, do you?'

'I liked Saffron. One day I'd like to get off with her.'

'You mean, kiss her and make babies and everything?' Charlie was disgusted.

'Not babies, no way. But she is sexy.'

'I don't think so.'

'Sexier than your sisters anyway,' Jamie said. 'Whoever marries them, it would be like marrying an orang-utan.'

Charlie laughed. Jokes about his sisters, Mary Jane and Annabel, were fair game. On the pin-board above his bed, where the boys at Broadley Court displayed photographs of their families, Charlie had four pictures: his parents, with his father wearing the uniform of the Royal Company of Archers; a photograph of Ardnessaig taken from the top of the drive; Nanny Arbroath with a don't-you-dare-point-that-camera-at-me expression on a picnic by a loch; and Mary Jane and Annabel Crieff as bridesmaids at a society wedding. These pictures of his sisters had long ago had moustaches and spectacles added to them, and tufts of underarm hair, and a bone inserted through Mary Jane's nose.

In class, the two boys had adjoining desks. Jamie Temple liked to construct elaborate runways in which a marble could be flicked along the pencil groove on the top of his desk, drop through the ink well on to the spine of Kennedy's *Shorter Latin Primer*, roll across the tin lid of his protractor case, down the slope of an exercise book – the *piste* – on to a French vocab dictionary, clatter across a bridge made with a six-inch ruler, bounce against a *laager* of rubbers – the pits – and travel down into the base of the desk where it emerged through a hole. He spent much of his time in lessons surreptitiously inserting his hands inside the desk, making minute adjustments to the gradient of the infrastructure. Despite paying almost no attention in class to anything he was taught, Jamie had a quickness that scraped him through exams. In tests, it was more likely to be Charlie cribbing off Jamie than vice-versa. Charlie, in any case, never sat any exam without a carefully prepared crib sheet up his sleeve, or inserted under the tongue of his shoe; he transcribed the dates and chronology of the Kings and Queens of England, and the books of the Old Testament, in microscopic handwriting in pencil on scraps of blotting paper – blotch – which could afterwards be chewed to pulp in his mouth.

The curriculum at Broadley Court was devised chiefly to fill up the day. Archie Trumper, who had been Headmaster and proprietor of the school since shortly before the Second World War, had a reputation as a classicist and teacher of genius; a reputation he ruthlessly protected by hiring assistant masters of the lowest available quality.

There was a chapel service every morning and another every evening at which Archie Trumper, dressed in the cassock and yellowing surplice that he almost certainly wasn't entitled to wear, lectured the boys on the decline of English test cricket and the iniquity of pop music ('They look like girls with their filthy dirty long hair, and sound like a cats' chorus'), or read aloud the Broadley Court roll of honour, the names and ranks of the old boys who fell in the Great War and the war against Hitler that followed. Or else he compered complicated Scripture quizzes, complete with trick questions: 'Name the six gifts that the Prodigal Son was given by his father upon his return home. Any boy? Any boy? A robe, a pair of sandals, a ring, music, the fatted calf and – Any boy? Any boy? – *a kiss*. Every time, why does nobody ever remember the kiss?'

It was during one of these twice-daily chapel marathons that Jamie Temple conceived the scheme that was to become famous as the Great Alarm Clock Episode.

Having thought of it, he confided in no one but Charlie who was sworn to secrecy. Thereafter, the two boys discussed little else, expanding and refining the plan and gleefully anticipating the pandemonium it would cause.

On the following weekend, while the whole of the school staff was standing on the touchline, watching the Broadley

First XI lose to St George's, Jamie sneaked back inside the building. By the side of Matron's bed, with its pink candlewick bedcover, he found a little brass alarm clock on three legs which he slipped into his pocket. Then, moving on to the modern bungalows where the assistant masters lived in a colony, he discovered a couple more alarm clocks by the beds of the French and Geography teachers. Finally, in the flat above the garages, where old Ma Marbles, the art teacher, lived alone with her cats, he found a further two. In all, he gathered half-a-dozen clocks which he secreted back in his dormitory.

That night, he and Charlie carefully synchronised every alarm to 8.35 a.m. Then, slipping out of Bermuda and down dark corridors to the chapel, they concealed the clocks inside the organ, behind the altar and under the pews, in a box of psalters and behind the wooden hymn board. Returning to bed, they felt an exhilarating sense of anticipation.

The next morning in chapel service, as Archie Trumper was gearing up for a broadside against the decolonisation of British Africa ('The blacks don't even want us to go; they know when they're on to a good thing'), his sermon was interrupted by the shrill ringing of a bell. 'What the devil is that? Where's that noise coming from?'

Just then, a second alarm went off – louder this time – quickly followed by a third. It could have been a fire alarm, had Broadley Court possessed anything so high-tech.

As it dawned on Archie Trumper what was happening, his face turned the colour of *borscht*. 'If this is some boy's idea of a joke . . .'

The fourth clock was activated – *dingalingalingaling* – then the fifth and sixth – *clangalangalang*. All over the chapel, alarms were ringing at different pitches as the Headmaster marched in one direction then another attempting to locate the source of the racket. Jamie and Charlie succeeded in looking as surprised as everyone else as the drama unfolded. Eventually all the bells had run their course. Archie Trumper, eyes blazing, hands tugging at the sleeves of his cassock, ordered the school prefects to search the whole chapel and locate the clocks. 'And I expect the boy or boys responsible for this outrage to identify themselves immediately.'

Jamie and Charlie joined the rest of the school in looking innocently around the chapel, to see who might own up.

'Very well,' said Archie Trumper. 'If nobody's going to own up, we'll simply sit here until someone does. All day if necessary. It doesn't worry me. I shall have my own lunch brought in, and you can watch me eat it. Nobody else will eat, of course. You can miss lunch, tea, breakfast tomorrow morning, whatever. We can stay here all night long. I have plenty of marking to be getting on with.'

For four and a half hours, the one hundred and twenty boys sat silently in the chapel, waiting for someone to come forward. Jamie and Charlie had agreed in advance that, whatever happened, they would never confess.

At one o'clock, the school cook carried in a slice of veal and ham pie and a scoop of coleslaw for the Headmaster. The six alarm clocks were lined up as exhibits on the altar.

At half-past two Jamie Temple stuck up his hand. A frisson of excitement passed through the school. Charlie was horrified. Had Temple gone barmy or something?

'Yes, Temple?' said Archie Trumper. 'Have you got something you want to tell us?'

'Excuse me, sir,' said Jamie. 'It's just that I think I recognise one of the clocks, sir, the brass one with three legs. I've seen it before in Matron's room.'

'Have you indeed?' said Archie Trumper.

'And I was just thinking, sir, that maybe it was Matron who left it in the chapel, by accident.'

The whole school erupted with laughter. It was Matron's alarm clock! She was the practical joker! It wasn't one of the boys at all!

The Headmaster demanded silence. 'Frankly I don't think it's very likely, do you, Temple, that Matron would initiate an idiotic prank like this?' But probably, after six hours, even Archie Trumper was searching for a face-saving exit from the impasse, so he said: 'I shall speak to Matron and, let me assure you, this investigation is by no means concluded. Make no mistake, the culprit will be caught and admonished. Meanwhile, you can all return to your form-rooms and resume your lessons.'

As they filed out of the chapel, Jamie was a hero. Boys were slapping him on the back: 'That was brilliant, Temple. Imagine it being Matron's fault all the time. Trumper was false accusing.'

Later, when they met in the bootroom to gloat over the enormous success of the escapade, Charlie said to Jamie, 'For one minute I thought you were going to own up. I thought you'd gone cuckoo or something.'

Jamie laughed. 'Not in a trillion years, no fear. But, you see, I just have this honest face. People always believe me, even when I'm lying.'

'That's so lucky,' said Charlie, enviously.

'My father has it too,' Jamie replied. 'He tells whoppers all day long, especially to my mother. And everyone just automatically believes him.'

In common with every other preparatory school in the late sixties, Broadley Court was in perpetual need of money. Although the constant round of fundraising had not yet reached the obsessive proportions of the eighties and nineties, there was still an expectation that everything to do with the school – a filter system for the swimming pool, upgrading the Nuffield science laboratories, even the replumbing of bathrooms and refurbishment of classrooms – should be achieved using funds specially raised for the purpose. For parents, this was infuriating. Having already paid over substantial fees, they were then suborned at every turn into giving more money. At sports day, at the Christmas carol concert, in the interval at the school play, Archie Trumper would vault on to the stage and cajole the captive parents on the progress of his numerous appeals. 'We are now more than a quarter of the way towards our target for returfing the First XI cricket square and reroofing the pavilion,' he would say, 'and I would particularly like to express my thanks to those parents who have so generously contributed. To those parents who haven't yet sent a donation – and you know who you are – I can only repeat that this is a very worthy cause, and one that will directly benefit the daily lives of your offspring here at Broadley.'

Michael Temple, while always being amongst the first to send a cheque for whatever came along, complained about it vociferously. 'You know what this is like,' he would tell other parents in his loud lush voice. 'It's like ordering the set lunch at some decent restaurant and then being told you have to pay a levy on top for the chief bottlewashers in the kitchen. Goodness knows why we all put up with it.' The Crieffs, meanwhile, made a point of ignoring all appeals for money, believing that their higher social status absolved them from impositions of this kind.

One sports day, on one of the hottest June days of the decade, the Crieffs were introduced to the Temples for the first time.

'You really have been so kind to Charlie,' said Lady Crieff, shaking Michael Temple tepidly by the hand, while thinking that his shirt collar and tie were several inches too wide, and his eau-de-cologne several degrees too pungent, to be worn by a gentleman. It was really quite surprising the other parents these days at supposedly good schools, she observed, taking in the trace of bright red lipstick on Margaret Temple's teeth.

'Oh, it's a pleasure,' said Michael. 'It's fun for Jamie having a friend to take out, otherwise he gets fidgety in the restaurants we enjoy. Incidentally, there's a new French place opening over near Cookham, which should be worth a punt.'

The Crieffs, who always brought a picnic down to the school, smiled patronisingly.

'It's great the boys get on so well together,' Michael went on. 'Especially as they both have Marcus as their godfather.'

Lady Crieff stiffened. 'Sadly we haven't seen Marcus Brand for a long time,' she said, in a voice that made plain it wasn't sad at all.

'He is a slippery fish these days,' agreed Michael. 'One has to book him up weeks in advance. With all these businesses he's gobbling up, it's like obtaining an audience with royalty.'

The Crieffs, who were only dimly conscious of Marcus's burgeoning business empire, and were hardly disposed to be impressed by it, looked nonplussed.

'Tell you what I'll do,' said Michael. 'Next time I run into Marcus, I'll tell him we were all talking about him and he should give you a bell. He'll probably give you a ride in his new chopper, if you're lucky.'

At the time in question, Broadley Court's latest appeal was for funds to repair the cricket nets. Every boy in the school was challenged by Archie Trumper to raise £10 by their own initiative: 'It's up to you how you achieve this. You might want to do caddying at your local golf club in the holidays, or get yourself sponsored for some activity such as polishing your parents' shoes.'

'I'll tell you something,' Jamie declared to Charlie. 'No way am I cleaning shoes. Anyway, my father has a man who comes in and does that for him already.'

'Then how will you get the money?'

'That's my great idea – write to Godfather Marcus and ask him for it! I bet he'll send us £20.'

The idea struck both boys as a stroke of genius. They wrote him a joint letter, explaining about the fundraising, and sent it off to his new headquarters in Pall Mall. 'Please send the £20 to us at Broadley Court as quickly as possible. Love from Charlie (Crieff) and Jamie (Temple).'

For ten days they received no reply, though each morning, when the school post was distributed, Jamie always said, 'It's bound to come today. It has to. I couldn't stand having to cart someone's golf clubs around, just to make more money for Trumper to spend on buying sherry for himself.'

'Twenty pounds wouldn't be anything to Marcus,' said Charlie. 'It would be like sixpence to anyone else. My mother says he's probably a Jew, but doesn't admit to it.'

On the eleventh morning, the letter arrived. They recognised it instantly because the address in Pall Mall was printed on the flap of the envelope. Jamie held it up to the light. 'I'm pretty sure there's money inside. It feels like there is. Didn't I say he'd send us some?'

They ripped open the envelope. Inside was a sheet of

thick cream-coloured paper, engraved with the name of Marcus's company. The letter itself was signed, not by their godfather but by somebody described as the Manager for Investor Relations. 'Your letter to the Chairman has been forwarded to my department. As you can imagine, we receive numerous requests of this nature from many different worthy charities and sadly cannot support them all. We do, however, wish you well with your endeavours, and hope that the Brand Group of Companies may be able to help on some future occasion.'

This was the first, but not the last, time that Marcus Brand's godchildren would solicit money from him. The difference being that, in the future, they would ask for considerably more.

4: November, 1968

Stuart Bolton was walking back from the bus stop after school with his friends Mick and Ginger. They were approaching the factory next to the old brewery, where it always stank of malt and hops, when they saw the big crowd of men outside the gates. There were about seven hundred of them, it looked like, standing about on the pavement in their donkey jackets, and three men were standing on crates addressing them through a megaphone. Some of the crowd were holding placards.

'What's going on?' asked Stuart. 'What are all the men doing?'

'That's where my dad works,' said Mick. 'He works in that factory.'

As they got closer, they noticed two police vans parked in the next street, full of men with riot shields, and there were more policemen lined up outside the factory gates.

'Look, that's my dad stood over there,' said Mick. 'We can ask him.' Mick's father, a bull-necked Brummie who had lived in the next terrace to Stuart for as long as he remembered, was smoking with a group of mates from his assembly line. When he saw the boys he shook his head despondently.

'They've only gone and locked us out,' he said. 'They've chained the gates against the whole workforce.'

'But why've they done that?' asked Stuart.

'New management. They want to put half the men out of work and replace us with robots.'

'It's disgusting,' said another man. 'No way is that going to happen, no way. If they try and do away with one single job, we're working to rule.'

From the back of the crowd, Stuart could just about make out what the shop steward was saying through a loud hailer. 'This action has the full endorsement of the national executive of the Amalgamated Engineering Union. If we come out, it's not just the Birmingham membership but the whole industry. There won't be a plant in production from Longbridge to Cowley. Every chapel will come out in sympathy.'

''Ow about a General Strike?' someone shouted out from the crowd. There was a cheer of support.

'If necessary, brothers, yes. We're going to teach this management a lesson that they won't forget. The Smethwick Chassis Works will not accept any reduction in the workforce. Not one job. This great industry of ours is going to fight to ensure its survival.'

'Who is that talking?' Stuart asked Mick's dad. The shop steward on the crate was broad-shouldered and determined. Stuart thought he was a brilliant speaker, like some Roman senator they learned about at school, addressing the populace in the forum.

'Father of the chapel,' said Mick's dad. 'The other bloke, the older man in the raincoat, he's the area convenor. He's the powerful one, they say.'

'They'll have to unlock the gates eventually,' said Stuart. 'If everyone sticks together, they won't have any choice. Otherwise they can't make anything.'

Mick's dad shrugged. 'I hope you're right about that, son. There's little enough work round here. Go on – you'd better run off home and get some tea inside you.'

As usual, when Stuart returned home, his mother wasn't back yet from work, so he found the front door key under the brick and let himself in. Then he took four slices of white bread from the bread bin, and the margarine and waxy red ball of Edam from the fridge, and made himself a triple-decker sandwich with cheese and jam and peanut butter. These sandwiches were the best thing about his mother not being there because she said they were totally disgusting and he wasn't allowed to make them when she was around.

After tea, before he started on his homework, Stuart went into his bedroom and got out his chest expanders. They looked like iron bedsprings with handles at both ends, and, according to the advertisement, you could double your muscle power in twelve weeks. In the picture, a Mr Universe had been shown stretching the springs to some incredible arm span. Stuart couldn't manage that yet but, little by little, he had felt muscles developing like ping-pong balls in his upper arms. In the two years since the holiday in Cap Ferrat, he had worked determinedly on becoming stronger. He had also learned to swim, and nothing had given him so much satisfaction as being picked to swim for the school under-13s at St Edward's Grammar.

After that Stuart settled down to his homework, which always took at least two hours. That term they were learning about the invasion of England in 1513 by an army of opportunist Scottish nobles, which ended with the great victory at Flodden Field, and the pig iron smelting process that had transformed the economy of the West Midlands. They set a lot of homework at St Edward's, which many of the boys resented but Stuart never really minded. When the whole school was set one of the new IQ tests, he scored unexpectedly highly. He was hungry for knowledge and his mother encouraged him too. He discovered that he was above average at languages and maths, and already they were talking about him at school as someone who might eventually go on to university.

At half-past six Jean Bolton arrived home with a bag full of shopping and the evening newspaper. As usual, she asked him about his day at school and gave him a piece of fruit that she'd bought in the Bull Ring market at lunchtime.

Stuart ate the apple and picked up the *Birmingham Post*. On the front page was a photograph of the lockout at the Smethwick Chassis Works; you could see the big crowd of men outside the factory gates, and the shards of jagged glass set into the top of the wall. Stuart was looking to see if he could spot Mick's dad anywhere when he noticed the picture of Marcus Brand underneath. At first, he could hardly believe it was him. He was standing at the head of a long, polished boardroom table, with two other men in suits sitting on either side of him looking very serious. Marcus was staring defiantly into the camera. Beneath the photograph, a caption read, 'Smethwick Chassis Works Chairman, Marcus Brand, said yesterday he would rather close the factory permanently than concede to AEU demands'.

Stuart read the news story, which jumped to a later page in the paper. He had had no idea that his godfather owned the factory where Mick's dad worked, and the fathers of many other boys in his class; probably about sixty boys at St Edward's had a father, uncle or elder brother employed at the chassis works. And he couldn't believe that Marcus would shut it down.

It was the biggest component factory in Smethwick, and it supplied all the most important car plants in the country. Hub caps, windscreen motors, dynamos, ignition coils: all through the day, trucks loaded with parts rolled out of the yard, bound for the Leyland plant at Longbridge and Ford at Halewood and Dagenham. You couldn't just shut down somewhere like that, which made all those things, could you?

Towards the end of the article, after they'd reported what the union was saying, and how job-losses were non-negotiable, the *Post* had interviewed Marcus. Questioned on how long he would be staying in Birmingham, he had declared, 'I shall base myself here for as long as necessary. I haven't booked into a hotel because I am making myself available to talk with the unions at any time, night or day. I am sleeping on a sofa in my office. But I should caution the membership that I am not infinitely patient. Nor am I interested in discussing anything other than an orderly reduction in manpower to meet the targets I have set within the declared timeframe, and an end to restrictive practices. Anything else is a waste of time.'

The interviewer then asked Marcus whether his threat to close the factory should be taken seriously.

'Believe me, I should hate to shut this business down, but faced with no other option, I will not hesitate. Compare our productivity with that of almost any other industrialised economy – and particularly those of West Germany and Japan – and you will see that we are woefully uncompetitive. Our present levels of overmanning are unsustainable. I urge the fathers of the chapel to recognise this, and come to the table before it's too late.'

He continued, 'It would be salutary for those shop stewards who tell me that the British component industry cannot or will not conduct itself in a sensible manner, to remember the recent fate of many great British companies that have either been taken over or gone to the wall. I am thinking of Fisher and Ludlow, Briggs Motor Bodies, Pressed Steel – those are only the most prominent. If SCW wishes to go the same way, then so be it, but I would sooner put it out of its misery now, like an old lame dog that must be taken outside and shot, than allow it to limp on to certain death three or four years down the line.'

Reading all this, Stuart felt a complicated divergence of loyalty and emotion. Never before, not in his whole life, had he seen a photograph of anyone he knew in a newspaper. Marcus Brand was famous and, as his godson, that meant he was famous too. Half of him longed to show Ginger and Mick this picture of the man who had flown him to France on an aeroplane and given everyone champagne out of golden goblets. It made him proud, too, to know that his father had worked for Marcus, the famous boss who was in the newspapers. Apparently he used to drive this brilliant Bentley, with all leather trim inside, which could go a hundred miles an hour or something. But Stuart also felt oddly ashamed. If the chassis works closed, all those men would be put out of work, and it would be his godfather's fault. Everyone knew that half the factories in Birmingham had shut down already. When you walked along the Birmingham and Fazeley canal, you passed factories and warehouses that were boarded up and all their windows smashed. Quite a few boys at St Edward's had fathers who were out of work. Stuart understood he had better keep quiet about his special connection to Marcus Brand, at least until after the dispute was over.

The next morning, as he walked to school, the crowd was still standing about on the pavement outside the works, and there were more policemen keeping them back from the gates. It looked to Stuart like there were more men outside today than there had been yesterday. Secondary pickets had been bussed in from other factories across the city. The strikers had lit braziers and were warming their hands against the bitter November cold. As he passed by, Stuart glanced up at the windows of the office block within the perimeter wall, where the managers worked, and wondered whether Marcus was somewhere inside. He imagined him eating a bowl of lobsters, breaking their pink claws with those special silver crackers.

He turned his face away quickly, half fearing to be spotted by Marcus through the window, half wanting to see him again.

In the school playground at break, Mick and Ginger and all the boys talked about the strike. According to Mick's dad, the new owner was like a slave driver; he smoked this big fat cigar all day while the men did all the work, and he was driven up from London in a Bentley. Stuart sucked his milk through a straw and said nothing.

'This bloke,' said Mick, 'he's so greedy for money, he doesn't even want to pay the men their proper wages. Dad says he wants to put in these new foreign machines, which do it all for you – you wouldn't need any people stood there minding them. They work by themselves and can think and all, like Daleks.'

Ginger said, 'Ex-ter-min-ate. Ex-ter-min-ate.'

'It's not funny,' said Mick. 'Dad's dead worried. He hasn't ever worked any other place except there.'

Stuart was doing his homework that night when he heard his mother come in and put down her bags on the table with a thump. A minute or two later the sound of a Chopin prelude began wafting through the flat. Jean Bolton loved classical music, and as soon as she got home put on the Third Programme. Ever since his ninth birthday, she had made a point of taking Stuart with her to concerts at the Birmingham Town Hall. Already he had heard an Artur Rubinstein recital of Chopin, Falla and Beethoven in the great municipal landmark with its soaring pillars and vast organ.

The evening paper was once again leading on the dispute

at the chassis works. This time there was a photograph of Marcus Brand's Bentley, taken over the factory wall, presumably from an adjacent rooftop.

'Mum,' said Stuart. 'Look at this, there's a picture of my godfather's car.'

'I saw it already, Stuart. And I think it would be a good idea if we didn't mention it to anyone else. A lot of people round here are upset, and it won't do to go round talking about Mr Brand.'

Already, Jean Bolton regretted her decision to allow Stuart to go to France. She sensed that he hadn't enjoyed himself, though he hadn't actually said as much. With her son, it was sometimes hard to know what he felt about anything, he could be that unforthcoming.

The lockout continued for twenty-three days. At first there was a conviction on the part of the workers that the dispute couldn't last much longer. The management was losing orders, and it was only a question of time before they capitulated. The shop stewards were even talking about a special payment for all the men before they'd return to work, as compensation for loss of wages. But by the end of the second week, with no paypacket, Mick's family were running out of money for food, and the corner shop wasn't extending any more credit. One teatime, Stuart took Mick back home for a triple-decker sandwich. 'Dad says the men are totally united,' Mick told him. 'They're roasting chestnuts on the braziers. They're really showing that Mr Brand, he's dead scared now. He's pissing himself.'

In the third week, the mood abruptly changed. Marcus Brand gave an interview to the *Post*, stating that if the men didn't return to work, he'd dismantle the assembly lines and sell the machinery for whatever he could get for it. 'Already we've had offers. We have received approaches from interested parties in India and elsewhere. We can ship the whole plant.'

Then tussling broke out around the gates, and a pile of tyres and petrol-soaked rags was set alight against the perimeter wall. The police presence increased. The local shop stewards, rattled by their lack of progress, became more militant in their demands, and executives from the Joint Negotiating Committee of the TUC were seen entering the works.

Stuart, Mick and Ginger were walking home from school on Thursday when they witnessed the fight. It had broken out twenty minutes earlier, with some of the younger lads pelting the police with lumps of brick. Matters had escalated from there. Pretty soon more than two hundred men had been drawn into it, and bottles and slabs of broken pavement were being pitched through the air at the line of police. Everywhere there was shouting and cursing as the frustrations of the long dispute spilled into violence. Already, Stuart could see one policeman, blood running down his face, being supported to a van between colleagues. Then part of the crowd surged forward, and the men were using placards as weapons and the police were responding with truncheons. Shop stewards were shouting through megaphones, half urging the men on, half calling them to order, but their words were lost in the scrap.

Watching from the hill above, the boys could see everything. They were cheering on the men like spectators at a wrestling match.

'There's Dad,' shouted Mick excitedly. 'Look, down there, he's got a metal pole.' They saw Mick's father and a crowd of co-workers running at the gate with a rusty girder as a battering ram. Stuart felt a surge of exhilaration. At that moment, he knew exactly where his loyalties lay.

The girder pounded against the gate, which shuddered but held. The line of men reversed, manoeuvring the girder for a second run-up. But then they were overwhelmed by police, who began laying into them with truncheons. You could see the men shielding their heads with their arms, and the girder dropped on to the ground with a metallic clang. Mick gasped as he watched his father take a direct blow to his skull and drop to his knees. The policeman hit him a second time, this time against his shoulder, and then he was dragged off by a couple of men, back into the safety of the crowd.

By the time the boys found him, he was stretched out on

the pavement, being tended by a group of strikers. His face was badly bruised. A shop steward – the one that Stuart had earlier compared to a Roman senator – was encouraging him to take a sip of tea. 'You're a hero, mate, no question, a ruddy hero.' And then he turned to the boys, who were standing back not knowing what to do, and asked, 'Any of you lads know where he lives?'

Mick shot up his hand, as he'd been taught at school. 'He's my dad.'

'Well, you'd better fetch your mum then,' said the shop steward. 'Tell her what's happened, and get her to come quick. And you can tell her nobody's ever going to forget what her old man's done today.'

Mick sprinted off, followed by Stuart who suddenly realised how late it was. His mother would be home soon and he hadn't started on his homework. But how could he think about schoolwork at a time like this, with history in the making? He felt proud at Mick's father's courage, and moved by the shop steward's eulogy and the way that all the men were working together to save the factory.

A white van was parked outside the flat with its rear doors open, and two men in overalls were struggling to carry a wooden crate to the front door. The crate was shaped like a large painting, encased in planks.

'You live here?' one of them asked. 'We've got a delivery for a Stuart Bolton.'

'I'm Stuart.' He couldn't imagine what it could possibly be, or who could be sending it to him. He had never been sent anything so big before.

The men somehow edged the crate up the narrow stairs, complaining all the way, and through the front door of the Boltons' flat. They left it, still unwrapped, in the centre of the living room.

Shortly afterwards, Jean returned and exclaimed when she saw it. 'There must be a mistake, I haven't ordered anything. They'll have to come straight back and take it away again, that's all.'

But the special delivery label read 'Stuart Bolton' clearly enough, so they set to work unpacking. After a few minutes, he shouted, 'Mum! It's amazing. I know what it is. It's table football! This is so amazing.'

They pushed back the sofa and tipped the giant table on to its side to attach the legs. There were two teams – Birmingham City and Aston Villa in their proper club strips – and each of the players was attached to steel bars, and there were goals at each end with netting and floodlights at each corner. It was the biggest, most incredible table football game Stuart had ever seen, far bigger than the one in the youth club which was spastic compared to this.

'Is it really meant for me?' he asked, suddenly anxious that it might be a mistake.

Jean opened the card, but she'd guessed already. 'It's a present from Marcus Brand,' she read. 'He says, "I've been thinking about you, Stuart, because I'm staying in your magnificent city. If I wasn't so occupied with work, I'd give you tea at the Metropole. Hope you still enjoy football, I remember you telling me you'd like one of these one day."'

When they heaved the table upright, it filled three-quarters of the surface area of the living room. There was hardly space to walk round it to reach the kitchen. And when you extended the steel rods, you had to press yourself flat against the walls.

Stuart beat his mother nine-games-to-nil on that first afternoon. He quickly got the hang of the wrist action, but the fact was, Jean Bolton didn't put up much competition. He found that, with a couple of hard spins of the handle, the white ball slammed into the back of the net every time and dropped into the pocket.

'Now, Stuart,' she said after a while, 'I can't stand here playing football all day long. Finish your homework and then, if there's time, ask one of your friends over for a match.'

But Stuart knew that he could never let his friends see the game. He could never admit that Marcus had sent it – especially not to Mick – and how else could he explain how he came by it?

The table stood like a reproach in the living room. It was the best present he'd ever had by miles, but when he thought of Mick's dad, bruised and bloodied on the pavement, it made him ashamed.

Later that evening he sat next to his mother on the sofa, drinking a mug of Ovaltine. The table football loomed over them. From their low vantage point, they could only see the base of the table with its steel rods protruding above their heads.

'Mum,' Stuart said, 'I really need to ask you something. When I was in France staying with my godfather, he said Dad had been a hero. What did he mean?'

'A hero? I'm not sure exactly. Your father was a very good man, probably that's what Mr Brand meant.'

'But how did Dad die anyway? You've never explained. Was he really killed in a car crash?'

Jean sighed. It was a conversation she would rather have avoided, but Stuart was eleven now, and she would have to tell him something one day.

'Yes, it was a car accident. It was very sad. You were only six weeks old when it happened, and we were living in Scotland in a cottage near to Mr Brand's house.'

'Was Godfather Marcus in the crash too?'

'No, but his wife was.'

'I didn't know Marcus even had a wife. When we were in France there was a lady staying called Clemence, but I didn't think she was his actual wife.'

'Mrs Brand died in the same awful accident as your father. It was the middle of the night, and the car drove off the road. It hit a tree.'

Stuart went very quiet, taking it all in. 'Was Dad actually driving when it crashed?'

Jean nodded. 'The hospital told us he probably died instantly. He wouldn't have been in any pain.'

Stuart was still thinking. 'Was Marcus really angry that Dad killed his wife?'

'Stuart!'

'But if it was Dad's fault. If he was doing the driving . . .'

Jean put her arms around her son and hugged him. 'Stuart, listen to me. It wasn't your father's fault. It all happened a very long time ago, a tragic accident, but he wasn't to blame. Your father was the most wonderful, kind man who loved you and it's so sad that he hasn't been here to see you grow up. He'd have been so proud of you. And you must always be proud of him.' She drew Stuart close to her, beneath the jutting overhang of the table football. 'He wasn't to blame.'

Stuart nodded, and smiled reassuringly at his mother. But in his heart he was not reassured.

It was a week after this conversation that two things happened at almost the same time.

The first, and more important, development was that the dispute at the Smethwick Chassis Works was resolved through arbitration. At the time, the unions hailed the result as a famous victory. Marcus Brand made several important concessions over manning levels and automation, which resulted in eighty per cent of the workforce keeping their jobs, though additional job losses were negotiated through natural wastage. Mick's father returned to the assembly line and remained with the company for a further twenty months, until his position was abolished in the next round of restructuring.

The same week, Stuart told his mother that he wanted to give the table football to the youth club. He said that it filled up the living room a bit too much, and there would anyway be more people to play against at the club. Jean Bolton was relieved to see the back of it. She arranged that it should be presented anonymously, and during the many matches that Stuart played on it against his friends, he never gave the slightest hint as to where it had come from.

5: July, 1973

The house in the Bahamas resembled something out of *Gone With The Wind*: a white plantation building with a double-height portico supported by six white columns, and a white cupola on the roof. From his bedroom window in one of the two pink-washed guest cottages, Stuart had a view of a perfectly manicured, brilliant green golf course, with raked bunkers and palm trees as straight as industrial chimneys.

Seven years had passed since the holiday at Cap Ferrat. Following the delivery of the table football, Stuart had received only one other communication from Marcus, when a thirteenth birthday card had landed on the mat with two £20 notes tucked inside. That was three years ago. Then the invitation to Nassau had arrived: 'Come and stay. Lyford Cay is meant to be an amusing place for teenagers, and most of you haven't seen each other since France. My secretary, Barbara Miles, will take care of the travel arrangements.'

Five of the godchildren had travelled out on the same flight, and been joined at Nassau International airport by Abigail Schwartzman, who had flown direct from New York. When her luggage appeared in the arrivals hall – five matching monogrammed Vuittons – Charlie Crieff turned to Jamie Temple and said, 'Good grief, look at all that. What do you suppose she's brought?'

'A week's supply of cream puffs probably,' replied Jamie. And they sniggered because Abigail at fifteen was undeniably fat.

Two open-topped jeeps were waiting outside for the godchildren and the suitcases. Two Bahamian drivers in white ducks swung the luggage into the boots. Mary Merrett, seeing her father's battered holdall that she'd borrowed for the holiday being squeezed in next to Abigail's

71

embossed portmanteau, fretted that she might not have brought the correct clothes.

Charlie and Jamie slipped into the front of one jeep, alongside the driver, with the three girls occupying the bench behind and Stuart on the jump-seat in the back. For most of the journey, he cast surreptitious glances at Saffron Weaver. When he'd seen her at the airport, he couldn't at first connect her with the little girl who'd been in France. She was now heartwrenchingly pretty with long fair hair and shapely bare legs emerging from her frayed denim shorts. Under the fierce, almost white sun which blazed down on their heads, Stuart watched her through eyes screwed up behind his glasses, and wished he had sunglasses like all the others.

They drove along the coast road, bordered on one side by a flat terrain of bush and scrub with billboards advertising lobster restaurants on the cays, and on the other by an emerald sea. A narrow sandbar lay fifty yards out from the shore; beyond it, the open sea in lakes of jagged blues.

Jamie suddenly spun round in his seat and said, 'Christ, everyone! Shark! It's a Great White attacking that woman.'

Abigail yelped, 'Where? I don't see anything.' She stared anxiously out to sea.

'Two hundred yards. You can see the fin, look, and blood on the surf. Jesus, it's taken her whole leg off.'

'Oh, please, no,' said Abigail, instantly filled with terror. 'My mom warned me this place was dangerous.'

Jamie's face broke into a huge grin. 'Sucker! You're so gullible.' He flicked his fringe out of his eyes with his fingers. 'Sorry if I scared you, I just couldn't resist.'

Charlie was snorting with suppressed mirth. He leaned over the seat-back. His pink striped shirt was damp with sweat where he'd been leaning against the leather seat, and he loosened his cufflinks and rolled up his sleeves. 'Jamie does that all the time at school. He's the house wag. He can forge our housemaster's signature and puts these fake notices up on the noticeboard in the slab.'

Mary, looking slightly horrified, asked, 'But don't you get into trouble when they find out?'

'No way, I just deny it,' said Jamie. He laughed and his eyes lit up his face. 'If you don't admit anything, they can't get you. Like, I did this great notice saying all boys had to go to the Blacktongue concert in Windsor Great Park, and signed it with Talbot-Jones's signature. One of my best forgeries actually. And some suckers actually believed it. They were going out of bounds to buy tickets.'

Charlie turned to face the girls, his right arm resting along the seat-back. At sixteen, his tightly curled fair hair was carefully cut so that it exactly covered his ears, and he radiated an overwhelming confidence born of knowing that he was at a best-of-breed public school, the son of a Scottish laird and heir to Ardnessaig. On his sockless feet he wore a pair of penny loafers with coins faddishly inserted into the straps. His pink New & Lingwood shirt was one of four, all striped, that he had recently bought on his parents' tab at the school outfitters in the High Street. At close quarters, he gave off an abrasive tang of the Eau Sauvage with which he patted his cheeks after his bi-weekly shave. Mary felt that Charlie was probably the most attractive boy she'd ever seen, and wished she could think of something to say, but felt unaccountably tongue-tied.

He said, 'Do you remember in France when we were towed on those tyres behind Marcus's speedboat?' He was addressing the girls but Stuart stiffened. 'There was some weird boy staying who couldn't swim. Who was that, I can't remember?'

'It was Stuart, of course, who's here in the back,' said Mary.

'Oh, awfully sorry, Stuart,' Charlie said languidly. 'No offence. I didn't notice you crouching behind Abigail's hand luggage. Anyway, that was years ago, I expect you've learned to swim by now.'

'Of course I can bloody swim,' replied Stuart, more aggressively than he'd intended. 'I could outswim you any day.'

'Certainly hope so,' countered Charlie. 'I only ever swim to cool down. Except at home in Scotland when you swim to warm up.'

The jeeps halted at a barrier and the driver spoke to a security guard in immaculate colonial fatigues. They heard him say 'Houseguests of Mr Brand', and the barrier was raised and the guard waved them through on to an asphalt drive lined with colonial mansions behind white brick walls. Seeing all the detached houses with their in-and-out drives, Stuart was reminded of the more exclusive residential streets in Solihull, except these houses were far bigger and had thirty-foot palm trees instead of pampas grass.

They passed a marina where moored white Sunseekers were being power-hosed by their crews, and then proceeded along a wide avenue past the entrances to more large mansions. The grass verges on each side of the drive were perfectly mown.

Jamie said, 'According to my father, you can only buy a house at the Lyford Cay Club by pulling strings. You have to go about cultivating the right people.' He shrugged. 'And be disgustingly rich like Marcus.'

From time to time, they overtook electric golf carts transporting very old people in sun visors and pastel chinos to the clubhouse.

'OK, ladies and gentlemen, this is it,' said the driver as he turned off the road on to the gravel sweep that was the approach to Sandy Cove.

'Not bad,' said Charlie as the jeeps drew up side by side under the portico. 'It's the White House on a golf course.'

'Hope he's got space for us all,' said Jamie. 'From the look of it, there's only twenty or thirty bedrooms.'

Two manservants in white jackets with livery buttons and black trousers appeared from a side entrance and began helping the drivers with the luggage. A matronly woman emerged from the front door and said, 'All arrived safely, I'm glad to see, no frightful hold-ups on the journey? I'm Barbara Miles, Mr Brand's secretary, and I hope you'll all enjoy a very happy time at Sandy Cove. If you'll follow me, I'll take you to your godfather who's waiting to give you a drink on the terrace. I expect you're all thirsty after the drive.'

'You bet,' said Charlie. 'And thank you so much, Mrs

Miles, for organising our flights and everything. It all went like clockwork. You did a marvellous job.'

Barbara Miles purred. Stuart felt a stab of irritation that Charlie Crieff's obvious insincerity had worked its magic so easily. Charlie was a git.

The hall echoed to their footsteps. A curved marble staircase with a polished steel handrail rose into the rotunda, its terracotta wall lined with three enormous eighteenth-century paintings by James Seymour of horses and their liveried grooms; in the middle of the hall was a round table, covered by a green tasselled cloth, on which stood a neo-classical torso on a granite plinth, an array of orchids in blue-and-white Chinese cachepots and a display of art books. Five tall doors opened on to the hall.

'It's freezing in here,' said Saffron, her bare legs goose-pimpled in a blast of air-conditioning.

'Mr Brand hates to be hot,' said Mrs Miles. 'The first thing we did when he bought this house was install the most efficient air-conditioning we could find. This system was shipped from Miami.'

They passed a drawing room and a billiard room and came to a covered courtyard in the centre of the house, which had been done out like an office with desks, type-writers and metal filing cabinets. Two secretaries were typing letters and a telex machine was disgorging a loop of ticker tape.

'Does Marcus have an office here too?' asked Mary. 'I thought this was supposed to be his holiday house.'

'Mr Brand needs to stay in touch wherever he is,' explained Mrs Miles. 'It isn't always possible, but we do our best. Problems start when the electricity goes off, which does happen here in the West Indies. There's not a lot we can do about it until the new telephone exchange arrives. Mr Brand is helping the government to purchase it.'

They approached a pair of high Georgian-style doors. Mrs Miles unhooked a house telephone from the wall and touched a number. 'Mr Brand? I have your godchildren outside.'

A moment later they were inside the inner sanctum, an

immense library, shelves filled floor-to-ceiling with matched leather-bound sets and French windows open on to a terrace. Marcus, who had been seated behind a large Carlton House desk, leapt to his feet. 'It's *wonderful* you all could make it! Can't tell you how happy you've made me. Well done. Well done all of you.' He embraced the children, beginning with Saffron. 'My God, Saffron – just stand there, don't say anything, I want to look at you. Godfather's privilege. Feast mine eyes. *Gorgeous*. Your mother's daughter. How old are you all now anyway? Sixteen, seventeen? Can't remember the girls looking so attractive in my day. There you are, you see, born too early, timing's everything in life.'

He moved on to Abigail, registering for the most fleeting of moments disapproval at her appearance. At sixteen, she looked forty-five with her blow-dried black hair, gold earrings, gold bracelet and blue and white seersucker trouser suit. Understanding his thought process, Abigail blushed. Desperately self-conscious about her figure, and full of self-loathing at her regular bouts of comfort eating, she had never wanted to come to Nassau. But her father, anxious to revive his business relationship with Marcus despite his previous bad experience, had bullied and bribed her to accept.

'Father fit, I trust,' asked Marcus.

'He says to send you his best,' replied Abigail. 'He's kind of busy right now on a scheme to redevelop the 20th Street wharf.'

'So he informs me,' said Marcus. 'Sent me the prospectus.'

'Hello, Godfather Marcus, I'm Mary Merrett. I believe you know my father, Derek Merrett.' Mary stuck out her hand.

'Mary,' said Marcus, kissing her on the cheek. 'Certainly I know your father. Work together, have done for donkey's years. Haven't seen quite so much of him lately, tell the truth, too much else going on. Dreadful habit, work. Bit like smoking – difficult to break once you've got the bug.'

Watching this exchange, Stuart was struck by how little

altered Marcus was from his mental image of him. Marcus in the South of France, Marcus photographed in the *Birmingham Post*, and now here in the Bahamas; his fellow godchildren had changed, physically anyway, almost beyond recognition, but Marcus had not. At forty-two, dressed in pale blue belted sailing trousers and a short-sleeved shirt with a monogram on the pocket, his hair remained thick and black and his eyes still burned into the skull of whoever he was addressing, exactly as Stuart remembered.

'Hell am I thinking of?' Marcus said suddenly. 'Bartholomew – bring champagne. Anything else you want, tell Bartholomew. Got most things hidden away in that cupboard of yours, haven't you, Barty?'

'Hope so, Mr Brand,' said Bartholomew the Bahamian butler, all white teeth, already advancing with a tray of frosted silver goblets of Veuve Clicquot.

Charlie Crieff was inspecting the paintings. By no means the possessor of a good eye, he could nevertheless identify anything old and prominent, particularly if similar examples hung at Arbroath Castle.

'Great to see you, Marcus,' he said, champagne goblet in his left hand, right arm outstretched to his godfather. 'Hope you don't object, I've been admiring your pictures. Am I right in thinking that's a Samuel Scott between the windows?'

'Haven't got an earthly,' said Marcus. 'Clueless about paintings. Girl who put the house together – came over from New York – she'd know. Lovely girl. Flying in tomorrow as it happens, delivering knick-knacks, whatever. Ask her.'

Jamie, standing next to Stuart, leaned towards him and said, 'I love it, don't you, when Charlie pretends to know about art? He always does that when he's trying to impress.'

'I didn't think he had to try,' replied Stuart.

'Who, Charlie? Oh, he tries all the time, though he'd hate anyone to realise.'

Outside on the terrace a table was laid for lunch under a white umbrella, with plates and side plates and a salad bowl all made of deep green glass the colour of emeralds. Around the table were canvas-backed movie producer's chairs, with the words 'Marcus Brand, Chairman, BGC' blocked on to the canvas.

'Tell you what,' he said, 'Bartholomew's going to show you where you're all sleeping. Sort yourselves out a bit, freshen up, and we'll meet back here again for lunch in about twenty minutes. Enough time for everyone? Abigail? Saffron? Good. Girls are sleeping over here in the main house, boys in the guest cottages out of harm's way. Take your drinks with you, if you'd like to.'

Jamie and Charlie were billeted together in the first pink cottage, with its tin roof and fretted veranda and patch of private garden front and back, and Stuart in the identical cottage next door. He discovered that his clothes had already been unpacked for him; his spare pair of jeans was on a hanger in the cupboard, amidst a thicket of empty hangers, his t-shirts and bathing trunks stacked on shelves. Through the open window he could hear Charlie saying something to Jamie about a girl: 'You can just tell she's on for it,' and Charlie's laugh – haw, haw, haw – echoed across the golf course. Stuart wondered, in a flash of jealousy, whether they could be talking about Saffron. Ever since they'd arrived, he had been unable to take his eyes off her. So far they hadn't exchanged one word, nor had she even glanced in his direction, but he was consumed by her. She was completely different from any girl he had seen in his life: girls like Saffron didn't exist in Birmingham. In Marcus's library, he had been conscious of her every movement around the room. Talking to Jamie, he had all the time been watching Saffron talking to Marcus.

Next door, in the bathroom, Charlie applied pressure to a small spot on his chin and anointed it with a pink dab of Germolene from a round tin. He threw on a blue and yellow striped shirt and a pair of white trousers, and considered whether his Panama hat would impress Saffron. Jamie, rooting about in the wardrobe for his swimming trunks, said, 'Hey, Charlie, come and look at this. There's a safe in this cupboard – empty, I've already checked. But look, a mini-bar full of drinks. Miniature bottles of everything . . .

78

gin, vodka, beer. They always have these in hotels in Jamaica.'

'You don't think they're rather common?' asked Charlie. 'I've always been told that it's nicer to be *brought* a drink, not make your own.'

'Don't be a complete fart. You don't get it, do you? We'll get the girls over here one night. Mix a few deadly cocktails and we're away.'

Mary standing in front of the long white-framed mirror in her bedroom, wondered whether she looked all right in the Laura Ashley sundress with the little spriggy flower pattern, or whether the white Laura Ashley with the lace collar would be nicer for lunch. They were the two most expensive dresses she had ever owned, and her parents had accompanied her to the shop in Guildford High Street to help choose them. They were only planning on buying one dress but then her father, unbelievably generously, had said, 'Go on, Mary, have them both. I know, Belinda, you don't have to tell me, but Marcus might take them to some smart places in the West Indies. It can be her birthday present in advance.' At the bottom of her spongebag, Mary found the pale pink lipstick that she'd smuggled into her luggage; her mother disapproved of make-up for girls until after they'd left school. She applied the lipstick, fastened the clasp of her charm bracelet and hastened downstairs so as not to be late.

Saffron lay down on a big white four-poster bed, with its white muslin nets, and worried about her mother. Yesterday, just before she'd left Knighton for the airport, Amaryllis had had an almighty bust-up with Bongo all to do with one of the girl grooms in the stable yard, and whether or not he had been flirting with her. There had been this big shouting match, which had ended with Bongo telling Amaryllis to clear out, which meant that once again they'd have nowhere to live. Saffron was praying her mother could make it up with him since Bongo wasn't such a bad guy if Masters of Foxhounds with cavernous nostrils were your thing. He had certainly come like a gift from God when Amaryllis and Trev had broken up so acrimoniously, and Trev had changed the locks on the house in Edith Grove and they'd drifted around London like gypsies for five months, sleeping on friends' floors. Amaryllis's modelling career had never quite taken off as predicted, and she had been working at a nightclub in Beak Street, the Pinstripe, where men paid money just to chat her up and buy her champagne. That was where she'd met Bongo Fortescue, who farmed outside Hungerford and had never been married despite being forty-six years old. A week later, Amaryllis and Saffron had moved into his large farmhouse with him and the golden retrievers, and had been there for three years. Saffron had learned to ride and went to school, when Amaryllis could get it together to drive her in, at a sixth-form college in Newbury. When she stopped to think about it, which was seldom, Saffron could see that her beautiful, chaotic mother had little in common with the loud, lecherous landowner, but it suited them to stay together.

The consequence of so much turmoil just before leaving was that Saffron had barely had time to pack. She had stuffed into her suitcase whatever she could find in her drawer and on the pulley in the bathroom. Her knickers, she realised, she'd left drying on the rail of the Aga. None of her clothes were ironed and now most had disappeared altogether.

Her bedroom was enormous, on the first floor of the house next to Godfather Marcus's. There were French windows open on to a balcony, and a view across lawns and palm trees to a private mooring on a canal and the sea. Since the holiday in the South of France, Saffron had never set foot out of England, unless you counted Scotland where Bongo had taken a fishing lodge on the Helmsdale last August. Saffron had mixed feelings about that episode, having no interest in salmon and having spent much of the holiday fighting off the attentions of Bongo himself who, fuelled with malt whisky, had twice tried to clamber into her bed after dinner. Saffron couldn't figure out whether this holiday to Lyford Cay had come at exactly the right or the wrong moment, with everything unsettled at home.

There was a tap at the door and an American voice asked,

'Saffron? Is this your room? Do you mind if I step inside for a moment?'

Abigail was enveloped in a pink towelling dressing gown and her hair, evidently just washed, piled on her head in a towel.

'Have you got a hairdryer? I can't seem to find one in my closet.'

'Take a look,' said Saffron. 'I don't own one. But if you can find one, take it.'

Abigail's jaw dropped. 'You mean, you don't use a hair-dryer?'

Saffron shook her head, sat up on the bed and pushed back the muslins. 'I suppose we should go and have lunch.'

'What are you wearing?' asked Abigail nervously.

'What I came in, I think. I didn't bring much. I could wear this pink bikini, I suppose. It's my mother's. It just happened to slip into my case by itself.'

Saffron peeled off her t-shirt and shorts and stepped into the bikini bottoms. Startled by her sudden nudity, Abigail averted her eyes several seconds too late to avoid registering Saffron's perfect figure.

'You're saying your *mother* wears a bikini like that? Your *mother*?'

'Amaryllis used to be a model. She buys clothes all the time, it's like a disease with her, even when we're broke which we are mostly. Shit, the top of this thing is loose! My tits are pathetic. Amaryllis has these amazing ones. I'm telling you, any man who meets her, it's like, "Well, hello there." They can't keep their eyes off them.'

'I hate mine,' said Abigail. 'They're so big, it's like carrying these two great sacks of *matza* around. Soon as I'm old enough, my mom says I can have them reduced. She has this incredible surgeon who did her eyes.'

Saffron padded over to the dressing table and put on a pair of feather earrings: they were like downy partridge feathers, painted yellow, green and red, and dangled from her lobes on tiny gold hooks.

'Those are cute,' said Abigail. 'Are they from Fiorucci?'

'Miss Selfridge.' Saffron was opening and closing drawers

81

in the dressing table. 'Thank God, here they are. I thought my fags had been nicked.' She removed a Marlboro from a packet and lit up.

'You *smoke*?' said Abigail.

'I keep trying to kick it, but it never seems to work. I'm back below a pack a day, it's better than it was.'

There was a second knock at the door and a voice said, 'Miss Weaver? Mr Brand says lunch will be served on the terrace in five minutes.'

'Oh, my God,' said Abigail. 'I'm not dressed and my hair isn't dry or anything. What should I wear, Saffron? I've been reviewing my choices, and nothing seems appropriate.'

'You had a trouser suit on earlier. Wear that.'

'I couldn't. That's for travelling and it's creased from the flight. I though maybe something short . . . or I have this Norma Kamali beach wrap from Bergdorf's.'

'Either sounds great.' Saffron took her cigarette into the bathroom and prodded the butt down the plughole of the basin. 'I'm not sure Marcus approves. Better not leave any evidence. See you outside.'

Marcus, the three boys and Mary were already sitting down. Charlie was telling Marcus that he was thinking of going into the Army for three years after school. 'A Short Service Commission. Obviously it has to be with a regiment stationed in London.' Two ample-hipped Bahamian cooks in pinafores and aprons were flipping grey hamburgers on a barbecue under the spreading branches of an umbrella tree, and Bartholomew the butler was circling the table with a bottle of Sancerre wrapped in a linen napkin.

Saffron, picking her way across the coarse grass in her bare feet and pink bikini, was only dimly aware of all four men at the table staring at her, with various degrees of appreciation, love, lust and regret. Marcus, sizing her up through half-closed eyelids, privately predicted that in three or four years' time his goddaughter would be one of the most beautiful and desirable women in the world. Stuart, unable to look directly at her owing to the sun's glare, gawped awkwardly at the approaching vision, knowing he was painfully in love, and that nothing mattered except somehow making an impression on her. Charlie stood up, pulled out the canvas chair next to his own with a flourish, and said, 'Saffron. Come and sit down here. You look terrific. What amazing earrings: did you shoot the birds yourself?' Jamie was thinking that Saffron had the best legs, and was wondering whether it would be bad form to have a crack at her himself, considering Charlie had already more or less bagged her.

Abigail's appearance on the terrace in a baby-pink one-piece swimsuit covered with tiny gold beads, floppy pink trousers and matching towelling turban, coincided with the arrival of lunch.

Looking round at the expanse of lawn, the private mooring, the cooks in their pinafores stationed behind the smoky barbecue, Charlie said, 'It's enormously kind of you to ask us all here, Marcus. You really are being amazingly generous. This is an incredible place.'

'I'm glad you think so.' Marcus's reply was chilly. A deliberate pause, then: 'Tell you what, Charlie, I wouldn't overdo the flattery if I were you. Has a way of being misinterpreted. Act too grateful, makes people think, "He's over-impressed. Maybe he doesn't deserve to be here".'

It took Charlie a moment or two to absorb the put-down, then he turned deep red and stared, stunned, down at his plate.

Mary, wanting desperately to say something in his defence, said, 'But isn't it good manners to thank people? That's what I was taught.'

Marcus tilted his head, considering the question. 'Depends on the situation, frankly. Chap who carries your suitcases, delivers your breakfast, thank him – her – certainly, bloody rude not to, providing you with a service. Same thing with a driver, caddy, tart come to that. But you wouldn't gush at your lawyer, would you? Stockbroker neither. Question of social parity. Doesn't do to be thanking your host all the time, only point I'm making, makes people think you're out of your depth.'

Over lunch, Marcus explained to the children the rules applicable to guests of members at the Lyford Cay Club.

He put on a pair of half-lens tortoiseshell spectacles and studied a small card of rules, with the badge of the club embossed in gold on the front, its crossed tennis rackets, golf clubs, sailing boat and blue marlin set into the quarterings.

'Main thing you need to grasp,' Marcus said, 'is that you can't pay for anything with cash. Anything you want to do, sign for it. Sign your name on the chit, then write mine – Brand – so they know to send the bill to me. Whatever you decide – tennis, diving, lunch at the club by the pool – sign away. And I'll tell you now, whichever one of you has the lowest bill at the end of the week, I'll be disappointed in them. I want you to have *fun*. Whole point of being here. Got that everybody? Abigail?' He smiled in her direction. 'They've got a beauty place here, somewhere up behind the croquet lawn. Do use it. Could be quite wrong, but I have the impression you rather go in for that sort of thing.'

Abigail flushed, wondering whether Marcus's crack implied he thought she needed to visit the beauty salon. At home, she went twice a week for hair and nails, but sun and salt water caused havoc on vacation.

'Other thing to watch out for,' he said, 'is the dress regulations. They do rather mind what people wear here, different times of the day – I blame the American members, much more formal than the Brits, whatever they say. Spend half their time fussing about, changing one outfit for another. I've asked Barbara to place a copy of the rule book in each of your bedrooms, so take a look at it, will you? Load of bollocks about whites on the tennis courts and ties for men in the clubhouse after seven o'clock.'

He addressed himself to Stuart. 'Don't know whether or not you've brought a tie along, but if not, ask Bartholomew, he keeps an emergency supply. Charlie I'm sure's brought plenty, ten at least. That right, Charlie? Brought plenty of ties with you to the Bahamas?'

'Actually yes, Marcus. I did bring a couple, just in case.'

'There you are, you see. Well-organised chap. I like that. Full marks.'

Charlie had by now recovered his brio, and was anxious to

re-establish himself in Marcus's eyes as the most worldly and sophisticated of the godchildren.

'How's your car business going, Marcus? I saw an article in the newspapers about you buying some factory up in Manchester or Coventry or somewhere.'

'Birmingham.'

'That's right. God, rather you than me. I hope you don't actually have to go up there too often.'

'Twice a year. In and out in a day. Lot more at the beginning, though. We had some teething trouble with the workforce, but that's settled down.'

'That's what I read. You smashed the unions after that strike. You really stood up to them. They were actually storming your factory, and the police didn't lift a finger to stop them.'

Marcus shrugged. 'It was quite hairy at the time. But I came to the conclusion that it was preferable to have one major confrontation, and try and win it, than get caught in an endless round of fruitless negotiations.'

'If everyone faced them down like you did,' stated Charlie, sounding suddenly very self-important, like a man forty years older, 'the unions could be emasculated for good. That's what should happen with the miners, car workers, hospital porters . . . whole damn' lot of them. They should all be completely smashed, only this government's too cowardly to take them on.'

Stuart, who had barely uttered a word during lunch, and was already mad at Charlie for manoeuvring Saffron so smoothly next to him, erupted, 'You don't know what you're talking about, Charlie. I bet you haven't even met a union member, not in your whole life.' His Birmingham accent became stronger and thicker as he got riled.

'Sorry, were you talking to me?' said Charlie, one eyebrow arched, a half-sneer playing on his lips. 'I didn't quite catch what you said there. My ears must still be blocked from the aeroplane.'

'You heard,' said Stuart. 'I said, you're talking through your arse. You don't know anything about unions, or what they do to protect working people against unscrupulous owners.' Stuart felt suddenly furious. Adrenaline was pumping around inside him; a muscle had tightened in his neck. People like Charlie understood nothing. His smugness was offensive. What did he know about good men like Mick's dad, who'd given fifteen years of his life to the chassis works and then, the minute he became dispensable, was kicked out without a second thought? Four years he'd been out of work now, and the local employment office no longer bothered to pretend they'd find him anything.

'You are, of course, quite right that I don't have first-hand experience of industrial relations,' said Charlie. 'But I do actually know about working-class people, or anyway Scottish working people who are admittedly a superior example of the species. Every Saturday from mid-August until October we employ more than eighty of them as beaters, and about twenty men on the estate all year round. Not to mention several of their wives who came up to Ardnessaig to help and have been with us, some of them, for more than twenty years. So please don't tell me I don't know any working-class types.'

Mary, rooting for Charlie, felt that he had come back brilliantly at the ghastly Stuart, and put him firmly in his place.

'Have you even visited an industrial town?' Stuart asked.

'I've been through Crewe on the train.'

'If you did, you might learn something.' Stuart wished he was more articulate, but the words wouldn't come. How could he hope to explain what he meant to anyone sitting in this tropical garden, with servants everywhere and butlers pouring wine? No way were they going to get it.

'He's right, you know.' Marcus, who had been watching the argument with detached amusement, waited while Bartholomew refilled his glass. 'Stuart's absolutely right about one thing. You've never been within a hundred miles of a factory, Charlie. Or down a mine.'

'Rather hope I never have to,' he replied. 'There was an old cellar at my prep school, Broadley Court, and they used to lock you down there for a couple of hours in the dark if you fooled about. Known as the Black Hole. Jamie was always in there, weren't you, Jamie? Anyway, that was as close as I've ever come to being a coal miner.'

'Your mother's family, the Arbroaths, made their money out of coal.'

Charlie looked flustered. 'I don't think so. Actually they've been at Arbroath since the thirteenth century.'

'And entirely rebuilt it in 1870 with their coal fortune. Your family were pit owners. Important to recognise in life where the folding stuff derives from.'

Then, switching his attention to Stuart, Marcus said, 'When you castigated unscrupulous owners, Stuart, I trust it wasn't your godfather you had in mind?' His eyes were twinkling, but the slight downward tilt of the head and those searching eyes expected an answer.

'Not especially,' replied Stuart. He had recovered his composure, and was wondering what Saffron had made of the spat. Sided with Charlie probably, since they came from the same class. 'I was making a general point.'

'Well, permit me to make a general point of my own,' said Marcus, 'and then we must allow these poor working people here to get on with their job of clearing the table. If you did have my stewardship of the Smethwick Chassis Works even half in mind during your disturbingly socialistic outburst, let me leave you with one thought. If I hadn't bought the business six years ago – and at that time there were slightly more than 2,800 employees and an almost full order book of exclusively loss-making work – then the whole bang-shooting match would be long over by now. Finished. Gates locked, plant hammered and nobody left beyond a night-watchman on a stool and a couple of loose dogs, hoping to take a bite out of some luckless trespasser's backside. As it is, we have 1,100 employees, a full order book of profitable work, a thriving business, state-of-the-art plant and a reputation for reliability that we never, ever had before. Can't pretend I relished booting seventeen hundred men on to the scrapheap of history, but nor did I have sleepless nights about it either.'

Marcus pushed back his chair, his pragmatics lecture apparently making him impatient to get on. 'Dinner at the club tonight at eight o'clock, be ready to leave at quarter to. This afternoon, do what you like. Swim, tennis, whatever. If anyone feels like a boat ride out to the cays, tell the boatboys. Fuck-all else they've got to do. There are beaches they know on the Exumas, if you want to dive.'

After he'd gone, the godchildren fell silent for a moment. His presence had been so overpowering, and so much the point of gravity of the lunch, it took time to adjust. Then Abigail announced that she was going inside to find a hairdryer, and Mary wondered whether they should all offer to help with the washing up, and Saffron, without saying anything, went down to the beach alone to smoke. Charlie, pointedly excluding Stuart, said, 'Jamie, come on, let's go out in a boat. Marcus said his people would take us.'

At the mooring, a white speedboat was lashed to the jetty and Carlton, head boatboy to Marcus Brand, sixty years old with skin like cracked rubber, was hovering by the door of his wooden boathouse. Inside, water skis, rods, tackle, wetsuits and oxygen canisters for diving were stored, in perfect order, on wooden pallets. Ten minutes later they were speeding out to sea, looking back at the receding white mansions of the Lyford Cay Club.

'So,' said Jamie, the wind blowing his hair back from his face, 'what do you make of our fellow godchildren?'

Charlie chuckled. 'I'd describe us as a bit of a mixed bag, wouldn't you? And that's the biggest understatement of the year. Starting with that communist – God knows what he's doing here, or why he's even Marcus's godson. Can't work that one out at all.'

'And the girls? Scores out of ten, please.'

'Ten for Saffron, no question. Jesus, she's a complete sexpot! At lunch, I started getting a hard-on just sitting next to her. Hope she didn't notice.'

'You should have put her hand on your lap,' said Jamie. 'Napkin on top, no problem.'

Charlie laughed.

'Why not?' said Jamie. 'I would have, in your position. Girls like Saffron, they expect it.'

'Seriously?' Despite his bravado, Charlie's romantic experience to date consisted of exchanging letters with several pretty schoolgirls at Heathfield, and a seven-minute deep-throat snogging session at the Feathers Ball.

'Sure. Quickest way of letting a woman know you fancy her. Never fails. Well, not that often.'

Charlie looked thoughtful. His mother, Lady Crieff, had never found it convenient to bath her children, and the only woman who had seen Charlie naked since birth was Nanny Arbroath. The prospect of getting off with Saffron Weaver during the holiday excited and rather scared him.

'Want some wine?' Jamie was drawing the cork from a half bottle.

'Where on earth did you get that?'

'Fridge in our room. I told you, it's crammed with booze.' He took a swig from the bottle and passed it to Charlie. 'Come on, stop drooling over Saffron. You haven't marked the other girls.'

'Now that's more difficult,' said Charlie. 'Are we allowed to award minus points?'

'Abby, you mean?'

'What a dog! Woof, woof. One out of ten . . . no, too generous. A half, more like.'

'I'd give her a three or four.'

'Four? You crazy? Imagine actually doing it with her, you wouldn't even be able to find the hole under all that blubber.'

'I quite fancy big women,' said Jamie carelessly. 'And you saw her tits?'

'You fancy everyone, that's your problem.'

'Probably. Apart from your sister. The one with the moustache and the bone through her nose.'

'Mary Jane? My mother's been trying to marry her off to some neighbour, but it isn't getting anywhere. Pity, he's got great shooting.'

'But is he blind?' asked Jamie.

'God, no. He's one of the best shots in Angus.'

'That's the trouble then, tell your mother. With Mary Jane, she wants to set her up with a blind man.'

Both boys laughed. They'd been refining their cracks

about Charlie's sisters for seven years, since their first term at Broadley Court. It was part of the infrastructure of their friendship.

'You haven't marked Mary yet,' Jamie said.

'Mary? I need to think about that.' Charlie ho-hummed as the speedboat puttered into a sandy bay, partly ringed by a coral reef.

'Quite a pretty face. Probably a bit thick, which is not a problem. Nice eyes. Couldn't really tell about her body under that white dress. I'm reserving judgement until we see her in a swimsuit.'

'That's cheating. You have to say.'

'OK, a six then. Seven with a good body. But next to Saffron, no contest.'

They waded ashore and mooched about the beach, tossing coconut husks into the sea and finishing the wine, and then the second bottle which Jamie had hidden in a towel.

'How come Marcus is so rich anyway?' Charlie asked. 'My parents say it came from his wife originally, the one who died.'

'I think it's mostly property, that's according to my father. And he owns a lot of factories now too. The car factory and all kinds of other things, biscuits and jam and so on.'

'What my mother calls dirty money.'

'Why dirty?'

'Biscuits and car factories – and property speculating? Come on, it doesn't sound particularly nice, does it? I mean, if someone asked you what you did for your living, you wouldn't want to admit to it, would you? "I bake biscuits".'

'It wouldn't bother me, not if I was loaded like Marcus.'

'You're only saying that because your father's a property tycoon himself.'

'I wish. He isn't such a tycoon any more. Divorcing my mother nearly cleaned him out. Anyway,' Jamie said, 'your parents have never approved of Marcus. I'm surprised they allowed you to come on this jaunt.'

'My mother's very anti-him. She says nobody knows anything about him or where he came from, which is the sort of thing that matters to her, bloodlines. But they don't object as much as they did, probably because he's done so well.'

'You mean, once there's enough of it, it doesn't matter where the money comes from.'

Charlie didn't reply directly but said, 'Marcus is obviously rolling. Some of those pictures in the library are really good, even if he did have to buy them.' Then he said, 'Jamie, do you remember in France, something Marcus said on the last day? We were all outside on the terrace, celebrating some deal he'd done.'

'He asked what we'd buy if we had a fortune. You chose an Aston Martin.'

'Yeah, but afterwards. Something he said later. About how, if he didn't have children, he might leave the lot to us, his godchildren.'

'Vaguely,' Jamie said. 'It was seven years ago.'

'He definitely said it. And he still doesn't have any.'

'Well, he probably will.'

'He might not. There's a chance. In which case . . .'

'You're so calculating, Charlie. Our godfather invites us to stay, and already you're eyeing up his stuff.'

Charlie laughed. 'But it's worth bearing in mind. Someone's going to get it all one day.'

Having no other plans, and finding nobody about at the villa, Stuart took a lonely walk around the perimeter of the golf course, watching decrepit old men in canary yellow trousers ease themselves out of golf buggies, stagger across the green and attempt a short putt while a caddy held the flag above the hole. Unused to being away from home, and conscious of how different he was from Marcus's other godchildren, Stuart already regretted coming to the Bahamas. He had accepted the invitation because, instinctively, he knew he should pass up no opportunity to expand his horizons. He had wanted to see the West Indies and this was his chance. But it was all quite different from his expectations. Instead of the open blue seas and pirate coves of his imagination, he was plodding around a fairway full of senile

Americans inside a concentration camp for rich idiots. This wasn't the real West Indies. On their way from the airport, they'd passed brightly coloured wooden shacks with corrugated roofs, and goats rooting about outside in the dirt, but that was as close as Stuart had come to real life. He felt ambivalent towards Marcus – half despising him for making the men redundant in Smethwick, half fascinated by his vitality and power. He was awkward in Marcus's presence, too, because Marcus's wife had died in that crash while his father was driving. Stuart couldn't help feeling that it must have been partly his dad's fault, and this made him uncomfortable and unworthy, a cuckoo in the nest.

The other godchildren mostly seemed OK, though he doubted they had much in common. Charlie he loathed for his snobbishness and, even more, for his self-assurance. If it wasn't for Saffron, he might as well go straight home to Birmingham and get ahead with his A-level syllabus reading. But Saffron was different. He felt if he could only sit down with her and have a really good talk, without any of the Lyford Cay crap going on, they'd probably get on really well, and then you never knew what might happen.

Having found a hairdryer and sorted through her clothes, Abigail was at a loose end. She was also starving. At lunch, she'd taken a small plate of salad with no dressing and a burger with no bun. Seeing Saffron in the buff had freaked her out, and she was on a crash diet. At fat camp in the summer the coaches taught them, 'Slow and steady, no sudden weight swings,' but they hadn't had to contend with Saffron. Feeling unbearably guilty, Abigail opened the mini-bar and removed the Fritos corn chips and Lays potato crisps. Then, just for good measure, she grabbed the Hershey bar. It was a long time till dinner.

Saffron, meanwhile, on her tenth Marlboro of the day, was thinking she quite liked Jamie. He was a laugh. His friend Charlie, she couldn't work out at all; he was like an old geezer in that straw hat of his, and slimy too. Stuart in the specs seemed all right, a bit nerdy maybe. As for Godfather Marcus, he'd do for her mum. Amaryllis needed a new sugar daddy.

Sharply at a quarter to eight, the jeeps were driven round to the front door for the short journey to the clubhouse. Stuart had been provided by Bartholomew with an embossed silk tie which looked oddly bulky over his denim shirt. The godchildren were directed into the second jeep while Marcus rode in the first, accompanied by a predatory young American, newly arrived, named Clayborne Dupuis. Abigail, who knew about such matters, identified her as Marcus's interior decorator, responsible for the furbishment of Sandy Cove.

'She's not bad either,' Jamie whispered to Charlie as they set off. 'Do you suppose anything's going on between her and Marcus?'

Charlie shrugged. 'I wouldn't chance it, if that's what you mean. Anyway, she must be nearly thirty.'

The bar and dining room of the club were packed, the air thick with the scent of Chanel No. 5, mint Juleps and old WASP money. Mary had never seen so much conspicuous jewellery; her little gold bracelet, with its prancing pony, lucky horseshoe and teddy bear charms, seemed pathetically thin and tinny on her wrist by comparison. Abigail's mother, Harriet Schwartzman, who had never been to Lyford Cay but read all about it in *Town & Country*, had informed her daughter that it was one of the only resorts in the Caribbean where it was obligatory to dress up to your wealth level. Consequently, Abigail was unique among Marcus's six godchildren in looking completely at home in the clubhouse, on account of her strapless Halston resortwear.

Several members eyed up Saffron and Clayborne as they arrived. Charlie was oblivious to this but Jamie, who instinctively read the sexual temperature, stuck close to Saffron. Marcus was standing at the bar with Clayborne, his hand resting lightly on her bottom. Watching him, Jamie noticed that while Marcus was ostensibly giving her his full attention, he was also sizing up the other people in room. Several of the older members were surreptitiously watching him; disapprovingly, Jamie felt. He got the impression that certain members were avoiding Marcus. If so, he wondered how his godfather had managed to become a member at all, since the Lyford Cay committee was notoriously tricky, regularly making borderline applicants wait for decades before turning them down.

Throughout dinner Marcus was in a haze of irritable preoccupation, hardly bothering with his godchildren. Mary, seated next to him, felt it must be her fault for being boring, as her various conversational sallies fizzled out, one after another. Charlie asked Saffron whether she knew anybody who lived in Scotland, and she replied that she didn't, and that she'd only visited once with her mum's boyfriend. Normally he would have interpreted this as a sign of massive social gaucherie, but with Saffron he saw it as a plus, since all girls wanted to get into the Scottish set and he could be the conduit. He suggested she should come north and stay at Ardnessaig for the Ball of Kirriemuir, but Saffron, oblivious to the honour, said she had no particular wish to revisit Scotland. Stuart, who still hadn't addressed a word to her, took heart from the rebuff, feeling that it cleared the way for him. Jamie, who had read somewhere that women found it sexy if you stared very hard at their lips without making eye contact, tested the technique first on Saffron, then Clayborne, with no visible results.

Their week in the Bahamas repeated the pattern of the first day. Jamie and Charlie spent their afternoons deep-sea fishing or scuba diving from the boat. Stuart rapidly came to despise the claustrophobic snobbery of the Lyford Cay Club with a passion. Refusing on principle to run up bills around the swimming pool, he swam alone in the sea, each day covering a greater distance. He would set himself goals, entering the water from the strip of private beach below Sandy Cove and swimming a couple of hundred yards out until he was clear of the line of buoys. Then he turned in a southerly direction, swimming parallel to the great white mansions along the shore until he had covered a distance of at least two miles. He swam steadily and mechanically, never hurrying. What was there to hurry for? All that awaited him back at the house were further fatuous remarks from that prick Charlie Crieff. The solitude of the ocean gave him space to think about Saffron, with whom he was by now •

obsessed. She was an angel, a goddess. There wasn't a hope she'd be interested in a bloke from the backend of Smethwick – but he did hope. Once, as he neared the beach after one of his marathon swims, he spotted Saffron smoking amidst the sea grape in the sand dunes, but by the time he'd waded ashore, she had vanished.

Mary and Abigail played tennis each morning with a handsome Danish professional, though Mary could think only of Charlie. When she had overheard him invite Saffron to Scotland, she'd thought her heart would break, though the sensation was, in itself, nothing new. At school, she was accustomed to being picked among the last for everything; prettier, more popular girls were always chosen ahead of her, but she was resilient. Her sweet nature led her to live in hope, but without undue expectation, that one day wonderful things would happen to her.

One hot afternoon, walking over the dunes in the hope of spotting Charlie, Mary almost tripped over Saffron who started and guiltily stubbed out a Marlboro in the sand.

'Oh, I'm sorry,' Mary said, blushing. 'I didn't realise anyone was here.' She began to hurry on, never quite knowing what to say to Saffron who always looked like a fashion model.

'Want a cigarette?' Saffron held out her pack.

'Oh, no, thank you. I don't really smoke. But thanks for offering.'

Saffron smiled. 'I always come down here for a fag after lunch. Well, three or four, let's face it. I asked Marcus if he'd mind me smoking up at the house, and he said he would. Don't let on, will you?'

Mary shook her head. But she felt uncomfortable at the thought of deceiving their godfather.

'Do you know him very well? Marcus, I mean.' Saffron was lighting up a fresh cigarette.

'Not that well. He's a friend of my father's. Used to be, anyway. I don't exactly know, I don't think they've seen each other much recently.' Mary felt confused. The whole business about Marcus Brand being her godfather was a slight mystery to her. Her father talked about him a great deal, but Marcus had never visited their house so far as she could remember. At her Confirmation, he had pulled out on the day of the service.

'What about you? I suppose your parents are great friends of Marcus's?'

'You must be joking. The only time I've even met him was that holiday in France.'

'How come he's your godfather then?'

Saffron shrugged. 'Amaryllis – that's my mum – said he was mates with my father before I was born.'

'Haven't they stayed friends?'

'God knows. I haven't clapped eyes on Dad for thirteen years. He walked out on us. He lives in Ireland somewhere, I think.'

Mary felt awful for asking the question. Loving and admiring her own father so much, she couldn't imagine what it would be like not having one. 'I'm so sorry. I didn't mean to pry.'

Saffron slowly exhaled smoke from her mouth. 'It's no big deal. I can hardly remember him actually, he left when I was two. He used to visit us sometimes, but then stopped coming. I don't even know what he does now. He's a gypsy, I think, or something like that.'

Mary squatted on her heels in the sand, trying to imagine how Marcus had ever come to be friends with an Irish gypsy.

'Anyway, we're very lucky to have a godfather like him, aren't we?' she said. 'It's so generous of him to bring us all here on holiday.'

'You don't think it's a bit weird?' Saffron replied. 'No, of course you don't, you don't think that at all. Forget I even said it. I've just had some bad experiences lately, and it's making me over-cynical, that's all.'

Marcus's attendance at lunch and dinner was unpredictable; much of his time he spent in his office negotiating, so he explained, the purchase of a manganese mine in Mexico. His lawyer Dick Mathias made fleeting visits, arriving with a briefcase full of documents for signature. Abigail, alert to slights, noticed that when Marcus did show up for meals, he invariably placed himself between Saffron and Clayborne, and never next to her.

Marcus announced that, in honour of their last night, he had ordered up a barbecue on the beach behind the house with a steel band that Mrs Miles had somehow located in the main town of Nassau. Jamie looked meaningfully at Charlie. 'This is it. Tonight, after the barbecue, we move.'

'How?'

'I told you, drinks in the cottage. They're total sitting ducks.'

Charlie nodded. Although far from convinced that he had made sufficient headway with Saffron for her to be regarded as a sitting duck, he didn't want to admit this to Jamie, Saffron having been designated 'his' for the duration of the holiday. Anyway, you couldn't tell with women. One minute they blanked you, the next they were tacit participants in a tongue sandwich. That, at least, had been Charlie's experience of the species in his life to date.

'What about you?' he asked. 'Who are you getting off with? You haven't said.'

Jamie smiled mysteriously. 'Playing this one by ear actually.'

'Come on, don't be a jerk.'

'I mean it, I don't know. I've been putting out feelers, nothing definite.'

Dozens of glass lanterns with candles inside were dotted in a crescent on the beach, and two large barbecue drums glowing with charcoal. Carlton and the boatboys, got up for the occasion in chef's hats and grinning sheepishly at the novelty, were taking directions from Bartholomew as the swordfish steaks and giant prawns were placed on the blackened iron grill. Just out of range of the heat was a long buffet table and the cooks from Sandy Cove in their pinafores and aprons were presiding over an array of elaborate salads: rice salad, lobster salad, fava bean salad, dishes of coleslaw, platters of yams and half coconuts filled with mayonnaise, blue cheese and thousand island dressing. The nine-man steel band had their oil drums and egg whisks set up under the floodlit palms, and embarked on a fairground cover-version of 'Barbados', bonging and donging beneath the stars.

Surf was breaking in fat white bolsters. Marcus, accompanied by Barbara Miles, Dick Mathias and the girls from the office, arrived on the beach to inspect everything.

'What have you got for us here, Carlton?'

'Dem's swordfish, Mr Brand.'

'Catch them ourselves, did we, or buy them in?'

'Catch dem, chief. Denzil went out early in the rigger.'

'Good man, Denzil,' Marcus said approvingly. Bartholomew, handing round rum punches in coconuts for the godchildren, broke off to deliver a flute of champagne to his employer.

'This band of yours capable of playing anything less dirge-like?' Marcus asked Barbara Miles. 'Sounds like they're burying a cat.'

Mrs Miles scurried over to the band and the music died away mid-beat to be replaced by a lively version of 'Brown-Skinned Girl, Come Home and Marry Me'.

'Come on, *dance* everybody!' commanded Marcus. 'Put your drinks down. These local boys – the band – they like to see pretty white girls dance, don't disappoint them.'

Stuart and Charlie both gravitated towards Saffron. Her long legs, brown as butterscotch from hours spent smoking in the dunes, looked ravishing that night in tiny yellow hotpants. Stuart, with half a glass of rum inside him, was determined not to chicken out.

'Saffron.' Marcus strode across the sand towards her. 'Come and start the dancing with me. Hardly seen a thing of you all week.' He draped his arm around her waist and manoeuvred her towards the patch of flat sand which was the dancefloor. Seeing the chief and this beautiful girl taking the floor, the band raised the tempo, egging them on as they began to rock and roll.

Marcus was a smooth and controlled dancer. 'Relax your wrists and allow yourself to be led,' he told Saffron, twirling her round for the third time.

'Are you always so bossy?' she asked, as he spun her back on herself. Her eyes sparkled with the exertion.

'Oh, yes, always,' Marcus replied gruffly.

Stuart asked Abigail to dance and they were bopping about on the edge of the floor. Abigail was a surprisingly nimble dancer, as fat people often are, prancing about on neat little feet, occasionally waving her arms above her head as she had been taught at the Mount Bethesda Academy of Dancing. Stuart considered this embarrassing and contrived, and tried to give the impression that Abigail was a totally separate entity from himself, refusing to catch her eye. At one point he sensed Saffron glancing at him, and did his best to smoulder like James Dean.

Charlie said to Mary, 'I suppose we'd better dance,' and boogied ahead on to the dancefloor, leaving her to follow. Overcome with shyness and happiness, Mary hopped from one foot to the other to the music, and shook her arms from side to side like someone sieving peas. Charlie, fists clenched and gyrating like a steam engine, watched Saffron entwined with Marcus. It shocked him that she and their godfather were slow dancing. Marcus leaned forward and whispered something into Saffron's ear. She giggled. Charlie wondered whether Saffron was flirting with Marcus. If so, she was a complete and utter tart.

Charlie wasn't the only person watching developments on the dancefloor. Clayborne and Jamie, bopping alongside, had both noticed Marcus's behaviour, and it was making Clayborne unhappy. Ever since she'd arrived, she'd felt him withdrawing from her and was aware her time was nearly up. Their afternoon love-making, though Marcus had been as technically attentive as ever, had lacked conviction, and he had even queried her latest, massively inflated invoice which he'd never done before. No question, the writing was on the wall. She'd miss all this: the jewellery and the rest of it.

She didn't believe Marcus would seriously try anything with the blonde – she was fifteen, for goodness' sake. But it was a humiliating finale all the same. Clayborne flung her arms round Jamie's neck, and he pressed his groin against hers, following his own excellent advice.

The band broke for supper but Marcus announced that

Saffron was feeling unwell and he was taking her up to the house.

'What's wrong with her?' Clayborne asked, sardonically. 'Love sickness?'

'Touch of sunstroke,' Marcus replied. 'Don't break up the party, I'll handle this.'

'I bet you will too,' murmured Clayborne under her breath.

Stuart and Charlie stood rooted to the spot as Saffron, head pressed into Marcus's shoulder, mounted the shallow stone steps from the beach and allowed herself to be led up the lantern-lined path to Sandy Cove. Speechless, they watched her go, until they saw the French doors from the terrace into the library open and close, while the steel band launched into the latest Bob Marley hit.

Jamie was already on his fourth rum and Coke which had stimulated in him a thirst for more, and different, alcohol.

'Party-time everybody,' he declared. 'We're all going back to our cottage. You coming, Clayborne?'

She shrugged. All too aware she'd let the big fish slip from her hook, she didn't see why she shouldn't have a bit of fun. At the very least it would annoy Marcus. Besides, the boy was cute.

Charlie, Mary, Stuart and Abigail arrived at the guest cottage to find the fridge door open and a cluster of miniatures on the glass surface of the bamboo dressing table. Jamie was swigging Curacao from the bottle.

'Help yourselves,' he told everyone. 'There's everything: brandy, vodka, whisky . . .'

Mary took a sip of the white wine that Charlie tipped into a toothmug with the words Sandy Cove painted into the glaze. She felt gloriously, impossibly happy. As they had walked together up from the beach, he had taken her hand. He had actually sought out her hand in the darkness, squeezed and held on to it for ten seconds. And she had returned the pressure. Charlie hadn't said anything, but the message could not have been clearer. He loved her. She felt delirious. For the whole week she had hankered hopelessly after Charlie, not knowing whether he felt anything for her at all. And all the time he did! She watched him joking with Jamie across the room. Jamie was mixing a deadly champagne cocktail with white rum and Courvoisier which he was assuring Clayborne would blow the top of her head off: 'Or, better still, blow your top off!' Charlie was laughing his wonderful, confident laugh. Mary felt so lucky to be going out with someone like him.

Over the subsequent months, whenever she relived the events in the pink guest cottage until they assumed a kind of cinematic intensity, Mary was amazed by how quickly everything had happened. One minute she was drinking her toothmug of wine, and the next Jamie and Clayborne were rolling about together on the bedcover, and Clayborne was actually topless. Mary had hardly been able to believe it: an *adult* undressing in front of everybody. She had turned her face away, shocked by what was going on.

'But what if Marcus comes?' she'd asked nervously.

'Believe me, honey, he will,' Clayborne replied, from somewhere underneath Jamie. 'But it takes him ages, smart guy.'

Then Charlie had clamped his arms around Mary's waist and said, 'Let's go outside.' They stumbled together to the edge of the golf course, not even holding hands, and then Charlie had stopped and looked at her and pulled back her head and, suddenly lunging, thrust his tongue inside her mouth and down her throat. For fifteen minutes they swayed together, joined at the lips, their tongues slithering and jabbing like two copulating lizards in a drainpipe. Twice, Charlie tried to slip his fingers inside the white lacey cups of Mary's bra, but she shook her head and he reluctantly retreated.

'We'd better go back inside,' Charlie had said eventually. 'Or they'll be wondering where we are.'

6: October, 1973

Mary's life at the Convent of the Perpetual Martyr, Chobham, was transformed; the fact that she had an official
boyfriend – that she was going out with Charlie Crieff –
altered everything utterly.

It was no exaggeration to say that, of her fifteen waking
hours a day, Mary devoted five to pondering her relationship
with Charlie. During lessons, she practised writing her
signature with the surname Crieff: Mary Crieff, Mary Crieff,
Mary Crieff. Over time, it became second nature. In her
dormitory, or perambulating the lacrosse pitch during
break, she discussed him *ad nauseam* with her friends. The
acquisition of a boyfriend, as news of him spread, actually
widened Mary's circle of friendship. Girls who had previously never bothered much about her, now included her,
either because they had boyfriends themselves at Charlie's
school, or wished they did. In chapel, Mary prayed for
Charlie, and prayed that she might receive a reply to her last
three love letters.

Their romance had assumed, in the constant retelling,
the quality of a fairytale: how they had danced together on a
candle-lit beach in the Bahamas, the lapping of the waves
on the sand, the amazing steel band that her godfather
Marcus Brand had specially hired for the barbecue (so
superior to anything you got in England), the moment
that Charlie first held her hand. She wished she had a
photograph of him. In each letter she asked him for one,
but he hadn't sent one yet. She hoped he'd be smiling in the
picture, because he was so handsome when he smiled, and
that he'd be wearing one of his stripy shirts and Panama
hat. The post at the convent was distributed shortly before
lunch, and she got butterflies every day at the thought of a
letter in his handwriting.

So far, Mary had written seven letters to Charlie and

received one reply. At the stationer's in Chobham they sold special envelopes and writing paper, pink and lime green, and she had walked into town one half-holiday and bought a whole stack. She had developed a new signature which incorporated a smiley face into the big, round 'a' of Mary. On the back of the envelope she printed SWALK – sealed with a loving kiss – but after she'd posted it, and it was too late, she wondered whether Charlie would like that, and regretted it.

His letter back to her – her most precious possession, with talismanic status – had been less forthcoming than her letters to him, probably because he was a man. He had thanked her for her correspondence, and said there had been a Scottish dance last Saturday against St Mary's; Jamie had got off with some scrubber and been gated for taking her into the music schools. He was playing a lot of squash. He hoped he would see her soon.

He hoped he would see her soon! Was there ever such unequivocal proof of their extraordinary love?

In the dormitory next to Mary's was a girl called Zara Fane and it turned out that she was a neighbour of Charlie's in Scotland. Mary had never liked Zara but, because of the coincidence, she started to get friendly with her, hoping to pick up any detail about her boyfriend. In return, she had to endure Zara's stories about her own horrible-sounding boyfriend, who rode a dirtbike and, according to Zara, had sex with her outdoors.

'Has Charlie had other girlfriends before me?' Mary asked, in trepidation.

Zara shrugged. She was applying black lipstick to piss off the nuns. 'Couldn't tell you. I doubt it, he's not that cool. He's mostly into shooting.'

'Does he have brothers or sisters?'

'Sisters. Both older. Quite ugly, like Charlie really.'

Mary wanted to protest, but couldn't risk a breach with Zara.

'Tell me again about his house.'

'Why do you want to know? You're not going to marry him or something, are you?'

Mary had thought of little else since their snog on the golf course. She would become Scottish and have his children.

'Just interested.'

'I've told you, it's got turrets and a long drive. The dining room is full of stags' heads. All the big houses round there are the same really.'

One morning a stiff white envelope arrived unexpectedly at school, addressed to Miss Mary Merrett and postmarked Bridge of Esk. The invitation from Lady Crieff to attend a discotheque party for Charlie at Ardnessaig House was the grandest Mary had ever seen. Tucked inside was a hand-written postcard: 'We do hope that you will be able to join our houseparty for this'. It was signed 'Verena Crieff'.

Mary read and reread the invitation a dozen times, scarcely able to believe it. She was going to stay with Charlie. Her boyfriend had asked her to stay.

At the weekend she was due to go home to Dorking for half-term. She longed to show the invitation to her parents, as she had shown it already to half the school. She was slightly anxious her mother wouldn't allow her to go, but she would be seventeen in six months' time, and it would be ridiculous if she couldn't. She wasn't sure either how she was meant to get to the party; she knew how pushed her parents were for money, with the school fees and everything, and the journey to Scotland would be expensive. She prayed it would all work out.

As it turned out, her worries were unnecessary. Both her parents were delighted by Mary's first formal invitation. If truth be told, Belinda Merrett was not unexcited at the thought of her daughter as a houseguest of people like the Crieffs. And Derek, having pretended to give the matter serious consideration, said that since young Charlie Crieff was a fellow godchild of Marcus's, he must surely be a good chap. Derek would be prepared to advance Mary the train fare to Scotland, to be deducted in instalments out of her pocket money.

'My goodness me,' said Belinda when everything had been decided. 'We can't keep up with you these days, Mary. Holidays in the West Indies, dancing with lords and ladies in Scotland . . . We shall have to start thinking about what you're going to wear, won't we, for your first big social occasion?'

7: December, 1973

Two miles before Ardnessaig, the taxi passed through a dour granite village where the only pub was named the Crieff Arms. Already torn between sheer terror about her trip to Scotland, and anticipation of seeing Charlie, Mary stared at the wonky pub sign with its painting of a ferocious clan chieftain in wig and dress tartan. It seemed to her a very impressive thing to have a whole pub named after yourself.

Up ahead lay the granite lodges that marked the entrance to Ardnessaig. The massive iron gates were, as ever, open, long ago collapsed on their hinges into the lawn. A couple of hundred yards beyond the lodges, the drive took a sharp turn to the left, past a bank of rhododendrons, then cut through a huge expanse of lawn – in spring a mass of daffodils but in December desolate and grey as a loch in winter. She could see Ardnessaig now across the lawn, with its crow-stepped gables and turrets. As the taxi drew up at the front door, a part of Mary wished she hadn't come at all.

She paid the driver and carried her mother's little blue suitcase into an outer hall. There were boots everywhere and, on a chest, cartridge bags and gun cases, and a framed Ordnance Survey map showing the boundaries of the Ardnessaig Estate, which was evidently vast.

Nobody seemed to be about, so she ventured further inside into a much larger hall, with shields and muskets fixed to brown panelling and a polished wood staircase leading up to a gallery. The hall smelt of breakfast and wet dog. In a corner stood a mahogany display cabinet containing a collection of old silver cups and horn flasks. Feeling that she shouldn't explore further on her own, Mary waited in the hall, her ears straining for any sign of life.

'Down, you filthy, filthy beast. You will *not* climb up on to that sofa.' A ferocious female voice came from behind a door, followed by several sharp whacks. 'Bad boy, Dougal.

Grrr . . . naughty boy!' The voice made a snarling noise, like someone clearing catarrh from the bottom of their throat. 'Look at that horrible damp place. Grrr . . . bad Dougal.'

Gingerly, Mary knocked on the open door. She was in a drawing room full of sofas and spindly tables covered by family photographs in silver frames.

'Excuse me, I'm Mary Merrett. I've just arrived.'

'Who? Who did you say you are?' A very large, formidable woman in a cardigan and tweed skirt, with a helmet of backcombed black hair and the chilliest eyes Mary had ever seen, peered at her across the room. In one hand she was holding a rolled-up newspaper with which she periodically chastised a black Labrador puppy.

'Mary Merrett. I'm staying with Charlie for his party.'

'Merrett? I don't know that I've ever met a Merrett before. Where are your people from?'

'We live in Surrey, near Dorking.'

'Do you indeed? Good gracious, Surrey. I know people used to live in Surrey once upon a time, but I didn't realise they still did.'

Not knowing how to reply to this, Mary asked, 'Is Charlie here? I'm dying to see him.'

'Out on the hill with everyone else,' said Verena Crieff. 'I'm sure they won't shoot late because of the light. I expect you'd like to be shown your bedroom.' She pressed a bell set into the panelling and eventually a severe-looking woman in black walking shoes appeared in the drawing room. 'Nanny, this is Miss Merrett. She has arrived to stay from Surrey, and says she's one of Charlie's friends. I wonder if you could show her to whichever room you've put her in.'

Mary followed Nanny Arbroath back through the hall and up the stairs. 'Is that all you've brought with you?' Nanny Arbroath said, eyeing Mary's little suitcase suspiciously. 'You do travel light.'

They walked to the end of a wide upstairs corridor with frayed carpets and watercolours of Ardnessaig, and through a door into a more spartan wing of the house, with linoleum on the floor and glazed arrow slits for windows.

'Was this once a castle?' Mary asked.

107

'A castle? Whatever put that idea into your head? The Victorians put this ugly place up, Lord Crieff's great-grandfather. If it's a castle you want, you need to visit Arbroath.'

They stopped outside a bedroom door with the number seventeen painted on it in red paint. A brass nameplate had a slip of card inserted. Mary saw two names: her own and Zara Fane's.

She unpacked, hanging up her new Monsoon dress in a vast wardrobe in which the coat hangers were the size and weight of crowbars. Several planks at the back of the wardrobe had come loose and crashed to the floor, revealing strips of flowery wallpaper, less faded than elsewhere in the room. On the bottom of the wardrobe, which was lined with old newspaper, lay an upturned tin containing yellow pellets of rat poison. It had slightly surprised Mary that Lady Crieff hadn't seemed to know she was Charlie's girlfriend, but it didn't really matter. At least she was here.

Mary examined her dress and was relieved to find it had survived the journey without much creasing. It was mauve and yellow tartan, with a ruffle at the neck, and it made her look taller and slimmer than she actually was. She hoped Charlie would like her in it.

Voices below and car doors slamming drew her to the window. Three Land Rovers had drawn up in front of the house and a dozen figures in shooting clothes were unloading guns and releasing dogs from the back. At first Mary couldn't spot Charlie among the guns, but then she saw him, his curly hair concealed beneath a tweed cap, standing with Jamie Temple. Next to Jamie was Zara Fane who, to Mary's astonishment, was also wearing a cap and carrying a shotgun.

She raced downstairs, her heart full of love. Charlie was distributing tips to the beaters. He turned and saw her. 'Oh, hi, Mary. I didn't expect you'd be able to make it, actually.'

She kissed him, but he shook her off. 'Not here. Later, maybe. We've got to go and get changed. People will start arriving soon.'

*

'Now *that* is a very unusual tartan,' declared Verena Crieff as Mary made her entrance in the drawing room before dinner. 'Do tell us what it is.'

Mary felt the whole room staring at her: the men in their dinner jackets and kilts, the women in long velvet skirts and tartan sashes standing with their backs to the fire, the young men in velvet jackets and open-necked shirts.

'It comes from Monsoon,' she said.

'But what *is* it?' Lady Crieff persisted. 'The plaid. Is it your clan tartan? Are you entitled to wear it?'

'I-I don't know. We bought it in Guildford, in a shop.'

'From a shop in Guildford? Extraordinary! I hope they have permission. Someone should look into this, don't you agree, Jock?'

'Looks rather like the Murray to me,' said Sir Jock Kerr-Innes, an amiable septuagenarian who was another of Charlie's godfathers. 'You're not a Murray, by any chance?'

'No, I'm called Mary Merrett.'

'Merrett? Merrett? I don't believe I've heard of a Merrett tartan. Someone's pulling your leg, my dear, if you ask me.'

Utterly humiliated, and wishing she was wearing anything except the Monsoon dress, Mary plunged into the throng of eighty or ninety teenagers congregating around a bowl of wine punch. The first person she saw was Jamie in black t-shirt and black velvet jeans.

'Hi, Mary. How are your legendary tonsils?'

Mary looked blank.

'Last time I saw you, you and Charlie were checking each other's out. According to Charlie, it was the longest unbroken tongue-sandwich in the history of snogging. You're going to be entered for the *Guinness Book of Records*. Twenty-five minutes without breathing – he said it was like inflating a lilo.'

Mary's cheeks burned. She was sure Charlie would never say anything like that.

'That was a classic last evening at Marcus's, wasn't it?' Jamie said. 'Wild. That American chick Clayborne . . . unbelievable slag. She gave me her phone number, for if ever I was in New York, but I left it behind on the plane.'

'Have you seen Charlie?' Mary asked.

'Somewhere over there, I think. We've been spiking the punch. It's got vodka and cherry brandy in it too now.'

A fork supper was laid out in the dining room, to be followed by dancing in the Ardnessaig cellars which ran under half the length of the house. A mobile discotheque, Northern Lights, had been engaged from Inverness and was setting up below; several miles of red and yellow electric cable trailed up and down the basement steps, taking power from the pantry to the turntables. 'We spent the whole morning dragging mattresses down there,' Jamie said. 'I'm telling you, once this party gets going, it's going to be wild. Charlie says at least three nymphomaniacs are coming.'

Looking around the dining room, Mary realised that, apart from Charlie, Jamie and Zara, she knew no one, and Charlie was perpetually surrounded by people. He looked devastatingly handsome in his tartan trews and pale blue shirt. Once he's finished saying hello to the other guests, he'll come and find me, she thought.

Enormous china dishes of grouse casserole and red cabbage and cans of Tennent's lager were ranged along the sideboard, watched over by stag trophies and a silver-plated capercaillie.

Zara Fane, in silver hotpants, black bustier and clogs, loomed up to ask Mary whether she'd seen Jamie anywhere. Blowsy, and already flushed with drink, she said, 'He's meant to be filching whisky for the punch. It still tastes like cat's piss.'

'We're sharing the same bedroom,' Mary said.

'Yah, right,' Zara said. 'Listen, if either of us wants to entertain later on, the other one dosses in the bathroom, OK?'

Somewhere beneath them, the discotheque powered up with a blast of Slade: '*Mama, mama, mama, we're orl crazee nahow*'.

Swept downstairs in a herd of other guests, Mary arrived in a long low chamber like an air-raid shelter, lined on both sides by arched Victorian wine bins. Several of these had been got up as snogging and heavy-petting pits with mattresses and rugs and posters of Led Zeppelin and Pink Floyd. Lady Crieff and Jock Kerr-Innes were making an obligatory appearance on the dancefloor, Sir Jock jigging about in his embroidered velvet slippers, while Verena Crieff made isn't-this-all-unbearable-and-loud expressions before retreating back upstairs. Alistair Crieff was doing his duty by his hefty daughter Mary Jane, gamely man-handling her about the floor, watched by a guffawing Jamie making chimpanzee noises.

Now the cellar was heaving with people. Acoustically unfeasible, the bass rhythm reverberated in waves of feedback off the low ceiling and in and out of the petting pits. With no question of conversation, Charlie's friends staggered about in dance movements that had their origins in rock and roll, reeling and semaphore. The uneven floor of the cellar made the needle jump on the turntable. Each time it happened, the disc jockeys from Northern Lights, two grossly fat and perspiring toffs in white dinner jackets, announced over the sound system, 'Sorry about that spot of turbulence back there, ladies and gentlemen. Groove on.'

Mary had been in the cellar for an hour and a half, and nobody, let alone Charlie, had asked her to dance. She glanced at her watch: ten-thirty. Far, far too early to slip upstairs. The muscles in her cheeks were beginning to ache from the fixed, unbothered smile she always put on in this predicament, indicating that she was quite definitely having a super time and nobody need feel remotely sorry for her. She could see Charlie across the floor, dancing with two pretty blondes at the same time, flashing his captivating smile from one to the other. The last time I saw Charlie dancing, she thought, he was dancing with me. The disco was playing the Stones' 'Sympathy for the Devil' when the strobes came on, illuminating the cellar with intense white pulses of light. Everyone began prancing about with exaggerated gestures to get the maximum mileage from the effect. Charlie was strutting about like Mick Jagger, puckering his lips as he mouthed, '*Pleased to meet yah . . . hope yah guess mah name*'. Overwhelmed by misery, Mary dived for cover into the nearest snog pit, but found Jamie there already, french kissing Zara.

She headed up to the dining room, but encountered Nanny Arbroath standing guard at the top of the cellar steps: 'If you could remain downstairs. Lady Crieff has particularly asked that Charlie's friends shouldn't wander about all over the house.'

In a corner of the cellar was a primitive brick lavatory which must, in an earlier age, have been used by the staff who stoked the old Ardnessaig boilers. Mary retreated inside and bolted the door. She sat down on the seat in her Monsoon dress and leaned her head against the lead plumbing. Outside, the base rhythm of T Rex's 'Telegram Sam' made the lavatory chain with its bulbous china handle swing like a pendulum above her head. If she could hide herself away in here for three more hours, she thought, it would all be over.

After ten minutes, she heard a rattling of the door handle. She kept absolutely quiet until whoever it was went away.

Soon after, the handle turned again. But Mary couldn't bring herself to give up her refuge, dreading the prospect of returning to the party.

A small queue had formed outside the lavatory. She heard a man's voice say, 'I believe there are people screwing each other in there, actually.' He hammered on the door. 'Look, bloody well hurry up, can't you? We all know what you're doing. Some people need a slash, you realise.'

Mary pulled the chain and a cascade of water thundered from the cistern into the pan.

'Sorry to keep you waiting,' she faltered. 'I wasn't feeling too well.'

The whole queue, convinced by now that sexual inter-course had been in progress, stared disbelievingly into the vacated lavatory, still half expecting a second person to emerge. As she scuttled past, they regarded Mary with suspicion.

With no place left to hide, she resumed her vigil on the edge of the dancefloor. She measured the passage of time by the three-minute segments of records; ten tracks meant thirty minutes, twenty was an hour. 'Hi Ho Silver Lining', 'All Right Now', 'Radar Love', 'Desperado', 'Won't Get Fooled Again' . . . it was edging towards midnight. Charlie was wiggling his hips at a bosomy redhead in a violet velvet boob-tube. The majority of the guests were, by now, paralytically drunk, the men swaying about with cans of Tennent's in both fists or leaning, pie-eyed, against brick pillars so the backs of their velvet jackets were covered with brick dust and cobwebs. Those that remained upright chanted raucously along to the records.

Now the music turned slow. Jamie had his arms round the redhead in the boob-tube and was expertly unzipping her one-handed. The disco was playing 'A Whiter Shade of Pale'. Noticing that Charlie was no longer anywhere in evidence, Mary reckoned she could slip away to bed.

Ardnessaig was in semi-darkness. She crossed the hall and made her way upstairs, past the watercolours and paintings of highland cattle, to her bedroom. As she opened the door and switched on the light, she heard groans and squeals and a flustered voice: 'Christ, who the hell's turned on the bloody lights?'

Charlie was sprawled on top of Zara on Mary's bed. In the two or three seconds that they all stared at each other, frozen in inaction, Mary saw Zara's mouth hang open in horror, black lipstick smudged on the pillow case, and Charlie's hand paralysed inside her black bustier.

'I'm terribly sorry,' Mary stammered. 'I didn't realise anyone was in here.'

As she pulled the door shut behind her, she heard Zara giggle, 'God, that's just so embarrassing, Charlie. Especially as she fancies you rotten herself.'

Reeling with despair, Mary went from room to room, searching for a vacant one with no sign of habitation. But each bedroom contained an entwined couple or else open suitcases dumped on bedcovers. Eventually, near the bathroom, she discovered a linen cupboard full of sheets and towels and, building herself a nest between the hot pipes and an immersion tank, counted off the hours until she would be home again in Dorking.

8: October, 1975

'Any idea why you're here? You'll notice I haven't asked the girls this time, just my three godsons.'

Marcus was ensconced at a table on the Place Vendôme side of the Hôtel Ritz when Charlie and Jamie were shown to it. Seated beside him at the dinner table laid for four was Stuart. For a moment Marcus's godsons stared at each other, assimilating the changes brought about by the intervening two years since Lyford Cay. Stuart had grown long sideboards in his first year at university, two inches below his ears, which Charlie considered typically common. His hair was longer, and he was wearing round wire spectacles like John Lennon's. Charlie and Jamie had grown their hair longer too. Charlie's tight curls now almost touched his collar, and there was a large red pustule on the back of his neck. Having drunk several free glasses of wine on the flight over with Jamie, his chilly pale blue eyes were already ringed with red. Jamie's eyes, by contrast, were sparkling and amused. At eighteen, he was strikingly handsome. His thick brown hair, which he had cut at a barbers called Sweeney's in Beauchamp Place, flopped in a springy centre-parting across his forehead.

'Nobody guessed? Shame on you. Your coming of age. You all turn eighteen this year. Big milestone, important to do the thing properly.'

The boys broke into grins, finally getting it.

'Hence Paris,' Marcus said. 'If you're going to become eighteen, Paris is the city to do it in. Best wine, best women . . . bloody useless city in which to make money but that's another matter.'

He insisted they chose the richest, most extravagant items on the menu, as being the only dishes that would go with the special wine he had pre-ordered.

The godsons couldn't remember having seen Marcus in

such exuberant form before. Outwardly, he showed none of the stresses and strains of his recent hostile takeover of British Consolidated Foodstuffs, which had dominated the business pages of the newspapers throughout the summer. He had a martini in a frosted glass in front of him and was smoking a Montecristo. Accustomed as they were to seeing him in holiday clothes, the double-breasted navy-blue suit and silk tie that were his working uniform added an additional dimension of gravitas. His aura of power was practically tangible and, Stuart felt, intimidating. It was when Marcus was at his most charming that you sensed how dangerous it might be to cross him.

Waiters brought the paraphernalia for flambéd Chateaubriand to the table, fussing around Marcus with the special deference due to great men who are also generous tippers. Several French businessmen came over to pay their respects and congratulate him on his recent business coup. Whatever misgivings the Lyford Cay set might have had about him definitely weren't shared by the French, Jamie noticed.

Marcus proposed a toast in Château Lafite. 'To the three of you. Sorry I haven't done more for you before now. Probably should have been giving you moral pep talks and taking you through the ten commandments, but not sure I'm qualified, frankly. I just want you to know that I'm very fond of you all, and proud to have you as my godsons.'

Charlie, replying for them, declared that Marcus had been an incredibly generous godfather. 'My other godfather, Jock Kerr-Innes, only ever gives me five pounds.'

'I'd wish you luck for the rest of your lives,' Marcus went on, 'but there's not a lot of point at this stage, so I won't bother.'

'Why's that?' Jamie asked.

'Far too late. Your characters are set in stone by now. Determination, drive – either you have them or you don't.'

'How can you tell?'

'Oh, it's instinctive more than anything else. When you've hired as many people for as many different positions as I have, it becomes second nature.'

'What about us three?' Stuart asked. 'Can you tell which of us will be successful?'

'Of course, Stuart. I know precisely. I wouldn't dream of telling you, though, ruin the suspense. Life's long enough as it is without giving away the ending before you've even got started.' He regarded his godchildren and they felt a stab of anxiety, realising they had already been judged.

'When you've completed your education, I hope at least some of you will come and work for me,' Marcus continued.

'Really?' Charlie replied, privately thinking he couldn't exactly see himself in a chocolate biscuit factory. 'That's an extremely generous offer.'

Marcus gave him a hard stare. 'There are businesses we're looking at – too early to say which at this stage – that might interest you more than you imagine, Charlie. You'd be surprised.'

'Are you just going to buy more and more companies?' Jamie asked.

'Only the right companies. But, yes, as a group we're in expansion mode. We're looking at a lot of different things, in Europe and Asia particularly. Not so much in Britain where wealth creation is a dirty term. I'll be disappointed if we don't triple group revenue in the next two years. We should achieve considerably more. Which is why I'd enjoy having you involved.

'Think about it,' he said. 'Standing invitation from your godfather, take me up on it or not as you like. Whatever you decide.'

The boys were left with the impression that, whatever Marcus said, he would certainly be offended if nobody took him up on the offer. Fleetingly, Jamie considered what it would be like to work for his godfather, and decided it might all be too much like hard graft. The whole idea of getting a job made him queasy. Ever since his predictably disastrous A-level results had come through, which put university out of reach, all anyone wanted to talk about was what he was going to do next, as though it was the most urgent thing in the world. What was the panic? He was living at home in South Eaton Place with his mother and their paths hardly crossed; Margaret put herself to sleep at nine o'clock each night with a cocktail of prescription sleeping pills, which was precisely when Jamie was getting up to go out. He recalled the morning the postcard had arrived from the exam board, with his three straight fails. It was a bit unfortunate he hadn't actually been there at the time; he'd been poking a girl in Trevor Square on her parents' immaculate king-sized bed. His father had been furious. Maybe if he'd revised he'd have done better; Jamie didn't care. He was sure everything would turn out fine.

Stuart had already rejected the idea of working for Marcus on moral grounds: he wasn't becoming an overseer in a factory. And, since starting at Birmingham University, he felt even more sceptical about everything Marcus represented. He was a control freak, and Stuart was sure that, in the future, he wouldn't have much to do with him.

Charlie, meanwhile, thought he'd wait and see. He was starting at Sandhurst next month. Beyond that, if his godfather really was buying some worthwhile companies, it mightn't be a bad long-term career move to keep in with him.

They were finishing a *tarte au citron* when three of the most beautiful and exotic women the boys had ever seen sat down at the next table. Jamie, who noticed them first, was transfixed. Impeccably turned out in little fitted Parisian suits, nipped in at the waist, and with legs that never ended, they ordered cocktails, occasionally throwing glances in the direction of Marcus's table.

'Those girls keep staring at us,' Jamie said to his godfather.

'They're waiting for the signal to join us, that's why,' Marcus replied. 'They're your birthday presents.'

The godsons looked astonished.

'I thought you might find them rather fun, but for heaven's sake don't tell your parents or they'll never let me buy you dinner again.'

'But where do they come from?' Charlie asked.

'Madame Claude girls. You must have heard of them, they're practically an institution in Paris. Lovely girls of bourgeois background most of them, or else do a highly convincing impersonation. They don't come cheap either. The blonde I've hired for you, Charlie, is a favourite with the Shah of Iran. Thought you'd enjoy that. Good provenance.'

'Christ,' said Charlie. 'You mean, they let you go all the way with them and everything?' For a moment, he was seized with panic; he had never slept with a woman. His social confidence masked a terror of not knowing exactly what to do in bed. At parties, when sufficiently drunk, he could snog and try to grope a girl's tits, but the prospect of being alone with a naked woman filled him with trepidation.

'They're yours till the morning.'

'Bloody hell.' Charlie looked bug-eyed. 'I mean, Christ.'

'Your girl, Stuart, is the little Haitian *culotte* in the Sonia Rykiel suit. Sweet little thing. I sat next to her at the Elysée Palace last week.'

Stuart gaped at the Haitian. She looks like Bianca Jagger, he thought. Was this a joke, or did Marcus really mean them to have sex? He found the idea shocking, but also exciting. He couldn't believe these amazing women were actually tarts.

'And for you, Jamie, a very special treat, the little Chinese. Connoisseurs' choice. Spends half the year in Castel's, the other half in Rabat with one of the Princes of Morocco. Tonight, for your birthday, all yours.'

Marcus beckoned to the girls who came to the table, radiant and smiling, while the waiters scurried about bringing extra chairs.

'They look like the finalists in Miss World,' Jamie whispered to Stuart. 'Only a lot sexier.'

Marcus introduced the boys with elaborate formality. 'This is my eldest godson, the honourable Charles Crieff. Now, Marie-France, he's from a very old and noble Scottish family; over here, you'd have packed him off to the guillotine long ago.'

The girl designated for him squeezed his hand. Charlie, blushing and puffing, shook it and said, 'Charlie Crieff. Good to meet you.'

Marcus introduced Stuart, exactly as he had done ten

years earlier in Cap Ferrat, as the son of a hero. Jamie he commended as an English playboy. 'I rather suspect he may be able to teach you a thing or two, Suki. Have an idea he's my most experienced godson. Behaved reprehensibly with a friend of mine in the Bahamas, which is something I shouldn't risk a second time if I were you, Jamie. Understood?' He regarded him sternly without a hint of a smile.

Pushing back his chair, Marcus tossed three room keys on to the tablecloth.

'The girls are paid up until noon tomorrow, so no need to bugger off too early in the morning. I'm leaving for Geneva at dawn, so I won't see you. One word of advice. I'd let the girls make the running if I were you. They're the absolute pick of their profession and don't come any better, as the expression goes. Enjoy yourselves.'

Jamie could hardly believe his luck. He loved the look of his bird, Suki, and his hands were already making a bee-line for her bum. Having never shagged an oriental before, but knowing their reputation, he couldn't wait to get started. When he blew into her ear, she giggled, and he knew he was in for the best time.

His face bright red, eyes bulging like a pair of poached eggs, Charlie gazed at the blonde designated for him and tried not to imagine her in the buff. At least she wasn't a wog like Stuart's. He still half hoped the whole thing was a wind-up, and he wouldn't have to go through with it. But it seemed real enough, and Jamie would tease him forever if he ducked out now. Awkwardly, nervously, and staring long-ingly into the hotel bar as they passed by, Charlie accompanied Marie-France in the direction of the mahogany-panelled lift.

Stuart, meanwhile, was in a lather of incredulity and anticipation. His girl was a complete knock-out. She was like a movie star. He could hardly believe she'd consent to go to bed with him. Apart from a few fumbles, he'd never got close to full sex before. He'd never even seen a female stripped off in real life. And yet . . . he didn't want to exploit the girl. Having been brought up to respect women, it didn't feel right, expecting her to do it for money.

Uncertainly, he appealed to Marcus. 'Er, I'm not really sure about this.'

'Not sure about what, Stuart?'

'Well, er, the ethics.'

Marcus roared with laughter. 'The ethics! My God, I do love the young. *Glorious*! If I told you these girls regularly earn five thousand pounds for one weekend's work – five thousand *minimum* – does that make you feel better about it? Enough to buy a small house in Birmingham. They probably make more over the summer than most people earn in a lifetime, so I wouldn't expend too much effort worrying about ethics. *They're* certainly not. Now, stop fussing, otherwise you'll offend your date. She'll start thinking you don't fancy her or you're queer or something. Go on, hurry up. Straight upstairs with you. NOW. Oh, and many happy returns of the day.'

9: July, 1977

The sun was shining for once, Polzeath was filling up with tourists and Niall McMeakin was confident they were going to have a great first season.

'We're going to be packed out from now till the end of October, no question, darling,' he told Amaryllis, celebrating in anticipation by uncorking one of the new consignment of Casablanca rosé.

He had borrowed the money to buy the popular Creel and Lobster restaurant overlooking Polzeath harbour twelve months earlier, and they'd spent the winter ripping out the old lobster pots and plastic crabs and replacing them with Moroccan lamps, kelims and camel saddles. Niall reckoned the Cornish fishing village had more than enough seafood and cream tea joints already, but nowhere where you could eat authentic Moroccan *tagines* and *couscous*. The Kasbah would fill the gap while providing himself and Amaryllis with a cosy little love-nest above the shop, plus a put-me-up for Saffron on the half-landing.

He had met Amaryllis down on the beach and they'd clicked just like that. She had moved in the same day, the sex was great, she could roll a joint and it was no drawback having Saffron around to help out in the Kasbah when the place got busy. So far, it had to be admitted, business had been below expectation, but things would hot up now that summer was here. Niall had owned or managed four previous restaurants, all slow burners at the beginning, all definitely picking up just as the banks had pulled the rug.

Saffron finished watering the herbs that Amaryllis was growing in the kitchen window box – the mint, chives and marijuana. Her part-time job in the gift shop didn't begin until the afternoon. Niall and her mother were well into a second bottle of the rosé and were starting to turn quarrelsome, which was a regular occurrence at this time of day. Saffron hoped nobody would venture into the Kasbah that lunchtime because nothing had been done about preparing any food.

Niall, with his orange hair and scrofulous goatee, wasn't her favourite among her mother's boyfriends, but she preferred him to Barney the Wiltshire kineseologist who'd preceded him, or the tractor mechanic with the motorhome outside Okehampton. There had been so many. Amaryllis was beautiful but too impulsive and trusting. In the end, nothing seemed to last.

Saffron supposed that, at some point, she had better find herself something proper to do. She couldn't stay in Polzeath all her life. After Amaryllis split with Bongo and they'd had to leave Lambourn, her education had drawn to its natural conclusion. For the present, she was content to take the summer as it came. She was friendly with the local surfing fraternity, and was seeing a boy from Trebetherick who liked to take her into the long grass on the cliffs above the town and described her as his girlfriend. It didn't bother her. She never made any special effort with men, or did anything to encourage or discourage them, but somehow they latched on to her. Most men made a pass at her eventually. She never thought much about it, before or afterwards.

The telephone began ringing at the desk and Niall, sitting just out of reach, shouted, 'Get the phone, won't you, Saff? It'll be someone wanting to make a booking.'

She picked up the kitchen extension and a female voice, fearsomely efficient and vaguely familiar, said, 'Is that Saffron Weaver? I have Marcus Brand for you.'

There was a series of clicks and Marcus came on. 'Saffron? What the hell are you doing down in Cornwall? Have you any idea the trouble we've had tracking you down? Practically had to hire private detectives.'

It was the first time she'd heard from her godfather since Lyford Cay. She had sometimes wondered what it would be like talking to him again, but he was charging ahead, oblivious to any awkwardness, taking command as he was accustomed to doing in every situation. The energy down the line was rather alarming, when directed at Polzeath.

'My American goddaughter, Abigail Schwartzman, is over in London, staying at Claridge's with her parents,' he said. 'Thought I should do something for her while she's here. How are you placed to come clothes shopping with us?'

'Clothes shopping?'

'You're my best-looking goddaughter, always look terrific in anything, thought of you immediately. Obvious choice.'

She heard Niall shouting from next door, 'If it's a party of six or more, Saff, tell 'em we can't handle it. We don't do mass catering.'

'Mrs Miles has booked your train ticket,' Marcus said. 'I shall hand you back to her in a moment and she'll give you the details. My driver will be looking out for you tomorrow at the barrier.'

Abigail and her mother were lunching together at Harry's Bar while her father entertained Marcus round the corner in the more masculine environs of Mark's Club. Zubin, having made a great fortune with his edge-of-conurbation shopping malls, which he had rolled out across North America and Canada, was now interested in exporting the concept into Britain. Despite having been double-crossed by Marcus once in the past, he still reckoned that, with all his connections, he was the obvious person to enlist as partner.

Of the two lunches, the business one at Mark's Club was the more convivial and productive. Marcus, having decided before he arrived not to participate in the venture, on the principle that he never became partners with people he'd previously betrayed, was smoking a cigar and thinking about Saffron. The prospect of seeing her this afternoon intrigued him very much. Although he had said on the telephone that he'd had no idea where to find her, he had known perfectly well. He made it his business to keep tabs on the movements of his friends, business rivals and girlfriends, as well as his godchildren. He had followed Saffron's progress from Hungerford to Middle Wallop to Okehampton to Polzeath. Eventually, he had plans for Saffron Weaver. The

Schwartzmans' arrival in London provided a convenient pretext to check up on her.

Picking miserably at an artichoke risotto, Abigail asked her mother for the twentieth time why she had to go clothes shopping with Marcus.

'Because your father wants you to, that's why.' Harriet was perched like a Pekinese on two linen-covered cushions, which were essential to raise her to the height of the table. On her ring finger she wore an enormous yellow diamond, the size of a golf ball, which threw all her surrounding fingers into shadow.

'I'm nineteen years old, Mom. Surely it's up to me to decide whether I want to go or not.'

'Eat your lunch and stop making a fuss.' Harriet waved away the Polish waitress who was hovering with a bowl of Parmesan cheese for the risotto. 'Marcus is a very busy man, he's sacrificing his afternoon to take you shopping. You should appreciate that and be grateful. Do any of your other godfathers take you shopping? I don't think so.'

'That's because I don't have any other godfathers. We're Jewish, remember.'

'No need to get smart with me, Abigail, you know what I'm saying. The reason you don't want to go is because you're fat. That's all it is. Next time we're in London, we stay at the Berkeley not at Claridge's, they have a spa there, you can swim. You should drop some weight, Abigail. I'm taking you to that dietician when we get home, the one they featured in *Glamour*. He even had Liz Taylor slimmed down for a while. The consultations cost a fortune, but you need help with those hips.'

Harriet Schwartzman frequently despaired. The daughter of Latvian immigrants, who had arrived penniless on Ellis Island from Riga fifty years earlier and built a successful business manufacturing pianos, she couldn't understand Abigail's lack of personal ambition. Harriet's life had been an unending odyssey of determined self-improvement: her marriage to Zubin, then beginning to make a name for himself in the real estate world, the succession of apartments and houses in better and better areas leading eventually to

Franklin Lakes, her passion for culture at which she worked with grim tenacity, seldom missing an important exhibition or concert and now widening her scope to include opera and ballet. Nobody read society and shelter magazines more closely than Harriet Schwartzman, or abided by their dictates more completely in the assiduous pursuit of gracious living. Having spent the first twelve years of her life in poverty, an experience which had simultaneously toughened her and left her with a metabolism that made her incapable of putting on weight, she couldn't see how Abigail would forgo the opportunity to be taken shopping by a prominent tycoon.

Although it was true that Abigail was painfully self-conscious about her weight, which seemed to pile on irrespective of her food intake, this was not the main reason she dreaded her afternoon with Marcus Brand. She had hated both the holidays with him, sensing his colossal lack of interest in her and not knowing how to talk to him as some of the other godchildren could do. Alert to slights, and with an almost perfect visual memory, she could remember every lunch and dinner in Lyford Cay and not once had Marcus put her next to him. Not just Saffron but even Mary had been placed next to him; Saffron all the time. And the worst of it was that, in spite of herself, she had to admit she found Marcus attractive. Back home in Franklin Lakes, in the new, much larger family mansion that Zubin had built on the site of the old one, Abigail often remembered her godfather dancing with Saffron at the beach barbecue. When she wasn't too busy hating him, she was fantasising about him dancing with her instead. Afterwards, she always reacted with total revulsion against these fantasies, which made her dislike Marcus all the more, holding him responsible for that, too.

Abigail's confidence plummeted still further when Marcus's Bentley, picking her up from the step of Harry's Bar, turned out to contain not only her godfather, but Saffron as well. Tell me this isn't happening, Abigail wailed to herself. Tell me I'm not schlepping round the stores all afternoon with this Cheryl Tiegs lookalike.

It was horrible, she felt, the three of them sitting in a line on the leather backseat: herself dressed up like a table decoration at a bar-mitzvah, in the floral Ungaro suit Harriet had made her put on; Godfather Marcus, enveloped in cigar smoke and insincerity, declaring what a lucky fellow he was to be playing hooky from the office with two such gorgeous young women; and Saffron almost wilfully under-dressed in a blue-and-white cheesecloth shirt and a long, slightly crumpled Indian skirt. Abigail had no way of knowing that they were the only clean garments Saffron could find in the whole flat when she'd hunted around that morning.

'I have a list of boutiques here,' Marcus said. 'One of the girls who works for Barbara in my office has compiled it.' He read from the list, which was typed on Brand Group writing paper. 'Fruit Fly, Ace, Antony Price. These are all down in the King's Road somewhere.' He altered his voice to the frequency on which Makepiece, the chauffeur who had succeeded Bolton twenty years before, understood that he was being addressed.

'King's Road, Makepiece,' Marcus ordered. 'We're going to buy some clothes for these attractive girls back here.' Abigail reckoned it wasn't the first time Marcus's driver had heard that particular instruction.

After they'd pulled up outside the first boutique, Marcus, striding ahead, instantly commandeered the manageress and all the sales assistants who clustered around him in their gold satin drainpipes, their cheekbones brushed with red and silver blusher. Saffron and Abigail felt overawed by the coolness of the shop, with its plastic and satin frocks stapled to violet walls and Roxy Music playing over the sound system. But Marcus, seeming completely at home between rails of disco clothes and metallic tote bags, had dresses removed from windows, stripped from mannequins and delivered, armfuls at a time, to the curtained changing booths. 'Here's another one for Saffron to try on, the silver thing, and the gold one there for Abigail.'

Once Saffron was dressed, he stood like a racehorse owner in the paddock, watching her parade up and down.

'That one looks marvellous on you, Saffron. Like a mermaid, perfect for Polzeath. Yes, we'll take that one. Abigail? You nearly ready in there? You're taking an awfully long time.'

Behind the curtain, struggling to tug a silver latex sheath over her shoulders, Abigail wanted to cry in despair. So far she tried on eight things, and none had come close to fitting. It was shaming.

To make matters worse, Saffron had undergone a remarkable transformation. Her blonde hair, bleached almost white by her summer on the beach, had been twisted on top of her head, accentuating her amazingly long neck. Free from cheesecloth, her figure was even better than it had been four years earlier in Lyford Cay; her slender giraffe-like legs made Abigail think of Jerry Hall's. And with their dramatic fish tails and draping for tiny waists, the Antony Price dresses could have been made for her.

Marcus applauded each time she came out in a new outfit. Abigail, grimacing, was now convinced Saffron was his mistress. They were probably at it night and day; no wonder Saffron's so thin, she thought bitterly.

Returning to the changing room in a gold lamé tuxedo, Saffron rolled her eyes and said, 'Jesus Christ, isn't all this ridiculous? What are we doing here anyway?'

Abigail, amazed, said, 'How do you mean?'

'When does Marcus imagine I'm going to wear clothes like these? I live in Cornwall, for God's sake. People wear bathing suits or jeans. If I went outside in this gear, I'd probably get arrested.'

'But you go to things all the time where you have to dress up, don't you? With Marcus.'

'With *Marcus*? I haven't seen him for four years. Not since that weird holiday in the Bahamas.'

'But I thought . . .' Abigail, confused, didn't know what to say next.

Saffron laughed. 'I know what you're thinking. He tried, of course, men are so predictable, but I told him I couldn't face it.'

'You did?'

'Come on. He's forty years old or something. Anyway, I don't know why you think I go to swanky parties. That's a laugh. You're the one who does that.'

'I am?'

'Your clothes are amazing. On that holiday, you never wore the same outfit twice.'

Abigail made a face. 'That's my mom, she buys them for me. I can't think why. The only place I ever get to wear them is in restaurants.'

'You should try our restaurant one day. Actually it belongs to my mum's boyfriend. You'd better be quick, though, because it probably won't last.'

'The restaurant?'

'The restaurant, the relationship, both.' Saffron shrugged.

'Then what happens?'

'Amaryllis finds a new boyfriend. She's very good at it. Usually it only takes a few weeks. She found Niall, the restaurant one, in three days. She picked him up on a beach. That was a record.'

'I think I'd find that kind of upsetting,' Abigail said, suddenly realising she actually rather liked Saffron.

'It is scary sometimes,' Saffron admitted. 'The night before Amaryllis met Niall, we slept in a bus shelter with our suitcases. Maybe she'll meet a really great guy next time, and it'll work out.'

'She should marry someone like Marcus,' Abigail said. Then added quickly, 'Not Marcus himself, of course.'

Saffron went red. 'That probably wouldn't be such a good idea.'

Marcus loomed over the curtain of the changing booths, suddenly as impatient to leave the boutique as he had earlier been impatient to initiate the shopping expedition.

'You know what, Abigail?' he said briskly. 'I suggest we call it a day. English and American sizing is evidently different. I've asked the people to wrap a couple of those gold handbags for you instead. Best get dressed, quick as you can, and I'll have you dropped back at the hotel. I'll get you to the station, Saffron, in good time for the train.'

'No, thank you,' said Abigail, 'Saffron and I are going to

hang out together this afternoon. We've got a lot to catch up on.'

'Goodbye, Marcus,' said Saffron sweetly, 'thank you for the clothes.'

Striding out to his car, Marcus was irritated to hear a loud peal of laughter from the changing room.

10: October, 1977

Barry Tomkins, Professor of Post-War Economics and Political Science at Birmingham University, was delivering his fourth lecture of the term. The Keir Hardie lecture theatre in the new Edgbaston Economics faculty was, as usual, less than a quarter full; having spent much of his academic career campaigning for a wider demographic intake at Britain's universities, it was a disappointment to Professor Tomkins that his working-class students found his lectures and seminars every bit as missable as their middle-class predecessors had done.

Scanning the hall, with its raked beechwood seats and Soviet-style community mural depicting scenes from Birmingham's industrial revolution, Barry Tomkins tried to ascertain how his new lecture series was going down with the students. He was particularly pleased with it, and had hoped that, with certain revisions and padding and a select bibliography which was always good for six pages, he might have enough there for a book – *The New Slavemasters: contemporary capitalists and their impact on the economics of industrialised and non-industrialised nations (1958–1978)*. In the second row, a student with a beard and a Ban Coca-Colonialism t-shirt was defiantly asleep, not even bothering to pretend, his bare feet dangling over the seatback of the row in front. Elsewhere, two Nordic girls were locked in a passionate and provocative embrace. Several students were openly rolling joints, and the theatre reeked of patchouli oil.

As usual, the only person who appeared to be paying any attention and taking notes was a local boy in his third year, Stuart Bolton, who Professor Tomkins had long ago identified as a high-flyer. A diligent student of few words, he appeared to think deeply about everything he was taught, as though testing the mainly left-wing economic theories that were the faculty's speciality. Disconcertingly, Stuart's questions, though always sympathetic to socialist precepts, often put his tutor on the spot.

'Those of you who have attended previous lectures in the course,' began Professor Tomkins, 'will know that we have been looking at Slater Walker, the negative long-term impact of asset stripping on British manufacture and the opportunistic break up of the Haw Par Company in Singapore, James Goldsmith and his detrimental policy for the branded foods and soft drinks industries at Cavenham Foods, and R.W. 'Tiny' Rowland whose Lonrho conglomerate has sought to impose a pernicious form of economic colonialism on the emerging African nations, appropriating and exploiting their mineral resources for the benefit of Western shareholders.'

Barry Tomkins rearranged his testicles inside his tight stonewashed jeans. Although nothing about his appearance, his brown corduroy jerkin and rats' tails of prematurely grey hair, suggested overweening vanity, he was nonetheless a vain man. 'Today,' he went on, 'we turn our attention to another nascent emerging group of contemporary capitalists. I like to refer to this lot as the "global pirates".' He paused, so that the audience could absorb the wit of the categorisation. 'One increasingly prominent example is Marcus Brand. His *modus operandi* is to acquire and exploit businesses across a wide range of different sectors and national frontiers. Characteristically, he will purchase these businesses at a discounted valuation, neutralise the unions where they exist and systematically downsize the workforce, laying off up to sixty per cent of the manpower, which was the unfortunate eventuality at the Smethwick Chassis Works here in Birmingham.'

Sitting in the sixth row, Stuart was stunned. He had had no idea his godfather was part of Tomkins's course, or that Marcus had reached this level of notoriety.

Professor Tomkins placed an acetate diagram on the overhead projector. 'As we can see,' he said, 'the Brand Group of Companies – BGC – had its origins in a small-to-medium sized property and shipping operation based in the City of London. Brand seized control of the business in the late 1950s, injected private capital, replaced the long-serving senior management with his own placemen and embroiled the company in a series of questionable redevelopment schemes, some involving bomb sites left over from the war.'

He went on to describe Marcus Brand's diversification into financial services, car parts and food manufacture, culminating in the 1975 acquisition of British Consolidated Foodstuffs and the takeover, three years earlier, of the Imperial Kowloon Trading Company in Hong Kong.

Stuart thought: That must have been the deal Marcus was referring to in Paris. He'd said he was about to buy some big company in Asia.

'Perhaps the most disturbing aspect of the rapid creation of this global conglomerate,' opined Professor Tomkins, 'is that Brand has managed to retain absolute control over the share capital. The company remains privately held, with no external investors. It would be legitimate to question how this feat has been achieved within such a short timeframe, without resort to dubious financial practices.'

Listening to this, Stuart experienced a variety of emotions. The first, taking him by surprise, was annoyance. He found Barry Tomkins's assault on his godfather unjust. Normally he relished the Professor's sly demolition jobs on prominent tycoons, with which he instinctively concurred. But the assault on Marcus irritated him, though he couldn't explain exactly why. Objectively, he could see that everything in Tomkins's lecture was true; Marcus was ruthless and greedy and all the rest of it. But that was only half the story. There was a compelling side to his godfather and, as he knew from personal experience, a generous one too. Next to Marcus, Professor Tomkins cut a drab figure.

Stuart's feelings about Marcus were so ambivalent that he could no longer analyse them. Politically, he knew their views were diametrically opposed. His time at university had strengthened, and added intellectual ballast to, his socialism. In his first week he had joined the University Labour Club, and in the October 1974 General Election canvassed enthusiastically to secure the re-election of the Labour candidate for Sparkbrook. When Tony Benn travelled up to Birmingham to speak in his support, Stuart was mesmerised by his oratory and was one of the last to finish applauding during the fourteen-minute standing ovation. His socialism was instinctive and idealistic. He saw himself as part of the fortunate first generation of working-class boys who were getting a decent education, and thus felt he had a moral imperative to help those that followed along behind. His encounters with his co-godchild Charlie Crieff had reinforced his belief that people of higher social classes – insular, selfish pricks – wouldn't put themselves out to help people like Stuart. They would have to help themselves.

Towards the end of his second term, he had fallen in love with a girl in his hall of residence, Lauren Webb, who was studying medical science. For eighteen months they were inseparable, eventually sharing digs in the top flat of a terraced house in Selly Oak. She was blonde and, in the murky half-light of the JCR bar, bore a remote resemblance to Saffron; the existence of whom Stuart had never mentioned, though he often thought about her still. In term time, Stuart and Lauren swam together four times a week in the local baths. Years of training had turned Stuart into an accomplished endurance swimmer, who regularly put in a hundred lengths before lectures. On Saturdays, he crossed the city to have tea with his mother, sometimes taking Lauren along too, sometimes alone. Jean still lived in the same small flat in Smethwick to which she'd moved when her husband had been killed in the car accident twenty years earlier. The main reason Stuart had elected to go to university in Birmingham was to stay close enough to visit his mother.

One vacation he travelled down to Yeovil to stay with Lauren's parents. Their arrival coincided with a family crisis. Lauren's father, who was employed as a financial controller at a neighbouring soft drinks plant, had that morning been handed his notice, along with six hundred other men. 'The writing's been on the wall for two years,' Mr Webb said, 'ever since our old owners, Consolidated Foodstuffs, were taken over by these new people. It's been an open secret they wanted to combine us with their other factory over at Castle Cary.'

'Who are the new owners?' Stuart asked, hoping he might be mistaken.

'Bugger named Brand. Couldn't tell you the first thing about him, because he's never graced us with his presence.'

Stuart was relieved that Lauren, in whom he confided everything else, was completely ignorant of her boyfriend's connection to Marcus. He had told no one in Birmingham. The luxurious holidays in Cap Ferrat and Lyford Cay belonged to a different and hermetically sealed part of his life. At times he found it hardly credible that they'd happened, so remote were they from his everyday existence. But sometimes, especially when swimming, memories of those holidays crowded in on him: his terror at being dragged through the sea on the tractor tyre, Charlie's condescension ('His mother's a charlady'), his enduring and insane hankering after Saffron.

Everything to do with Marcus provoked guilt. Either he felt guilty about having a hard-nosed tycoon as his godfather at all, or guilty that it was a secret source of pride to him, or guilty about his father's involvement in the death of Marcus's wife. Stuart had another secret he had never told Lauren, and which he regarded as the deepest of all. This concerned the episode in Paris when Marcus had supplied his godsons with hookers at the Hôtel Ritz for their eight-eenth birthday present.

Stuart's moral confusion was intense as he was torn between powerful erotic memories of the Haitian girl and shame at his own sexual exploitation of a Third World migrant. The fact that Talita had told him what she earned, which was more in a single night than Stuart's grant from the local education authority for the entire year, only partly salved his conscience. Stuart's first proper sexual encounter had been so passionate and prolonged that he couldn't think back to it without becoming aroused. And yet that night, after he had come, he had been overwhelmed by guilt, and found himself apologising to Talita for making her go through with it.

In the end, they had curled around each other and gone to sleep and, in the morning, she had taken him to an exhibition of Degas paintings at the Grand Palais. Returning to the Ritz to collect his luggage, Stuart had run into Jamie in the lobby. 'How was yours?' Jamie had asked. 'We did it eleven times, no kidding. And guess what, Stuart? She said my dong's two-and-a-half times bigger that Adnan Khashoggi's.'

Professor Tomkins was wrapping up his lecture on global piracy with a few sarcastic digs at Marcus's record on shrinking workforces. 'It might be salutary before next week for you to tabulate the total number of job losses across all Brand's companies since he made the remorseless pursuit of profits his only consideration. Now,' he said, looking around the room, 'I think we have a couple of minutes left for questions, if anyone has any.'

The student in the Ban Coca-Colonialism t-shirt shook himself awake, and the Nordic girls began a loud, slurping process of oral disengagement. All over the lecture theatre, seatbacks slammed upright as everyone started for the exits.

'I have a question,' Stuart said.

Reluctantly, some students sat down again while others, ignoring him, pressed on through the doors.

'Barry, you pointed out in your lecture that Marcus Brand made sixty per cent of the workforce redundant at the Smethwick Chassis Works when he took it over nine years ago. Some people believe that, in doing this, the factory was actually saved from closure. If he hadn't made those tough decisions, it would have gone bankrupt. Instead, there are eleven hundred men working there today, new plant and a thriving business. How do you react to that interpretation?'

Barry Tomkins looked dumbfounded, then aghast. 'I don't believe I've ever been asked a question like that in my life before. In fact, I'm not even sure it merits an answer, with its ugly capitalist sophistries. If you'd been speaking to Marcus Brand himself, I doubt he'd come up with a better exculpation himself. Where do you get your facts from, as a matter of interest?'

Stuart, reddening, shrugged. He didn't know what had

come over him, defending Marcus. He despised everything his godfather represented.

'No problem, Barry,' he said. 'I was just interested in your reaction, that's all.'

: November, 1977

When Marcus Brand bought West Candover Park in Hampshire for the then astronomical sum of £7 million, it marked a turning point in his public profile. Until that time, his reputation had been confined to the City; specifically, to that part of the City which could never be categorised as Establishment. But in becoming the owner of West Candover Park, which many people consider the most beautiful house in the South of England, Marcus inevitably attracted widespread recognition. For more than two hundred years it had been the seat of the merchant banking Poole family; a perfect Georgian mansion of mellow grey stone, with a Doric portico, orangery and famous water gardens fronting a tributary of the River Test. During the long period of the Pooles' occupancy, West Candover Park had become famous as the setting for important houseparties; the second Viscount Poole liked to boast that no political appointment of significance had been made by the Conservative Party between the wars without the candidate first spending a weekend on approval in Hampshire. And when one of the royal princesses had required a discreet but well-staffed house in which to pursue her notorious alliance with a negro jazz pianist, West Candover Park provided safe harbour. The news that Marcus had bought the estate meant that items about him began to surface for the first time in the gossip columns.

Verena Crieff, spotting one of these in her morning newspaper as she ate breakfast under the glassy-eyed surveillance of the stags' heads in the dining room at Ardnessaig, read the paragraph aloud to her husband.

'It's quite monstrous,' she said. 'Seven million pounds! What I'd like to know is how much of that came from poor Lucy Macpherson's trust.'

'People do say Marcus has done rather well for himself through his businesses,' replied Alistair Crieff, wistfully.

'I wouldn't be at all surprised,' snorted Lady Crieff. 'When Charlie went all that way to stay with him in the West Indies, Marcus spent half the time having business meetings, or that's what Charlie said.'

Nevertheless, when they learned shortly afterwards that Marcus had decided to hold an enormous dance at West Candover Park, and that it was to be given in honour of his six godchildren, Verena Crieff agreed, with misgivings, that they should probably accept. 'I would like to see the gardens,' she explained, 'before he has an opportunity to ruin them.'

The invitation had come, as all Marcus's ideas came, without warning and delivered as a *fait accompli*.

A letter in the form of a round robin, with the godchildren listed alphabetically, began: 'I have decided I would like to give a joint dance to celebrate your twenty-first birthdays, to be held on Saturday 22 November. I suggest the invitation reads, "The Godfather At Home" and that it takes place at my house in Hampshire. I have instructed a firm of party planners to arrange everything. All they need from you all as quickly as possible is a list of the names and correct addresses of *one hundred guests each* who you would like me to invite on your behalf.'

The reactions of the godchildren, on receiving the circular, differed widely.

'This idea of Marcus's is all very well,' complained Charlie to Jamie in the fashionable nightclub Françoise, known as Frankie's, which occupied a basement off Sloane Square opposite Peter Jones. 'But how the hell are we supposed to keep our lists down to a hundred? My party at Ardnessaig, there were almost a hundred people at that, and that was just the Scottish contingent.'

'It's definitely tight,' Jamie agreed. 'I began making a list of good-fun women and got to ninety and was only on the letter K.'

Charlie felt a stab of envy. Everything came easily to Jamie. He only had to smile at a girl and she jumped into bed with him. He had the use of that huge house in South Eaton Place as a knocking shop, and he didn't even work. At some level, Charlie had been jealous of his best friend for years.

In Polzeath, where Amaryllis had torn open Saffron's letter from Marcus because it looked interesting, there was fevered activity on the half-landing. Amaryllis was trying to decide which of Saffron's Antony Price creations suited her best. By the time Saffron arrived home, discarded frocks lay in heaps on the floor while her mother paraded around the almost-empty dining room of the Kasbah dressed as a silver mermaid.

Saffron, drawing up a list of her surfing crowd, suddenly realised she had no idea of their surnames or addresses. She wondered whether it would be all right to put c/o the Beach Café, North Beach, Polzeath.

Mary, in the middle of a Cordon Bleu cooking course in Godalming, was horrified by the whole idea. Still holding a candle for Charlie Crieff and badly bruised by his betrayal at Ardnessaig, she could think of nothing she wanted less than a joint party. Zara Fane would doubtless be there, and Mary couldn't bear it. After a week of acrimonious argument with both her parents, she admitted defeat and agreed that her mother could provide the names of suitable neighbours' children and old Perpetual Martyr convent girls.

In Franklin Lakes, NJ, Abigail Schwartzman, who had resumed fantasising about Marcus ever since her return from London, accepted the invitation fatalistically, as the latest, inevitable chapter in her hopeless obsession.

Stuart laughed when the letter arrived. It was too much. Who had a hundred best mates anyway, unless they were George Best or Mick Jagger? Apart from Lauren Webb, from whom he'd split six weeks earlier, and his neighbours on the corridor at the hall of residence, and the lads from the swimming group and the Student Union bar, and the Labour Club of course, he didn't know anyone. That was only about twenty-five people. Plus Mick and Ginger, his old school mates; Mick was working behind the bar of a big pub in Bromwich now, and Ginger had found a job on the assembly line at the Smethwick Chassis Works. He would get the shock of his life if an invitation arrived to his boss's place down south.

Stuart reread the letter. What was 'a firm of party planners' meant to be? Didn't the rich even organise their own parties? And he wondered whether West Candover Park was like Cannon Hill Park, where he and Lauren had clambered over the railings late one night and made love underneath the kids' swings. He liked the touch about 'The Godfather at Home'. That was classy. Francis Ford Coppola was Stuart's favourite director.

And Saffron would be at the party. She was one of Marcus's godchildren; she'd be there, no question.

The next morning, Stuart made a list of his twenty friends and posted them off to the party planner's office in Brechin Mews. If Marcus Brand wanted to invite his friends, he wouldn't look a gift horse in the mouth. In a final flash of bravado, he added the name Professor Barry Tomkins to the list.

The entire length of the drive was lit by torches from the Doric lodges to the sweep of gravel in front of the portico where a long line of cars was dropping off guests before being directed, by a dozen villagers in caps and raincoats, to temporary car parks in the watermeadows. Stuart, who had arrived at the dance on the back of Ginger's Enfield motorcycle, gazed up at the house in astonishment. Illuminated by floodlights, it looked like the ruddy Parthenon, he thought, with a great wing stuck out to each side. He had never imagined West Candover Park would be so overwhelming. He wondered what Professor Tomkins who, to his surprise, had been the first of Stuart's guests to accept the invitation, would make of it all.

'There you go,' he said to Ginger as they chained up the bike. 'Capitalism in action. This is what you get if you put enough men out of work.'

Ginger whistled. 'It's fucking brilliant, innit? I wouldn't say no, if someone gave me a pile like that.'

All around them, guests were streaming towards the house from the car park. Stuart eyed them suspiciously. In their dinner jackets and bow ties, they looked like so many Charlie Crieffs. The invitation had stipulated black tie and Stuart had hired the whole rig for the occasion from a men's outfitters in the Bull Ring. Ginger and Mick had borrowed theirs from pals who worked in the functions suite of the old Midlands Hotel. Each time Stuart caught sight of Ginger, he cracked up laughing, he looked that different and posh. His velvet bow tie was so big it looked like a dead rat pinned to his throat.

They reached the steps and joined a queue of people waiting to file inside. Stuart couldn't see any of the other guests he'd invited himself. Maybe they wouldn't show up, which suddenly seemed no bad thing. He couldn't spot Saffron anywhere either, or Marcus come to that. The other guests all looked like they'd been invited by Charlie Crieff or Jamie Temple; they spoke with the same accent, and seemed to know each other already. Ginger elbowed Stuart in the ribs. 'There's great crumpet here. Look at 'em, prize totty everywhere.'

As they entered the house, three coaches full of guests drew up outside. Marcus's party planners had organised a shuttle service from London for those who preferred not to drive, picking up in Eaton Square with champagne served all the way. Another ninety hoorays and army officers, led by Charlie, staggered out on to the gravel.

Stuart and Ginger passed through a hall, where their names were ticked off by secretaries sitting behind a desk, then through a drawing room full of Old Masters, and across the terrace via a tented corridor into a marquee. In fact, it was three enormous interconnecting marquees, two erected on the lawns leading down to the river, the third encompassing the tributary itself and a gilded ornamental bridge.

Far into the distance, across half an acre of yellow and white striped tenting, Stuart could see a dancefloor and discotheque, dozens of round tables laid for dinner and a second, larger dancefloor where a fifteen-piece dance band, Lester Lanin and his Orchestra, were getting into their swing. Already, there must have been five hundred people inside the tents, and more arriving all the time. The opulence of the scene left Stuart stupefied. Twined around the tent poles were elaborate arrangements of yellow roses, ivy and white lilies. A yew hedge and several classical garden statues had been embraced by the marquees, with champagne bars installed in bowers carved into the yew. Waiters were circulating with trays of cocktails. In the middle of the throng, Stuart spotted Marcus. He was standing four-square in a maroon-coloured velvet smoking jacket, cigar clamped between his teeth, addressing a rather earnest-looking woman in navy blue taffeta. To Stuart, he looked more powerful and substantial than ever, as though taking up more space than anyone else. He reminded him of the dominant stag in an oil painting by Landseer he'd once seen, surveying the glen with absolute assurance and arrogance.

'Stuart!' Noticing his godson, Marcus was summoning him over.

'Stuart, I want to introduce you to the next Prime Minister of England. Margaret, this is Stuart Bolton, my godson and one of the hosts of tonight's party.'

'Come now, Mr Brand,' replied Margaret Thatcher. 'Isn't it tempting fate to describe me as the next Prime Minister?'

'Not at all,' he replied smoothly. 'This Government's finished. Callaghan's a busted flush. Come the election, you'll get in with an overall majority of between forty and fifty seats, that's my prediction. Don't you agree, Stuart? No one's going to vote socialist next time.'

'I don't know about round here, but in Birmingham they are,' Stuart replied. 'Labour's doing a grand job. I don't know anyone who's planning on voting Conservative, as a matter of fact.'

Marcus threw him a quizzical look, which managed to convey both displeasure and amusement.

'You should meet Ginger here,' Stuart went on. 'He works for you, Marcus, at your chassis works in Smethwick. You should meet him too, Mrs Thatcher. He's getting to be an endangered species in Britain – someone who works in industry.'

Margaret Thatcher grasped Ginger by the arm. 'Marvellous decision,' she said, her voice dropping an octave. 'You have made the *right decision*. Britain's prosperity was founded on its industrial revolution – we applaud industry. We must embrace it and invigorate it, to make Britain *great* again. Great Britain! That's the mission of the Conservative Party. To put the *great* back into Britain.'

'Mrs Thatcher is absolutely right,' Marcus said, addressing Ginger. 'Without a sustainable industrial base, the economy will be permanently constricted. I am glad to have you in my company.' He wrung Ginger's hand.

Marcus gave Stuart a nod which signalled that they were dismissed, and they backed into the crowd. Clustered around the bar they found Mick and Lauren, and half the inhabitants of Stuart's hall of residence.

'Get this,' Mick said, 'it's a completely free bar all night. Even shorts are on the house.'

Lauren addressed Stuart reproachfully. 'You never told me your godfather was the guy who shut down Dad's factory. I never would have come, if I'd known that.'

Ginger interjected, 'He's all right, Mr Brand is. He's an all right bloke. Have you seen the buffet? You can have anything you want – cold meats, steaks – this whole big spread.'

'Mary?' Stuart recognised her at once. She had hardly altered in the five years since Lyford Cay; her wary English prettiness was unmistakable. Her cheeks remained slightly plump and soft, and she had lovely white skin. She was wearing a turquoise strapless dress made of raw silk, which didn't quite fit, and almost no make-up apart from lip gloss and a dab of dark blue eyeliner. Her brown fringe was flicked up at the sides.

'Stuart? Is it really you under all that hair?' He thought she looked anxious, like a startled deer ready to bolt. She introduced him to a dozen girls from her old school, the Convent of the Perpetual Martyr, and from the cookery school in Godalming where she was learning to prepare directors' lunches.

'Do you always go around together in this big gang?' Having never encountered southern girls before, Stuart was almost alarmed by these tall, gawky Surrey belles, who said they came from Leatherhead, Haslemere and the Hog's Back.

'They're my bodyguards,' Mary said. 'Protection against Charlie Crieff. If we see him, they're going to surround me.'

'I thought Charlie was a mate. In the Bahamas . . .'

'Don't remind me. I was completely taken in. It's a bit of a sore point. Anyway, I know what he's like now. I'm completely over him.'

'I saw him getting off a coach when we arrived, looking typically pleased with himself.'

'Oh my God, oh my God, he's here!' Mary was suddenly animated. She turned to her friends. 'Lottie, Laura, Nipples, everyone – he's *here*. We've got to find him. But for God's sake, don't let him see me.'

Saffron, Amaryllis and ten members of the Polzeath surfing club had been driven to the dance by Niall McMeakin in a rented Dormobile. The journey from Cornwall to Hampshire had taken seven hours and, somewhere around Micheldever, they had changed into their party clothes in a lay-by. Amaryllis was wearing the Antony Price mermaid dress. Saffron didn't think she'd ever looked more beautiful; more like an elder sister than a mother. Amaryllis, however, was unusually agitated about her appearance, spending the last twenty miles repeatedly fixing her make-up in the driving mirror.

On the dancefloor, Jamie was having a great time. He was bopping with a girl he'd met five minutes earlier, and she was giving him all the signals. He couldn't decide whether to snog her right away or have another drink; probably a drink, there was no hurry. Looking around the tent, he recognised half the people there. Since Marcus's other godchildren had failed to invite enough guests, he and Charlie had ended up with three hundred friends each. It was going to be a wild night. Earlier on, he'd spotted some incredible girls arriving in a transit van – they looked like lifeguards or beach-bums – he'd have to check them out later on.

Abigail mooched gloomily round the party, knowing nobody and realising she was trapped until both her parents, with whom she had arrived in a chauffeured limousine, were ready to leave. Probably that wouldn't be until five or six o'clock in the morning. Harriet had already recognised a prominent, much-married duke and his new American wife across the tent, and was in ecstasy. Zubin had flown the Atlantic with the express purpose of finding investors for a new development project and reckoned Marcus's dance would be a promising hunting ground. He was prowling between the tables in a white tuxedo, trying to identify the money.

Abigail doubted she had ever looked less attractive. She felt a complete frump. She had grown fatter since Lyford Cay, and would have chosen to wear something plain and black to disguise her weight, but her mother had forced her into the showiest dress in the tent, a gold ballgown like a Marie Antoinette shepherdess with bows, ribbons and frills. The only battle Abigail had won was over her hair, which was elaborately blow-dried into a Farrah Fawcett flick.

Queues were forming at the buffets and guests were bagging places for dinner. A top table had been reserved for Marcus, the Leader of the Opposition, several members of her new Shadow Cabinet, the Duke and Duchess and various prominent businessmen, with the remainder of the seven hundred guests left to sit where they liked. Already, distinct cliques were taking up positions around the tent: Charlie and a riotous table of army officers, Jamie surrounded by pretty London girls, Stuart and his Birmingham lot, Mary's Surrey set, Saffron's surfers. Returning from the buffet with a plate of cold salmon and cucumber, Mary spotted Charlie for the first time. In his midnight blue mess jacket and gold epaulettes, he was even better looking than she remembered. For four years she had tried to dispel him completely from her mind, but in those few seconds she knew it hadn't worked and she was still utterly fixated.

Verena and Alistair Crieff were at a table with Jamie Temple's mother Margaret, her ex-husband and Michael's latest squeeze, Yvonne, a stroppy, deeply tanned fitness instructor twenty-seven years his junior. The conversation was not exactly flowing easily. Margaret Temple, unused to staying up so late, had been supplied with powerful uppers by a society doctor in Basil Street and, in her anxiety at seeing Michael and his new piece, had wolfed half the packet, washed down by several glasses of champagne. As a result, she was finding it difficult to form words successfully.

Verena Crieff, having spent the entire journey down from Scotland predicting that they wouldn't know a soul, and that they'd be surrounded by the most ghastly, common people, was furious to have been excluded from the top table. Staring around the vast marquee, and taking in the conspicuous expenditure, she sniffed, pursed her lips and guessed that it must have cost fifty thousand pounds, which was just so vulgar. Had she known the real cost, which she had underestimated by several hundred per cent, she would probably have collapsed.

'If I was going to spend this sort of money,' she declared to Margaret Temple, 'I would much rather buy a painting – something that lasts – than waste it on a party.'

Alistair Crieff, recalling his wife's predilection for lovely paintings, felt a sense of foreboding. The estate accounts had recently been presented to him, and it had been another terrible year. Already he owed more than sixty thousand to the Inland Revenue, Ardnessaig needed a new roof, and the only solution lay in selling pictures. He dreaded telling Verena that the Lely would have to go. It was either that or the Ramsay in the dining room. Nor had Alistair been reassured by a recent visit from Christie's. According to the auctioneer fellow, the pictures at Ardnessaig were worth much less than Alistair had hoped, sporting pictures and family portraits being currently out of fashion.

'You're absolutely right about paintings,' Michael Temple agreed, leaning across the table to Lady Crieff. 'As an investment, they're out-performing the equity market by thirty per cent. Paintings and vintage wine, can't go wrong. That's my tip for tonight.'

'How fascinating,' said Verena, making it plain that she was not fascinated.

'That's where the clever money's headed,' said Michael, unabashed. 'Marcus is buying paintings by the shed load. I saw his dealer earlier on. Said he's bought several Constables on Marcus's behalf already this year, Stubbs too, you name it.'

Just then, bearing plates piled high with langoustines and beef Wellington, a beautiful, ethereal blonde arrived at their table, accompanied by a craggy-faced hippie in a Moroccan kaftan. Michael Temple's eyebrows shot up half an inch. He liked what he was seeing. The blonde was a knockout. He'd had it up to here with Yvonne's moods and hamstring stretches in his bedroom, and was on the hunt for the next big thing.

'Amaryllis, is it? Now you just sit down here next to me and tell me how you came by such a beautiful name,' said Michael, licking his lips like a fox in the hencoop.

Over on the dancefloor, Lester Lanin was belting out a convincing cover-version of Frank Sinatra's 'New York, New York'. 'You have to hand it to Marcus,' Derek Merrett said, as he whisked his wife across the parquet in a good old-fashioned waltz. 'I hear he flew the entire band over from America, just for this evening. That's fifteen aeroplane tickets. Everything Marcus does, he does it with tremendous style. It has to be the best.'

For the briefest of moments, Belinda Merrett wished that Marcus paid her husband more generously instead. But the treacherous thought was quickly suppressed.

At a table surrounded by a dozen of his brother cavalry officers, Charlie was drinking too much. Having spent half the previous week commanding a bunch of squaddies in manoeuvres on Salisbury Plain, and the other half propping up the bar of the Antelope pub in Belgravia, the booze was slipping into his bloodstream more rapidly than usual. Lately, his evenings had all ended the same way. Plenty of alcohol, food fights, some seriously hilarious practical jokes, like the time they'd set up roadblocks overnight on the King's Road and diverted several hundred vehicles into a cul-de-sac at the end of Oakley Street. There had been a frightful stink when it turned out that the adjutant's wife was in one of the cars.

He was pouring himself another large glass of claret when

he noticed Stuart, surrounded by a table of unsavoury specimens. The last time he'd seen Stuart had been in Paris, during the episode with the hookers that Charlie preferred to forget. In his excitement and embarrassment, he had blown off before he'd even got inside his. Then, having nothing to say to the tart, her being foreign, he'd quickly hustled her out of the room.

He remembered that Stuart had just gone to some frightful left-wing, northern university. The others must be his fellow students, judging by their long hair and National Health glasses. Charlie felt an instinctive revulsion, affronted that they should be at Marcus's dance at all.

Spooning up a gobbet of beef Wellington, he flicked it across the tent. 'Grockle alert, everyone! Grockle alert!'

The meat landed on the tablecloth, splattering Lauren's white dress with droplets of gravy.

But when Stuart looked round to see where it had appeared from, Charlie stared innocently down at his plate.

It was approaching midnight and the dance was hotting up. Juliana's Discotheque was pounding out record after record by Blondie and Elton John. The Perpetual Martyr girls were bopping together in a pack to 'Crocodile Rock', while keeping a sharp eye out for likely men to draw into their orbit. Jamie, to his delight, had run into Clayborne Dupuis and was taking up with her where they'd left off in Lyford Cay. Harriet Schwartzman dragged a reluctant Zubin on to the dancefloor, and was shamelessly rubbernecking the Duke and Duchess as they edged closer and closer to them. Michael Temple was pressed up against Amaryllis, his paw-like hands moving on oiled palms from the small of her back to her buttocks.

Stuart, dancing with Lauren for old times' sake, was scanning the tent for any sign of Saffron. To his relief, all his mates appeared to be having a whale of a time. Mick and Ginger were grooving away with Mary's girlfriends. The Surrey contingent, delighted by the novelty of a bit of rough, were throwing themselves at the Birmingham boys, who were amazed by how much more promiscuous posh birds were than their normal women. Out of the corner of his eye, Stuart could see the secretary of the university Labour Club enthusiastically necking with Nipples from the Hog's Back. And Professor Barry Tomkins, noticeably plastered, was prancing about with a bottle of Muscadet in one hand and a balloon of brandy in the other.

Mary hadn't taken her eyes off Charlie all evening. She was watching him now, still at his table, surrounded by subalterns telling blue jokes. Too shy to approach him, she longed for him to come over to the dancefloor, so they could meet by accident. Charlie, meanwhile, giddy with drink, was telling his friends about 'this incredible woman, and I mean really incredible woman, with these incredible long legs. And she's really on for it, OK? Saffron . . . that's her name, Saffron. Bloody stupid name for this really incredible woman. And she's here in the tent, somewhere. And when I've had just one more drink – one more whisky – I'm damn' well going to find her, OK?'

Jamie was thinking what a really classic party this was. He'd been dancing without a break for two hours, with Clayborne, Zara Fane and a dozen more. He'd even had a duty-bop with his younger sister, Lucinda, now a juicy fifteen in violet eyeshadow. There were so many fanciable women, his Marlboro packet was covered with scrawled names and telephone numbers. But when he spotted Saffron on the dancefloor, everyone else was forgotten. She was dancing with a suntanned guy who Jamie reckoned looked a bit of a dork.

'Hi, Saffron. Want a bop?' He cut in, expertly separating her from her partner.

'Er, sure, Jamie,' she replied, as he directed her into the writhing interior of the dancefloor. Soon they were entirely screened by other couples; Jamie preferred to do his dirty work discreetly.

'You look totally, completely, fucking amazing,' he said. 'Why don't I ever see you?'

'Probably because you don't live in Cornwall!'

'*Cornwall?* I thought you'd become a model in Paris or something.'

Saffron smiled. 'It's my mum who looks like a model. That's what people say anyway.'

'We should have dinner one night in London. How about Monday?'

'I can't. We're driving back to Polzeath after this.'

'When then?'

Saffron shrugged. 'I can't really get away. I have a job in a gift shop.'

Heading towards them across the floor came Michael Temple in a sweaty clinch with Amaryllis.

'That's my mum over there. That dirty old bloke's got his hand on her bum.'

'That dirty old bloke's my father, actually.' Jamie roared with laughter. 'He has too – the lucky sod. And you're right, your mum's a cracker. Like mother, like daughter.'

Saffron felt a sudden wave of anxiety. Whenever Amaryllis found a new man, it made her insecure.

'You OK, Saffron?' Jamie asked. 'You've gone white.'

'I'll be fine in a moment. I need some water, that's all.'

'Listen, come with me,' Jamie said. 'To the cloakroom. I think I've got something that might help.'

Across the dancefloor, Marcus was slow-dancing with Clayborne Dupuis, closely watched by Abigail who was dancing stiffly with Dick Mathias. She was thinking, I hate Marcus, I hate him so much. But if I could swap places with Clayborne, I'd pay a million bucks. All round her, men with flushed faces were whirling their partners faster and faster. Her parents, she could see, were performing a perfect foxtrot on the edge of the floor, from which vantage point they could monitor what was happening across the whole marquee. Harriet was bitterly jealous of the American Duchess's diamond choker, which she'd been busy memorising with the intention of commissioning a copy as soon as possible. In general, however, Harriet had been disappointed by the English women at the dance, whom she regarded as underdressed, underjewelled and undercoiffed.

The tables were thinning out, some already abandoned. Weaving between them in search of the loo, a pixilated Barry Tomkins stumbled against a table full of old people.

A woman with a helmet of backcombed black hair and a tartan balldress was saying, 'The man's a complete disgrace. So ostentatious! What I'd like to know is where Marcus came from in the first place. The Macphersons didn't know the first thing about him when he married poor Lucy.'

Professor Tomkins, boss-eyed, fell into a chair next to her and slurred, 'You're absholutely right, Marcush Brand is jusht a pernishous Capitalisht, exshploiting the workersh. Come the revolushion, we'll shtring him up together, you and I.'

Breakfast was being served from silver chafing dishes kept warm over gas burners. Outside on the lawn, a Portakabin ladies' loo was filled with girls repairing their make-up. The army officers were lined up, peeing in unison into a flowerbed. Charlie, shaking himself dry, thought the moment had arrived to find Saffron.

Back inside the marquee, Zubin and Harriet Schwartz-man had forged an introduction to the Crieffs. As a British aristocrat with a large spread in Scotland, Zubin reckoned Lord Crieff would be an ideal investor for his Gramercy Park development.

'It all sounds jolly exciting, I must say,' Alistair replied when Zubin had outlined the opportunity. 'And very decent of you to consider letting me in on it.' He felt pathetically grateful to the worldly American, seeing in him a solution to his money troubles. 'The thing is, you see, we have to put a new roof on Ardnessaig.'

Harriet brightened, having something to contribute to the conversation. 'Why stop at the roof?' she asked. 'We knocked our old house down and started all over. We had it rebuilt to our exact specifications. Zubin wanted a steam room and I have these wonderful walk-in closets. We've got this fabulous architect, I could give you his name.'

Mary found herself trailing Charlie. She had followed him outside and watched as he watered the flowerbed. Not quite daring to say hello, and determined not to be spotted, she nevertheless hoped he would somehow notice her, and everything would be all right again.

Jamie, returning to the marquee from the garden, stopped

and spoke to Charlie. Whatever it was he said seemed to make Charlie angry, and he strode impatiently down an avenue of pollarded limes. They passed the wall of the orangery and along a gravel path which ran parallel to the largest of the three tents, in the direction of the river. Charlie was swaying from side to side. Mary couldn't think where he was going.

In the distance, leaning against the canvas wall of the marquee, she saw someone else, their face obscured by shadow. The moon moved out of cloud, and she realised it was Saffron; but something was wrong with her, her head rolling forward and her movements unco-ordinated. At first, as Charlie approached her, she didn't seem to see him.

Mary stopped. She felt guilty snooping on Charlie, but was unable to back off. She knew he had fancied Saffron in Lyford Cay, but thought all that had finished the night of the beach barbecue when he had chosen her instead.

Charlie went up to Saffron and grasped her roughly by the waist.

'I've come for my snog.'

'Who is this? Oh, it's you, Charlie.' She sounded woozy, not quite sober. 'Don't be an idiot.'

'I mean it. I've been looking for you all night.'

'Let go of me, Charlie. You're being ridiculous.' She tried to push him away.

His voice sounded harsh and slurred. 'I know you want to. I've got a hard-on just thinking about you. Don't you realise that?' His hair was sweaty and she could smell drink on his breath.

'Charlie, I want to go back inside.'

He wrenched her arm behind her back, hurting her. 'You're not going anywhere. You only want to go inside to find Jamie. Or Marcus. You're such a fucking tart, Saffron. Everyone knows that. You do it with anyone who asks. So why not me? Come on, you know you want it.'

'Let go of me, Charlie. Let me go.' Saffron's voice was rising. From inside the marquee, there was music: the Eagles' 'Hotel California'.

Mary tore back through the garden. She had to fetch help.

She was horrified by Charlie, having never seen him drunk before, and felt foolish and naive and scared.

Guests were rock 'n' rolling on the lawn. Several had removed their shoes and socks and were dancing in their bare feet. Mary looked round desperately for anyone she knew.

At a table just inside the entrance to the tent was Stuart. Breathlessly, she said, 'Quick, you've got to come. Outside . . . Charlie and Saffron . . . It's horrible. You've got to do something.'

Stuart leapt up. 'Where are they?'

'Down by the river, I'll show you. He's hurting her.'

Stuart was already outside, sprinting down the lime avenue. He felt surprisingly clear-headed and in control. As he rounded the orangery, he saw Charlie and Saffron tussling against the furthest tent.

Catching him unawares, Stuart lifted Charlie into the air and threw him down on to the wet lawn. 'Saffron, are you all right? Did he hurt you?'

She stared at him, glassy-eyed. She was shivering. Her pupils wouldn't focus. 'Yeah, I'm fine. I'll be fine.'

Charlie's head was spinning with drink and the shock of being knocked down. The knees of his trousers were soaked with dew.

'What the hell did you do that for, you bastard? How dare you?'

'You're completely pissed, Charlie. I'd go back to the party if I were you.'

'Why don't *you* go back to the party?' He was staggering to his feet. 'Saffron and I were having a private conversation. It's none of your fucking business. Go and look after those northern hags you invited.'

'I told you already, Charlie, you're not wanted here. Go back to the tent.'

'Bugger you! I'm not being told what to do by a cleaner's son. And take your dirty paws off Saffron too. You're out of your league, Stuart, always have been.' He was swaying towards them, his face contorted with malevolence. He couldn't believe Stuart had the presumption to interfere. 'Is your mother working here tonight then, clearing away plates?'

'Ignore him, Saffron,' Stuart said. 'He's drunk. Let's go.'

'Go jump in the lake, peasant. That's if you've learned to swim yet.' Charlie lurched forward, tried to swing a punch, stumbled and fell on to his face.

Stuart took off his jacket and draped it over Saffron's shoulders. 'You sure you're OK?'

'I said I'm fine, didn't I? Don't go on about it, that's all.'

Mary took her other side, and together they supported her along the gravel path back to the dance.

Far away, inside the tent, the discotheque was playing 'Silver Machine'. Watching Stuart's broad, shirted back, with his ghastly hired dinner jacket resting across Saffron's shoulders, Charlie considered him the most obnoxious individual he had ever met. And he vowed that, some day, one way or another, he would make that jumped-up little prole squirm.

Part Two

12: September, 1979

Charlie Crieff was hazy about the geography of Hong Kong on Kowloon side; without his Brand Corporation driver, he would never have been able to find the bonded warehouses where the company's one hundred and ninety Chinese employees worked in a maze of sheds and godowns out beyond the airport in the district called Kwun Tong.

For the seventeen weeks he had been employed as a trainee manager in the wine and spirits division of the Brand Pacific Trading Corporation, Charlie had visited the Kwun Tong godown every Tuesday afternoon. These visits were largely a matter of ceremony. Day to day, the warehouse was run with exemplary efficiency by a local foreman of thirty years' experience named Frankie Li. But on Tuesday afternoons, Charlie Crieff, the young *gweilo* bossman from head office, arrived in his stone-coloured tropical suit, striped shirt and Panama to give the place the once-over and ensure everything was ship-shape.

His driver pulled up in the parking space reserved for the emissary of the *taipan*, and held the door open for him to get out. Charlie wrinkled his nose and felt his stomach turn. This area of Kowloon always stank of dried fish and drains. Today, he really thought he might throw up. He had been drinking at the Jockey until two or three o'clock in the morning. The boys had been *roaring*, totally roaring, and his brain was fried. An artery in his forehead throbbed beneath his Panama. He paused for a moment outside, to pull himself together. His stomach muscles were contracting and looping the loop as he fought back the urge to chunder. But to do so in front of his Chinese driver was inconceivable.

He swallowed hard and looked up at the Brand warehouse. It occupied a whole block, a two-hundred-yard stretch of windowless brick, punctuated by grey galvanised air-conditioning ducts. God, this place is a complete and utter hole, he thought, as he picked his way across the broken pavement. He could almost hear the stale alcohol sloshing about inside his legs.

Frankie Li greeted him deferentially, offering the 'small beer' – the bottle of Tsing Tao in a half-pint tankard – which was part of the ritual of the weekly inspection. Mr Li himself never took a beer, and Charlie had never suggested that he might. At that particular moment, the last thing in the world Charlie needed was more alcohol, but to reject the 'small beer' would be to depart from long-established tradition and risk losing face in front of his Chinese subordinate. So they stood awkwardly in the hallway while he drained the tankard and wiped the froth from his upper lip with his sleeve, and then said, 'Right-ho, Mr Li, let's take a look around, shall we? I think we'll begin with the cognacs today.'

Each visit, Charlie made a spot inspection of a different section of the vast warehouse; sometimes it would be the imported French wines and champagnes, sometimes London gin or the wooden pallets loaded with fourteen different Scotch malt whiskies bound for Tokyo and Manila. In four years, the Brand Corporation had become the second largest importer and exporter of European spirits into the Far East after Jardine Matheson.

Mr Li led Charlie between the walls of wooden crates, which rose on either side of them to a height of ten or twelve feet. Each crate had been issued with a docket number which recorded the shipment and port of embarkation as well as its ultimate destination. One of Charlie's jobs was to select random crates and check that their paperwork was in order. Behind their inscrutable exterior, Charlie knew the Chinese were congenitally untrustworthy, and perfectly capable of fudging the dockets and stealing the booze.

As they made their way along the aisles, the Chinese coolies who manoeuvred metal trolleys about the warehouse shrank back into the shadows. Each man was wearing a grey sleeveless vest with BRAND blocked on the back in big black letters. On his early visits, Charlie had made a point of acknowledging the workers, wishing them a patrician good afternoon in the same spirit that he greeted the tenantry on the Ardnessaig Estate when he happened to run into them, but these overtures were met with blank incomprehension, so he no longer bothered. Instead, he followed Mr Li between the canyons of pallet slats, trying to look like the man in charge and not like a twenty-four-year-old with a major-league hangover.

Almost the first thing Charlie had learned when he joined the company was the Chinese taste for premium cognac. Privately, he thought Chinks shouldn't be drinking expensive French brandy; he reckoned it was a status thing for them and doubted they truly appreciated the taste. Cognac was the highest-ticket commodity in the godown, and consequently the most prone to theft.

'OK, Mr Li. Let's have that box out here, shall we?' Bloody-mindedly, Charlie pointed to a crate three rows deep into the stack, and four feet down from the top.

'That one, Mr Clieff?' The Chinese foreman looked dismayed.

'No, one row further in. Watch where I'm pointing, won't you?'

Half a dozen warehousemen began the job of dismantling the tower of crates in the restricted space. The men were soon sweating and cursing as they heaved them on top of neighbouring stacks, to liberate the one Charlie had indicated. It took almost twenty minutes to reach it. Charlie, still feeling nauseous, tapped his foot as a sign of irritation.

'OK, give me the docket,' he commanded Mr Li. Cursorily scanning it, he saw that it had arrived at the port of Hong Kong from Le Havre twenty-six days earlier, and was bound for Kao-hsiung in Taiwan on a shipment the following week. Then he asked for the crate to be opened. A coolie produced a crowbar and prised open the wooden lid. Charlie removed a bottle from its bed of straw and examined it in the half-light.

'That one seems to be in order. Now that one, please.' He pointed to a box on the very bottom row of the adjacent pallet, on to which the coolies had been shifting the overspill crates from the first tower. To reach it would involve moving twice as many boxes as before. Frankie Li stared flatly at Charlie before relaying the order in Cantonese.

Not for the first time since he'd arrived in Hong Kong, Charlie was grateful for his officer training. He felt that it had imbued him with a confidence about giving orders and an expectation that these commands would be obeyed. He could appreciate why the great companies of the colony – Swire's, Jardine's and the Brand Pacific Trading Corporation – employed British recruits of appropriate background to run their businesses. It was largely a question of attitude. A fellow like Frankie Li was a first-rate individual, but in the end you needed a white man, and preferably a public school white man, to keep them on the straight and narrow. Charlie hadn't the slightest doubt that Mr Li felt exactly the same way.

It took the coolies half an hour to reach the second crate. The foreman tore off the docket and presented it to Charlie.

'Actually, Mr Li,' said Charlie, 'I'm not going to bother to look at that one. So long as you know that I *could* look at it, nobody will try any funny stuff. The men can put the crates back as they were now.'

Whatever misgivings Charlie had once had about working for his godfather had long since disappeared. His position as Marcus's godson had, in fact, conferred on him a status he was quick to capitalise on. The job itself was not taxing. His office in Ice House Street, situated in an annexe of the local Brand headquarters in Chater Road, was two minutes' walk from the Captain's Bar at the Mandarin Hotel. He shared a Brand company mess on the Peak with two other trainees and a hoop-backed Chinese amah, Betty Woo, who stirred the dust about with a bamboo broom and took care of the laundry. At night, she slept on a roll-up mat on the kitchen floor so was liable to be woken up whenever they fetched San Migs from the fridge. There was a company junk moored in Aberdeen Harbour, which could be borrowed for expeditions across to Lamma or around the coast to Stanley. There were even several company cottages on the underpopulated neighbouring island of Lantau, which could be rented for weekend parties. Charlie soon discovered that, as Marcus's godson, he could jump the queue for these sought-after cottages, if he spoke to the right people and made sure they were fully in the picture.

Early on, Charlie found that life was sweeter if he implied that he was closer to Marcus than he actually was. If truth be told, he had not seen his godfather for almost two years, since the great dance at West Candover Park. When, on completing his Short Service Commission, he had written to Marcus asking for a job, the letter had been answered by some grey man in the personnel department, who had insisted Charlie be subjected to the whole rigmarole of interviews and aptitude tests, including an exceedingly tedious 'Assessment and Orientation Weekend' at a college outside Brackley. Once installed in Hong Kong, however, things looked up considerably, and Charlie allowed it to be understood that he had a direct line to Marcus, and had to some extent been posted to the Colony to act as his second pair of eyes. This did not particularly endear him to his superiors, but made sufficient impression to secure him plenty of leeway. Nobody ever made an issue of it when he arrived late in Ice House Street after a heavy night, or failed to complete his routine reports on time. And as far as invitations were concerned, Charlie's special relationship with the owner meant that he was asked to more, and better, parties than would ever otherwise have come his way. In his first twelve weeks, he was asked up to play tennis and swim and have lunch by half the local directors of BPTC at their houses on the Peak, and the view took hold that Charlie Crieff, eldest son and heir of Lord Crieff of Ardnessaig, cousin of the Earl of Arbroath and godson of Marcus, was a sound addition to the Hong Kong expatriate community. Granted, he didn't particularly put himself out in terms of conversation and charm, nor was he conspicuously grateful for the efforts made on his behalf, but he was young, tall, single and well-connected, and this alone was enough to guarantee his social success.

It was fortunate, from Charlie's point of view, that Marcus was spending so little time in the Far East. Having bought a controlling interest in the Imperial Kowloon

Trading Company four years earlier, he had devoted eighteen months to conducting a reign of terror, winkling the last of the founding Dumfermline family from the board of directors, changing the name to the Brand Pacific Trading Corporation and restructuring the business from top to bottom. It had been Marcus's personal decision to tear down the nineteenth-century headquarters building, with its wide verandas and famous tea gardens fronting Victoria Harbour, and to replace them with the Hung Hom Lucky Plaza shopping mall. He had ordered the string of company racehorses, the pride and joy of old 'Whitey' Dumfermline and stabled up at the Imperial yard in Happy Valley, to be sold and the site built over by an apartment block and Porsche showroom, for which BPTC had recently become the local concessionaire. Since his return to London, Marcus's control of the company was exerted largely by memo and telex. But the anxiety in the eyes of his managers and directors was manifest, and Charlie was quick to work it for all that it was worth.

During this period, long-serving executives existed in a climate of fear. Any day they could be called to one of the penthouse suites at the top of the Mandarin that Marcus used as his corporate offices, and be summarily fired. In these situations, Marcus was reluctant ever to pay more than the minimum compensation; his preference for long and expensive legal action to even the barest acknowledgement of contractual obligations was legendary.

One evening, eight months after his arrival in Hong Kong, Charlie received a surprise telephone call at the mess from Barbara Miles.

'Is that Charlie? This is Mrs Miles speaking. I'm ringing you from Marcus Brand's office at the Mandarin Hotel.'

After a brisk exchange of pleasantries, she said, 'Mr Brand is in Hong Kong on a two-day visit, and hopes you can have breakfast with him tomorrow morning here at his suite.'

Somewhat less than nine hours later, Charlie found himself sitting across a cloth-covered room-service wagon from his godfather, eating a plate of bacon and fried eggs. It was the first time Charlie had seen Marcus in work-mode, and he found the experience alarming. Breakfast was punctuated by a stream of telephone calls, during which he barked peremptory orders to unidentified subordinates. He was jacketless, wearing the trousers of a navy blue suit and reeked overpoweringly of a citrus-based eau de cologne. Twice he interrogated Charlie – 'Making me any money yet?' – but moved on before he could answer.

There was a tap at the door and Barbara Miles entered, saying, 'Mr Russell has arrived for his eight-thirty appointment, Mr Brand.'

Charlie had met Rory Russell on several occasions. A well-loved, bumbling veteran of Imperial Kowloon with thirty years' service, he had lately been sidelined in the business and now largely occupied himself by running the colony's annual croquet tournament. Like Charlie, he originated from the east coast of Scotland, and Rory and his wife had been among the first to invite Charlie to lunch when he'd arrived.

'Should I leave?' Charlie asked, not unhappy to have an excuse to get out.

'No, stay. This won't take long.'

Rory Russell entered the suite, brimming with respectful goodwill towards his ultimate boss. He hoped Marcus had had a comfortable flight from London, that the Mandarin was pulling out all the stops for him, that he would have time to watch some racing at the weekend.

'Look, never mind all that,' Marcus replied, curtly. 'The fact is, there isn't a job for you here any longer. You know that, I know that, we all know that. You're a busted flush, Russell, and we don't have room for passengers in this organisation. Sorry to be blunt, but I would like you to leave at the end of this month.'

Rory Russell's affable face collapsed in shock and dismay. Having never exchanged an intemperate word with anyone in his life, he could hardly cope with what he was hearing. He stood in the middle of the room, gaping for air like a beached fish.

'I'm sorry you feel that way,' he replied at last. 'I have always tried to serve this company loyally, and to the best of my ability. I have been stationed out here for more than thirty years. Couldn't you just give me a couple more years, old boy? Both my sons will be finished with school by then, and I promise I'll go quietly.'

Under the terms of their original contracts with Imperial Kowloon, senior expatriate managers had the larger part of their children's school fees paid by the company. Rory, Charlie knew, had two teenage boys at Oundle.

Marcus, picking at a fruit platter at his desk, gave the man a bored, distracted look.

'There are, presumably, free schools back in England. That's what I've always heard. Though, frankly, if your sons are anything like you in terms of intellect, I seriously doubt they're capable of reaping the benefits of education.'

'I always had an understanding with Whitey Dumfermline . . .' Rory began. Tears were pricking his eyes now, and his face had drained of colour.

'Don't you dare quote Whitey Dumfermline at me! It was Whitey Dumfermline and the dim-witted, inadequate managers he surrounded himself with who damn' near did for this company. I've spent the past several years clearing up the mess they left behind. That's my final word on the subject. Now, get out of this suite, please, before I call security to throw you out. And I expect you to vacate your company house by midday on the thirty-first or I'll send the police round to help.'

Charlie's charmed life in Hong Kong was marred by only one shortcoming: he never had enough money. As a trainee manager in the wine and spirits division, he was on the bottom rung of the Brand Corporation salary scale, and the company made deductions every month for his (heavily subsidised) messing arrangements and share of the amah. Although it was widely supposed that he had a generous monthly allowance from his parents – and capital – this was not in fact the case. The Ardnessaig Estate was continuing to struggle and, for the third year running, had actually recorded a loss. In a recent letter from his father, Alistair Crieff had mentioned that he was considering selling Invercairn, a farm on the edge of the estate. He was still depending on things coming right in New York, and mentioned that he was hearing encouraging noises about the Gramercy Park development in which he had become an investor. Referring to Zubin Schwartzman, he described him as 'that clever American Jew I met at your godfather's dance down south'.

Charlie soon realised that he was spending much more in Hong Kong than he earned. Not by nature extravagant, he nevertheless felt there were minimum standards by which he should live – and be seen to live. If it was assumed that he was well off, he saw no reason to disappoint public opinion. He ordered himself suits, shirts and pyjamas at Sam's forty-eight-hour tailor in the Miramar Hotel Arcade (another establishment that expected gentlemen to sink a 'small beer' when ordering clothes) and from A-Man Hing Cheong at the Mandarin. At lunchtime and after work, he drank at the Bull and Bear at the bottom of Hutchinson House or at the Godown in the basement of Sutherland House behind the Hong Kong Club. Quickly tiring of the food that Betty Woo served up in the mess – the roast chicken and stir-fry vegetables, the lychees in syrup – he took to eating out every night in restaurants. Hong Kong in the late seventies was full of itinerant English girls – backpacking Sloanes – passing through on their way to Thailand or Bali. They flitted into town for a week or two to buy cameras before striking out for Chiang-Mai or Chiang-Rai. (Charlie never fully got his head round where these exotic places actually were; all he understood was that, while they were in Hong Kong, these tantalising pretty girls in their tight pink trousers expected to doss down on the sitting-room floor of his mess, and be taken out to dinner – and paid for.)

Six months into his posting, just as he was about to slope off from work for the night, Charlie took a telephone call in Ice House Street.

"Allo? 'Allo? Is that Charlie Clieff? I like to order two Number Four, yes, please, with special flied lice, egg lice, prawn clacker . . .'

The voice was unmistakably that of an English public schoolboy attempting a comic Chinese accent.

'Who is this?' Charlie was hungover and not completely in the mood.

'Me Chinese laundly. Ah so, you want me teach you sexy Chinese bledroom tricks, yes, please?'

'Look, cut it out, will you? It's not that funny.'

'God, keep your hair on, Charlie. What happened? Have you turned into a stuffed shirt?'

'Jamie? Fuck, I should have guessed! Where are you, for Christ's sake?'

'The airport.'

'*Here*? You mean Kai Tak?'

'Where do you think I mean, you git? Moscow? Actually, that's where I just was. I flew Aeroflot.'

'But what are you doing in Hong Kong?'

'Complicated story. I'll explain at dinner. Well, are you picking me up from here or aren't you? I am coming to stay with you, you realise.'

It was great to see Jamie. Charlie hadn't even realised how much he had missed his best friend. They had supper at a Mongolian barbecue place in Wanchai on their way in from the airport, and didn't miss a beat. All their old banter resumed as though they were back having a drink in London.

The teenage Chinese waitress who took their order was stunning in a white blouse and pencil-thin black skirt, and while she was oiling up the iron barbecue and lighting the burner, Jamie ran his hand up her skirt, making her jump with shock. Later, when she took their order, he asked, 'Have you any goose on the menu tonight?'

'Gloose?' She tittered nervously.

'Goose? Do Chinese peoples like to be goosed?' He gave her one of his most charming, flirtatious smiles. 'Very nice goosing.'

'I find out,' replied the waitress, hurrying through the swing-doors into the kitchen.

A minute later, a huge Chinese matron appeared at the table with wrestler's muscles and a tuft of black underarm hair sprouting from a tear in her blouse. 'Yes?'

'My God, Charlie, you never told me your sister was

working here.' Jamie smiled up at the waitress. 'Two chicken barbecue. Two large beers. Oh, and your daughter to take away after the meal.'

When they'd finished laughing and the beers had arrived, Charlie said, 'Well, what *are* you doing in Hong Kong then?'

'Skipping the country.' Jamie rolled his eyes. 'Not seriously, I mean I'm not wanted by the police or anything. Nothing heavy. It just seemed advisable to get out for a few weeks.'

'But why? What have you been up to?'

'It's no big deal. It's these people I'm sharing a flat with. You don't know them, but they sometimes use stuff, just for themselves, and the fuzz were starting to poke their noses in.'

'You mean drugs? You should be careful, Jamie.'

'Honestly, Charlie. I don't even do drugs, hardly ever. Nothing hard anyway. It's the other people in the flat. I couldn't afford them, even if I wanted any. I'm broke.'

They ordered another round of beers and Charlie, laughing, said, 'For God's sake, don't buy any here. They hang drug smugglers in Hong Kong. Didn't you see the notices at the airport?'

'No way would I do them here. Especially when I'm staying with you. You're practically running Hong Kong now, aren't you? Or that's what I heard.'

'Hardly,' Charlie replied, though he liked the compliment. 'Who did you hear that from, incidentally?'

'Oh, Dad ran into Marcus somewhere and he mentioned something about it. Said you're doing very well.'

'*Marcus* said that?'

'You're the blue-eyed godson. That's according to Dad.'

Charlie felt a glow of self-satisfaction. So his efforts had been noticed after all. In a way, it didn't surprise him. He had certainly sharpened things up at the Kwun Tong warehouse and, socially, he reckoned he was operating at a higher level than the other management trainees. By the time they had finished dinner, and were sharing a cab up the steep lanes to the Peak, Charlie had come to see Marcus's appreciation as no more than his due, which would no doubt shortly be reflected in a pay-increase and promotion. The more he thought about it, the more he saw himself on the fast-track to the top.

It was incredible how many people knew Jamie, Charlie thought, after only a few days in Hong Kong. Half the backpacking Sloanes in pink trousers were friends of his from London, and they were so pleased to see him. He had schoolfriends who now worked at Jardine Matheson and Swire's, and they were pleased to see him too (much more pleased than they had ever been to see Charlie when he arrived). All day, while Charlie was out at work, Jamie rang friends and made plans. Betty Woo, who had never been seen to smile before in her life, was instantly charmed by him, scooping all his dirty washing from his suitcase and returning it with a blush, washed and ironed, without being asked.

Every evening they ate out in parties of sixteen or more people. It seemed that the whole colony couldn't get enough of Jamie Temple. But whenever a bill arrived, he left Charlie to pick up his share, promising to pay him back later.

'This can't go on, you know,' Charlie said one evening. 'Me paying for everything. I've almost run out.'

'Leave it to me tonight,' Jamie said mysteriously. 'I'll show you a good trick.'

That evening, an even larger party than usual went to a Szechuan restaurant on Nathan Road. There must have been twenty-four of them, and their noisy table occupied the entire window. Jamie, in jeans and an open-necked shirt, held court, surrounded by five of the sexiest and most sought-after girls in Hong Kong. Charlie, in cords and a tweed jacket, watched his friend in envious admiration and tried to work out what it was women saw in him.

It wasn't that Jamie said anything interesting. He just laughed a lot, and ran his fingers through his fringe. And he had the knack of touching girls without its being a big deal. Right now, Jamie's left hand was resting on Georgie's wrist, and his right arm was draped round Rachel's shoulder. Neither was objecting.

Whenever Charlie attempted physical contact with women, they recoiled as though he was making a move on them.

The bill arrived and Jamie raised his hand to the hovering waiter and said, 'Over here, please.' He took the bill, studied it and looked round the table counting heads. Picking up a pen from the saucer, he began a long-division sum.

He addressed the party: 'I take it the men are all paying for a girl each tonight, and I've added a tip. So that's two hundred Hong Kong dollars for each man.' Then, turning to Charlie, he said, 'I'm doing your share tonight, Charlie, so I'll pay for four.'

He collected together the money – a stash of red and green dollar bills – and carefully counted it. 'There we go. All done. No one needs to wash dishes.'

As they headed down Nathan Road, dodging the oncoming pedestrians, Charlie whispered, 'I don't get it. I thought you said you didn't have any cash.'

'I don't. I just excluded us when dividing up the bill. We didn't pay a bean.'

Charlie looked at him in a mixture of horror and respect. 'Bloody hell. Do you do that a lot?'

'Almost never, actually. I prefer to borrow from my friends.'

'What if the others find out?'

'They won't. They never saw the total. And asking them to pay for a girl helps, it confuses things. No one disputes a bill when they're paying for a bird.'

They were approaching the Star ferry terminal to re-cross to Hong Kong side when Jamie shouted, 'Mary – Mary?' A girl in a velvet jacket and an older man in a blazer were standing in line by the gangway.

'Jamie! How amazing. Have you met my father, Derek Merrett?' Then Mary noticed Charlie behind Jamie. She coloured and introduced him as well.

'What are you doing here?' Mary asked Jamie.

'Staying with Charlie. How about you?'

'Staying with Dad. He's working out here at the moment. He works for Marcus, remember. In shipping.'

'We should all get together one evening,' suggested Derek Merrett, rubbing his hands together and with a slightly ingratiating, lop-sided smile. 'You're all three god-children of Marcus's, aren't you? Perfect excuse for a little get together.'

'Give me your number,' Jamie said to Mary, 'and let's meet up for a drink or something.'

After they'd boarded the ferry, Charlie asked him, 'You're not really intending to ring her?'

'Why not? She's looking great or didn't you notice?'

'Her father's awfully charlie. Don't you despise men who wear Hush Puppies and have leather patches on their elbows?'

'Didn't notice. Too busy ogling Mary. She's got really pretty.'

Charlie shrugged. 'She's OK, I suppose.'

'I thought you fancied her. You used to. In Nassau, on that golf course . . .'

'Forget it, Jamie. That was nothing. It was just tongues.'

'You should have another crack. Why not? She's here in Hong Kong and gagging for it.'

'Don't be stupid.'

''Course she is. Don't you notice anything? Minute she saw you, she went red as a beetroot. I'm telling you, it's there for the asking, I can always read the signals. Ask her out for dinner, you'll be in her knickers in no time.'

Charlie looked thoughtful. Until Jamie pointed it out, he hadn't registered how much Mary had changed. Objectively, he could see that she had, indeed, become quite fanciable. Her black hair was shining with health, her skin pink and pretty; she had nice, even white teeth and, so far as he could tell under the velvet jacket, good firm tits. If truth be told, Charlie had been feeling shifty about his behaviour to Mary at his birthday discotheque at Ardnessaig. Not so shifty that he had considered doing anything about it, like apologising; but, dimly, he knew he had behaved reprehensibly, and had tried to expunge the memory from his mind. He had spotted her in the throng at Marcus's dance, but had pretended not to. What was the point? Mary and he came from different parts of the country and, he assumed, moved in rather different circles. Like his mother, he had an instinctive contempt for Surrey, a county he had never visited. He knew it to be full of mock-Tudor villas with in and out driveways, birdbaths and crazy paving. His fleeting introduction to Mary's father at the Star ferry terminal only confirmed his prejudice about the calibre of the people who lived there.

However, Jamie's crack about Mary dropping her knickers in exchange for dinner played on Charlie's mind.

He realised that, in terms of sexual experience, he came nowhere next to his friend. It was an area that filled him with confusion and embarrassment. When he remembered the night at the Hôtel Ritz, he blanched. Afterwards, when Jamie had regaled him with graphic details of his own non-stop antics with the Chinese *culotte*, Charlie had fallen silent. There were some episodes too sensitive to focus on without a shudder.

'Well?' Jamie asked, as they shared a nightcap back at the mess. 'What have you decided? Are you going to get your leg over Mary Merrett or aren't you?'

Charlie shrugged.

'Because if you're not, I might have a crack.'

Charlie regarded his friend with surprise. '*You* might? You said on the ferry it was me she fancied.'

'I've told you, you can have her any time you want. I'm just saying, if you decide to pass, I'll give her one myself. But it's your call.'

Charlie opened a beer and tipped it over the dregs of his whisky. He had to admit that the idea of rogering Mary, if it really was on a plate, was worth considering. She wasn't bad-looking and if Jamie was right, and she really was on for it, then why not? He had no intention of putting himself out, or shelling out a load of expenditure in terms of dinners and flowers, but if it was a simple matter of a roll in the sack, then he might as well have a go. And he certainly didn't like the idea of Jamie getting in there instead. Charlie reckoned the Jamie Temple fan club was large enough already, without adding Mary to his roster of conquests.

So he said, 'Actually, Jamie, I think I might as well shag her myself.'

'Good man.'

Before they turned in, they resolved to invite Mary that weekend to one of the Brand company cottages on Lantau. 'I'll see how I feel about her once we get there,' Charlie said. 'So long as she doesn't wear Hush Puppies like her frightful old man.'

'The extraordinary thing about these Chinese islands,' Charlie declared, as the ferry backed up to the pier in Silvermine Bay, 'is that they're identical to Scotland. That view over there of the peak – it could be the view towards Ardnessaig from Invercairn.'

They had caught the Friday evening sailing to Mui Wo from the Outlying Islands Ferry Pier in Central. For Mary, it was the first time she had left the centre of Hong Kong since arriving there, and she spent the journey peering through steamed-up windows, watching the junks ply their course across the South China Sea, and staring at the dark, rocky islands that littered the channel. Charlie was explaining to Jamie the responsibilities of his job in the wine and spirits division. As he told it, he was a merchant adventurer in a perilous sea of yellow faces; only by living on his wits, and relying on the innate respect of the native for the *gweilo*, was he able to deter the Chinks from raiding the cognac and running amok.

'It's essential they see you in a certain way,' he said. 'The thing about your average Chinaman is, left to his own devices, he'll happily sit on his backside smoking opium and playing mah-jong all day. That's when he isn't part of some Triad. But point him in the right direction and he's bloody resourceful, works hard, hates trade unionism as much if not more than we do, detests communism. Ask Johnny Li what he thinks of Chairman Mao and his little red book, and he'll tell you. They're scared shitless the People's Army will march across the border one fine morning, and they'll all be dragged off to some collective rice paddy in the Pearl River delta.'

Mary had been in a state of excitement and anxiety since Jamie had suggested the weekend on Lantau. Seeing Charlie at the Star ferry terminal had reawakened feelings in her that she had thought were long dead. Six years had passed since the momentous holiday in Lyford Cay, and any residual yearning for him had been ruthlessly suppressed. It was a fact that, for almost four years following her humiliating dumping at Ardnessaig, she had been gripped by a destructive obsession. She would wake up in the night, remembering the exact expressions on Charlie's and Zara's faces when she had disturbed them in her bedroom: Charlie's popping eyes, Zara's black lipstick, Charlie's hand paralysed inside Zara's bustier. Throughout her Cordon Bleu cooking course, she had thought about Charlie every day, picturing him with Zara and making herself miserable with fantasies about their happiness. She had found it impossible to blame Charlie for what had happened, seeing Zara – treacherous, sluttish Zara – as the villain of the piece. Mary had confided in her all her most secret feelings about Charlie, and all the time Zara had been planning to seduce him away from her. In Godalming, when other boys had asked her out, she gave signals that there was already somebody else in her life, and consequently had no boyfriends. Only when Charlie betrayed her for the second time, as she saw it, at West Candover Park with Saffron, was she able to break the cycle of obsession, and shrug off the hope that he would one day return to her.

She had been deeply shocked by the episode behind the marquee at Marcus's dance. Charlie had seemed like a different person that night, drunk and overbearing. She didn't like to think what might have happened if she hadn't fetched help, and yet she felt embarrassed about her part in that too. Stuart must have guessed she'd been following Charlie. And she had mixed feelings about Stuart's assault on him, throwing him on to the ground like that. Had he needed to be so rough when it was obvious Charlie was drunk? Even at the time, a part of Mary had wanted to rush forward and wrap her arms around him and look after him.

They disembarked on to the pier at Mui Wo, carrying

their weekend bags. The sea in the harbour was murky and choked with floating plastic debris. Along the front, past the barrier, was a Chinese market and various food stalls and seafood places. Charlie strode ahead in his cords and tweed jacket, searching for a taxi. Watching him, Mary again thought how good-looking he was. Now that he was out of the Army, he had grown his hair slightly longer. But he hadn't lost his erect bearing: chest out, shoulders back.

They were dropped at the Brand Corporation cottage, and hunted about for the key kept under a stone Buddha by the back door. Architecturally the cottage, one of three built by the Dumfermlines as a staff amenity, reminded Mary of the estate cottages at Ardnessaig, and the association was uncomfortable. Inside were three large, underfurnished bedrooms, and a sitting room with a nineteenth-century print above the fireplace of a tea clipper entering Victoria Harbour.

Jamie collected some cold beers from the kitchen and they sat outside on a stone bench, taking in the view. Away in the distance they could see the pitched rooftops and prayer flags of the Po Lin Monastery and a dramatic peak enveloped in mist.

'Does this cottage really belong to Godfather Marcus?' Mary asked.

'To the company,' Charlie said. 'But since he owns BPTC outright, you could say it's his cottage. They all are.'

'Does he stay here much, do you know?'

'God, no. I doubt he even knows it exists. When he comes to Hong Kong, he stays at the Mandarin or the Peninsula.'

Cracking open a second San Miguel, Jamie said, 'This would be a great place to grow hash, you realise. You could cultivate the whole hillside and make a fortune.' Then, noticing Charlie's horrified face, he said, 'Just joking. Probably Marcus wouldn't find it funny either, if his place was busted.'

Charlie had preordered a box of provisions from the amah who took care of the cottage, and Mary volunteered to make supper. As she unpacked the food, she wondered by what criteria Charlie had chosen it; there was a scrawny white chicken wrapped in newspaper, two plastic bags full of large white radishes, a tin of beef in oyster sauce and three bottles of Glenfiddich. In the back of the larder she found rice, left behind by previous weekenders, a wok, soy sauce and a jar of mint jelly. She considered what her teachers on the Cordon Bleu course would have suggested in this predicament. For her directors' lunches, she generally produced a salmon and leek roulade, followed by boeuf-en-croûte. She would love to have cooked an equally delicious meal tonight, if only she had the ingredients. (What were you supposed to do with giant radishes? Fry them? Add them to a casserole?) The act of preparing dinner, and being in sole charge of this strange kitchen, made her feel busy and happy. Outside on the terrace, Charlie and Jamie were laughing and drinking beers. When he smiled, Charlie was incredibly handsome. Through the open window, she heard him drawl, 'Still haven't made up my mind actually, Jamie. Could go either way.'

Mary laid the table in the sitting room. She found candlesticks, and tablemats with pictures of Regency bucks shooting snipe in the drawer of a dresser. The serving dishes looked as though they hadn't been washed properly for forty years; dust ran off them in rivulets under the tap. Miraculously, the dinner was starting to come together too. When she called the men in from the terrace to eat, she was quite proud of the civilised scene she had somehow managed to conjure up.

Throughout dinner, Charlie went out of his way to be amusing and attentive. He made Mary laugh, describing some of the characters on the Ardnessaig Estate, like the old ghillie who lived in a cottage by the top loch and stubbornly refused to allow any liquid to pass his lips except whisky. Lord Crieff had had to write a special letter on his behalf when he'd gone into the cottage hospital for an operation. And he related the idiocies of the amah, Betty Woo, at the mess. Asked to make Yorkshire pudding, she had produced something resembling a swollen doughnut. When they cut into it, soy sauce had spurted all over the ceiling.

Jamie, for once, was almost subdued, leaving Charlie to

make the running. After dinner, explaining that he didn't feel too great, he disappeared to bed.

Charlie poured a couple of whiskies and carried them outside on to the terrace. 'They have amazing stars in this part of the world. You can really see them clearly.'

They sat side by side on the stone bench, looking up at the inky black sky. A couple of miles away across the valley, they could hear the tinkling of wind chimes from the monastery.

As she gazed up into the night, Mary became conscious of an arm, a long serpentine arm, sneaking along the back of the bench. It began its mission covertly – Charlie was ostensibly stretching his arms – but, surreptitiously, like the tentacle of an octopus closing on its prey, it edged behind her back and a large hand encircled her shoulder. All the while, Charlie continued to stare intently upwards, as though nothing was quite so fascinating to him at that moment as Chinese astronomy, and the hand by now gently massaging Mary's shoulder was an independent phenomenon for which he had no responsibility.

Mary felt her breath quicken. She hadn't expected this, and hardly knew how to react. There was a time – such a long time – when she had yearned for Charlie, and she had tried so hard to suppress her feelings for him.

The hand moved away from her shoulder and gravitated towards her left breast. The fingers were marching like an army of ants across her blouse. So far, Mary had given no indication that she had even noticed them. Charlie was still gaping at the stars.

'Charlie? Should you be doing this? What about Zara?'

'Zara? Who's Zara?'

'Zara Fane. I . . . You're going out with her, aren't you?'

'Oh, that Zara. God, no. Whatever gave you that idea?'

Mary felt a wave of confusion. 'But in Scotland . . .'

'That was nothing, it never was. The thing about Zara is, she isn't even properly Scottish. She pretends she is, but they only bought that house twenty years ago. Anyway,' he said, suddenly lunging to kiss her, 'who cares about Zara? You're much prettier.'

Mary found herself kissing him back, far more passionately than she ever would have expected, and then Charlie said, 'Come on, let's go to bed. Time for some action.'

The invitation was delivered as an order, and Mary obediently followed him back into the house, past the debris of dinner still on the table, and into his bedroom. His shirt was already off, and he had one foot up on the bed, untying the laces of his brown brogues.

'Buck up and get your kit off, Mary,' he said as he stepped out of his tan-coloured cords. 'Let's not hang about.'

Mary peeled off her dress and dived under the bedclothes in her underwear. The sheets felt cold and damp against her back. Charlie joined her, still wearing his Sam's boxer shorts.

He yanked her knickers down round her ankles, pulled down his own boxers and was in. Mary closed her eyes and bit her lip. Charlie thrust painfully half a dozen times before suddenly pulling out and coming over her bush. Mary's first real sexual experience was all over in under a minute.

Afterwards, she lay uncertainly in the bed while Charlie took a noisy pee in the bathroom next door. When he returned, he said, 'Any chance you could fetch me a whisky, Mary? There should be some around somewhere.'

She put on his dressing gown and went through to the kitchen to find the Glenfiddich. To her dismay, Jamie was getting a beer from the fridge.

He raised his eyebrows meaningfully and asked, 'So?'

Mary, mortified, pretended she hadn't understood, and began stacking dishes in the sink.

'I'm curious. Does Charlie fuck with his socks on?'

She didn't reply.

'You never really know, you see, with your best friends. You go to the same school, go on holiday, stay with Marcus, but when it comes to screwing, you haven't a clue what they're like at it. And no way of finding out, unless you're queer, or sleep with the same women. So, go on, give us the low down.'

Mary dropped the dishes into the sink with a clatter, and ran, crying, into her own room and slammed the door.

13: October, 1979

In a first-floor office above a bathroom appliance showroom near the S-bend of the King's Road, Jamie had his feet up on his desk and was smoking a Gauloise. The phone was jammed under the crook of his neck while he held on for Fringe Benefits, a hairdresser's in Putney High Street. He had already been holding for ten minutes and could hear the manageress in the background, helping a customer on with her coat.

Eventually, and with obvious reluctance, she came to the phone. 'Hello?'

'Good afternoon, Mrs Blanco. This is Jamie Temple from *World's End* magazine and I have some very good news for you.'

'Oh, yes?'

'Fringe Benefits has just been nominated as one of the ten best hairdressing salons in our distribution area. Congratulations, Mrs Blanco, on a well-earned victory.'

'Oh, yes?' The manageress sounded cautiously pleased, but non-committal, as though she didn't know quite what value to attach to the accolade.

'Mrs Blanco, we're going to be publishing a special feature about the winners in our next issue mentioning, er, Fringe Benefits. I wondered whether you might like to take an advertisement in the magazine, to capitalise on your success?'

This time, the reaction was suspicious.

'Where did you say you're ringing from again?'

'*World's End*. We're a controlled-circulation publication covering Chelsea, Fulham, Putney, Parson's Green, Hurlingham and Earl's Court. Very upmarket. Seventy thousand circulation.' Jamie winked across the desk at Wanda and made a face. 'And, as I say, you've been voted one of the top ten salons, Mrs Blanco.'

Wanda was a fellow salesman at *World's End*, an Australian from Perth or maybe Adelaide. Most of the sales team were Aussies or Kiwis, doing the job for a month or two before moving on.

'I'm sorry, Mrs Blanco? You're saying you don't want to advertise? I can assure you, all your competitors are going to be in the feature.' He consulted his list of prospects. 'Hair Today is coming in. So's Curl Up And Dye. Comb Hither in the Brompton Road. Captain Backwash in Gunter Grove . . .'

Jamie held the receiver away from his ear, and took a drag on his fag.

'Well, I'm sorry you feel that way, Mrs Blanco. But if you're not able to support us with an advertisement then I'm not sure we'll be able to keep you in as one of our winners. It would be very disappointing. Most of our award winners are very keen to participate, for all the extra business it brings them. A half-page only costs £140, which is a bargain for ninety-thousand circulation.'

He took a pair of scissors from the desk and, rolling his eyes at Wanda, pretended to cut through the telephone wire. He mouthed, 'What are you doing after work, sweetheart? Fancy a drink?'

Wanda mouthed back, 'Sure. Who's paying?'

'You. But I'll pay you back tomorrow, when we get our commission.'

He tuned back into the phone. 'Tell you what, Mrs Blanco. You sound like a very nice person and I want to help you. I'm going to make you an offer; £80 for a half but you have to promise to keep that a secret. If your competitors found out, they'd throttle me. We have a deal? We do? Great news. And congratulations again to you and your, er, salubrious establishment.'

He replaced the receiver and said, 'Christ, what a stroppy old cow! I wouldn't let her near my hair.'

A Kiwi salesgirl called Josephine, who worked nights in the paediatrics ward at St Mary's Hospital, said, 'Did I hear that right, Jamie, or were you claiming ninety thousand back there?'

Jamie laughed. 'Did I say ninety? I don't know what came over me, Jo. Think I should ring her back?'

There was an unofficial contest between the sales staff of *World's End* to see who could make the most audacious circulation claims with a straight face. The magazine, as they were aware, printed about fifteen thousand copies, half of which got pushed through the letter boxes of local residents. The remainder were delivered in huge piles to anywhere that would take them, or dumped by the entrance to the tube.

'You know something, Jamie?' Wanda said, as they prepared to set off for the pub. 'You are so, so wicked. You look like a little cherub, like butter wouldn't melt, but you are such a naughty boy. Has anyone ever told you that?'

'Only about twice a day for twenty-three years. Tell you what, Wanda, buy me a double vodka and I'll show you exactly how naughty I can be.'

On the stairs they ran into Piers Anscombe, the owner of *World's End*, returning from lunch. In addition to his responsibilities as proprietor, he was also the magazine's restaurant critic. Much of his week was taken up with eating enormous free meals as the guest of local Italian trattorias, from which he seldom returned before five o'clock.

'Leaving already?' he asked, clutching unsteadily on to the banisters. His camel-coloured overcoat with its brown velvet collar more or less matched his teeth, Jamie noticed.

'That's right, Piers. We've had a bonanza day. Sold a shed load of space. You'll be shelling out a fortune in commission tomorrow, you realise?'

'It's a marvellous little business this,' replied Piers, stumbling slightly as he passed by. 'Did I mention Seymour Beaverbrook once offered me two million pounds for it over a drink in the American Bar at the Savoy?'

'Worth twice that, Piers, easily,' Jamie said insincerely. 'Could be worth ten for quality like ours.'

Jamie had been working for *World's End* since the summer, or more accurately had been rolling up with reasonable frequency, utilising the phone for personal calls, charming the girls in the office, arriving late and bunking off early. His pay, which was entirely based on commission, was handed over in cash on Friday afternoons, dependent on Piers getting to the bank before it closed. In a good week, when Jamie made it into work for three or four days and really hit the phones, he could walk away with three or four hundred pounds, quickly spent on drinks, Gitanes, Gauloises and a growing appetite for cocaine. When he put in the effort, nobody sold advertising more effectively than he did. On the telephone, he came over as so friendly and guileless that clients ate out of his hand. His speciality was cold-calling the dozens of small businesses up and down the New King's Road – the lighting and vintage clothes shops – and persuading them to take quarter-pages. At lunchtime, he patrolled the pavements in his oversized black trenchcoat and vertically striped trousers, to meet girls at Pucci Pizza or the Phene Arms.

In theory, at least, Jamie lived with his mother in Clancarty Road, in the damp Victorian house to which Margaret Temple had moved following her divorce from Michael. It was an area of Fulham populated by dumped wives, part of a grid of redbrick terraces known as the Wandsworth Bridge Road toast rack. Margaret had found the downgrade from South Eaton Place to Clancarty Road hard to accept, and had crammed into the smaller house as much of her old furniture and paintings as possible. Every surface was covered with Herend ornaments of parrots and toucans, Staffordshire figurines and silver boxes. The walls of the tiny dining room overlooking the patio were hung with a patchwork of oversized oil paintings – mostly views of the Seine and Dutch still lives of fruit and insects – that she and Michael had bought during their marriage. Jamie found the whole place unbearably claustrophobic, and spent as many nights away as he could.

He began living a nomadic existence, sleeping on the bedroom floors, or more usually inside the warm beds, of dozens of different girls. One night he would be in Bina Gardens, the next in some nursery at the top of a house in Markham Square. He knew girls who shared basement flats in Lexham Gardens who were always glad to see him, and girls with mothers who didn't bat an eyelid when they discovered him in the morning bunked up with their seventeen-year-old daughter in Flood Street. And then there were the girls he met late at night at Wedgie's, the King's Road nightclub, who invited him home on the spur of the moment.

There was something about Jamie that made it easy for women to go to bed with him, even when they hardly knew him. He was handsome and carelessly charming, and he exuded a kind of hopelessness that was completely non-threatening, which made them want to look after him. He was vague and sweet and unreliable and invariably late for everything. If you lent him a front-door key, he lost it. He couldn't drive a car, never having got round to taking lessons. He had a well-founded reputation for being a wonderful kisser and took the virginities of a whole generation who hung around Chelsea, many of whom remained slightly in love with him for years afterwards. For several months, he lived in a cupboard beneath the stairs of a house in Glebe Place. The house belonged to a girl named Fleur Ayrton-Phillips and she shared it with three girlfriends. Jamie was adopted as the house pet: 'He's so sweet.' After they had cleared out the Hoover and cartons of spare light bulbs, and installed a mattress and duvet, Jamie took up residence. This low, fetid space, hardly bigger than a coffin, in which it was impossible to sit upright, soon came to be known as the Tunnel of Love; to this day, if you mention the Tunnel of Love to several respectable married women in Wiltshire, Gloucestershire and Oxfordshire, they colour slightly, and smile enigmatically, and cast anxious glances in the direction of their stockbroker husbands, to make sure you weren't overheard.

Although most of Jamie's girlfriends were young and blonde, he by no means confined himself to his own generation. For a while, he became the toyboy lover of the wife of the prominent racehorse trainer, Honkie Gilborne. Jamie met her in the Justin de Blank café in the General Trading Company in Sloane Street, where he was hanging out with a cigarette, and Lavinia was enjoying a quick coffee having just ordered several expensive wedding presents upstairs in the gift registry. Jamie had begun eyeing up Lavinia straightaway – a feisty blonde with highlights and tight suede trousers, who smelt alluringly of Cristalle. For some reason she could later hardly explain, Lavinia allowed herself to be chatted up by this good-looking boy at the next table who was barely older than her son at Eton. She soon found herself inviting him back for a drink and lunch at their flat in Cadogan Gardens. Two hours later, when she handed him the money for his taxi home, she knew she'd just had the best sex in twenty years.

They fell into a routine of meeting at the flat every Tuesday afternoon. In no time, Jamie was bringing round his washing for the Gilborne's Portuguese daily (Lavinia explained that the filthy jeans and crumpled shirts belonged to her son, Hugo). Once, in a moment of reckless passion, and knowing that her husband was at the flat, Lavinia even crawled inside the notorious Tunnel of Love, and wondered what she thought she was doing as Jamie bonked her expertly in the confined space.

One weekend, four months into their relationship, she invited him to stay for the weekend in Berkshire, outside Lambourn. There was to be a large houseparty and Jamie would be introduced as a muralist and the godson of their neighbour Marcus Brand, who had, coincidentally, recently sent some of his horses to be trained at the Gilborne yard.

Lavinia drove Jamie down to Lambourn herself, using the journey to perfect their story that he would shortly start work on a trompe l'oeil for the dining-room niches in Cadogan Gardens. When they drew up outside the large flint and brick manor house, a string of ponies was being led through the yard by two girl grooms. 'Be careful, darling boy,' Lavinia had said, spraying herself with Cristalle to cover the faint aroma of sex that still hung around them both from their explosive quickie before setting off. 'Honkie would go ape shit if he ever discovered.'

Henry – Honkie – Gilborne was a bull-necked Old Etonian with one of the most successful and profitable racing stables in England. One of the first trainers to cash in on the emerging passion for racing among oil-rich sheikhs, he spent a month every year in the Gulf, flying between Dubai, Sharjah and Abu Dhabi to persuade Arab princes that bloodstock racing had a hell of a lot more to it than camel racing. As a result, he had over a hundred horses in training, thirty stable lads, two dozen different owners to juggle and a string of major wins, including the Oaks (twice) and the St Leger, to his credit. He ruled the yard with a rod of iron, regularly appearing on the gallops at six o'clock in the morning. In his limited spare time, he liked to drink claret heavily and, occasionally, clamber on top of his still attractive wife, in which position he generally nodded off before completing the job.

There were three couples staying for the weekend, as well as Jamie, and others invited for dinner on Saturday night. Jamie spent Saturday shooting rabbits on the Downs with Hugo Gilborne, who was home for Long Leave, and lightly flirting with his sister Arabella, over from St Mary's, Wantage. He was conscious of furious glares from Lavinia as he giggled with Arabella over the fish pie at lunch.

Dinner was a heavy-duty event. The men rolled up in full Berkshire dinner party kit: claret-coloured velvet smoking jackets with silk lapels, cream shirts, bow ties, velvet slippers embroidered with whatever family crest, racing colours, fox mask, leaping salmon, military badge or entwined initials they could muster. Lavinia looked ravishing in a black velvet skirt and lacy low-cut top which showed off her terrific breasts to advantage. Watching them across the polished table through a forest of silver candlesticks and wine glasses, Jamie had to restrain himself from reaching out and helping himself.

At the end of dinner, the women left the men in the dining room to their port and to discuss the newly elected Conservative government, now in its fifth month of office. Several of the merchant bankers and landowners expressed the view that Margaret Thatcher was only a caretaker leader. 'Strictly *entre-nous*,' confided a senior partner at Cazenove's, 'the party's already well down the road towards identifying a suitable candidate to take over, probably Willie Whitelaw or Peter Carrington.'

A man with enormous nostrils named Bongo Fortescue, who farmed over at Hungerford, said, 'The only person round here who seems to be at all enthusiastic about Thatcher is Marcus Brand.'

Several of the bankers exchanged meaningful glances and one said, 'Well, yes, that isn't altogether a cause for surprise, Bongo. Marcus is always rather, er, unorthodox in his approach, wouldn't you say?'

Honkie Gilborne, decanting a third bottle of port, said, 'Jamie, didn't someone say Marcus is your godfather?'

Jamie nodded, and the bankers regarded him with curiosity.

Bongo Fortescue, suddenly interested, asked, 'Ever come across a girl called Saffron Weaver? She's his goddaughter. Bloody attractive. Haven't seen her for about six years – used to shack up with her mother, matter of fact. Ever met Saffron?'

Jamie said that he had, and that she was still very pretty.

'Bet she is,' said Bongo wistfully. 'Mother wasn't bad either. Did a runner on me, never knew why.'

Later on, in the chintz-filled drawing room, with its racecourse sketches by Sir Alfred Munnings and bronzes of dozing gundogs, Lavinia and her daughter were pouring coffee. The men were playing backgammon. Honkie was drinking heavily, refilling his glass with port, claret or J&B, whichever came to hand.

Lavinia whispered to Jamie, 'Honkie will be out like a light in fifteen minutes. When everyone's gone home, come to my bedroom. We'll leave him down here.'

Not long afterwards, having checked that his host was snoring peacefully in an armchair, Jamie slipped along the corridor to the master bedroom. Lavinia, clad in a lacy pink nightdress, was waiting for him, stretched out on a glazed bedcover printed with a pattern of honeysuckle and ribbons.

'Promise me I'm prettier than Arabella,' she said as Jamie peeled off his dinner jacket trousers and boxers and joined her inside her Monogrammed Linen Shop sheets. Jamie,

185

who had just invited Arabella to Wedgie's next time she was up in London, blushed slightly.

'You know you're the most gorgeous woman I've met in ages,' he quickly reassured her, turning a chintz-covered photograph frame on her bedside table to the wall so as not to stare at three oval-shaped snaps of Hugo, Arabella and a sloppy-tongued King Charles spaniel. 'Bella's sweet but you're a cracker. I could hardly take my eyes off you at dinner.'

'We really shouldn't be doing this,' Lavinia said without much conviction, running her fingers across Jamie's smooth stomach and marvelling at its washboard flatness compared to Honkie's pot belly.

'Don't see why not,' he protested. 'I mean, it's not like Honkie wants to himself. He can't be dog-in-the-manger about it, not with top-class totty like you. If you were my wife, I wouldn't let you out of bed all weekend. We'd be shagging each other stupid.'

All would have been well if he hadn't fallen asleep afterwards. He had intended, after their hour of joyous lovemaking, to slip back to his own bedroom, but somehow it never happened. The next thing he knew, he was being shaken awake by an enraged Honkie Gilborne, standing over him in a smoking jacket and raining blows on to his head. Jamie felt horribly vulnerable, stark naked in the marital bed. All he could see was a huge muscle in Honkie's bull neck, thick as electric cable, throbbing with fury. 'You can clear out of my house right now, is that understood?' he stormed, booting Jamie across a needlepoint rug. 'I don't want to find you here tomorrow morning.'

It was unfortunate for Jamie that he had never learned to drive. At three o'clock in the morning, no taxi would have come out from Swindon, even supposing he had the money to pay one. Concluding there was nothing to be done about it, he went to bed, resolving to hitch-hike home early the next morning before anyone was up.

At eight o'clock, awakened by breakfast smells from downstairs and realising he was ravenous, he decided to chance his luck before hitting the road. He was sitting alone at the dining-room table, being served a large plate of scrambled eggs and grilled bacon by the Gilbornes' cook, when Honkie entered the room. For a moment he stood still in disbelief.

'I thought I told you last night to get out of my house.'

'God, I'm so sorry,' Jamie replied. 'But the thing is, you see, I haven't passed my driving test yet, so I don't have transport.'

'Jesus *Christ*!' To be cuckolded by a learner driver was the last straw. 'Have you got your bags packed ready? Well, get them – fast – and I'll run you to the railway station. You can catch a train.'

Five minutes later, they were driving in silence in Honkie's shooting brake through the winding country lanes. They arrived at Swindon station and he said, 'I don't know when the next London train is, nor do I care. You can ruddy well sit here and wait for it.'

'Thank you for a fantastic weekend, sir,' Jamie said, with boyish enthusiasm. 'I really did enjoy myself. But I wonder if I could borrow some cash for my ticket? I don't seem to have any on me. Obviously I'll pay you back.'

With a huge sigh, Honkie peeled off a twenty-pound note and handed it to the young man who had so recently rogered his wife. At that moment, he felt incredibly tired and old and hungover and, unequal to facing Lavinia and their other guests just yet, he wondered whether the pub in the village might be open to serve him a hair of the dog.

With final cheery exclamations of farewell and thanks, Jamie dodged past the guard at the barrier of the sleepy Sunday-morning station and hopped on to the train. Entirely oblivious of the mayhem he'd left behind him, the weekend had already become a huge joke which he looked forward to relaying to Charlie in all its hilarious detail. Happily, unthinkingly, and with the clearest of consciences, Jamie made his way along the carriages to the buffet car, where he bought himself a large gin and tonic and a bag of peanuts with Honkie's cash.

14: October, 1979

From his table in the alcove, which he shared with two other management trainees, Stuart had a ringside view of Shiplake & Clegg's staff canteen. At one minute past noon, the cavernous hall with its linoleum floor and dozens of Formica-topped tables was heaving with workers on their lunch break. One entire wall of the room was occupied by Bangladeshis, who in those days represented half the eleven hundred-strong workforce. Elsewhere he could see tables of Bengalis and Tamils and – an ever-declining minority – blue-collar English Brummies, some of whom had had fathers, and even grandfathers, who had worked at Shiplake & Clegg. At the furthest end of the hall, in an alcove reserved for middle and senior management, were tables spread with cloths and laid with real Sheffield cutlery and glass beakers (as oppose to the china mugs used by everyone else). While the manual workers collected their own food on plastic trays, senior staff were entitled to 'silver service' and were waited on by a variety of nice old dinner ladies in overalls. As a management trainee on the graduate scheme, Stuart was expected to have lunch in the alcove, but never did so without feelings of acute embarrassment. He would much sooner have sat out on the floor along with everyone else. Segregated dining struck him as symptomatic of everything that was wrong about British industry, and about Shiplake & Clegg in particular.

He had joined the company straight out of university, because a management traineeship in a broadly based local industry seemed like a gift from God and enabled him to live at home with his mother. Shiplake & Clegg was one of the longest-established manufacturers in the West Midlands, founded in the mid-nineteenth century by two legendary burghers of the city, Josiah Shiplake and Ebenezer Clegg. Originally a smelting works and foundry, it had diversified over the years into light industry, and by the late seventies specialised in the assembly of electrical goods. There were still two Shiplakes and a Clegg on the board, great-grand-children of the founders and, on the wall of the canteen, a sepia photograph of Josiah and Ebenezer wearing side-whiskers and stove-pipe hats at the grand opening of the Birmingham-to-Coventry canal.

During his first few months, Stuart had been almost overawed by the deeply engrained traditions and procedures of the company. Every four weeks he was attached to a different department – starting on the shop floor where he shadowed an assembly-line supervisor, then moving on to accounts, personnel, and domestic and overseas sales. In each department he struggled to master the complex customs and practices which had grown up over genera-tions, and the strict job demarcations, jealously enforced, which prevented even the smallest alteration in any employ-ee's job specification. Among the clerical staff, who in those days were still predominantly white, there were people who had been at Shiplake & Clegg for thirty or even forty years, performing the same tasks, day in, day out, for the whole of that time. The shocking thing, as Stuart saw it, was that they seemed perfectly resigned to their lot, and violently hostile to any suggestion of change. In his tenth week, noticing that two women at opposite ends of the department were recording almost identical sales information in different ledgers, he pointed this out to the Deputy Chief Clerk, with the proposal that much of the duplication could be eliminated. Within minutes, he had been summoned into the office of the Chief Clerk, where it was patiently explained to him that, 'If you ever make a Smart Alec suggestion like that again, laddie, the entire clerical depart-ment will probably down pens and walk out, and then where will we all be, eh?'

By the end of six months, Stuart realised the business was in deep trouble. He didn't need to see the results, which as a private company were closely guarded, to know that it was in terminal decline. Morale in the sales department was at rock bottom. For twenty years, the company had specialised in manufacturing electric hairdryers, heated rollers and curling tongs, blow heaters, low-cost radios (or wirelesses as they were still known internally), as well as acting as a supplier of electrical components to other manufacturers in the West Midlands. In recent years, however, competition from abroad was lacerating. How could they possibly compete with the goods coming in by the shipload from Hong Kong and Taiwan? As the despairing Sales Director explained, the wholesale price of a Shiplake & Clegg two-speed hairdryer was dearer than the retail price of the same thing from the Far East. One by one, the department stores that had for years been their principal market cancelled their orders and switched to foreign makes instead.

Stuart also guessed that the design of some of their products might have a lot to do with the sales decline too. Although it was mandatory within the company to deride the poor quality of the imports ('You'd likely electrocute yourself and all if you plugged them in, 'orrible Chinese rubbish'), when Stuart made a trip one Saturday morning to the electrical department at Rackham's to inspect the competition, he thought the goods looked neater, smaller and undeniably more sophisticated.

This conclusion depressed him. Still a conviction socialist, who had been horrified and genuinely surprised by Thatcher the milk snatcher's arrival at Downing Street, he feared that the new government, with its bloodless commitment to supply-side economics, would be reluctant to bail out Shiplake & Clegg, even if it meant the loss of eleven hundred jobs. Once or twice, however, as he swam his regular forty lengths at the local baths, Stuart did allow that Shiplake & Clegg in its present form might not be a particularly deserving charity case, and he wished that he could do something positive to help.

Giving up his university digs and moving back in with his mother had not been in all respects an easy transition. He had always got on well with Jean, and was glad to be able to contribute to the housekeeping and bills, but reoccupying his boyhood bedroom with his old Aston Villa football posters on the wall, and the chest expanders like iron bedsprings in the back of the wardrobe, made him feel he had reverted to an earlier stage of development. Only the shelf full of economics text books and course notes were evidence that he had recently gained a first-class honours degree in Economics and Political Science. Jean had been promoted to senior secretary at the local firm of solicitors where she had worked for twenty-five years. Her boss, the senior partner, spent three days a week on the golf course now as he neared retirement, and Jean, with her fierce efficiency and common sense, ran the whole practice in his absence, without ever making an issue of it. For the first time in her career she was fairly paid, but lived as frugally as ever. She was known to every trader in the market for her insistence on buying the freshest fruit and vegetables at the cheapest prices. 'Here she comes again, look,' they would shout out as she carefully inspected the produce at the various stalls. 'It's the flamin' Sergeant Major on her rounds.' But they said it affectionately and with respect.

Partly as a means of avoiding eating tea with his mother every night, Stuart enrolled in an evening adult education accountancy course, where he learned about cash flow and how to decode a balance sheet. He also became a devotee of the self-help business manuals that had begun flooding into the bookshops, mostly written by American motivational gurus and celebrity CEOs. In one of these books, he came across the word 'marketing' for the first time, and wondered whether Shiplake & Clegg (where the concept was unknown) could benefit by adopting the new science.

Of his old friends only Ginger was still living in the area (Mick having quit Bromwich for the oil rigs of Aberdeen). Once a week they kicked a football around after work in a floodlit indoor sports centre, followed by a couple of lagers and a curry at one of the new balti houses springing up all over the city. Ginger had been promoted to assembly-line supervisor at the Smethwick Chassis Works (lately renamed Brand HGV) and told Stuart, in high excitement, that they were installing a plant to manufacture a new mechanical digger to go up against JCB. The works employed fewer than five hundred men now, but Ginger was more fired up about it all than Stuart had ever seen him. 'I'm telling you, Stu, nobody's making vehicles like these. Not in Europe, not in America.'

Eighteen months into the management scheme, Stuart made a decision. It was something he'd been thinking about for several months but had never had the bottle to follow through. But one lunchtime in the canteen, feeling like an Afrikaaner beneficiary of apartheid as he ate his meat and two veg in the roped-off alcove, he knew the time had arrived. That afternoon, he put in a call to the office of Terence Clegg, joint Managing Director of Shiplake & Clegg, requesting a personal interview. When Clegg's secretary asked him dubiously what the meeting was concerning, Stuart replied, with uncharacteristic recklessness, 'Rescuing the company from bankruptcy.' A time was pencilled in for late the following week, though this was, she emphasised, only a provisional appointment. 'Mr Clegg is extremely busy at the moment and might not be able to see you.'

Stuart made his preparations meticulously. He knew he wouldn't be given long with the boss, and there was so much he needed to say. His diligent study of American business manuals, his evening classes, and most of all his personal experiences around the company, had bred in him a passionate conviction that the whole business – the strategy, the culture – had to change from top to bottom, and change dramatically, or face certain extinction. Management was old-fashioned and inaccessible, almost wilfully backward-looking in its approach. There was no mechanism for good ideas to filter upwards from the shop floor; in fact, there was a culture that positively stifled suggestions from the work-force, on the grounds they were incendiary and sure to cost more. Everywhere he looked, he saw stagnation and ineptitude. Most of their products were built to a higher standard than their competitors', but while superior in function were deficient in design and unattractively pack-aged. It was no wonder they were consistently losing market share. The company had its fair whack of loyal employees, but the more ambitious managers were bailing out, frustrated by the *status quo*. In particular, Stuart had derived the impression that many of the Indian workers employed on the assembly lines were under-utilised in the organisation. He had noticed how numerate some of them were, and felt sure they would flourish on the clerical side. But, out of time-honoured prejudice, few immigrants from the sub-continent ever made the transition to white-collar positions.

On the Saturday before his audience with Terence Clegg, and accompanied to the city centre by his mother, Stuart bought his first proper suit at Burton's. His shoulders and back had become so muscular from swimming that it was difficult finding a cut to accommodate them. In the end, they chose a three-piece grey pinstripe model with padded shoulders and a special internal pocket in which to keep train tickets. Surveying himself in the fitting-room mirror, with his new, shorter haircut and thick-rimmed glasses, he hoped that he would never run into his old Labour Club chums while in this rig. To spend eighty pounds on a suit, more than a week's wages, struck him as embarrassing and unnatural.

The crucial day arrived, and five minutes before the appointed hour Stuart found himself hovering in Mr Clegg's outer office under the stern eye of three secretaries. No one invited him to take a seat so he remained standing, clutching the ring-file of notes he had prepared for the session. From behind a double set of mahogany doors, the muffled tones of a racing commentary were just audible. Some horse trained by Honkie Gilborne, with Lester Piggott in the saddle, had just won the Cesarewitch by a length. As the minutes ticked by, Stuart's trepidation mounted, and it required all his resolution not to slink away.

Forty minutes after the appointed hour, an intercom crackled on the foremost secretary's desk and a voice said, 'If that cheeky young fellow who wants to see me is out there, you can send him in.'

Stuart had never really seen Terence Clegg. Occasionally he had spotted him driving through the factory gates in his burgundy-coloured Roller, which he parked in a named space around the side of the building. At close quarters, he was unexpectedly small, barely five foot three, with truculent gunslit eyes, the mashed nose of a boxer and what looked suspiciously like a well-sprung toupee on his fat head. He waved Stuart to a seat across a desk which was partially covered by a collection of replica veteran cars on veneered wooden stands.

'Now, young man,' he said in a Birmingham accent much thicker than Stuart's own. 'My secretary, Miss Bossy Boots out there, gave me a message you want to save this company of mine from going under. On the face of it, that's a pretty bollocksy message to receive from a trainee who's been with us for only a year, wouldn't you say?'

'Eighteen months,' said Stuart. 'I've been working here eighteen months.'

'Have you, by gum?' said Terence, jabbing at a briefing paper with a short, stubby finger. 'Well, Miss Bossy Boots has slipped up for once, she's put a year down here.' He chuckled, pleased to have caught her out. 'How long, as a matter of interest, do you think I've been in this business myself?'

Stuart had no idea. 'Twenty years, Mr Clegg?'

'Forty-three. I began on my sixteenth birthday, apprenticed to my Uncle Billy in the old sheet metal works at Edgbaston. That's gone now. We had to shut it down, you see, it stopped being viable.'

Stuart wondered whether the moment had come to launch into his much-practised speech, which he had boiled down and down until the whole thing could be delivered in under ten minutes.

But before he could take the plunge, Terence Clegg continued, 'You may think we don't know about change at Shiplake & Clegg, but we do, you know, which is why we've survived for more than a hundred and fifty years and still going strong. This is the first time we've met, you and I, but from what I've been hearing, you're an out-and-out clever clogs. That's what they're telling me about you, the other managers. I've been asking, you see, checking up on you. Not that I hold it against you, being clever. We like to employ clever people, always have, providing they keep their noses to the grindstone. But there's cleverness and cleverness, and you may have the wrong kind of cleverness for Shiplake & Clegg. You're a smartarse, aren't you? Too clever by half.' He stared at Stuart through mean little eyes. 'That's what people are saying anyway – always wanting to change things that have worked perfectly well for a hundred years, simply because you think you know better.'

Stuart was tongue-tied; the meeting wasn't going as planned. Mr Clegg wasn't giving him a chance. He could feel the sweat running down the inside of his suit.

'This may come as a surprise to you,' Terence Clegg said, 'but I don't appreciate receiving messages from my junior staff, telling me I'm going belly up. I don't appreciate it at all. Cocky's one way of putting it. Some bloody nerve is another. And I wanted to tell you that personally before handing you your walking papers. See Miss Bossy Boots on the way out, she'll give you an envelope with your final wage packet inside. Always assuming we don't go bankrupt in the next two minutes, of course.'

And that was that. Fifteen minutes later, Stuart had left Shiplake & Clegg for the last time and was heading for the bus stop, still clutching the file which contained his radical blueprint for saving the company.

When no bus came, he decided to walk home, right across the city. His shock at the outcome of the interview was turning into anger, and he needed to work off his aggression with exercise. He felt a greater sense of frustration than he had ever experienced before. He had worked so hard on his presentation and, despite Terence Clegg's crass contempt, he knew his ideas were valuable. He resented being described as a clever clogs. He hadn't asked to see Mr Clegg out of personal vanity but to help the company, and maybe safeguard the jobs of hundreds of honest, diligent workers. That was what he told himself anyway as he crossed the city in his Burton suit, past the Indian restaurants and discount white goods emporiums which increasingly seemed to dominate Birmingham.

He paused at a tobacconist, feeling the need for a cigarette. He hardly smoked – and never at home, Jean disapproving strongly – but sometimes, in moments of stress, nothing worked like a hit of nicotine. It was while paying for the cigarettes that his eye was caught by a magazine amongst the serried ranks displayed above the counter. It was the new issue of *Management Today* and one of the coverlines read: 'The Building of Brand. Profile: Marcus Brand, Eighties Expansionist'. Stuart bought a copy, parked himself on a bench in a churchyard, lit up and began to read.

The four-page profile was accompanied by a colour photograph of Marcus behind a massive and elaborate desk in his London office, supremely confident and affluent-looking in a navy blue suit. A certain impatience in his expression made you guess that he had been giving the *Management Today* photographer a hard time, pressing him to hurry up. Inserted in the succeeding spread was a half-tone diagram illustrating the corporate structure of the Brand Group, with squat grey arrows showing how the constituent divisions – Brand Pacific Trading Corporation (BPTC), Brand HGV, British Consolidated Foodstuffs, Brand Shipping and Aviation, Brand Financial Services and Brand Commercial Estates – slotted together. At the bottom of the page a block of smaller photographs included the exterior of West Candover Park, Dick Mathias (here described as Marcus's chief acquisitions officer) and a snap-shot of Marcus on his wedding day, emerging from the porch of a church with a ravishing young bride on his arm.

Having attended Professor Tomkins's lecture on his godfather, much of Marcus's story was already familiar to Stuart. He had hoped the article might tell him something about his godfather's origins and how he'd got started in business. But, as with the lecture, the journalist's knowledge did not pre-date Marcus's late-fifties takeover of the prop-erty and shipping company. It was as though he had been born fully formed as a mini-tycoon; his background and education remained a blank.

Towards the bottom of the fourth page was a paragraph that halted Stuart in his tracks: 'In 1958, aged 26, Brand married Lucy Macpherson, the only child of Scottish landowners with estates in Angus and Sutherland. After less than a year, the marriage came to a sudden and tragic end when Lucy was killed in a car accident. It later emerged that the driver, Marcus Brand's company chauffeur, was three times over the legal limit for alcohol. Brand has never remarried.'

Stuart stared at the page in disbelief. His father drunk? His father personally responsible for Mrs Brand's death? He found the news staggering, and also shameful. He understood now why his mother was so evasive on the subject. Jean had told Stuart the car had spun off the road and hit a tree, but she hadn't mentioned his father was pissed as a newt.

Stuart's next thought was that he could never see Marcus again. Out of the question, now he knew the full story. He couldn't understand how his godfather had stomached him on those holidays; a living reminder of what had happened. In the South of France, all those years ago, and at the Paris Ritz, when Marcus had introduced Stuart as the son of a hero, he must have been taking the piss. Had he lived, they'd have prosecuted Ron Bolton for manslaughter.

Stuart arrived home in a state of shock, with no job and with a lifetime's illusions shattered. He could understand why Jean had covered up for his father, but he still felt betrayed.

His mother was in the kitchen, frying onions for steak and onion pudding. Stuart dropped the magazine on to the table, open at the article.

'I know about Dad,' he said flatly. 'He was drunk, wasn't he?'

Jean turned to look at him and replied, 'Yes, I'm afraid he was. He had no business to have been driving that car.'

'Why did he then?' Stuart was suddenly furious. 'He only killed Marcus's wife. It says here he was way over the limit.'

His mother wouldn't meet his eye. 'Stuart, don't let's go into it. It won't do any good. I've spent the last twenty years trying to forget. There's no point dragging it all up again.'

'I wish you'd told me, that's all.'

'Perhaps I should have. It never seemed the right moment.

You're doing so well in your career, and working so hard, I didn't want to upset you.'

'That's ironic,' he replied. 'That really is ironic, after what happened today.'

Suddenly remembering his important interview with the boss, Jean asked, 'Of course, your meeting, how did it go? Did Mr Clegg like any of your ideas?'

'He liked them so much he sacked me. On the spot. I've been told never to darken the doors of Shiplake & Clegg again.'

'Oh, Stuart pet. And after you'd worked so hard on it all.' Jean Bolton felt a moment of sheer anguish on his behalf and, longing to console him, hugged her beefy son in his new three-piece suit; she knew that if anybody deserved good fortune in the world, it was he.

That evening, Jean and Stuart sat up later than they had ever done before, talking about what he should do next. It had always been Stuart who had taken the decisions about his future. He was bad at accepting advice, and when he had elected to go to Birmingham University to read Economics, and later to enter the management traineeship at Shiplake & Clegg, he had done so without reference to Jean.

This time, however, it was his mother who came up with the idea that shifted the course of his life. While dusting his room, she had picked up some of the business books and noticed an interesting thing. Many of the writers – the bosses of big American corporations – had been to business school. They always mentioned it in their biographies: 'He studied business management at MIT', or Harvard or Wharton. Jean had no idea what any of this entailed, but thought that, if anyone would get something out of it, Stuart would. Now here was the perfect opportunity. They should look into the feasibility of his studying business in America.

When Jean told him her plan, he laughed. 'Nice idea, Mum, but have you any idea what these places cost? You have to be a millionaire or something to go to them. Even most Americans can't afford them, and they're pigs in clover next to us.'

'I think I may have enough money,' his mother replied calmly.

'That's very kind of you, but I'm quite sure you haven't.'

'I've been careful over the years, I've put some aside. So much a week into a special account at the post office, in your name. I think you might be surprised.' She mentioned a figure and his jaw dropped.

'It's amazing, isn't it, how it tots up, when you buy all your vegetables in the market and neither drink nor smoke?' She said this last bit meaningfully, having smelt cigarette smoke on his suit.

'I could never use your money, Mum. They're your life savings.'

'No, they're not. They're *your* life savings. I told you, the account's in your name. I was putting the money by for the day you got married, but if you want to spend it on business school instead – which sounds a much better idea to me – so be it.'

15: November, 1979

Slightly stoned, and getting ready for bed in the third-floor flat in Gledhow Gardens, Saffron stared at herself in the bathroom mirror and made a solemn promise. Tomorrow, she vowed, I am giving up. From Monday to Friday I'm going to be completely clean and find a job. If I ever take anything again, it will be strictly at weekends. And no way – *no way* – am I going to break that promise.

In the five months she had been living in South Kensington, Saffron had made several similar promises. But life in Gledhow Gardens made it difficult to stick to them. For a start, she invariably woke up drowsy, having put herself to sleep with a late-night Mogadon or a couple of smokes of heroin to get her down after the coke. Nobody surfaced in the flat much before noon and then they would pad around the kitchen – Peregrine, Rupert and Sim – making coffee and wondering about someone going out to buy milk. Callers dropped round incessantly to buy stuff from the boys; the entryphone buzzed all afternoon. In that respect, Saffron thought, it was the total opposite of the Kasbah, Niall's Moroccan restaurant in Polzeath, which had finally gone out of business at the end of the summer.

She had met Peregrine on almost her first night in London. He had taken her to a nightclub, the Embassy in Albemarle Street, where she had been exhilarated by the chrome and leather glamour of the place, the music, the long bar, the sophistication of Peregrine and his mates which made the Polzeath crowd she'd been part of seem like Cornish yokels. She moved into Gledhow Gardens immediately, with the understanding that she was Perry's girl, though sex hardly came into it. Every evening, they drove down to the river to a pub called the Common Vole in Milman's Street, where the dealers hung out and the boys did their business.

With incredible speed, Saffron became integrated into the wider Gledhow Gardens set. It helped that she was beautiful. At twenty-two, in her Jean Machine dungarees and R. Soles cowboy boots, she looked like a softer, more vulnerable Marianne Faithfull. On the nights that they piled into a taxi and headed, already half out of it, to the Embassy Club, Saffron wore the tightest velvet drainpipes in bright red, orange or turquoise, with Perry's old motorcycle jacket pulled over the top. After six lines of coke in the basement cloakroom, she could dance until four in the morning, never once leaving the dancefloor, high on the music ('Cel-e-bration time . . . *Come on!*'), white powder and sheer glamour of being young and in London.

Despite being with Peregrine for nearly six months, Saffron knew surprisingly little about him. She vaguely assumed he must be rich, because he owned the flat and never worked (unless you counted the low-level drug deals he conducted to subsidise his own habit). She thought his parents lived out in the country somewhere, in Buckinghamshire, but he seldom went home, and when he did, he didn't take her with him. She guessed he was thirty or thirty-one, but had never asked him. In a curious way, the routine of drug-taking – the getting high and coming back down, the procuring of supplies, the ritual of inhaling heroin from tinfoil and the mellow feeling of oblivion it produced – was all-consuming and conspired against everything else, including curiosity.

To have moved so rapidly into the world of drugs seemed, at the time, seamless and inevitable. Cocaine and heroin were as intrinsic a part of the culture she now inhabited as the bottles of San Mig Charlie Crieff was downing eight thousand miles away in Hong Kong. And, it must be stated, Saffron needed no encouragement. In Polzeath, she had regularly smoked dope on the beach late at night, rolling joints as the waves lapped against the sand of Padstow Bay. But the immediate, seductive hit from harder drugs was a revelation. One smoke of heroin and all the anxiety in her life was taken away.

The final few months of the Kasbah had been tense and

upsetting even before the bank had broken its word and sent in the receivers, and everything – the tables, cutlery, kelims and camel saddles – was removed in a van to be sold. Amaryllis had discovered she was pregnant which, far from being a cause for joy, had precipitated violent rows with Niall. One evening, late at night, following a drink-fuelled argument that seemed to go on for three full days, he had lashed out with a kitchen knife. There had been a tussle, with chairs and crockery crashing on to the floor, as he chased her round the table. Eventually Amaryllis had screamed, 'I'm sorry, Niall, but that's it. We're off. Pack your suitcase, Saffron, we're out of here in ten minutes.' Niall, pleading with her to reconsider, had driven them and their baggage to Trebetherick and they had caught the last bus – the only bus out of town that evening – to Port Isaac. The next morning mother and daughter both took jobs at a private hotel on the cliff. Within a week Amaryllis had moved in with the owner, an alcoholic widower with jet black hair and a military provenance, named Major Victor Bing. 'For Christ's sake, Saffron, don't mention the baby,' her mother had hissed after her first night with the Major. 'He hasn't noticed the bump yet, the pissed old fart. I'm going to tell him it's his.' Shortly after this domestic arrangement took hold, Saffron left Cornwall and moved to London.

The blizzard of drugs that swirled around Gledhow Gardens absolved her of all the pain and worry she felt about her mother and everything that had happened. It had been Saffron's ambition – was still her ambition – to find a job in one of the boutiques or antique markets in the King's Road. Ever since the shopping trip with Marcus two and a half years earlier, she had longed to work at Antony Price, selling leopard-skin sheaths, or in Antiquarius at one of the stalls selling antique lace dresses. Once she got as far as obtaining a Saturday job in Fiorucci, but overslept and never showed up. Furious with herself, she vowed never to touch drugs again, but the unexpectedly painful process of with-drawal – the stomach cramps and shivering – was unbear-able, and she lasted barely a day.

The telephone rang one afternoon and Peregrine, looking slightly annoyed, said it was for her. Saffron was surprised since nobody she knew, not even Amaryllis, had the number at Gledhow Gardens.

'Saffron? This is Barbara Miles speaking, from Marcus Brand's office,' a familiar brisk voice greeted her. 'You're keeping well, I trust? I don't believe we've heard from you since your godfather's dance.'

Saffron felt a moment of embarrassment. It was true that she had never written to Marcus to thank him, though she had meant to. Somehow, in the chaos of the Kasbah, it had never seemed possible.

'Have you got your diary to hand?' Barbara Miles was asking. 'Marcus would like to take you out to dinner on the seventeenth, which is next Thursday. He will collect you from your flat at eight o'clock, if that's convenient.'

'Er, sure,' said Saffron. 'I'm sure that's fine.' She had no diary, or any other engagements come to that. Everything that happened at Gledhow Gardens just happened, nothing was planned in advance.

The reappearance of Marcus in her life jolted her, filling her with excitement and dread. She had still not come to terms with the episode six years ago in Lyford Cay, which she had revealed to nobody, not even Amaryllis. At the same time Marcus occupied a special, almost heroic, position in her psyche: bigger, richer, more powerful and, at some level, more dangerous than all others. She realised that, by next Thursday, she needed to be totally clean, and thinking straight, and looking her best for him.

As it turned out, the next few days were particularly heavy at Gledhow Gardens. Perry and Sim took delivery of a consignment of Iranian brown, much larger than usual, and the flat heaved with callers. For every packet they sold, there was a free smoke or a big fat line of coke for the inmates. The days and nights passed in a blur. People came and went, the entryphone buzzed and the sitting room was like a doctor's surgery. A six-foot-six Nigerian named Dr Gregory arrived to score and sat up with Sim through the night, smoking their way through a lump the size of a hen's egg. When Jamie Temple dropped in to buy coke from Perry, it seemed to Saffron the most natural thing in the world.

'Hey, you look great,' said her godbrother. 'This where you're living now?'

Saffron nodded.

'We should have a drink sometime. Do you know the Common Vole in Milman's Street?'

She had never before used so much heroin in such a short period. She lost all sense of time. For four days, she never once left the flat, as she rode heroin high after heroin high. She used coke to get her up, heroin to bring her back down, and Temazepam or Rohypnol, three or four tabs at a time, to get off to sleep. One afternoon when she overdosed on bad heroin, which must have been cut with Vim or talcum powder, neither she nor anybody else even noticed.

Marcus's Bentley was double parked outside the flat, and the tycoon dispatched his chauffeur to ring the entryphone. For five minutes Makepiece stood on the front steps.

'I don't know what's going on inside there, Mr Brand,' he reported through the car window. 'A gentleman did answer, but he said Saffron isn't available to come out.'

'All right, Makepiece,' Marcus said, climbing out of the back. 'Evidently we have a problem here. Help me break down this door, please.'

Marcus stood on the pavement in his navy blue suit, directing operations, while Makepiece put his shoulder to the outside door. On his third run at it, the frame splintered and it collapsed on its hinges into the common parts.

'Thank you, Makepiece. Now a repeat performance upstairs, please.'

The sudden appearance of Marcus in the flat, following the violent demolition of the front door, left its inhabitants stupefied. He stood at the entrance to the room, his eyes sweeping the scene like the beam of a lighthouse, taking everything in. His sheer bulk was intimidating. Dr Gregory, who had been warming a nugget of heroin in tinfoil with his lighter, attempted to conceal the evidence behind an arm-chair.

'Where is Saffron Weaver?' Marcus's voice radiated authority.

Sim pointed to a heap on the hearth rug.

'Makepiece, call an ambulance. Tell them it's an emergency and that Marcus Brand insists they get here in under three minutes.' He turned on the others, eyes blazing with fury.

'Which of you is the owner of this disgusting hovel?'

Reluctantly, Peregrine admitted that he was.

'Let me make one thing clear,' Marcus said icily. 'If my goddaughter dies, I'll have you put away for life. For *life*, God damn you. And don't think for one second that I can't arrange it.'

Peregrine stared at the carpet, avoiding Marcus's eye.

'*Look at me* when I'm talking to you, you bloody imbecile.'

Peregrine raised his eyes to meet Marcus's, but withered beneath his stare.

'Let me tell you something else,' Marcus said. 'If for any reason you don't get life, I'll have your damn' legs broken.'

An ambulance, siren blaring, pulled up behind the Bentley and paramedics ran, panting, up the stairs. They examined Saffron and reported, 'She's breathing, sir. We'll take her down to Casualty at St Stephen's. She's going to be OK, I think.'

'She'd better be, for all your sakes,' Marcus said, addressing Saffron's flatmates. 'And if any one of you ever – *ever* – so much as speaks to her again in her life, or makes any kind of contact, I'll have you killed. And that is a promise.'

'My name is Saffron and I am an addict. I am a worthwhile person and my recovery must come first.'

Saffron was in her sixth week of group therapy and the daily affirmations no longer surprised or embarrassed her. There were ten others in her group, all alcoholics or drug addicts, and their public declarations of weakness and rebirth were the first item on the daily agenda. Ever since Marcus had had her delivered direct from St Stephen's hospital to Broadway Lodge, a rehab clinic in the seaside town of Weston-super-Mare, Saffron's life had been given over to protestations of self-worth. In her first six weeks, she had progressed through the Twelve Steps of Recovery from powerlessness and damage sessions, at which her Counsellor and the group had broken down her denial systems, to the bluer skies of hope and recovery. ('We made a decision to turn our will and our lives over to the care of God as we understand him.')

She shared a dormitory with five other women, all older and, she felt, sicker than herself. And, never having been away to boarding school, she felt horribly constrained inside the Victorian building on the top of the hill, from which you could sometimes smell, but never see, the sea.

But as the therapy progressed, Saffron found herself increasingly absorbed by it. In her first few days, she was told to write her life story, describing her childhood, schooling and how she had got into drugs, which she read out to the group. Until she wrote it all down, she had never appreciated quite how many times they had moved house, or the number and variety of Amaryllis's boyfriends. She enjoyed the sensation of being the centre of attention, as each episode unfolded. One consequence of having led such a rackety life was that she had never had a best friend to tell all this to before, and it came tumbling out – Trev the photographer, Bongo Fortescue's sexual overtures in Scotland, her initiation into smack at Marcus's dance, Niall and the kitchen knife, and the boys at Gledhow Gardens – acting like a wonderful release.

Afterwards, the group was invited to send her letters, describing their reaction to her autobiography. Feeling that it had gone down well, and utterly caught up in her own tragic story, Saffron expected plaudits. Instead, she was rocked by the severity of their appraisals, as they accused her of selfishness, arrogance, manipulation and 'thinking of yourself as special and different'.

In time, she became resigned to the institutionalised self-abasement and introspection that underpinned the Twelve Steps. A feature of the treatment was consideration of 'family of origin': what messages had her family sent out, overtly and subliminally, while she was growing up? What kind of role models had been available to her? She was encouraged to confront the impact of her father's abandonment of his family for Limerick; and the influence of Amaryllis, who used her sexuality to get attention from men. The soul-searching was cathartic and, Saffron felt, enlightening. She found herself becoming increasingly candid with the group and nobody was happier when, at the weekly 'Change of Objective' sessions, she was deemed ready to progress from one step to the next. In one respect only did she hold back, and this was in relation to Marcus. Not once during her treatment at Broadway Lodge did she refer to the holiday in Lyford Cay, or to the long shadow of her charismatic godfather.

Free from drugs, and thinking clearly again for the first time in months, Saffron began to plan her life after therapy. She would find a job, probably in a clothes shop, and steer clear of everyone she had known before, including Peregrine. It would be a fresh beginning, with new friends. She would apologise to Marcus and thank him for saving her life, by spiriting her away so dramatically from Gledhow Gardens. (When she learned how he had smashed down the front door, his status as hero was enhanced still further.)

She longed for him to visit her at one of the family groups, when friends and relations arrived at Broadway Lodge to listen to the affirmations, and were encouraged to contribute uncomfortable observations of their own. But she knew that he would never come. Instead, Amaryllis and Major Bing drove up from Cornwall one Saturday, arriving halfway through the session having stopped for a quick drink in the town. Watching Victor's watery eyes and unsteady step as he searched for a place among the moulded plastic chairs, Saffron thought he was a natural candidate for treatment himself. Amaryllis, of course, looked beautiful in a long purple coat and carrying her new baby, Lorcan, in a sling. With his furze of bright orange hair and thin, anaemic face, Lorcan was a miniature version of Niall.

Throughout the session, Amaryllis sat with a serene, far-away expression on her face, as though she was watching a school play rather than participating in her daughter's group therapy for drug addiction. Even when Saffron was encouraged to enumerate the long list of her mother's past lovers, and the feelings of insecurity they had produced while she was growing up, she didn't seem to mind. Saffron was pleased that Amaryllis had come but, equally, was relieved when she left. She didn't feel her mother appreciated the circumstances that had made her daughter's treatment so necessary, and viewed it as an indulgence.

'When you've had enough of this place,' Amaryllis said afterwards, without much enthusiasm, 'I suppose you could always come down to the hotel. Vic would let you help out. He has an awful job keeping staff.'

Outside in the car park, in the narrow turning place, he backed up his Rover into the steep terracing with a metallic thud.

'I think I'll probably go back to London, Amaryllis,' Saffron said. 'But thanks anyway for the offer.'

'Probably that would be best,' her mother replied. 'I'm not sure the hotel's doing that well, as a matter of fact.' She cast a meaningful glance at Victor. 'This might not be a forever situation.'

'Will you be OK? I mean, with Lorcan to look after and everything.'

'I expect something'll come up. One just can't be so picky as one approaches forty.'

16: December, 1979

Derek Merrett, notably more stooped than three months earlier, was making his fourth journey up to Mary's new flat from the car which was parked on the far opposite corner of Nevern Square. As there was no lift, he struggled up eight flights of stairs with her box of Kate Bush and Abba records, record player and speakers, a basket of winter produce from the garden in Dorking, a chocolate cake and a bottle of Tio Pepe as a housewarming gift. Strictly speaking, Mary had moved in with two girlfriends six weeks earlier, but this was the first time her parents had visited. With characteristic thoughtfulness, Mary wanted to get the place straight before inviting them to supper.

Upstairs in the sitting room, already prettified by Indian bedspreads on the sofa and Athena posters of French Impressionists, Belinda Merrett was having an anxious word with her daughter. She wanted to get it out of the way before Derek joined them.

'I don't want to say anything in front of your father,' Belinda said, 'but he's had a bit of an upset at work. He doesn't want you to know about it, but I think it's better that you do because things are going to be rather difficult, I'm afraid.'

'What's happened? Daddy hasn't lost his job, has he?'

'Not lost it, no. But they've given him a less important job and cut his pay.'

'Is he very upset?'

'He says not, and is putting a good face on it, but he feels awfully let down. I don't think they did it in a very nice way either. He was almost the last person in the office to know.'

'Did he think of leaving?'

'I think he would have done if they'd suggested better terms, but Daddy said they didn't offer much. The money wouldn't have lasted long, he's fifty-three now, and he wasn't sure there'd be other jobs out there.'

'So he's going to stay? Well, that's something.'

'Yes, that's something. But it's humiliating for him and we're really going to have to watch the pennies.'

'I'm off your hands now anyway,' Mary said. 'You don't need to help me any longer. I can pay my own rent. And I've had a pay rise at the agency, did I tell you? I earn five and a half thousand now.'

Her mother smiled. 'That's wonderful news, darling, and very well deserved. You know how your father loves helping you, and always will if he can. But it might just not be possible for a bit.' Outside on the half-landing they heard Derek's heavy footsteps as he trudged up the stairs. 'He's coming now so shush, and don't let on I've told you. But the person I'm furious with is Marcus Brand. I'd like to know what role he played in all this. Your father tried to ring him, and Marcus wouldn't even take his call. So much for your godfather.'

Mary showed her parents around the flat which took all of two minutes. Aside from the sitting room, there was a large bedroom with twin beds, where two of the girls slept, with the third flatmate sleeping in rotation on a sofa bed next door. There was a bathroom with a drying rack suspended above the tub on ropes, from which a selection of bras dripped like the tentacles of a dead octopus. The grim galley kitchen had been jollied up with a poster of French cheeses.

'If you climb out of the window,' Mary said, 'there's a fire escape which leads to the roof. In the summer, we're going to sunbathe up there.'

'Please be very careful, that's all I ask,' her father implored her. 'It's really rather a dodgy area, Earl's Court. I don't really like you living here.' One of Derek Merrett's saddest realisations about his change of circumstance was that he would probably never now be able to afford to buy Mary a flat of her own. It had been his dearest wish for as long as he could remember that, once his daughter left school and moved to London, he would somehow help her get a foothold on the property ladder. His inability to achieve this ambition was a personal reproach.

'Don't be silly, Daddy,' Mary said brightly. 'Everyone lives in Earl's Court. Tons of girls from school live round here.'

Mary and Belinda went into the kitchen to put the final touches to supper, then laid the table in the sitting room. Since Mary's flatmates were both expected home, she showed her mother how they elongated the table by erecting the ironing board next to it, and covering the whole thing with a tablecloth. 'We've worked out that when we give dinner parties we can seat ten people. You have to watch your knees, though, in case you knock the lever and the ironing board crashes down.'

Meanwhile, Derek had gone out in search of a late-night hardware store selling carpet tacks. 'Someone's going to trip up over that join and hurt themselves. I don't know, three young ladies sharing a flat together. You need a handyman.' When Mary's flatmates arrived half an hour later, they found Derek on his hands and knees, hammering the underlay back into position.

It was a comfort to the Merretts that Mary's flatmates were two of her oldest girlfriends, Sarah Whitley and Nicola 'Nipples' Ayrton-Phillips. Both girls had been brought up within fifteen miles' drive of the Merretts, and had been regular visitors for more than ten years. It was consequently a happy and familiar party that sat down to supper that evening, full of high spirits and easy chatter, as Mary served up her famous boeuf stroganoff with paprika, followed by a chocolate roulade.

All the girls were full of their new jobs and new lives in London. Sarah had found a position as departmental secretary in the country properties section of Savills, where she ran the diaries of five fanciable estate agents and tried to write down telephone numbers in the correct order. Nipples Ayrton-Phillips, an adorable blonde of infinite sweetness and patience, had achieved her lifetime's ambition of teaching three-year-olds at a Montessori nursery in Pimlico. Nobody who heard her describe the 'little people' she looked after, and her evident joy in their simple songs and potato prints, could doubt her suitability for the task. Mary herself had put aside her cooking for the time being and found a job at a secretarial employment agency in New Bond Street, which supplied temps to desirable local companies including Sotheby's, Agnew's and Thomas Goode.

It was the urgent ambition of the three flatmates to hold a joint dinner party as soon as possible. The only hitch in their plan was the fact that they didn't know any men. Nipples had an older brother, but he was with his regiment in Osnabrück. Sarah had been introduced to a Lloyd's broker at the Antelope, who had written down her number, but so far he hadn't called. There were the estate agents, of course, all great fun, but Sarah felt shy of inviting just one of her bosses to dinner, in case it was misinterpreted, and she couldn't very well ask them all. None of the girls felt confident of the party's success unless there were ten people, which meant five men. And they didn't know five men in London.

'You know who you could ask,' Derek suggested. 'What about those nice boys you met staying with Marcus Brand? You know the ones I mean, Marcus's godsons. You introduced me to them on the ferry in Hong Kong.'

Mary could think of nobody in the world she wanted to see less than Charlie Crieff and Jamie Temple, and said, 'I think they're still out in Hong Kong, Daddy.'

'Pity,' said Derek. 'They're exactly the sort of chaps you want to have round for supper. You stayed with them one weekend, didn't you, at one of the company cottages?'

Mary felt herself blushing. That weekend had been one of the worst experiences of her life. She couldn't think of it without a hot flush. She hadn't seen or spoken to Charlie since they stepped off the ferry in Central that Sunday evening, and she hoped she'd never have to again. It was true that, in the back of her stocking drawer, she still kept a photograph of him; she never looked at it, but couldn't quite bring herself to throw it away. But she knew she hated him.

'I haven't seen either of them since Hong Kong. We've lost touch.'

'And there was me imagining you were sweet on the curly-haired one. What was his name, Charlie someone or other?' Derek addressed himself to her friends. 'Mary never tells us a thing about her boyfriends, you know. Secretive girl is our Mary.' He gave his daughter a look that radiated affection. 'Anyway, you're all still far too young to have boyfriends. Plenty of time for that by and by.'

'Oh, don't say that,' protested Belinda. 'Don't leave it too long. Mary is nearly twenty-two, Derek. By the time I was her age, I was already married to you, and Mary was on the way.'

Much later that evening, after her parents had gone home and she had cleared up the dinner and dismantled the ironing board, Mary lay awake on the sofa bed listening to records. Outside, the yellow glare from the street lamps and the headlights of cars cutting through Nevern Square cast strange shadows across the sitting-room ceiling with its central rose. There was a particular Kate Bush track on the *Kick Inside* album called 'The Man with the Child in his Eyes', and whenever she played it she automatically thought of Charlie. Tonight, she played it over and over, listening to Kate warble that maybe he didn't love her, and just took a trip on her love for him. The poignancy of the lyric reduced Mary to tears.

Not long after the Merretts' visit to the flat in Nevern Square, a development occurred that transformed the girls' social prospects: Sarah Whitley received an invitation to buy tickets to a charity ball at the Café Royal in Piccadilly. The event, which was named the Thunder Ball and held jointly in aid of Westminster Conservatives and Afghan Refugees, was taking place in two weeks' time, with after-dinner tickets available at £20 each. In addition to dancing to Joffins Discotheque, there was to be a tombola and a lucky programme. But, from the girls' point of view, the Thunder Ball promised something rarer: an opportunity to meet hundreds and hundreds of men.

'Listen to all these people on the Junior Committee,' Sarah said, reading her way through a list of names set in microscopic type. 'Nick Bamburgh-Wilson, Mark Cavendish, Ralphie Arbroath, Hugo Gilborne, Flea Strutt . . . This is going to be such an amazing party.'

'Do you know any of those people then?' Mary asked in surprise.

'No, but they *sound* amazing, don't they?'

For two weeks the flatmates eagerly anticipated the event which was to launch them into London society. They bought silk taffeta dresses and, at lunchtime on the day of the ball, met up at a salon called Comb Hither in the Brompton Road to have their hair done. According to a magazine Nipples had picked up at the tube station, Comb Hither had recently been voted one of the best in the area.

By the time they spilled out of a taxi into Piccadilly Circus, they looked like the Three Degrees in pink and blue taffeta with their hair blown dry and lacquered like *bombes glacées*.

The first thing they saw as they approached the Café Royal was a crowd of two or three hundred people fighting to get in. A cordon of bouncers was surrounding the entrance and repelling all comers. Behind them on the front steps an agitated Sloane in a dinner jacket, stick-ups and a red diamante bow-tie was shouting, 'Please get *back* from the doors, ladies and gentlemen, right back on to the pavement. Nobody – NOBODY – is coming in until we have some ORDER.'

There was a howl of protest and the crowd surged forward. People were waving their invitations in the air, demanding to be let in. 'This is fucking *ridiculous*,' someone shouted. The crowd was growing in size all the time as taxis deposited more guests on to the pavement, and those at the back were pushing forward, compressing the people in the middle. A girl began screaming, 'Flea's fallen over, she's going to be *crushed to death*.'

The Sloane organiser was still bawling for calm. 'We have to check everybody's TICKETS. Please bear with us, ladies and gentlemen. There are *counterfeit tickets* in circulation, and we need to check every invitation before anyone can come in.'

'For Christ's sake, let us *in*, you bloody poof,' yelled someone else, and there was a cheer of agreement. 'Listen,' said the Sloane, vainly appealing to the crowd's finer feelings, 'this party's in aid of *charity*. Counterfeit tickets won't help the *charity*.'

Then, with one almighty push, the crowd broke through the thin black line and stormed the entrance, trampling over each other as they flooded up the wide stone staircase to the ballroom on the fifth floor with its patterned carpet of silver fleur-de-lys on royal blue pile. As the flatmates entered the lobby, the Sloane was still trying to rally Security who had sloped off to the bar for a beer.

Whatever expectation Mary, Sarah and Nipples had harboured of their first London ball, it wasn't this. At a glance they could see they were way too uncool. They also appeared to be the only people in the ballroom who weren't drunk or drugged. Cadaverous Harrovians, barely older than fourteen, lurched around the room with their jackets off, swigging lager from bottles or yanking at the strapless dresses of strangers who didn't even object. Nigerian chieftains' sons, fresh out of Lancing, snogged stockbrokers' daughters on red plush banquettes. Bottle-blondes with pinprick pupils and rodeo boots downed shots of tequila before throwing up into the Café Royal's bucket-sized bronze ashtrays. As far as suitable spare men for their dinner party were concerned, they'd have had more chance of finding them in the Earl's Court Europa.

Mary was considering joining the three-deep mêlée at the bar when she saw Zara Fane, tits bursting out of their tiny leather nests, heading in her direction. Rapidly moving into reverse, Mary, Sarah and Nipples headed for the Ladies.

There, in the relative calm of this sugar-pink oasis, with its rows of marble basins and stacks of linen hand towels, the girls laughed their heads off. 'Honestly, what *are* we doing here?' Mary asked, as she fixed her make-up in the mirror. 'With all those people being sick out there, they should call it the Chunder Ball.'

Behind them, in one of the pink stippled cubicles, they heard a high-pitched squeal followed by a rhythmic banging against the door. The cubicle was shaking so much, they thought it would fall down.

'You don't possibly think, do you . ... ?' asked Sarah, her eyes widening in astonishment. 'It *can't* be.' And the three girls convulsed with laughter, imagining what must be going on inside.

A couple of minutes later, the bolt shot back, and two furtive-looking teenagers scuttled out of the cloakroom. Although the flatmates didn't know it, they had just witnessed the first glorious coupling of Hugo Gilborne and Lucinda Temple.

'If this is what London's like all the time,' said Nipples, 'I'm not sure I can handle it. And me a convent girl too.'

They were considering a return to the ballroom when they heard a loud tapping noise. 'Not another one,' said Sarah. 'This whole cloakroom's turning into a knocking shop.'

'I think it's coming from outside the window,' said Nipples. 'Someone's trying to get in.'

Gingerly, she released the handle. The pebble-glazed window flew open and a young man in a dinner jacket was visible hoisting himself on to the ledge from the internal well of the hotel.

It was Jamie Temple.

Seeing Mary, he flashed her his most charming smile while clambering across the basins and down on to the floor.

'God, thanks for letting me in, girls. It was getting quite hairy out there. The drainpipe was coming away from the wall and it's a five-storey drop.' He kissed Mary on the cheek. 'It's so great to see you. You look terrific. Like, er, Cinderella.'

Feeling flustered, Mary introduced him to her friends, Sarah Whitley and Nicola Ayrton-Phillips.

'Anything to do with Fleur Ayrton-Phillips?' asked Jamie, eyeing Nipples up and down.

'Fleur's my cousin,' she replied, blushing slightly.

'I sometimes live under her stairs in Glebe Place. It's called the Tunnel of Love. You should visit sometime.'

'Can you please explain why you've just come in through that window?' demanded Mary.

'Why? Oh, I always come in that way. That's half the fun of these events, gatecrashing them. The Café Royal's the most difficult though. You have to come in through the kitchen entrance, into the staff lav, climb out of the window and then shin up the drainpipe. They should hold these parties at the Savoy, that's a cinch.'

Then, heading for the door, he said, 'See you around, girls. And if you see my sister Lucinda, tell her I've made it.'

17: June, 1981

'I hope you don't mind my saying this, but you look exactly like someone I used to know.'

Stuart had walked past the opulent gallery on the Upper East Side four times already, and each time noticed the same woman inside, sitting behind a desk, who was a dead ringer for Abigail Schwartzman. Except that the gallery assistant was half Abigail's weight, with a terrific figure and perfectly straight, beautifully cut hair. He had gawped at her through the window, pretending to admire the Matisses and Pissarros, but still couldn't be certain. In the end he thought, What the hell? I'll ask.

'Stuart?' Abigail leapt to her feet. 'Hey, I just can't believe this. I hardly recognised you. You've changed.' His chest had filled out a lot, she noticed, and he walked with a slight Californian roll. He looked suntanned and fit in clean jeans and a bomber jacket.

'You too,' said Stuart. 'I was trying to decide if it was you. I almost didn't come in.' He looked round the gallery with its silk moiré walls and discreetly lit minor masterpieces. 'These are the real McCoy, aren't they? I always wondered who bought this stuff. Now you can tell me.'

'You'd be surprised. Marcus Brand for one. It's the main reason I got this job, I think, he's one of the gallery's best customers.' Then, giving him a hug, she said, 'It really is good to see you, Stuart. It must be four years . . . longer really because I hardly saw you at Marcus's dance. Wasn't that one gross evening?'

Stuart laughed. 'I won't forget it in a hurry, that's for sure. You know I live in America now?'

'I don't know anything. I'm totally out of the loop. The only place I get to go these days is right here to the gallery. You know what,' she said, 'it's near enough to closing time.

What do you say we shut this place down and go get a drink? I want to hear everything.'

They walked the few blocks to the Carlyle Hotel and ordered Bloody Marys in the bar. Looking round at all the bejewelled late-life anorexics, and the pianist tinkling away in the corner, Stuart was immediately worried about the bill.

'This place isn't going to cost me an arm and a leg, is it? Sorry to mention money, but I'm still a student.'

'No problem, the gallery can pay,' Abigail replied. 'I'll say a big shot came in, they'll think I've done them a favour.'

'So it's not your own gallery then?'

'I wish. It belongs to Mr Gluckstein. Hershel Gluckstein. He's kind of the main man for selling French Impressionists in the city. Nothing much changes hands without his knowing about it first.'

'Good to work for?'

'Not especially. Though he's nice enough to me because of the Marcus connection. Especially lately when he's hoping to sell him a Corot.'

'Sorry to be ignorant, but what's that? Art history was never my strong point. I'm a Birmingham lad, remember.'

'Just another dead white male. Boring, boring. Actually, the picture Marcus might buy is OK. It's a little sketch of a ballerina, done in red chalk. The kind of thing my mother would appreciate, if it was in colour.'

'It sounds like you don't like the paintings much.'

'Just not my taste. I prefer modern stuff. Pollock, de Kooning . . .' She shrugged.

The drinks arrived and Abigail, who really had become very attractive, Stuart decided, asked the waiter, 'Hey, what's happened to all the chips and olives?' He went off to fetch snacks and Abigail said, 'They're for you. I can't touch them myself, I'm on the Scarsdale. But if you're a student, you'd better eat as much as you can.

'Now,' she said, 'I need to know what I've been missing. How's Jamie? And Charlie – still obnoxious as ever?' She laughed. 'Do you remember how Jamie used to wind me up in the Bahamas? Like that time he pretended he'd seen a shark taking someone's leg off? I was so gullible in those days, the wide-eyed teen from New Jersey. But Jamie was cute.'

They talked about Jamie and Charlie, neither of whom Stuart had seen since Marcus's dance, and he told Abigail about the incident behind the marquee, when a drunken Charlie had forced himself on Saffron.

'No surprises there then,' Abigail said. 'Charlie had the hots for Saffron right from the word go.'

'I thought it was Mary Merrett he fancied,' Stuart said, too quickly.

'Oh, get real, Stuart. You were there, weren't you? He couldn't take his eyes off her. None of you guys could. You were all besotted. How is Saffron anyway? Marcus took us both shopping last time I was in London and I found I quite liked her. I hadn't expected to but she's a nice kid. A bit mixed up. There's something kind of tragic about her.'

Stuart, who was still more interested in Saffron than he cared to admit, said, 'I'm sure she'll be fine. She'll end up marrying some rich git and that'll be that. She might have done so already, for all I know. Let's not talk about Saffron, I'd rather hear your news. Have you been working at the gallery all that time?'

'Women in America are allowed to go to college, you know. I was at Brandeis. In my sophomore year I studied law, hated it, and switched to Women's Studies.'

Stuart stared at her in alarm. 'Isn't that feminism and all that?'

'All *what*, Stuart? Burning bras and strapping on dildos? Oh, sure it is, and learning how not to make our husbands' Erev Shabat supper when they come home from a hard week at the office.' She laughed. 'That's what my parents think Women's Studies are about anyway, which is probably why I didn't tell them I'd switched courses. I'm such a militant feminist, aren't I, I couldn't even tell my own parents? When they came up for my graduation, I was freaking out they were going to realise.'

'And did they?'

'Luckily my mother had eyes only for what people were wearing, and how they measured up against her Commencement Day couture. Dad was working the room for investors, so he didn't notice either. The story of my life. So that's me, how about you?'

They ordered more drinks and Stuart gave her a precis of the last few years – his university course at Birmingham, moving back home to mother, the unhappy episode at Shiplake & Clegg and Jean's incredible generosity in putting him through business school at Stanford Institute of Technology. He told her how the MBA programme was everything he'd hoped it would be, and how it had opened his mind to so many possibilities that he never could have experienced in England. 'I'm sharing a dorm on campus with four great guys – one's from Seattle, one's a Korean student from Seoul, one's from West Germany and the other's Bolivian. We study together, we attend lectures together, we swim together. We spend so much time together, we even think alike now. We're practically psychic. That would never happen in England. The whole country's stuck in the dark ages.'

'But that's changing, isn't it?' said Abigail.

'Not that I've noticed.'

'Marcus says Margaret Thatcher is transforming Britain. He told Hershel Gluckstein she's a revolutionary, which didn't exactly impress him. She sounds like Fidel Castro.'

'I'd prefer Castro any day,' Stuart declared, but with slightly less conviction than he might once have managed.

'The one thing you haven't told me is what you're doing in New York?'

'Being a tourist. I hate to admit it, but this is my first time ever in the city. I flew over from California for the weekend. I thought I'd better do the sights while I'm in America.'

'Need a guide?' asked Abigail. 'I've nothing planned for tomorrow. I'd be happy to show you the cool stuff.'

'You mean it? I'd love that. But only so long as we can see some uncool stuff too. I can't go home without going up the Empire State Building. And seeing the Statue of Liberty.'

'It's a deal. We'll do the tourist beat, buy the t-shirt, then you've got to promise to come to some galleries in Soho. I'd like to show you some real art.'

'Sounds fantastic.'

'If you want to,' Abigail said, sounding suddenly nervous, as though half expecting to be rebuffed, 'you can come and have dinner with my parents tomorrow, too. I always go home Saturday night, it's like a family tradition.'

'That's a really kind offer. But won't your parents mind?'

'Put it this way, they'd like it even more if I brought home a good Jewish *Nebbish*. But they'll like you, and you can talk to them about Marcus. Dad hates him, by the way, whatever he says. But my mother's a devoted fan. She was totally over-impressed by some duchess she saw at his party.'

Every once in a while, and usually when you least expect it, life delivers a day so exhilarating, so completely enjoyable, that it can only be a gift from God. The Saturday that Stuart and Abigail spent together in New York was just such a day. It was perfect New York summer weather with a sky as clear and blue as a duck's egg, and without a trace of humidity. The sun refracted off the skyscrapers and lit up the plate-glass canyons, yellow cabs drew up on cue, muggers stayed in bed, joggers in Central Park waved cheerily as they loped by, even the taxi drivers spoke broken English and knew their way around the city. And Abigail had planned the tour skilfully, beginning the day with bagels and lox at Dean & DeLuca and timing it just right to make the first ferry from Battery Park to Liberty Island, skipping the long queues up to the torch. They took photographs of each other with Stuart's Instamatic and, years later, finding the prints tucked inside a file marked SIT, he was reminded how alluring but also vulnerable Abigail had looked that day in her yellow dungarees and flowered shirt, squinting into the sun with the towers of Lower Manhattan behind her. As they passed Ellis Island on their way back to the Battery, Abigail pointed out the spot where her maternal grandparents, Israel and Batya Volovskaya, had landed in the United States from Riga, more than fifty years earlier. She said they had lived in a *shtetle* in the countryside until they'd been driven out in a pogrom and arrived without ten dollars to their name. 'I guess they always felt like outsiders,' Abigail said.

'I know the feeling, growing up in the Midlands.'

'Maybe that's why we get along so well. We're both outsiders in a way. I certainly felt that on those vacations with Marcus. You were so kind in Nassau. You were the only person who asked me to dance, remember?'

'You were the only one who'd have accepted, remember. Apart from you and Mary, everyone ignored me.'

They visited the Empire State Building where, from the panoramic viewing terrace, Abigail pointed out the landmarks of the city and Stuart fed quarters into a misted-up telescope to peer at them at closer range. And afterwards, from a parade of gift shops so tacky that you had to laugh, he bought 'I love the Big Apple' baseball caps and, back at ground level, hot dogs from a stall on 44th Street. They had lunch at a bistro in Greenwich Village where, even at midday, there was live jazz, and then Abigail took him to a dozen small galleries where she was greeted like an old friend. As far as the paintings were concerned, which consisted mostly of squiggles, blobs and big expanses of spray paint on canvas (and which Stuart privately believed could have been churned out by the paint shop at Marcus's carworks with no trouble), he was unimpressed, but Abigail's enthusiasm for them, and for the whole downtown art scene, was infectious, and he found himself quite caught up in it by the end of the day.

The vibrancy and energy of Manhattan – of America – with its apparent classlessness and endless opportunities, had made an immense impression on Stuart. Everything about America was bigger and better than its British equivalents. Having been brought up in Birmingham, with its desolate city centre and gimcrack sixties buildings, he fell passionately in love with the soaring New York architecture. American industry was confident and meritocratic. The country was facing up to its race issues and really doing something to fix them, unlike England where immigrants were segregated in a cafeteria. Even the hamburgers at lunch bore no relation to the dry, cardboard Wimpys back home. A part of Stuart would have liked to have become an American citizen, but he knew his mother would never agree to leave England, so the idea was a non-starter.

In the evening they picked up Abigail's car from a garage near her parents' apartment and headed out of the city across the George Washington Bridge. 'You know something,' Stuart said. 'I've been here a year, but this will be my first time in a private home. I'm honoured to be invited.'

'Hold the gratitude until after the visit,' Abigail replied cryptically. 'My parents are – how shall I phrase this? – an acquired taste. Not everyone acquires it.'

Stuart noticed that, the closer they got to the Bergen County line, the more anxious Abigail became. All her *chutzpah*, so evident during the tour of the galleries, was ebbing away. It was as though, mile by mile, she was reverting to her allotted role of dutiful daughter. As they approached the ornate wrought-iron gates of her childhood home, he saw her hands were shaking at the wheel.

Whatever demons they held for Abigail, Harriet and Zubin Schwartzman were welcoming hosts. Stuart felt almost overwhelmed by the warmth and generosity of their hospitality. 'Abigail has told us so much about you,' said Harriet, proffering a crystal candy dish full of Godiva chocolates. 'I'm sorry we didn't meet before at that wonderful party Marcus gave for you all.'

'Well, Abigail's told me a lot about you too,' replied Stuart.

'Abigail's told you about us? Then you're luckier than we are. We never hear from her. Now she's living in the city, she's forgotten her parents.'

'That's not true at all,' protested Abigail, hovering nervously at her mother's elbow. 'I call you every day.'

'Mostly when she wants something,' said Zubin, handing Stuart a tumbler of bourbon. 'I don't know what is it with daughters. They want an allowance, they want new clothes all the time, they want a car, they want credit cards . . .'

'What are you saying, Daddy? You're giving Stuart quite the wrong impression. I have a job at the gallery.'

'I know you have a job at the gallery. How could I forget that? I had to buy Hershel Gluckstein three lunches at the

Four Seasons to land it for you and, let me remind you, lunch at the Four Seasons doesn't come cheap.'

Stuart understood that Zubin took a perverse pleasure in shelling out for his daughter, and that the ribald kvetching was mostly play-acting, to preserve his parental leverage.

Judging by the drawing room, with its rose velour Louis Quatorze sofa set with a dozen brocade cushions, each one positioned at a perfect point, Stuart didn't think he'd ever been in a tidier or more beautiful house. The place was immaculate, as though the room was permanently off-limits.

There was a smoked glass credenza containing a display of crystal dishes and figurines, a three-tiered crystal chandelier, an arrangement of silk dried flowers on a marble-topped coffee table with claw legs and, above the fireplace, an oil painting of a pretty girl which looked like it might be famous. If I ever become rich, Stuart thought, I'd like to have a home like this.

They ate a delicious dinner in an equally immaculate dining room, served by a silent Dominican maid who Abigail said had been her childhood nanny.

'Do you remember how adorable you were as a little girl?' Harriet said. 'That was when I liked you best, when Carmelita used to bring you down to us, all dressed up in those marvellous Baby Diors with all that heavenly smocking.' Addressing herself to Stuart, she said, 'Abigail always had such beautiful clothes. Why do daughters have to grow up? They grow up and never want to see their parents any more!'

Zubin asked Stuart what he did in life and, hearing he was at business school, told him about his own businesses, the shopping malls and real estate. The way he told it, the Midas touch was dingy by comparison to Zubin's. 'Right now, in this city,' he said, 'you've got to be stupid not to make money. A schmuck could make money. Abigail could make money.' A development he was involved in at Gramercy Park was going to make a fortune, he said. 'Actually an English guy's one of our investors, we met him at Marcus Brand's place. Lord Crieff of Scotland. He's going to be one very happy man.

225

'Did you ever hear how Marcus and I became friends?' Zubin continued. 'It's quite a story.' Stuart would willingly have forgone the anecdote, but it was plain that Zubin couldn't be stopped. Ever since his discovery of his father's culpability in Lucy Brand's death, Stuart couldn't hear Marcus's name without blanching. He had long ago resolved to have nothing further to do with his godfather – it would be far too embarrassing – and the less he heard about him the better. But Zubin, alert to Marcus's ever-increasing wealth and influence, now liked to present his earlier falling out with the tycoon as the inevitable cut-and-thrust between two ambitious and fairly matched business monoliths, and Marcus's double-crossing as a badge of friendship.

'He didn't know anyone in this city, not when I first met him. He'll tell you that himself if you ask him. "Zubin introduced me to everyone." He acknowledges it. What's the name of that club in London . . . you know the place. The guy who has it also owns that nightclub . . . Harriet, help me.'

'Mark's Club, Zubin.'

'Mark's Club. Marcus has never forgotten. "You introduced me to all the right people, Zubin." He told me that over lunch there.'

Suddenly curious about Marcus's life in those early days, and reckoning Zubin might be able to throw light on it, Stuart asked, 'Where did he come from originally? In all the newspaper articles about him, it never says.'

'Search me,' said Zubin. 'I don't know too much about him. By the time I met him, he was living in London and building his business. I heard he was married once but the wife died, which was too bad.'

'He's Jewish, we know that,' said Harriet.

'He is? I never heard that before,' said Zubin.

'Of course he's Jewish, he told me that himself. He doesn't go to temple, but his family were Jewish. They observed all the holidays. He told me at Harry's Bar.'

After supper, as they were driving back into the city, Abigail said, 'So, you survived my parents?'

'I like your parents. It was a great evening.'

'It's different for you, you're a guest. With me, they just get under my skin.'

'They dote on you. Anyone can see that.'

'That's half the trouble, they have this knack of making me feel guilty all the time. Like, whatever I achieve, it's never enough.'

'A lot of parents are like that, I think,' said Stuart, thinking how very lucky he was with his own mother who, while ambitious for him, had never once confused high expectations with love.

'I spend my life trying to win people's approval,' Abigail said, 'I can't help it. The more demanding they are, the more I want to please them. I do it at the gallery with Hershel, with my parents, even with Marcus. Actually, with Marcus more than anybody.'

'With Marcus? Why bother?'

'Probably because he totally ignores me,' Abigail said. 'He always has. I'm his least favourite godchild. In Nassau, he never once sat next to me at lunch or dinner. Not one time. I don't mean to sound paranoid, but it really freaked me.'

'You shouldn't let it. What's Marcus to you? It's not like you have to see him much.'

'That's just it,' Abigail said, her voice becoming rapidly hyper. 'I *want* to see him. I want him to approve of me. Stuart, I haven't told this to anybody before, but I think about him all the time. I guess I'm in love with him. I know it's ridiculous, I can't explain it. When I hear he's coming to New York, I can't think about anything else, I get so excited. I've dropped fifty pounds for him, not that it's done any good. At that dance, when I went to say hello to him, he practically blanked me. And the worst thing about it is, the more he ignores me, the more I want to impress him. What should I do, Stuart? I need your advice. Should I tell him?'

'Blimey,' said Stuart, rather disconcerted by this stream of confessional psychobabble. 'I don't really know what to suggest. But I certainly wouldn't tell him if I were you.'

'That's what my shrink said, but I'm not sure. Last time

Marcus was here, I rang his hotel three times, but when they put me through to his suite, I put the phone down.'

'Christ! That bad, is it?'

'Sometimes I think the only way out is to kill myself. But then I think, what's the point? He probably wouldn't even notice. Tell me honestly, Stuart, am I completely nuts?'

He stared out of the window, feeling unequal to the situation. 'I'd say obsessed more than anything else,' he said. 'I'm sure you'll get over it in time.'

'But that's just it,' Abigail replied, suddenly breaking down. 'I don't want to get over it. All I want is to make Marcus proud of me.'

18: July, 1981

Hurtling down the Fosse Way between Northleach and Cirencester, Jamie tossed a fag-end out of the passenger window of Nipples Ayrton-Phillips's yellow Ford Fiesta. He watched it bounce a couple of times on the road before being lifted into the air by a gust of tailwind, and into a meadow full of ragwort and Friesian cattle.

'We're going to be frightfully late,' Nipples said. 'They asked us to arrive by tea time.'

'We'll be fine. It's only eight o'clock. Dinner won't be for ages.'

For a whole variety of reasons Jamie was feeling cool about life. In his pocket was a nice fat envelope of cocaine, enough to get him and Nipples through tonight's dance with some left over. Then there was Nipples herself. He had been three-timing the pretty Montessori teacher for several months now but she was fun to have around, not least as a driver. They had spent last night together in the Tunnel of Love. Nipples's flatmate, Mary Merrett, didn't approve at all, but probably she was just jealous, Jamie reckoned.

And then there was the dance itself. Jamie loved dances. He scarcely knew the people who were giving this one, and had never heard of the people who were having him to stay in their houseparty. As far as he was concerned, it was very decent of all these strangers to invite him into their homes, with so many tempting trinkets left lying about.

They pulled up outside The Manor in West Cerney in a screech of rubber on raked gravel. Glaring out through a sash window was the mistress of the house. (Jamie hadn't bothered to check out her name on the postcard as yet – a Mrs Michael Bembridge.)

'We didn't know what on earth had happened to you,' said Mrs Bembridge crossly. 'Go and get changed. There are still a few people upstairs. Jamie, I've put you in Michael's dressing room.'

Jamie carried his suitcase up to the dressing room and quickly cased the joint. On the mahogany chest-of-drawers was a pair of ivory-backed hairbrushes, which he reckoned might fetch fifteen quid at Antiquarius; it was a pity they had initials set into them because it reduced their value. Most of the small pictures in the room were photographs of school rowing eights, with the young M.G. Bembridge balancing in a scull with an oar. Worthless. But in a box in the top drawer were several pairs of gold and silver-plated cufflinks.

Jamie didn't feel proud of his recent light-fingered proclivities. Each time he nicked something, he swore this was the very last time. Not naturally devious, he would rather have had limitless money of his own to spend on girlfriends, drinks and cocaine. But the fact was, he could no longer bring himself to roll up at *World's End* more than one or two days a week, and his commission had plummeted. To lift the odd watercolour or Georgian serving spoon along the way was his only means of making ends meet. Somewhere in the back of his mind, he nursed the chivalrous notion that, one day, when he got more together, he would buy back all the cufflinks, silverware and watercolours and return them anonymously to their owners.

He upturned his suitcase on to the bed and began to get changed. Where the hell was his dinner jacket? Blast, he thought, I've left it behind in the Tunnel of Love. Big problem. He wondered what to do.

There was a wardrobe in the room containing Michael Bembridge's own clothes, tightly packed together on a rail and smelling of mothballs. Jamie saw an array of City suits, shooting suits, sports jackets and skiing gear. Down below, in serried ranks, were two dozen polished brogues with cedar shoe trees. And at the end of the rail, still in its dry cleaning bag, he spotted a dinner jacket.

Seven minutes later he was downstairs in the drawing room, drink in hand, admiring the view of parkland and horse chestnut trees through the open windows, while enjoying the sensation of being eyed up by so many pretty girls.

'Darling, have you seen my dinner jacket anywhere?' Michael Bembridge appeared at the door in pleated dress shirt and bow tie.

'In your cupboard,' said his wife. 'I collected it from Sketchley's for you yesterday.'

'How strange, I couldn't see it. I'll have another look.'

Jamie accepted a refill of champagne, and flirted gently with Joanna Bembridge and Zara Fane. Both girls were putting out sexual vibes like bitches on heat. There was no doubt about it: with his cowlick brown hair, sweet smile, snake hips and perfectly-cut DJ, Jamie was the most desirable man in the room by miles.

'This really is most odd,' said Michael Bembridge, returning to the drawing room looking perplexed. 'I've looked absolutely everywhere. There's nothing else for it, I'll have to wear a blue suit with my bow tie. Can't be helped.'

During dinner, Michael several times eyed Jamie's dinner jacket as though dimly recognising it.

'This may seem an odd question, Jamie,' he said eventually. 'But you didn't accidentally put on the wrong dinner jacket, did you? That one looks awfully like mine.'

'Definitely not,' replied Jamie, without missing a beat. 'This was my grandfather's.'

'I see, fine. Hope you didn't mind my asking?'

But later, when the women had left the room to take a pee, he returned to the subject.

'You're going to think me an awful old bore,' he said, 'but you wouldn't mind letting me see the label inside, would you? Mine's a Tom Brown. I've had it for years, and it really is identical to the one you've got on, even down to the repair on the sleeve. Be a good man and put my mind at rest, won't you?'

Jamie frowned and, sounding genuinely affronted, said, 'I'm awfully sorry, sir, but are you accusing me of stealing your clothes? I mean, it's a bit much, isn't it? I've been sent to stay at your house for a friend's dance, and the next thing

I know I'm being asked to turn out my pockets. Do you normally accuse your guests of theft?'

Michael Bembridge, recognising that his question had been taken in the wrong way, was overcome with regret and embarrassment.

'My dear fellow, of course I didn't mean to disbelieve you. I wouldn't dream of it, it was unforgivable of me. And please don't show me the label, I don't even want to see it, I absolutely refuse.'

'You quite sure?' Jamie asked, innocence seeping out of every pore. 'It's got my grandfather's tailor's label inside.'

'Under no circumstances will I look at it. I don't know what got into me. I insist you have another glass of wine and forget all about it.'

Fifteen minutes later, as they were driving cross-country to the dance, Jamie said, 'Listen, Nipples, after the party let's head straight back to London. They can send our stuff later. I really can't face going back to that house.'

Hovering outside Jamie's bedroom door in Clancarty Road, Margaret Temple wondered whether it would be all right to go in. She knew he was sleeping at home for once, because she'd heard the front door slam at four o'clock in the morning. Whether Jamie was alone, or had a girlfriend in there with him, she couldn't tell. But it was after twelve o'clock and he must be awake by now. Margaret was anxious to have a heart-to-heart with her elusive son about his future.

For well over a year she had been worrying about Jamie, but then she worried about so many things. She worried about money, she worried about Jamie's sister Lucinda who was behaving so inconsiderately, she worried about her house which had subsidence and which the insurance company refused to put right because she had excluded it from her policy, and now she was worried about her little collection of Victorian silver boxes and napkin rings which seemed to be disappearing one by one. She supposed it must be the cleaning lady, but was reluctant to confront her in case she gave in her notice. Margaret was worried she would never be able to replace her at the same low hourly rate. Were it not for her wire-haired Jack Russell, Cadogan, which demanded to be walked twice a day without fail, Margaret would have sat at home all day worrying. Instead, she worried while beating the boundaries of Eel Brook Common and South Park, occasionally pausing to wish good afternoon to one of her nice doggie friends.

It went without saying that she would rather have been walking Cadogan in Hyde Park or the Royal Hospital Gardens. A day never passed without her regretting the move from Belgravia. What wouldn't she give to be back within walking distance of the greengrocer and butcher in Elizabeth Street ('my spiritual home') or the cheerful Italian restaurants, decorators and present shops along Walton Street? There were times, more than she cared to admit, when she wondered whether she should have stayed put with Michael, and learned to turn a blind eye to his serial philandering. Then perhaps they would still all be living in South Eaton Place. The thought of that lovely stucco house with its perfect proportions and faultless address almost set her off crying again. The most upsetting news she'd heard recently – and this really worried her – was that Michael was having to put the house on the market. Some co-development he had underwritten with Marcus Brand had come unstuck, and Marcus had called in a huge loan. Michael had rung to warn her that his finances were temporarily in a dicky state, and she might have to whistle for her maintenance for a month or two.

Having listened at his bedroom door for fifteen minutes, Margaret tapped lightly and called, 'Jamie? Jamie darling, it's me. May I come in?'

He groaned and turned over. 'Go away.'

'I do need to talk to you, Jamie. It's important.'

She crept into the room, stepping over the mound of discarded clothes, and perched on the edge of the bed. To her immense relief, Jamie was alone; she had her son all to herself. He turned over on to his back, stretched, revealing a furze of chestnut underarm hair in each pit, and whispered, 'Can't it wait? What's the big hurry?' Watching him waking up, his naked body hardly covered by an Asterix the Gaul duvet, Margaret thought how handsome he was, and was hardly surprised all the girls were dotty about him.

Jamie heaved himself up in bed and said witheringly, 'Thanks, Mother. I was out at a dance last night, you do realise. In Gloucestershire.'

'Was it lovely? Whose was it?' Since her divorce from Michael, Margaret was seldom invited to anything smart any more. Her social life had fallen like a stone into the deep, dark pit of eternal oblivion reserved for Fulham divorcees. Instead, she lived vicariously through Jamie who was her only remaining link with the world she had once inhabited.

'It was OK. At some Priory with a moat. There were fireworks. Can't remember the people's name.'

'That's very ungrateful of you,' Margaret said, suddenly bitter. Increasingly, her hunger for news of parties and high life was tainted by anger that she was no longer part of that world.

'Who was there?' she asked, unable to restrain herself.

'Loads of people.' He yawned. 'It's always the same crowd anyway. I saw Marcus Brand, but didn't talk to him.'

'Oh, I do wish you had,' said Margaret. 'Marcus is one of the reasons I wanted a word with you. I think you should ask him for a job.'

'I have a job.'

'A proper job. I'm sure if you write to him he'll come up with something. He is your godfather. And didn't you say Charlie is working for him already?'

Jamie felt a moment of panic. Having no inclination to slave in one of Marcus's dull-sounding enterprises, and guessing he would in any case never be capable of holding down a serious job, he cast about for a way out.

'It's funny you should be bringing this up, Mother,' he said, wildly extemporising. 'I was reading about this course at Westminster Polytechnic.'

Margaret looked doubtful. 'Is it very expensive? I'm not sure your father or I can really afford much at the moment.'

'I did have one idea,' he said carefully. 'You know your Staffordshire figures? They'd fetch quite a lot these days.

What I was thinking was, I could flog them for you, use the money for the course and then pay you back when I get a great job afterwards. It would be like a loan for my education.'

Margaret closed her eyes. Of all the worldly possessions left to her, nothing gave her so much pleasure as her sixty Staffordshire figurines. They lived in a special backlit display cabinet in the drawing room. She had been collecting them for more than twenty-five years, beginning with Little Bo Peep and her flock of bone china sheep, gravitating to the more serious, scarcer pieces like Falstaff and Lord Raglan. To dispose of the collection would break her heart.

But, there again, was there anything more important than your children's education? And hadn't she been worrying herself sick for months now about Jamie's lack of ambition, and what would become of him? To turn down his own idea of higher education for the sake of some pottery ornaments couldn't possibly be the right decision. How could she face herself in the mirror? And so, with awful sadness, mitigated only by the certainty that she was doing the right thing by her son, Margaret agreed to his proposal.

'I must say, Jamie, I'm proud of you,' she said, as she crept out of the room. 'Now, try and go back to sleep if you can, darling. You deserve a proper lie-in. You won't get many when you start your studies.'

Jamie waited until he heard her footsteps disappear down the passage, then sprang out of bed. To his horror, a small packet of coke, two pairs of gold cufflinks and the ceramic snuff boxes with armorial crests he had filched from last night's dance had been lying in full view on the seat of a chair. The Tom Brown dinner jacket belonging to M.G. Bembridge Esq. was flung across its back.

Jamie bundled the suit into a carrier bag, which he would shortly dump in the nearest municipal rubbish bin. The snuff boxes and cuff-links he would sell tomorrow at an antiques market, whichever would take them off his hands.

19: February, 1982

At a St Valentine's Night dinner party on 14 February 1982, on an evening so icy that several cars skidded into each other while attempting to park outside the flat in Nevern Square, Mary met the man she would become engaged to only four weeks later, and who would become her husband in June the same year.

Crispin Gore was tall and conventionally handsome, good-humoured and honourable. The youngest of three almost indistinguishable red-headed brothers, he had been raised on the rolling prairies of the family cereal farm near Fakenham in Norfolk, educated at Radley where he captained the golf team, spent six months on a sheep station outside Canberra owned by a distant cousin, joined Savills and had worked his way up through his department. At the age of twenty-nine, he was number two gun on the country properties side for much of the South West of England, covering an area encompassing Basingstoke to Bath, Bridgwater to Blandford Forum. He was 'fortunate enough' (as he invariably put it) to have as his secretary 'the invaluable' Sarah Whitley, on whom he had harboured vague designs until he met her flatmate, Mary, at the St Valentine's Night dinner party.

It was love at first sight in the English manner. Which is to say that neither Mary nor Crispin gave the slightest indication to one another of their massive and immediate mutual attraction. Crispin was entranced by Mary's soft prettiness. Within minutes of meeting her, sensing her shyness, he had an extraordinary urge to envelop her in his own natural self-confidence, and protect her. Instead, he helped her to erect the ironing board extension to the dinner table, and to open the mis-matched bottles of sparkling pink wine brought along by the guests.

Mary recognised in Crispin Gore a man of utter integrity

and kindness. She also found him attractive. Probably even Mary herself couldn't have said which of these attributes carried the most weight in her thinking. But long before the pasta bowls for the main course had been cleared away, Mary knew Crispin was the first man she was truly interested in since Charlie.

She found him incredibly easy to talk to, feeling no obligation to be either clever or witty. She described her day at the employment agency (they had recently gained Asprey's as a client which was fantastic) and Crispin told her about his day selling houses (an Arab was buying some great Palladian pile near Bicester, which was a tragedy, but who in England needed or could afford twenty-five bedrooms any more?).

'Maybe he's got twenty-five wives?' suggested Mary.

Crispin roared with laughter. 'Maybe he has. It must be ghastly. One wife will be quite enough for me, if ever I'm lucky enough to meet the right person.'

Thank goodness, was Mary's first thought, he hasn't found anyone yet.

'I've been hearing about this flat for ages from Sarah,' Crispin said. 'Which of your flatmates is the one known as Nipples?'

'I wish you hadn't asked that, it's rather a sore point. We had to ask her to move out, she went a bit druggy.'

'Ah,' said Crispin, shaking his head in a wordly-wise way.

'We have a new flatmate now, Jo Bembridge. She lives in Gloucestershire.'

At twenty-five minutes to ten the next morning, before Mary had even had time to take off her coat, Crispin had rung her at the office to invite her skiing in a fortnight's time.

'There are going to be ten of us in the chalet. Do say yes. It will be miles more fun with you there too.'

When they returned from Val d'Isère engaged, nobody was more delighted than Mary's parents. They took an instant liking to Crispin when she brought him down for lunch at Fircones, and whatever apprehension they'd had about the speed of it all was entirely dissipated. 'I know Crispin won't be embarrassed by my saying this in front of him,' Belinda Merrett declared, having drunk a second glass of white wine and feeling uncharacteristically tipsy, 'but you've chosen very well, Mary. Crispin's a lovely young man. He reminds me of your father when we first met all those years ago.'

Tactfully disguising his slight horror at being compared to Mary's stooping, ingratiating father, Crispin replied, 'That's entirely undeserved, Mrs Merrett. It's jolly decent of you to welcome me so warmly into your family.'

'I do hope you'll call me Belinda,' she said. 'There's no formality in this house.'

Congratulations poured in from all sides. There was a drinks party in Nevern Square, parties at Crispin's bachelor flat in Shawfield Street, impromptu drinks in the office after work when the girls presented Mary with a special wedding planner with spaces to list bridesmaids' dresses and favourite hymns. It seemed to her that, for a whole month, she was never without a glass of champagne in her hand. All Crispin's family wanted to meet her, including great-aunts who would surely never live long enough to make the wedding. One of them, living all alone in a flat in Burton Court, was so doddery that at first she failed to hear the door bell and then forgot to give them a drink.

'You're so wonderful to put up with all my funny old relations,' Crispin said.

'I love meeting them,' replied Mary, who genuinely did.

As an only child, with hardly any family of her own, she was entranced by the great rambling infrastructure of cousins and aunts she was marrying into. She adored Crispin's parents and brothers and their long, tile-slung farmhouse surrounded on all four sides by vast flat ploughed fields. Immediately welcoming, and taking it for granted that as Crispin's choice they would all love her, they made Mary feel instantly at home. She couldn't help contrasting the easy warmth of the Gores with her chilly reception all those years before from the Crieffs at Ardnessaig. Defiantly unpretentious, there was nothing the Gores liked better as a family than eating supper all together in front of the television on trays, watching *Dad's Army* or *Are You Being Served?* It was only during Mary's third weekend at Fakenham, when Crispin's father, Robin, was bouncing her across the farm in his mud-spattered Land Rover, that he let slip they had seven thousand acres.

All three of Mary's godparents wrote to say how delighted they were for her. Marcus dashed off a telex from Hong Kong declaring, 'You are the first of my six godchildren to become engaged. Congratulations. Please advise Barbara of the date of the wedding as soon as possible, so she can incorporate it into my schedule.'

'Oh, God, we don't really have to invite him?' Mary shuddered when it arrived. 'I don't want him to be there at all.'

Crispin, finding the telex amongst the pile of post Mary had put aside for him, asked, 'This isn't from Marcus Brand, is it? How on earth do you know him?'

'He's my godfather.'

'Really?' Crispin looked amazed. 'We acted for the Pooles when he bought West Candover Park from them. I have to say, he was the trickiest individual we've ever dealt with.'

Belinda turned the organisation of her daughter's wedding into a full-time occupation, and there were moments when Mary felt compromised by the stream of telephone calls to the office. How did people plan weddings and work at the same time? Only her determination not to be seen slacking off, or for the other girls to be landed with any of her workload, enabled her to juggle the continual questions about flowers, bouquets and orders of service with the demands of her clients.

Church and vicar were booked for the second Saturday in June; Mary was to be married in the same Norman church in the Surrey village where she had been christened twenty-four years before. Afterwards, the reception would be held in the Merretts' garden in a marquee on the croquet lawn. Worrying about the expense of it all, and desperately conscious her parents couldn't really afford it, Mary suggested they'd be every bit as happy with something simpler. 'Nonsense,' Derek had replied. 'If I can't send my only daughter off in style, I wouldn't be much of a father, would I? I'm going to be so proud, darling, walking with you down the aisle on the big day.'

As the preparations gathered pace, Mary began to feel disembodied, as though everything was whirling around her and she hardly counted any more. Events took on a life of their own. A wedding cake was ordered, caterer booked, wines selected and menu approved. Being almost the first girl in her generation at school to get married, there were no friends with small children to sign up as bridesmaids. The story of my life, Mary thought: first a chronic man shortage, now a bridesmaid shortage. But she was deliriously happy and nothing could deflate her for long. In the end, half a dozen pages and bridesmaids were identified among the ranks of Crispin's cousins.

Miraculously, Mary and her parents managed to get through all the arrangements for the wedding with only one argument. This was over the guest list. Mary remained determined not to invite Marcus, but Derek was immovable; to exclude the man who was variously his Chairman, his old friend and Mary's godfather was out of the question. 'I must say, Mary,' he said, 'I find your attitude on this inexplicable, especially as Marcus has always shown such an interest in you. I won't hear of his not being asked.'

Belinda, who secretly sided with her daughter but felt that they should do nothing to rock the boat apropos Derek's job, retrieved one of the stiff invitations from the box, shook out the interleaf of tissue paper, and inscribed Marcus's name.

As far as the other godchildren were concerned, Mary had lost touch with Saffron Weaver and Abigail Schwartzman, neither of whom she felt it necessary to ask. Jamie she supposed she ought to invite despite his disgraceful corruption of poor Nipples which had started all her problems in the first place. Charlie she didn't want at all, but it would be rude not to ask him, though since he was safely in Hong Kong he almost certainly wouldn't be able to make it. Somewhere, in an old address book, she still had Stuart Bolton's address in Birmingham, or maybe it was his mother's. She hadn't seen or heard anything of him since Marcus's dance five years ago when he'd been such a hero. She decided to invite him on the off-chance.

Eventually getting round to opening his invitation eight weeks later, which had been sent to Clancarty Road, a place he had been studiously avoiding because he couldn't face his mother, Jamie learned that Mary Merrett was getting spliced the very next weekend. This is rather sudden, he thought suspiciously. Oy, oy, what's naughty Mary been up to then? Someone's put her up the duff.

Everybody agreed, as they turned to watch Mary process so solemnly down the aisle on the arm of her father, that few brides ever looked quite as radiant as the soon-to-be Mrs Crispin Gore. Her appearance at the West Door in a 'Princess Diana' dress with puffy sleeves, full train and a big bow at the front, copied by a local dressmaker in Godalming from the wedding pictures of the Prince and Princess of Wales, sent up gasps of admiration. And when the organist launched into 'The Entrance of the Queen of Sheba' with a blast of trumpets, and Mary, trailed by six of the sweetest small children in peach dresses, peach silk knickerbockers and broderie-anglaise shirts, could visibly be seen blinking back tears of joy, at least half of the congregation felt like joining in.

As she walked towards the altar, it seemed to Mary that her entire life was flashing before her eyes. The pews were overflowing with friends and familiar faces. Most of her year from the Convent of the Perpetual Martyr were there, looking amazing in raw taffeta suits and straw hats they'd decorated themselves with flowers and ribbons. She spotted her parents' old friends the Whitleys and Mount-Joneses, and Mr and Mrs Dodd-Harvey, and Miss Green, her old riding school teacher, hot and uncomfortable in a cerise-coloured suit that clashed with her red face. Out of the corner of her eye, she saw Jamie Temple looking debonair in a morning coat with his hair slicked back and, next to him, Charlie Crieff, who had never replied to the invitation. For a moment she caught his eye and he nodded at her in a condescending manner. Mary realised, to her immense relief, that Charlie no longer meant anything to her at all; the spell was finally broken. She could see both her flatmates, Sarah and Jo, standing with Nipples close to the front, Reverend Mother, her old school headmistress, and two of her godparents though no sign of Marcus.

The broad back of Crispin was waiting for her at the altar, flanked by his elder brother, Rupert, who was best man. Mary could see her mother in a front pew, in the royal blue suit and matching hat she had bought at House of Fraser and, across the aisle, her future parents-in-law and all Crispin's family smiling at her as she passed. Crispin's mother looked incredibly chic, Mary thought, in powder pink. 'You look beautiful,' Crispin whispered to her when she reached his side, and gave her hand a reassuring squeeze.

The service passed in a blur. Afterwards, she could remember almost nothing of the vicar's homily about marriage being something you have to work at, or the passage from Khalil Gibran's 'The Prophet' read by Crispin's eldest brother, Guy. She knew only that she and Crispin had exchanged their vows firmly and clearly, and Rupert had slipped the wedding ring to his brother at exactly the right moment, and that the vicar had duly pronounced them man and wife, and soon afterwards everyone started singing 'Jerusalem'. In what seemed like no time at all, she was retracing her steps back up the aisle, with Crispin by her side, and then out into the blazing heat of the churchyard on what would later be confirmed as one of the hottest June days of the decade.

After photographs outside the porch, they were driven the half-mile to Fircones for the reception. Inside the marquee, its sides left open to the garden owing to the incredible heat, everything was in readiness; the garden itself prinked to within an inch of its life. Derek had taken two days off work to achieve the perfect vertical stripes on the uneven lawn leading down to the stream and the paddock beyond. A decorative wheelbarrow on the terrace was planted with pink and red fuchsias. The flowerbeds were a riot of colour, with clusters of floribunda roses and delphiniums. Some of the Gores' Norfolk friends, accustomed to rather larger, wilder gardens, remarked that they had never seen anything so immaculate.

Several delightful old ladies were pouring out tea, and waitresses circulated with champagne and plates of vol-au-vents, bridge rolls, finger sandwiches and sausages on sticks coated with honey and mustard. As a means of keeping the budget down, the timing of the day had been carefully worked out, so the Merretts wouldn't need to feed their guests with anything more substantial than canapés. The wedding had therefore been set for two o'clock, with the reception at three, speeches and cutting of the cake at half-past four, and the departure of the bride and groom at half-past five. The scene was, however, idyllic and, standing at the head of the receiving line greeting their guests, Mary felt incredibly grateful to her parents for putting on such a beautiful wedding.

Derek Merrett was becoming agitated by the non-arrival of Marcus. 'It's very strange,' he kept saying to Belinda. 'His office confirmed on Monday he was definitely coming. They asked me to send a second map.'

'I really wouldn't think about it,' she said. 'If he doesn't come, he doesn't come. He's only one person.'

But Derek did think about it. The absence of his boss was a snub and a bad portent. Besides which, he had told everyone at work Marcus would be a guest at Mary's wedding.

Jamie was checking out the talent and, so far, had been disappointed; the girls at this reception looked significantly less louche than he was used to. He'd spotted Nipples in the church, but her parents were there too, and Jamie was keen to avoid them. He was considering slipping inside the house and casing the joint for knick-knacks when a raven-haired girl whose pretty face was dimly familiar approached him.

'Don't you recognise me?'

'Er, of course, yes. But remind me . . .'

'Jo Bembridge. You were going to stay at our house for that dance, but you went back to London. We've still got some of your stuff.'

Jamie flushed. It always made him uncomfortable being reminded of the scenes of his crimes.

'While we were at the dance, a burglar must have broken into the house and stolen Dad's cufflinks. The police couldn't understand how they got in, though, because the alarm was on.'

'Doesn't really surprise me,' Jamie said coolly. 'Gloucestershire's a hotbed of crime. They even nicked your father's dinner jacket, didn't they?'

Charlie was feeling sweaty and fat. He was wearing his old school tailcoat and his stomach was straining the waistband of his trousers; he must have put on weight in Hong Kong. Looking around the garden he reckoned the Merretts' set-up was pretty much as predicted. He'd half-expected gnomes on the front lawn, this being Surrey, but at least they were spared that. Some of the guests were fearfully naff, but others were better class; the Gores' friends, he imagined. Mary had done well for herself. For an instant, he wondered whether he should have put in more effort with her himself, until he remembered how frigid she'd been in bed. The only reason he'd come to the wedding was to see Marcus, and Marcus wasn't even here. It would have suited Charlie to bump into his boss in a social setting.

Mary and Crispin circulated around the garden, hand in hand, trying to greet those guests who, feeling they were not close enough friends to talk to the bride and groom, had been carefully avoiding them throughout the reception. When Mary saw a broad-shouldered figure in a lounge suit and horn-rimmed glasses, she was thrilled when she realised it was Stuart.

'I can't believe it's really you, you look so brown and fit. Where've you been?'

'The States. I'm studying over there.' His manner seemed different too, Mary thought, more relaxed and confident.

'Stuart saved my life,' she told her husband. 'We were on holiday together in the Bahamas, and he was the only person who was kind to me.'

'Anyway, it was nice of you to invite me to this,' Stuart said. 'You never know, our paths might cross again one day.'

His accent has gone all American, Mary noticed; it hardly sounded Birmingham any more.

As Stuart left, she found herself face to face with Nipples who she had barely seen since her ejection from Nevern Square.

'You look fantastic,' Mary said. 'Are you completely recovered now?'

'So long as I stick to Coca-Cola. I meant to tell you, I met a friend of yours when I was in Broadway Lodge – Saffron.'

'Saffron? She used to be so beautiful, I was quite scared of her. Is she OK?'

'She sends her love. She said you had some really good talks in the Bahamas.'

'Did she really say that? How embarrassing. I wish I'd invited her now.'

The reception was bowling along and it was almost time for the speeches. The men, sweltering inside their tailcoats, were unfastening the buttons of their waistcoats. Two little pages, having kicked off their shoes, were tearing about the garden. Crispin's four pale-faced nieces, with their Norfolk complexions, were sheltering under a tea table. Derek Merrett wondered whether they should delay the cutting of the cake by a further five minutes, in case Marcus still made it.

At that moment they heard a distant hack-hack somewhere above them, and a helicopter, still hardly larger than a dot in the sky, was circling the garden, apparently searching for a place to land.

'Good God,' Derek said to Belinda, 'that's Marcus's chopper.' And then to Crispin, 'I think that's Mary's godfather, Marcus Brand, trying to land. I'd better wave him down in the paddock.'

Two minutes later, a snub-nosed Bell with black titanium rotor-blades was hovering above the meadow, blowing back the long grass as it came down. Red lights were blinking on the roof and tail. Almost all the guests, excited by the arrival of a helicopter, had gathered on the edge of the field and were hanging on to their hats as they waited for the rotors to stop.

The pilot climbed out and ran round the front to open the passenger door. Then out stepped Marcus, mesmerising in a mother-of-pearl waistcoat and tails. The pilot handed him a top hat which seemed taller and glossier than anyone else's top hat. He stood for a moment in the meadow, appraising the scene and waiting for the rotors to come to a stop. Recently, his face had become a little bit fleshy around his jowls. He still had wonderful posture, Mary noticed, and held himself in a way that made everyone around him appear smaller and rather shrivelled and stooped and poor.

'Forgive me for being late,' he said to her, enfolding her in a bear hug. 'I've come straight from Paris.'

The arrival of Marcus in such exhilarating circumstances altered the dynamic of the afternoon. What had hitherto been a charming, if slightly parochial, Home Counties wedding reception, took on a glamorous edge, as though they had suddenly been joined by royalty. It was an indication of Marcus Brand's increasing celebrity that so many people, men and women alike, wanted to get close to him and gawp. Derek ushered him gingerly round the garden, introducing him to the Gores with elaborate explanations of their respective status and importance.

Watching the charade across the lawn, Jamie said to Charlie, 'You know what he looks like, Mary's dad? He's like some old stockman at an agricultural show, parading his prize bull around the ring.'

'Let's hope he doesn't get gored,' Charlie said. 'From what I hear, Derek Merrett's career's on the skids.'

Jamie was drinking heavily. The champagne had long since been superseded by white wine, but he drank as fast as the waiters could pour. 'Have you noticed the way Marcus is looking at Mary?'

Charlie peered across the garden, where their godfather was standing four-square by the rockery, surrounded by some of the Merretts' dimmer neighbours. Marcus, he could see, was paying no attention to them at all, but staring intently at Mary in her wedding dress. His expression seemed to combine disapproval with scarcely concealed sexual longing.

'What's got into him?' Charlie asked. 'He doesn't look too happy.'

'Jealous probably. Jealous Mary's happy and it's nothing to do with him. I bet he secretly hates it she's got a husband. Anyway, it's obvious he fancies her.'

'Has he always?' Charlie asked in surprise.

'Not that I noticed. Probably it's seeing her in virgin white. Most men fancy brides.'

Charlie decided the moment was opportune to suck up to Marcus. After three years in Hong Kong, he was beginning to wonder if his career was stuck in a rut, and whether he was due a transfer back to London.

'*Charlie!*' True to form, Marcus greeted his godson with an extraordinary initial show of enthusiasm, which quickly evaporated. 'What are you doing here anyway? Thought you were supposed to be working for me in Asia.' He glared, as though he'd caught Charlie absent without leave.

'Actually, Marcus, I thought I'd better put in an appearance at a fellow godchild's wedding.'

'Yes, indeed,' Marcus replied dryly. 'You always were very friendly with my goddaughter Mary.'

Charlie flushed. 'I like almost all your godchildren,' he began. 'You've given us some incredible holidays . . .'

'And, of course, you took Mary to Lantau for that weekend. I hope you found plenty to amuse yourselves with at the cottage.'

Charlie wondered how he could possibly have known about Lantau, and precisely what he knew.

'Yah, it was a great weekend. We visited the Buddhist monastery.'

'Splendid,' said Marcus. 'I'm glad you have an interest in Eastern religions.' And then, turning on his heel, he headed off in the direction of Mary, leaving Charlie bemused and irritated.

Jamie, scouring the party for another drink, didn't notice Stuart until he bumped into him.

'You OK, Jamie?' Stuart asked, shocked by his dissolute appearance. 'I haven't seen you for years. What are you up to?'

'I was meant to be going to some polytechnic, but then I didn't,' he slurred, and laughed. 'Little problem about blowing my fees on certain substances.'

'You sure you're OK?' Stuart asked again. He thought Jamie looked terrible. He must have lost two stone and his eyes weren't focusing.

'I would be if I could find a drink round here. Haven't seen anyone with a bottle, have you?'

'Listen, Jamie, this is none of my business – I don't even live in England any more – but you should see a doctor. I mean it, you look ill.'

'Maybe I will.' Jamie pulled a face. 'But first I need a drink.'

The cutting of the cake was long overdue, and Rupert Gore and Derek Merrett were delving about in their tail-coats for their speeches.

'Regrettably, I won't be able to stay for the speeches,' Marcus told Derek. 'Work calls me back to London. But I wonder whether I might make a short public presentation of my wedding present before I leave. It's rather fun, you see.'

'Er, of course, Marcus,' said Derek, rather thrown by this unexpected alteration to the plans.

Derek called for silence and the two hundred guests formed a semi-circle in the tent.

'In a moment, ladies and gentlemen, we will have the ceremonial cutting of the cake followed by speeches,' he announced. 'But before that I am delighted to introduce my very old personal friend Marcus Brand. Marcus is certainly my oldest work friend, since we started out together more than twenty-five years ago sharing a little office in Broad Street. Since then, of course, Marcus has gone on to become one of our most successful tycoons, running a business empire so big I can't even keep track of half of what he owns these days. But he has remained a loyal friend to the Merretts, and a wonderful godfather to Mary, and I am personally very honoured that he has made the considerable effort to be here this afternoon. So, Marcus, over to you.'

Marcus stepped forward and regarded the crowd, moving his big head very slowly as he waited for silence. Standing with Crispin at the front of the circle, Mary was reminded of an adult tiger she had once seen in a zoo, immensely powerful and sleek, appraising the trippers through the bars of its cage with indulgent disdain. Stuart was watching Marcus too, trying to figure out what he felt about him these days. Since Stanford, his opinion of business entrepreneurs had become more tempered as he'd learned how hard it was to start and run successful enterprises. At least Marcus was someone who made things happen. Stuart remained profoundly suspicious of him, but had to admit he was impressive.

'You must forgive this unscheduled intrusion,' Marcus said. 'I promise I will not detain you for more than a minute. But I would like to say how pleased I am for Mary on this momentous day, and to wish her great happiness for the future. Mary, I hope you will allow your godfather to say that you are an exceptionally beautiful young woman, and your husband is a very fortunate fellow.' Then he said, 'I have a wedding present for you that I regret I have been unable to have gift wrapped, but if the driver could bring it round on to the lawn, I would like to present it to you both with my fondest wishes.'

There was the purr of an engine somewhere behind them, and the crowd turned to see a little green open-topped MG drawing up alongside the tent. Marcus led Mary by the hand, withdrew the keys from the ignition, tossed them to her and said, 'For you and Crispin. From The Godfather.' Then leaning so close that his words were inaudible to anybody else, he whispered, 'One day, Mary – not now, but one day – I would like to get to know you much better.'

Five minutes later, as Rupert Gore was midway through an entertaining anecdote about Crispin's schooldays, his story was drowned out by the roar of a helicopter taking off from the paddock.

20: October, 1982

'My name is Saffron and I am an addict.'

'Hello, Saffron,' intoned the group.

'My name is Jamie and I am an addict.'

'Hello, Jamie.'

Fourteen people were sitting in a semi-circle in a church hall in Radnor Walk, a narrow Chelsea terrace full of brightly painted, bijou houses off the King's Road. This particular Saturday midday meeting, ironically known as the 'Early Risers', was the two-hundred-and-twenty-third that Saffron had attended. For Jamie, it was his fourth meeting, and he still needed convincing.

He hadn't seen Saffron for almost three years and she looked sexier than ever. She had grown her hair and wore it in a long, blonde braid. She had shadows under her eyes, but her figure, in the tightest blue jeans and leopard-skin jacket, was incredible. He remembered seeing her last at Gledhow Gardens, but then she had abruptly disappeared from the scene. He wondered what she'd been doing.

Saffron, watching Jamie, knew exactly what he'd been doing. Since returning to London, she had severed all ties with her old life, but she still heard things. When Jamie had dropped into the jeans shop where she had a job, Midnight Cowboy in the Fulham Road, she had avoided him. She had been clean of drugs for more than two years. She had achieved this by steering clear of everyone and everywhere that might put her in the way of temptation: Peregrine, Rupert, Sim, the Common Vole, the flats in Redcliffe Square and Harrington Gardens where gear was always available. She now shared a flat in Beaufort Street with three other ex-junkies, worked at Midnight Cowboy and attended meetings. Although there were times when the thought of never having another drink in her life, let alone a line of coke, made her feel like a shadow of her old self, she tried to live day by day. Now, seeing Jamie, she felt a moment of trepidation.

At the end of the meeting he said, 'Hi, Saffron. Want a drink?'

'Of course I want a drink, but you know I can't. Nor can you.'

'A Coke. Or a coffee,' he said innocently. 'I thought you'd like to hear about Marcus, I saw him at Mary Merrett's wedding.'

They sat outside a coffee bar called Picasso, watching the crowds of Saturday morning shoppers in the King's Road. Jamie described Mary's reception as being 'like a vicar's tea party' and then the arrival of Marcus by helicopter. 'I'm telling you, Saff, it was like the Vietnam War or something, with this dirty great chopper dipping over the garden. He gave her an MG as a wedding present. Charlie was really pissed off. He wants to get married himself now, just to get the car.'

Saffron laughed. She had forgotten how much she liked Jamie, and how easy he was to have around. He had got very thin, and lines were beginning to be etched on his face, and his teeth weren't great. But he was attractive and funny and, more than any of Marcus's other godchildren, could relate to what she'd been through.

'Do you go to a lot of those meetings?' he asked.

'Three or four a week. More when I need to.'

'They must work for you, you look fantastic. I'm not really into them myself.'

'Why go then?'

'Dad and Mum got together and forced me into it, otherwise they were threatening to send me somewhere.'

'Perhaps they should.'

'Not you too! Jesus, I'm sick of being given advice. At Mary's wedding, Stuart Bolton of all people said I should get help. I'm perfectly OK. It's just London that's the problem – there's so much stuff around, it's difficult to stop.'

'Why not get out then?'

'I'd like to. It's just getting it together. I want to go to India. I've heard it's incredible, you can live on five pounds a week out there.' He was going to add something about the price of hash, but decided against. 'We should go together, Saff. Wouldn't that be great? We really ought to do it. For two months or something.'

To Saffron, who hadn't left England for ten years since the holiday in Lyford Cay, the prospect of going to India was thrilling. Ever since she was a child, she'd loved the whole idea of India. She was owed holiday by Midnight Cowboy but had deferred it, not wanting to spend it with Amaryllis and Lorcan at Major Bing's hotel, and having no other plans. To go abroad with Jamie wasn't ideal, but he was a safe escort, she had known him almost all her life – he was her godbrother – and they were both recovering addicts attending the same meetings. In a way, it could be good for both of them.

'I'll have to ask at the shop about time off,' she told him. 'But if you start using, the trip's off.'

On the large, flat sandstone roof of the Hotel Vishnu in Jaipur, Saffron turned the pages of the *Lonely Planet* guidebook and wondered whether they ought to do any of the tourist sights before moving on. They had been in Rajasthan four weeks and, so far, had visited nothing. Her eyes glazed over at the names of temples and palaces. Jamie should be back soon from his shopping trip.

Rock music was blaring from the hotel snack bar. 'I shot the sheriff . . .' Always at the Vishnu it was Eric Clapton or Simon and Garfunkel. Three Dutch travellers were eating omelettes and banana *lassis*, their backpacks piled up around their table. Saffron was drinking a Thumbs Up cola through a straw. She had long ago lost all sense of time passing; they had been staying at the Vishnu for ages, and the days folded into each other. She hoped Jamie wouldn't be too long because she really needed something now.

The sun was directly overhead, which must mean it was already one or two o'clock; the walls and floor of the rooftop shimmered in the fierce light. One of the reasons they never saw anything was because they never got up until midday. They made love when they awoke, and showered in the fetid communal washroom, and then Jamie went out to buy dope. In the afternoon they got stoned. Last night they had sat out on the roof almost until dawn, smoking and hanging out with other Western travellers. Saffron's hands and feet were traced with hennaed patterns, and she wore beads and toe-rings.

Before leaving London, she had not expected to become Jamie's girlfriend, nor to start using drugs again; both just happened. Their induction into India had been so traumatic and haphazard that all her best intentions were abandoned. They had arrived at Delhi airport in the middle of the night, with no hotel booked, and been delivered by a taxi driver through dark streets to a doss house in Old Delhi which probably belonged to his cousin. A very dirty man in a vest with very dirty feet was asleep behind reception. He had led them up a foul-smelling staircase to a room with three iron bedsteads and no bedding and no lock on the door. The walls were streaked with red gashes of betel juice. Desperately retching, rather frightened, and miserable that India had turned out to be so different from her expectations, she felt like going straight home. But her air ticket (and the ticket she had bought for Jamie, for which he was going to pay her back) could not be altered. In the morning, having slept not a wink and bitten by bed bugs, they had ventured outside in search of breakfast. By the time they returned to the hotel, their luggage had been ransacked and half their stuff stolen.

It had taken them four days to get out of Delhi. The complexities of buying bus tickets, and even of finding the bus station, posed immense difficulties for someone as inherently casual as Jamie. Had it not been for Saffron, whose beauty drew crowds of hopeful admirers, they would probably never have left the city at all.

Jaipur and the Hotel Vishnu had come as an oasis. With its large bare bedrooms, Karma Cola culture and Western snack bar, they felt a wave of relief and joy to be there. For two days they wandered the streets of Jaipur, wherever chance took them, buying Rajasthani jewellery and saris. On the second evening, Jamie had produced some dope.

'You're not going to smoke that?' Saffron asked, horrified and simultaneously yearning for a drag herself.

'It's only a joint. A joint doesn't count.'

'It does. You've got to stay clean of everything.'

Jamie shrugged and gave a mischievous smile. 'Not in India. Everyone does it. The bloke I bought this off, he must have been a hundred and he was high as a kite. Go on, Saff, have some.'

She weakened, and the glorious, mellow feeling began to steal over her. It was like being back on the beach in Padstow, when she'd sneak some of Niall's dope and roll joints in the dunes. She had practically grown up with marijuana; Amaryllis used to keep it in the salad box of the fridge. And after all, Saffron reasoned, it was heroin she was meant to be keeping clear of. It was heroin that had sent her to Broadway Lodge, not dope; Jamie was right, a joint hardly counted. Later that same evening, not exactly burning with passion for one another, but strongly attracted by their respective good looks and being together in India and anyway half out of it, Jamie and Saffron made love for the first time, on a Rajasthani bedspread sewn with a pattern of orange and pink lozenges and bright mirrored decals.

For Saffron, soporific with dope, the rooftop of the Vishnu became her world. Gazing out over the parapet, she saw the flat roofs of the pink city, with laundry flapping in the wind and old men dozing on *charpoys* in patches of shade. Occasionally a flock of pigeons would rise up into the air with a great beating of wings. In the distance, she could see the honeycomb façade of the Hawa Mahal – Palace of the Winds – and wondered what it might be. Her excursions were limited to jewellers and boutiques in the vicinity of the hotel, where she invariably picked out the most interesting and pretty pieces on offer. Her one regret was not having more money to buy things, but Jamie had arrived in India practically penniless and she was paying for them both.

She wondered whether she might be in love with him. He had the kind of skin that goes brown quickly, and looked healthier here than he had in London; he had given up shaving and was growing a beard. As a lover, he was exuberant and jokey. Returning to their room from the communal washroom, wrapped only in a sarong, he said, 'Jesus Christ, Saff, there's an ugly-looking Italian bird in there – she must weigh twenty stone. I nearly gave her one, just to help her sleep.' He made Saffron laugh, telling her about his scams at *World's End* and his escapades with women, which he made sound light and joyful. 'Did I ever tell you, Saff, about Whitney? She's so great. Comes from Ghana, I think, or Nigeria. I was staying with her over at her dad's place – some mansion up in Holland Park – when he turns up unexpectedly and he's only the tribal chieftain, you know, and starts chasing me round the house with this dirty great spear. Thought he was going to castrate me.' At night, Saffron and Jamie slept curled round each other on the hard Indian bed, and Saffron, waking first, could feel the beat of his heart against her back and wondered at how untroubled he looked, fast asleep under the bedspread.

Slowly, very slowly, they travelled through Rajasthan, to Pushkar and the *puja* lake, to Ajmer, to Udaipur. They had an idea, never entirely articulated, of reaching Jaiselmer and the Thar desert. Long-distance coaches in India depart early, too early for Jamie and Saffron. Consequently they travelled on local buses that took twice as long, rattling from village to village, Hindi music blaring, regularly breaking down and waiting on roadsides while barefoot welders, sparks flying in the darkness, fixed broken camshafts. Men in orange and yellow turbans loomed over them as Jamie tried to sleep stretched out on the seats; or they stared at Saffron in her beads and toe-rings, blonde hair streaked with henna, and pressed against her whenever the bus lurched to a halt.

They arrived at Udaipur and found a room, the cheapest available, at a guest house called Lalbagh at the north end of Lake Pichola, close to the Jagdish Temple. As soon as they arrived, Jamie set off to the bazaar on a mission, while Saffron sat on the whitewashed roof of the Lalbagh, staring across the lake at the Monsoon Palace on its great spur of rock, and at the two islands, Jagmandir and Jagniwas – the second, she read, now taken over by the Lake Palace Hotel.

Jamie returned, patting his pockets, and said, 'Guess what? They filmed *Octopussy* at the Lake Palace. That was just one of the coolest James Bonds. We have to go and see it.'

Later that evening they walked along the edge of the lake, past the bathing *ghats*, to the jetty where the launch departed for the Lake Palace. Slightly intimidated by the turbaned concierges at the jetty with their swirling Rajput moustaches, Saffron said to Jamie, 'I hope it isn't really expensive to have a drink, I've only got about a hundred rupees.'

'Should be plenty. We just want to see it. Do you remember, in the film, that great bit when all the women storm the parapets, practically naked, with daggers stuffed into their knickers?'

They stepped off the launch and, feeling suddenly grubby, headed for the bar. After the Lalbagh and the Hotel Vishnu, the five-star Lake Palace was almost overwhelming with its white marble floors, arcade of jewellery shops, Moghul fretwork and tinkling fountains. A barman in a red frockcoat handed them a drinks menu.

'Great, *cocktails*!' Jamie said. 'I've been dying for a margarita.'

'Have you seen what they cost?' Saffron said. 'They're two hundred rupees each.'

They ordered Cokes for fifty rupees each, Jamie grumbling at the unfairness of not being able to afford a proper drink. When they asked the waiter for a bowl of nuts and Bombay mix, like they'd seen on the next table, he stared at their hippie clothes and, with obvious reluctance, produced a half-empty bronze dish. They sprawled side by side on a sofa, spinning the drinks out, Saffron's long legs draped across Jamie's knees, and Jamie's arm resting across her shoulder.

In an alcove of the bar, unnoticed by either of them, was a large party of Indian and British businessmen. Waiters were serving them whiskies and Screwdrivers, and trays of *Bhelpuri* and samosas on toothpicks and dishes of hot almonds wrapped in napkins. Marcus Brand was experiencing, at that moment, feelings of intense jealousy and an almost intolerable sexual excitement as he watched Jamie stroke Saffron's hair and her golden-brown legs gently move against Jamie's thigh. She looks filthy, Marcus thought, but my God, she's sexy.

For fifteen minutes he made no effort to greet his god-children but continued charming the representatives of the Eastern Gujarat State Government from whom he had hopes of a $70 million hydroelectric project to dam the Narmada River and submerge twenty tribal villages in the process. His chief negotiator, Dick Mathias, had already been in India for a month, accompanied by three members of the Brand Group treasury department. Tonight Dick was knocking back martinis like he needed them. Two fat and jowly Indian middlemen, retained by Marcus to grease palms without compromising him personally, were lounging on the banquettes, sausaged into tight shiny suits. The representatives of the State looked vaguely furtive and monopolised the snacks.

The waiter brought Jamie and Saffron their bill in a vellum-covered folder, and she said, 'I can't understand this. It's a hundred and ninety rupees. The Cokes were only a hundred. How's this happened?'

Jamie studied the bill. 'State tax, Government tax, Expenditure tax, Service. They've added another ninety.'

'I haven't got that much. Have you got any?'

'Nothing. I spent it, you know what on.'

'Now what do we do?' said Saffron. She looked desperately around the bar.

'I suppose we could swim,' Jamie said. 'Climb out of the cloakroom window, slip into the lake and make for the shore.'

A heavy proprietorial hand settled on Saffron's shoulder. 'Anything I can do to help?' Marcus was towering over them in a light suit and blue and white gingham shirt. He allowed a five-hundred-rupee note to flutter on to the bill. 'I'm delighted to see you both, even though you look like tramps. What the hell's that you've got round your head, Jamie?'

'Er, a bandana, Marcus.'

'You look like one of the more disreputable inmates in a

lunatic asylum. Take it off at once before you come and join us. I'm with some important Indians, not that you'd know to look at them. The cocktails are perfectly safe, they make their own ice.'

Jamie got his margarita. Within minutes he was regaling the fat Indians with tales of his travels while the business-men, horrified by his descriptions of the flea pits he and Saffron had been staying in, muttered plaintive rejoinders: 'Next time you really must put up at one of the Taj hotels, or stay at our place in Delhi.' Marcus, hardly bothering to disguise his interest in Saffron, unsuccessfully urged her to order a Screwdriver instead of fresh orange juice. She was feeling rather thrown by the sudden appearance of her godfather and wishing she didn't look so dishevelled and dirty. Something about their relationship made her want to look her best in front of him; she understood that he expected this of women and, having been raised by Amaryllis to equate the approval of men with personal security, she longed to please him.

She hadn't seen him since the seminal night when he'd smashed down the door at Gledhow Gardens and had her admitted to Broadway Lodge. The drama of the episode, combined with her conviction that Marcus had saved her life, had further boosted his status as hero and man of action. Even though she had committed herself to living as simply as possible, to keep clear of temptation, she instinctively responded to his power. And she was aware, too, from Amaryllis, that Marcus had picked up all her medical bills at rehab, arranging for them to be sent direct to his office. Her feelings about him, at this point in her life, were intensely complex; she felt grateful, and almost hero-worshipped him, but she was also wary. She wished that he, who of all people knew she mustn't touch alcohol, wouldn't keep pressing it on her.

Jamie was on the whisky: crystal tumblers of Johnnie Walker, served on damp linen doilies. He was enjoying himself, this was his best day in India. He hadn't realised how much he had missed drinking spirits. And he was becoming bored with the hassle of the trip, he missed the

King's Road. Recently, even dope had been losing its kick for him; this afternoon, in the bazaar, he had got hold of a small lump of heroin which he looked forward to smoking back at the hotel.

'How is your mother?' Marcus asked Saffron.

'She's fine. Lives in Devon with Victor, and Lorcan who's three now.'

'Your mother was beautiful when she was your age. You look very like her. It's striking, the similarity.'

Saffron was flattered, having always thought herself nowhere near Amaryllis in the looks department. She asked, 'Did you used to be mates with her, when you were young?'

'Everybody knew your mother. She had a lot of admirers,' Marcus replied, slightly put out by the implication that he was past it.

Drinks over, and with no intention of inviting them to stay for dinner, Marcus escorted his godchildren to the landing stage where he tipped the hotel boatman to drop them on the north shore of the lake, near to the Lalbagh.

'Next time I see you,' he said, as they stepped on to the launch, 'I trust you won't be wearing fancy dress.'

'Marcus is great, isn't he?' Jamie said, as they recrossed Lake Pichola. 'That was lucky running into him. I had five drinks.'

'He's always been kind to me. I haven't told anyone this, but he paid for my treatment.'

'He can afford it. He's rolling. Charlie says he's worth fifty million quid. Maybe a hundred.'

Saffron shrugged. Stone cold sober, and conscious that Jamie wasn't, she experienced a momentary feeling of depression at leaving the glamour of the Lake Palace and Marcus for the squalor of the Lalbagh and Jamie.

'You all right, Saff?' Jamie asked, wrapping his arm around her back.

She shook him off. 'I'll be fine in a minute.'

'You will be, I promise, when I show you what I bought this afternoon.'

Afterwards, when she tried to make sense of what

happened, Saffron was never able to explain why, on that night of all nights, she should have broken her heartfelt promise never to touch heroin again; the promise repeatedly and publicly reaffirmed at hundreds of NA meetings. She reckoned her resolve, already fatally undermined by dope, had finally collapsed under the proximity of so many cocktails.

Jamie was warming the second lump of heroin on the piece of tinfoil with his lighter, inhaling the smoke deep into his lungs, when the police burst in; three Indian policemen wielding *lathis*, raiding the hotel bedroom, seizing the incriminating ball of heroin, throwing Jamie to the floor, clutching at Saffron. 'Jesus Christ,' she heard Jamie say, 'we've been busted.' The manager of the Lalbagh hovered in the doorway, assuring the officers he had no idea what had been going on under his roof.

They were taken to a police station in handcuffs and gave a written statement that was later typed, two-fingered, by a policeman in a vest. An officer with a lazy eye kept eyeing Saffron up, staring at her bare legs and midriff. Their passports were confiscated, the heroin sealed in a brown envelope and signed, then countersigned, by everyone in the station. It was after midnight when they were taken to the lock-up – a barred cage – from which a dozen other prisoners stared out at them with mad, malevolent faces (or so they appeared to Saffron), murderers, vagrants with withered arms, all holding on to the bars of the cage, grinning through blackened and broken teeth at the new arrivals. A policeman unlocked the door and steered them inside. Jamie and Saffron hardly dared look at the other prisoners, who stared hungrily at Saffron. The entire floor of the cell slanted in towards a drain in the middle which, judging by the stench, served as a lavatory. The prisoners were huddled under grey blankets, draped across their shoulders. Still partly insulated by the effects of the heroin (though this was beginning to wear off), Jamie and Saffron squatted together on the floor, scared stiff, trying not to catch anyone's eyes. Jamie kept muttering, 'Jesus, this is a mess, a total cock-up. We've got to say we found the smack in the room, Saff, and didn't know what it was. If we both stick to the same story, they can't do a thing.' Saffron wasn't so sure. And she felt that Jamie in a tight corner wasn't going to be completely reliable.

The horror of their predicament was coming home to them. They were in an Indian prison! Arrested for drug offences! What was the penalty for taking heroin in India? Twenty years? Life? Death? A man with a lean, hard, dark face approached them, moving on all fours like a langur monkey. He had a head like a walnut, a little potbelly and a crazy expression. Out of the folds of his dhoti he produced a small knife, a penknife with a rusty blade. Saffron thought: He's going to kill us. She glanced towards the bars; not a policeman in sight. He's going to murder us in this cage and nobody will lift a finger to save us, or even know about it. The man showed the knife to them, running his fat thumb across the blade, gave a high-pitched monkey laugh and bounded off.

'Saffron Weaver?' A guard was calling out her name. 'Please be coming this way.' He unlocked the cage. Saffron wondered what might happen to her, all alone in an Indian jail at night. Why were they separating her from Jamie?

Jamie, who had inhaled more heroin than Saffron, was slumped against the wall of the cell, his head in his knees. She tried to shake him awake, but he was out cold.

She trailed the guard along dark corridors, their walls scarred with betel juice like the hotel on their first night in Delhi. She wished she was wearing something more substantial than her batik sarong and beads: she felt vulnerable. It occurred to her that the officer with the squiffy eye might have asked for her to be brought to him, and the thought made her shiver.

The first person she saw in the office was Dick Mathias. He looked very tall, surrounded by the Indian policemen.

'Good evening again, Saffron. Time to go, I think. The launch is waiting at the ghats.'

She looked round in disbelief. Was she really free to leave?

'What about Jamie?'

'He'll be released in the morning. Marcus says he should spend the night here.' Dick Mathias shook hands with the officers in turn, all of whom looked pleased by whatever arrangement had been struck.

They rode back to the Lake Palace in silence. Saffron knew from past experience Dick never made small talk. At the hotel, he led her along marble corridors and across marble courtyards to a room designated the Maharani Suite.

The suite was immense. Saffron was conscious of a little white swing in the corner, suspended on ropes from a Moghul arch. A canopied bed with a carved bedhead dominated the room. Marcus was working on papers behind a desk.

'I do hope,' he said, 'that my godfatherly duties won't always consist of rescuing you from misadventures with narcotics. It's becoming rather tedious and predictable.'

'I'm so sorry, Marcus.' Saffron began to explain herself, trying to remember the story Jamie had cooked up, her brain fuzzy with exhaustion and fear of the prison and relief at being out of it.

'I think we all know what happened,' Marcus said. He was very stern. His eyes showed not a glimmer of amusement or forgiveness as he rose and walked slowly towards her. 'What you deserve, of course, is a good spanking. I will consider imposing other sanctions as well. If the Police Superintendent hadn't been so co-operative, you would be facing a sentence of between ten and fifteen years.'

'I'm sorry, Marcus. I really am.' Saffron started to cry.

'Don't snivel please, I do hate that. We can discuss all this further in the morning, before your flight back to England. That was part of our agreement with the police. That and a substantial bribe. Tickets are being organised for both of you. Meanwhile,' he said, suddenly solicitous, and drawing her to him, 'it's getting late. Time for bed, Saffron. You're a more grown-up girl than you were in Nassau. If you're grown-up enough to come to India with Jamie, and disport yourself so flagrantly all over the bar of this hotel, then I think you can earn a little redemption from your godfather too, don't you?'

21: January, 1983

Mary didn't believe anyone in the world was so lucky or felt
so happy as she did. Eight months into her married life, she
still woke up each morning thanking God and Crispin for
her good fortune. The better she knew him, the more she
adored her husband. They lived in a pale blue cottage like a
doll's house near Stamford Bridge, in a cul-de-sac named
Billing Road, with two bedrooms and a sitting room with an
Adam-style fireplace. Mary devoted herself to making it
charming and comfortable. The kitchen cupboards were full
of their wedding presents: asparagus steamers, bright orange
Le Creuset casserole dishes, white china ramekins and gravy
boats embossed with a pattern of root vegetables from the
General Trading Company. The sitting room featured
several round tables covered by long cloths, displaying
silver-framed photographs of their wedding and of Crispin
skiing in Val d'Isère. Parked outside the house in a residents'
bay was the green open-topped MG, which had seemed
embarrassing when Marcus gave it to them, being so flashy,
but made them feel glamorous and carefree whenever they
went out in it.

Every evening Mary cooked Crispin a delicious dinner,
having bought the ingredients during her lunch hour. And
every evening he declared, 'Honestly, Mary, I must be the
luckiest man in Fulham. I don't think the other chaps at
work get given dinners like this by their wives.' Mary
thought those other wives must be very selfish, or perhaps
they simply weren't married to men like Crispin.

Sometimes they gave little dinner parties, to show off
their new china. Mary took special pride in these dinners,
wanting everything to be exactly right, rinsing the glasses in
boiling water and polishing them with a glass cloth until
they sparkled. Twice a week she waxed and buffed the
various pieces of good furniture her parents-in-law had

loaned them from Fakenham. Their bedroom curtains, with a pattern of green humming birds, were hand-me-downs from the Gores, altered by Belinda Merrett to fit the smaller London windows. When Mary's ex-flatmates from Nevern Square were among their first dinner party guests, she couldn't help feeling slightly sorry for them, still living in that messy flat, and not realising how wonderful it is to live with someone you really love. If Sarah Whitley (who still worked for Crispin at Savills) detected a slight smugness in the newly married Mary Gore, she was too generous-spirited to mention it.

Their favourite evenings, however, were the ones they spent alone: when Crispin arrived home in the MG from his long day showing country properties, and they sat down together to supper, just the two of them, wonderfully content. 'You're so good at everything,' Crispin would declare as his wife served up salmon-*en-croûte* with new potatoes and sugar-snap peas. 'We must have six children. My grandmother was one of six.'

And Mary would blush sweetly, 'What? *Six?* And where are we going to put them all, I'd like to know?'

'Obviously we won't live in London for ever,' he replied. 'There are plenty of nice old rectories around us in Norfolk.'

At night, and sometimes even in the morning, they made love which cemented the tender and straightforward nature of their marriage. Within six months, they had stopped using contraception, leaving things to nature to decide.

Meanwhile, Mary continued to work at the recruitment agency in New Bond Street, but secretly knowing that it wouldn't be for ever; the focus of her life had already shifted away from her career to Billing Road and Crispin.

On Thursday 27 January, at 4.25 in the afternoon, Mary received a telephone call at the office that changed her life for ever. Sarah was ringing her from Savills. Thinking it was a social call, Mary said, 'Can I ring you back in ten minutes, Sarah? It's rather hectic here just now.' But Sarah said, 'It's Crispin. There's been an accident. I've just been rung by the hospital. They said he's been involved in a car-crash.'

Mary felt her mouth go dry. 'Oh my God, what's happened? Where is he?'

'Some hospital in Reading, I've got the address and everything. They didn't say much, except he's been in a collision. He was driving back from Dorchester. They've taken him to Casualty.'

Mary pictured the little MG with its tin-thin bodywork; it wouldn't give much protection in a crash.

Sarah heard the rising hysteria in her voice. 'Why couldn't he ring me himself? Is he badly hurt?'

'I don't know, Mary. I'm sure he's OK, they're probably just checking him over. But I'll drive you down to the hospital, if you like. I could be outside your office in ten minutes.'

All the way to Reading, Mary had terrible premonitions. She kept asking Sarah, 'What *exactly* did the hospital say?' as though her friend must have more information, and was withholding something.

'He's been involved in a crash, he's in hospital, truly that's all they told me.'

Why did they even have to have an MG? Mary was thinking. Why had Marcus given it to them? Crispin had joked, 'You can open one of these with a can opener.' But he had relished the speed and acceleration. 'I've a lot to get home for these days,' he had told her. 'You, darling.'

'Don't worry, Mary, really don't worry,' Sarah said. 'It'll be fine, I promise. There are loads of crashes every day. They probably won't even keep him in overnight, we'll take him straight home.'

'I love Crispin so much,' Mary said. 'He's my whole life.'

'He adores you too. He talks about you all the time in the office. Mary this and Mary that. It gets quite boring for the rest of us.'

They reached the outskirts of Reading, a city which seemed to consist largely of roundabouts and pedestrian precincts, but the hospital was well signposted. Sarah dropped her at the entrance and went to find a place in the car park. Mary ran through the doors, almost unbearably anguished when she had to queue for information.

'Crispin Gore,' she said. 'Apparently he's in here some-where. We had a phone call.'

Very slowly, the receptionist consulted one list, then another. 'Second floor, Block E. That's Intensive Care. There should be a nurse in the dispensary.'

Mary ran along the half-mile of corridors, following green toytown signs to Casualty and Intensive Care. It must be serious. Please, please, let everything be all right. She was hyperventilating. By the time she found Block E, she was in tears.

A sister was watching out for her. Reception must have rung ahead to alert them.

'I've come to see Crispin Gore. Where is he?'

'And you are?'

'Mary Merrett . . . Mary Gore. I'm his wife.'

The sister looked grave. 'You'd better sit down. Have you got anyone with you?'

'My friend Sarah's just coming. She's parking.'

'Sit down, love, I'll get you a cup of tea.'

Afterwards, Mary could recall the trauma of the succeeding days only in fits and starts; mostly it was obliterated by blank shock. She had no memory of being driven home that evening by her parents to Dorking. The hospital had given her a sedative when she became hysterical. For days, she sobbed and sobbed, or stared numbly into space. When the facts of the accident eventually emerged – Crispin had been driving much too fast, the head-on collision with a lorry on a blind corner – she could scarcely take it in. Derek Merrett identified the body and, as he said to Belinda, was glad Mary hadn't seen Crispin in that condition. The little soft-topped sports car hadn't stood a chance; it had been crushed on impact. Crispin's parents drove over from Norfolk to see her, on a visit that was unbelievably poignant for everyone. Mary, with characteristic selflessness, said that it must all be much worse for the Gores because they had loved Crispin for all his life and she hadn't even known him for one year. In fact it had been eleven months; they had met on 14 February 1982 and he had died on 27 January the following year. Eleven months and thirteen days of unbelievable, undeserved happiness.

Her misery was all-consuming. Only her enormous self-discipline enabled her to crawl out of her childhood bed in the mornings, and go for long walks alone across the dead brown bracken of the South Downs, numb with grief. She could not bear at that time to return to Billing Road, so Sarah and Nipples went over to the house for her, and collected photographs and some of her clothes. She asked Sarah to fetch Crispin's jerseys and these she wore every day – his big baggy jumpers and cardigans – for comfort. She decided too to stick in their wedding pictures which she had never quite got round to doing before. Her mother found it heartbreaking, watching Mary sort them into piles – setting off for the church, the bridesmaids and pages, the reception – and glue them into the beautiful album, a wedding present, covered with marbled Italian paper and embossed with their initials; but Mary found it cathartic, as though bringing some archival order to the wildness of her mourning. She scrutinised every picture of Crispin for some expression, some particular way of standing, that would bring him back to her. Sometimes, staring at the photographs of this handsome red-headed man in his morning coat, she could hardly believe he had ever been her husband and that she was his widow.

So many letters arrived, from her own friends and from Crispin's; letters of condolence from people she had never met, or only at the wedding. Crispin's old housemaster wrote from Radley. The vicar who had married them sent a letter of great wisdom and compassion, not even trying to explain how God in his mercy could ever have allowed such a terrible thing to happen; but none of these well-meaning letters could help her, lost as she was in her grief.

A date was set for the funeral. It was decided this should be held at the Gores' local parish church near Fakenham, where the vicar knew the family well. On the morning of the service, a bleak and bitter Saturday, Mary was driven by her parents from Surrey to Norfolk. She wore an old black coat, a black hat and no make-up. She had lost so much weight that her mother was terribly worried about her; her skin, white as chalk, was stretched taut and almost translucent. Her eyes looked huge, with big dark circles under them.

The church was packed, with a cast that closely repeated that of the wedding eight months before. Everyone looked sombre, many were in tears. As she took her place in the front pew, between her own parents and Crispin's mother, she recognised most of his ushers in the congregation, as well as Crispin's colleagues from Savills and many of the Gores' farm workers. The ushers, last seen in their fancy Favourbrook waistcoats at the wedding, were now in dark suits and dark ties. The coffin was carried into the church by Crispin's two brothers, his father and his best friend from Radley. Seconds before the service was due to begin, Mary saw Marcus arriving in a long black overcoat with beaver lapels. As he made his way down the aisle, several people whispered to each other, 'That's Marcus Brand who gave Crispin the car.'

Crispin's father looked ten years older, his hair turned from grey to white. His wife was hollow-eyed. Several of Crispin's nieces, the same pale-faced little girls who had so recently been their bridesmaids, began howling at the sadness of it all, and had to be taken outside the church. Rupert Gore, his voice faltering, read a poem which began, 'Death is nothing at all, I have only slipped away into the next room,' and then Guy Gore read Rupert Brooke's 'The Soldier': '. . . And laughter, learned of friends, and gentleness, in hearts of peace, under an English heaven.' An old farm worker, who had allowed the ten-year-old Crispin to ride with him on his combine during harvesting, blew his nose noisily into a huge hankie. And when they sang one of the hymns from the wedding, and reached the bit about building Jerusalem in England's green and pleasant land, everyone's voices broke and no one could reach the top notes.

Mary twisted her wedding ring round and round her finger, thinking about when they had chosen it together, and trying not to cry; she knew that, once she started, she'd break down completely. She clenched her engagement ring quite viciously into her palm and stared straight ahead at a stained glass window of spring lambs and primroses. The vicar of St Ethelreda's did his best, inviting the congregation to remember the kind and sincere person Crispin had been, and not to see his life cut short as a waste, but as a wonderful example of a life lived to the full. It was typical of Crispin, he observed, that he should have been racing back to town to have supper with his beloved wife. When he said he was sure that everyone's hearts had gone out to Crispin's widow, Mary, it provoked such a wave of sobbing and tears from every part of the building, and in particular from Mary's old schoolfriends, that he thought it sensible to wind up his homily without further ado. Turning round and seeing so many of her convent friends, Mary thought, Isn't life strange? I was the first in the class to get married, and now I'm the first to be widowed. It will probably be forty years before the next one loses her husband.

Jamie Temple, who arrived after the service had already started and was sitting up in the gallery, was trying not to be noticed by Marcus, whom he hadn't seen since Udaipur. Jamie wasn't ready to face his godfather just yet.

Marcus, meanwhile, having positioned himself prominently in the second row, was making a note on the leather-bound jotter he kept in his inside pocket. It was a note reminding himself to fire the Managing Director of Brand HGV, whose quarterly earnings had fallen for the second successive reporting period. He paid no attention to the funeral service, but found himself paying almost obsessive attention to Mary. He had noticed at her wedding how attractive she was looking these days. It had annoyed him at the time, seeing her commit herself to another man – and such a dull young man too. Marcus had felt piqued that she could prefer any man over himself. He had had it in mind, once the rosy glow of the marriage began to wear off, say in eighteen months to two years' time, to make overtures in that direction. But Mary in her widow's weeds was even more enticing. He could scarcely take his eyes off her. With her white skin and tiny, fragile figure, she looks virginal, he thought, like a Madonna in a painting. With Crispin off the scene, he couldn't see any reason to delay.

Strategies for her pursuit and eventual seduction flowed through his mind. The prospect of taking her to bed excited him considerably, not least because he knew it wouldn't be easy. His goddaughter, he realised, was a prude, the worst kind of parochial English convent girl. And he guessed that her over-developed sense of propriety and decorum would inhibit her from yielding too readily. Most women were only too pleased to become the mistress of the great Marcus Brand. Had Mary been a little French widow, he reflected, her seduction would have been a simple matter. But with Mary, it required guile and careful planning. Already, he had half an idea of how it might be achieved. The prospect of the pursuit – and eventual conquest – made him happy to be her godfather.

22: February, 1983

'Is that Mary Gore? I have Marcus Brand for you.' Barbara Miles had tracked Mary down to Billing Road where she had recently returned after Crispin's funeral.

Marcus came on the line. 'Mary, how's Saturday looking for you? Thought you might enjoy a day's racing at Newmarket.'

She was speechless. 'It so kind of you to think of me, but I'm just not up for anything at the moment. Much too soon.'

'Do you good, a day out in the fresh air with your godfather. We should have some fun. I've got some ponies running.'

'Really, truly, Marcus . . . I couldn't.'

'Nonsense. I'll pick you up at eleven o'clock. Be looking out.'

And so she acquiesced, as it seemed she always must where Marcus was concerned. But she did so reluctantly. It occurred to her, in a rare moment of self-indulgence, that everything bad that had happened in her life was somehow connected with Marcus. It was through Marcus she'd met Charlie. And Marcus had humiliated her father at the office. And it was Marcus who had given them the sports car that had killed Crispin. Whenever he comes anywhere near me, she thought, something awful happens.

The Brand Group had a corporate box overlooking the winning post. Mary, in the same black coat she had worn to Crispin's funeral, was already regretting being there. Not having regained her appetite, she couldn't face the platters of cold roast beef, lobster, cress salad, hard-boiled eggs and gloopy mayonnaise being handed round by pinafored waitresses. Marcus was in overpowering form, clearly irritated by her low spirits. His trainer, Honkie Gilborne, had dropped by for a drink with his glamorous wife Lavinia to discuss the prospects for Marcus's colt, Shanghai Jock, in the 3.30. Dick Mathias was speaking very quietly on the telephone to a business associate in Bermuda. An unwatched television was broadcasting results from another race meeting at Uttoxeter.

Marcus took her with him into the paddock, where they stood in the middle while the runners were led around by the stable hands. Honkie, Marcus and two of the Maktoum brothers discussed the unrealistic level of prize money in English racing, and how it would have to change if the French and Americans were to be kept involved. Then the jockeys entered the paddock, and Marcus introduced Mary to Willie Carson who would be riding Shanghai Jock in the big race. His silks were in the maroon and light blue colours of the Brand Corporation.

'Willie, I'd like you to meet my goddaughter Mary Gore,' Marcus said. 'If she gets any thinner, she'll be in line for your job soon.'

'Hope not, Mr Brand.'

'Better keep on your toes then, hadn't you, Willie? Mrs Gore's prettier than you as well.'

'Right you are, Mr Brand.'

They returned to the box to watch the race from the balcony. For some reason, Mary felt uncomfortable at the attention Marcus was paying her. She was sure he only meant to be kind, but his arm kept moving behind her back and circling her waist, and when he placed his binoculars around her neck, his hands brushed against her breasts.

The horses were lined up in the starting gates, then they were under starter's orders and they were off. Marcus, Honkie, Lavinia and even Dick were cheering next to her on the balcony: 'Come *on*, Shanghai Jock. Come *on*, Shanghai Jock . . .' And when the maroon and light blue colours moved into the lead in the final furlong, and then won by half a length, the whole party was ecstatic.

'This way, Mary,' Marcus said. 'You must collect the cup with me. We'd better give the photographers something attractive to point their cameras at.' Twenty minutes later, she was standing alongside her godfather in the Winner's Enclosure, accepting a giant gold trophy from the wife of the Chairman of the Newcastle and Mutual Assurance Company. Mary hoped it was only the exhilaration of victory that made Marcus kiss her on the lips.

'There's one thing I do need to talk to you about,' he said in the by now deserted box. 'It's to do with your father.'

'Dad's been so brilliant since everything happened. He's such a kind man.'

'We nevertheless have a situation at work that's becoming a problem.' Marcus sounded very serious. 'To be blunt, we don't have a role for him any longer in the organisation. We pretty much arrived at the conclusion three or four years ago. But Derek and I go back a long way and, for your sake as much as anything else, we came up with something else for him. We created a job, if you like, hoping he'd make a go of it. Unfortunately it hasn't worked out. Frankly, he's sitting in an office counting paper clips, not doing himself or anyone else the slightest good. My managers are fed up, and want him out.'

'Marcus, he'd be devastated. Dad's so loyal to the company and to you. I can't bear it. There must be something he can do, isn't there?'

'Believe me, I've looked everywhere, all the divisions. The fact is, nobody will accept him. I suppose I could insist and impose him somewhere, but I can tell you now it won't work, not in the long run.'

'But Dad works so hard. He always has.'

'He turns up at the office in the morning, certainly. I'm sure you know your father well enough to realise he's no brain box. The company's changed, the world's changed. People like Derek have no place in business any longer.'

'But what else can he do? I know he thinks he wouldn't be able to find another job. All he's ever done is work for you.'

'I don't know, Mary. I'd need to think about that. One thing I do know is that we can't fill the organisation with dead wood indefinitely.'

Angry at hearing her father so dismissed, she said, 'If you'd paid him properly in the first place he could afford to retire.'

Marcus glared at her, tilting his head. 'Sure you know

what you're talking about?' he asked, pouring them both a glass of claret.

'What I mean is, Dad's never earned much, compared to other people. You've made millions and millions, but he hasn't made anything.'

'Mary, I wasn't going to tell you this, but now you've provoked me. I appreciate you're still upset about your husband and by what I've just told you, but that's no reason to abuse me, especially when you haven't the slightest idea about it. I've helped your family a lot over the years, a lot. Who do you think paid your school fees at that convent? Derek? He couldn't have afforded it on his salary. And who do you imagine paid for your wedding? You ask your father if you don't believe me. So please don't tell me I haven't done my bit.'

Mary sat for a while in stunned silence. But not for one moment did she disbelieve anything Marcus had told her.

'Forgive me,' she said after a while. 'You have been very generous to us. I shouldn't have said any of that, it was totally wrong. You've been much kinder than you needed to be, much kinder. I see that now.'

Marcus put his hand to her cheek and stroked it. 'Of course you're upset,' he murmured. 'You've had a hideous time. And you're so beautiful. An attractive girl like you shouldn't be all on her own. Everything should be lovely for you.'

He moved his fingers to her mouth and traced the outline of her lips. 'You need somebody to take care of you, someone strong, someone powerful . . .' There was something feline and seductive about him. His face was suddenly very close to hers, she could feel him enveloping her.

'What are you doing, Marcus?' She pushed back her chair and stood up.

'Don't be alarmed, Mary, I think I can help you. You need a protector. Your whole family, your father too.'

Mary stared at him. His steel-blue eyes were locked on to hers. She found him revolting, but also, she hated to admit, handsome and mesmerising.

'I understand your grief,' he went on. His voice was silky

and soft. 'My own wife also died in a car accident. Lucy and I had been married only a short time. She was the most exquisite creature and she meant everything to me. I thought I would never get over her. Maybe I never have got over her.' He took Mary's hand and she found herself unable to push him away.

'I'm sorry,' she said. 'I didn't know. You've never mentioned her before.'

'I've tried to put her behind me, bury myself in my work. If Lucy were still alive, I doubt I would have created the Brand Group, or not on the same scale anyway.' He shrugged, and smiled at her. 'You remind me of her in many ways – your hair and your eyes. She also had those wonderful, candid brown eyes.'

'How did it happen – the accident, I mean?' Mary was anxious to move the conversation away from herself.

'In the worst way, a drunk behind the wheel – my own chauffeur who was driving Lucy. It was late, a farm vehicle came round the corner, the car spun out of control and hit a tree. They died instantly. At the post-mortem, they discovered the chauffeur was several times over the limit. His blood was three parts Scotch.'

'I hate people who drink and drive.'

'You can imagine how I felt. I've always felt partly responsible, though, because Ron Bolton was my chauffeur. If I'd only known he had this problem with booze.'

'Bolton? That's Stuart's surname.'

'Ron was his father. That was another tragedy. Stuart was only a month or six weeks old. It wasn't the child's fault, the whole ghastly mess. I was sorry for him, which is why I took him on as a godson.'

Mary felt a new admiration for Marcus. She didn't think many people would be big enough to adopt a godchild whose parent had killed their own wife. She realised she had underestimated him. And she felt they had a special bond, since both had lost spouses in similar circumstances.

'Incidentally,' he said, 'I'd be grateful if you didn't tell Stuart about his father being inebriated. I don't believe he knows, and it's probably as well if he never does.'

'Of course, Marcus. I won't say a word.'

'I always assumed I'd remarry, but it didn't pan out that way. But I'm fortunate to have godchildren instead who are prepared to put up with me from time to time.'

Then he said, 'On Thursday I want you to come to dinner in London, at my flat.'

'I couldn't possibly . . .'

'Don't refuse, it would be helpful to me to have you there, I'm giving a little party. Fifteen or twenty people, mostly business, I'm afraid. Some Americans, Brazilians. I would like you to be there as my . . . hostess for the evening. You look wonderful, you *are* wonderful, it would be a help to me.' He squeezed her hand.

'Marcus, I'm sorry, but it's out of the question. Crispin only died last month, I couldn't get through a dinner party.'

'Very well,' he said coolly. 'I had hoped that, after dinner, when the others had left, we might have got to know each other better. And decide what to do about your unfortunate father.' He stared at her meaningfully. 'You don't need to decide now. Think about it. Leave a message with Barbara in my office on Monday, yes or no.'

There was no mistaking the implication: the choice, Mary understood, could hardly have been starker. Either she turned up at Marcus's dinner party, and accepted the inevitable consequences, or her father got the chop. Her fury and disgust at his presumption were savage. She couldn't believe he would even make a suggestion like that – to someone whose husband had recently died, to his own goddaughter – it was revolting, contemptible. Of course she had not the slightest intention of accepting. The idea of going to bed with anyone ever again, let alone Marcus, made her flesh crawl. She would never betray Crispin's memory. And she couldn't get over Marcus's cynicism at inviting her to go racing – forcing her to go against her will – with the sole purpose of trying to seduce her.

Her first reaction was to tell her parents everything; not over the telephone, she'd go down the next day for Sunday lunch. Her father would be horrified. When he heard about it, he wouldn't even want to work for a pervert like Marcus. She went to bed that night shaking with anger, and vowing never to see Marcus again.

In the morning, however, she woke up with different worries: how would her father manage without a job? She had no illusions about the father she loved, and realised that Marcus's assessment of Derek's contribution at work was probably accurate. He had never been any good at selling himself; he was neither persuasive nor pushy by nature. When he had attended parents' evenings at the convent, he was always last in line to speak to the teachers; stooping and over-deferential, he hung back, allowing others to edge ahead. And once at a drinks party in Hong Kong, while she was talking to a young man who had no idea who she was, Derek had approached them across the room. 'Don't look round,' she'd been warned, 'the biggest crashing bore is heading this way.' Sacked from the Brand Group, would her poor father ever find anything else?

Collecting her from the station in the Rover, Derek asked with mournful jocularity whether she was feeling slightly better about life, and Mary, anxious not to worry him, assured him that she was. On Monday she'd be restarting work, which would keep her busy and help draw her out of herself.

'Your mother and I are so looking forward to hearing all about your day at Newmarket,' Derek said. 'I was delighted when you said Marcus was taking you.'

Mary didn't reply, but smiled wanly at her father.

'Did you know,' Derek went on, 'that we almost didn't ask him to be your godfather? Got cold feet because he was shooting up through the ranks at work. Exceptional brain, that was obvious even then. Lucky thing we stuck to our guns: marvellous godfather he's been to you, marvellous.'

Belinda was in the kitchen, putting the final touches to lunch. Throughout Mary's life, there had always been a joint of roast beef on the table on Sundays. 'Roast beef with all the trimmings,' Derek invariably proclaimed, rubbing his hands together. 'Go on, breathe deeply, best smell in the world, the roast beef of old England. Nothing to beat it. Some nice roast potatoes and carrots, bit of Yorkshire pud, horse-radish, gravy . . . and you're all set.'

And, before that, the mandatory visit to the sitting room for a glass of pre-lunch sherry. The delicate-stemmed schooners, each one engraved with a picture of a different garden bird, had been a present at the Merretts' own wedding, twenty-seven years earlier, and still brought out every Sunday on the same silver-plated tray. Mary, in her present mood, would have preferred a glassful from one of her own larger but suddenly redundant wedding glasses. A photograph of her and Crispin encircled by bridesmaids and pages was prominently displayed on the piano. Already, she thought, Crispin belongs to another era of my life. I will never, ever forget him, but every year I will remember him a little less clearly.

'So, how are you, Dad?' Mary asked. 'Had a good week?'

'Known better, known worse,' Derek replied in the jaunty tone he always adopted when asked anything about himself. 'Not a bad result down the old sweatshop. I'm working on a few little schemes *entre nous* that might make a difference in the old efficiency stakes. That's the name of the game these days, so they tell me. I'm looking at how some of the admin departments relate to each other, and will shortly be putting pen to paper in the form of a memorandum. Copies all round, right to the very top, not excluding Marcus, though that might raise a few eyebrows in certain quarters.'

Derek had never directly alluded to his diminished status within the Brand empire, though it was understood he no longer ran a part of the shipping division. He referred to his new smaller office, a glass box situated in an annexe of the accounts department. 'The Financial Controller has become a good mate,' he said. 'Never even knew him by sight in my old job. Lovely fellow, we play the odd round of golf together over at Epsom.'

'I'm glad it's going well,' Mary said, realising her father had no inkling of the thread by which his job hung.

'Well, it would go even better if only I had a little more co-operation from the boys in operations. They're giving me a bit of the old run around. I pencil a little meeting into their diaries, weeks in advance, having first checked with their PAs they've nothing on, and then they blow me out at the eleventh hour. Fair dos, say I, nothing's set in stone, we can always reschedule, but it's happening again and again. Sometimes I wonder whether I should tell Marcus, but I don't like to drop anyone in it.'

Belinda said, 'Come on, Derek, don't go on about work. Give poor Mary a top-up, her glass is empty.'

'Right you are, no sooner said. No empty glasses at Fircones, please.'

Circulating with the sherry bottle, he said, 'Speaking of Marcus – the Great White Chief to us humble mortals – we want to hear all about your day at the races, Mary. Didn't he have some big winner yesterday?'

'Yes, in the biggest race. I had to collect the cup with him.'

'Did you indeed?' Derek said, exhilarated by the news. 'If they took a photograph of you and Marcus together, we must get hold of a copy. That would be something: Marcus and Mary with the winner's trophy. If I can lay my hands on an extra print, I'll have one for the office as well.'

During lunch Mary twice had it in mind to unburden herself of Marcus's Faustian pact. Twice she was ready to tell everything. But each time, her father launched into some new rhapsody on the wonders of his boss: how Marcus had dropped everything ('rescheduled the entire European quarterly reviews') to be at Crispin's funeral, and his extraordinary generosity and commitment as a godparent. In the end, she couldn't bring herself to say anything. She left Dorking without breathing a word.

Long before the taxi dropped her at the front entrance, Mary could see the limousines double-parked along St James's Place. Marcus's London flat was in a sixties apartment block opposite the Stafford Hotel, in a discreet cul-de-sac of Queen Anne townhouses and Palladian palazzos, all now corporate headquarters for American and European investment companies. Two security guards in the lobby checked her name on a typed guest list before allowing her to proceed to the bank of elevators.

The door was opened by Bartholomew, the butler who travelled everywhere with Marcus, dressed in a white jacket. 'May I bring you a glass of champagne, Mrs Gore? Mr Brand and his other guests are through in the drawing room.'

'Just something soft, please, Bartholomew. An orange juice would be lovely.'

Her overwhelming impression of the flat was of sleek executive opulence. Had Mary been the sort of person who read international decorating magazines, she would have recognised the distinctive hand of David Hicks in the geometric-patterned carpets, smoked-glass tables, giant obelisks on the mantelpiece and symmetrically hung paintings. Above the sofa was a display of drawings by Chagall, each individually lit with its own bronze picture light. A giant smoked-glass coffee table was arranged with art books and fragments of marble sculpture, Renaissance hands and Hindu *lingams*. One whole wall of the drawing room consisted of a plate-glass window overlooking the treetops of Green Park.

Already there must have been a dozen people in the room, of whom Mary recognised only two, Marcus and Dick Mathias. Marcus, in a black velvet smoking jacket, was locked in conversation with a steel-haired American banker and his dolled-up wife, but he bounded over and steered Mary into the group. 'This is Mrs Gore, my gorgeous goddaughter.' The dolled-up wife, buckling under the weight of her frosted hair, beaded Saint Laurent cocktail frock and door-knocker sapphire earrings, looked Mary up and down, clearly unimpressed. Mary didn't care. Having accepted the invitation under duress, she had intentionally turned up in a shapeless blue shift which she knew didn't suit her, without jewellery and almost without make-up. She couldn't have known that, by dressing as a chaste sixth-former, she would excite Marcus even more.

He threw her a knowing look, to show her he understood exactly what her game was, and said, 'I'm so happy you decided to come tonight. I hoped very much that you would.'

Mary was about to favour him with her frank opinion of blackmailers when he took her arm and led her around the room. 'Some of the people this evening are quite, er, challenging,' he whispered. 'I'm depending on you to leaven all this Eurotrash with your wholesome English loveliness, you wonderful creature.' He introduced her to a Brazilian couple with flashing, egregious smiles and capped teeth, who said they had mining interests outside Sâo Paolo, and to a silent South Korean with whom the Brand Group had a joint venture in an electronics components plant. 'Mr Kim is our partner in North East Asia.'

Marcus had a gift, Mary realised, of making everyone he spoke to feel interesting and indispensable. As he moved around the room, from cluster to cluster, he touched them with the bright beam of his charm. When he cared to, he had the ability to make ignorant men feel clever, dull women amusing, plain women desirable, number-crunchers crea-tive, the ministers of small, poor nations feel like world statesmen. Never before having witnessed Marcus's power to manipulate in a business context, Mary now understood why he was so successful. His energy was dazzling.

They went into dinner in a dining room done up like the inside of a tent, with a canopied ceiling of red-and-white-striped silk. Marcus had placed himself directly opposite her at the centre of the long table. As the lengthy meal progressed, she was aware of his eyes resting on her, appraising her. Unable to eat more than a mouthful, she left her food virtually untouched on her plate. What was she even doing at this ludicrous party? She missed Crispin so much, she wanted to cry.

The Korean seated on her right asked, 'Whad id mean eggshactly "Godfarder"? Mishter Brand is vehry spiridual persun?'

'Absolutely correct, Mr Kim,' Marcus said, leaning across the table. 'A lot of English parents, they know I'm such a fine upstanding fellow, they ask me to stand as godfather to their children, teach them right from wrong. Ideal role model, you see.'

Mr Kim, looking suitably impressed, bowed his head respectfully.

During pudding, Mary became conscious of a socked foot rubbing against her ankle. Glaring at Marcus, she pushed it away; a few seconds later the foot returned, softly massaging her thigh. The minute dinner's over, she thought, I'm out of here.

Bartholomew circulated with a box of cigars and Marcus and the American banker lit up. A waitress brought fresh glasses for champagne. Accidentally catching Marcus's eye, Mary was annoyed to find it twinkling at her. 'Not too bored?' he mouthed. 'They'll be gone soon.'

She never did work out how Marcus achieved the instant evacuation of his flat. No sooner had his guests left the dining room than they were out of the door and into the lift, as though in response to some covert signal, possibly delivered by Bartholomew.

'You do realise I won't go through with this?' Mary said firmly, finding herself suddenly alone with Marcus.

'Darling Mary, please don't come over all moral on me, you're far too pretty. Have a glass of champagne. You haven't drunk anything all evening, I've been watching you. Take it, I insist. I've got some good news.'

'Good news?'

'I may have found something for Derek, up on the seventh

floor with me. Nice big office in corporate, interesting assignment.'

'What is it?'

'"What is it?" she asks, looking at her godfather with rum scepticism as though he's selling her a lemon.' Marcus laughed and put his arm around her shoulders. 'As a matter of fact it's a new position, created specially for him. International Liaison Director. There you go, jolly fine title it is too. What does it involve? Simple. Say I've got some bloody tiresome business people coming in from overseas – Indonesians, Malaysians, whatever – all jolly important to the organisation, expect to be buttered up while they're in town, but not frankly the sort of individuals I can endure sitting through three courses with. Here's the solution: a night on the tiles with our very important International Liaison Director. Drinks, showtime, dinner, talk about Marcus and what a clever chap he is, goodnight. Derek will love it. They can bore each other's pants off and everyone's happy.'

'Please stop mocking my father,' Mary said. But she knew Marcus was right: the job was perfect for him.

'Pays quite well too,' Marcus said airily. 'Remind me, what does Derek make at the moment?'

'I've no idea.'

'Twenty or thereabouts at a guess. This job carries a hundred.'

'A hundred thousand pounds a year?'

'Why not? Two grand a week to have dinner with arseholes. I wouldn't do it for less. How's the champagne?'

'Fine, thank you. No more for me.' Too late: he'd refilled the flute.

'So that's the Derek problem resolved. Now what can I do for his beautiful daughter?'

'I have to go home.'

'I don't think so, Mary. I don't think so at all.' He clasped her around the waist and pulled her very gently towards him, enveloping her in the folds of his smoking jacket. One hand began stroking her hair and caressing her shoulders. 'You're very beautiful, I don't think you realise what an attractive woman you are.'

'You shouldn't say things like that, Marcus, when you don't mean them. I really have got to go home.' She tried to pull away, but he held her close, massaging her shoulders, her back; his hair smelt faintly of some delicious citrus-based eau-de-cologne. It was the first time anyone had touched her like that since Crispin died. His fingers moved so gently to her cheek, stroking her face, stroking the back of her neck, then he was pressing his lips to her forehead, kissing her very softly and tenderly, kissing her hair. This was so wrong, it was all so wrong, but Mary's strength to resist was ebbing away; she was like a tiny meteor drawn into the orbit of some great planet. 'Don't fight it,' Marcus murmured. 'I can make you happy again. Trust me, Mary. I understand how you're feeling, I can heal you if you allow me.' Slowly he moved her face towards his until their lips met. She was surrendering; even as she struggled against him, she felt her powerlessness.

He scooped her up in his arms and carried her to his bedroom, still stroking and caressing her, and lowered her on to a vast bed, its sheets turned down in readiness on both sides. Very slowly and gently, he undressed her, covering her white skin with kisses while he caressed her back. To her complete astonishment, she felt herself becoming aroused.

'Shhh, shhh . . .' Marcus was brushing her breasts with his fingertips, all the time shushing and stroking her like a groom reassuring a frightened foal. The palms of his hands were moving all over her now, stroking her buttocks, her pubic bone. She shuddered when he gently parted her legs with both hands because it felt so good and she was so wet. Waves of guilt coincided with her orgasm; an extraordinary release of emotion washing over her like breakers across a tide barrier.

Marcus, until this point still fully clothed, quickly undressed. For a man approaching fifty, his figure was in perfect shape without an ounce of surplus fat.

'Keep your knees exactly two feet apart,' he told her, 'and now, slowly, slowly, draw them up into your chest.'

'Are you always so bossy?' Mary asked. 'Or is it just with me?'

'Bit of a bad habit, I'm afraid,' he replied, thrusting deeper inside her than she'd ever thought possible. 'Got rather accustomed to telling other people what to do.'

The second time she came she thought it must be over for both of them, but Marcus went on and on until, to her utter amazement and for the only time in her life, she climaxed a third time. With Crispin it had all been over in ten minutes and he'd never kissed her there, but Marcus did and afterwards kept going for forty.

Once finished, he slipped on a silk dressing gown and said, 'That was a lot of fun, Mary. Going home time, I think. Get dressed and I'll have Makepiece bring the car round to the front.'

Peremptorily dismissed, she gathered up her clothes and dressed in the bathroom. Catching sight of herself in the mirror, she hurriedly looked away.

The fact that she'd enjoyed it quite so much, and that this had been evident to Marcus, only increased her feeling of self-disgust.

She woke up feeling sick and shortly afterwards was sick. When she remembered what had happened last night she froze. It was horrifying, shameful. At each new memory she felt worse: Marcus kissing her nipples and touching her between her legs. She was utterly ashamed. She lay in bed, immobile. She blamed herself. Marcus's behaviour was, of course, beyond the pale, but she should have resisted more strenuously. She could have walked out of the flat. But why had she been there at all if she wasn't always intending to go to bed with him? What had she imagined she was doing?

She went downstairs to make coffee. Passing through the drawing room, she felt reproached by the wholesomeness of her wedding photographs. She prayed that Crispin hadn't been looking down at her last night, and that nobody would ever, ever find out. She lay in the bath for over an hour, washing every inch of herself, scrubbing away her self-loathing. Marcus had realised she'd enjoyed it, that was the worst part. It went without saying she would never see him again. If he ever tried to invite her to anything, she'd refuse.

She was a twenty-four-year-old widow; she had no god-daughterly obligation to Marcus. He had extracted a shameful bargain for which he would never be forgiven, and she would have nothing further to do with him.

The doorbell rang and, wrapped in a dressing gown, she went downstairs.

'Who is it?'

'Makepiece, Mrs Gore. Mr Brand's asked me to deliver something to you.'

Reluctantly, she opened the door. Marcus's Bentley was double-parked in Billing Road, and Makepiece was handing her a flat square parcel wrapped in brown paper.

She carried it into the house and unwrapped it. There was a picture inside with a note taped on to the glass: 'Your husband was a lucky fellow. Hope you like this little Corot.' It was a drawing of a ballerina in red chalk.

Feeling horribly insulted, and not wanting anything around to remind her of Marcus, she thrust it against the wall behind the sofa where it was to remain, forgotten, for almost a year.

Mary was still at home that afternoon when the telephone rang. She almost didn't pick it up, afraid it might be Marcus. But it was her mother, sounding upset.

'Darling, I hate to tell you bad news, but I've just had your poor father on the phone from the office. He's been sacked. Those horrible personnel people called him in and said they're making his job redundant.'

Mary's legs began to shake. 'I don't believe this, Mum. Marcus told me . . .' And then she saw it: he had tricked her.

'Your father's trying to speak to Marcus at the moment,' Belinda said, 'but I've warned him it won't do any good. Marcus won't give a damn. He won't lift a finger.'

24: March, 1983

For several weeks Mary had woken up each morning feeling queasy. She attributed this to the natural process of grieving which could plunge her without warning into deep depression. These feelings descended on her anywhere: at the office, on the bus, but usually at Billing Road where she spent her evenings as a virtual recluse. When Sarah and Jo invited her round to Nevern Square, she said she wasn't ready to see anyone. At weekends, she went home to Dorking because she knew it helped her mother to have her around; though he made light of it, Derek was desperately hurt by his ejection from the Brand Group, and showed no sign of finding another job. For her own part, Mary remained so disgusted by Marcus's double duplicity that she couldn't hear his name without shuddering. She considered him wholly evil. The fact that she could never tell anyone what had happened that night only made it worse; and, in some horrible way, even her marriage to Crispin had been contaminated by the episode. Invited to spend a weekend with the Gores in Norfolk, where his parents and brothers had been kindness itself, she'd felt unworthy, knowing she had sullied Crispin's memory with Marcus.

There was a Health Centre in World's End and one morning, feeling exhausted and lethargic, she booked an appointment on her way into work.

The doctor who examined her spent a long time pressing her stomach. 'You couldn't be pregnant, could you?'

'That's impossible.' But she thought: My God, it is, isn't it? She was so thin and run-down that, when she'd skipped her period, she'd thought nothing of it. She couldn't even remember when she'd last had one, it had been so long ago.

'I really do think you might be pregnant, you know,' the doctor said. 'I'd like to send you for a scan.'

She lay beneath the scanner, stomach larded with green gel, praying it wasn't true. And yet, even before the technician told her, she knew that it was.

'It's quite far gone too,' he said. 'I'd say anywhere between four and seven weeks.'

The devastating significance of the timescale was not lost on her: the baby could be either Crispin's or Marcus's.

She felt her legs buckle beneath her as she removed the gel with a paper towel.

'Er, thank you,' she said. 'It's come as a bit of a surprise, but thank you all the same.'

Noticing her wedding ring, and thinking Mary was exactly the sort of woman who'd make a natural mother, he said, 'You'll get used to it. If I were you, Mrs Gore, I'd go straight off and ring your husband. I bet he'll be over the moon when he hears. And many congratulations to you both.'

Part Three

25: December, 1983

From his desk in the dealing room on the third floor of 191 Gresham Street, Charlie could see more than a dozen varieties of pinstripe: there was muted grey chalkstripe with quarter-inch stripes (this was favoured by the partners), gangster black with the full, spivvy one-inch repeat (dealers), broken tramlines like morse code on a light grey twill (research), dark grey cablestripe (senior equity salesmen), grey-black, half-inch, two-vent jobs (Charlie and his mates); there must have been a hundred men in the room, ninety per cent of them pinstriped. The first thing Charlie had done on returning from Hong Kong was to head straight down to Billings & Edmonds and invest in a pair of bog-standard, double-breasted, single pleat, two-vent pinstripe suits. Having secured a job as a junior equity salesman at Cruickshank & Willis, one of the oldest-established blue chip stockbrokers in the City of London, Charlie marked his change of career with the new school uniform.

It had been a wrench leaving Hong Kong but, taking the long view, he knew his career wasn't motoring. If Marcus had been based out there full-time, things might have been different. But the men he had put in to run the Brand Pacific Trading Corporation – bean-counters and bureaucrats, in Charlie's opinion – had failed to promote their owner's godson with the speed he regarded as his due. In particular, the new Scottish Chief Executive, Callum MacKay, who came from Paisley of all places and had previously worked for Shell, had formed an unfavourable opinion of Charlie, considering him lazy and insincere. Nor had it helped when he overheard Charlie describing him as 'a common little man' at the opening of the new Brand hoverport in Causeway Bay. Shortly afterwards, Charlie had been told he was in line for a transfer to the Seoul office – social Siberia – and had promptly quit. To his chagrin, he had copied the archly polite letter of resignation to Marcus in London but had heard not a squeak from his godfather; he had been looking forward to telling him exactly where BPTC was going wrong, and how jumped-up middle-managers like Callum MacKay didn't understand the Chinese mentality.

In other ways, too, he was pleased to be back in London. After such promising beginnings, his social life in Hong Kong had diminished as hostesses, discouraged by his rudeness in neither replying to invitations nor thanking them for them afterwards, dropped him from their lists. He was asked less frequently to swim or play tennis on the Peak. And as it slowly became understood that Charlie wasn't particularly competent in his job, his constant references to 'my godfather Marcus Brand' took on a desperate edge, inviting pity more than admiration.

He bought a flat in Knightsbridge, in Ennismore Mews, using money from a family trust. This trust, which had been frequently alluded to over the years, being part of the estate of Great-aunt Mollie Arbroath, had disappointed Charlie by being smaller than anticipated. But it enabled him to take a lease on a two-bedroomed shoebox in the cobbled mews close to Harrods. He quickly equipped the place with two dozen tumblers from the Reject China Shop and several cumbersome pieces of furniture from Ardnessaig, including a tallboy emblazoned with the Crieff crest, which had to be swung through a window by a crane.

Charlie found his new job congenial and soon discovered he was passably good at it. As a junior equity salesman, he had been given three or four small institutional clients to look after and, at lunchtime, he duly took care of their junior fund managers at various pubs and wine bars within walking distance of Gresham Street. In no time, he became a face at Sweeting's and the City Pipe, with its sawdust floor and champagne bar. His natural confidence and insincerity gave him an edge in talking up stocks, and he had a sharp ear for market-sensitive information. In those pre-insider trading days, Charlie saw it as part of the job to pay attention at drinks parties and weekends away for titbits to push to his clients. When he overheard two City blowhards at the urinal of the Turf Club discussing a possible bid by BTR for Thomas Tilling, he bought a quarter of a million shares on behalf of clients the next morning, ahead of the formal announcement.

He sat at a black-and-white screen with twenty channels showing price changes for the main companies, but never saw research as something to detain him. The research department, which led off the dealing room, was staffed by grey men and grey women, analysts who would never secure a cubicle at the City Pipe. Charlie defined himself as a business getter and people person. Let others deal with the backroom stuff, the sending of confirmatory telexes, the grubbing through annual reports and research documents; Charlie's gift was for sniffing the air, detecting the cooling or quickening of sentiment for a stock which would drive the price. His bonuses, paid quarterly, soon doubled his starter salary. And in time he began to introduce private clients of his own, whom he entertained over long, alcoholic lunches. When Honkie Gilborne, the racing trainer, became a client, having met Charlie at the Cheltenham Gold Cup, Honkie staggered home afterwards from the celebratory piss-up.

Charlie had one great ambition, and this was to secure Marcus as a private client. He had, of course, heard the negative stories about his godfather, and realised he was likely to be bracketed with Robert Maxwell and Jimmy Goldsmith – as a character considered not altogether reliable by the blue-blooded mandarins of Cruickshank & Willis. But he also knew that it would be a considerable feather in his cap if he could bring in the great tycoon, and that whatever reservations they might harbour about Marcus would soon disappear with a few decent-sized orders. Marcus, Charlie knew, was a serious punter, who played the stockmarket as he did everything else, restlessly, recklessly, continually shuffling and cutting his portfolio, acting on tips and wild hunches. And Charlie was astute enough to realise he must seduce his godfather with some mega, unmissable opportunity, something that would really grab his attention.

His chance came six weeks later. It so happened that Charlie was ending the day with a couple of bottles of Becks at the Jamaica Wine House (the 'Jampot'), a popular watering hole off Cornhill with a covered alleyway which linked two open-air courtyards. Charlie had it in mind to prime the pump a bit at the Jampot, then head into town to another pub in Mossop Street called the Admiral Codrington (the 'Cod') where you could rely on finding a few Sloane slappers who might let you throw a leg over in exchange for dinner. He was ordering at the bar when he overheard a piece of news that stopped him in his tracks: the City pirate James Hanson was looking at London Brick as a potential takeover target.

Bright and early the next morning, Charlie dialled Pall Mall and asked for Marcus Brand. The call was intercepted by Barbara Miles.

'Oh, hello, Charlie,' she said brightly. Ever since Nassau, when he had sucked up to her so successfully, Mrs Miles had always had a soft spot for Charlie. 'I'll put you through to Mr Brand. He'll be pleased to hear from you. He was so disappointed when you decided to leave the Brand Group.' Charlie was astonished, but definitely gratified, by this intelligence.

A moment later Marcus came on the line. 'Charlie? What are you ringing me for? Want your old job back?'

He explained he was now selling equities at Cruickshank & Willis, and offered Marcus his tip on London Brick. 'I'd be delighted to place your order, if that would help.'

Marcus sounded thoughtful. 'I'm looking at today's price on the screen,' he said. There was a long pause. 'All right, Charlie, I'll give you a shot. I'll take a million at 192p. Ring me every morning before the market opens and we'll review the situation.'

A million shares: it was a huge position. Charlie was already working out the brokerage and the implication for his own bonus.

'God, thanks, Marcus, thanks a lot. Christ, I'd better get my skates on.'

'Don't let me down,' Marcus said, cutting him off before he could reply.

That week, when the price of London Brick stock shot up

to almost £2.70 on takeover rumours, Charlie made three-quarters of a million pounds for his godfather, and twelve thousand quid for himself.

When the senior partner of the firm personally congratulated him on signing up Marcus Brand, who began to place almost half his orders through Cruickshank & Willis, Charlie knew his career was really taking off. He marked the occasion by ordering a third suit, this time lined in Dracula red silk.

As he told Jamie later that evening over a drink at the Cod, 'Old Wanker Willis came over to my desk, parked his fat bum topside, and asked how I'd pulled in Marcus. I couldn't decide whether to admit he's my godfather. In the end, I decided against, just said I'd cold-called him. Wanker was bloody impressed. Big brownie points all round for yours truly.'

Jamie said, 'If you've made Marcus a million quid, Charlie, you'll be in line for a stonker of a Christmas present this year.'

'I was thinking that. He does rather owe me.'

'Doubt I'll even get a card, after that balls-up in India. Marcus went ballistic. Told me I was a layabout and a menace to women.'

'That is a pretty accurate assessment.'

'No, it isn't,' Jamie replied, grinning. 'I've got a job, decent money, steady women . . . well, fairly steady.'

'What job?'

'If I told you I made two grand last week, what would you say?'

'I'd be amazed. What are you doing?'

'It's a bit of a laugh, actually. Women, er, pay me to sleep with them.'

'You're kidding?'

'No, I've joined an agency. It's based in South Ken, behind the tube station. I have to ring in each morning at eleven o'clock and they give me my list for the day. It's quite classy, seriously, they only cover Chelsea and Kensington. We don't touch south of the river or anything cheesy like that.'

'God, you're depraved,' Charlie said, secretly rather envious. 'It would only happen to you, getting paid to shag frustrated housewives. Aren't they total dogs, most of them?'

'No, they're really nice people. I've visited some lovely houses. Some of those places in the Boltons, it's like being in the country. And these birds are really generous, they give me tips if I do a good job.'

'Christ, Jamie, you are such a jammy bastard!' Then, suddenly serious, he asked, 'But can you always get it up? To order, I mean. What if you're not in the mood?'

Jamie looked surprised. 'Oh, that's not a problem. I mean, my contract says I only have to do it three times a day – professionally, I mean. Obviously I still see my girlfriends.'

'What would Talbot-Jones say, if he got to hear about it?' Charlie was laughing. 'You know, some questionnaire arrived from the careers department at school the other day, asking what everyone's doing eight years on. What'll you put: male escort?'

'Funny you should mention school,' Jamie said. 'Do you remember a boy in our house called Silcox? Used to cox the Eight? Well, I had his mother as a client the other day.'

'Lady Silcox? Her husband's a partner at Cruickshank & Willis.'

'She's a real goer. Tore my back to shreds with her nails. But she's a great tipper.'

Charlie looked astonished. 'Aren't you ever going to settle down, Jamie? You can't spend your whole life screwing around.' And both of them roared at the unintentional pun.

'Actually, I am settled down,' Jamie said coolly. 'I haven't told you before, but I'm married.'

'You're *what*? Who to, for God's sake?'

'Oh, she's called Jurgena. She's from Czechoslovakia.'

'Why haven't I met her?'

'We don't see that much of each other, actually. She's got a boyfriend, they live in Acton.'

'Sorry, Jamie, but I don't get it.'

'It was a passport thing. Jurgena needed a passport and

work-permit and I married her to help her out. At Chelsea Register Office.'

'But – *why*? Why did you agree?'

'Three grand. It's no big deal. You pole up at the registry office, do the business, have a celebratory lunch just in case anyone's suspicious and they're following you, and that's it. Cash only. Not bad going for one morning's work.'

'You're unbelievable.' Charlie stared at his friend in grudging admiration. 'Is there nothing you wouldn't do?'

'How *are* your ravishing sisters?' Jamie asked.

26: December, 1983

Clara Belinda Gore was born three weeks before Christmas at Queen Charlotte's Hospital in Hammersmith, weighing 6lbs 4ozs. As the midwife handed the still blood-spattered baby to the mother for the first time, Mary stared anxiously at her daughter's face, searching for some resemblance to Crispin. She studied the half-closed eyes, the strangely flattened face, the tiny mouth and lips but, to her dreadful disappointment, could see nothing of her husband. Clinging to the back of Clara's tiny, delicate head were several strands of jet-black hair. The determined jaw clamped voraciously around her gingerly inserted nipple also reminded her uncomfortably of Marcus. As Mary suckled her new baby, she felt devastated she hadn't given birth to a sweet-tempered redhead.

She had been exhausted by the delivery, which had lasted almost sixteen hours and been achieved without pain relief. The hospital had offered her an epidural, but she had refused everything, even gas and air. Part of her was afraid that, under the effect of anaesthetic, she might burble her guilty secret about Marcus. And, at some level, she didn't think she deserved any surcease from pain, believing she had betrayed Crispin. She felt that giving birth naturally, and facing up to the pain all on her own, would partly exorcise her guilt.

Having no previous means of comparison, Mary was not at first disquietened by the succession of doctors, paediatricians and specialists who came to examine Clara in the first few hours. They checked her reflexes, measured her limbs and shone torches into her eyes. Eventually a senior paediatrician sat down by her bedside and said, 'Mrs Gore, your daughter is beautiful, but I must tell you that there may be a problem. We have reason to fear that she may have Down's Syndrome.'

Mary, who had heard of the condition but been considered too young for amniocentesis, was immediately anxious. 'What is that exactly? Is she deformed?'

'It does mean she may not be one hundred per cent co-ordinated. It's a chromosomal abnormality that occurs once in approximately nine hundred births. We'll need to do many more tests before we can tell how serious it is. I don't want you to worry too much at this stage, but I did need to inform you that we have these concerns. Many Down's babies lead nearly normal lives, and they are usually extremely affectionate children. It's just that they need a lot of special love and care.'

A nurse brought Clara back to Mary for further feeding, and this time she saw that the folds of skin around her slightly slanted eyes were different from those of normal babies. The paediatrician pointed out how Clara had a single deep crease across the middle of the palm of her tiny hand, which was often an indication of Down's Syndrome, and how her tongue was slightly enlarged to the shape of her mouth, which might lead to speech difficulties later on. Mary felt an incredible wave of relief because she realised the lack of resemblance to Crispin could simply be the result of Down's Syndrome. At that moment, her heart filled with compassion for this tiny, damaged baby girl, and Mary vowed that, whoever the father was, it didn't matter and she didn't care, she would always adore her and protect her.

She telephoned her parents, and then the Gores, to tell them the news, and soon her bedside was filled with flowers which arrived, it seemed, simultaneously from everyone she'd ever met. An arrangement of pink carnations and white chrysanthemums came from the girls in the office, and a white hydrangea from Sarah and Jo along with a tiny knitted bobble-hat, and then a lovely bunch of pale pink and white roses from her parents-in-law. A hugely expensive arrangement of Casablanca lilies, roses and stephanotis was sent by Marcus from Moyses Stevens. Mary hadn't told him about the birth, and wondered how he'd found out.

Derek and Belinda drove up from Fircones with a large rabbit with a pink ribbon around its neck and a bottle of champagne 'to wet the baby's head'. Then Belinda asked, 'Have you any ideas yet about names for her?' and when Mary replied, 'I want to call her Clara Belinda,' tears poured down her mother's cheeks, and she said, 'We were talking about this in the car, darling. If you don't think you can manage her – Clara – on your own, I suppose we could take her on ourselves and look after her for you.'

'That's so kind,' Mary said, 'but I want to look after her myself. I'll manage.'

'Well, the offer stands,' Derek said. 'You're very young. It'll be quite a tie for you, having a, er, mongol round your neck, day in day out, all on your own.' Then he said, 'That's a magnificent bouquet from Marcus. I don't suppose he knows that your baby isn't quite . . . ?' He tapered off unhappily.

Mary remained in hospital for a further two weeks, more for Clara's sake than her own. During those early days she learned a great deal about Down's Syndrome, and how Clara might be expected to develop over the years ahead; how she would probably have some level of mental retardation, but how this wouldn't necessarily be serious, she would learn to walk, talk and play exactly like other children, only somewhat later than her peers. Clara would go to school, make friends, probably find a job when she grew up, and would live to the age of forty-five or fifty. Some women with Down's Syndrome eventually got married and even had children, Mary learned, though, there was a fifty per cent chance of a Down's mother giving birth to a Down's child. The only difference between a Down's child and a normal one was the exhaustive level of supervision and care which Down's Syndrome necessitated. Until she was at least sixteen, Clara could never be left alone in a room, even for an instant, and certainly never in a kitchen or a bathroom where accidents were most likely to occur.

Every afternoon the Merretts visited their daughter and grand-daughter in hospital, bringing fruit and baby clothes that Belinda had knitted herself, sugar-pink booties with white ribbons. Derek, who at first felt uncomfortable around an imperfect child, learned not to call her a 'mongol' and even steeled himself to pick her up from her metal cot and joggle her about. The first time he did this he said, 'Good heavens, Mary, she looks Chinese this close up, with these slitty eyes. Her father's not a Chinaman, is he?' When Mary burst into tears, and Belinda glared at him, Derek adopted an incredulous what-have-I-done-wrong-now? expression, genuinely not getting it.

Mary spent hours scrutinising her adored daughter, looking for facial or physical characteristics that could have come only from Crispin. As the days passed, she became depressed, failing to detect a single familiar gesture or expression. In fact, the more she looked at Clara's flat face, the more sure she was that Clara's father was Marcus. It was a ghastly realisation, and she vowed never to tell anyone, particularly not Marcus himself. Nor would she ever tell Clara. She could grow up believing she was the daughter of an honourable estate agent, not the reptilian tycoon.

Twice the Gores drove up from Norfolk to visit their fifth grandchild, and both of Crispin's brothers came too, filling the hospital room with their noisy, tweedy bonhomie. Crispin's brother Guy brought his four whey-faced daughters, and they gazed in wonder at the sleeping Clara in her cot, asking, 'Were we that small when we were babies? She isn't even as big as a puppy.'

Mary found her parents-in-law's visits uncomfortable, convinced as she was that Clara wasn't their granddaughter at all. She felt unworthy of their easy sympathy and kindness. When Davina Gore said, 'I hope you'll bring Clara down to stay with us when the weather gets warmer. We'd love to have you, and you can have a bit of a rest,' Mary wished she hadn't asked. And when her father-in-law took the opportunity of his wife leaving the room – in what was manifestly a pre-planned manoeuvre – to mention that he intended setting up a monthly allowance for Clara, Mary felt penitent and panic-stricken, not wanting to be the fraudulent recipient of her in-laws' benevolence.

Although Mary was, by nature, soft and yielding, and wanted above anything to please, there was also a stubborn side to her character and once she had made up her mind about something, particularly on a question of right and wrong, she was almost impossible to shift. Her determination not to depend on the Gores increased every day. Hers was a devastating dilemma as she realised that, with her parents-in-law's help, Clara's life would be far easier and happier, and that, moreover, she risked cutting her daughter off from a family of exceptional warmth. Nor did she want to offend Robin and Davina Gore, who were being so practical about Clara's future. When she was older, how Clara would love playing in the huge barns and walled gardens at Fakenham, and swimming in her grandparents' pool! And yet Mary knew she could never accept their money. Every time she saw her mother-in-law, her guilty conscience chafed her like a hair shirt. How could she allow the Gores to support a child who might well have no possible connection to them? The fact that Mary couldn't share her doubts with anyone made her suffering even worse.

A letter arrived from the Gores' family solicitor in Kings Lynn informing her that, under the provisions of her deceased husband's will, the freehold on the house in Billing Road had passed to her, as well as eleven thousand pounds lodged in a deposit account. The same letter formalised Robin Gore's suggestion of a monthly allowance which would be reviewed upwards when Clara started school. That same morning, without giving herself a chance to reconsider, Mary replied to the solicitor, thanking him for the news about Billing Road, but politely declining the monthly allowance. 'Please say that I am truly grateful for their kind and generous offer,' she wrote, 'but I have decided to support Clara on my own.'

As news of Clara's Down's Syndrome spread among her group, Mary received more letters than she did visitors. All but her closest friends were embarrassed about seeing her, being uncertain how deformed Clara actually was, and how they would react to her weird looks and over-large tongue. One of the very first letters came from Stuart Bolton, who had heard the news from Abigail Schwartzman. Mary found Stuart's letter kinder and far more eloquent than she would have expected. He said he was returning to England in a few weeks' time, and hoped he could come and visit her and Clara then. Sarah Whitley also behaved like a star, coming round to the hospital most evenings with little presents for Clara – a gingham dress or a ragbook – and magazines for Mary. Once, flicking through a copy of *Harpers & Queen*, she came across a photo of Charlie Crieff dancing at the Caledonian Ball at the Grosvenor House Hotel. He looked rather stout and bloated, she thought, reeling with Zara Fane.

Mary spent her days reading up on Down's Syndrome. To her surprise, she learned that it had only been identified a hundred years earlier, by an English doctor named John Langdon Down. Throughout the twentieth century, medical advances had enabled researchers to investigate the disease's characteristics, and in 1959 a French physician, Jerome Lejeune, diagnosed it as a chromosomal anomaly. Instead of the usual forty-six chromosomes present in each cell, Lejeune observed forty-seven in Down's Syndrome patients. The syndrome was usually caused by an error in cell division called non-disjunction, and all people with Down's have an extra, critical portion of the number twenty-one chromosome present in some, or all, of their cells. Eighty per cent of children born with Down's Syndrome are born to women under thirty-five years of age. Her own twenty-fifth birthday, Mary realised with a start, was looming; more had happened in her life in the last eighteen months than in all the rest put together.

One afternoon, the telephone rang and it was Abigail, calling from Hershel Gluckstein's gallery in New York.

'Mary? I heard the news and had to call you. This is *so exciting*.'

'Yes, she's beautiful,' Mary replied, cradling Clara in her arms. 'I'm besotted with her. But how did you hear?'

'From Marcus. He's been over in the city. He was so happy for you. He was telling everybody he's a grand-godfather.'

Mary tensed. 'I can't believe Marcus was too bothered.'

'Oh, but he was. He's so proud of you. He talked about

you all the time. Mary, I'm sorry, I haven't even said anything about your husband. That was so terrible, I couldn't believe it when Marcus told me. We've lost touch. But you're so lucky to have a daughter. I wish I had a daughter.'

Mary laughed. Abigail sounded so sincere on the phone, and it was kind of her to bother to ring. They hadn't even clapped eyes on each other for five years.

'Has Marcus been to visit Clara yet?' Abigail asked.

'No.' Mary didn't elaborate, but if their godfather did ring up, she'd tell him he wasn't welcome.

'He's in Nassau now, but I bet the first thing he does when he gets back is give you a call. I can't give away the secret, but he's bought you a wonderful baby gift.'

'There's something you should know, Abigail. I haven't spoken to Marcus for months and I don't expect to speak to him ever again. I don't want to go into it, but Marcus isn't someone I really expect to be part of my future plans.'

'It's OK, Mary.' Abigail rushed on, 'I have the same problem. I just wait and wait for him to call. But, Mary, when you do next see Marcus, put in a good word for me, won't you? Tell him to take me out for a drink one evening. You're so lucky having a baby. He'll definitely come and see you. He could walk in any day. You're so lucky, Mary, you're so lucky! He'll definitely come and see you.' Abigail was so wrapped up in her own obsession she could not begin to guess the feeling of dreadful misery that was enveloping Mary. Marcus was like an indelible black stain on her memories of Crispin – and she hated him.

27: January, 1984

Saffron was painting a picture of the Matterhorn. Two mornings a week were art therapy at Chesa Glüna, when patients were supplied with big sheets of cartridge paper, poster paints and crayons. Saffron had never seen the Matterhorn and, the way things were going, probably never would. She felt she might spend the rest of her life at Chesa Glüna.

Her fellow patients – *inmates* – came from everywhere and were all ages. There were French heroin addicts, a Peruvian cokehead who was only fifteen (his parents were diplomats in Geneva), rich Belgian anorexics, African mental patients, old guys in wheelchairs with late-age depression. The only thing they had in common was that someone, somewhere, had exiled them to the Swiss clinic and agreed to underwrite the substantial medical bills.

Saffron had been admitted to Chesa Glüna not once, but twice. On her return from India, twelve months earlier, Marcus had insisted she go straight back into treatment. He had rung Amaryllis, informed her that Saffron was a serious heroin addict and insisted steps be taken. Only by pulling strings, he explained, had he kept her out of an Indian jail. He had located Chesa Glüna in a suburb of Basle, somehow secured a place (the clinic was full) and volunteered to pick up her bills. Within three days of returning home, she was admitted.

From the first, Saffron bitterly resented her incarceration. She considered herself much less ill than the other patients, many of whom were genuine schizoids, shuffling about in pyjamas and varying states of undress. A former nineteenth-century lunatic asylum with high walls and tiny louvred windows, Chesa Glüna was a cross between a prison and a spa. The patients were kept heavily sedated; twice a day they were issued with little yellow tabs of largactil or valium to keep them docile and compliant. Saffron felt keenly the injustice that Jamie had got off scot-free and was racketing around London while she, who had tried so hard to stay clean, and so nearly succeeded, should be sent away.

Her love affair with him hadn't survived Udaipur. Without anything ever being said, it was understood that the episode of the Indian jail had drawn to an abrupt close a relationship already practically played out. Afterwards (and this was actually a characteristic of all Saffron's love affairs) she hardly spared a thought for her time with Jamie; it was consigned to a remote quarter of her memory in which experience was stored but seldom revisited. The journey through India, so lightly undertaken, evaporated like breath on the surface of a mirror.

Her feelings about Marcus were more complex, but these too she chose not to confront. Even as a child she had developed an ability to blank everything disquieting from her mind. The ever-present fear of homelessness, and the realisation that their survival as a family depended entirely on Amaryllis's success rate in picking up and retaining sugar daddies, had made Saffron stoical about the inevitability and unreliability of men. Even while she was with Jamie, she understood that if you lean on a reed, it bends. Since they were travelling together, and he seemed so positive that they had to get it on, she couldn't really be bothered to object; but the affair had hardly touched her. The instant Marcus appeared at the Lake Palace, Jamie had faded from view; her attention immediately sharpened and focused on her god-father. In Marcus lay the quintessence of everything she had been brought up to admire: hunter and provider, power-house and protector, philanderer (of course), prince among men. She noticed the way other people automatically deferred to him, even when they had no need to, being neither in his employ nor in any way beholden to him. And she instinctively recognised the effect she herself had on Marcus. She had always understood, from the age of twelve or thirteen, that she was prettier than anyone else, and that men quickly fell in love – in lust – with her. She had known this for so long that it was a natural condition of life. Even in

Nassau she had realised without really thinking about it that all three boys were falling for her. And, had it not been for Marcus's intervention, she would have gone along with any one of them, had they pressed the point. But when her godfather had steered her indoors, on the night of the beach barbecue, she had respected his *droit de seigneur*.

In India he had arrived, as he had earlier arrived in Gledhow Gardens, as both saviour and judge, rescuing her from the worst consequences of her own folly, and so increasing her feeling of obligation to him. That night, after her release from prison, when she had been delivered by Dick Mathias to his suite, Marcus had received her with a strictness and, afterwards, passion that had both bewildered and oddly aroused her. He had ordered her to bend over the end of his bed and punished her lingeringly with a leather-soled slipper; then he had made love to her with a tenderness and energy that made Jamie's efforts seem half-hearted.

On her first admission to Chesa Glüna, Saffron had railed against Marcus. He had betrayed her: he had promised she was forgiven, but had banished her to Switzerland. Unable to interpret his motives, she wondered whether she had disappointed him in bed, or whether he simply intended to keep her apart from Jamie. And, if so, was this for her own good – because Jamie was a bad influence – or out of jealousy? For two months she was diagnosed as clinically depressed. Dispirited, lonely and, she felt, abandoned by her family, she plodded listlessly around the clinic, or lay in bed, seeing no reason to get up.

Eventually, however, she began to recover. Unlike Broadway Lodge, with its structured recovery programme of groups and affirmations, Chesa Glüna's regime was based on medication (in increasing or decreasing quantities depending on progress) and occupational therapy. Art therapy alternated with cooking therapy – she learned to bake cakes. In the evenings, she played Ludo and Snakes and Ladders with the children of millionaire German industrialists and Kuwaiti sheikhs. At night, the doors of their bedrooms were locked from the outside. During this period, she reflected on people and events which she imagined had left her life for ever. She thought about Amaryllis's lovers, about Trev and Bongo and Barney the kineseologist, and Niall and Major Bing, and her own father in Ireland who had abandoned her. And she thought about Charlie Crieff, and Stuart Bolton who had rushed to her rescue at that posh dance of Marcus's, when Charlie had come on to her so roughly. She was grateful to Stuart for that, and thought about thanking him some day. She even considered writing him a note, but never got it together.

She knew she was making progress when other patients began to fall in love with her; a Belgian student named Thierry asked her to marry him and come and live with his parents in Liège. And then a young Swiss doctor, who ran the dispensary, promised to leave his wife for her, and surreptitiously prescribed Mandrax to help her sleep. By the end of her fourth month at Chesa Glüna, Saffron felt interested enough in her own future to start wearing make-up again and carefully launder her clothes. And finally, having passed a range of psychological and psychometric tests, she was deemed sufficiently recovered to be discharged.

She returned to England to discover that her mother had off-loaded Major Bing and drifted back to London. She and Lorcan were now living with a reflexologist named Paul in a basement flat in Queens Gate Gardens. Amaryllis, while genuinely pleased to see Saffron looking so much better, made it clear there was no room for her at the flat. It was a hard enough job keeping five-year-old Lorcan absolutely quiet in his bedroom while Paul's treatments were in progress next door. His sideline as a healer required total silence, and he became violent if disturbed.

Finding that her old job at Midnight Cowboy had been swept away by the mid-eighties jeans recession, Saffron landed a job in a shoe boutique, Sole of Discretion, in South Molton Street and, shortly afterwards, moved into a flat with one of the other salesgirls, Francine. The routines of regular work and ordinary life at first made her supremely happy. She resumed her attendance at NA, transferring her allegiance from the Chelsea meetings where she might run into Jamie, to more anonymous groups near the flat in Camden Town. On Sunday afternoons, she got into the habit of collecting Lorcan from Queens Gate Gardens and taking him for a walk in Hyde Park, enabling Amaryllis and Paul to enjoy a couple of hours of sexual healing together in bed.

It was during one of these Sunday afternoon walks, while Lorcan was playing on the grass behind the Serpentine, that Saffron ran into Peregrine. It was the first time she had seen him for more than four years.

'Hey, Saff. Christ, sunshine, whatever happened to you? You disappeared.'

She thought how little changed he was; even his jacket was the same.

'I've been . . . cleaning up. You know I'm clean now.'

He looked at her, one eyebrow raised. 'This your kid?'

'My mother's. My half-brother, I guess you could say. Lorcan, come and say hello to my friend Perry.'

'Hi, Lorcan. You like ice cream? I'll bet you do too. Come on, I'll buy you a cornet.'

Somehow or other, they ended up back at Gledhow Gardens. It was like a homecoming. Rupert was in rehab now, Perry said, but Sim was still there, sitting on the old sofa, smoking Iranian brown.

One puff was all it took to decimate her good intentions.

'Promise us that crazy godfather of yours won't show up here again,' Perry said, on Saffron's third or fourth visit to Gledhow Gardens. 'He's a fucking lunatic, seriously. He threatened to kill me.'

'Marcus? I haven't seen him for months. He doesn't even know I'm in London.'

After the second overdose, when Francine felt compelled to ring Amaryllis, who told Marcus, it was decided Saffron should return to Chesa Glüna but this time for longer.

'If it takes a year – five years – we have to try everything, otherwise she'll be dead by Christmas,' Marcus said. 'I've told them to send all bills directly to me.'

28: February, 1984

Stuart had arrived fifty minutes early for the interview – much too early to make himself known at reception. Having located Brand House, Marcus's corporate headquarters in a Pall Mall townhouse opposite the Royal Automobile Club, he resolved to walk several times around the block before his twelve o'clock appointment. London seemed conspicuously depressed and rundown after America; the buildings shabby and low-slung, many of the shopfronts shuttered and To Let boards everywhere. Stuart held the opinion that the British recession was largely self-induced, the inevitable consequence of years of inept management by a clapped-out, class-bound Establishment. Turning into St James's in the direction of Piccadilly, he shook his head at the smug-faced gentlemen's clubs that lined the street, with their pillared porticoes and rows of sash windows. It was incredible such places still existed. And his lips curled at the Regency shopfronts of the wine merchants – *merchants*! – and bespoke cobblers – *cobblers*! – their bow-windows displaying trilby hats, shoe lasts, badger-hair shaving brushes, snuff boxes and wooden cases of port. Who bought this stuff? What were they thinking of, if they thought at all? Couldn't they see it was all totally, laughably, irrelevant?

Wheeling up Duke Street, he passed art galleries selling old cracked paintings of haywains and sea battles, each uglier than the one before. A greengrocer described itself as a purveyor – *purveyor*! – of fine foods and spirits. There were shirt shops selling hideously garish striped shirts that could have appealed only to Charlie Crieff and his ilk. Arriving at the entrance to an auction house in King Street, he wandered inside and, hurrying past intimidatingly smart girls behind the front desk, climbed a flight of stairs to a gallery where an auction was in progress. He stood at the back and watched a plum-voiced auctioneer sell an enor-

310

mous painting of highland cattle for £960. The catalogue entry gave as the provenance: The Property of Lord Crieff of Ardnessaig.

Marcus's telephone call had caught Stuart unawares. He had returned to England from America a couple of days earlier and was visiting his mother in Smethwick. He had no idea how Marcus had even known that his course at Stanford was over.

'You may have all sorts of jobs fixed up already,' his godfather had said, 'but before you commit to anything, come and talk to me first.'

A board in the lobby of Brand House listed the names of over eighty companies in the Brand Group. There were divisions and subsidiaries he had never heard of before: Brand Air Freight, Brand Car Parks, Brand Natural Resources and Mineral Extraction. Stuart read them while he waited . . . and waited. At half-past twelve he checked with the receptionist that Mr Brand's office realised he was still there. 'I'll let them know,' she said, 'but there are several other gentlemen waiting ahead of you.'

At ten past two he was called up to the seventh floor. The lift doors opened into a spacious reception area. Six secretaries – mostly stunners, Stuart noticed – were stationed behind modular desks, murmuring softly into telephones. He hovered for a moment by the lift doors, uncertain where to go. Then Barbara Miles appeared, bearing down on him out of nowhere, apologising for the delay ('It's been quite a day, I'm afraid') and saying she'd take him directly into Marcus. 'He's awfully proud of you, you know,' she said. 'You did very well in your final grades.' Not for the first time, Stuart wondered how he could possibly have known.

Marcus was finishing a call, but beckoned him into the office, pointing at a chrome and leather swivel-chair. He was speaking emphatically in some Hispanic language, Spanish or Portuguese. He made a face at Stuart, indicating the conversation was tedious and that the person on the other end was banging on a bit. Occasionally he made notes on a leather-trimmed jotter.

The call ended and Marcus said, 'Brazilians! That was my old pal the Minister for Greased Palms and Backhanders in São Paolo, asking for his consideration to be paid in Zurich in Swiss francs. Says the peso's about to be devalued, can't accept payment in local currency this time.'

Uncertain how to respond, Stuart said, 'I didn't realise you did business in South America.'

'Forestry. We have the contract to clear an area of rain forest approximately the size of France. Big idea is to find copper at the same time, extract that too providing it's in economic quantities.'

Stuart stared at the godfather he hadn't seen since Mary Merrett's wedding two years earlier. As usual, he was struck by Marcus's restless energy and staccato manner of speaking, as though he were in a permanent fever of impatience to plunge ahead. Physically, he had scarcely altered since Lyford Cay; if anything, he looked fitter, browner, richer. Stuart wondered to what extent he was aware of Abigail's massive crush on him. Lately, Stuart had started screening many of Abigail's calls, particularly the late-night ones, when her fixation about Marcus could spiral into hysteria.

'My congratulations, incidentally, on your marks at Stanford. Straight As in every subject. Kudos.' Marcus stared at him over his spectacles. 'How do you feel about working for me? Need some clever chaps with business school disciplines, frankly, keep everyone on their toes. Plenty of experienced managers in the company already, loyal as they come – my God, are they loyal, worship at the shrine. But we need fresh blood and real balls.'

'What would the job consist of?' Stuart asked.

Marcus shrugged. 'Take your pick. Enough things going on, heaven knows. Find something that interests you, go in there as Business Strategy Development Officer or some such, ferret about a bit, tell me where the problems are, *who* they are, sort them out.'

Stuart looked doubtful. 'I'm not sure I've got the experience for that yet, Marcus. At Stanford, it was mostly theoretical.'

'Whole point,' Marcus replied. 'Test some of it out while

it's fresh in your mind. God-given opportunity. Go anywhere you like – Indonesia, Mexico, not bothered which – see if it works in practice. We have mines in Angola where productivity's so low they must be digging with their fingernails. More likely sitting on their big black backsides. Sort it out for me. Kick some ass. Tell them I sent you, so they'll sit up and take notice.'

Stuart winced at this casual racism and, picking up on it, Marcus said, '*Mea culpa*, I was forgetting you're my socialist godson. Didn't mean to disparage the Kaffirs, nothing personal. In fact, I've got a lot of respect for the coloured workforce – some of them work a damn' sight harder than the brothers do in this country.'

'I thought you'd derecognised all your unions, Marcus.'

'Have. Rather miss them too, in some respects. Used to look forward to my monthly stand-offs with Red Robbo and the rest of them. Least they knew what they wanted and stood up for themselves. I respect that. Nothing worse than a man who doesn't know what he wants.' Then he said, 'Come on, Stuart. Stop messing about, tell me you're joining. It'll be good having another Bolton in the company. Your father was here at the beginning, one of the first. Now, God knows, there are something like thirteen, fourteen thousand people in the organisation. Wouldn't recognise most of them if I passed them in the street. Nice to have a bit of continuity: father and son, second generation coming through.'

At the mention of his father, Stuart reddened. It was an area he found desperately uncomfortable.

'Think about it,' Marcus said, pushing back his chair and standing up. 'Let me know your decision, and I'll get our Human Resources people on to the paperwork. We didn't talk money, did we? Entry level graduates normally come in at around £25,000. Shall we say £60,000?'

Ringing the following morning to punt him a serious position in British Land, Charlie was disconcerted when Marcus said, 'Tell you who I saw yesterday, Charlie, your fellow godchild Stuart.'

'Stuart Bolton? I thought he was abroad, skiving at some foreign university.'

'He's back, with a brilliant degree too. Came to see me and I've offered him a job. He'll go places that boy – he's an impressive individual.'

Charlie stiffened. Instinctively competitive, it annoyed him to hear Marcus praising Stuart. Although Stuart couldn't possibly be thought of as similar calibre to himself, Charlie nevertheless valued his special access to Marcus and wanted to see off the prodigal godson.

'Has he accepted this job?'

'He's thinking about it.'

Charlie found this surprising, even impertinent. A grockle like Stuart should be grateful to be offered a job at all. He assumed it was a position in the post room or transport.

'I've proposed a management assignment in the Far East or South America, reporting directly to me,' Marcus went on.

Charlie endeavoured to stay cool. At moments of tension, he drawled, as a technique for sounding unconcerned. 'That's incredibly generous of you, Marcus. I doubt many people in your position would do that for their godchildren. You're sure he's reliable though?'

'Reliable?'

'Look, it's not my place to say this, and do for God's sake disregard it if you want to, but Stuart is a communist, isn't he? He certainly was last time I heard. And a union activist.'

'Really? I never knew that.' Marcus, being several times cleverer and more wily than Charlie, was enjoying playing him along.

'Don't you remember in Nassau he was always whingeing on about the workers? And at that amazing dance you gave for us, he actually slugged another guest, just because they were slightly better class than he is.'

'Good heavens. Who was the unfortunate fellow he punched?'

'Oh, just some . . . friend of Jamie's. He was very decent about it, didn't press charges. But, seriously, you want to watch out with Stuart. He isn't one hundred per cent. He'll probably end up leading a mineworkers' revolt or some-thing.'

'Well, thank you for the warning,' Marcus said. 'And if you ever run into the young man Stuart hit at my dance, apologise to him from me, won't you? I dimly remember hearing something about it at the time. Took place down by the river, didn't it? Goodbye, Charlie.'

It took Stuart a further two weeks to decide not to accept Marcus's job. Normally decisive, he found himself confused and vacillating. The money was much better than he was likely to get elsewhere, and he relished the prospect of putting his management theories into practice, particularly overseas. In that respect, Marcus had known exactly how to tempt him. But another part of Stuart was wary of getting too involved with his godfather. His ambivalence about Marcus's business philosophy had become, if anything, even more pronounced since his time at Stanford. The Brand Group's aggressive programme of global expansion, and almost Darwinian commitment to free market econom-ics, exemplified everything he'd been taught to admire at business school. But his residual socialism, homegrown in Birmingham, made him question Marcus's ethics.

He asked his mother for her advice, and was surprised by the strength of her reaction, which was unequivocally negative. 'Work for whoever you like, Stuart, but please, not for Mr Brand.' When he asked why not, she said she couldn't go into it.

Barbara Miles rang him a couple of times, pressing for a decision, but the night before his self-imposed deadline Stuart still hadn't made up his mind. That evening, he went to have supper in Billing Road with Mary, who he hadn't seen since his return from the States.

She was putting Clara to bed. The second bedroom under the eaves had been decorated as a little girl's room, with mauve wallpaper and a frieze of Beatrix Potter characters. In one corner stood a child's table from Dragons and a miniature chair with Clara's name stencilled on the back. She was less obviously disabled than Stuart had expected; an endearing little thing, with a flat plain face and a head of lank black hair. Only her slanted eyes and flattened features hinted at her Down's Syndrome.

'Would you like to read her a story?' Mary asked.

Stuart must have looked uncomfortable because Mary said, 'She'd love it if you could. She can't understand much, but she adores being read to, especially by men. She doesn't get to meet many, sadly.'

Stuart sat Clara on his knee and read from a picture book about an owl and a towel. 'Big Owl, Little Towel. Little Owl, Big Towel. There you are, look, there's the little owl wrapped up in a big towel.' Having no experience of babies, he felt self-conscious, uncertain what to say.

Clara, absorbed by it all, jabbed delightedly at the book with her stubby finger.

'She's bright,' Stuart said to Mary when they'd put her into her cot. 'I'm sure she understood that story. When I asked her "Which one's the owl?" she always got it right.'

'You were sweet with her. She loves attention. And dogs. In the park, whenever she sees a dog, she points and makes a barking noise. Her speech probably won't ever be very good. But usually I can work out what she's trying to tell me.'

They went down to the kitchen and made pasta. While waiting for the water to boil, they had a glass of wine in the sitting room. Stuart, who had only met Crispin briefly at the wedding, picked up a photograph of him in skiing gear and was embarrassed when Mary saw him studying it.

'Oh, sorry,' he said, hurriedly putting it down.

'It doesn't matter,' Mary said. 'I stare at those photographs for hours. Trying to keep him alive in my mind, I suppose.'

'It must have been terrible. I should have said something before.'

'You wrote the sweetest letter. I've kept all the letters. People said such kind things. Yours was one of the nicest actually, you know how to put things. I've kept your other one too, the one about Clara.'

Unaccustomed to praise, Stuart made a face.

They put on the spaghetti and he told Mary about his

dilemma over the job. She listened until he had finished, then asked, 'Have you any alternatives? I mean, is Marcus's job the only one on offer, or are there others?'

'Nothing definite, but I think I might be offered a place at McKinsey's. Management consultancy.'

'It sounds very intellectual. Is it a good company?'

'Yeah, I think so. In a way it's a bit obvious, a lot of business school graduates go to McKinsey. But I like what I've seen of the culture. The people there are all from different nationalities. I was interviewed for the job by an American, a Brit and a Dane. It's completely international, with intake entirely on merit.'

'I'd go there then, if I were you.'

'You would? I was sure you were going to tell me to work for Marcus.'

'No, take this other one. It's just a feeling I've got that you'll prefer it.'

'The money's better at the Brand Group.'

Thinking of her father, Mary replied, 'Believe me, they're not a trustworthy place. There's something about them, I can't explain. You asked for my opinion, and that's it.'

Stuart, watching her across the kitchen table, thought how pretty Mary looked when she was serious, and how, out of all the people he knew of his own age, her advice was probably the most reliable.

'OK. You've decided me. I'll ring Marcus first thing.'

That night, Stuart and Mary sat at the kitchen table until after midnight, talking about Clara and Crispin, and Mary's worries about her daughter as she grew up and became less easy to carry around; Stuart, in return, told her all about his time in the States, his enthusiasm for American culture, and how he'd spent part of his summer vacation driving right across the country from the East to the West Coast. 'Until you've driven across it, you have no idea how enormous America is.' He told her about running into Abigail in the art gallery, and how she had developed an obsession about Marcus. 'I think, given half a chance, she'd actually have a love affair with him,' Stuart said. 'It's that bad. Imagine, going to bed with your godfather.' Hearing this, Mary experienced a wave of self-disgust and hurriedly stood up to clear away the plates.

When it was finally time for him to go, she said, 'Stuart, there's something I've been meaning to ask you. Do feel free to say no, but I wondered whether you'd agree to be one of Clara's godparents? She's a year old already but with all her problems, I haven't done anything about having her christened. Until now, that is. I thought of asking you and an old school friend of mine, Sarah Whitley. What do you think? I won't be the least bit offended if you can't.'

'Mary, I'd be honoured. But are you sure? I can't pretend to know much about God, or even whether I believe in him really.'

'All I'm looking for is someone who can be there for Clara. Who'll take an interest in her and, I don't know, come and visit her once in a while. You probably want to think about it, before committing yourself.'

'I don't need to think at all. I'd love to be Clara's godfather. I'm really chuffed. It's the nicest thing that's happened for months.'

29: July, 1984

The first office of Merrett & Associates, recruitment consultants, occupied half of the top floor of a building in Knightsbridge Green above the Bally shoe shop. To reach the office, the visitor pressed the entryphone in a wooden door between a glass shopfront and a bureau-de-change, entered the dingy common parts, pressed the light-timer and raced to climb the eight half-flights of stairs before being plunged back into darkness. Merrett & Associates (there were no associates) rented the front office and shared a galley kitchen with the financial recruitment consultants next door.

When Clara was eighteen months old, Mary decided she must return to work. Crispin's money had virtually run out and, while they lived free in Billing Road, she urgently needed income. The Gores continued to press her to accept an allowance, but Mary continued to refuse, even though she knew her intransigence must be inexplicable and hurtful to her parents-in-law. But month by month, as Clara grew bigger, any resemblance to Crispin became less and less evident, until Mary was almost surprised no one else commented on it.

Her first thought had been to return to her old job in New Bond Street, which had been held open for her. But the more she thought about it, the more convinced she became that she should set up on her own. As her own boss, she would have more flexibility over time off if Clara became ill. And if she made a go of it, and the business did well, she might actually have some security. In the short term, of course, it would be risky starting her own business, especially in the middle of a recession.

Drawing on the last of her savings to employ a morning nanny, she spent a month inspecting premises with appropriate addresses. In the recruitment business at that time, there were only half a dozen streets in London where an agency such as hers might respectably open up: Beauchamp Place, Bond Street (Old or New), Dover Street, Albemarle Street, Montpelier Street and Knightsbridge Green. The offices themselves could be as small and grotty as you liked (clients, after all, never saw them) but the address, as posted in *The Times*'s Crème de la Crème section every Wednesday, was all-important. She visited three dozen top-floors (all recruitment consultants are top-floors) before finding Knightsbridge Green, which was the cheapest on offer, a short let on a property soon to be redeveloped by the Cadogan Estate. The office was very dark, much of the window being blocked by a galvanised iron fire escape used as a preening-post by fat grey pigeons; the brown carpet didn't quite fit the room and rose from the underlay in a series of spectacular rucks.

Mary did her sums and worked out that, provided that she placed four recruits in the first four weeks, she could just about cover the first month's overheads. However, when the landlord asked for a three-month deposit in advance, which she hadn't anticipated, she almost had to pull out, until she remembered Marcus's Corot drawing of the ballerina, still hidden behind the sofa, face to the wall, where she'd thrust it in anger two years earlier.

Feeling horribly furtive, and praying no one would ever find out, she sold the picture for a quarter of its true value to a gallery in the Pimlico Road which she had spotted from the top of a bus. This money, combined with a £2,000 loan from Stuart who came in as a fifteen per cent shareholder, was enough to secure the office, buy an IBM self-correcting golfball typewriter, stationery, a telephone, a jar of coffee, J-cloths and a box of tea bags. On the surface of her second-hand desk, she placed a framed photograph of Crispin and several small pictures of Clara. On the Sunday night before Merrett & Associates opened for business for the first time, Stuart came round to Knightsbridge Green with a hammer and carpet tacks and relaid the underlay, then stretched the fetid brown carpet almost flat on new batons. And then, delving into his briefcase, he produced a bottle of almost-cold champagne which they drank out of coffee mugs to toast the new venture.

It was his advice and support during those early months which kept the business above water, Mary would later say. It was Stuart who helped her employ a bookkeeper – a feisty Irishwoman from Dublin, who came in three afternoons a week to do the payroll and pay the temps – and Stuart who helped her find some of her first accounts. And regularly, after work, when Mary was tidying around the office before hurrying home on the bus to bath Clara, he would draw up outside the office in his black Datsun, press the entryphone and ask, 'Need a lift home, Mary? And maybe a quick drink on the way?' But most evenings she spent alone in Billing Road with Clara, reading the bedtime stories that were part of her daughter's routine, even though she hardly under-stood them. As Mary became more and more convinced that Clara was not Crispin's child, she hardly dared to think about her dead husband. It was too painful.

The business took longer to get going than she'd planned. The recession was deepening, and the demand for temps and permanent secretaries dipped. All over London, staff were being let go. Whenever she had a spare moment, Mary cold-called every company she'd ever heard of, badgering their personnel departments for business. Had it not been for Savills, who started to use her for part of their work, Merrett & Associates would probably not have survived its first six months. Gradually, however, Mary established a reputation as a reliable supplier of intelligent personal assistants. She had an ability to interview two dozen girls and correctly identify which ones had their heads screwed on, and which would never show up on Monday morning for work. (She once fired a temp over the phone when she rang in claiming to be sick; Mary could hear boarding announcements from Geneva airport in the background.) She learned to conduct shorthand tests in her sleep. And she became wise to the sliding scale of commissions and split-commissions (boring companies – i.e. financial services – paid twenty per cent of first-year salary; Christie's, Sotheby's, Bond Street jewellers and art galleries paid fifteen; registered charities like War on Want and the Musicians' Benevolent Fund expected to pay only ten).

In her first six months of trading, Mary placed only eleven people in permanent jobs. In her second six months she placed thirty-four and, after much discussion with Stuart, felt the business was now big enough to take on a second consultant. And at the close of the first year, after costs and Mary's own modest salary, Merrett & Associates was able to declare a profit of £1,800.

30: June, 1985

As he trailed the Deputy Chief Executive, the Marketing Director, the Brand Manager and the Logistics Director of MegaSave Freezer Centres down the steep basement steps to the entrance of Annabel's, Stuart realised this was his first ever visit to a London nightclub. They had been working late at the McKinsey & Company offices in St James's Place. MegaSave was Stuart's most important retail client, and together they had been devising a new strategy for squeezing suppliers' margins, which should have the effect of moving two additional percentage points from the garden pea producers to the cash-and-carry wholesaler. It had been an intense day's work in an airless meeting pod and Stuart's brain was aching. He would have preferred to have gone home to bed, but then MegaSave's Deputy Chief Executive, Paul Cheeseman, had suggested a nightcap at Annabel's and it had seemed impolite to refuse.

A uniformed porter held an umbrella over them as they climbed from the taxi into Berkeley Square. A gaggle of rich-looking Greeks were disgorging from a limousine, and Stuart half wondered whether the MegaSave party would be allowed in, but Paul appeared to be a member and they were waved through by the doorman.

Stuart's eyes were on stalks. Pushing through a crowd of members loitering in a narrow corridor, they emerged into a series of claustrophobic drawing rooms, lavishly festooned with Turkish carpets, leather and tapestry-covered armchairs and oil paintings of King Charles spaniels. Paul ordered a bottle of champagne and the MegaSave party were allocated a corner banquette and several low stools. Stuart couldn't help feeling they looked slightly out of place, being almost the only people there not wearing dinner jackets. He had never seen so many beautiful sexy women in one room before. There were immaculate Italians with jet black hair and bead-encrusted evening dresses slashed to the hip, affording tantalising glimpses of long brown legs. All the women, he noticed, were wearing amazing jewellery – chunky gold rings and bracelets, and earrings with enormous precious stones – and as they passed by on the way to their own tables, they wafted trails of expensive scent. Despite knowing almost nothing about the social scene, Stuart nevertheless recognised a tall English duke leaning against the bar with a South American playboy, both of whom were regularly pilloried in the newspapers for their serial infidelities. A boisterous party of American bankers emerged from the dining room to order after-dinner drinks. Greek and Panamanian shipping millionaires were arriving with their hookers (or so Stuart supposed), enveloped in Valentino and clouds of cigar smoke. A party of stunning, slinky and very young English girls (including, though he was unaware of it, Jamie Temple's sister Lucinda) surfaced from the dancefloor hanging on the arms of several raffish property spivs. The club was becoming fuller by the minute, and Paul said they'd been lucky to secure their tiny, stunted table.

The Deputy Chief Executive of MegaSave, oblivious to the spectacle around him, said, 'Basically, Stuart, there's not a lot the Federation of Garden Vegetables and Perishable Goods can do about it. These trade organisations are only waffle shops. If the suppliers resist, we'll delist them. If there's a referral to the OFT, we'll argue consumer choice.'

But Stuart wasn't paying attention. He had been astonished to spot Marcus entering the club, dressed in a dinner jacket and puffing on a cigar, strolling past the bar in the direction of the dancefloor. Following two feet in his wake, and looking more beautiful than ever, was Saffron.

'Excuse me one moment, Paul.' He could see the back of Saffron's head twenty yards in front of him, passing though a dimly lit dining area. Had you asked then what his intentions were, Stuart couldn't have told you. But in one split second all his old feelings for Saffron had been rekindled; it was seven years since Marcus's dance but nothing that had happened in between – his time in America, his job at McKinsey – had altered anything.

Of what had happened to Saffron in the intervening years, he had almost no clue. Mary had mentioned hearing something about drug problems, but he could see nothing of that. She glowed with good health. She was wearing a butterscotch-coloured slip dress with spaghetti straps that was almost translucent. Her skin was tanned; her blonde hair completely straight, one side tucked behind her ear.

Marcus and Saffron arrived at a tiny dancefloor patterned with fairy lights. The discotheque was playing Madonna's 'Like a Virgin'. Saffron shimmied on to the floor, lifting her arms high above her head and undulating her body, but Marcus, indicating he preferred to slow-dance to the fast record, encircled her in his own massive arms, one palm pressed into the small of her back. Stuart ventured as close as he dared, half concealed by a pillar on the edge of the dining area, and watched Saffron dancing with their godfather.

He was hopelessly smitten. Saffron's every gesture made his heart lurch. Her hair fell across her face and Stuart felt breathless when she pushed it back behind her ear. With her soft brown shoulders, long neck, incredible legs, Saffron was perfect, he couldn't take his eyes off her. He realised he was completely and utterly in love.

Marcus's hand was travelling south from the small of Saffron's back, massaging her arse. '*You better knock, knock, knock on wood . . . baybear*'. Stuart could only stare at his long surgeon's fingers as they traced the contours of her bottom. Saffron herself seemed oddly oblivious to it all, staring into the middle distance, practically disengaged. Stuart found it impossible to work out what she was thinking or feeling. Was she Marcus's girlfriend? The fact was, he simply couldn't tell.

'*It's like thunder . . . lightning . . . the way you love me it's frightening . . .*'

Marcus was leaning towards Saffron. For a dreadful moment it looked like he was going to kiss her, but he was whispering something into her ear. He raised an eyebrow as though waiting for a reply. Saffron shrugged, and he appeared annoyed.

In fact Marcus was more than annoyed: he was furious.

For the six weeks that his goddaughter had been back in London from Chesa Glüna, he had placed her under sexual siege. He had asked her out to dinner more than a dozen times, of which she had accepted on only three occasions. He had invited her to Nassau, he had invited her to the South of France. He had invited her on his plane. He had offered to buy her jewellery. Marcus had an account at Cartier, which was settled each month by Barbara Miles. Over the years, dozens of pretty girls had found their estimation of Marcus Brand clarified by the existence of this account. But none of these blandishments had, so far, done the trick with Saffron.

In the end, of course, he knew she would submit, as all women eventually submitted. But, for Marcus, submission was not in itself enough; after all, she had submitted to him before. It was necessary for Saffron to fall in love with him – with Marcus and his world. The two entities – Marcus the man and Marcus the tycoon, with his planes, yachts and houses – were, he understood, indivisible in the eyes of most women. He liked his women to become dependent on him, and the life that surrounded him, until they almost took it for granted – and then he took it away. The jewellery, holidays, racehorses, the circle of rich friends – he withdrew them like a rug pulled from under their feet. Like many rich men, he chose needy women over strong ones because their deference was greater, and he could see reflected in their eyes the magnitude of his own success. With Saffron, this reluctance to submit made him think she lacked gratitude. After all, he had twice picked up her medical bills. And, having seduced her before, he found her glazed intransigence the more discourteous because he was famously good in bed. At the same time, her very coolness excited him; he knew she was worth waiting for. And when she did eventually yield, he would exact appropriate retribution.

'I want you to join me on the boat this weekend,' he said. 'It's at Cannes. We can fly down on Friday in the Cessna.'

'I can't. Sorry, Marcus, but I've promised to help Amaryllis with Lorcan this weekend.'

To Marcus, this sounded the most ludicrous and inadequate excuse he'd ever heard.

'Can't your mother look after her accidents herself, for God's sake?'

'Oh, you know Amaryllis, she's never really looked after either of us. She's better at looking after her men really.'

31: September, 1986

The flotation of the Brand Group on the London Stock Market was one of the largest and most high-profile public offerings of 1986.

For years afterwards, Charlie Crieff liked to take full credit for it, having introduced Marcus to a senior partner at Cruickshank & Willis and secured their appointment as brokers to the float. Strictly speaking, Cruickshank & Willis were joint brokers with Rowe & Pitman, but Charlie would always say, 'It was our issue. We bought the other guys in, just returning a favour.'

Whatever the circumstances, the debut of such a powerful conglomerate – headed by an elusive, glamorous figure like Marcus Brand – dominated the financial pages for several weeks. And not just the financial pages: the gossip and social columns, electrified by the realisation that Marcus would shortly be worth more than two billion pounds, could not get enough of the tycoon, his houses and his holidays, his horses and his girlfriends.

Even Professor Barry Tomkins, who lectured on the flotation as part of his 'New Capitalists' course at Birmingham University, conceded it was the slickest share placement of the decade. Personally masterminded – some would later claim manipulated – by Marcus down to the last detail, the Brand flotation was a model of its kind. The prospectus was a triumph of style over substance. Nobody reading the eighty-page document could fail to be impressed by the Group's dizzy rate of growth and diversity. Revenues, projected three years ahead, were shown to rise incrementally. The list of subsidiary companies and branch offices filled more than eleven solid pages. The proposed board included, as non-executive directors, several distinguished former Cabinet ministers and ambassadors, as well as a professor of economics at All Souls College, Oxford.

Cruickshank & Willis furnished potential investors with glowing research reports. Under Marcus's dynamic leadership, the Group had significantly increased its margin of profit in every sector it had entered. Its market position in the areas of vehicle manufacture, branded biscuits and savoury condiments, Far East distribution and mineral extraction, could be classified as dominant.

No company used the new alchemy of public relations with more conviction. Dewe Rogerson were retained as external consultants, and the whole of the sixth floor of Brand House was cleared to make room for a new, enlarged in-house Investor Relations department. Fourteen PRs were employed specifically to handle national and international press. One of the very first people to be signed up for the department was Marcus's godson, Jamie Temple.

For Jamie, the opportunity came about entirely by chance. He was now in his third year as a male escort, and the job had long ago acquired a routine, even humdrum, aspect. After a leisurely breakfast with the newspapers at the Brasserie in Brompton Cross, he would stroll up the road to Pelham Crescent for his first appointment with the permatanned wife of the European VP of an American investment bank. At lunchtime, he serviced a popular television presenter. Then he had a couple of hours off before various teatime assignations, depending on the day of the week, in Tregunter Road or Markham Square. The women, as he often told Charlie, were touchingly appreciative of his efforts, taking him clothes shopping or to lunch in restaurants. 'It's really educational,' he once said. 'I've learned so much about art. Some of my clients have amazing paintings in their bedrooms, like French Impressionists.'

Throughout his career, Jamie's most faithful client had been Camilla Silcox, wife of the Cruickshank & Willis partner, Sir Iain Silcox. One evening, at a dinner given by the stockbroker in honour of Marcus, to celebrate their appointment as brokers to the flotation, Camilla had been seated next to the great tycoon. At some point during dinner, Marcus mentioned having six godchildren. Jamie's name came up. Camilla had a hot flush while admitting that she knew him ('He was a friend of my son at school'). Marcus gave her a long, hard stare, implying he possibly knew more.

'The only thing wrong with my godson Jamie is he can't keep his dick inside his flies,' Marcus said. 'That and a craving for illegal drugs.'

'I'm sure that's not true,' Lady Silcox replied, cheeks reddening. 'He seems a very conscientious young man. I'm sure he's only waiting for the right opportunity.'

Marcus rolled his eyes.

'You said earlier you were looking for young people to work in your publicity office. Why not Jamie?'

Marcus looked thoughtful. 'If I thought he could get out of bed before lunchtime, I might let him have a crack. Strangely enough, PR is something he could do quite well at. He's a convincing liar.'

And so it was decided. The following morning Jamie was summoned to Brand House and offered a job as PR co-ordinator. And, having talked it through with Camilla, and promised to visit her twice a week after work, Jamie wrote charming letters of resignation to his eleven other regular customers, explaining he was pulling out of the business ('if that's the right expression') and hoping they would find a satisfactory replacement before too long.

From the start, he proved to be a natural PR. His easy charm and plausibility made people want to help him. He rapidly discovered he could say anything at all, right off the top of his head, and journalists would write it down in their notepads, and there it would appear, word for word, in the next day's business sections. It amused him to see himself described as a 'spokesperson' for the Brand Group. The job seemed, if anything, even easier than shafting frustrated housewives, and the fringe benefits were better. 'It's great,' he told Charlie, 'I can take whoever I want to lunch, whenever I want.' He quickly became a regular at the River Room of the Savoy, where financial journalists liked being buttered up.

In the office, he was popular. Always a brilliant mimic, his impressions of Marcus made the department roll about with laughter. He took to referring to Marcus as 'The God-father', but did so in such a way that no one could have accused him of showing off. In no time at all, half the women in the office were in love.

The only person dismayed by the turn of events was Charlie, though he did his best to disguise it. Having successfully blocked Stuart's job at the Brand Group (or so he imagined), the last thing he wanted was Jamie cosying up to their godfather. He found the idea of his friend actually working in Marcus's building irksome; they might bump into each other in the lift, several times a week. And he resented Jamie muscling in on 'his' flotation. It was Charlie who had teed the whole thing up, not Jamie, and he hoped people remembered that. One morning, when Charlie rang Marcus with a share tip, Jamie was actually sitting in the office too, and Marcus put them on the conference speaker so they could say good morning to each other. 'There you go, you see,' he said. 'Now I have two-thirds of my godsons working for me.'

As the day of the flotation approached, Marcus became visibly tense for the first time in his life. Always alert to aspersions cast on his business ethics, he threatened several journalists with legal action when they questioned certain aspects of the Group's accounting policy. There was a suggestion that profits had been overstated, and concerns were expressed over the cat's cradle of cross-shareholdings between subsidiaries and complicated arms-length trusts. Charlie was quick to reassure institutional investors that everything was above board: 'You know, when you're as successful as Marcus is, you're bound to have detractors. People are frightfully envious. Frankly, with someone like Marcus, who's made as much money as he has for as long as he has, the numbers speak for themselves.' And when Jamie pulled off the biggest coup of all, securing Marcus a laudatory cover profile in *Fortune* ('Brand Value: Can you afford to ignore Marcus Brand?'), he was called up to the seventh floor and given an envelope containing a thousand pounds in cash.

Marcus, assisted by Dick Mathias, Wanker Willis and Sir

Iain Silcox of Cruickshank & Willis, Charlie, Jamie and representatives from Dewe Rogerson and Samuel Montagu, the merchant bankers to the issue, gave general presentations to groups of analysts and investors. Each time he watched him in action, Jamie was impressed by how good Marcus was on his feet. He had a gift for anticipating awkward questions, even before they were posed, and was shameless in his flattery of the analysts, somehow turning a hostile line into a friendly one with effortless ease. At the end of each presentation, Charlie was gloating: 'This one's definitely going to fly.'

On Thursday 30 September 1986 the Brand Group issued 250 million shares, being 25 per cent of the Company, at £2.30p for each common share, valuing the group at £2.3 billion. By the end of the first day's trading, the stock had touched £3.05 before easing slightly on profit taking.

Charlie Crieff, who had stagged the issue, made a personal profit on the turn of £131,000, which he regarded, if anything, as a little less than his proper due.

32: September, 1986

Six weeks after Abigail Schwartzman moved to London from New York to enrol on a Sotheby's Fine Art course, she met Jamie Temple at the number 19 bus stop opposite Chelsea Old Town Hall. It took them a moment to recognise one another, it being almost ten years since Marcus's dance at West Candover Park, and thirteen since the holiday in Lyford Cay when Abigail had binged on potato crisps and Hershey bars.

'Abigail? Abigail Schwartzman?'

'Jamie? I don't believe this. That's *you* inside that suit?'

Physically, both godchildren had altered in the interim almost beyond recognition. Abigail at twenty-nine was thirty pounds lighter than she'd been at sixteen; her figure, encased in black Donna Karan sports pants and an un-structured DKNY jacket, was voluptuous but no longer fat. Even at half-past eight in the morning, she was perfectly groomed, her short black hair freshly washed and shining, her make-up carefully applied. With her slightly olive skin and big brown eyes, she was very pretty, Jamie decided. He, for his part, was dressed for work in a slightly rumpled grey Piero de Monzi flared suit with a bright turquoise shirt and knitted dark blue tie. His complexion, especially in the early morning, hinted at a rackety past. But his eyes darted with mischief and charm, and he made her laugh on the top of the bus all the way to Piccadilly.

'I don't even know what you're doing these days,' Abigail said, as they got out at Green Park.

'Working for our famous godfather. It's a long story. But basically I'm employed to make sure he comes over like Margaret Thatcher and Mother Teresa combined, when-ever he's written about.'

'You work for *Marcus*? Ohmigod, I didn't know that. I haven't seen him for ages. How is he?'

Abigail's heart was pounding. The Fine Art course was a pretext; the reason she had moved to London was to be closer to Marcus. Her obsession with him had hardly lessened. Years on, ever unrequited, he remained the principal love interest in her life. At college, she had gone through a phase of jumping into bed with anyone who asked her. Recently, eschewing the sons of her parents' friends, she only ever seemed to accept dates with older men who resembled either Zubin or Marcus.

'Marcus? Oh, exactly the same as usual, just slightly more so since he took the company public. Rolling rich, a despot, what else can I tell you?'

'Listen, I have to go,' Abigail said. 'But give me your number. I'll call you, I'd love to catch up. I want to hear more about Marcus . . . and everybody.'

They took to meeting for lunch and drinks after work in cocktail and champagne bars around Jermyn Street, of which Jules's and Green's were their favourites. Although Abigail was careful never to confide in Jamie about her obsession with Marcus, their conversations invariably headed in that direction. She was hungry for the slightest titbit of news about him. Was he in the country at the moment, or was he travelling? Had Jamie seen him? Did Marcus have a girlfriend?

'You should ring him up. I'm sure he'd be pleased to hear from you,' Jamie said.

'Do you think I should? Really, do you? Jamie, I don't know. I can never think of anything witty enough to say to him.'

One evening, Jamie said, 'I had a meeting with Marcus today. Channel 4 wants to interview him for *The Money Programme*. Afterwards, I mentioned I'd seen you.'

'You did?' Abigail's mouth went dry. 'What did he say about me? He probably can't even remember who I am.'

'He sends his love. Said to tell you he'd heard you're in London, and why haven't you rung him?'

'Ohmigod, he didn't say that? That makes me feel so

terrible. Oh, why didn't I call him when I first got here? Now it's embarrassing.'

By the second or third lunch, Jamie decided he really rather fancied Abigail. Although she obviously had a serious hang up about Marcus, she was in other respects a fun girl and a life-enhancer. He rather enjoyed being bossed around by her, finding it liberating. When they went out to restaurants, she booked the table and generally picked up the bill afterwards. And she could drive: one of her first acts on arriving in England was to lease the blue Golf GTi in which she took Jamie clothes shopping on Saturday mornings. The fact that she was rich was also a consideration. She seldom mentioned her parents, but Jamie remembered the Louis Vuitton luggage she'd brought to Lyford Cay, and Charlie had said her father was a multi-millionaire businessman in New York: 'You should have seen her mother at Marcus's dance. This tiny shrivelled Jewess with this fucking great diamond knuckleduster.'

Gradually, the idea took root in Jamie's mind that it might be advantageous to marry Abigail. This was not entirely a cynical ploy: he genuinely enjoyed her feistiness, wisecracks and still fleshy body. Marriage to Abigail would be a positive and timely solution to a growing sense that he was drifting. He was approaching thirty and hadn't five hundred pounds to his name. He was living, rent free, in a mews cottage in South Kensington, lent to him by a former client. But every penny he earned at the Brand Group, he spent. His father's business had gone under for the second time, and his mother's house in Clancarty Road wouldn't fetch much, assuming he eventually inherited half of it with his sister. Anyway, that might not be for years. Objectively, he would be doing himself a favour if he settled down with an attractive, competent, stinking rich American heiress.

Jamie had another motive too for pursuing Abigail, which was Marcus. Having correctly gauged the level of her obsession with their godfather, he felt a competitive need to displace Marcus in her affections. For the first time in his life he'd be able to put one over on him. Jamie suspected that, somehow or other, Marcus had sabotaged his affair with Saffron. He had no evidence, but guessed they'd had it off that night while he was holed up in the Indian jail. To turn Abigail's fixation on Marcus into a fixation on himself would be some sort of reparation.

Her feelings about Jamie were, if anything, even more diffuse. Initially viewing him only as a conduit for news about Marcus, she rapidly found herself falling in love with him. His sweet hopelessness aroused her maternal instinct, she loved fussing over him, sorting him out. She also found him exhilarating in bed. Having lived her first twenty-nine years as a virtual virgin, unable to find a man who could simultaneously satisfy herself and her parents' expectations, Jamie's sexual dexterity was a revelation. It turned her on to have him describe previous girlfriends. 'Tell me how many women you've slept with altogether,' she asked him, and he replied, 'Charlie once asked me the same question, and I lost count at four hundred. But who cares about them? It was only practising for when I met you.'

To be in love and in London, with four thousand miles between herself and New Jersey, was a wonderful thing. For the first time in her life, she was under nobody's thumb. She felt her lifelong anxieties and need for approval – from Zubin and Harriet, from Hershel Gluckstein, from Marcus – melt away as her relationship with Jamie intensified. At his instigation they developed a taste for making love in the open air, in locations where they risked being caught. They did it in the bracken in Richmond Park, in the bell tower of a church in the Cotswolds and on Holkham beach. 'For God's sake, don't make that dreadful moaning when you come,' he told her. 'People will think there's a seal cull going on.'

Four months after their chance meeting at the bus stop, Jamie and Abigail announced their engagement. When they informed their respective parents, none of whom had the slightest inkling such a development was on the cards, reactions were polarised. Margaret Temple dissolved into tears of relief that her only son had finally made good, which quickly turned into bitter complaints against her ex-husband, whom she assumed she would have to confront at the wedding. Michael Temple himself viewed an alliance with the Schwartzmans as a possible life-saver, and immediately began planning a new joint venture property company, with finance arranged by Zubin. He and Harriet, meanwhile, were enraged that Abigail should become engaged without their permission and to a *goy* boy as well.

'Far as I'm concerned, she's no longer my daughter,' Zubin stormed at a weeping Harriet. 'No way is either of us attending that wedding, or having anything to do with it. Abigail won't get another cent of my money. I'm stopping her allowance. Let's see how she gets along then, shall we? When I think of everything we've done for her, and *this* is how she repays us.'

Abigail organised the whole wedding with ferocious efficiency. Wounded but unsurprised by her parents' reaction to her engagement, she compounded their dismay by electing to marry in a church not a synagogue. Even this, however, posed problems when Jamie remembered he'd been married before, to the Czech migrant Jurgena, which ruled out a full church service. Abigail was temporarily rather stunned by news of this previous marriage, which her fiancé had never thought to mention, but he said, 'Honestly, Abby, it didn't mean a thing. We weren't in love or anything. We only ever went to bed once, and that was just for laughs.' In the end, Abigail managed to fix a quiet blessing at the Savoy Chapel, behind the Strand, to be followed by a lunch for twenty people in one of the private dining rooms at the Savoy.

With space for only eighteen guests, invitations were carefully rationed. Jamie was determined to have Charlie as his best man, and Abigail wanted Stuart to be there too as chief usher. They had the idea of asking Clara Gore to be a bridesmaid, but Mary, while delighted by the offer, felt Clara's co-ordination wasn't really up to it, but said they'd love to be part of the congregation ('We'll sit at the back'). Jamie couldn't decide whether or not to invite Saffron. For some reason, he'd never got round to telling Abby about their disastrous trip to India, and he knew his wife-to-be found Saffron's beauty undermining. On balance, he decided against. Marcus, of course, had to be asked, not least because of Jamie's job. Both Abigail and Jamie had serious misgivings, and it was a relief when he sent a charming, handwritten letter of refusal explaining he'd be in Los Angeles on business. He did, however, suggest the loan of his house in Lyford Cay for their honeymoon, an offer Jamie instantly accepted.

Both Jamie's parents were coming, and his sister Lucinda who asked to bring her new boyfriend, Rupert Lumley, a reformed coke addict turned property developer. Jamie, who remembered Rupert as one of the three suppliers of Gledhow Gardens, reluctantly agreed. Abigail, having no-body of her own in London to invite, asked her tutor from the Sotheby's course. The remaining nine places were filled by a selection of Jamie's old flames and landladies, including Nipples Ayrton-Phillips and her cousin Fleur, Lavinia Gilborne, Arabella Gilborne and Camilla Silcox.

As the day of the ceremony approached, Abigail became increasingly dispirited by her parents' determination to stay away. Although she had never exactly envisaged herself as a full-blown Jewish bride, vows taken under a decorated *chuppa* followed by a lavish banquet in a hotel ballroom, she still keenly felt the snub. So she was thrilled when, on the night before the wedding, Harriet rang her.

'Mother? You sound close, where are you?'

'Where I always stay when I'm in London. The Claridge's.'

'You're in London?'

'And why shouldn't I be in London? My only daughter is getting married tomorrow so they tell me. You're still my daughter, even if you have broken my heart.'

'How's Daddy?'

'If you ever called home you wouldn't have to ask a question like that!'

'Is he here in London too?'

'You think your father wants to see you marry a boy who isn't even Jewish? Your father?'

'Well, it's great you'll be there anyway. That makes me so happy.'

338

'So, what are you wearing tomorrow? And who's coming to this gentile wedding anyway? Is Marcus going to be there? You did get a party-planner for the reception? You haven't told your mother a thing about it.'

Afterwards, in their many post-mortems on how the wedding had gone, Abigail and Jamie felt that, all things considered, it had gone off a lot more smoothly than they'd dared hope. There had been moments, certainly, of high tension. Harriet, having turned up at the church an hour before the service in a little yellow and black Adolfo suit, with matching yellow and black crocodile shoes, had been horrified by the simplicity of the flowers and tried to order larger, gaudier arrangements; later, she had been outraged by Abigail's white trouser suit with its plunging neckline: 'To think, my daughter gets married in slacks! I'll never be able to display the photographs.' Margaret Temple, wearing a hat from Peter Jones of terminal insipidity, remonstrated with her ex-husband about maintenance arrears. Nipples Ayrton-Phillips kept disappearing throughout the service, and later throughout lunch, for extended visits to the Ladies. Lavinia Gilborne and Camilla Silcox, both beautifully turned out in almost identical Bruce Oldfield suits, eyed each other suspiciously across the pews. The star of the show, everyone agreed, was Clara, who played so beautifully and quietly in the back row with some little toys and books Mary had brought along. When Abigail processed back down the aisle with Jamie on her arm, Clara shouted out, her words as distinct as anything, 'That-lady-pretty,' and the congregation dissolved into laughter.

At lunch, where the seating plan was sabotaged when Harriet insisted on being placed next to her daughter, there were some unfortunate juxtapositions. Margaret, increasingly sour and belligerent, was trapped in a corner between Michael and Nipples, while Charlie was annoyed to find himself sitting next to Stuart.

'Didn't I hear you were turned down for a job at the Brand Group?' Charlie drawled.

'That's almost right,' Stuart replied, oblivious to the

intended slight. 'Marcus offered me a job after business school. It was tempting, but in the end I decided to go to McKinsey instead.'

'Christ, you're not a dreaded management consultant? They're always pitching for work at Cruickshank & Willis, but we wouldn't dream of allowing them in. Total leeches. I mean, if you don't know your own business better than a bunch of outside consultants, you might as well pack up and go home.'

Ignoring the barb, Stuart said, 'I'm enjoying it. I've been in the retail practice for a couple of years and it's been interesting. You really get to understand how different business models work. Now I'm moving over to financial services.'

'Yah, well, we don't have "business models" as you call them in the City. I was talking to Gordie White the other day, and he said they don't allow consultants within five hundred miles of any of their businesses. He who can, does; he who can't, consults.'

Stuart was disappointed Saffron wasn't at the lunch. Ever since that evening in Annabel's, when he'd seen her dancing with Marcus, he had been unable to get her out of his mind. He remembered how much he'd fancied her in her denim shorts in the Bahamas; half a lifetime later and he still fancied her, even though he probably still didn't stand a chance. Girls like Saffron inhabited a parallel universe. What would she see in someone like him?

Sitting on Stuart's other side was Jamie's sister, Lucinda, an achingly pretty blonde in a leopard-print hat. She had spent the whole summer in Italy, she said, helping run a discotheque in Porto Ercole. It occurred to Stuart she might be a good person to ask about Saffron.

'Saffron Weaver? I hardly see her these days except occasionally at Annabel's with Marcus.'

'Is she Marcus's girlfriend?' Stuart probed, full of trepidation.

Lucinda Temple shrugged. 'He has so many girls, I couldn't tell you. Probably. When she was going out with Jamie, Marcus really fancied her, Jamie said.'

'I hadn't realised Saffron went out with your brother.' Stuart felt he had been dealt a body-blow.

'Oh, God, they were together for ages – three months, I think. They went to India.' Then she added: 'Anyway, Saffron's been out with everyone. It's like *take a number* in the deli line.'

Stuart left the wedding lunch, his head full of competing emotions: jealousy of Jamie for having made it with Saffron, jealousy of Marcus, despair that Saffron would never look twice at him. Years ago, at Marcus's dance, Charlie Crieff had taunted him by saying she was out of his league and, having watched her at Annabel's, he reckoned it was true.

And yet Saffron had been out with Jamie. That alone was grounds for hope. If she'd been out with Jamie, why not him? And now Jamie was married to Abigail, it seemed to Stuart only Marcus stood between himself and his godsister.

33: April, 1987

Ten weeks after returning from honeymoon at Marcus's house in Lyford Cay, Jamie handed in his resignation at the Brand Group. Were it not for trepidation about his god-father's reaction, he would have resigned sooner. But with Marcus away travelling more than half the time, and Jamie's natural inclination to put off the moment for as long as possible, the weeks slipped into each other.

It had been Abigail's suggestion that her husband should leave the world of financial PR, and Jamie, already stifled by the routine of regular work, was happy to agree. His five months at Brand House had seemed like five years. Having never experienced full-time employment before, he was horrified by the reality. His colleagues found it normal to turn up to work five days a week, month in, month out, with only four weeks' holiday a year to look forward to. On those mornings when he couldn't get it together to crawl out of bed, and bunked off work, he found it intolerable to be asked for a doctor's note. The job itself, once the exhilaration of the float had subsided, struck Jamie as fairly mindless. And he felt increasingly hypocritical, being paid to tell everyone Marcus was a saint, when he suspected he was a complete shit.

Abigail, besotted with her handsome young husband, came to resent the time he spent working for Marcus. Having finally overcome her long obsession with their godfather, she wanted to sever all ties. As far as her own studies were concerned, she worked energetically and conscientiously; her passion for twentieth-century painting deepened with her knowledge. Her tutors, having initially pigeonholed her as another braindead American heiress looking for any excuse to hang out in London, recognised her genuine ability. Jamie loved to tease her when she was writing her essays late at night on Rothko and Motherwell.

'Who on earth painted those, darling? Clara Gore? Come on, Abby, let's go to bed.'

Abigail came increasingly to view her husband as a creative soul, whose potential could never be fulfilled in an office, and set about helping him find a new career. As far as money was concerned, they were all right for now. Zubin stubbornly refused to reinstate Abigail's allowance, but Harriet, having been charmed by Jamie at the wedding, and seeing with her own eyes how much he and her daughter were in love, secretly wired them pocket money every month which kept them in fags and groceries. Periodically, in his heart of hearts, Jamie couldn't help feeling he'd been sold a bit of a lemon in marrying Abigail; he was poorer than ever, and old man Schwartzman was showing no signs of coughing up the anticipated dowry. But Abigail was fun for now, and he was content to live from day to day, rising late and watching a gratifying amount of afternoon television while mulling over a change of career.

Disenchanted by office life, he thought he would be happier working outside in the fresh air, and Abigail paid for him to attend a short course on garden design at the Inchbald School in Pimlico. For ten weeks, he studied technical drawing and basic plantsmanship, learned how to survey a garden, take levels and the rudiments of practical landscaping (York stone, crunch gravel and where to buy it). Most of the other students were women of a certain age, who owned large gardens themselves or were approaching garden design as a second career. Instantly taking a shine to Marcus Brand's good-looking godson, they vied to sit next to him on the coach expeditions to Kew Gardens.

By the end of the course, Jamie felt he knew more than enough about the social hierarchy of English flowers and shrubs, box balls and hedges, and the pink and blue herbaceous borders ('loo paper colours' as he called them) that became so fashionable in the late eighties. He saw a congenial career stretching ahead of him redesigning patios and back gardens in Kensington and Fulham, supervising a couple of labourers, a glass of wine in one hand and a pair of secateurs in the other.

'I'll tell you who I'm going to ring up for commissions,' he told Charlie. 'All my old clients from my escort days. I mean, they already know I'm good with my hands in beds.'

34: May, 1987

Feeling desperately harassed, and coated with dust from the dozens of boxes and files she was humping up four flights of stairs, Mary could have sat down and wept. Clara's au pair, with hideous timing, had chosen today of all days to call in sick, which meant Mary had to supervise her daughter as well as the move. A traffic warden had given her five minutes to unload, and was hovering sadistically over the hired van with his book of tickets. She had left the front door on the latch to speed things up, but Clara kept staggering out into Beauchamp Place and Mary was terrified she'd get run over. She was right at the end of her tether when, like an angel of mercy, Stuart appeared on the pavement. 'Which would be more helpful, Mary? If I carried up the rest of these crates, or got Clara out of your hair for half an hour? I could take her round the corner for a milk shake.'

Merrett & Associates' relocation from Knightsbridge Green to larger premises in Beauchamp Place had been made necessary by the recruitment of two more consultants and a full-time receptionist. The company now employed six staff, including the Irish bookkeeper, and the new top-floor office comprised two large rooms above a couturier and a colonic irrigation clinic. By its third year in business, Merrett & Associates was firmly established as one of London's more reliable secretarial recruitment consultants, with a reputation for matching good applicants to suitable vacancies. Mary had devised an almost infallible coded system, based largely on instinct and first impressions, for who would fit in where. Ditzy blonde Sloanes were sent to estate agents, earnest dullards to charities, discreet daughters of service families to the Royal Household. The roster of permanent temps had grown to forty, and required a temps specialist. For an agency, the provision of last-minute temps was the most lucrative side of the business, but also

345

the most frustrating. Temps were famously unreliable, regularly struck down with shellfish poisoning on Monday mornings, caught in traffic, snowed in on summer days. Mary was pleased to be able to pass the burden to somebody else.

Her spread of blue-chip clients continued to expand. After eighteen months of hard slog, she finally began to crack the City, placing PAs at Cazenove's, Hoare Govett and Baring's. But the bulk of her business remained in the West End, with the Bond Street jewellers, art galleries and auctioneers.

Having started the agency at the bottom of the recession, she realised that, in order to win clients, she had to offer better services than her competitors. Early on, Merrett & Associates promised to supply substitute temps in emergencies. If one of their girls was struck down by a sudden migraine in the middle of the day, a replacement would be installed at her desk within an hour. Mary liked to joke that often their bosses didn't even notice there'd been a switch.

Looking back on those first two years, Mary was surprised they'd even come through it. She had never thought of herself as a businesswoman, and she was still occasionally overcome by shyness. But with tragedy had come courage, and the conviction that nothing worse could happen to her, and anyway, she had to support her daughter. So she worked away quietly and meticulously, quickly learning that in her job it was a greater advantage to be a good listener than the centre of attention. Nevertheless, had it not been for Stuart pumping another £3,000 into the company at a crucial moment, they would have been unable to meet their payroll and gone out of business. And, working so hard, she felt dreadfully guilty spending so much time away from Clara, and wondered why she couldn't swallow her pride and accept an allowance from the Gores. Sometimes in the afternoon the au pair had brought Clara round to the old offices in Knightsbridge Green, where she did colouring in a shorthand pad while her mother conducted interviews in the same room. Now that she was three-and-a-half, however,

Clara went to a special needs playgroup three mornings a week which took some of the pressure off.

Around the time of the company's third birthday, they received an unexpected accolade. An article appeared in the *Guardian*'s Appointments Section, naming Merrett & Associates as one of the five top small recruitment consultants. There was a large photograph of Mary, taken in the office surrounded by all her staff, accompanied by several paragraphs of laudatory copy. 'With top quality links to the leading secretarial colleges,' the piece said, 'the company has built a niche for itself providing high-calibre personal assistants.' Although Mary half suspected the feature was a cynical ploy by the section's advertising department, to thank her for using their classified columns, it was nevertheless an excuse for a joyous office party. Stuart, who had spent the day working with McKinsey colleagues at Citibank, pitched up late with two magnums of champagne from Oddbins. 'You look a dish in your picture,' he said, examining the article. 'I'll take a bet you get business out of this.'

Stuart's prediction turned out to be correct. Several new clients began using Merrett & Associates on the strength of the article, including a life insurance company called BFP based in St James's Square. Pretty soon, Mary was supplying BFP with all of their temps, up to twenty a month, and won the contract to provide permanent staff. At their next quarterly board meeting, when Mary, Stuart and the bookkeeper sat down to review the figures, he said, 'BFP have come from nowhere to become your biggest client. You do realise who they are, don't you?'

'They sell financial services, I think. I've met their Personnel woman a few times. Why?'

'The company's one of Marcus's. Brand Financial Planning.'

'I don't believe you.' Mary was aghast.

'Seriously, they're very well thought of. Probably the most interesting part of the whole group at the moment. A nice account to have.'

Never having confided in Stuart or anybody else about

her terrible experience with Marcus, Mary felt obliged to play down her disgust at having him as a client. But after the meeting, when everyone had gone, her anger was all-consuming. For four years since that night in St James's Place, which she couldn't even think about without feeling sick, she had ruthlessly cut Marcus out of her life. Neither she nor Clara would have any kind of contact with him ever again. She was reasonably certain Marcus had no idea he was Clara's father, and she wanted it to stay that way. Marcus had ruined her father's life, had ruined hers, but she would make damn' certain he didn't contaminate her daughter's. At Christmas she had received a card from him – a mean-ingless corporate card featuring Victorian children in fur muffs skating on a frozen river. The signature inside looked like a rubber stamp. Nevertheless, she had scrawled on the envelope 'Not Known Here. Return to Sender' and thrust it into the nearest post box. The last thing she needed was Christmas greetings from Marcus Brand.

She hadn't the slightest doubt the BFP contract had come courtesy of Marcus. It would be typical of him to imagine that by sending business her way, he would make her beholden to him. And typical to approach it covertly. No wonder they'd won so much business so quickly, she should have smelt a rat. He must have ordered BFP to become her number one client.

Her immediate reaction was to phone her contact in Human Resources and resign the account. But, the more she thought about it, she could not escape the conclusion that she had to face Marcus directly, tell him personally to stay out of her life and stop playing games. Although the prospect of being in the same room as her godfather almost brought on a panic attack, another part of Mary rather relished the prospect of a showdown. How dare he interfere with her business! She would tell him precisely what she thought of him.

She got the number for the Brand Group from directory enquiries and asked to be put through to his office.

'I would like to speak to Mr Brand. This is Mary Gore speaking.'

'Mary? My goodness, you sound fierce. This is Barbara Miles – we haven't heard from you for ages. How's little Clara getting on?'

Rather thrown by Barbara's friendliness, Mary replied, 'She's doing fine, thank you. She goes to morning school now, she's really growing up.'

'I'm so glad to hear it, we've all been thinking about you here. We did rather hope you'd send us a photograph, if you've got one, it would be lovely to see her.'

Mary said she'd see if she could find one, though she had no intention of sending Clara's picture anywhere near Marcus's office.

'Now, your godfather is away in Madrid until tomorrow evening. I can give you the number for the Ritz, if you like, or I can pass him a message.'

'Just tell him I want to see him,' Mary said. 'He'll know what it's about.'

'He'll be very pleased you rang,' Barbara said. 'We were only saying the other day, "What's happened to Mary?" '

As was usual with any arrangement involving her godfather, Mary quickly lost control of the agenda and a table was booked for lunch at Wilton's for the following Wednesday. She had envisaged seeing him in his office, saying her piece and then leaving; instead, there was the prospect of sitting across a table from him for at least an hour. Somehow, she felt she had already conceded the psychological high ground.

As the day of the lunch approached, she half wished she had never initiated it. The thought of Marcus made her nauseous. Try as she might to blot him out of her life, she had nevertheless been all too conscious of him. The excitement surrounding the flotation had established him as a constantly recurring figure in the newspapers. Whenever she opened her *Daily Mail*, there was Marcus in the Nigel Dempster column, squiring a new girlfriend or ordering a new plane. At the hairdresser's, she saw pictures of him in *Hello!* arriving at charity parties. Recently she had come across a photograph taken at a Conservative fundraiser, with Marcus standing between Margaret Thatcher and the Party Chairman, Norman Tebbit.

Not wanting to be wrong-footed by arriving late, she arrived far too early. Wilton's turned out to be an old-fashioned fish restaurant in Jermyn Street, with an oyster bar in the entrance hall manned by elderly waiters in white jackets. The panelled walls were decorated with paintings of dead salmon. The whole place, Mary thought, smelt vaguely of stale cigar smoke and sea water.

'I'm lunching with Marcus Brand, but I'm very early, I'm afraid,' she told the manager at the front desk.

'With Mr Brand? Oh, yes, indeed.' He was almost comically deferential. 'Would you care to wait at the table until Mr Brand arrives? May we bring you a drink?'

As the restaurant filled up, Mary realised it was almost exclusively a male hang-out; she was virtually the only woman in the place. Grossly fat, opulent-looking tycoons, some with cigars, greeted each other as they padded to their tables and booths. From her cursory reading of the social columns, she found herself recognising some of them, including Lord Weinstock and Jimmy Goldsmith. The waitresses were like old-fashioned nannies in white pina-fores, unfurling linen napkins for their charges and offering baskets of white bread.

Mary spotted Marcus being ushered through the restaur-ant by the manager. He looked tall and in perfect shape, his eyes almost imperceptibly scanning the other tables, regis-tering who was there. As he passed the table of Sir Evelyn de Rothschild, who was lunching the Editor of the *Economist*, he slowed down to solicit their opinion on that morning's statement from the Chairman of the Federal Reserve.

Seeing Mary, his broad face broke into an immense smile like the crocodile in one of Clara's picture books, and he said, 'My God, you do look lovely. That picture in the dreaded *Grauniad* did you no justice. Typical of a commu-nist rag like that. You should have sued them for every penny they're worth.'

Before she could reply, he pulled back his chair, sat down, noticed her glass of mineral water, and said, 'Waiter, bring my goddaughter a large glass of champagne and – why not? – the same for me! My goddaughter thinks she's a fish, likes to drink water. Ask me, there's only two things water's much good for: fill up your pool and something to float your yacht on. Wouldn't put it in my mouth, except occasionally in whisky in small quantities. Trouble with water is, fish fuck in it.'

The waiter, nodding vigorously at Marcus's *bien pensant*, hurried off to fetch the champagne before Mary could countermand the order.

'I needed to see you . . .' she began.

'And I'm very glad you have,' Marcus broke in. 'Couldn't think what had happened to you, you'd disappeared. Sent you a Christmas card, it gets sent back, not known here, return to sender. Thought you'd gone into a convent or joined the Moonies, some religious cult.'

'Actually, I've been working. I'm trying to run a small recruitment company.'

'And not that small either. You've done a first-rate job. Not easy to launch any business from a standing start, but you've done jolly well, full marks. I see you've co-opted Stuart on to your board which was a smart move. A lot of time for Stuart. Tried to bring him into my own company but timing wasn't right.'

'It was about the business I wanted to talk to you.' Mary was shaking. She dreaded the impending confrontation. But whatever happened, she mustn't dodge it.

'Thought it might be,' Marcus said. 'And the answer's yes. Frankly, we can structure the deal any way you want to play it. We can take forty-nine per cent, fifty-one, buy the whole thing if you'd like us to. Only two stipulations: you stay on as Chief Executive for a minimum of four years, and we have representation on the board. Don't worry, it won't be one of my rottweilers. I see this as a passive long-term investment, chance to get into a small tightly run outfit on the ground floor.'

'Marcus, I'm afraid you've misunderstood, I'm not inter-ested in selling the company.'

''Course you're not, Mary. You're probably thinking,

"Oh, Lord, here comes my notorious godfather up to his usual tricks. Wants to buy Merrett & Associates for a song. Six months down the line I'll be out on my ear in a widows and orphans hostel." Isn't that what you're thinking? Fact is, Mary, there's no timeframe on this, no gun to either of our heads. We could buy in this year, next year. It's your company, you're in the driving seat. All depends how quickly you want to expand. At the moment you've got how many branches? Two, isn't it?'

'One.'

'Well, why not ten? Why not thirty? Merrett & Associates in Edinburgh, Bath, Guildford – Cheltenham, for God's sake. And internationally. Whole world needs attractive, clued-up PAs. That's your speciality, isn't it? Bloody efficient girls, five hundred words a minute or whatever, who are easy on the eye and keep their bosses in a permanent state of sexual frenzy. All relate to that. Let's have a Merrett & Associates on Fifth Avenue. Why not? Washington, Chicago . . .'

Mary felt flattened. When Marcus was like this, ideas sparking, he was unstoppable, steamrolling every obstacle. 'I wanted to ask you about BFP,' she stuttered.

'So you *have* worked out who they are! Well done, that was a test. Wanted to find out how well you know your major clients. Spoke to them this morning, matter of fact, checked up on your performance. Anyway, they were all praise, think you do a grand job. We'll be punting a lot more work your way. Several other divisions coming on board.'

Utterly crushed, Mary could only nod mutely and prong the dozen Claire oysters that had appeared, without her asking, before her.

'Do think carefully about that offer,' Marcus reiterated at the end of lunch. 'Talk it over with Stuart. All about cash flow, you see. We're strongly cash-positive at the Brand Group at the moment. If you need five, ten million to fund a roll-out, plenty of worse places to come.'

35: September, 1987

For reasons of temperament, Jamie soon learned that a career as a landscape gardener did not agree with him. The job consisted mostly of loading and unloading paving stones from white vans, manoeuvring them through clients' houses and into small back gardens. Or else erecting screens of brown trellis around narrow yards in Battersea, and helping their owners buy giant terracotta pots at wholesale. Furthermore, it was difficult to make money. By the time he'd paid his two Irish labourers, Seamus and Padraig, who earned seven pounds an hour each, there was almost nothing left; the alternative, which was to do the heavy lifting himself, struck Jamie as too much like hard work. As a means of making a living, it certainly took longer, and involved more strenuous effort, than his previous vocation.

As predicted, several of his former girlfriends and clients volunteered to support his new venture. Lavinia Gilborne retained him to plant and maintain the window boxes in Cadogan Gardens. Camilla Silcox commissioned a trellis bower, which would eventually be covered by rambling roses, for their garden in the Little Boltons; there was talk of a special meadow of rare wild flowers for their country house near Malmesbury. In six months, Jamie embarked on eleven different projects, none of which gave him much satisfaction. 'You know what the problem is with this job,' he told Abigail. 'If I'm good at anything, it's talking to people and buttering them up. The only people I get to talk to these days are Seamus and Paddy. Half my clients don't even ask me inside for a cup of coffee.' He thought, but didn't say: In the old days I was a welcome visitor to the bedroom; these days, I'm lucky to make it as far as the kitchen.

Abigail agreed it was madness for Jamie not to be playing to his strengths and so, at the age of thirty, he began looking around for something else. This time, as he said to his wife, he had a much clearer idea of what would and wouldn't work for him; he needed a job involving people, definitely not a desk job or outdoors, with a lot of variety and based in London. When, some weeks later, he heard through Camilla Silcox that a new hotel in Montpelier Gardens was looking for a personable Assistant Manager, he decided it would suit him perfectly.

The vogue for discreet boutique hotels, which had begun in Paris, had recently come to London, and 60 Montpelier Gardens had been conceived as one of the discreetest and most expensive. Fashionably, instead of a name, it was known only by its number in the quiet garden square opposite Harrods. A pair of boxed bay trees was the sole indication of the front entrance. There was no reception desk, only a small painted table and pair of chintz-covered chairs where guests could perch while someone unobtrusively took an imprint of their credit card. Upstairs, the sixteen large suites had each been done over by a different fashionable decorator of the day, including Christophe Gollut, Joanna Wood and Jean Munro.

Having been set up for a job interview by Camilla, Jamie charmed his way into the position in fifteen minutes flat. The hotel's manager, Billy 'Bender' Barraclough, having worked his way up through the Berkeley in Wilton Place and the Mandarin Oriental in Bangkok, was entranced by Jamie and couldn't wait to see him in a tailcoat. When Jamie mentioned he'd worn one for five years at school, Bender hired him on the spot. 'It will be a wonderful asset having someone of your background in the team,' Bender assured him. 'A lot of well-known personalities stay with us, and they do like to be welcomed by someone who thinks in the same way.' Then, spotting Jamie's soil-encrusted fingernails, he added, 'Before you begin work, Jamie, I should like you to have a manicure. Naturally, the hotel will be happy to meet the expense.'

Slinking around 60 Montpelier Gardens in his dove-grey tails, Jamie was sure there was no more congenial job in London. His routine was gloriously free from urgency; Bender Barraclough believed it set a mood of relaxed elegance for the hotel if the Assistant General Manager – so handsome and well-connected – was seen tooling about in the lobby. On wet mornings, it was his duty to intercept guests as they headed towards the front door, and ask if they would care to borrow an umbrella. At midday, he strolled into the tiny chintz-upholstered drawing room to check that fresh ice had been delivered to the honesty bar. Periodically, he straightened up a copy of *Tatler*. In the afternoons, he would instruct the doorman to find Elaine Stritch a taxi. Aside from dodging Bender Barraclough's regular sexual overtures, and resisting the temptation to take forty winks in one of the bedrooms in the afternoon, his days were free from incident or pressure.

He had been in the job for about a month when he first became aware that Marcus regularly made use of a suite in the afternoons. Bender, having somehow missed Jamie's exciting connection to the tycoon, asked him to receive a guest 'with maximum discretion' at the staff entrance. The existence of this back way into the hotel, accessed through a cobbled mews, was one of the special features of 60 Montpelier Gardens. Madonna once evaded the entire British press corps for four days by entering and exiting via the kitchens.

When Bender called for 'maximum discretion', there were well-laid procedures that were put into action. Five minutes before the celebrity was due to arrive, Jamie would shepherd the kitchen staff – the chefs and washers-up – away from the area of the back door and into the pantry. He would then hover by the entrance until the car or taxi containing the celeb pulled up by the mound of black bin liners, and they scuttled inside unseen by prying eyes.

One afternoon, having watched a black Bentley arrive in the mews, he opened the kitchen door to Marcus.

'Any particular reason you're wearing a tailcoat, Jamie?' his godfather asked, not missing a beat. 'Not getting married again, are you?'

'Actually, I've got a job here as an Assistant Manager.'

'Well, try and stick with it a bit longer this time. Last time I heard, you were becoming the new Roddy Llewellyn.'

Jamie escorted Marcus, to the door of his suite and handed him the key. One of the rules of 'maximum discretion' was that no staff member ever entered a room if the guest was inside. If they requested room service, the tray was left outside the door. As far as was humanly possible, no hotel employee ever knew what or who the guest was doing.

Retreating downstairs, Jamie was filled with curiosity. What was Marcus up to? He would have liked to have asked the doorman whether anyone else had arrived by the front entrance, but the hotel's policy of *omerta* forbade it.

Two hours later, the doors of the elevator opened in the lobby, and out stepped Saffron. She was dressed in a gabardine raincoat and tweed hat, apparently disguised but unmistakable.

'*Saffron?*'

She stared blankly for a moment, not recognising him out of context.

'Jamie? It's so great to see you. God, this is just so weird.' She sounded like she was on something, not quite making sense. In the five years since their disastrous Indian holiday, she had lost weight; still devastatingly beautiful, but jumpy and all over the place. She had wrinkles around her eyes from sunbathing, but in some ways, Jamie thought, she was actually more beautiful than ever. Her face, with its more prominent cheekbones, was ravishing.

'What are you up to? You know I'm married now – to Abigail.' He felt the slight awkwardness between them. 'You should come over one evening.'

'I'd love to. Yeah, call me. And give my best to Abby. Tell her from me she's a lucky lady, I mean it. You look great, Jamie, really together.'

'You look amazing yourself, Saffron.'

She laughed. 'I'm OK. Really, everything's fine.' For a moment, it looked like she was going to say more, but she thought better of whatever it was and tottered to the front door and out into the street.

Shortly afterwards, Bender Barraclough appeared in the lobby looking pleased with himself.

'You did recognise who that was arriving earlier?' he whispered conspiratorially.

Jamie nodded.

'I thought you would. It is such a privilege having people of Marcus Brand's calibre using the hotel. It's what 60 Montpelier Gardens is all about.' Then he said, 'Jamie, I hate to ask you this, but where Mr Brand is concerned one can't be too careful. His room needs changing, and I don't want to ask the housekeepers to do it, it's too sensitive. I wonder if I could ask you to take care of it personally? We need a change of linen, tidy around the bathroom . . .'

Jamie unlocked the door of the Brompton Suite. The sitting room appeared totally untouched, neither of the salmon-coloured sofas had been sat on. In the bathroom, on the marble surround of the double basins, he found traces of cocaine. Venturing into the bedroom, he saw that the king-sized bed was a mass of rumpled sheets and towels, pillows all over the bed and carpet, the glazed, chintz bedcover with its pattern of birds of paradise hanging off the end of the bed, as though the occupants had been in too much haste to remove it properly. An empty bottle of champagne was thrust, upended, in a cooler. Two pillows placed at the foot of the bed still bore the imprint of a female backside; a third pillow on the floor was indented with the shape of kneecaps. On two of the bedposts were knotted hand towels, still attached to the posts, as though they had been used for restraint. Gathering up an armful of linen, he noticed several stray pubic hairs drifting on the undersheet, three fine blonde ones, like threads of gold silk, and a single coarse black one, curly as a corkscrew. The violence of his jealousy caught him unawares. He couldn't bear the idea of Marcus in bed with Saffron. He should never have finished with Saffron himself. He still adored her. But now it was too late, he was married to Abigail. He felt guilty, thinking this way, but the fact was he had married the wrong godchild.

Carefully gathering up the pubic hairs with his fingertips, he slipped them inside a matchbox. In a macabre way, he thought they made a nice memento.

'But why Wyoming, of all godforsaken places?'

Jamie had rung Charlie at Cruickshank & Willis within a few minutes of receiving the invitation. Abigail was sitting at the kitchen table in a pink dressing gown, waiting for coffee to percolate and studying the letter and its enclosures.

'Because he's bought a ranch out there. It's bloody enormous apparently. A hundred and fifty thousand acres outside Jackson Hole.'

'Any idea why, though? What does Marcus need a ranch for? I don't exactly see him as a cowboy.'

'Come on, Jamie, why does anybody need anything? A lot of tycoons buy ranches. It's one of those things they get, after they've bought the jet. Somewhere to fly to.'

'And we're expected to travel all the way to America to be impressed?'

'Godchildren's reunion. Fifteen years since the last one. It's very generous the way he keeps on inviting us.'

'Abby and I aren't sure we can face it.'

'You're kidding? You might not go?'

'We haven't decided. It's a long way and . . . I don't know.'

Charlie sounded shocked. 'From what I hear, the place is incredible. There's a private landing strip, horses, tennis, something like ten thousand cattle.'

'We'll think about it,' Jamie said. 'Abby's not sure.'

'Marcus will be furious if you don't go. It's like a three-line whip, all godchildren expected to attend. For heaven's sake, do come. Otherwise it'll just be me and Che Guevara – Stuart, I mean – plus Mary and Saffron.'

Jamie promised to consider it seriously. But at the mention of Saffron his own mind had suddenly been made up. He wanted to see her.

*

'I assume you've got one too,' Stuart said on the phone. 'Mine arrived this morning.'

Mary laughed. 'Not that I've had time to read it all. I've never seen so much bumph. Air schedules, visa forms – typical Marcus.'

'He hasn't half pushed the boat out this time. I read it coming in on the tube. First-class flights all the way. Then we get picked up in a private plane and land at the ranch.'

'You do, I don't. I'm not coming.'

Mary was adamant. No way was she going anywhere as Marcus's guest. Having singlemindedly avoided contact with him for more than five years, she had no intention of turning the clock back, and pretending nothing had happened. Apart from that one infuriating lunch at Wilton's, she hadn't seen him since her daughter was born.

'Why not? Hasn't Marcus invited Clara?'

'That's one reason – I can't leave her behind for a whole week. But I don't want to go anyway. I didn't enjoy either of those other holidays. Never felt particularly comfortable. In fact, I don't mind admitting it, I was thoroughly miserable. Apart from you, the other godchildren mostly ignored me. And every time Marcus spoke to me, I was petrified.'

'But that was years and years ago. I was pretty windy myself. If you felt scared, how do you imagine I felt, the boy from Birmingham? Charlie took the piss out of me all day long. He made me feel like that lad from the Hovis commercial, with his flat cap and wooden clogs. It won't be like that now, we're all adults. With the possible exception of Charlie.'

'Maybe. But I'm still not coming. I always had to go before because of my parents, but now I don't. You can tell me all about it when you get back. With any luck, Charlie will get thrown off by some bucking bronco and land on a cactus.'

'Goodness, Mary, you are down on him. Is he the reason you don't want to come?'

Charlie, Marcus, take your pick: Mary could think of a dozen reasons for taking a rain check on Wyoming. Only the slight feeling that, in declining, she was somehow landing Stuart in it, made her feel guilty.

'You know something, Mary?' he said. 'I think you should come, for lots of reasons. You need a holiday. You haven't been away since Clara was born and she's almost five. You've started a business and work your socks off, you deserve a break.'

'Stuart, I can't. There's no one I can leave Clara with, and I can't abandon the office.'

'Wrong on both counts. Clara can stay with your parents. They told me at her christening how much they wanted to have her on her own, and how you never let them. They'd love it. As for the business, it's rubbish to say you can't leave it. That's just the typical megalomaniac attitude of all founding entrepreneurs. We're warned against managers like you at McKinsey. You start these small businesses and can't let go. It's very dangerous, not delegating properly. It demotivates the staff. You've got two great deputies in Gilly and Louise. Use them, give them some space, get out of their hair.'

Still Mary sounded unconvinced. 'I'm still not happy, Stuart.'

'Then let me take the decision out of your hands. As a non-executive director of Merrett & Associates, I'm ordering you to take a holiday. And as Clara's godfather, I'm ordering you a second time. So you have no choice. I mean it, Mary, when we last had supper you looked washed out. I was worried about you. A week in the desert will do you good. And it won't be that bad anyway: I'll be there, and Jamie and Abby are friends of yours. And the blonde one, whatshername, Saffron, she's OK too.' Stuart was purposely vague. 'It could be a laugh.'

'I just wish Marcus would stop interfering in our lives, that's all. I thought godparents were meant to stop at your confirmation.'

'Think of him as a client then. He does give your company fifteen per cent of its turnover. And you might want to take him up on that buy-out one day. As fellow directors, we almost have a duty to go to Wyoming.'

*

The eight-seater King Air propeller plane flew around in a wide circle, to enable the godchildren to see the whole spread.

Charlie leaned forward to the second pilot and shouted above the engines, 'How far does the ranch extend? Where are the boundaries?'

'See that blue ridge over to the north? That's where the property starts. Then if you look way over there, beyond the pastureland, that dried-up watercourse marks the south perimeter.'

'It's bloody huge,' Charlie said, basking in the reflected glory of being the godson of the laird of this vast estate.

The pilot shrugged. 'There's a lot of big cattle ranches in Wyoming. Reckon it would take near enough three days if you rode the perimeter on horseback.'

As the plane banked, Mary could see a ranch house surrounded by green lawns and white post-and-rail fences, and several smaller log cabins spread out along the banks of a river. Various hay barns and a wooden bunkhouse stood on the edge of a dried-up floodplain. Then the plane straightened up for the descent, and a landing strip and metal hangar rose up ahead of them. Parked next to the hangar were several station wagons and Land Cruisers – the reception committee – and a string of quarter horses held by cowboys.

Marcus was waiting for them, wearing a Stetson and chaps, mounted on a sixteen-hand bay.

'Hope you had a good flight, not too bumpy,' he said. 'Can get a bit turbulent up there, hot air rising and so forth. Anyway, welcome to the MB Ranch. Splendid you're all here.' He greeted his godchildren while the suitcases were unloaded from the hold and on to a station wagon. 'I want to introduce you to the hands.' He signalled to the cowboys. 'Boys, I'd like you to meet my godchildren: Mr and Mrs Temple here – Jamie and Abigail – Mary Gore, Charlie Crieff, Saffron Weaver, and, over there, Stuart Bolton. And these good ole boys,' he said, indicating the cowboys, 'are Jim, Troy, Clarence, Sandy, Red, Johnny Two Moons and Zach. Now, who wants to ride up to the house and who wants to go in one of the pick-ups? Saffron, I think of you as a horsewoman. And how about you, Charlie? You grew up on an estate.'

'But not quite so large as this one, Marcus,' he replied ingratiatingly, as he was helped on to the back of a frisky roan. Still dehydrated from the six double whiskies he'd drunk on the overnight flight, he would have preferred to have gone by car, but felt obliged as senior godchild to meet the challenge. He also wanted to look good in front of Saffron who at some point during the journey he had decided was definitely attractive and worth another crack.

The other godchildren went on ahead in a convoy of Land Cruisers, leaving a trail of dust in their wake, while Marcus, Troy, Sandy, Zach, Saffron and Charlie set off over the parched terrain. At first the horses walked, picking their way down the steep side of a gorge to the basin of the dry floodplain. A narrow stream trickled along the middle of the riverbed, meandering between large smooth stones. Acid green cottonwood trees, with gnarled trunks and blowing puffs of fluffy white cotton, somehow clung on to the rocky riverbed. Miles away, on the horizon, they could see the blue mountain range that marked the perimeter of Marcus's land. Above them, an immense blue sky, without a cloud in sight, stretched infinitely in every direction.

They crossed the river, climbed the opposite bank and on to a prairie. Marcus broke into a gallop and the other horses followed suit. Saffron, having been well schooled by Amaryllis's old boyfriend Bongo Fortescue, had a perfect seat and moved up to ride alongside Marcus, her blonde hair streaming out behind her. Charlie noticed Zach exchange lascivious glances with Troy as they watched her move ahead. Charlie himself was finding the going tough. As a child, it had been his sisters who were the gymkhana stars; Charlie had actually been rather afraid of horses. It seemed they were going faster and faster. Without a riding hat, and dressed in the white chinos and blue blazer in which he'd travelled, he felt horribly vulnerable. The ground was rushing past beneath him, a dangerous-looking terrain of sharp stones and cacti. He wished he'd drunk less on the flight. He moved the reins into one hand and clutched on to the saddle with the other; not daring to look up, he kept his eyes fixed on the horse's hooves as they drummed across the prairie.

He couldn't believe how far it was to the ranch. From the air, it had appeared that the house and landing strip were practically adjacent, but it was almost twenty-five minutes before they arrived, steaming and sweating, at the stable yard. The scale of the ranch was awesome. The Ardnessaig Estate would fit into it seventy times; in fact, more like ninety times since Lord Crieff had recently sold off three hundred acres to a golf course consortium. Even his cousins the Arbroaths' fifteen thousand acres of prime Angus moorland seemed paltry next to this.

'Enjoy that?' Marcus asked when they'd dismounted.

'Amazing,' croaked Charlie. 'This is the most incredible country, especially seen from a horse.'

'Thought we might do quite a bit of riding while you're here. Boys can show you the grazing to the east of the spread. Totally different thing all together, lush like Switzerland, where we put the steers out to summer pasture.'

The other godchildren were sitting outside on a covered porch drinking coffee and cold beers. The ranch house was got up like a superior log cabin, with the porch rails and posts built of whole logs, and wide wooden planks in the veranda that ran the length of the building.

'Did you build this place yourself, Marcus?' asked Jamie. 'It's really cool.'

'The main house was built in the thirties by an industrialist from the East Coast. He used to come out on summers. But I've had a lot of work done. Not sure the original owner would recognise much, tell the truth.'

He gave the godchildren a tour of the inside, which was organised around a single great room with a stone fireplace. A staircase made of logs led up to a mezzanine gallery, with a long railing draped with Navajo rugs. Downstairs, four large sofas were upholstered in buffalo hide. A collection of Indian Acoma jars, arrowheads and Pueblo pots was displayed along a shelf. A beachwood stand held a Sioux headdress.

Lifting the headdress from the stand, Jamie placed it on his head and began whooping Red Indian-style. 'Me Big Chief Thrusting Dick. Me read heap good smoke signals from OK Corral.'

'For Pete's sake, put that thing back at once, Jamie,' Marcus said sharply. 'It's worth ninety thousand dollars.'

He showed them the new kitchen – 'The Cookhouse' – with its scrubbed wooden table, log chairs and gleaming battery of electric ovens and spits, and then they trooped outside, still clutching their drinks, to see the guest cottages. There were half a dozen of these, each designed as log cabins with stovepipe chimneys, though their interiors and bathrooms reminded Abigail of Ritz Carlton hotel suites. Behind each cabin stood a hot tub on a redwood deck screened by a stockade of tall, rare cacti.

As Marcus marched them all from guest cottage to guest cottage, extolling the wonders of prairie life, Stuart felt himself and the other godchildren regressing in age by fifteen years. It was hard to believe they were now all thirty. There was something in Marcus's attitude towards them, and in the echoes of earlier holidays, which made them revert to their teenage personas as all the old rivalries and insecurities reasserted themselves.

'Now, I've got a surprise which I think might be a bit of fun,' Marcus said. 'There's one for each of you, so you can use them to get around the ranch.'

Stuart was uncomfortably reminded of the tyres behind the speedboat in the South of France, and wondered what fresh humiliation Marcus had devised this time, but just then Jim, Troy, Clarence, Sandy, Red, Johnny Two Moons and Zach roared along the cinder path on seven gleaming red quad bikes.

'Now these really *are* quite fun,' Marcus said. 'They're yours for the duration of your stay. Use them to come over for breakfast, dinner, whatever, and take them wherever you like. They should touch about eighty on the flat.'

The cowboys dismounted and handed the bikes over to

Marcus and the godchildren. Then, having given them a few minutes to get the hang of them, Marcus led a tour of inspection of the outbuildings: the barns full of alfalfa and tractors, the corrals where they were raising Arab horses, the foreman's house and new bunkhouse for the hands. Then they looped back on themselves, up beyond the ranch, to a compound containing a swimming pool and three all-weather tennis courts. 'They're floodlit,' Marcus said, 'so if anyone's up to it, we can play after dinner. Otherwise it can be a bit sticky in the middle of the day. Sweat like a sow in this heat.'

As they cut back to the ranch, still in single file, Marcus out front, Jamie asked Abigail, 'What do you think would happen if one of us pulled out in front of him? Are we allowed to overtake The Godfather?'

'I wouldn't,' Abigail replied. 'I don't think it would go down too well.'

Jamie laughed and hunched over his handlebars. 'Yeah, this is like *Easy Rider*. No, we're Hell's Angels, the God-children Chapter.'

'More like the Q-Bikes,' said Stuart. 'Does anyone else remember the Q-Bikes? They were in the *Dandy* or the *Topper*, I think. They were this great gang of Scouse kids who had these wizard scooters.'

'Sorry, can't help you,' said Charlie squashingly. 'Comics were banned from the nursery.'

Jamie had been watching Saffron, who he assumed was still having a roaring affair with Marcus though neither gave the slightest indication of it. Greeting her at the airstrip, Marcus had been no more effusive than he'd been to anyone else. There was certainly no public display of affection. Right now, Saffron was riding fifth in the line of bikes, looking particularly juicy in the tan Stetson she'd borrowed from a cowboy. She seemed much more together than when he'd last seen her in the lobby of 60 Montpelier Gardens. After less than three hours in Wyoming, her face had caught the sun, which reminded him of how beautiful she'd looked in Rajasthan.

Stuart, too, had been watching Saffron, trying to establish

whether anything was going on between her and Marcus. Lucinda Temple had only said at Jamie and Abigail's wedding that it 'probably' was, because Marcus was such a randy old goat. Nothing definite. If they weren't, then Stuart would take his chances.

Charlie, meanwhile, had slowed down so he was riding parallel with Saffron. 'I haven't seen you for ages,' he said. 'I can't even remember when the last time was.'

'I can. At Marcus's dance.'

Reddening, he blustered, 'Oh, God, bloody years ago. So what are you doing with yourself? Modelling?'

'Charlie, I cannot believe you're coming out with that terrible old chat-up line. You should be ashamed of yourself.' But she smiled, and her eyes were friendly.

'Well, yes,' he said. 'Trouble with working in the City is you don't meet that many drop-dead-gorgeous women. I mean, there are compensations, you make an indecent amount of money, but it's pretty much a male bastion.'

'I didn't know you worked in the City. What are you? A trader?'

Charlie was astounded, and rather put out, that Saffron was unaware of his considerable recent success.

'Actually I'm a stockbroker.'

'Bad luck. Is that as boring as it sounds?'

Charlie revved the engine to cover his irritation. 'I'm a partner in Cruickshank & Willis, the outfit that took the Brand Group to market. It's generally regarded as one of the best; a sort of upmarket Cazenove's. As a matter of fact, I've just been made the youngest partner in the firm.'

He didn't mention that only by his threatening to quit, and take Marcus's business with him, had the other partners been forced to acquiesce against their better judgement. Nevertheless, having made it almost to the top of that blue-chip organisation, Charlie had started to earn serious money for the first time. In the aftermath of Big Bang, bonuses for business-getters were becoming, as Charlie put it, 'meaningful'. Last year he had taken home more than a quarter of a million pounds. If all went well, he expected to double that this year. He had bought a small Mercedes with leather seats and an in-car quadraphonic stereo system with graphic equalisers; the garage he felt compelled to rent to prevent the car being stolen or vandalised cost more per year than his starting salary at the firm. Finding his old accommodation in Ennismore Mews no longer reflected his new status, he sold it at an agreeable profit and bought a larger, nicer, third-floor flat in Egerton Place, where he filled the fridge with Parma ham and Bollinger. Showing it off for the first time to Jamie, who had walked across Brompton Road from 60 Montpelier Gardens in his tails, Charlie had said, 'The only drawback with this flat is the wall space. There's so much of it, and I never have a minute to look for pictures.'

'Perhaps you should ask Abby,' Jamie had suggested. 'She knows about art.'

'Modern or normal?'

'Contemporary. Big canvases painted all one colour, that sort of thing.'

'God, how gross. I want real pictures like we have at Ardnessaig. Actually, Marcus has some fairly attractive ones in the drawing room at West Candover Park, of Greek temples and maidens dancing about. I might ask him where he got them.'

'Old Masters? You must be doing well, Charlie.'

He preened. 'Put it this way, when you're producing a lot of cash for the firm, under a hell of a lot of pressure, they like to keep you happy.'

In his rare moments of self-doubt, however, when he arrived home from work to an empty flat, Charlie understood he needed a wife. He was almost thirty-two years old, conspicuously eligible, and it struck him as inappropriate that he wasn't yet married. Jamie was married, though Charlie had guessed what that was all about. For his own wife, he demanded someone rather tastier than Abigail, though admittedly she looked better these days than she used to. It surprised him, given his credentials, that more girls weren't beating a path to his door; in fact, on the sex and relationships front, he had been passing through a dormant patch that had lasted longer than he cared to admit.

Seeing Saffron on the plane to Wyoming had reawakened all his old lust for her, though this time he saw in her the possibility of something more significant and long-term.

Lunch had been set up under a grove of sweet tamarisk trees. Zach and Johnny Two Moons, the Apache, were flipping steaks on a metal grill and stirring a pot of moose beans. Mary, in white t-shirt and blue denim skirt, had finished her unpacking and was considering how she felt about being here. Seeing Marcus at the airstrip had made her feel uncomfortable, and already she was regretting her decision to come. The office in Beauchamp Place seemed a long way away, though she wasn't worrying about it as much as she'd expected. She had rung her parents and everything sounded OK with Clara, who was about to have her bath. Her talking had come on so much that, even over the telephone, Mary could understand most of what she was trying to say. Clara told her they'd been for a walk in some woods and had an ice cream.

The barbecue smelt deliciously of woodsmoke and grilling meat. The view towards the mountains fifty miles away was breathtaking. Mary consoled herself that she would at least get seven nights of unbroken sleep in her cabin, without having to keep half an ear open for Clara. She would keep her distance from Marcus and try not to get too paranoid.

Jamie and Abigail arrived for lunch, followed by Charlie, Stuart and Saffron, still wearing Zach's Stetson.

'Have you seen the soap in the guest bathrooms?' Abigail asked. 'Each piece has the letters MB burnt into it.'

'That'll be the cattle brand,' said Zach. 'They do that with a running iron, same as we use to brand the steers.'

'How horrible,' said Mary. 'Do you really brand cows? Doesn't it hurt them?'

'It hurts all right,' Zach said. 'They holler and bellow. It blisters the hide. You put the brandin' iron on the rump and count one, two, three, four, five. I can show you ladies how it's done, if you like.'

'No, thank you,' Mary said firmly, but Saffron, who'd

been helping the cowboys turn the steaks, said, 'I'd find that interesting, I'd love to see it one day.'

'Right, ma'm,' said Zach. 'We'll set that up for y'all.'

Charlie whispered to Jamie, 'I wouldn't mind branding Saffron myself. A nice hot poker on her bare arse.'

'You keep your poker inside your trousers, Charlie. Saffron's Marcus's bird, or didn't you know that?'

At precisely that moment, however, Marcus appeared in the garden clutching a Bloody Mary in one hand and a pert young blonde in the other. By the look of her, Charlie reckoned she was twenty-three, self-evidently American, a cheerleader type with a mouth full of pearly white teeth and legs like a Charlie's Angel.

'Uh-oh,' said Jamie. 'What have we here? Christie Brinkley's kid sister?'

'Whoever she is, I think she's chewing gum, unless her mouth always moves like that.'

'I don't think any of you has met my other house guest, Christina,' Marcus announced. 'Christina comes from Las Vegas.'

'I knew it,' Charlie muttered. 'He won her from a one-armed bandit. She fell out of the slot.'

'Or he fell into hers,' Jamie replied. 'She's a knockout.'

'Shhh,' said Charlie, as Marcus and Christina headed their way. He stuck out his hand. 'How do you do, Christina? Good to meet you. I'm Charlie Crieff, one of Marcus's god-sons. We also do a lot of business together back in London.'

'And I'm Jamie,' said Jamie, muscling in.

'Well, it's great to meet you too, boys,' said Christina. 'Marcus has told me a lot about you. You have quite a reputation to live up to, you know. Now, which one of you is the married one?'

'He is,' Charlie said quickly. 'Jamie's wife Abigail is the one over there in the cowgirl dress.'

'Well then, I'd better make her acquaintance and learn all your wicked secrets,' Christina said.

'You do realise this is a potentially disastrous situation,' Charlie said to Jamie.

369

They were hanging behind the others on the afternoon ride. Marcus and Christina were a couple of hundred yards ahead, leading the posse, with Johnny Two Moons and Jim slightly behind them.

Stuart and Abigail were taking lessons from Clarence and Troy, their horses attached to leading reins. Mary was pleased to discover she hadn't forgotten everything she'd been taught at Miss Green's stables. Jamie, in chaps and spurs, was doing his best to slouch like Clarence. Saffron and Zach were riding way off to one side, deep in conversation.

'What's disastrous?' Jamie asked.

'Christina.'

'I think she's rather good news. I approve of brassy blondes. Good on Marcus.'

'You don't get it, do you?'

'Get what?'

'How old would you say Christina is?'

'Twenty-two, twenty-three. You're not going to tell me seventeen?'

'She's twenty-three, I asked her. And you realise where all this could lead?'

'Not a clue.'

'God, Jamie, I'm sorry but you are a serious moron. She's *twenty-three*. What do women do when they're twenty-three? They have babies. Or at least they're perfectly capable of having them, which is the point.'

'So?'

'Do I need to spell this out syllable by syllable? Christina from Las Vegas is twenty-three. She is the girlfriend of Marcus Brand who is a billionaire. He is also our godfather. He also doesn't happen to have children of his own. Now, pay close attention because we're getting to the bit when it all becomes clear. If Marcus died – which we all hope and pray he doesn't – he would, as things stand, have nobody to leave his money to. There's no heir to the Brand Group, to the houses, nothing. Except us, his godchildren. Still with me? So, chances are the whole lot will come our way. Who else would he leave it to? The cats' home? It's pretty obvious he sees his godchildren as his surrogate family, otherwise why invite us to stay all the time? It's like he's showing us what's going to be ours one day.'

'You're unbelievable, Charlie. I remember you saying something like that in Lyford Cay. But you've expanded the theory since then.'

'Marcus has come a long way since then too. Don't you read the papers or follow the markets? He's probably one of the ten richest men in Europe. You worked for him, you should know. We're sitting on a goldmine. If he leaves two billion quid – and it could be more by then – that's about two hundred and fifty million each after tax. That's in cash and stocks. Then there's the properties, all this . . .' He waved at the Wyoming prairie. 'We'll be multi-millionaires, many times over.'

'I must admit, that would be a turn up for the books.'

'You could quit that menial job at the hotel for starters.'

'I'm rather enjoying it as a matter of fact.'

'You won't want to be handing out umbrellas when you're fifty, surely? You can buy a fabulous house, change wives, whatever you want.'

'And you think Christina might screw it all up?'

'If she becomes pregnant and has Marcus's baby, the whole thing's up the spout, literally. What if she produces a son? Well, any kid at all, it doesn't matter. Instantly there'd be an heir. Everything would go to them. We'd be lucky if we got left a painting to remember him by.'

They rode on in silence, the horses' bits jangling in the stillness of the desert. Charlie was sweating and his body odour rose with the heat. In the distance, they could see Marcus and Christina riding side by side. Charlie was thinking: Am I the only person round here who thinks these things through? Jamie and Abigail stood to inherit twice as much as he did, yet they didn't seem to have given it a second thought. They were talking half a billion pounds for the Temples! It struck him as unjust that, by marrying each other, Jamie and Abigail should inherit a double helping, but maybe there was some way around that.

Jamie asked, 'Tell me something, Charlie. Do you even like Marcus?'

'What an extraordinary question. Of course I do. I have enormous respect for everything he's achieved. He's built a global empire.'

'But do you like him?'

'Sure. He's tough and he can be a complete bastard. But he's bloody amusing too. When you see him in his own set, and he's on top form, Marcus is unbelievable.'

'You didn't used to like him though, did you?'

'What do you mean? Of course I did.'

'In the Bahamas, when we went over to that island to swim, you said you didn't approve of him because his money came from biscuits and car factories. I remember you saying nobody knows where he comes from.'

'I certainly didn't say anything of the kind.' Charlie looked flustered. 'I absolutely did not, and you must never repeat that to anyone. It would actually be slander, and I would have to consider legal action.'

'For Christ's sake, Charlie, keep your hair on. No need to get all pompous.'

'I'm sorry, but you obviously don't understand. Marcus is one of our biggest clients. If you start spreading malicious falsehoods about me, it could be very serious.'

'Come on, I only said you used to disapprove of him. So, you've revised your opinion. What's the big deal?'

'Just fuck off, Jamie. You don't get anything.'

'Maybe not. But at least I'm not wetting myself about Christina becoming pregnant.'

'You should be. She could even be pregnant already. If she goes swimming, try and get a look at her stomach.'

Saffron and Zach were getting on famously. A twenty-four-year-old farmboy who had never travelled further than Jackson Hole in his life, there was nothing Zach liked more than to be around pretty ladies, and he knew how to charm them, the ones from the city especially. Slouched low in his rattlesnake-trimmed saddle, he was becoming more laid-back by the second as he bullshitted Saffron about life on the range.

'Bunch o' people come up here one time,' he said, 'and a

rattler scared a lady's horse and threw her to the ground. She was screamin' and hollerin' like she was going to die or somethin', and ah pulled out mah pistol and blasted the sonofabitch through the brains.'

'Are there a lot of rattlesnakes around here?' Saffron asked excitedly.

'Y'all don't want to go walking in the rocks, not without a pistol anyways.'

'What about other wildlife?'

'There's coyote. When we go up to the line shack in the hills, they like to come see what we're about. But we reckon on shootin' them first before they get themselves into too much mischief. And there's plenty of antelope running wild across the range. Moose. And bears. And beavers. One thing you can say about them, they're destructive little varmints.'

Saffron was conscious of Marcus turning round to see where she'd got to. He looked annoyed at finding her still with Zach. Well, let him be annoyed, she didn't care. Whatever she'd had going with him was dead and buried for more than three months now since Christina had appeared on the scene. She had few regrets; this time she was determined there would be no reprise. She and Marcus were history, period. She was here to enjoy herself.

They arrived at pastureland where, as far as their eyes could see, big black Baulie beef cattle with white faces were roaming the prairie. Each cow was surrounded by a halo of gnats, which soon swarmed over the godchildren.

'Ow! Damn these things, they're all in my hair,' Saffron cursed.

'You want to put kerosene on your wrists to keep the bugs off,' Zach said. 'Them critters, they sure can bite.'

'Are these the cows you said you branded?'

'Most of these are steers – that's bulls with their nuts cut off.'

'You castrate them?'

'Sure thing. Gets their mind off of ass and on to grass.'

Saffron wondered whether the hunky cowboy was teasing her. She decided she didn't mind if he was. There was something refreshingly wholesome about Zach. And he was a lot more interesting than most of the men she'd met at Annabel's and Chesa Glüna.

'You're kidding?'

'They get mighty frisky before we take their nuts off. Rocky mountain oysters, that's the name for them round here.'

'I'm surprised you can catch the bulls, if they think you're going to castrate them.' Saffron was privately thinking Marcus might benefit from the same treatment. He was frisky enough.

'We use a rope. Catch the sonofabitch round the head or round the back heels, which we call heeling. Bring it down and stretch it out. Then take a rubber band, put it round their nuts. Cuts off the blood supply. They take three weeks to shrivel, then they drop off.'

Saffron was convinced that Marcus could only benefit from such treatment. She could see him up ahead, patting Christina on the seat of her Levis.

'Some fellers don't bother with the rubber band,' Zach went on. 'They take a knife to them. Some guys do it with their teeth, spit 'em out and have an oyster fry.'

'They *eat* them?'

'Sure, ma'm. Deep fried calf nuts, beans, some sweet bourbon . . .'

Stuart was observing Saffron and the cowboy, with whom he would have given a lot to change places. He was not however downhearted, still believing he was in with a chance. The existence of Christina as Marcus's girlfriend meant the affair with Saffron (if it had ever existed) was finished. All he needed was to spend time with her alone.

He realised that, at some level, he had been in love with her since 1973, which was fifteen years. Physically, she came closer to his ideal of feminine beauty than anyone he'd ever met; his knees actually went weak when he looked at her. However, he no longer felt shy of her as he once had. His time in the States, and three years at McKinsey, had given him a new confidence. As he reminded himself, he had three women working for him in the financial practice, all round about Saffron's age, and he got on fine with all of them, so what was the problem?

His opportunity came the following afternoon. Saffron and Stuart were heading back to their log cabins on the quad bikes after lunch. He suggested a burn over the prairie. 'Let's really hit it, full throttle.'

'OK,' said Saffron. 'I'll race you. See that water trough in the distance?'

They revved across the pasture, touching eighty, swerving to dodge the occasional huge boulder. As they approached the trough, Stuart slowed to allow her to sneak ahead.

'Cheat,' Saffron said. 'You let me win.'

'Not really. But we can call it a dead heat, if you prefer.'

'Dead heat's the right expression. I'm sweltering. It must be a hundred degrees out here.'

Stuart dismounted and examined the trough. 'I wouldn't drink this, it's full of bugs. But there's a tap, maybe it works.'

It did, and they perched on the metal rim drinking water from the faucet.

'Don't say anything,' Saffron said. 'It's so empty and peaceful here. I want to hear what it's like with no talking.' They sat in silence for a moment, listening to the wind whipping across the prairie. 'I could live here, you know,' she said. 'If Marcus said I could stay on for ever in my cabin, I would.'

'Wouldn't you get lonely? Marcus was saying he only spends three weeks a year at the ranch.'

She shrugged. 'There's the cowboys. And it would keep me away from temptation. The nearest place you can buy gear is Jackson Hole, and that's about a hundred miles away.'

'You don't still think about drugs?'

'Always will probably, you never stop wanting them. But I've been clean for a year now.'

'Drugs passed me by. At college, I could never afford them.'

'If you'd wanted them, you'd have afforded them. I've never had any money, and I've always got them.'

'How?'

'Mostly through friends. Some friends!' She pulled a face. 'Anyway, let's not talk about me, it's too depressing. What's your news? The last time I saw you was at that dance, when you rescued me from Charlie. I never thanked you.'

'No need.'

'But I was grateful. You were my knight in shining armour.'

'It was nothing. Any bloke would be only too pleased to rescue you.'

'Actually, they don't. They pretend they're rescuing me, then turn into monsters and lock me away in their castles.'

'Who does?'

'Marcus for one.'

She told Stuart about her two incarcerations at Chesa Glüna and how she'd felt she'd never get out again. 'Especially the second time. Marcus told them to throw away the key.'

'But I'd heard he was your, er, boyfriend or something. It's none of my business, but that's what people said.'

Saffron stared into the distance, towards the blue mountains. 'I guess you could say he was in a way. More of a lover than a boyfriend. Boyfriend sounds committed, and he was never that.'

'But it's over now?'

'Thank God, yes. It ended horribly, but you probably know that.'

'I don't know anything.' He wanted to say, All I know is I'm crazy about you. I don't care about your past, it's irrelevant. But he sat on the edge of the trough, watching her beautiful mouth as she talked.

She looked at him, as though having second thoughts. 'I haven't told this to anybody. Can I trust you?'

'Anything you tell me, I promise not to repeat. You have my word.'

'OK, well, Marcus made me have an abortion. This was last autumn. I was four months pregnant with his baby. He sent me to a clinic in Lausanne.'

'Oh, God, I'm so sorry.' Tentatively, he wrapped his arms

around her. It was the first time he had ever dared to touch her.

'I hadn't even realised I was pregnant. I hadn't been having periods anyway because of the drugs I was using.'

'And you didn't consider having the baby? Sorry, I don't mean to pry.'

'Marcus wouldn't let me. The minute he heard, he sent me off to this horrible place. He was furious with me. He said I was careless, and it's the woman's job to make sure she doesn't get pregnant, and he didn't want my fucking baby – those were his exact words. He wouldn't even come with me to Switzerland – his pilots flew me over in his plane.' Saffron was in floods, burying her face in Stuart's shoulder.

'I'm really sorry, Saffron. You're such a lovely person, I don't know how Marcus could be such a bastard.'

'Because he *is* a bastard.'

'Look, do you want my handkerchief? You'll feel better in a minute.' But he was thinking: I'd love to look after you. I could be your knight.

Stuart realised he was still desperately in love with Saffron, had always been so, and there was nothing in the world he wouldn't do for her, if only she'd let him.

'Let's go back to the ranch now,' Saffron said, smiling weakly. 'Zach's promised to show me how to rope a steer.'

It was late, very late after dinner on the fifth night of the holiday, and only the three of them were still up: Stuart, Saffron and Charlie, sprawled around the remains of the campfire under a big starry Wyoming sky.

Surreptitiously, Charlie glanced at his watch: 1.38. He was horribly tired and longed for bed, but he was damned if he was leaving Stuart alone with Saffron. He was sure Stuart was only waiting for him to turn in before moving in on her.

Saffron was looking unbelievably juicy tonight, he thought, with her long brown legs protruding from frayed denim shorts and a white shirt knotted under her tits, showcasing a sexy brown midriff. No way was Charlie handing her to Stuart on a plate. He would sit this one out. If anyone was having Saffron tonight, he was.

Stuart gazed longingly at her. She was perched on a log, a Marlboro between her lips, staring into the embers. If I don't make a move this time, he told himself, I never will. The second Charlie gets out of here, I'm going for it, no messing.

Stuart must be out of his tiny mind if he thinks a classy girl like Saffron would fancy him, Charlie assured himself. Ghastly, gauche, gormless Stuart? I don't think so. There again, you couldn't always tell with women, they were unpredictable; maybe Saffron liked a bit of rough. But Stuart was bound to turn in before long, and then Charlie would pounce.

Charlie had to go to bed soon, Stuart told himself. Toffs have no staying power, everyone knew that. And he couldn't be so deluded as to imagine Saffron fancied him, could he? Why would she fancy a chinless git like Charlie? On the other hand, he was stinking rich and women routinely sacrificed their true prospects for happiness on the altar of security, that was one of the great injustices of the capitalist system and always had been. Stuart didn't feel absolutely confident that, if Charlie came on to her, Saffron would have the strength of character to resist.

It was 2.55. Charlie's head was cloudy with exhaustion, his eyes kept closing. Wearily, he cracked open another Bud. Stuart would surely crash out soon.

With a superhuman effort, Stuart willed himself to stay awake. 'Don't you think the stars are incredible out here, Saff?' he asked. 'That's the Plough up there, and over there, look, that's Orion's Belt.'

Saffron shrugged, absorbed in her own thoughts.

I simply don't believe he's still hanging in here, Charlie cursed, glowering at Stuart. Don't they ever go to bed, the working classes? What's wrong with these people?

Can't he tell when he's not wanted? Stuart fumed. It's 3.45, for Pete's sake. Get out of here, get out of here . . . It would be starting to get light soon.

'God, look at the time,' Saffron said. 'Is that really what it is? I don't know how you do it – I'm shattered. See you both at breakfast, guys. 'Night, Charlie. 'Night, Stuart.'

And, before they could say a word, she was out of there.

Each day lunch was set up in a new location. Tables and chairs were transported to some picturesque spot on the ranch: to Elk Ridge where the caves in the canyons were full of prehistoric Indian wallpaintings or to a bend in the river on the prairie. The godchildren would ride out on horseback or on their quad bikes, whichever they chose, while the picnic, and the tented canopy Marcus insisted be strung between the cottonwood trees for shade, arrived by station wagon. He and Christina would roll up late by Land Cruiser, smelling of sex. In the afternoons, the entire party returned to the ranch to lie by the pool and sleep off the lunchtime wine. Later, when it became cooler, they played set after set of tennis, with Marcus, Charlie and Stuart becoming unbearably competitive as the evening wore on.

'You'll be pleased to hear,' Marcus announced at their penultimate dinner, 'I haven't forgotten our tradition of a last-night hooly. Can't pretend it's been so easy to get it organised this time, not like Lyford Cay, and especially without Barbara out here to arrange everything. But we've made a stab at it. So, tomorrow night's party night. Thought we might do a little square dancing, which is what they rather go in for round here.'

Whatever pretence Marcus made to the contrary, the party was meticulously organised with nothing left to chance. A vast barbecue had been erected over a stone firepit which blazed like the flames of Gehenna. What looked like a whole cow, skinned and trussed, was roasting over coals on a giant spit. Clarence and Red were grilling T-bone steaks and ribs on a second barbecue. A six-man bluegrass band, flown in that afternoon from Jackson Hole on Marcus's plane, was playing underneath the cottonwood trees, from which were suspended dozens of tiny storm lanterns. A wooden dancefloor had been laid close to the band. Zach, Jim and Johnny Two Moons were stationed behind a bar, dispensing tequila, bourbon and iced beer.

The godchildren stood around with drinks while the hands tended the barbecue. Zach was teaching Saffron how to chew snoose, Wyoming tobacco, oblivious to Marcus's frosty glares.

They collected their food and sat at a long table under the stars. 'Well, I must say, it's been a lot of fun having you all out here,' Marcus said. 'Jolly kind of you to make the effort. I know how busy you all are.'

There were murmurs of 'No, thank *you*, Marcus' and 'It's been amazing'.

Charlie, as self-styled senior godchild, was in a dilemma. He felt it was appropriate for him to stand up and say something, but remembered Marcus's sharp rebuke in Lyford Cay, when he'd been accused of being over-grateful. But if he stayed put and said nothing, someone else – Stuart, for instance – might take the initiative and usurp his position.

In the end, he decided to deliver an informal vote of thanks from a sitting position, praising the ranch and the Wild West scenery, Marcus's enduring generosity and the incredible time they'd all had. 'If I might add one last thing, Marcus, I'd like to pay public tribute to you as a business tycoon. I think I'm the only one of your godchildren who's fortunate enough to see you in a business environment on a regular basis. And I want to say, both as a business associate through Cruickshank & Willis, and as your eldest godson, how much I admire your whole approach, your sense of honour, your absolute integrity, the employment you've created, not just in Britain but all over the world.'

'Oh, for heaven's sake, Charlie, put a sock in it, won't you, you pompous ass?' Marcus lobbed a napkin at him across the table but didn't sound over-offended by the slew of praise. 'I don't want Christina hearing any of this, it'll start going to her head.'

Christina, missing the intended irony, asked, 'Don't you mean *your* head, Marcus?'

'I mean exactly what I said. Unlike Charlie, judging by all that nonsense. Sounds like the sort of platitudinous speech you give at a leaving dinner, when you've just given some bloody fool the boot.'

Mary, remembering her father, stared down at her plate.

Annoyed that his speech had been cut off mid-flow,

Charlie attempted to recover the high ground. 'Some people at a City lunch the other day were saying you're in line for a K, Marcus. Margaret's put you up for a New Year's Honour.'

'If she has, it's the biggest waste of time. I've told her twice already I don't want a knighthood. Wouldn't accept one. Not interested.'

'Seriously?' Charlie was shocked.

'All bullshit, the honours system. Two ways you can get one. Do fuck all in the Civil Service, don't rock the boat and be a good boy for thirty years of unremitting tedium and non-achievement, or else write out a whopping great cheque to a political party.'

'I thought you did give money to the Tories,' said Charlie.

'I do, lots of money. Give it to Labour too. I'd give it to the Liberals if they weren't a bunch of complete jerks.'

'What's the point of that?' Jamie asked. 'They cancel each other out.'

'Back both ponies. Crazy not to. Only worthwhile thing you learn from history is that nothing stays the same. Wherever we do business, number one rule is fund the government, fund the opposition.'

'But surely,' Charlie said, 'you don't think Labour will ever get back in again in England? Kinnock's a complete joke. Anyway, Thatcher's changed the country for ever, the public mentality's different, we're all into home ownership now. No one's going to vote to bring back the unions. People's main memory of socialism is the winter of discontent and unburied bodies.'

'Wouldn't be so sure. Democracies have short memories, and history is against you.'

'I'd take a bet if I didn't think I'd be fleecing you. There won't be another Labour government this century, or the one after.'

'Stuart? What's your reading? What are the soothsayers at McKinsey saying?'

'We're certainly predicting a third Conservative term, but beyond that, it's up for grabs.'

'Oh, come on,' Charlie said. 'Isn't that just classic management consultant speak? Sitting on the fence. Mathematically, it's impossible for Labour to get back in. All the boundary changes in the constituencies favour the Tories. And the population's ageing, which predetermines a drift to the right. Your problem, Stuart, is you want Labour to win. Go on, admit it. You'd love the unions back in Number Ten, all pally-pally.'

Stuart, no longer sure he desired anything of the kind, merely shook his head.

'We'll see,' Marcus said, pushing back his chair. 'Meanwhile, I'm still going to send off my fifty grand a year to the working-class heroes. They'll only waste it, of course, but that's not the point. Now – dancing. Red!' He called out to the senior of the seven cowboys, 'We're ready for some square dancing. Strike up the band! "Take your partners by the hand" – isn't that what they say? Everyone, over to the dancefloor. Christina, stand over there. No, not there, for goodness' sake, opposite me. Come on, you're supposed to be an American, you should know how to do this. Didn't they teach you anything in Las Vegas?'

Charlie gave Jamie a meaningful look. It sounded like Marcus was already becoming exasperated with her. If so, that was good news all round.

'Who are we missing?' Marcus asked. 'There should be eight and I can only count seven. Saffron? Where's Saffron?'

'She was here a few minutes ago,' said Mary.

'Maybe she's gone to the bathroom,' suggested Abigail.

'Well, someone go and find her, please. Red's going to walk us through this thing, and we all need to be here paying attention.'

Jamie, Charlie and Stuart hastened towards the ranch, searching for her. 'Saff!' shouted Jamie. 'Where are you? The dancing's about to start.'

The French windows from the great room were open on to the veranda, white cotton drapes billowing in the breeze.

Charlie, Jamie and Stuart arrived at exactly the same moment, just in time to see Zach leap to his feet, Levis at half-mast, while Saffron rolled off a buffalo-upholstered sofa and tugged down her skirt.

It was impossible to say which of Marcus's three godsons was most horrified.

Part Four

37: March, 1989

'I've got something here you're really going to love. You have to guess what it is.'

Jamie handed Charlie a clear-plastic orb, flat at the base, with what resembled a small piece of bristle suspended in aspic.

'Looks like a paperweight. What's so great about it?'

'It *is* a paperweight. It's what's inside that's interesting.'

'The curly black thing?' Charlie examined it under a lamp. 'Might be a dog hair. Or a big fat pube.'

'Right second time. It's a pubic hair. But whose pube exactly? That's the billion-dollar question. Look more closely, there might be more than one in there.'

Charlie tilted the paperweight this way and that. He had called round at Hillgate Place for a drink on his way home from work.

'There is a second one,' he said at last. 'Blonde. I almost didn't see it, it's so fine.'

'So? Any guesses?'

'Come on, Jamie, don't wind me up. I haven't a clue. Princess Diana? It could be anyone.'

'Someone you know, actually. In fact you know both parties. I'll give you a hint. The big one's male, of course, randy as hell, rich as Croesus . . .'

'Not Marcus? Christ, Jamie, how the hell did you get hold of it? And who's the blonde? No, don't tell me, not Saffron?'

Jamie nodded and laughed and told Charlie about discovering them amongst the bedclothes at 60 Montpelier Gardens.

'And you kept them? Why, you perv? What on earth for?'

'No reason. For a laugh. To show you, I suppose. I came across this matchbox I'd kept them in for ages, and thought they'd make a really cool paperweight. You remember those kits? They were the big craze one term at Broadley Court.'

'Jamie, you're too much. What are you intending to do with that thing? I wouldn't show it to too many people if I were you.'

'No fear. I'm not crossing Marcus now I know he's got a brute of a pube like that. But Saffron's is cute, no? I might take the odd peek at it occasionally, for old time's sake.'

38: June, 1990

On the evening of his thirty-third birthday, at a summer drinks party given by Camilla Silcox, wife of Cruickshank & Willis's senior partner Sir Iain, in the back garden of their house in the Little Boltons, Charlie met the woman he would marry in the autumn of that same year. For both halves of the couple, the timing of their meeting could not have been more opportune. Having reluctantly ruled out Saffron after the episode in Wyoming, he was seriously on the prowl for a wife. And for Miranda van Haagen, who had recently become divorced from the popular Dutch banker Boobie van Haagen, there was nothing to be gained by hanging about.

With four large Bellinis inside him, Charlie's first glimpse of Miranda, standing in a group of friends under Camilla's recently installed rose-covered bower, made him think his hunt might just be over. She was beautiful in the glossy, expensive, sophisticated way he adored. Her thick shiny blonde hair glistened with highlights and was crowned with a pair of Cartier sunglasses. Although wholly incapable of identifying an Hermès Kelly bag and a Ralph Lauren slip dress, he nevertheless recognised a quality woman when he saw one, and fought his way across the garden.

Bumping into his host en route, he asked, 'Iain, tell me, who's the blonde over there, the one in the middle?'

'In the pink frock? Miranda van Haagen. All rather sad, she and Boobie have just done the splits.'

'Van Haagen? What is she, Belgian or something?'

'Boobie's Dutch. Miranda's English. Can't remember what she was called before. I believe she grew up in Jersey, actually.'

They had dinner together that night with a group of friends, then again the next evening on their own. The following afternoon, which was a Saturday, they met for a long boozy lunch at San Lorenzo and went shopping afterwards in Beauchamp Place. By tea time they were in bed.

From the beginning, Charlie was captivated by Miranda, and slightly in awe of her. Six months older than himself, her life had been so much fuller and richer in experience than his own. She had stayed everywhere: in the smartest hotels in the Caribbean, in schlosses in Germany and Austria, on the largest yachts. A fully paid up member of the international set that she gaily referred to as Eurotrash, she appeared to have spent half her winters in Gstaad and her summers in Sardinia. At weekends, she flew to weddings in Rome. She had friends in the Hamptons. As a teenager, she had spent two seasons staying in Paddy McNally's chalet in Verbier, and was consequently a brilliant skier. She followed polo, and asked Charlie whether he was going to the Cartier day next month. A past boyfriend, she mentioned, pre-Boobie, had taken her to the Prix de L'Arc de Triomphe at Chantilly, and they'd had lunch in the Aga Khan's tent.

'One place that's always fun,' she said, 'is Lyford Cay. I've got so many good friends in Nassau.'

'My godfather has a house there,' Charlie replied, happy to have an opportunity to compete for once. 'Did you come across Marcus Brand?'

'Oh, God, we went to Sandy Cove all the time! I *adore* Marcus. I had no idea he's your godfather.' From that moment on, Miranda's interest in him moved up a notch.

For Charlie, having Miranda van Haagen as a girlfriend was the fulfilment of a dream. Smart, confident and fabulous-looking, she opened up a new world to him; a world which he felt should already have been his by rights, but which had somehow never quite opened its doors to him. He could see now that, pre-Miranda, his life had lacked pizzazz. He had been making all this money but had no one with whom to spend it. Miranda changed all that utterly. Within eight weeks of moving into his flat in Egerton Place, she had ripped out the old bathroom and created in its place a wonderful chrome and marble-lined palace; she re-sited the furniture, consigning to the skip his Ardnessaig nursery bed, replaced his clouded bachelor glasses with cut-crystal pieces from Villeroy & Boch, and networked with various Green Street galleries to supply Old Master drawings on approval. Soaking in his new film-star bath, with a major Bloody Mary in one of his new fishbowl-sized tumblers balanced on the edge of the tub, Charlie acknowledged that Miranda had transformed his life for the better.

In her wake, he now went out every evening to gallery openings and dinners, socialising with people he had previously encountered only in the faster social magazines. Together, they went to Ascot in the Sangsters' box and to Vienna for the wedding of an Austrian countess to an Italian playboy banker. As a partner in Cruickshank & Willis, who had brilliantly brought his godfather's conglomerate to market, Charlie was quickly accepted by Miranda's set as one of their own, and soon found himself dispensing financial advice to people many times richer than himself. Miranda was a tireless PR for him, constantly telling her girlfriends over lunch how successful he was, and how his 1990 bonus should top a million pounds. The message soon spread. As a non-working lover, Miranda had plenty of time for lunches.

For her own part, Miranda saw the potential in Charlie. Once she'd got him out of tweeds and cords and into the Italian smart-casual look her group favoured, he wasn't bad-looking; a little overweight, receding slightly at the temples, but definitely presentable. He was successful, which she liked, and, she supposed, clever, though he never said anything noticeably witty or intelligent. On the other hand, nor did the other financiers and bankers who married her girlfriends. In Miranda's set, the women were flirtatious and outrageous, the men sleek, silver-haired and frequently morose.

Quite early on in their relationship, when she was boring Charlie with stories about some German princess she knew called Marie-Christine Schoenmann-Ausberg-Konwitz, or Sherman-Auschwitz-Kronenburg – Charlie didn't care – he said, 'These German titles are two a penny, aren't they? I don't know why you bang on about them so much.'

Hating to be criticised, Miranda scowled at him. 'And I suppose you're not interested in titles?'

'Not especially. Well, I mean, I suppose I'm quite interested in my own title. When my father eventually drops off his perch, I won't object to being Lord Crieff. But that's different. It's recognition for our family for hundreds of years of, uh, living at Ardnessaig.'

Miranda, who hadn't realised Charlie was heir to a title and a family seat, imagined herself booking restaurant tables as Lady Crieff, and thought how that would annoy Boobie. Her feelings about her ex-husband were still unresolved. Wonderful in bed, far better in fact than Charlie who was positively gauche, Boobie nevertheless had an effeminate side which Miranda had done her best to ignore. But one Sunday afternoon, returning earlier than expected from Hurlingham, she had surprised Boobie sitting at her dressing table in bra and knickers, coated in her make-up and masturbating into the mirror. What had annoyed her most was the sight of all her new Krizia cocktail dresses, in which he had evidently just been parading, crumpled on the bed.

They had separated and a divorce, as amicable as these things can be under the circumstances, followed two years later. But she still heard about Boobie all the time, through others in their set, and occasionally they spoke on the telephone. Miranda was sure Boobie had heard about Charlie, and longed to know what he thought.

Miranda having been married before, they decided on a low-key ceremony at Chelsea Register Office followed by a lunch for a hundred and eighty friends at 30 Pavilion Road. Jamie was best man, wearing his hotelier's tails and a buttonhole filched from a breakfast tray. Marcus and the Silcoxes sat at the top table with the bride and groom and their families, and Charlie's other godfather, Sir Jock Kerr-Innes, now almost a hundred. Lord and Lady Crieff, suddenly looking much older themselves, flew down to London for the wedding with Mary Jane, Annabel and Nanny Arbroath and put up at the Basil Street Hotel where Alistair Crieff had secured a special weekend rate. Financially, they had recently had a bit of a knock-back, Zubin Schwartzman's Gramercy Park development having hit the buffers. Alistair didn't understand it all, but it seemed that the company had failed and been taken over by a new company, also owned by Zubin. As an investor in the original company, the Crieffs lost their entire stake. Alistair was in discussions with Christie's local man about another sale of sporting pictures from Ardnessaig, though most of the good ones had gone last time round.

Verena Crieff was full of misgivings about Charlie's choice of wife, having failed to find any trace of Miranda in her various reference books. 'I've never heard of anyone coming *from* Jersey before. One's heard of people going *to* Jersey, but not coming from there.'

'You'll meet Miranda's father at the wedding, Mama,' Charlie said. 'He's called Bryan Parkin. He's a very success-ful tax lawyer in St Helier.'

Verena made a face. 'It's such a pity you can't have a proper wedding in a church. Will none of my children give me a proper wedding? Neither of your sisters is married, I don't know why. You can't expect the Arbroaths to come all the way down just for a register office wedding.'

'I've told you, Miranda's been married already.'

'To a Mr van Haagen. I couldn't find anything about *him* either.'

On the evening before the wedding, Charlie took his parents and sisters out to dinner to meet his fiancée for the first time. Considerable thought was paid to the choice of restaurant, Charlie wanting somewhere not too noisy so they could hear themselves speak, smart enough to point at his recent success, sufficiently lively to keep them all going, and with food to suit both his own family (plain) and Miranda (modern Italian). In the end, probably pleasing nobody, he chose an expensive French place called Walton's in Walton Street which was the very restaurant, Miranda mentioned in the taxi on the way, where Boobie had proposed to her six years earlier.

The dinner was not a success. Mary Jane and Annabel, grown enormous on a diet of roast game and baps, were too fat for the small brittle chairs, and the waiters had trouble squeezing past them on their way to the kitchen. Verena glared disapprovingly around the restaurant, saying she didn't recognise anybody and who were all these people? Alistair, spotting the prices of the main courses, lapsed into a stunned silence.

Verena and Miranda squabbled on sight. When Miranda lit up a cigarette before the waiter had taken their order, Verena's nostrils flared and she fanned herself with the menu. When Miranda ordered lobster and avocado terrine, Verena exclaimed, 'Goodness me, lobster! How very extravagant.'

Miranda, prettier and sexier than ever in a beige suede dress, hardly bothered to disguise her colossal lack of interest in her future parents-in-law. Quickly marking Verena down as the original mother-in-law from hell, and Charlie's sisters as too gross to count, she interrogated Alistair about Scotland and found his replies unsatisfactory. The Ardnessaig Estate was smaller than she'd envisaged and, she soon established, run down. Nor did the Crieffs seem to know Miranda's Scottish friends with houses in Lyford Cay. She had assumed, since Charlie's parents must be old friends of Marcus Brand's, that they moved in similar circles, but now was beginning to doubt it.

Verena turned to Miranda. 'Do you shoot?'

'Only boar.'

'Do you indeed? Where do you do that?'

'In the Ardennes. With Philippe Fontainebleau.'

'And who is Philippe Fontainebleau when he's at home?'

'We met when he was working at Merrill Lynch in New York. He's such fun. His cousin would be the King of France if they'd kept their royal family.'

'And you come from Jersey yourself, Charlie tells me.'

'My father lives outside St Helier. My mother's married to an American reinsurance broker and lives in Bermuda.'

'Gracious.' Verena made her disapproval felt. 'And remind me where you met my son? He did tell me, but I seem to have forgotten.'

'At cocktails with the Silcoxes.'

'The who? I don't believe I've heard of them.'

'Sir Iain and Lady Silcox? He's made millions in the City. In fact, they've just bought a sporting estate in Scotland themselves, right near the top, for stalking parties. Nina Campbell's doing up the lodge for them, from top to bottom.'

Verena Crieff assessed her daughter-in-law anew. After forty minutes of sparring, each knew that in the other they had met their match. Both realised they disliked and distrusted each other, and that the feeling was mutual. Verena regarded Miranda as several notches too common for her son, and later described her to Charlie's sisters as 'an adventuress'. Miranda, in turn, regarded Verena as a pathetic old snob, totally out of the loop socially, and liable to be a burden on them in the future.

The house Miranda persuaded Charlie to buy in Upper Phillimore Gardens was one of the largest and most expensive in the cherry-lined Kensington street. But as she said at the time, 'If you can borrow the money from Cruickshank's at a low rate of interest, it makes sense to do it. The way house prices are moving in London, we'll be getting richer every day.'

The great white stucco mansion, detached and double-fronted, with a Greek family living on one side and Iranian exiles on the other, at first struck Charlie as ludicrously big for them. 'What the hell would we do with nine bedrooms? And the survey is terrible. The whole place is falling down.'

Miranda was reassuring. 'Two bedrooms are in the basement, so they don't count. The maid will be living down there. Anyway, you choose houses for their reception rooms and these are perfect. You do want to give dinner parties, don't you? I thought you wanted the Silcoxes to come to dinner, and Marcus?'

'Yes, yes, of course I do,' Charlie hurriedly agreed. He was particularly anxious to entertain Marcus. Ever since Wyoming, he'd been worrying about the continued presence of Christina in Marcus's life. They had been together for more than two years now, and each day he feared he might wake up to hear she was pregnant. It made sense to stay very close to his godfather at the moment. At the wedding lunch, he had split Marcus and Christina up, placing her at a distant table full of young, spivvy lechers in the hope one of them might get off with her, but it hadn't worked. In Nassau, where Marcus had lent them Sandy Cove for their honeymoon, Charlie had one day asked the old boatboy, Carlton, whether he thought the chief and Christina would ever get hitched, and he'd replied, 'Don't ask me, Mr Crieff, I don't know nothin'. But dem's a mighty fine pair of yams dat lady's got on her chest.'

Charlie had no conception of how expensive it could be to renovate and decorate a London house. It was, as their architect put it, a total gut job. Six months after he'd borrowed almost two million pounds from Cruickshank & Willis at two-and-a-half per cent, all that was left of the place was the façade, shored up by steel girders. Even as his admiration grew for Miranda's fiercesome efficiency, he began to worry about the state of his finances. It became clear he had married a woman with standards, a perfectionist for whom no detail could be resolved without the advice of an acknowledged expert. Lighting consultants were engaged to work with the interior designer devising mood lighting for every room and corridor. Sound engineers installed an integrated stereo system that pumped perfectly balanced music throughout the house. Specialist kitchen designers planned and built a high-tech version of a peasant's kitchen in Provence. Four French craftsmen arrived from Toulouse to lay flagstones in the hall. A company that specialised in the fitting of temperature and humidity-controlled wine cellars was commissioned to install a giant glass-fronted cabinet that held four hundred bottles. As the house took shape, Charlie came to see that it expressed in bricks and mortar everything he had achieved in his career; the lavish comfort of the interiors – the gas log fires in every room, the banks of halogen lights, the incredibly thick chintz curtains, lined and interlined, and their majestic swagged pelmets, the tapestry-covered stool in the library arranged with all the newest magazines, the needlepoint cushions with their facetious mottoes ('Good Girls go to Heaven, Bad Girls go Shopping'), the marble steam room, power showers and deep cedar-lined clothes cupboards – all these were the visible manifestations of his success, just compensation for his hard work. By an interesting psychological sleight-of-mind, the very fact of living in such a large house in Upper Phillimore Gardens convinced Charlie he deserved to live there. That his borrowing exceeded one hundred per cent of the house's market value was a detail he chose not to focus on.

Miranda's passion for experts extended into everyday life. Soon it seemed to Charlie that half the domestics in London were on his payroll, and half the alternative health quacks too. In addition to Maha, their Filipino housekeeper, and her friend Conceptia who came in to help with the ironing, there was the man who did the window boxes, the girl who delivered flowers once a week for the hall, the retired Guardsman who polished his shoes and sponged his suits. When they gave dinner parties, they hired a chef and a butler to hand around, plus – for some reason lost on Charlie – significant tips for Maha, Conceptia and any other Filipinos in the Kensington area who fancied wielding a dishcloth. During the day, Miranda was a magnet for masseurs, yoga and Pilates teachers, manicurists and shiatsu experts. One afternoon, returning home early from work, Charlie found a reflexologist with his portable table and a personal trainer waiting on the doorstep for his wife, who was late back from a tennis lesson.

She had a gift for running comfortable houses. When he arrived home in the evening, gas fires blazed in every fireplace. Ice was waiting for him in the bucket by the little sink in the walk-in drinks cupboard, the door of which was cunningly disguised as a wall of books with dummy leather spines. If they were going out later on (which invariable they were), his evening clothes had been laid out in readiness by Maha on the bed in his dressing room. Charlie's only complaint about life in his marital home was the sweltering hothouse micro-climate. Having been brought up at Ard-nessaig without central heating, he found the perpetual ninety-degree temperature unbearable. Radiators emitted stifling vapours twenty-four hours a day; towel rails were scalding. He slunk about the house late at night turning down thermostats, but by morning they had been turned back up.

Increasingly, they became embroiled in London's charity circuit, taking tables at balls and fashion shows. The Hon Mrs Charles Crieff was invited to join the committee for a film premier at the Odeon, Leicester Square to benefit an AIDS charity, the other members of which included Lady Weinberg, Mrs Wafic Said, Mrs Vivien Duffield, the Hon Mrs Rocco Forte, Emma Thompson and Kenneth Branagh, a gay decorator, a fashionable florist and a society couturier. The Princess of Wales agreed to be Patron of the evening. In no time they were attending a fundraiser every fortnight, as word got out that the glamorous Crieffs were always good for a £5,000 table. When Miranda was appointed a Vice Chairman of KidZone, a fashionable charity set up to convert a church hall in Ladbroke Grove into a performing arts centre for multi-cultural disadvantaged children, she knew she'd arrived.

Charlie remained determined to get Marcus over for a dinner party, preferably without Christina. Liaising with Barbara, they eventually identified a date four months ahead when Marcus would be stopping over in London for one night between Singapore and New York.

'We've got to make sure this is a really great evening,' Charlie told Miranda. 'We need to think carefully about who else to invite with him.'

'What about that friend of yours with the American wife? The one who was your best man. He's another of Marcus's godchildren, isn't he?'

'Actually I don't think that's a particularly good idea. Jamie's a bit juvenile. We need slightly heavier hitters, with Marcus coming.'

In the end they invited Sir Iain and Camilla Silcox, the German Princess Marie-Christine Schoenmann-Ausberg-Konwitz, a French banker who worked at Paribas and his English wife who Miranda knew from Hurlingham, and the youngest daughter of a Greek shipping dynasty with her latest husband, who they'd met through the KidZone committee.

As the day of the great dinner approached, Miranda's list of things they still needed for the house grew and grew. Although by returning most of their wedding presents to Harrods and trading them in for cash, which they put towards better tableware than they'd been given, they were well provided with china and glass, there remained many glaring omissions. 'Do you realise we haven't got a single pudding glass?' Miranda asked, almost accusingly. 'And we need cut-glass bowls for the raspberries and *tiramisù*. And scented candles. It's all right for you, Charlie, you'll be at your office all day, but I'm going to have to rush about all over London, buying all this stuff. The only place you can get raspberries out of season is Harrods Food Hall. And if it's raining you can never find a taxi.'

By the time he got home, however, the house was immaculate. The hall smelt overpoweringly of scented candles and stephanotis. A pair of very camp hired butlers were decanting claret in the kitchen, a chef was preparing a crown of lamb, and Maha, assisted by three Filipino friends, was filling water jugs with Badoit. Of Miranda, there was no sign.

'Evening, Maha. Everything under control, I see. Seen Mrs Crieff anywhere?'

'Very sorry, sir, madam is upstairs. Foot man comes.' Charlie never understood why it was necessary for Maha to apologise every time he asked her a simple question, and he glared crossly. It had been a trying day at work and he wished this dinner wasn't happening, except it was so important.

Upstairs in their bedroom, Miranda was stretched out on a massage table in her underwear, having her feet pressed by an elderly reflexologist with a white goatee.

'Hi, darling. You've met Paul, haven't you? Ow! Yes, press that bit there – just there – a bit deeper. It's my kidney, I think, or the gall bladder.'

Charlie hardly bothered to acknowledge Paul. 'We met

on the doorstep when my wife was late.' He wanted to add 'as usual' but bit his tongue. He didn't want this evening to start on a sour note.

'You'll never guess,' Miranda said, 'but I was telling Paul about tonight, and why my feet were going to be particularly tense because of all the organising, and he knows Marcus. Or at least his girlfriend does. Isn't that an amazing coincidence?'

'Really?' said Charlie, who hardly thought it so amazing. 'How's that?'

'My partner's daughter, Saffron, is his goddaughter,' said Paul. 'She went to stay with him a couple of years ago in America.'

'God!' said Charlie. 'I was staying there too, I know Saffron.' Even now, when he heard her name, his heart fluttered. 'Er, how is she these days?'

'Definitely on the mend. Which is a relief for everyone after her recent setbacks.'

As the guests started to arrive, and were shown to the drawing room by one camp hired butler to be handed a glass of champagne by the second, Charlie and Miranda stood against the fireplace in satisfaction, knowing everything was perfect. Miranda looked sensational in a backless silver Moschino cocktail dress worn with the giant Theo Fennell earrings Charlie had given her for her birthday. Charlie himself wore the navy blue suit, white shirt and dark tie that had become his standard dinner party uniform. Marcus and Iain, recognising in each other players of similar weight, had gravitated together to discuss the American economy. Charlie thought he would leave them undisturbed for a few more minutes, before introducing his godfather to the Greek shipping heiress. At dinner, Marcus would be sitting between the princess and Miranda, and he wanted to ensure Marcus met Helena – as another prize exhibit – before they went through to eat.

At nine o'clock, Maha hovered at the drawing-room door to indicate they were ready. Already on the table were bowls of cold vichyssoise, each decorated with a sprig of dill and a dollop of caviar. Charlie, who had placed himself on the other side of the Princess, so as to be near Marcus, was sure that the gleaming table, with its orchid centrepieces and successful worldly guests, must be making a good impression on the tycoon. He had always identified with the biblical maxim 'To the rich it shall be given', and trusted Marcus would abide by it when making his will.

Charlie's reward came over the raspberries. 'Are you managing to spend much time in Nassau?' he asked Marcus. Then, for the benefit of Marie-Christine, he added, 'Marcus has the most wonderful house in Lyford Cay, which he very generously lent us for our honeymoon. But he's so busy flying around the world buying new businesses, I doubt he gets there that often, do you, Marcus?'

'Actually we were in Nassau in September. Christina and I squeezed in a week, largely to keep the staff on their toes. They become idle if you neglect them for too long. Start thinking it's their own house.'

At the mention of Christina, Charlie stiffened. 'And how is the lovely Christina?' he asked casually.

'History. Thing ran out of juice. So it was 'bye-bye Christina.'

Charlie felt exhilarated. Marcus and Christina were no longer an item and the danger was over, at least for now.

'You'd better have another glass of champagne, Marcus,' he said. 'Christina was marvellous-looking, but it was pretty common knowledge around town that she was in it for the money.'

Wonderfully light-headed and, he supposed, tens of millions of pounds richer, Charlie instructed a hired butler to open several more bottles of Krug as they all went back through to the drawing room for coffee.

As she led the way, Miranda's eyes darted critically across the sofas and armchairs, checking that their cushions had been properly replumped by Maha and her helpers during dinner, and that the dirty before-dinner glasses had been cleared away and replaced with clean ones. While she supervised the distribution of coffee and camomile tea, Marcus took up a position on the club fender in front of the fireplace, and all the women of the party sat at his feet on the carpet, or perched on nearby chairs, eager to catch every *bon mot* from the famous and brilliant tycoon. Several of the women, including the French banker's wife, the Greek shipping heiress and even Camilla Silcox, were gently flirting with him, and the Princess, who had drunk too much at dinner, became outrageous, angling for an invitation to his yacht.

'I am so impressed you actually bought your own yacht, Marcus,' she declared. 'I have heard this crude saying – if it flies, floats or fornicates, it is better to rent.'

Marcus gave her a hard stare. 'Whole point of owning a plane or a boat in the first place. Increases your rate of fornication. Never yet invited a woman on to either one of mine who didn't end up in the owner's cabin. No doubt I'm too cynical about the female species. You'll have to come and stay yourself one weekend and then we shall see.'

The Princess coloured, but promised to give him her number before she left. 'I live in a little cottage just behind Harrods,' she volunteered. 'It is very quiet and private.'

Suddenly anxious that she was blatantly offering herself up as Christina's successor, and might actually pose a greater long-term threat than the Las Vegas showgirl, Charlie waded in. 'Marie-Christine lives in the most lovely little mews with a charming paved garden. You probably know Erskine Greer, the entrepreneur, who pays her rent for her?'

Princess Marie-Christine shot him a venomous look. 'You are too generous about my little cottage, Charlie. It is so small, it is nothing. And the garden is a mess. I employed this cute young gardener, Jamie someone-or-other, to take care of it for me, but he never came back to finish the job.'

39: June, 1990

Jamie sat in the cubicle, trousers round his ankles, reading a dirty magazine. It was his fifth visit to the clinic in three weeks, and the limited selection of pornography was beginning to lose its punch. The nurse had placed copies of *Mayfair*, *Penthouse* and *Club International*, all horribly dog-eared, on a plastic stool to help him along, but they were the same issues as on previous visits. Unsure he could reach orgasm staring at the familiar beaver-shots, he closed his eyes and thought of Saffron, stark naked and smothered in baby oil, grinding against his groin.

They had been coming to the clinic in Welbeck Street for six months, ever since Abigail, anxious at not being pregnant after three years of trying, arranged to see a fertility doctor. They had been married four years and, at thirty-three, she longed for a baby. There seemed no reason why she couldn't have one, she was healthy and vivacious. Her GP told her to stay calm, not to overdo things and to keep trying. 'I'll be very surprised if nature doesn't take its course. You and your husband both look like respectable citizens. Not heavy drinkers, are you, no drug abuse?'

Jamie found it almost ironic Abigail couldn't get a bun in the oven. For fifteen years he'd been busy shagging everything that moved, praying he wouldn't put anyone up the duff. There had been a couple of near misses, the odd split condom in the Tunnel of Love, but nothing drastic. Then, after all that, he ended up with a bird with unripe eggs or whatever.

He could hear the nurse pacing the corridor outside, waiting for him to hand over his offering in the plastic receptacle. The moment he came, he had to unbolt the door, pass it round and she'd scuttle off to the refrigerator while it was still piping hot. The nurse was a fanciable Australian – Jodie – and Jamie enjoyed flirting with her. It

403

struck him as a rotten waste, expending all this energy on a hand-job with Jodie standing outside. The first time he handed her the receptacle, he asked, 'Hey, Jodie, what if I want to come a second time?'

Abigail's anxiety over her failure to conceive became more manic as time went by. She consulted a fertility specialist in Upper Cavendish Street who sent her to have her tubes blown, and another in Harley Street who prescribed two weeks of bed rest every month around ovulation. Jamie noticed that, in place of the Courtauld Institute art books by Ernst Gombrich and Bernard Berenson, her bedside table was filled with self-help manuals on conception and pregnancy. At Abigail's insistence, they began to follow rigorous regimes, sometimes making love three times a day for a month, sometimes abstaining from sex altogether for weeks on end, to lull her womb into a state of benign relaxation before going at it hammer and tongs. Despairing of conventional medicine, she tried alternative therapists, including a Chinese herbalist in Gerrard Street who prescribed snake venom. An acupuncturist claimed to have released an energy blockage in her ovaries, and a reflexologist with a goatee recommended by Miranda Crieff stimulated her adrenal gland. Every month, when her period came, she was overwhelmed by sadness.

Transfixed by *Club International*, Jamie was thinking that the girl leaning across the bamboo hanging-chair looked awfully like Zara Fane used to, though Zara would, of course, be twenty years older than the tart in the picture. The bird in the next story reminded him of Arabella Gilborne. There were times, he had to admit, when he found monogamy a struggle. It was as though, after years of grazing a sexual smörgasbord, he was suddenly expected to eat the same set meal night after night.

Calling out over the top of the cubicle, he said, 'Jodie! Be a sport, love, and come in here with your top off. I need something real to gawp at.'

'You behave, Mr Temple,' Jodie called back. 'And get a move on in there, there are others waiting at reception.'

As it happened, it was a health article in *Vogue* which

alerted Abigail to the possibilities of IVF. Pioneered by Dr Patrick Steptoe and Dr Robert Edwards at Oldham General Hospital near Manchester in the late seventies, she read, In Vitro Fertilisation or pre-embryo transfer had made it feasible for hundreds of childless couples to conceive a child. Within twenty-four hours, Abigail had secured a referral from her GP and booked an appointment for herself and Jamie.

He had an irrational fear of hospitals, particularly fertility hospitals. Like all men, he was freaked out by the possibility that their failure could be his fault, that he was shooting blanks. Outwardly confident, he accompanied her under protest, saying he couldn't keep leaving 60 Montpelier Place and why was he needed to come along anyway?

A consultant surgeon explained to them the principles of IVF: how the woman's eggs were extracted at the right time from the ovary, injected with the father's sperm and left to divide for a few days in a nutrient solution in a laboratory petri dish. Then the fertilised egg was implanted in the womb and, with luck, would grow into an embryo. The success or otherwise of the transfer could be assessed in thirteen days, and the chances of success were about one in seven.

At the end of his explanation, the consultant turned to them and said, 'I'm sure you must have lots of questions, Mr and Mrs Temple, which I'm happy to answer now or, if any come to you later on, feel free to ring me.'

'Is this what they call test-tube babies?' Jamie asked.

'That is indeed the popular term for it. We tend to use less sensational language.'

'If Abby goes ahead, does that mean we might end up with septuplets like that old woman in the newspapers?'

'I don't think that's very likely,' replied the consultant reassuringly, 'I'm sure we'll all think we've done a good job if you produce one healthy baby.'

'Pity,' said Jamie. 'I hoped the *Daily Express* might pay for their education. It costs a bloody fortune, you know.'

Jangly and exhausted from the massive course of hormonal therapy that preceded her monthly visits to the clinic,

Abigail felt she was cracking up. The injections made her irrational and, however much she told herself it was a side-effect of medication, she still spent a week every month in tears, raging at Jamie, raging at the world, and generally being impossible. She was obsessed by the notion that, unless she produced a baby, he would leave her, and that he would be justified in leaving her. As she told Mary on the telephone one afternoon, while Mary was desperately trying to track down a temp to cover in the Senior Partner's office at Goldman Sachs the next morning, why should Jamie be condemned to spend his life with a barren wife, when hundreds of women would love to bear his children? In these moods, she was inconsolable. Nor were matters made easier by Harriet, who took to ringing her daughter while Zubin was out of town, hinting it was high time she produced a grandchild, and how she was sure that would be enough to heal the rift with her father. Frequently, when he arrived home from the hotel, Jamie would find Abigail hunched up in bed with the light switched off, unwilling or unable to talk. He tried to be sympathetic, reminding himself it was all the fault of the monkey glands, but it was tough.

Nor did it help that the hormonal injections made her bloat. After six months of IVF, she had put on twenty-five pounds and none of her dresses would do up. In her misery at her ballooning figure, she took to comfort eating, buying Hershey bars ten at a time from Selfridge's food hall. As Jamie confided to Charlie, during one of their increasingly infrequent after-work drinks, 'My wife's fatter than she was on that holiday in the Bahamas. I'm telling you, Charlie, when she rolls over in bed, I'm scared of being flattened.'

40: June, 1990

Saffron was sitting on a swing-seat on the flagstoned terrace of Nick Blackwater's faux-Elizabethan mansion on the St George's Hill Estate, Weybridge, in Surrey. She was wearing a headset plugged into a Sony Walkman, listening to her new boyfriend's classic album *Next Best Thing (to Paradise)*. Although the album had sold more than seventy million copies worldwide since its release twenty years earlier, and turned the four members of the supergroup Blacktongue into multi-millionaires, Saffron had never in fact listened to it properly before, something she'd wisely concealed from Nick. As the band's bass guitarist and lyricist, beneath his self-deprecating, working-boy-made-good persona, Nick Blackwater expected the recognition.

She closed her eyes, trying to decipher the words, and sipped the glass of iced coffee Nick's driver-cum-butler, Harrison, had brought out to her. Dimly, she recognised some of the tracks from her Gledhow Gardens days; Perry and Sim were always playing Blacktongue. To Saffron, some of the lyrics about blind men seeing with the eyes of small children seemed rather ridiculous, but the tunes were good and catchy. She could have done without the guitar solos.

It was a perfect English summer's afternoon and the warm breeze felt good against her bare breasts. Despite its location in the middle of an exclusive residential estate, Nick's house was completely private, surrounded by a dry moat and fifteen acres of topiary and beautiful walled gardens. The rock star himself had driven over to the Royal County of Berkshire Polo Club at Winkfield for some practice chukkas before the big tournament on Saturday.

Sometimes it seemed weird to Saffron that she was living with Nick at all. He had pulled her at a music industry event, driven her down that same night, and here she still was five months later. Something else she'd never told him was that, at the time they'd met, she hadn't a clue who he was. She couldn't decide whether or not he'd appreciate knowing that, it could go either way.

He was twenty-three years older than she was, fifty-five or fifty-six she reckoned, though it was a touchy subject, a bit overweight, especially in jeans. But the first thing she'd noticed about him was his wonderfully soft leather jacket. 'Go on, try it on,' he'd urged her. 'You'll look better in it than me, babe,' which she did. 'Come down to my place,' he'd said later. 'I've got cupboard-loads of clobber down there.'

She had drifted into living with him, almost without noticing. He'd said, 'Why not stop over Monday, Saff?' Then: 'Why not stay Wednesday? You can see me fall off my horse.' At some point Harrison had collected her stuff from London and they were an item.

Occasionally curmudgeonly and introspective, Nick's dark moods seldom lasted longer than half a day, and he was around all the time. Once every two years Blacktongue reformed for a farewell world stadium tour, otherwise he was at a loose end. He pottered about the grounds, inspecting his collection of veteran Bristols, sometimes taking one out for a spin with his mechanic, or practising his polo swing on the wooden horse in the refectory. Periodically he drove up to London for the day, to check out his Covent Garden burger restaurant, Riffs, decorated with rock memorabilia. Three afternoons a week he practised with his polo team, Blacktongue Blues, which he sponsored to the tune of two million pounds a year, including the hire of two deadly Colombian nine-goal assassins.

As Saffron quickly discovered, it was a sore point for Nick that nobody listened to or bought his new records. Blacktongue had produced seven albums since *Next Best Thing* (*to Paradise*), one every three years, but sales were diabolical. The most recent release, despite a torrent of hype and cover stories in *Q* and the *NME*, failed even to make the top one hundred. *Next Best Thing*, however, continued to shift in hundreds of thousands. In a recent poll, it had been voted one of the fifty greatest albums of all time, two places ahead of *Imagine*.

Nick had installed a recording studio in the old kitchens, with their enormous floor-to-ceiling mullioned windows, and still jammed several nights a month with session musicians and various iconic rock celebrities. Saffron grew used to finding Sting and several former members of Pink Floyd, bleary-eyed in the kitchen, when she surfaced in the morning, having jammed through the night. But she knew it infuriated Nick that the public was indifferent to his new music, only buying more and more copies of *Next Best Thing*. The average age of his fans was pushing fifty, and having first bought the album as teenagers in vinyl, they had bought the cassette several times more for the car, and later the CD. Blacktongue's record company made a fortune releasing as many obscure 'Collectors' recordings as they could exhume – *Next Best Thing (to Paradise)* performed live at the Key Arena, Seattle – which sold like hot cakes. When she went to watch Nick play at the Albert Hall, Saffron was amazed by the sea of bald heads in the audience.

The person who'd been most excited by the advent of Nick Blackwater in her life was Amaryllis. She told Saffron, confidentially, that she thought she'd had a thing with Blacktongue's drummer at one time, though it might not have been him. Nick was cool about Amaryllis, Paul and Lorcan coming down for Sunday lunch at the mansion, when they were also joined by Nick's parents, Elsie and Bert, a retired stationmaster, who lived in the gatehouse at the top of the drive. Amaryllis secretly resented being lumped in with the other old parents ('It's like a senior citizens' club, darling') but didn't say anything to Nick, in case they weren't invited back.

The only awkwardness in Saffron's thing with Nick lay in her relationship with his truculent, fucked-up daughters, Leah and Calypso. The children of his first marriage to his childhood sweetheart, who had been brought up by their mother in Camden Town, the girls bristled with needy contempt for their famous father, and instantly resented Saffron who was closer to their own age than their mother's.

Their first encounters had been agony, with Leah cutting her dead and Calypso's constant references to Nick's exes, all of whom, she inferred, they'd seen off. But to Saffron's enormous credit – and to Nick's astonishment – she quickly won them over, lending them her groovy new clothes and organising tickets for their dad's concerts. Within a couple of months, Calypso was ringing Saffron for girlie chats.

When Saffron was asked by her mother, who'd drunk far too much Chablis one Sunday lunchtime, what the sex was like with Nick, Saffron didn't reply. The fact was, there wasn't a lot of it. Having slept indiscriminately with hundreds of groupies after concerts for two decades, mostly when pissed, and having consequently caught every venereal and urinary disease going, Nick's enthusiasm for screwing was severely impaired. When he peed, he experienced pain in his penis and, one way or another, he got a bigger buzz these days from a great first-growth St Emilion. He was considering buying a vineyard in the hills behind Grimaud in the South of France, just to see how they made the stuff.

He was in love with Saffron, of course – she was the classiest bird he'd been with since Angie walked out on him. But he valued her most for her availability, and for being easy on the eye.

As for Saffron, coming after the turbulence of her manipulative relationship with Marcus, she was glad to be with a man who was more insecure than herself. To keep him happy, she told him, 'You know, Nick, your new music's much better than your old stuff. It really gets it.' Nick Blackwater's face lit up. But a few minutes later he asked suspiciously, 'You aren't saying you don't rate the early albums, Saff?'

Nick was in a filthy mood, not helped by a long tailback of cars ahead of them at the pump. They had been forty minutes late setting off, and would now be pushed to reach Midhurst in time for the match. Blacktongue Blues were in the semi-finals of the Veuve Clicquot Gold Cup at Cowdray, and he was playing.

'Jesus Christ, what are those people *doing*?' Ahead of them on the forecourt, an elderly couple in a Hillman Hunter were tooling about with the pump, apparently having trouble releasing it from the holster.

'And *now* what's their problem? I don't fucking believe this, they can't find the key for the petrol cap. Go on, hoot them, Saff.' He drummed his fingers on the walnut dashboard of the black Range Rover.

'Nick, why don't you just get out and go look round the shop or something? You're making me tense. I'll do the petrol.'

She edged the Range Rover into the adjacent bay and began filling the tank, watching the digital display pass forty pounds, then fifty. The way these machines guzzled juice, they'd probably have to fill up again on the way home.

Next to her, the elderly lady was also watching the display, as her husband pumped petrol in little fits and starts into the Hillman. 'Stop! Stop there, Derek. No, ten more pence to go, slowly now. Whoa! That's five pounds exactly.'

The lady had been watching Saffron curiously. 'Excuse me for asking,' she said, 'but aren't you Saffron Weaver?'

'Er, yes, how very clever of you,' she replied uncertainly.

'You don't know us,' said Belinda Merrett, 'but I believe you're friends with our daughter, Mary. Mary Gore. Merrett as was.'

'Mary? Of course I know Mary. How is she? I haven't seen her since America when we were staying with Marcus.'

'She's just about coping, I think,' said Belinda. 'Clara's become quite a handful these days, as she gets bigger. She's nearly eight now. Well, I'll tell Mary we saw you. She'll be so interested. You didn't mind us saying hello?'

'It was lovely to meet you,' Saffron replied warmly. Then she asked, 'How did you even know who I was, by the way?'

'Oh, goodness me, your picture was in the local paper with your popstar friend, when you opened the garden for the nurses. I cut it out and sent it to Mary.'

'Here comes Nick now, Mrs Merrett, let me introduce you.'

'Can you fucking believe this?' he stormed, climbing into the car and slamming the door. 'Someone's going to get the fucking bullet for this. The only Blacktongue tape that Texaco shop sells is *Next Best Thing*.'

The Lodsworth River Ground had seldom looked more bucolic. The lawns swept down to the River Rother, bordered on two sides by sweet chestnut trees and on the fourth by the ruins of old Cowdray Castle. The stands were packed with spectators in Panamas and pretty summer dresses. The last stragglers were reeling out from the sponsors' hospitality tents, where they had eaten an elaborate four-course lunch prepared by the celebrity chef Anton Mosimann, and were now being harried to their seats by public relations people. The match was due to start in five minutes, and an Australian commentator was building up the suspense over a crackling tannoy.

Down at the pony lines, there was consternation. Where the hell was Nick? Two girl grooms in Blacktongue t-shirts were holding his ponies in readiness. Another was standing by with his sticks, helmet, knee guards and boots. Carlos Ingracias, the elder of the two devastatingly talented and arrogant Ingracias brothers, looked at his watch and said, 'We should play anyway, with three players. It won't make any difference, it might help in fact.'

But they knew that, without the patron, they wouldn't be going anywhere. He may only be a one-goal player, but he paid the bills. One of the grooms went in search of the umpire, to warn him there might be a slight delay.

A mobile telephone went off, and Nick's voice, loud enough to be heard forty yards away, boomed around the grounds. 'We are stuck, you might like to know, in a traffic jam in Midhurst-sodding-High-Street. Bumper to bumper. Can someone kindly get us out of here?'

'Where are you exactly?' asked one of the grooms.

'Christ knows. I can see a Chinese take-away, the Peking Dog or something. And, hold on, a school coming up on the left.'

'I know. I'll be right with you, Nick,' said the groom, galloping off across the watermeadows with a spare pony, in the direction of the traffic.

Five minutes later, when Nick Blackwater cantered on to the ground with Carlos and Gracida Ingracias, and the young British professional Hugo Gilborne, there was a roar of approval for the rock star, and the Midhurst town band struck up the title track from *Next Best Thing*.

By the time Saffron, who had been left to inch through the traffic in the Range Rover, arrived at the ground it was half-time, Blacktongue Blues were three goals up, all scored by the Ingraciases, and Nick was sweating like a pig and mopping his neck with a towel.

Still annoyed with him for bailing out of the car, and knowing Nick was always tetchy between chukkas, Saffron went to tread divots. The ground was thronging with spectators, all dutifully pressing the churned turf with the soles of their loafers. As she reached the middle of the ground, a familiar voice called out, 'Saffron!'

Charlie was striding towards her with a haughty blonde in a huge hat, flashing lots of cleavage. My God, he's put on weight though, Saffron thought; he didn't have that paunch in Wyoming. It was true that Charlie in his early thirties was looking ten years older; his hairline had receded a further two inches from an already-high forehead, and his white chinos strained at the waistband. His face, beneath his Panama, was red and bloated.

'I don't think you've met Miranda, my wife.' They shook hands, and Miranda looked Saffron up and down, noting the short Versace dress, a present from Nick.

Having heard a lot about her from Charlie, and suspecting she might have been a girlfriend somewhere along the line, Miranda regarded her with suspicion. Not much character, she thought, but she had to admit Saffron was fabulous-looking with legs almost as good as her own.

'What brings you to polo, Saffron? I've never seen you here before. That cowboy friend of yours isn't playing, is he, Red or Zach or whatever his name was?' Charlie said it lightly, but meant it to hurt. He still hadn't forgiven her for choosing the ranch-hand over himself in Wyoming. Since then, she'd dropped totally out of his life, and he assumed she was back working as a counter-jumper in a shoe shop or jeans boutique. He was keen she should realise she'd backed the wrong horse with Zach, and looked for ways of alluding to his own big house and smart new friends.

'How are you getting back to London after the match?' he asked. 'If you don't mind perching on the jump seat, I can run you back in the Aston Martin. We're heading for Upper Phillimore Gardens.'

'Thanks, Charlie, but I'm going back to Surrey afterwards.'

'Not staying with Mary Merrett, are you? She's the only person I've ever met who lives in Surrey. It's all a bit chi-chi round there for me.'

'Well, it's where I'm living.'

Better and better, Charlie thought. She can't even afford to live in London. 'Most of our friends seem to live in Gloucestershire or Oxfordshire, I don't know why. Miranda and I have just spent a very amusing weekend near Chipping Norton, Sonny and Rosita Marlborough came over for dinner on Saturday night.'

'Sounds posh,' said Saffron. 'We had scrambled eggs in the kitchen and went to bed.'

'Maybe see you later,' Charlie said, delighted with himself. He reckoned he had made the point.

The second half reversed Blacktongue's lead. Kerry Packer's Elliston White team scored four goals in succession and moved ahead in the seventh chukka. Nick was agitated, charging about the field, cutting across his own players and cursing Gracida Ingracias who threatened to flounce off the lawn in a huff. Only two brilliant long shots by Carlos secured victory in extra time.

Nick was ecstatic. Scooping up Saffron at the pony lines, he led the team to the picket enclosure to collect the trophy from Viscount Cowdray and the wife of the Managing Director of Veuve Clicquot, the sponsors. As he held the cup above his head, and the Ingraciases sprayed jeroboams of champagne over the spectators, Saffron noticed Charlie and Miranda staring at them. His mouth hanging open in astonishment, Charlie was trying to fathom what the hell Saffron was doing in the enclosure with Nick Blackwater of

Blacktongue, whose *Next Best Thing* album was one of the few records Charlie had ever bought. And why, he wondered, was Nick's arm wrapped around Saffron's waist?

Bolstered by the good news of Marcus's split from Christina, Miranda persuaded Charlie they should look for a house in the country.

'You do realise,' she said, 'we are the only people we know who spend every single weekend in London?'

'No, we don't. We've been away virtually every weekend all summer.'

'That's staying with people, it's different. I mean it, Charlie, it's getting embarrassing. We can't spend our lives cadging off friends, we've got to invite them back sometimes.'

'We're already borrowing a lot on Phillimore Gardens, I'm not sure about taking on a second mortgage.' Charlie felt uncomfortable. He hated to deny his wife anything, knowing it spelt trouble. As she frequently reminded him, when she'd been married to Boobie, he'd indulged her in everything. 'Charlie's such a skinflint,' she liked to proclaim at dinner. 'It's his Scottish ancestry. It's like getting blood out of a stone.'

'I just think it would be better if we waited two or three years,' Charlie said. 'Two decent bonuses and I'll begin paying off the capital loan on this house. At the moment, we're only covering the interest. Anyway, the time for a country house is after we have children.'

'We should start looking now. You know how long it takes to find the right place. The Silcoxes looked for six years.' Miranda would not be fobbed off. When she was like this, Charlie knew she was implacable. He hadn't forgotten the tantrum when he'd suggested Scotland for a fortnight in the summer, rather than the three or four weeks she was accustomed to in Soto Grande.

In the end, Charlie conceded it could do no harm to get a feel for the market, and what was out there, leaving the decision on whether or not to buy until they saw the right house. Privately, he hoped it wouldn't be for a long, long time.

He had reckoned without his wife's astonishing energy and thoroughness. Within three days, every country estate agent had been contacted and the hall table in Upper Phillimore Gardens was piled high with details of Queen Anne manor houses and Georgian rectories. Tucked inside one sixteen-page full-colour brochure, he found a letter to Miranda from an agent confirming the hunt for a suitable house 'in the million-plus bracket', but respectfully suggesting they might need to go slightly higher to secure the right property.

One evening, he arrived home to find two smart young men from a property search company, Estate Locate, sitting in his drawing room. Road maps of England lay open on the tapestry-covered stool, and they were helping Miranda pinpoint the areas of the country where she most wanted to live. Miranda explained that Estate Locate, for a fee of four per cent of the purchase price plus an upfront retainer of three thousand pounds, helped buyers secure the house of their dreams.

'Almost invariably the best properties don't come on to the open market at all,' explained Algy Thistlethwaite, who had a canary yellow silk handkerchief bursting out of his top pocket. 'If a house makes it into the front of *Country Life*, you know it's a dog.'

'And how do you get to hear about them first?' Charlie asked.

'Entirely word of mouth,' Algy assured him. 'It's all about networking. We make it our business to know every potential move, generally several months before it becomes official. Off the top of my head, I can think of four or five properties that'll be coming on to the market next spring, all of which might be exactly right for you.' Warming to his theme, Algy went on, 'Actually, one of our secret weapons is knowing in advance whose marriages are in trouble. When a couple hit the rocks, that's three potential pieces of new business for us. We sell the marital home, then help both parties locate a new one.'

'Charming,' said Charlie, who wanted a drink and a bath, preferably simultaneously, but sensed Miranda expected him to stay.

'I know it sounds callous, sir,' said Roly Touche, the junior of the two agents, 'but it's a jolly effective way of getting in first. I don't know whether you know the racing trainer Honkie Gilborne, but when we heard he was splitting from his wife, we put the whole deal together in four days, from flash to bang. That was a stud near Lambourn. Sold it sight unseen to Malaysians for three point six.'

'We've been talking to Mrs Crieff,' Algy said, 'and have established you don't want to be more than ninety minutes drive from your London residence.'

'I expect we could probably go a bit further, if necessary,' Charlie said.

'No, we couldn't.' Miranda spoke sharply. 'I imagine I'll be the one expected to collect the children from school and drive them down on a Friday night, right through the worst traffic, while you saunter down later on the train. Ninety minutes in the car is the absolute limit.' She glared at him.

'We gather you're looking in the Oxfordshire, Gloucestershire direction, sir,' said Roly. 'Nothing south or east of London – Essex, Suffolk, Kent?'

'Well, Suffolk's a possibility, I suppose. Convenient for the City.'

'No!' said Miranda firmly. 'No way.'

'And we understand you've ruled out Berkshire and Surrey?'

'God, yes,' Charlie said. 'If we're buying somewhere in the country, I'd prefer to be in the country, not some glorified golf course.'

'Totally understood,' said Algy, who shared a top-floor flat overlooking Clapham Common South Side. 'How about Hampshire or Wiltshire?'

'If we see the right house, we'll consider it. All we really need is a bedroom for us, some children's bedrooms, two or three decent-sized spare rooms and ideally a cottage for some help.'

'So that's seven bedrooms, in the main house?'

'Seven or eight, yes. Plus a room for Maha, our Filipino, which can be downstairs if necessary.'

'What about land?' asked Roly Touche, writing it all down.

'Not an issue,' said Charlie. 'Thirty, forty acres? The house ought to sit in the middle of its land. And a decent drive. One thing I definitely don't want is a house in a village. No Old Rectories next to the church, please.'

'We'll need a paddock,' Miranda said. 'And stables.'

'And a swimming pool and tennis court,' said Charlie. 'Don't mind if it's grass or hard,' he added flexibly.

'Hope you don't mind my being frank,' said Algy, 'but if you're looking for all this in Oxfordshire and Gloucestershire, I'm not sure your present budget is realistic. You did mention a guide price of one to one point five, Mrs Crieff? That whole Oxford-Cirencester-Tetbury triangle has gone through the roof. If you want to stay below one point five you'll need to go beyond the Escarpment, out beyond Evesham. We sold a fairly standard manor house near Cirencester for some people called Bembridge recently, and realised one point six. They were splitting up, so were delighted to get that price.'

'Seriously,' said Roly Touche, 'we have more than fifty instructions at the moment from clients with budgets north of one point seven, all looking for properties in the Oxfordshire area. Including one very famous rock star – actually it's Nick Mason, but I didn't say that – and there's a lot of silly City bonus money around.'

'I work in finance myself, actually,' nodded Charlie, feeling suddenly competitive. He didn't want these pipsqueaks to imagine he couldn't afford a proper country house. 'If we have to go higher, that doesn't present a prob.'

'Shall we say a ceiling of two mill then?' asked Algy, amending his briefing notes.

'Fine,' said Charlie. 'And make sure you show us the good stuff first, OK? Don't send any crap.

'Oh, and one last thing,' he added, as he poured a large whisky to take upstairs. 'If we're talking that kind of money,

I want a house with a decent name. Something Manor or Park. Hall and Priory are acceptable too. But I'm not living in a Meadowbanks or Cosy Nook, so don't bother sending the pretty pictures.'

Having embarked on the hunt for the perfect country house, Charlie soon found his enthusiasm matching, even exceeding, that of Miranda. He spent hours studying the brochures of ever-grander properties. Having established the Crieffs' financial ceiling as two million pounds, Estate Locate tantalised them with details of houses costing two-and-a-half million upwards. Charlie could now see they'd been totally unrealistic in imagining they could buy a country house for as little as a million quid. Some of the houses being offered at that price were little more than farmhouses; if you drove past them, you wouldn't look twice. He became expert at detecting the drawbacks of properties from their photographs and floorplans, without bothering to view. Either their halls were too small and mean, or the arrangement of reception rooms too pokey (he hated the 'railway carriage effect' of rooms leading into each other), or the ceilings too low and the approach unimposing. It was astonishing how many houses in Oxfordshire and Gloucestershire had beams and ghastly mullioned windows, or nowhere to park cars. Accompanied by Algy Thistlethwaite or Roly Touche, Charlie and Miranda criss-crossed the golden triangle, inspecting houses that invariably disappointed. And Algy unnerved them with stories of properties fetching dizzier and dizzier prices. The market was moving so quickly, he said, they were regularly receiving instructions from American and Far East clients impatient to spend four or five million, and they still couldn't find anything.

Charlie's list of essential attributes grew longer as his hubris increased. He felt that an orangery – or anyway a large conservatory – was vital, preferably with under-floor heating. A dovecote, he told Algy, was desirable, as was a good range of traditional outbuildings. The swimming pool should have a decent changing hut. He wanted smart entrance gates, such as he had grown up with at Ardnessaig.

He wanted a walled garden. He wanted a library. He desired 'mature woodland', as the brochures described any copse of brambles and mixed deciduous trees. Having read a newspaper article about the President of the Board of Trade Michael Heseltine, and how he was planting an arboretum of rare trees to enjoy in his old age, Charlie decided he would like to establish an arboretum himself.

He came to the conclusion that, if they were buying in the country at all, there was no point going for a second-rate set-up, which would last them only a few years. They should be investing in a 'house for life'. It would make better financial sense to really go for it this time – and pay later – rather than keep trading up with all the attendant moving costs.

His 1991 bonus promised to be his biggest ever. Marcus continued to use Cruickshank & Willis for his personal portfolio management, and Charlie jealously guarded every transaction. As the firm's largest private client, Marcus provided Charlie with his powerbase and security. Convinced his godfather would never consider switching his custom elsewhere, Charlie's arrogance grew, and the back-office staff in particular found him insufferable.

Where money was concerned, Charlie could no longer determine whether he was actually rich or poor. They lived incredibly well, but slightly less well than others in their set. His salary and bonuses, as they doubled and trebled, hardly seemed to keep pace with their expenditure. Sometimes it worried him that, two years after buying Upper Phillimore Gardens, he still hadn't paid off a single penny of its purchase price. But, in other moods, he felt unassailably rich and clever. Lauded by his friends as brilliantly successful, married to a stunning, well-dressed woman, the owner of a huge and impeccable Kensington house and heir to the Ardnessaig Estate in Angus, Charlie could be forgiven a measure of smugness. And always, in the back of his mind, was the prospect of a massive inheritance from Marcus. The difference between son and godson struck him as a question of semantics in the case of a childless, unmarried tycoon. To all intents and purposes, he was Marcus's heir. And Marcus had a personal fortune of two thousand million pounds. Put in that context, Charlie did not feel reckless in upping the ante in his search for a country house.

As it happened, the appearance of Old Testbury Hall on the property market coincided with the arrival of a letter from Alistair Crieff. While Miranda sat beetle-browed at the breakfast table studying the lavish brochure for the Hampshire estate, Charlie struggled to decipher his father's handwriting which seemed much shakier than he remembered. The pale blue writing paper was engraved, in a darker shade of blue, with the address and coat of arms of the Crieffs of Ardnessaig, and the old three-digit telephone number and exchange. Charlie experienced a moment of guilt, not having seen or spoken to his parents for many months. Recognising their hostility to Miranda, whom they had never invited to Ardnessaig, and anyway being far too busy to make the long journey north, Charlie had allowed them to fade out of his life.

The news from his father was not good. His mother, he read, was ill and had been unable to leave her bed for five weeks. Nobody knew what was wrong with her. Their GP wanted to send her to hospital in Dundee for tests, but Verena was reluctant to go, having heard the screening equipment was shared by National Health patients. There was talk of having to employ full-time round-the-clock nurses at home: 'Dr Bannerman says we will require two of them – young Australian girls apparently – since your mother needs constant care. The expense is almost unbelievable.' The billiards room at Ardnessaig had a leak in the ceiling, the carpets had been rolled up and pails permanently positioned, since there was no spare money to repair anything. Alistair hoped to sell part of a field on the A90 to a company wanting to build a Little Chef service station: 'That might be our saviour.'

'What's prompted this letter,' his father wrote, 'is the hope that you might be able to help us out a bit with the nursing bills. To be perfectly honest, we have very little free money left at all, and these Australian nurses expect three

422

hundred pounds *a week* each. According to Dr Bannerman, this is normal. It's crippling, but what else can we do? Your mother is in a certain amount of pain, poor thing, and can be short with people. Apparently colonial girls will put up with it better than local Scottish help. I hate asking you for money, Charlie, but I hear you're doing very well for yourself down in London, and Ardnessaig will pass to you one day (not long either, the way we're going!) so I hope you'll see what you can manage.'

Miranda was frowning over the floorplan of Old Testbury Hall. Some of the bedrooms on the second floor didn't appear to have en-suite bathrooms, and the kitchen would need to be knocked through into the breakfast room, but in other respects it was her dream house. Six miles from Newbury, with gardens sweeping down to the River Lambourn, it was a perfect scaled-up Georgian doll's house with nine bedrooms, a stable block with a glass octagon on the roof, a half-mile drive lined with espaliered lime trees, well-established herbaceous borders originally designed by Lanning Roper, and a brick and flint summerhouse adjacent to the swimming pool. The terrifying price, which was three million pounds, almost struck her as a bargain, so inured had she become to astronomical valuations.

'Listen, Charlie,' she said, 'I'm ringing Algy. We need to see this place today.'

'You'd better read this first,' he said. 'It's from my father.'

Miranda skimmed the letter while Maha brought Charlie a fresh pot of coffee.

'Well, I call that the absolute limit,' Miranda said when she'd finished reading. 'Your father wants us to pay for two permanent live-in staff? We don't even have that ourselves. Poor Maha's worked off her feet and been asking me whether she can have some extra help, and now your parents expect us to subsidise their living in that great big ugly castle . . .'

'Hang on, hang on. Ardnessaig isn't ugly and it will be ours one day. I don't want to send them money any more than you do . . .'

'Then don't. Say no. For God's sake, Charlie, take a

stand. If you do it once, it'll never stop. Your mother might live for years and then what are you supposed to do? Carry on paying those Aussie nurses? And then your father will become ill. This could go on for ever.'

'I ought to do something about that ceiling, it can't just be left to deteriorate.'

'You want to repair a ceiling in a billiards room in Scotland? This is unreal. I thought you said we couldn't be extravagant? You never stopped complaining when I bought that Fendi coat. You don't even play billiards.'

'When I'm up there I do.'

'You never are up there.'

'I will be one day. Obviously.'

'Well, don't expect me to come. That whole place sounds like it's falling down. Think what it would cost to heat. I know you love Arctic temperatures, but I don't.'

Charlie had never actually discussed Ardnessaig with Miranda, automatically assuming that at some still-distant moment in their lives they would move north, for at least part of the year, when he would assume his responsibilities and perquisites as laird of the family estate. As he had grown older and richer, however, he realised his feelings about Ardnessaig were ambivalent. As a schoolboy, and later in Hong Kong, his self-image was to a large part dependent on the existence of the estate which had seemed, at the time, almost impossibly impressive. Now he wasn't so certain. His childhood memories of growing up there were mostly unhappy. If Marcus left him a couple of hundred million quid, he wasn't sure he'd want to spend much time there.

'What do you suggest?' he asked Miranda. 'That I write and say no?'

'Up to you. I'm just pointing out we can't do everything. If we're going to buy this country house – and, God knows, we've been searching for the right one for long enough – we can't be expected to give non-stop handouts to your parents as well. What about your sisters? Surely someone else can chip in for a change. What's happened to that frightful old nanny who came to our wedding?'

424

Charlie looked thoughtful. 'Nanny Arbroath? She's retired. Lives in Perth.'

'Then unretire her. She'll be much cheaper and she knows the house.'

'She must be eighty,' Charlie said doubtfully.

'All the better, she won't expect much. Do you realise the Silcoxes are paying their Haitian housekeeper three hundred and sixty a week, and that's cash in hand?'

Verena Crieff was propped up in bed against four large worn pillows, each embroidered with the elaborate coronet and 'A' for Arbroath that identified them as part of her original marriage trousseau. It was a bleak November Sunday morning, and Lady Crieff was perplexed. She was reading a special supplement that had arrived with *The Sunday Times* listing the Thousand Richest People in Britain. As in previous years, she found the idea of the list unbearably common and intrusive ('How *dare* they publish how much money people have? And how do they even know?') but this time she thought there must be a mistake. So far as she could see, there was no mention of her cousins the Arbroaths on the list. It was bewildering. The Arbroaths were one of the richest families in Britain, weren't they, with fifteen thousand acres and a dining room hung floor-to-ceiling with Gainsboroughs and Van Dykes?

Her eyes moved down the pages of microscopic type, recognising almost nobody. Occasionally they alighted on a familiar landed Duke – Westminster, Buccleuch – but the majority of the names meant nothing to her. She read a paragraph about a quick-fit exhaust entrepreneur, who was apparently 'worth' £110 million, and an Indian lady with a factory preparing packaged *balti* and samosas – whatever they were – who had £92 million. The unspeakable Marcus Brand was put in at number five, one place ahead of the Queen and two behind Robert Maxwell. Of the Crieffs' old friends and neighbours, whose land marched with their own, there was no trace.

Nanny Arbroath staggered into the bedroom carrying a bamboo bed-tray on which sat a Welsh Rarebit, a selection of multi-coloured pills and a large, iceless gin and tonic with which to wash them down.

Since being lured from her retirement flat by Charlie with the promise of fifty pounds a week clear, Nanny Arbroath had sought to re-establish her authority in the household. Without small children on whom to exercise her bad temper, she turned it on her employers, terrorising the bedridden Lady Crieff and refusing to provide anything but the simplest snacks for Lord Crieff, who subsisted on boiled eggs and cheese.

'I've taken His Lordship his supper in the library,' she said. 'I don't know how I'm expected to manage all these stairs with my legs. I've forgotten your sweet, but you'll have to do without, I can't go all that way again.'

42: October, 1991

On those Sundays when Jamie was on duty all day at 60 Montpelier Gardens, Abigail would often ring Mary at Billing Road and make a plan to have lunch followed by a walk in Hyde Park. Five years after moving to London from New Jersey, her circle of friends remained surprisingly limited. Jamie's long hours at the hotel, and regular evening shifts, made it difficult to construct a social life; his address book was comprised, in any case, entirely of old girlfriends whom Abigail had no desire to know better. Consequently, her days and weekends were rather lonely. Particularly since giving up her art studies to concentrate on becoming pregnant, she found herself gravitating towards Mary for friendship and reassurance.

It became their routine to leave their cars in the car park on the north shore of the Serpentine, then walk past the boathouses up to the head of the lake, call at the playground on the Knightsbridge side of the park and end up having tea in the Lido café. Clara would walk for as long as she could manage, then move into a pushchair. At the age of eight, she was becoming sensitive to the fact she wasn't like other children, and easily upset by taunts and snubs. The first time Mary and Abigail took her to the playground, some small boys refused to play on the roundabout with her, saying 'That girl looks funny.' It took several Sundays before she could be coaxed back again for another try.

Over the course of many long walks, which her friend was inclined to monopolise as a freeform psychotherapy session, Mary saw what a wonderful mother Abigail had the potential to be. Even when apparently absorbed in some saga about her mother, or what her latest alternative healer had said about her reproductive aura, she would dart forward to wipe Clara's nose, or break off to point out a string of horses trotting past on Rotten Row. It seemed dreadfully unfair to Mary that, eighteen months after embarking on IVF, Abby was still unable to conceive.

Then, early one morning, Abigail rang Mary at work and insisted on being put straight through. Hardly able to contain her joy, she said, 'I'm pregnant. It really is true, it's been confirmed.'

'That's *wonderful*, Abigail. I'm so happy for you.' Mary smiled at the four clients sitting in her office. 'Listen, I've got some people here now, but I'm just so pleased for you. Can I ring you later on, and maybe drop by after work? Clara will be thrilled too, she loves babies.'

'I'm ringing my mother as soon as it's time. It's four a.m. in America, I'd better leave it 'til six, don't you think?'

'Well, congratulations – and to Jamie. How's he taken it, by the way?'

'Shell-shocked. He's such a big baby himself, he can't imagine being a dad.'

But then, four days later, she started bleeding, and doubts were raised over whether Abigail had ever been pregnant at all. Sometimes, with IVF, the signals are difficult to read, and the consultant suggested the implanted egg had never properly made the transition to embryo.

Her disappointment was shattering. Having told the good news to everybody she knew, she found it almost impossible to accept this reversal. The fact that Jamie seemed to take it so much in his stride, and to carry on going to work as though nothing had happened, only added to her misery, because it made her think he'd never wanted the baby in the first place. And when a huge parcel of pregnancy dresses arrived by Fedex from her mother in Franklin Lakes, which had been dispatched before she'd heard the sad news, with a She's-having-a-baby card inside saying how happy Zubin was, and how she and Jamie must come and stay with them soon in America, Abigail wondered whether she could even survive it.

Mary, during those desperate days, visited her every evening, filling the fridge with milk and juice and pre-cooked dishes from Marks & Spencer. Abigail lay in bed, rigid with unhappiness and sense of failure, crying and crying and insisting it was all her fault. Mary did her best to comfort her, promising her next time it would all work out, and this was nature's way of ensuring only a healthy child would be born. 'It obviously wasn't meant to be,' Mary assured her. 'I bet you anything you like, in a couple of months time you'll be having a perfect baby. Believe me.'

'I don't care if it's perfect or not,' Abigail wailed. 'I just want a baby. Clara isn't perfect, and you still love her. I want a baby so much and I know I'm never going to have one.'

As Mary told it to Stuart, when they met for a late supper at Pizza Express in the Fulham Road, Abigail was so distraught she didn't like to leave her. 'I almost think she might do something stupid.'

'God, I hope not,' Stuart said. 'She's always been a little crazy, but I doubt she'd go that far. Anyway, Jamie's there, isn't he?'

'He wasn't back when I left. He's not exactly hurrying home at the moment. He's naughty, but I don't blame him. It can't be easy, living with Abby in her present state.'

Slowly Abigail recovered, and re-embarked on her fertility course, though with less optimism than before. Mary detected a resignation in her attitude, as though she now believed she would never become a mother.

One Sunday afternoon, as they dodged the rollerbladers and cyclists on the asphalt path round the Serpentine, Abigail asked, 'Tell me truthfully, Mary, did Jamie take a lot of drugs in the old days?'

'I honestly couldn't tell you. I reckon so, but I don't actually know that for a fact. A lot of people did. I was never part of it. I was too boring, I suppose.'

'I've been thinking . . . maybe the drugs affected our chance of being able to have a baby.'

Mary shrugged. 'I'm not a medical expert.'

'He was a heroin junkie for five years, he admits that. And took a lot of coke. It could have killed his sperm, or enough of them anyway. If you pump yourself full of chemicals . . .'

'What does your doctor say?'

'Doesn't know. Jamie has a low sperm count. But they can't say if it's because of drugs.'

429

They arrived at the old Festival of Britain self-service cafeteria, and carried a tray of tea and pastries out on to the terrace. Clara, bundled up in a green duffel coat, was drinking a mug of hot chocolate. Lately she had learned to distinguish hot from cold, and to drink from a cup on her own, holding on to the handle; to Mary, it felt like real progress.

'You know what I'm beginning to think, Mary? That maybe it's for the best in the long run that we haven't had a child.'

'Don't say that. I've told you, you'll have one soon. You mustn't give up hope.'

'It could be an omen that we're not meant to be together. Doesn't that sometimes happen – unsuitable couples can't have kids? It's God's way of saying you're incompatible.'

'You and Jamie? Oh, Abby, that's not true. You're a great couple. At your wedding, everyone was saying how perfect it was. You've been fantastic for him, look how he's settled down.'

'He didn't come home last night.'

'Really? Where was he then?'

'God knows. He said he was working, but when I rang the hotel they said it was his night off.'

'What did Jamie have to say about it?'

'Said he'd been so tired he'd crashed out in one of the bedrooms. He'd meant to put his feet up for a few minutes, but dropped off and didn't wake up till the morning.'

'You believe him?'

'I don't know. I genuinely don't. He made it sound convincing, but Jamie's always convincing. Maybe he's got someone else.'

'You don't really think that.'

'You couldn't blame him. Look at me: I'm so fat again, he probably wants to be with someone else.'

'It's only temporary, while you're having the treatment.'

'Maybe I should just forget this whole baby thing and try and lose weight. I mean it, I'm beginning to think it's not worth it. It's all become such a procedure. All I do is have ovulation scans and drink pints and pints of water. It's not exactly sexy.' She laughed shakily. 'The other day I had to ring Jamie at lunchtime at the hotel and tell him to come straight round. My ovum was ripe. That's what they said at the clinic. We had to do it immediately. He was in a meeting and was very grumpy about being dragged out.'

'I thought that's what men liked: instant gratification.'

'But not with me, it seems. Not any more. Oh, God, Mary, I don't know what to do. I know I've disappointed him horribly. I'm fat and I can't have children. And Jamie won't even talk about it. He's such a great liar, I don't know what he thinks about anything or even when he's telling the truth.'

Mary laughed. 'I just remembered something, it flashed into my head – in Nassau, when he pretended he'd seen a shark in the bay, biting a woman's leg off.'

'And I fell for it hook, line and sinker. I was such a sucker, and my mom had been on at me for weeks about not swimming in the ocean. She'd been watching *Jaws*, I guess. That's what I mean about Jamie, he says something and you believe him. We're a couple of misfits, I reckon. That's probably why we hitched up in the first place.'

Mary smiled at her friend. 'I've never known anyone who's less of a misfit than you are.'

'That's because you don't realise how screwed up I really am. You know I've been seeing psychiatrists since I was sixteen.'

'All Americans do that, don't they? It doesn't mean anything.'

'I started after that vacation in Nassau. It left me with low self-esteem. Well, I guess I had that already. The experience made it worse.'

'I probably needed therapy myself after that holiday. The combination of Marcus and Charlie . . .'

'How is Charlie? Jamie sees him sometimes, but I refuse to. He kind of depresses me each time.'

'Living in a huge house in Kensington with his very expensive wife. Apparently they give grand dinner parties to which you only get invited if you're very rich.'

'Have you been to one?'

'You joking? You think they'd ask a single mother with a Down's Syndrome child who runs an employment agency? No, I heard from Stuart who had lunch with Marcus. Marcus had been to dinner – natch. It was full of millionaires and foreign princesses.'

'You're seeing a lot of Stuart, aren't you, Mary?'

'He's a director of my company,' she replied quickly. 'He's been incredibly kind.'

Abigail scrutinised her across the table. 'You two aren't an item, are you? Why am I suspicious all of a sudden?'

'Of course not. Whatever made you imagine that?'

'Because it's a great idea. And you're both so secretive, I wouldn't put it past either of you, stepping out on the sly.'

'I can assure you we're not. We've been friends for a long time, that's all. Stuart is Clara's godfather.'

'It would be perfect. Stuart's such a workaholic, he's never going to meet anyone else. Don't take that the wrong way, he'd be lucky to marry you. Ready-made family and all that. Then you could have some more kids together.'

'Have you finished, Abigail? Well, it's a nice idea, but there's one big problem you've overlooked, quite apart from the fact there's never been the slightest glimmer of romance between us. Stuart's in love with someone else.'

'He is?'

'You know her. Saffron.'

'*Saffron?* Get out of here! When did all this start?'

'It hasn't. Nothing's happening. I said Stuart's in love with her. He has been for ages.'

'He told you that?'

'Doesn't need to. I can tell. He's always had a thing for her. Since Nassau probably. Mention her name and he goes scarlet.'

'But it's crazy. They're totally unsuited. I mean, Saffron's beautiful.'

'And Stuart's not?' Mary laughed.

'I didn't mean that. Stuart's fine. In fact he's almost quite good-looking these days. I don't know what's happened, contact lenses or being successful. But he and Saffron have nothing in common.'

432

'Nothing. But it's love.'

'Anyway, Saffron was with Marcus, wasn't she? Jamie says they used to meet in his hotel for afternoon sex.'

'Complicated, isn't it? And that's why nothing's going on between Stuart and me. Anyway, even if he was available, I'm not sure I'm ready. You know, I still think about Crispin every day. Looking after Clara's a full-time job, never mind a new husband.'

43: January, 1992

'Saffron, you're late,' Marcus said. 'We were beginning to think you weren't coming in today.'

Barbara Miles and the other girls in the office pretended not to hear the rebuke, busying themselves with the post.

'I'm sorry, Marcus.'

'Don't be sorry. Get up earlier. And don't be late again.'

Saffron, who had left her godfather's flat in St James's Place ten minutes earlier, and watched him climb alone into the back of the Bentley for the short journey to Pall Mall, felt the injustice of the situation. Had he offered her a lift, she'd have been on time.

'Don't stand about like a spare prick in a bordello, Saffron, there's plenty to do. I have to fly to São Paolo tomorrow and you're coming with me. There's cocktails to organise for Saturday evening.'

Two weeks after her eighteen-month relationship with Nick Blackwater of Blacktongue drew to a close, and she had cleared her possessions from his mansion on the St George's Hill Estate, Saffron had accepted the position of social secretary to Marcus. As he explained the job to her, her duties would focus on the personal and business aspects of his social life: replying to and issuing invitations, ensuring the correct mix of guests at his parties, liaising with Barbara over his travel arrangements and occasionally acting as hostess at business dinners. 'Help me a lot,' he told her, 'to have someone keeping tabs on what's going on, who's where at any particular time. Next weekend I'm with Jimmy and Laure in Mexico, then flying straight up to Vancouver to entertain various members of the provincial government there. Need someone to take care of the details: is the private room all right at the Pan Pacific Hotel, enough chairs, nice soap in the ladies' loo? You'd do it standing on your head, Saffron. Doesn't hurt you're decorative either.

434

Giving a dinner for President Suharto of Indonesia next Thursday at Claridge's, he'll appreciate being seated next to you.'

Having no alternative offers of employment, and undermined by the generosity of the salary, Saffron overcame her instinctive misgivings about working for her godfather. Of course she realised, even as she accepted the job, that her role as social secretary also implied a resumption of her earlier role as Marcus's mistress. The prospect, which she saw as inevitable, made her feel like an escaped convict being returned to a particularly comfortable and well-appointed jail, where the system, though certainly abusive, was at least well understood by her, and where the foibles of the governor could be managed. On her second day in her new role, Marcus took her to dinner and later to bed. Shortly afterwards, he handed her the keys to a company flat in Arlington House, a block of service apartments above Le Caprice restaurant, which became her home.

Her life assumed a pattern of intense activity interspersed with days, sometimes weeks, of emptiness and solitude. Travelling with Marcus, she arranged his breakfast meetings, lunches, drinks and dinners. In hotels, they were booked into communicating suites. It was never clear to Saffron to what extent Barbara Miles was party to this arrangement; Saffron assumed she knew everything, though Barbara never acknowledged as much, and in the office at Pall Mall her attitude to Marcus's goddaughter was benignly professional.

When they flew anywhere in the new Gulfstream III, it was Saffron's job to brief the stewardesses on the menus; when any foreign dignitary passed through town, she worked her way through the Rolodex, contacting a dozen suitably weighted couples to dine at St James's Place. She soon became familiar with the assistants to all the prominent socialites, tycoons and press proprietors of the city.

Marcus liked her to be available for him twenty-four hours a day, seven days a week. He would call her without regard to time zones, from anywhere in the world, and expect to find her either in the office or at Arlington House.

If she was out, he left message after message on the answerphone: 'Where the hell are you? Ring me immediately you get in.' Sometimes he arrived home from a trip in the middle of the night, and would summon her round to St James's Place, or would turn up himself without warning at Arlington House and press the intercom, randy from the flight and raring to go. Consequently, it was difficult for Saffron to make other plans. Her days, when Marcus was out of town, were lonely. She had, in any case, spent much of the last seven years away from London, first in Switzerland, then with Nick Blackwater, and most of her friendships had drifted. At the age of thirty-four, there was almost nobody in her address book she could call and suggest supper. There were times when she wondered whether she'd been too hasty in walking out on Nick; his morose silences in front of the golf on television were hardly worse than the silence of her flat. And when she thought of the baby she might have had with Marcus – it would have been five now – she buried her face in the sofa cushions and wept. One evening, turning the pages of an old address book and realising the extent to which she'd lost touch with her past, she dialled the number of one of her old surfer friends in Polzeath. To her delight, the number still rang and her friend, Carol, was at home. They talked for twenty-five minutes, as Carol told her about her life in Cornwall, and her eleven-year-old daughter, Jazzy, already at the local secondary school. Saffron was glad to have made contact but knew she would never do so again.

Her state of mind increasingly depended on Marcus's own moods. Sometimes he would ring her from Hong Kong or Sydney after a successful day's business, eager to confide, brimming with charm, telling her he wished she was there with him, and how much he was looking forward to being with her again. 'We must take a holiday, just the two of us. Where do you want to go, Saffron? Come on, there must be somewhere. Think about it, tell me when I get back. We'll set it up.'

He would return with presents, generally jewellery: a little velvet box from a hotel mall. Inside would be gold or diamond earrings. His taste in jewellery was not Saffron's own taste, which was for simpler, less conspicuous pieces. For her birthday, he presented her with a pair of yellow diamond drop-earrings from S.J. Phillips of New Bond Street which later, finding the receipt beneath a pile of post in the flat, she learned to her amazement had cost forty thousand pounds.

On several occasions, over dinner, he said, 'I'd thought you'd like to know that I'm proposing to make some provision for you in my will. I do want to see you well provided for. I must ask Dick to make arrangements.'

It turned Marcus on to have Saffron dance around the apartment wearing nothing but her Manolo Blahnik mules and diamond earrings. When he visited Arlington House, he liked first to shower, then put on the patterned silk dressing gown he kept on the back of her bathroom door. Then, as he lay on the bed, resting against the pillows, he made telephone calls while she danced, reviewing the details of a negotiation or bawling out subordinates for some aspect of their performance. If she slowed the tempo of her dancing, he mouthed, 'Don't stop. Keep going.' The combination of the erotic dancing and aggressive business always had the effect of arousing him. Finishing his calls, he would stand up, his erection springing through the folds of his dressing gown, and pad across the bedroom. Then he would run his hands over her body, and Saffron would take hold of his erection and lead him towards the bed. She knew without asking, from the intensity of the gleam in his eyes, whether he wanted to play it gentle or rough. He liked her to talk dirty to him, the filthier the better, using all the basest words, but after he had erupted inside her his mood changed abruptly, and he talked about paintings he was considering buying. Flying at high altitude supercharged Marcus's sex drive; stepping off Concorde, he would ring her from the carphone on the way in from Heathrow, having first closed the privacy glass between himself and Makepiece, ordering her to be ready and naked for him.

But when he chose to, he could make Saffron miserable. Without warning or pretext, he withdrew his support, omitting to ring her for days at a time, and sending only aridly professional faxes about upcoming diary dates. Or he would return after a long trip and pay her no visit. She knew from the bustle in the office that he was back in London, but was not summoned into his office.

She came to detest the service flat, with its beige walls, beige carpets, beige curtains and smoked-glass coffee tables. She had never lived anywhere so soulless. But her attempts to brighten the place up, draping coloured throws over the beige armchairs, were constantly frustrated; the cleaners, who arrived each day to tidy the place, carefully removed them all and left them neatly folded in the louvred airing cupboard.

Almost her only expeditions were to NA meetings, and to hairdressers, manicurists and spas. Marcus expected her to be well-groomed and picked up all her bills which were sent directly to Barbara at the office. Twice a week she had her hair and nails done at Michaeljohn; she swam in the rooftop pool at the Berkeley. As a result, she looked amazing. Running into her at one of Marcus's corporate drinks parties, Charlie and Miranda Crieff were struck by how much more sophisticated she appeared, compared to their previous sighting at the polo.

Charlie regarded Saffron's renaissance in Marcus's life as bad news. Immediately interpreting her position as social secretary as a synonym for hooker, he sensed danger. 'God knows why Marcus is back bonking Saffron,' he said to Miranda. 'I thought he'd got that out of his system.'

'Didn't I tell you that woman's a tart?' Miranda replied. 'You saw her earrings? You don't need to ask how she earned them.'

'So long as she doesn't get pregnant. She's stupid enough, that's for sure.'

'Girls like that: if they can produce a kid, it's a meal ticket for life.'

'Maybe I should warn Marcus. If I get the chance, I'll tell him she tried to pull the same stunt on Nick Blackwater.' Charlie consoled himself that Saffron's rackety past might have affected her ability to conceive. He certainly hoped so.

The one area of joy in Saffron's life lay in her job, or at least part of her job. She derived huge satisfaction from organising Marcus's corporate dinners, finding ways of transforming the tables with the imaginative use of flowers and glass. She loved the challenge of devising new schemes for hotel dining rooms. At one party she ordered thousands of rose petals skewered on to joss sticks, which lay across the napkins; she sourced coloured water glasses and frosted glass bowls, which she filled with coloured candles floating in lavender oil. She bought bolts of sari material in Southall, in vibrant oranges and flaming reds, to use as tablecloths at a dinner for the Indian Minister of Finance. Among the stockmarket analysts who were regularly entertained by the Brand Group, the corporate hospitality earned a reputation for being more fun and more glamorous than that of competitive conglomerates.

Her life, she felt, existed in a vacuum, frequently put on hold while Marcus was away. Sometimes she realised she despised him, and that she must break free of the cycle of dependency; other times she longed for his return. She was mesmerised by him, but also scared. As time went by, she felt trapped by his insistence on knowing where she was every minute of the day. If she deliberately avoided telling him, he had ways of finding out, which made her believe she must be being followed. When he provided her with a car and driver, she guessed this was primarily as a means of stepping up the surveillance.

She took to asking the driver to wait for her outside Harrods while she pretended to shop. In fact she would cut through the store to another entrance, hail a taxi and grab an hour or two of unmonitored freedom. But she couldn't pull the stunt too often.

At the same time, she thought her telephone at Arlington House had a tap on it. Sometimes, lifting the receiver, she heard inexplicable clicking sounds and once, playing back at her down the line, was the echoing blowback of a call she'd made earlier that same day. Had there been anyone special to ring in her life, she'd have done so from a public phone box.

44: June, 1992

Two years almost to the day after they had met, Miranda produced a son and heir, the Hon Pelham Alistair Arbroath Crieff, at the Portland Hospital in West London.

Charlie, who was not present at the birth, followed the action from an adjacent waiting-room where he enjoyed a plate of smoked salmon from the Portland's extensive bilingual menu printed in English and Arabic. The date and timing of the birth were predictable, Miranda having chosen to have the baby delivered by caesarean section. Her obstetrician, 'Fingers' Ringland, certainly the most fashionable and reputedly the most expensive of London's society gynaecologists, had agreed to the operation to save her pelvic floor muscles; he preferred, in any case, to deliver babies midweek, thereby freeing up the weekend for golf.

Charlie's satisfaction at producing a son was clouded only by creeping unease at the cost of the hospital. Miranda's caesarean, being elective, was not covered by his company health scheme. The daily room rate, once extras were taken into account, was running at over a thousand pounds a night. And, nine days after the operation, his wife was showing no signs of checking out. Instead, she was sitting up in bed, surrounded by baskets of flowers, entertaining her many smart girlfriends who arrived laden with smocked shirts and nightclothes from the White House and Anthea Moore Ede. When he suggested it might be time to go home, Miranda bit his head off: 'In case you've forgotten, Charlie, I've just been *cut open* and *stitched up* again. This is not the time to be acting like Scrooge, thank you very much.'

He wished his parents were alive to hear the good news about Pelham, but neither had survived an outbreak of listeria brought on by eating very old pâté. It turned out that Nanny Arbroath had failed to notice the date on the tin, which was eighteen years beyond its recommended sell-by period. Charlie had made several trips to Ardnessaig since February, arranging both funerals with his sisters and trying to sort out the chaos of his father's finances. It was evident the estate was effectively bankrupt. Not having visited the house for several years, he was horrified by the number of gaps on the walls where pictures had once hung. The stairwell, once a close patchwork of portraits and sporting paintings, resembled a mouth full of broken teeth, there were so many odd white spaces. The muskets and pikes in the hall had all been sold, though the hooks and lengths of chain that had displayed them remained, dangling like in some medieval torture chamber. Having reviewed the estate accounts for the last five years, and talked it over with Miranda who refused even to fly north to see the house, invoking her pregnancy, Charlie decided he had no choice but to put Ardnessaig on the market.

There was no doubt they needed the money. Old Testbury Hall was straining his finances almost to breaking point. His loan from Cruickshank's now slightly exceeded five million pounds. Having assured him their new country house needed almost nothing done to it ('We can move straight in'), Miranda had embarked on a major programme of works: stripping out the nearly new Smallbone kitchen and replacing it with an almost identical one (Charlie felt) by Mark Wilkinson, knocking down internal walls, moving doors, turning bedrooms into bathrooms and bathrooms into bedrooms, always at scarcely believable expense. The final straw came when she insisted on rebuilding the swimming pool, installing one with an electric 'jelly' cover which was safer for children. 'For heaven's sake, Charlie, we are only talking twenty-five thousand pounds here. I am not going to the considerable discomfort of bearing your child only to have it drown in an unsafe pool, simply because you want to save yourself a few quid.'

To make matters worse, the house was not going to be ready for occupation much before October, which meant they'd had to rent another house in a nearby village for the summer, so Miranda could oversee progress on a daily basis.

One of the reasons for the delay, Charlie understood, was that his wife kept changing her mind on what she wanted. She found it difficult to visualise anything from plans and swatches alone, only able to determine whether something was 'right' when she saw it in situ. Consequently they were blowing thousands of pounds on relaying flagstones and rethinking curtain pelmets. Earlier that week, a brand new, just-installed basin and its marble surround had been removed from a spare bedroom, Miranda having decided a double basin was more desirable.

'No way can we change that,' Charlie had remonstrated. 'It's utter madness. Have you *any idea* what this'll cost?' He had stood in the entrance to the bathroom, blocking the builder's way, while the architect and surveyor looked on.

'Charlie, we are talking about a principal guest bedroom here,' Miranda had replied. 'The bedroom in which Marcus Brand will be sleeping, if we ever ask him to stay, which I assume you'll want to. Do you or do you not want it to be right?'

As usual, Miranda had located his Achilles heel, and Charlie withdrew with a shrug. It was true, the prospect of entertaining Marcus for an entire weekend was one of his principal motives in buying a country house. He envisaged Marcus arriving by helicopter from West Candover Park, landing in one of the paddocks beyond the walled garden, and their arranging a special dinner party in his honour on Saturday night, drawing on all the local grandees. They would invite the local Tory MP, who would be eager to meet the tycoon. As his finances became daily more strained, Charlie would do anything to curry favour with his godfather.

The stress of renovating Old Testbury Hall, of Miranda and Pelham, of Ardnessaig and of his horrendous borrowings, made Charlie volatile. His mood swings, in which he alternately imagined himself brilliantly successful or broke, became more extreme. At the office, he was quick to blame subordinates for his own mistakes, and nursed a grievance that Cruickshank's undervalued and underpaid him. He took to lingering in bars after work before going home to face his wife, with whichever colleagues could be persuaded to join him. One evening, shortly after Miranda had brought Pelham home from the Portland, he invited his departmental secretary, Heather Holt, out for a drink at a new Vietnamese cocktail bar, the Hanoi in Moorgate, known for its explosive tequila-based slammers. Heather had been working at Cruickshank & Willis for ten months, initially temping between departments before landing a permanent position on the equities desk. Despite having never previously shown her any attention at all, Charlie nevertheless dimly fancied her, misinterpreting her willing helpfulness as a sign of availability.

Arriving at the Hanoi, he drank six margaritas in sixty minutes. Heather, while flattered to be bought a drink by her fat boss, had promised her boyfriend she'd be home to cook supper in Colchester before eight o'clock; on the floor by her feet lay two plastic bags of groceries she had bought during her lunch break at Tesco. The cavernous bar, with its bamboo walls and photographs of American B-52 bombers, was heaving with young traders and bond dealers; perched unsteadily on a wooden stool at the bar, Charlie was unaware of how incongruous a figure he appeared with his red face and thick pinstripes. His head cloudy with alcohol and exhaustion, he knew only that he was desperate to impress this pretty young girl.

'How often are you up in Scotland?' he asked her. 'You should come and spend a weekend at Ardnessaig. Have you stayed in a stately home before?'

Heather said she had not. She also asked, rather pointedly, whether Mrs Crieff would be there too.

'Lady Crieff actually,' Charlie replied. 'You may not know this, but I'm a lord these days. My father's just snuffed it. Not that I'm going to play on my title in the office, but it does grease the wheels booking restaurant tables.'

Heather nodded while surreptitiously looking at her watch. Her train left Liverpool Street in twenty minutes. It was, in any case, difficult to hear what Charlie was saying. The music at the Hanoi was deafening, and he was slurring his words.

'Thing about Miranda – Lady Crieff – is she isn't a country girl. I mean it, she's a pavement princess. Comes from Jersey which is terribly common, don't you think?'

Heather shrugged. 'I've never visited.'

'I wouldn't go if you paid me. Not for a million pounds, thank you very much. Have you ever been to Nassau? Well, you should. I'll take you one day. My godfather Marcus Brand has a house there, actually it's the biggest house on the island. We could have a great time together, sherioshly.'

Heather was wondering if it would be impolite to stand up and leave.

'Maybe you should be the next Lady Crieff, er . . . Heather,' Charlie said. 'Marcus is going to leave me a couple of hundred million quid and then I'm jacking in work to spend time with a really beautiful woman like you.' Without warning he lunged and tried to kiss her. 'Has anyone ever told you you're a stunner?' He kissed her a second time, on the mouth. 'Look, I don't want you to be in awe of me, Heather. I know I'm your boss and bloody rich and successful and everything, but I don't want you to think of me as Lord Crieff. Underneath it all, I'm just an ordinary bloke. Let's get out of here, shall we? I know a hotel where no one will recognise us.'

'I don't think that's a very good idea. In fact, I have to go now.' Heather stood up, gathered her shopping bags and bolted for the exit.

'Don't you dare fucking leave!' Charlie called after her. 'Stay – have another drink. I want to tell you about Ardnessaig . . . '

Astonished, he watched her disappear into the street. 'Stupid cow,' he muttered. If she'd played her cards right, she could have done very nicely for herself.

The disposal of Ardnessaig, on which Charlie increasingly depended, was presenting unforeseen problems. Stubbornly, it refused to sell. Dozens of prospective purchasers came to view, and the estate agents were at first optimistic. A write-up in the *Sunday Telegraph* property pages emphasised the house's noble provenance; the full-page advertisement in *Country Life*, with photograph taken in springtime across

444

a lawn bristling with daffodils, brilliantly obscured the crumbling brickwork. A Chinese couple flew all the way from Hong Kong to view the place, raising prospects of a healthy premium, but returned home without making an offer. In due course, the estate agent recommended dropping the asking price by forty per cent. 'The problem's the survey,' he told Charlie. 'Anyone who takes the property on will have to spend a fortune on it. You know it's riddled with dry rot.' Reluctantly, Charlie agreed to the lower price. Until he could get rid of Ardnessaig, he was lumbered with paying the wages of his parents' old gardener and ghillie who kept the place ticking over.

Meanwhile, in an attempt to stem expenditure at home, Charlie discouraged Miranda from employing a nanny for Pelham from the Norland training college. Although he actually rather hankered after a brown-uniformed nurse in the house, to lend an impressive air of smartness to the nursery floor and to open the front door at parties, he was horrified by the salary Norland nannies commanded. Instead, he persuaded Miranda that old Nanny Arbroath, with her decades of experience with the best families, was a more appropriate candidate. 'At least she won't want to go out to Stringfellow's every night,' he declared. 'The thing about having a proper old-fashioned nanny is you get seven nights' free babysitting thrown in. These young girls expect to be paid on top for everything.'

A week later Nanny Arbroath, now almost blind, was helped out of a taxi in Upper Phillimore Gardens and huffed and puffed her way upstairs to the top floor. Having allowed herself to be made a cup of tea by Maha, she complained to the new Lady Crieff that this was the only position she'd ever accepted where there wasn't a nursery maid to assist her. Later that evening, while bathing Pelham for the first time, she allowed him to slip under water while she searched the bathroom cabinet for gripe water; had Maha not been on hand to rescue him, he would certainly have drowned.

After eight months on the market, an offer at last came through in December for the Ardnessaig Estate. Disappointingly, it did not approach the revised asking price and, at three hundred thousand pounds, was less than a third of the initial valuation. Charlie was nevertheless advised to accept the offer. 'We've marketed it pretty comprehensively,' he was told, 'through all our international offices. The fact is, it's proved a very difficult sell.' Faced with mounting bills for the renovation of Old Testbury Hall (his builders wanted five grand a week in cash), Charlie felt he had no option.

'Who's buying the place anyway?' he asked when the deposit money came through. 'Some ruddy Dutchman, I suppose. Or a stinking rich Chink.'

'No, the purchaser's English actually. Works down in London. A Mr Bolton. Stuart Bolton.'

'Christ, not him!' Charlie exploded down the telephone. 'You don't mean a prole with a Birmingham accent? Complete know-all who works for some management consultancy?'

'Mr Bolton's office is at McKinsey.'

'I knew it! Bloody hell, the deal's off. I'm not having that turd living in my house. Tell him his offer's been rejected.'

'I'm afraid that's not possible, Lord Crieff. The solicitors have already exchanged.'

Charlie was incandescent. This was absolutely typical of a conniving, lying, wretched git like Stuart, who had no idea how to behave. He had obviously planned the whole thing. He'd waited until the price hit rock-bottom, then put in an opportunistic offer. And Charlie had no doubt why he'd done it: to insult his family. For seven hundred years the Crieffs had lived at Ardnessaig, uncomplainingly fulfilling their obligations to the local community, opening the local highland games and giving employment to half the village, and then along comes a cleaner's son, chortling at his own impudence, having duped some mortgage house into lending him the cash, and thinks he's jack-the-laird all of a sudden. At that moment, all kinds of wild schemes ripped through Charlie's head: he would set fire to the house, burn it to the ground if necessary rather than see Stuart have it; he would contact every neighbour for miles around Ardnessaig, warning them what kind of man Stuart was, and advising them to have nothing to do with him; he would insist the old ghillie and gardener refuse to work for the new owner out of loyalty to his family. He felt sure that, having met Stuart, they wouldn't want to in any case.

In a fury, Charlie stormed into the bedroom. Miranda looked displeased to see him. Lately, their relationship had been going through a rocky patch. In her opinion, all Charlie did was lecture her about money, telling her to cut back on this, cut back on that, she had never known anything like it. Recently he had even questioned whether it was necessary for her to have her hair done twice a week at Michaeljohn, even though everyone else did. She never went near the place without seeing Charlie's old flame Saffron in there, having her nails polished or a pedicure. If Charlie had wanted a cheap date as a wife, he should have married one.

'What are all those?' he asked accusingly. Miranda was sitting up in bed, underneath scalloped sheets and a white eiderdown, surrounded by an immense heap of cards.

'Christmas cards.' For a moment she refused to catch his eye. 'Aren't they lovely? They're of Pelham. John Swannell's done a studio shot.'

Charlie extracted a card from the pile. A charming black-and-white portrait of his son, posing on a pillow, was spray-mounted on stiff card with a red border. At the top of the card was a little bow in Crieff tartan. Looking at the cascade of cards on the bed, some written, others not, each interleaved with sheets of tissue paper, Charlie asked, 'How many are you sending?'

'They're baby announcements and Christmas cards combined, so it's not as bad as it looks.'

'How many, I asked?'

'A thousand.'

'*A thousand*? Jesus, do we even have a thousand friends? They must have cost a bomb. How much were they, as a matter of fact?'

Miranda shrugged. 'I've no idea.'

Suddenly spying the invoice at the bottom of a cardboard box, Charlie scooped it into the air with a flourish. 'I don't believe it. They're more than two pounds each! And that's just printing and envelopes. It doesn't include the photograph or the stamps.'

'I know it's a lot,' Miranda replied guiltily. 'But Pelham looks so adorable, you have to admit. It was the tartan bow that pushed the price up. I thought you'd be pleased. You keep saying how you love Scotland.'

'Who's being sent these things anyway?'

'Everybody. The Silcoxes. Marcus. All our friends.'

He picked up a card at random and opened it. Inside, a typeset message read, 'Season's Greetings and Best Wishes for 1993 from Charles, Miranda and Pelham Crieff'. Underneath, in her own expansive script, Miranda had written, 'To dearest Boobie. Thank you for everything. With all my love and lots of hugs, Always, Randy?'

'Randy? Who in God's name is Randy?'

Miranda reddened. 'Just a silly name he used to call me when we were married. Only as a joke. Oh, for heaven's sake, Charlie, you're not jealous? I don't believe it. I *divorced* Boobie, didn't I? To marry you. What more do you want? Listen, chill out, won't you? I'm Lady Crieff these days, in case you've forgotten, not Mrs Boobie van Haagen.'

Exasperated and confused, Charlie slammed the bedroom door and stamped downstairs. On the hall table was a pile of post, mostly brown envelopes indicating bills, but one proper letter with handwriting on the front addressed to him. Standing next to an array of orchids left over from a recent dinner party, he tore it open. For some reason, the writing was vaguely familiar. The letter, he noticed, had been forwarded from Ardnessaig several days earlier.

'Dear Charlie,' he read, 'You may not realise this, but I recently made an offer on Ardnessaig. To be honest, I had no idea it was your parents' place until after I'd fallen in love with it. It is the most fantastic house in a spectacular position, and nothing would make me happier than to spend time up there. But I wouldn't feel comfortable unless I felt I had your blessing. Please call me at my office and let me know your thoughts. I'm not, as you well know, a natural-born lord of the manor, and there may be all kinds of factors that make me quite unsuitable. But I do assure you that, if you allow me to buy the estate, I will do my best to take proper care of it. My solicitor is making a formal offer, but ring me before the end of the week if you disapprove. Yours ever, Stuart.'

Charlie read the letter twice, screwed it into a ball, and tossed it into the bin. If there was one thing he couldn't abide, it was being patronised.

Stuart came round to Billing Road to deliver the big parcel from F.A.O. Schwartz, which he had bought the previous afternoon in New York and lugged back with him on the redeye overnight. Being slightly too large for the overhead locker, the parcel had spent most of the journey at his feet, hogging the legroom and digging into his ankles.

He pressed the bell and, a few seconds later, the front door was opened by Clara. 'Godfarva Stew! It's Godfarva Stew!' Her face lit up with happiness as she threw herself into his arms.

'I'll put this box down first, Clara. You're so grown-up now, I can't hold you *and* the present.'

'Is it for me?'

'What do you think?' Stuart smiled. 'Of course it's for you. It's your Christmas present.'

'Mummy, Mummy! Godfarva Stew's got me a present.'

Mary appeared from the kitchen, drying her hands on a dishcloth. 'Stuart, you really shouldn't have. Look at that huge box, Clara. Aren't you a lucky girl? And it comes from America too.' She kissed him. 'It's lovely to see you. You really do spoil her. She's been so excited ever since you rang.'

'I hope you didn't mind my calling from the airport. I thought it would be easier to drop it off now, rather than take it home first.'

'We always love seeing you. Have you time for a cup of coffee? Or breakfast? I can cook you an egg.'

Stuart looked at his watch. 'Well, a quick coffee would be great. And a piece of toast, if you've got it. I need to be at the office in an hour.'

'Straight off the flight? You'll be shattered. What were you doing in New York anyway?'

'Seeing clients. One of the British clearing banks is

considering opening up in the States. I'm helping them tackle some of the regulatory hurdles.'

'Sounds deadly.'

'Well, I was only there one night. It was in and out. And I got to bunk off for half an hour to get Clara's present.'

'Don't burn yourself out.'

Stuart laughed. 'I'm fine, really. They do work you hard at McKinsey, but it won't be for ever.'

'Why? Are you thinking of leaving?'

'Half. Beginning to think anyway. I'd like to get stuck in to one business and work for it full-time, rather than all this company doctor stuff. It's interesting, but you never feel one hundred per cent involved. And the permanent staff never trust you either, because they think you're going to restructure them out of a job.'

'So what's next? But before you answer that, please have an egg. And I've some bacon here too. It won't take five minutes and you'll feel better after a fry up.'

'OK, you've talked me into it. Bump up my cholesterol.'

'You can handle it. Do you still swim?'

'Most days, whenever I can. I've joined the RAC Club in Pall Mall. They've got this whopping great pool.'

'You've joined a stuffy old club? *You?* I can hardly believe it. Isn't it full of peppery old colonels?'

'The RAC isn't like that, it's quite meritocratic, really. I only joined so I could use the Olympic-sized pool.' Stuart laughed. 'OK, I admit it, I'm a total hypocrite, I've joined this big expensive club with pillars and libraries and whatnot. I'll be voting Tory next – and that's a joke by the way, just in case you believed me.'

'Don't worry, I won't tell anybody. Your secret is safe with me. One of my temps was at McKinsey's last week. I told her to look out for you. She said she never saw you but reported back you've just been made a partner. That's fantastic.'

Stuart grimaced. 'They made me a partner but that doesn't mean much. My latest client is a South African-owned telecoms group in Finland, so I spend most weeks commuting between Jo'burg and Helsinki. I'm not surprised I never met your temp.'

'Don't overdo it. You're too conscientious. I bet, when you're not at work, you mostly sit in your flat in the Barbican reading work stuff.'

Stuart looked embarrassed. 'There is a fair bit to read.'

Mary handed him a plate of eggs, bacon, fried bread and baked beans. 'There you go, compliments of the greasy spoon. Clara, fetch Godfather Stuart the tomato ketchup. It's in the larder, darling, that's right.' Turning to Stuart, she said, 'She's so sweet, loves being helpful. Last night we put all the washing into the machine together, and she sorted out the whites and coloureds for me. She's really coming on.'

'I've got a worse secret even than the RAC,' said Stuart, piling beans on to his fried bread. 'I've been dreading telling anyone, in case they laugh.'

'Go on. Try me.'

'Well, I've bought a place up in Scotland.'

'In *Scotland*? Why?'

'I saw a picture in a property magazine that got pushed through the letterbox. It was of this Victorian castle surrounded by daffodils, and they weren't asking a lot for it, considering the size of the place, so I decided to check it out.'

'And?'

'I loved it. It's so peaceful, right away from any other houses, and you can see for miles across the moors. It's in terrible condition, the roof and all that, but I just thought, why not? I can put it straight bit by bit, it'll be somewhere to escape to.'

'Whereabouts in Scotland is it?'

'A couple of hours' drive north of Edinburgh. The nearest village is called Bridge of Esk.'

'God, I haven't heard that name in years. You realise who's going to be your neighbour? Charlie Crieff.'

Stuart went red. 'Well, in actual fact, it's Charlie's old house I've bought. His parents died and he decided to sell up.'

'You've bought Ardnessaig? I don't believe this.'

'How do you know what it's called? You haven't been there, have you?'

'Haven't I just? You've bought Ardnessaig . . . I'm sorry, Stuart, but I've got to have a shot of coffee now, even though I'm trying to kick my caffeine habit. I stayed there for a party a million years ago. One of the worst experiences of my life, I still get the shivers remembering it. I thought I was going out with Charlie at the time, and it was all excruciating. How extraordinary – Ardnessaig. Has it still got that mouldy hall full of armour, and those turrets?'

'The armour's been sold, but the turrets are still clinging on. It needs a lot of work doing. It does look a bit like Wormwood Scrubs, but the countryside's incredible round there.'

'To be honest, I can't remember much about it. I've spent twenty years trying to blank the whole thing. But with you living there, the atmosphere will lighten up, I'm sure. The time I went, I was wearing this tartan party dress I'd got from Monsoon, and Charlie's mother, who was a monster, a complete *monster*, and incredibly grand and intimidating, kept asking which clan I belonged to.'

'If she'd asked me, I'd have told her the Angus Steak House. I worked in one in Birmingham one summer during college. Blue and green tartan carpet. The manager was Turkish, quite a decent bloke. That's my only connection with Scotland before now.'

'What does Charlie think?'

'Good question. Before I put my offer in, I did drop him a note, asking if he minded. We've never really hit it off, Charlie and me, and I thought it best to tell him first.'

'What did he say?'

'Never replied. So I went ahead and did the business. The cheque mustn't have bounced or I'd have heard something.'

'Rude of him not to answer.'

Stuart shrugged. 'I considered ringing him but thought better of it. He was probably still cut up about his parents dying. I don't think he spent all that much time at Ardnessaig anyway, or that's what the ghillie said. They hadn't seen him for a few years.'

'Stuart, did I hear you correctly, *you* have a *ghillie*?'

This time Stuart went beetroot. 'Well, he came with the

house. I couldn't take away his livelihood. Anyway, he's a good bloke, he's teaching me to fish, not that there's many in the river to catch.'

'You are fast becoming my smartest friend, you do realise?'

'And you, Mary, are taking the Michael. If you saw the place, you wouldn't say that. Anyway, I hope you and Clara will be my first guests when it's all fixed up. That's if you can bear to return.'

'For Clara's favourite godfather, I'd go anywhere. Even Ardnessaig.'

During this period when he was a partner at McKinsey, running a section of the financial services and telecoms practice, which he would afterwards say was the most intense and remorseless time in his working life, Stuart came increasingly to rely on Mary and Clara as a kind of surrogate family. At weekends, when he was at a loose end or had no food in the fridge, he would drive over to Billing Road to be fed and fussed over by Mary and afterwards take Clara out to play in the park. As she grew older and more confident, he started taking her to the zoo or to the Science Museum in Exhibition Road. Often they ended their afternoons together at Pizza Express, where her greatest treat was a chocolate milkshake with ice cream. Her physical co-ordination continued to improve, though her volume control remained erratic, her voice sometimes coming out much too loud, almost as a shout when she was excited, causing other people to turn and stare. One afternoon in the pizza place, two smart old women at an adjacent table summoned a waitress and complained about her, saying she shouldn't be allowed in if she 'wasn't all there'. The kindly waitress, who had served Clara several times before, relayed their message with apologies. Stuart, furious on Clara's behalf, stood up and confronted the women. 'I hear you think my goddaughter should be banned.'

The women looked embarrassed. 'She was making rather a lot of noise, you know. I'm sure it would be kinder to her if

454

you took her somewhere else, maybe to McDonald's. She could shout to her heart's content down there.'

'Well, it may interest you to know that even the sight of you two nosey-parkers sitting here has ruined my tea, and I've no doubt it's spoiled Clara's too. Next time, I suggest you go to McDonald's yourselves. Or try the local primary school, I'm sure it's full of small children for you to scold, so you'll have a lovely time.'

Once a month, Stuart still met Mary and her accountant for a Merrett & Associates board meeting. The consultancy continued to expand despite the latest recession which was, once again, forcing companies to cut back on temporary staff. Panicked by a small drop in turnover, Mary asked Stuart whether she should sell up: 'I was probably crazy not to sell to Marcus when he asked.' But Stuart was reassuring. 'This business is cyclical – in fact you're probably more vulnerable to economic downturns than most. Don't worry about it, it'll come back. And if you survive, which you will, you'll be stronger. Less well-run agencies will go to the wall, so you'll finish up with more market share.'

As so often, Stuart's prediction was spot on. Outgrowing Beauchamp Place, Mary took a lease on the top three floors of a building above a sandwich shop in Dover Street. The price, negotiated by Stuart, was a steal. 'You see,' he told her, 'good things do come out of recessions.' Her staff doubled from ten to twenty and the agency regularly placed eighty temps a week. One week in early December they placed a hundred for the first time and held a party. Recognising early on that the secretarial world was about to undergo a seismic shift owing to the introduction of computers, Mary had ordered every variety of new machine and software – Word Perfect, IBM, Uniplex and Multimate – to help her army of temps make the transition from typewriters. As a result, Merrett & Associates gained a reputation for providing the best-trained temporary staff, and a dozen new clients shifted their business to Mary's consultancy.

She still continued to interview many of the candidates herself, particularly for senior positions. One afternoon, while compiling a shortlist to run the London office of the CEO of J.P. Morgan, Mary was impressed by a pretty young PA named Heather Holt.

Noticing she'd quit her last job at Cruickshank & Willis after less than a year, Mary asked her why.

'It was rather embarrassing,' replied the girl, colouring. 'I don't really like talking about it, but one of the directors made a pass at me. After I turned him down, he turned really nasty in the office, always criticising my work and victimising me. I knew I'd never get a promotion, so I left.'

'I hope you informed someone at the company? I know some of their Human Resources people over there, they'd be horrified.'

'I did consider it, but this director's quite important and I didn't think they'd believe me. And even if they did, there was nothing they could do. He looked after the biggest client, you see – Marcus Brand.'

Mary stiffened. 'Just between ourselves, who was the director?'

'I'm not sure I should give his name. I really do want to forget it.'

'It's important, Heather. You see, I might be asked to supply a PA for the same man one day, and I'd rather know.'

'All right then, so long as it stays between us. He's called Charles Crieff. He's got a very loud voice and a fat stomach, and he's really creepy.'

46: June, 1993

'Is that Marcus's yacht, do you suppose?' asked Abigail, pointing at a handsome wooden *gulet* moored in Istiniye Bay. The six godchildren, their spouses and luggage, were being sped along the Bosphorus in a pair of launches from Atatürk airport.

'Come off it,' Charlie said. 'That's a fishing boat. *Market-maker*'s the big white job behind.'

Abigail and Mary stared up at the hundred-and-eighty-foot yacht, with its four decks and helipad. To Mary, it looked like a cross between a cross-channel ferry and a wedding cake.

'That one? You can't be serious. It's *enormous*. What on earth does Marcus use it for?'

'Business and pleasure,' said Charlie airily. 'He holds meetings on board with foreign heads of state, etcetera. You've got to hand it to him, it's an impressive piece of kit.'

The launches drew up alongside a swimming platform at the stern where four deckhands in white ducks and t-shirts were waiting to help them disembark.

'Do please be careful with my face case,' said Miranda Crieff, passing it to a deckhand. 'It's fragile.'

'Me too,' said Jamie. 'I played a blinder last night. Only just made the flight.'

'And I'm so mad at him,' muttered Abigail, which explained her filthy mood all morning.

So far, Mary thought, the Istanbul jaunt had got off to a terrible start. Jamie and Abigail hadn't addressed a word to each other since leaving London, Charlie and Miranda were tense too, Saffron seemed withdrawn and disengaged, and Charlie was making an obvious point of avoiding Stuart, which Mary assumed was to do with Ardnessaig. According to Stuart, Charlie had never referred to the purchase, and cut him dead at the air terminal.

A deckhand threw a switch and the swimming platform began to ascend hydraulically towards the veranda deck. As they gained height, they could see the shores of the Bosphorus spreading out to either side of them, the villages with their minarets, the coastal highway and, just visible on the horizon, the hazy domes of the city.

'God, this is all so James Bond,' Jamie said. 'Do you suppose Marcus will be waiting in his cabin like Blofeld with his cat?' He put on a sinister Blofeld voice. ' "So, godchildren, I haf gathered you all here for a reason: tomorrow at noon we at SPECTRE will be nukeing six capital cities and installing ze new world order . . ." '

'Don't be juvenile,' Charlie snapped. 'Personally, I think it's bloody decent of Marcus to invite us all.'

For Charlie, the long weekend on *Marketmaker* had assumed a significance far greater than for the other godchildren. He had got it into his head that, over the course of the next five days, Marcus was going to make an important announcement. And this announcement, Charlie felt sure, involved making over a large sum of money to each of them. He had several good reasons for believing this. For a start, he had been told by Barbara Miles, who always knew what was going on, that Marcus was determined to find a date that all his godchildren could manage – which also fitted in with his own schedule and *Marketmaker*'s itinerary, of course. With Stuart away travelling on business so much, it had been a problem nailing everyone down. Charlie had floated the idea to Barbara that perhaps they could go ahead without Stuart, if he was the awkward one, but she had replied, 'No, Marcus insists you're all there together, he wants to explain something to you.' Charlie couldn't imagine what this could be other than an announcement about money.

The more he thought about it, the more likely it seemed. To the best of his knowledge, Marcus had been born in 1932 which made him sixty or sixty-one, which was exactly the moment you'd begin planning the orderly handover of your affairs. And with an empire on the scale of Marcus's, it would take an immense amount of planning. Nothing would make better sense than for part of the capital – or, say, equity in the Brand Group – to be assigned to the godchildren now, while Marcus could still be expected to live another seven years, to reduce inheritance tax. When Charlie subsequently established that Dick Mathias was going to be on board too, he became even more sure his theory was correct. Why else invite your lawyer-cum-accountant? It wasn't as if Dick would be a social asset on a cruise. As he explained to Miranda over dinner, 'It would actually be irresponsible of Marcus not to put a proper plan in place. Otherwise the tax liability's going to be punitive. Having said that, the whole company's set up to avoid tax. From a regulatory standpoint, it doesn't exist.'

As the date of the holiday approached, Charlie felt himself becoming anxious and irritable. He couldn't work out how much Marcus would give them. Some days, he felt sure it would be a minimum of twenty million each as a first instalment, possibly gifted in the form of a trust. Other days he felt more pessimistic, and thought it could be as little as five million. He became anxious, too, about how equitable the division of the spoils might be. He had always assumed the six godchildren would receive equal shares. But now terrible scenarios presented themselves to him. His spies within Marcus's office had confirmed Saffron was definitely reinstated as Marcus's mistress, and actually lived in a company-owned flat above the Caprice restaurant. It sickened Charlie to think of her in bed with him (in his imagination, she was always up on top, grinding away on Marcus's groin), making herself pleasing to him, with a level of access that, by simple virtue of being a hooker, was never available to himself. He took it for granted Saffron would use her position to try and engineer a larger share of the inheritance, and this made him feel vulnerable. He worried too about the frightful Stuart Bolton. Marcus seemed to have a totally unrealistic picture of Stuart, which probably went back to his genesis as the chauffeur's son. Charlie was sick of being told how decent and hardworking Stuart was. Charlie knew all about Stuart. He worried that Marcus had some mad romantic idea in his head about Stuart's working-class origins, and would leave him extra money out of pity. From everything Charlie heard, Stuart was stinking with it these days; management consultants knew how to charge. He hoped Marcus hadn't got the erroneous impression Charlie didn't need money himself, imagining he was making enough already at Cruickshank & Willis. That would be a disaster. Charlie now almost regretted inviting Marcus to dinner that evening, and showing off the splendours of Upper Phillimore Gardens.

He felt the potential injustice, too, of Jamie and Abigail's situation. As married godchildren, they stood to receive a double portion. Assuming each godchild eventually ended up with two hundred million, that made four hundred million for the Temples! It was intolerable. Why did they need so much? It wasn't as if they had decent houses to keep up, or a child to put through education. Charlie had recently embarked on a school fees scheme for Pelham, and was under no illusions about what it would all cost. And Abigail was already rich in her own right, wasn't she? Presumably that gross Semite Zubin Schwartzman had looked after her. On the flight to Istanbul, Charlie glared at his old friend Jamie, and Jamie's fat wife Abigail, and brooded on how unfair it would be if they inherited twice as much as he did. If anybody deserved a double share it was him – Charlie – who had actually worked for the Brand Group in Hong Kong, and played a big part in building it up, and had furthermore introduced Marcus to Cruickshank & Willis which had successfully handled the flotation on the stock-market. All these thoughts weighed on Charlie's mind as he anticipated the Black Sea cruise in Marcus's new yacht, *Marketmaker*.

A small reception committee awaited them on the veranda deck: two stewards bearing trays of drinks, *Marketmaker*'s Captain in white uniform with gold braid, Dick Mathias clutching a frosted martini glass, a beautiful Chinese girl dressed entirely in black . . . and Marcus. As the hydraulic platform jerked to a halt, Marcus, who was reading a pile of marked-up financial weeklies while speaking into a GSM cell phone, thrust them aside and bounded across the deck.

'Welcome, welcome, all of you! Can't tell you how delighted I am to have you here on my tub. Trust the journey wasn't too painful, boys waiting for you all right at the airport?'

'Absolutely, Marcus,' said Charlie. 'Went like clockwork. I must say, it's terrific to be here. This is a magnificent vessel.'

'Glad you approve. You have such high standards these days, you and Miranda, I was quite nervous inviting you. Thought it might not be smart enough.'

Charlie guffawed, though the remark worried him. It was essential Marcus didn't misread their situation.

'Now, who else have we got here? Jamie and Abigail, *wonderful*. I wish all my godchildren married each other, so much simpler for allocating cabins. Isn't that right, Alun?' He addressed this remark to the Chief Steward.

'Quite right, sir,' replied Alun, smiling.

'Put 'em in together, you see, married couples,' declared Marcus. 'Saves on cabins, bedding, doubling up.'

'We can squeeze Saffron and Mary in with us, if you're short of cabins,' said Jamie, ignoring his wife's furious face.

'I'm sure you'd enjoy that, Jamie, but luckily for the girls there are eight cabins. Eight or nine. Plus the owner's suite, as they insist on calling it. And half a dozen cabins for the crew on the lower deck. So we should just about manage at a pinch.'

He advanced on Mary who felt all her old anxieties rushing back.

'Mary! Mary, Mary, never contrary. You look peaky, Mary, must be that company of yours taking it out of you, the one you refused to sell to me. Well, you can rest here. Sleep, sunbathe, nothing planned for five days, hope you don't all die of boredom.'

He shook hands with Stuart – rather respectfully, Charlie noticed to his irritation – and pecked Saffron cursorily on the cheek. Miranda, watching him, wondered whether anything had happened between Marcus and Saffron, they seemed awkward together and she had hardly uttered a word since leaving London. Miranda would have to get to the bottom of it.

'First things first,' said Marcus. 'Grab a big drink, most important, then the stewards will show you where you're sleeping. There are telephones in all the cabins, in case you need to stay in touch with your offices. It's a Siemens system, seems to work reasonably well. If you want cell phones or satcoms, ask Alun here, he's the expert.

'Other than that,' Marcus went on, 'it's just the six of you staying this week. Thought we could have more fun that way, godchildren's benefit. Plus Dick, of course, who you all know, and Flora here, who I don't think you have met before. Flora Huang. Comes from Communist China. Flora's very attached to her Chairman Mao jacket. Been trying to coax her into a bikini, but no joy so far. Regards it as capitalist decadence, isn't that right, Flora?'

Flora Huang, who was really incredibly pretty, Mary thought, with her teenager's figure and shiny black hair, smiled at Marcus and shook her head. Then, in perfect English with the slightest trace of an American accent, she replied, 'No way am I parading about in a bikini. My chest is too flat and sunshine's bad for the skin, very ageing. Look at you, Marcus.'

'How the hell does the Chink fit into the picture?' Charlie asked Miranda, the minute they were alone. Miranda was inspecting her rail of dresses, which had been unpacked by a steward and hung up in the cabin, deciding which needed to be taken away for pressing.

'Search me. She looks about fourteen.'

'Twenty-two,' said Charlie. 'I asked.'

'She's quite cute in a skinny kind of way.'

'If you like shopgirls. When I lived in Hong Kong, the department stores were full of girls like that, working behind the cosmetics counters. Rich Chinese used to take them as concubines.'

'You think that about everyone, Charlie. You're always saying women are prostitutes.'

'You don't think she is then? Come off it.'

462

'I've absolutely no idea. And nor have you. You don't know anything about her. She looks all right to me, quite pretty and bright.'

'Bright? Oh, please.'

'Her English is excellent. You can't speak Chinese.'

'That's totally different. Anyway, what else would she be doing on board? She has to be Marcus's latest. And Saffron's looking pissed off. Bet you anything he's chucked her and moved on to this slanty-eyed Flora.'

'If that's true, you should be happy. You've been banging on about Saffron for months.'

'I don't know. Flora could be more dangerous, in actual fact. Marcus has always had a sick thing for young girls.'

'Have you seen the list of toys?' Jamie asked.

'What toys?' replied Abigail, raising her voice above the noise of the shower. She was washing her hair in the enormous walnut-panelled bathroom of their enormous stateroom, having already checked that the hairdryer worked perfectly.

'There's a list on the dressing table of all the things that come with the yacht. Listen: two Kayak canoes, one Sport Nautique ski boat, two Yamaha waverunners, one wave-blaster, two jet skis, two windsurfers . . . it goes on and on, this is incredible. There's more over the page. One inflatable Suzuki tender, one Boston Whaler – not sure what that is exactly – one four-person banana boat . . .'

'I hope we're not expected to go out on those things. I was planning on spending five days flat on my back, addressing my tan. Summer in England has been a wash-out. I'm practically suicidal.'

'This yacht is something else, isn't it?' Jamie said. He pressed a button and Burt Bacharach flooded the cabin: '*What the world needs now . . .*'

'These bathrobes on the back of the door, they're really nice quality,' Jamie went on. 'I'm sure Marcus won't miss them.'

'Jamie, *no!*' squealed Abigail.

He flicked another switch and electrically operated curtains began their slow journey across the windows.

'Abby, this is so cool, you've got to look. It's unbelievably naff, but I love it.' Flicking the switch on and off, off and on, he was completely absorbed, watching the curtains advance a few inches along their tracks, then shift into reverse.

'Oh, Christ, what's happened now? It's jammed. I can't move it. Look, it's stuck.'

'You'd better call a steward,' Abigail snapped. 'You know, you're so annoying sometimes, Jamie, why can't you just leave things alone? You break everything.'

'No need to bite my head off. It's not my fault.'

'You do it every time. You broke the radio in the new car the first day we got it, and it's still not fixed, two years later.'

'God, you're uptight. You know what you need, don't you? Come on, lock the door. We can do it right now if we're quick.'

'I'm afraid I don't know much about ships,' Mary said to Marcus during lunch on the main deck. 'Did you buy this one like this, or did you have to decorate it?'

'Had her built at the Nishii shipyards in Japan. Fellow named Jon Bannenberg came up with the design to my specifications.'

'It must have taken ages, it's enormous.'

'Put it this way, it was a lot quicker at Nishii with the Nips in charge, swarming over the hull on twenty-four-hour shifts, than if we'd had her built on the Clyde.'

'If you'd done that,' chortled Charlie, 'you certainly wouldn't have taken delivery yet. The brothers would still be on their tea breaks, if they weren't out on strike.'

'There barely is a shipbuilding industry in the north-west these days,' Stuart said. 'Aside from the occasional commission from the MoD, the whole place is a graveyard. We helped a client buy one of the old warehouses for a DIY superstore.'

'There's a moral there somewhere,' Charlie said. 'But I expect we're all too politically correct to recognise it. And, speaking of politics, I seem to remember last time we were all together in Wyoming, certain people who shall remain nameless predicted a Labour landslide at the General

Election. I hope those certain people now accept they have egg all over their faces, and that not all of the British population happens to be comprised of left-wing, mentally subnormal, crippled, lesbian communists from Islington or Camden or wherever it is you choose to live, Stuart.'

'Thank you, Charlie, for managing to insult at least three of my guests in one sentence,' said Marcus dryly. 'I think you might apologise to Mary, don't you? Her daughter is disabled, far as I remember.'

'Lord, I'm so sorry, Mary. I'd completely forgotten you've got a spastic, otherwise I wouldn't have said anything.'

Mary shrugged. 'You're forgiven, Charlie, you weren't to know.' But she was thinking that, once again, she'd made a colossal mistake in coming on a Marcus jaunt. She'd intended to refuse but, as always, had capitulated. Proximity to Charlie and Marcus made her miserable, she should know that by now.

'And how about apologising to Flora next?' Marcus was helping himself to *mezze* from a large dish. 'She probably doesn't appreciate communism being employed as a term of abuse.'

'Well, sorry about that too, Flora. Though I don't imagine you're a particularly rampant commie, all things considered.' He indicated the yacht with its prettily laid dining table under a white awning, and the four stewards circling with dishes of food.

'Oh, I definitely regard myself as communist,' she replied. 'I've been a member of the party since school. In fact it was the local party that sent me to college in the States.'

'But you don't actually believe all that one-man-one-ricebowl claptrap? I used to work for Marcus in Hong Kong, and anyone could see the free market works better than Mao's cock-up on the mainland. If it doesn't, how come about sixty thousand people a year try to jump the fence? I've never heard of anyone going the other direction.'

'I don't pretend everything in our system is perfect. No system is. But I saw more poverty in New York while I was studying there than I ever saw in Beijing.'

'Well, I go to Manhattan fairly frequently and never see any. Admittedly I avoid the subway.' Anxious to divert the conversation away from the tedious subject of socialism, he said to Marcus, 'Miranda and I stayed at the Carlyle when we were last in New York. That's where you stay too, isn't it?'

'Did,' said Marcus. 'I like it because your driver can wait outside on 76th Street. A lot of the hotels, they're moved on all the time. But I keep an apartment now on Sutton Place. In fact I lent it to Flora for the last term of her studies.'

At the end of lunch, the Captain of *Marketmaker* explained to the godchildren the schedule for the next five days' sailing. For the remainder of the afternoon, the yacht would stay at anchor in Istiniye Bay; transport was standing by for anyone who wanted to sightsee in the city, otherwise the top deck and veranda deck were set aside for sunbathing. That evening, the party would be taken across the bay in launches for dinner at Club 29, a recently opened Istanbul restaurant-cum-nightclub. ('The nearest thing the Turks can provide to Jimmyz in Monte Carlo,' noted Marcus.) Then, shortly before dawn tomorrow morning, *Marketmaker* would begin its journey up the Bosphorus to the Black Sea. They would stop for lunch at a fish restaurant called Anadolu Kavagi in the last village on the Anatolian side, and would then spend five days cruising the north Turkish coast as far as Sinop. 'At Sinop,' said the Captain, 'you will disembark and Mr Brand has arranged for you to be flown by private jet back to Istanbul for your connecting flights.'

'What about you, Marcus?' Saffron asked, addressing her godfather for almost the first time. 'Are you flying back to London with us?'

'Regrettably not,' he said. 'Dick and I will be extending our cruise over to Odessa. There's some business I have to sign off. You know the Soviets, nothing's official without a great banquet and vodka toasts. They're as bad as the Chinese in that respect, which is why Flora's coming with me, to keep an eye on protocol.'

Charlie, Miranda and Jamie all turned to Saffon to see how she was taking this news. She stared down at her coffee cup, temporarily frozen. Abigail and Mary both looked at Flora as the implication of the announcement sank in. Charlie nodded meaningfully at his wife, as if to say 'I told you so'. Stuart tried to think of something reassuring to say to Saffron, whose long brown legs were disturbingly close to his white hairy thighs, but could think of nothing appropriate.

After a long silence, Jamie asked, 'What's it like doing business with the Russians, Marcus? Aren't you worried they're going to set you up all the time? You know, a sting. They get some drop-dead-gorgeous blonde, Svetlana or whoever, to pick you up and then, while you're going at it hammer and tongs, the KGB are photographing you through a two-way mirror to blackmail you with the pictures.'

Feeling Saffron's discomfort, Stuart said, 'I'm sure that doesn't happen any longer. Post-*perestroika*, the KGB's virtually been disbanded. They don't spy on foreign businessmen, they're too desperate for inward investment.'

'You're absolutely correct, the KGB as an organisation has been significantly degraded. But I wouldn't write it off completely.' Marcus allowed Alun to top up his wine glass. 'The contacts I used to have inside the KGB have all become colossally rich, involved in the various industrial-criminal oligarchies. In many ways their power is greater now than it was before. I certainly feel I have to do more for them, not less, because it's essential to have them on side if you want anything to get done over there.'

'And you genuinely believe there's money to be made in the old Soviet Union?' Charlie asked, sounding sceptical. 'We've been approached over various deals at Cruickshank's, but can't see the profit. They always want to settle our fees in local currency or cucumbers.'

'Never been so convinced of anything in my life,' Marcus declared. 'Ask me my strategy for the next five years and I'll reply in three words: Russia, Russia, Russia. Get it right now and there are fortunes to be made five years out. Obviously you need to take the long view. This is a situation where the premium on first-mover status will come through in spades.'

'That's a really good tip,' said Charlie. 'Actually a mate of mine in the City is starting a business importing Russian caviar, and I thought I might become one of his backers.'

'I'll tell you an amusing story about caviar,' Marcus said, 'which also has the distinction of being absolutely true. Last time I was over in Moscow, five or six weeks ago, I had an invitation to call on Mikhail and Raisa Gorbachev out at their *dacha* in the country. Anyway, as you can imagine in a society like Russia, the whole expedition quickly turned into a massive bloody hoo-hah with outriders escorting the limousine front and back, armed security and God knows what else. Eventually we arrive at this *dacha* in the middle of a forest, which was pleasant enough if you appreciate that sort of thing – a lot of heavy furniture, antimacassars everywhere, half the Soviet Army lurking outside in the undergrowth – and the first person I see is Mikhail tooling about in a pair of Levis with his big red strawberry-mark on his forehead, and Raisa in what looks like a C&A housecoat, and they offer me a big dollop of caviar on a cracker. I make some friendly remark about how he must get unlimited supplies of caviar as General Secretary of the Communist Party, and you know what he says? "The thing Raisa and I love in your country is Marmite." That's right, Marmite. Apparently someone had given them a taste of the stuff in London, and they can't get hold of it in Moscow, not even in the *berioska* shops, doesn't exist. Minute I arrived home, I got Barbara to send off two big boxes to the Kremlin. Raisa said she was delighted. They eat it on black bread with little sticks of cucumber. Can't stand the stuff myself, but out there they prefer it to caviar.'

As soon as they had been dropped off in the Sultanahmet area of the city, where, alone of the godchildren, Mary and Stuart had elected to spend the afternoon visiting the Aya Sofya mosque and Topkapi Palace rather than sunbathe on the yacht, Mary said, 'I didn't want to talk in the car with the driver there, but what on earth's going on?'

'Between Saffron and Marcus?'

'Between everyone. I've never known it this tense before. Charlie's so uptight and so's Miranda. Jamie and Abigail aren't much better. I adore Abigail, but I know she's very unhappy at the moment. As for Saffon, I'm really worried about her, she's obviously miserable.'

'I tried to cheer her up at lunch, but failed dismally. It's Marcus, presumably. I've never really understood that situation, the way it drags on and on. Saffron should get out and find someone else.'

Mary glanced at Stuart to establish whether he could be referring to himself, but his face was impassive. When he chose to, he gave nothing away.

They bought tickets at a kiosk for the Topkapi Palace and ambled through the labyrinth of courtyards and harems, inspecting the treasury with its giant bronze braziers and Iznik faience, and the sleeping quarters of the eunuchs and concubines. Stuart was thinking, 'This is my big chance. If I don't grab it, it'll never come again.' He imagined a future for himself with Saffron at Ardnessaig. Hundreds of miles from temptation – and Marcus – she could make a new beginning. She must be thirty-five but she was wearing much better than he was. Sometimes, after an arduous week in the office, Stuart felt himself to be quite middle-aged. He was just about keeping his weight under control, through a disciplined regime of jogging, swimming and regular work-outs, but it was a constant battle. As for Saffron, he thought she was more beautiful now than when he'd first met her. He had no illusions about what he could offer her, compared to Marcus, but he would cherish her, and rescue her from all this.

'Did you talk to Flora?' Mary asked.

'Only for five minutes. But on first impression, I like her.'

'Me too. And she's incredibly on the ball. When you and Marcus were talking about the American balance of payments or whatever it was, she was so well informed. How does she know about Alan Greenspan and everything?'

'Listens carefully to Marcus probably. I don't want to be nosey, but how do you suppose they know each other? He mentioned she'd been living in his New York apartment, but you don't think . . . do you?'

Mary shrugged. She didn't want to be drawn on Marcus's sexual proclivities, it was too close to home.

'Flora doesn't seem his usual type,' Stuart said. Then, thinking of Saffron, he added, 'Not that Saffron was either. What I mean is, she's not like that girl he had in Wyoming, the Las Vegas one – Christina – or the one in France years ago, Clemence. Or those Madame Claude girls he went in for.'

'Madame Claude girls? I don't know about them.'

Stuart coloured. 'Oh, just something I once heard.' He had never mentioned to anyone his birthday present at the Hôtel Ritz, which still had the power to mortify.

'It might be entirely innocent with Flora,' Mary said. 'Marcus is probably just being kind.' She didn't buy into this theory herself, but said it anyway. 'Flora told me she was brought up in some really poor part of China. Her parents worked in a rice paddy and didn't even have any tools. She's done it all on her own. Getting to America, and everything.'

'Maybe it is all innocent,' said Stuart, who didn't believe it either. As if reading his mind, Mary said, 'Do you think anyone in the world has such a weird godfather as we do? I was thinking about that on the plane on the way out. He invites us on all these amazing holidays, but he's not exactly godly, is he? I mean, "godfather" has to be the worst description for him in the Christian sense.'

Stuart smiled. They were staring over the parapet of a courtyard at the top of the palace, watching the dozens of ferries and small boats plying their course beneath Galata Bridge. 'I sometimes wonder what Marcus gets out of it all,' he said.

'In what way?'

'Inviting us here, there and everywhere. This time it's Turkey. It must have been a big effort getting it together, even with Barbara on the case. Before that it was Wyoming. Before that, the Bahamas, France, that party for our twenty-firsts. Normal godparents wouldn't do that, even if they were as rich as Marcus is.'

'That's true.'

'What I reckon is he loves showing off his homes and all the gadgets – you know, those quad bikes at the ranch, and the jetskis on the yacht. Maybe he doesn't have that many friends to invite, apart from business people. His god-children are like this permanent mutual admiration society, who he can summon whenever he likes, and he gets all this reflected glory. It's a big ego trip for him, having us here.'

'I think you're being generous,' said Mary. 'I've thought about this a lot, and it's more complicated. In fact his motivation's really warped. You know how manipulative he is. He gets his kicks from interfering in our lives.'

'Come on, that's a bit melodramatic.'

'Think about it. We've all become more and more dependent on him. We're all involved with him one way or another. The only person who isn't is you, and that's only because you said no when he tried to get you into his company. Then you'd have been beholden too. Charlie used to work for him, still does really, he's at his beck and call twenty-four hours a day. Miranda says Marcus rings in the middle of the night to talk to Charlie about stocks and shares. Jamie used to work for Marcus and, according to Abigail, still has to sneak him into his hotel through the kitchens to meet girls. Then there's Abigail. She had a massive complex about him for ages, which her psychiatrist says was really damaging. And Saffron we've already talked about. He's been ruining her life for fifteen years – longer, actually – since the Bahamas. She's totally screwed up, and Marcus has a lot to answer for. Even with me, as you know, he's managed to worm his way into my business. He's my largest client and I can't walk away. And I'll never forgive him for what he did to my father. Do you realise, Dad hasn't even got a pension from the Brand Group, not a proper one anyway? I was seething about that at lunch today, as we sat about on that yacht. What do you think it cost to build? Five million pounds?'

'More like forty million, I'd guess. At least forty.'

'You're not serious? Christ! I'm sorry, Stuart, I don't want to be like this, but I can't help it. I get so angry when I think about it. Marcus uses people. He picks them up and spits them out.'

'Without being pedantic, he doesn't spit out his god-children, does he? As we've just observed, he goes on and on inviting us.'

'Only to keep tabs on us. He enjoys stirring it up, controlling us. Like at lunch today with Charlie, telling him to apologise to me and Flora. In a way, it would be better to be one of his employees – at least you get sacked and are out of it. But his godchildren don't get sacked. That's the ghastly thing. It never ends.'

'Mary, I've never heard you bitter before. You shouldn't have come if you hate it so much.'

She shrugged. 'I felt I had to, because of my business.' But her real motive, she knew, was more personal. Marcus was Clara's father, and she wanted to stay close to him for her daughter's sake. And she liked to study him: to try to recognise physical traits and gestures that had passed through to Clara. When she scrutinised her daughter, she could see nothing of Crispin, only her flattened, oddly featureless Down's characteristics, which made all Down's children look so alike. But watching Marcus at lunch raising a wine glass to his lips, frowning over the rim, she fancied she was reminded of Clara with her plastic beaker. She was here for Clara's sake, she told herself; for Clara, she would do anything.

'Meanwhile, we still have five more days to go,' said Stuart.

Mary laughed. 'You're right, we've got to make the best of it. It's just I hate the way his tentacles are everywhere, making us do what he wants. And the awful thing is, whatever he wants, we go along with it.'

How perfect is this? How happy am I? Saffron was sunbathing, topless, on a white sunbed next to the helipad on the top deck of *Matchmaker*, soaking up the last evening rays which fell, with delicious warmth, across her back. The top deck, off-limits to all crew-members other than Alun, had been designated a bare-breasts zone. Alun, as a self-declared homosexual, had special dispensation to deliver drinks.

Saffron would gladly have killed herself. She felt despair on a scale that was unimaginable. After lunch, Marcus had drawn her to one side and said, "Fraid I'm going to have to ask you to clear out of that flat when you get back. It's needed for someone else in the organisation.'

Saffron knew instinctively who that someone else would be.

'Will I see you again?' she asked him desperately. Having longed for her freedom, now that it was upon her, she felt only panic.

"Course you will. Hell are you talking about? You work for Barbara, don't you? Plenty still to organise in the office.'

Above her head, the giant titanium arms of *Marketmaker's* communications antennae moved to lock on to some space-bound satellite.

It had been Marcus's coldness that had shocked her. His distance had been brutal. 'If you could pack up your personal possessions by the end of the week, I'll have Makepiece deliver them wherever you choose.' She understood from his voice the finality of the situation. After nine tortuous years, it was all irrevocably over. At that moment, she could think only of the good times: dancing in Annabel's, the foreign trips, the exhilaration she felt when he directed his charm at her, and how she craved it as a small child craves sweets. She could no longer remember her transition from cool, disengaged girlfriend, almost dismissive of her godfather's early overtures, into needy mistress, jealous of his every absence, utterly in his thrall. She couldn't believe it had all ended. She saw no need for it to. She would willingly share Marcus with Flora, if it meant she needn't lose him completely. He handed her a gold Must de Cartier bracelet, less extravagant than other pieces of jewellery he had given her in the past. 'You mustn't go away empty-handed.'

Twice during the course of their long relationship, the subject of marriage had been raised, always obliquely. In her unworldly way, Saffron had never bothered making an issue of it. Now she wondered if she'd been stupid. She had given herself to two rich men, Nick and Marcus, but had nothing to show for it beyond a roll of jewellery and a cupboard full of clothes. She had no idea where she'd be living a week from today. Maybe Amaryllis and Paul would take her in, until she found a place of her own.

She had been conscious of Flora's existence for several months, originally by intuition: Marcus had been spending more and more time in Manhattan, and seldom invited her to join him there. The apartment on Sutton Place South, which she had helped choose and furnish, was out-of-bounds to her. When they spent an April weekend together in Rome, Marcus's love-making was more perfunctory than usual and once, meeting him at a restaurant after a shopping trip, Saffron saw him talking softly into a mobile telephone, as though not wanting to be overheard. Later that afternoon, back in their suite at the Hassler, she had pressed the Last Number Redial button and the name Flora Huang flashed up on the panel.

'Who's Flora?' she had asked casually, when they were in bed.

'Flora?' he answered too quickly. 'Flora? I don't know what you're talking about.'

'The Flora you rang from the restaurant.'

'Oh, that Flora.' His voice was full of bluster. 'Flora Huang, you mean. She's Chinese. She's someone who may be joining the company, to help advise us on opportunities in Red China.'

'And why is she at your apartment in New York?'

For the second time, Saffron sensed deceit.

'Why is she at the apartment?' Marcus played for time. 'Oh, she's studying for her master's degree over there – at Colombia. I said she could stay for a month. Coming from mainland China, she's not exactly long on dollars, poor little thing.'

'So Flora's a student. How old is she then?'

Saffron despised herself for asking, knowing it was the wrong way to handle Marcus. He hated to be cross-questioned.

474

'Twenty-five, since you ask. I believe so, anyway. Could be a year or two younger, never easy to tell with orientals. Why do you want to know? Not jealous, surely?'

'I just wondered who she is, that's all.'

'Because I do detest jealous females. Told you that before. Christina was jealous, always wanting to know where I was, who I'd seen, who I'd had lunch with. I told her: Mind Your Own Beeswax. She didn't – or couldn't – so out she jolly well went.'

Saffron thought this ironic, coming from Marcus, but said nothing, simply stared at him with one eyebrow raised.

'Another thing,' he had said, eyes blazing. 'Touch my telephone again and I'll break both your arms, understood?'

Later that afternoon, enticing her to sexual frenzy, Marcus had temporarily erased her worst suspicions; but Saffon understood that in Flora she had a serious rival.

Even now, after so long, she knew she didn't completely understand Marcus. There were areas of his life – of his heart and past – that remained closed to her. She knew nothing of his upbringing. She had met no members of his family, if he had one. Once, flying in his jet across the brown Central Massif of Anatolia, he mentioned spending time there as a young man, but said it in a tone that discouraged supplementary questions. She understood that, buried beneath the terse bonhomie, was a darkness of the soul. Emotionally reticent, he preferred to probe the feelings of others until he had located their epicentres of vulnerability.

Familiarity had not lessened his ability to undermine her; if anything, it had increased it. Sometimes, in his mental sadism and cold-bloodedness, in his desire to dominate everyone and everything around him, Marcus made Saffron physically sick. But when he chose to, he could make her feel more prized, and more beloved, than any man in the world could. After a period of neglect, he would love-bomb her, enveloping her with attention, sympathy and presents. Even when he strayed, as with Christina, Saffron had no doubt she remained the most important woman in his life. She could hardly believe he would now abandon her.

The evening sun began to lose some of its heat as it

descended into the hills. Saffron shivered, wondering whether to go below and change for dinner. She didn't know how she'd get through the evening, but didn't want to give Marcus the satisfaction of having her cry off. Dimly, she became aware of someone watching her.

'Who's that? Oh, it's you, Miranda.' She had appeared on deck in a long, strapless, turquoise Belville Sassoon evening dress, holding a flute of champagne. 'You look amazing.'

'Oh, thanks.' Miranda closed her eyes and bathed her face in the sun. 'Charlie allowed me to buy this dress for the cruise. You've no idea how out of character that is. He's as mean as bird shit.'

Saffron draped herself in a towel.

'Actually, I was looking for you,' Miranda said. 'I wanted to make sure you're OK.'

'I've had better days, but don't worry, I'm fine.' She thought the floodgates might open any time, but didn't want to break down in front of Miranda, whom she neither liked nor trusted.

'Charlie says if you're feeling down, come and have a drink in our cabin. We'd like to look after you. I mean, if Marcus has dumped you, you must feel ghastly.'

'I'm sure I'm not the first girl he's dumped,' Saffron replied wearily. She longed for Miranda to stop invading her space and go away. The Crieffs were the last people on the yacht she'd pour her heart out to. 'Truly, I'm fine. I'll see you at supper.'

Returning to the cabin with a look of triumph, Miranda announced to Charlie, 'OK, it's official. Straight from the horse's mouth. Marcus and Saffron are history. He's given Little Miss Golddigger the heave-ho.'

Charlie chuckled and poured himself a whisky. 'One down, one to go. Now all we need is to get rid of Suzy Wong. Drink?'

'No, thanks. I've been feeling queasy all day. You'd think a boat this expensive would have proper stabilisers, wouldn't you?'

*

Marcus chose the second night of the cruise to make his great announcement.

During the day, *Marketmaker* completed her journey up the Bosphorus and into the Black Sea. They had dropped anchor for the night at a place called Riva where a beautiful Genoese castle stood on a headland above the bay, and a river meandered across a wide beach into the sea.

As they entered the Black Sea, the waves became higher and the sea rougher, and Miranda, who had already been feeling sick for twenty-four hours, retreated into her cabin, and would have preferred to skip dinner altogether if Charlie hadn't forced her to get up.

'Sorry to hear you're feeling below par,' Marcus said. 'The Black Sea does have rather a treacherous reputation. The rollers regularly break the backs of ships, snap them in two. Three big rollers in a row, the third one does it for them. Snap! The longer Mediterranean hulls can't take it, you see. That's why Black Sea boats tend to be short and stocky.'

'We'll be all right, won't we, Marcus?' Abigail asked nervously. 'This yacht isn't particularly short or stocky.'

'Hope so,' he replied, roaring with laughter. 'Isn't that right, Captain? We're not going to snap in half, midway through our dinner? Mrs Temple's worried we might all end up in the drink.'

'I think we should be OK, Mr Brand,' replied the Captain, coming in on the joke. 'Providing we don't all stand on the same side of the deck at the same time, and tip ourselves over.'

'Excellent advice, Captain. You'd better make sure we've got equal numbers on either side of the table. Or perhaps we should weigh our guests first, balance out the fat ones with the skinny ones. What do you think of that idea, Abigail?'

Desperately self-conscious about her ballooning figure, Abigail flinched and didn't reply.

Stewards circulated with cocktails and tiny Turkish *mezze* while the guests waited for Saffron and Flora, who were the last to arrive. Jamie was drinking martinis with Dick Mathias who, ever the loyal major-domo, was talking about Marcus, describing him as the most brilliant and visionary business-man in the world today. Jamie was already on his third martini, Dick was two ahead. Jamie hoped that, by putting in the hours with Dick now, he wouldn't have to sit near him at dinner. Jamie was hoping for either Saffron or Flora, both of whom he fancied in different ways.

Dick was saying, 'If you could bottle and market Marcus's drive and ambition, you'd be a rich man.'

'Sure,' replied Jamie, only half listening. 'I used to work for him, remember. I know how ruthless he can be.'

'Ruthless is one word I've heard attached to him,' said Dick, who Jamie suddenly realised was half-cut. 'Ruthless, determined, call it what you like. Whatever he wants, he has to have it, no matter what. Believe me, nothing stands in his way, whether it's a business he's interested in buying, or a house, or this magnificent yacht. Or pussy.'

'Really?' said Jamie. 'I rather thought he didn't have to try too hard in that department.'

'One occasion,' Dick said, slurring his words now. 'I heard there was this young lady who'd caught his eye, and she was with this no-hoper at the time, and Marcus wanted him out the way to get a clear run at the broad. Do you know what he came up with, the crafty dog?'

'No idea. Tell me.'

'He fitted up this guy on a drugs rap. Tipped off the police who raided his hotel, and got him busted. Those are the lengths Marcus will go to when he wants something badly enough.'

Suddenly sobered up, Jamie asked, 'Where did this take place, this charming ruse of Marcus's?'

'Oh, some place in the tropics. India, I think it was. With the other guy safely inside the local jail, Marcus moved in and got the girl. That's what I mean by determined.'

Everyone having now surfaced on deck, Marcus was rallying the guests for dinner, admonishing Saffron and Flora for keeping them all waiting, before placing them on either side of himself. Saffron looked terrible, her eyes red and puffy; Mary could see she'd been crying. Miranda, surreptitiously watching Flora, thought she looked ridiculously underdressed in a black Commes des Garçons slip, but reluctantly conceded she was pretty, if androgynous teenagers were your bag. Charlie felt sick with anxiety, correctly predicting tonight was the night of their god-father's great proclamation. Abigail was still feeling crushed by Marcus's crack about overweight guests. Mary wished she was home with Clara. Stuart wished he was sitting closer to Saffron, so he could comfort her. Jamie was seething over Dick's revelation before dinner, which finally explained why the Udaipur police had chosen to raid his room that night ten years ago.

Marcus tapped the rim of his wineglass with a fork for silence. 'Seems to have become a tradition for me to stand up on my hind legs and formally welcome my godchildren, wherever we happen to be. I always say how happy and honoured I am you still agree to come and visit your increasingly elderly godfather' – shouts of 'Not so!' from Charlie – 'when, God knows, you have plenty else to be doing in your busy lives, what with work, wives, offspring and all the rest of it. Anyway, I'm genuinely delighted to have you all to stay once again, particularly aboard this yacht, which is a bit of a passion of mine at the moment and, I hope you'll agree, not too unbearably uncomfortable as these things go.'

Afterwards, when she tried to remember how Marcus had appeared on that decisive evening, Mary could only think of his silhouette outlined against the blackness of the Turkish night; the rails and rigging of the yacht lit up by hundreds of small white bulbs, the dark outline of the castle on the hill across the bay, waves breaking against *Marketmaker*'s carbon-fibre and aluminium hull. Marcus stood at the head of the table, restless, magnificent, faintly supercilious, addressing his godchildren like a board meeting, as though they were the bone-brained aristocrats, deposed and neu-tered politicians, sundry chancers and egregious yes-men who comprised the non-executive directors of the Brand Group.

'Now there are two important parish notices I do want to mention this evening . . .'

Charlie and Miranda stiffened. Here it came: they were about to learn whether it was five million or twenty.

'The first concerns breakfast. Ladies can have breakfast brought to their cabins in the morning. Press four on the telephone and it rings in the galley. Tell 'em what you'd like and they'll bring it to you. They should have most things down there. *Godsons*, however, I expect to see you on deck for breakfast any time after eight-thirty. Follow me so far? Splendid. Brilliant.

'The second announcement is something that gives me special satisfaction, since it concerns my godchildren who have, as I've frequently declared, provided me with more pleasure over the years than I can possibly say.' He beamed in the direction of Mary and Saffron, who both felt queasy at the reminder of the pleasure they'd given him.

Charlie felt himself relax. It was the big one.

'For several months now, I've been thinking long and hard about the future. All of you sitting around this table are fast approaching forty, children no longer. I would almost say you are grown-ups, or at least some of you are.' He allowed his eyes to move around the table, as if deliberating which of his godchildren might still be regarded as children, and which as adults.

'It has occurred to me that these regular gatherings we all so enjoy – the godchildren's summits – are in danger of becoming a little stale, with the same faces appearing year after year, all of us grow slightly older, if not always wiser. Consequently I have decided to adopt a seventh godchild, to introduce some fresh blood.'

Charlie and Miranda stared at each other, aghast.

'I first met Flora Huang in New York six months ago, and was immediately impressed by her intelligence and resilience. She was brought up in Communist China in the province of Guangzhou. She is an orphan and the story of how she made her way to the United States, via Hong Kong, is really something quite remarkable, and an inspiration to us all. During recent months I have come to know Flora fairly well, and regard it a privilege to call her a friend. From today, I will also call her my goddaughter. I asked Flora two weeks ago whether she would like to become a member of our club. Prudently, she suggested she first join us on *Marketmaker* and meet her fellow godchildren; see what she was getting herself into. I'm very glad to say that, shortly before dinner this evening, she told me that you've passed the test, and she has agreed to be co-opted as my seventh godchild. As she said herself, seven is considered an auspicious number in China, so the signs couldn't be better. Isn't that right, Flora?'

'Quite correct, Godfather Marcus.'

'There you are, you see, she's one of us already. Well, that concludes my announcement, and I'll let you all get on with your dinner. First, though, I think it would be a nice idea if we all rose to our feet and drank a toast to ourselves – the ever-expanding Cosa Nostra of godchildren.'

As the renovation of Ardnessaig neared completion, Stuart found himself spending every available weekend in Scotland. He tried to organise his working week so he could make the last shuttle to Edinburgh on Friday evenings, pick up a hire-car at the airport, drive north to Angus and put up at the Crieff Arms, an uncomfortable granite coaching inn in the main street in Bridge of Esk, now mostly frequented by travelling salesmen. As word got out that he was the new owner of the Ardnessaig Estate, he found himself an object of curiosity in the local town. Dropping into the public bar for a pint and a sandwich for the first time, he was mortified when the whole place fell silent as the locals stared at him – the new laird – hardly disguising their surprise and disapproval that he should enter the bar at all.

Saturdays he spent up at the house with his surveyor who was overseeing the works and the teams of foremen, electricians, plasterers, stonemasons, roofers and carpenters who were repairing every part of the house and outbuildings. The scale of what needed to be done was far greater than he had first envisaged. Almost all of the woodwork, on all four floors, was riddled with dry rot. The panelling in the drawing room, billiards room and dining room had to be stripped out and, once removed, the stone walls behind were discovered to be running with water, and had to be tanked and sealed. Large areas of the slate roof were taken up and replaced, and the turrets partially rebuilt. The wiring was so old and precarious that the electrician, Laurie McCraig from Dunkeld, marvelled that the whole place hadn't burned to the ground years before. After several failed attempts at jump-starting the hot water system, it had to be written off and every inch of piping in the house renewed.

Then most of the floorboards in the Victorian wing were found to be rotten, as was the central section of the main staircase. It seemed to Stuart that half the Scots pines in Angus were felled to provide replacement floorboards.

He rationalised the lay-out of the house, particularly of the domestic offices as the estate agent described the vast kitchens, pantries, larders and cold rooms beyond the green baize door. Doubting he would ever have servants himself, he had the door removed from its hinges and thrown on a skip, and the old morning room converted into a modern kitchen-cum-breakfast room, with a pine table in the window bay and pine units mounted on the walls. There were still half a dozen large downstairs rooms he had no idea what to do with, and seventy windows without curtains. For the dining room, he had managed to purchase the Crieffs' enormous dining table and twenty-four matching chairs from the Ardnessaig Estate sale, as well as a highly polished mahogany sideboard with a deep scratch across its surface. Otherwise, the place was conspicuously lacking in furniture and pictures. He planned on picking up as much stuff as possible at local sales. More than once, he wished Mary was there to help him. There were times, such as when he had made his ninth consecutive weekend visit to the Crieff Arms, that he wondered what he thought he was doing there at all, a working-class bachelor with this huge baronial home, and felt lonely and slightly pretentious.

He spent his Sunday mornings getting to know the half dozen tenants on the estate, the ghillie and gardener and the families who lived in the few remaining stone cottages that hadn't been sold off by Lord Crieff. Initially he felt slightly awkward about these relationships, not wanting to be viewed as some species of absentee gentry, but in time relaxed into his new role, conducting himself with friendliness and a certain understated authority. The condition of several of the cottages appalled him, with their leaking roofs and medieval plumbing. As he told Mary, 'Callum the ghillie lives in a croft with no inside toilet. He told me he's been asking for one for twenty years, but the Crieffs did nothing about it.' Recognising that he would never feel comfortable living up at the big house, with his seven en-suite bathrooms, unless the estate cottages were modernised too, he instructed the surveyor to draw up plans for them, starting with a new bathroom and central heating for Callum. He took out a second mortgage from Barclays to pay for it all, but viewed it as a moral imperative.

On Sunday afternoons, he loved to stride alone across the hills above the estate, listening to classical music on his Walkman, before catching the last shuttle south to London and reality.

It became his ambition to persuade his mother to quit Birmingham and move permanently into Ardnessaig. But Jean Bolton, at the age of seventy-three, was reluctant to leave her cosy Smethwick flat, her friends and the concert halls of the city. For reasons that Stuart didn't fully understand, Jean had misgivings about returning north. He assumed that she did not want to revive unhappy memories of his father's death in Scotland while driving Marcus's wife under the influence of alcohol. 'I know what you want, Stuart,' she joshed him. 'You're just looking for an unpaid housekeeper to keep that ridiculous big place of yours tidy.' Privately, she was touched her son should want her around to share some of his material success. In the end, it was agreed that she would spend half the year up at Ardnessaig, in a self-contained turret flat with its own separate entrance, keeping an eye on things, and helping Stuart make the place habitable.

After more than a year of builders, the house at last reached a point at which guests could be invited to stay. For his first-ever weekend houseparty, Stuart invited Mary and his goddaughter Clara, plus Jamie and Abigail Temple who, following the Black Sea cruise, were all enjoying an upswing in their friendship. The four of them flew north together on a British Midland morning shuttle, and Stuart collected them from the airport.

'This is a bit of a let-down,' Jamie teased him when he met them at the barrier. 'I thought you'd be wearing a kilt at least: the Royal Stuart. And where's your sporran? You're meant to be some great Scottish landowner these days, aren't you?'

'Hardly,' laughed Stuart. 'The estate was down to three

hundred acres by the time I came along, which is peanuts round here. And most of it's bog and heather.'

As they approached Ardnessaig, Mary thought she recognised some of the towns and landmarks from her previous visit, twenty years earlier, and experienced an extraordinary feeling of dread. When they drove through the massive iron gates, now back on their hinges, and past the granite lodges at the head of the drive, she felt as though she was returning to some ancient boarding school, at which she had been notably unhappy, as all her old insecurities rushed back.

'Bloody hell, what have you done to the place?' Jamie gasped as Ardnessaig came into view across the lawn. 'It's like Disneyland. The Magic Castle.'

'The pink, you mean? I decided to have the outside painted. Cheers it up, don't you think?'

'It's blinding. You have to shield your eyes.'

Stuart looked crestfallen. 'You don't think it's a mistake? Tell me truthfully. It's authentic, you know, several of the old places round here are painted white or pink.'

'Clara likes it anyway,' laughed Mary. 'Look at her. She's saying Mickey Mouse lives here. And I like it too, as a matter of fact. It feels like a different house.'

'It's a great pink,' Abigail said. 'Monet used a pink like that on some of the waterlilies.'

'But not on a ruddy Scottish castle, I'll bet he didn't,' said Jamie. 'I wish Charlie's mother was still around to see it. It's like Barbie's palace or something.'

They entered the hall into a wall of heat.

'It's *tropical* in here,' Abigail said. 'I love it.'

'It's for Mary,' Stuart said. 'She told me, the last time she was here, the place was freezing. So I've turned the heating on full blast. I can turn it down if you like.'

'No, don't,' said everyone at once.

'It's like a country house hotel.' Jamie made for a tray of drinks on a hall table, with spirits and mixers laid out, and pewter bowls filled with Ritz crackers and cheese footballs. The Great Hall of Ardnessaig, stripped of its shields, muskets and brown panelling, was now painted a pale shade of magnolia, and two large sofas, upholstered in new glazed chintz with a pattern of pineapples, stood opposite each other in front of the fireplace, in which stood a display of dried bulrushes in a ceramic vase.

Jean, who had never before met any of Stuart's guests, though she had heard plenty about them all, appeared in the hall wearing an apron over her dress, and making a great fuss of Clara, for whom she produced special toys and books. Having been introduced to everybody, she took Clara away into the kitchen with her, to help her prepare lunch, while Stuart took the grown-ups on a tour of the house.

The whole place, Mary saw, was transformed out of all recognition. Apart from the great height of the rooms and the Victorian cornices, and the positioning of the windows, she would never have known this was the same house. The gloomy drawing room in which she had encountered Lady Crieff smacking the Labrador puppy with a rolled-up newspaper, was now painted Dulux beige, with suede-covered sofas and chrome-and-leather armchairs, and a four-deck Bang & Olufsen music centre winking and blinking on a pine trestle. The original dining room, in which the buffet supper had been served before Charlie's eighteenth birthday discotheque, was occupied by a ping-pong table, the vast baronial dining table and matching chairs having been shifted to the library on the sunnier side of the house, overlooking the terrace, on which Jean had erected a bird table festooned with nuts in rope bags.

'Now this I do have to show you,' Stuart said, throwing open the door to the cellars. 'When I bought this place, I don't think anyone had set foot down here for about twenty years. There were Led Zeppelin posters on the walls and piles of rotting mattresses.'

'Too right,' said Jamie. 'I had a major tongue sandwich with Zara Fane on one of them.'

Stuart led them down the steep cellar steps, now carpeted with coir matting and smelling overpoweringly of fresh paint and eucalyptus.

'It's a bit of an indulgence this, I have to admit,' he said. 'Gym and sauna. I've only got three pieces of equipment so far, but there's a rowing machine on order.'

Mary, Abigail and Jamie stared in astonishment at the low-ceilinged cellar, arranged with Cybex dips and abs frames, a Nordic Wendy house containing a sauna, and a smoked-glass shower unit. The arched Victorian wine bins, once monopolised by snogging pens, contained piles of fluffy beige towels on pine shelves.

They had shepherd's pie and apple tart with cream in the kitchen, cooked by Jean, and afterwards Stuart suggested a long walk across the hills. 'If we're lucky, we might even see a few deer. There's usually a few up near the top loch.'

Mary suggested she should probably stay behind at the house with Clara, worried she might not be able to keep up.

'Nonsense,' said Stuart. 'Of course Clara's coming. When you get tired, Clara, I'll carry you on my shoulders. Anyway, we'll take the Land Rover to the end of the road, let's do this the easy way.'

They climbed up the steep side of a heather-clad hill, then walked along the spine between two deep glens, looking down on several small lochs where a herd of roe deer were grazing. 'You can think of me,' Stuart said. 'Every weekend I walk along here, it's my favourite hike, I do all my best thinking on this track.'

'What's that pretty house down there?' Mary asked, pointing to a large gabled manse across the valley, in the direction of Ardnessaig.

'That's the old Estate Manager's house, from the days when the estate was large enough to need a manager. You know who lives there now? Mary Jane Crieff, Charlie's sister. I met her the other day in the village, she came up and introduced herself. Seems quite a pleasant lady, nothing like Charlie.'

'God, I remember Mary Jane,' said Jamie. 'Does she still look like a gorilla? That's what we used to think, anyway.'

'I wouldn't say that. She's no beauty, but she's OK-looking. She's what I'd call a proper country lady, loves her dogs and horses, doesn't put a lot of effort into her personal appearance.'

'So she never married?' Mary asked.

'Apparently not. She runs a kennels from her place,

people leave their dogs there when they go away on holiday. And she breeds terriers.'

'I'd be curious to see her again,' Jamie said. 'Can't we drive by her house or something? At prep school, Charlie had photos of his sisters pinned above his bed, and we drew bones through their noses and underarm hair.'

'Sounds sophisticated,' said Stuart sarcastically. 'I knew I missed out on something not going to private school. Anyway, if you want to visit Mary Jane, that's no problem. I've got an open invitation to drop round anytime. I'll call her.' He produced a mobile from the pocket of his waxed jacket and scrolled through the address book. In a moment a plan was fixed. 'We're invited to tea. She says she's looking forward to seeing you, Jamie, and are you still as handsome as you used to be?'

The Honourable Mary Jane Eloise Crieff, elder daughter of the late Lord and Lady Crieff of Ardnessaig, had inherited almost nothing from her parents, either materially or in her character. Having spent her childhood being lectured on her noble lineage, and her twenties being pushed towards one suitable marriage or another, she had stubbornly remained single and was devoting the remainder of her life to doing what she enjoyed best, which was breeding Border Terriers in her cold, untidy house.

At the age of fifty, she was wonderfully indifferent to the opinion of the rest of the world. When she had visitors, it did not occur to her to straighten the sitting room or clear away the old coffee mugs and remains of her lunch which still sat on a tray on a footstool. Her smart neighbours, who had grown up with eccentric, outspoken Mary Jane, were not in the least perturbed. At least twice a week she hurtled off in her ancient shooting brake to dine with old friends. But on the other nights she was just as happy on her own with the dogs and a good detective novel, eating supper in bed with the television on. The hearth in front of her fireplace was spread with sheets of old newspaper, on which stood a dozen tin dog bowls filled with smeary scraps of meat and dog biscuits.

'So you're Jamie?' she boomed as Stuart's party filed into her hall. 'Well, you've kept most of your hair, I see.'

As she led them through into her chaotic, cosy sitting room, where the faded chintz covers were covered by a thatch of dog hairs, half a dozen terriers shot across the room, yapping and wagging their tails and jumping up at the visitors.

'*Down*, Errol. *Down*, Fergie. Get *down*, you naughty beast.' For a moment, Mary was reminded of Lady Crieff, and felt rising panic. But she soon realised that Mary Jane with her big tweedy legs, sagging bosom, uncombed hair and chapped red face, was as unlike her mother as it was possible to be.

'Well, Jamie, do you still see anything of that pompous ass Charlie?'

He replied they occasionally had lunch together.

'You were great muckers once upon a time. Always staying at the big house. I remember thinking then: what does he see in Charlie? He's always been sneaky, my brother. You know he put Ardnessaig on the market before our parents were even buried? Sold the lot. He'd have sold this house too if he'd been allowed to. Luckily it had been given to me for my lifetime. And that's in writing.'

Feeling he should say something in defence of his old friend, Jamie said, 'He was on quite good form, last time I saw him.'

'Can't think why, with a wife like that. Miranda. They deserve each other. Much too grand for me.'

Mary Jane, Mary and Clara went into the large, icy kitchen to put on the kettle and lay a tray with the unmatched mugs and tea cups, some of which were original Wedgwood, Mary noticed, others promotional tat from the local garage shop. 'Don't mind builders' tea, do you?' Then, pointing at Clara, Mary Jane asked, 'What does it eat?'

'Just about anything, don't you, Clara?'

'Good. Can't stand fusspots. There should be some doughnuts in the bread-bin. Best check they're not stale.

'So how do you lot all know each other?' she asked when the tea had been carried through into the sitting room.

489

'Oh, we've known each other for years,' Jamie replied. 'Originally through someone called Marcus Brand. We're all his godchildren. Actually that's how I first met Charlie too, through Marcus.'

'Marcus Brand? That stinker! Good Lord, how perfectly frightful. My parents wouldn't have him in the house.'

'Then how come they chose him as Charlie's godfather?' Abigail asked. 'That seems kind of contrary.'

'Oh, God, it was during all that business about Lucy Macpherson. I don't know the whole story, no one ever really talked about it, but I do know Marcus behaved very badly, something to do with siphoning money from Lucy's trust. And then she was killed in that ghastly motor accident which conveniently got Marcus off the hook, otherwise he'd have ended up inside – that's what people said, anyway.'

'Who was Lucy Macpherson exactly?' Mary asked. 'I've never really heard about her before.'

'Lucy? Sweet girl. Her parents lived up the road at Tolquhoun House. Wonderful place, now turned into a police training college. Anyway, she met Marcus when she was seventeen or eighteen, fell madly in love and married him against her parents' advice. She really was the prettiest thing, half the young men round here were absolutely spitting. I was a bridesmaid at their wedding, as a matter of fact.'

'And then what happened?' Stuart asked, suddenly full of trepidation.

'Couldn't tell you the details, because Jock Kerr-Innes, who was Lucy's trustee, hushed the whole thing up. Silly old fool! Marcus ran rings around him. It was something to do with Lucy's house down in London, which her parents had given her as a wedding present. Marcus mortgaged it and put the money into his business without telling her, or anyone else for that matter. Totally outrageous because the house was held in trust. When it all came out, the Macphersons wanted Lucy to leave Marcus, and I gather she was on the point of doing so, too. Then they were going to have him prosecuted for fraud.

'Poor Lucy, she was so in love with him, even though he was completely unfaithful, put it about like a tom cat. She didn't know what to do. The Macphersons summoned Marcus up to Scotland for an explanation, and Lucy was desperate about it all, not knowing whether to side with her parents or her husband. Then, in the middle of the night, Marcus got his chauffeur to drive her down to Edinburgh. God knows why, it was a filthy night in the middle of October. He said she was pregnant, or thought she was, and insisted on seeing her doctor. Never made any sense to me, but that's what he said. And the chauffeur turned out to be rat-arsed; been drinking whisky all evening. Drove into a tree and got them both killed instantly. Just outside Forfar. Terrible tragedy, her parents never really recovered. Hector Macpherson went ga-ga soon after. But convenient for Marcus, because Lucy had left him everything in her will.'

'So the fraud case and all that was dropped?' asked Abigail.

'Jock felt pretty miffed about it, so did Hector. Nobody round here knew anything for ages, which was why my parents appointed Marcus as one of Charlie's godparents. Lucy was going to be a godmother, but they transferred it over to Marcus after the accident. He was banished by the Macphersons, of course, they never saw him again. But by then he'd got his mitts on poor Lucy's capital.'

'That *was* lucky,' said Jamie.

'Lucky my foot! If you ask me, Marcus and the chauffeur were in cahoots. The whole thing was a set-up, he wanted her out of the way.'

'But why would the driver agree to that?' asked Stuart. 'He was killed, for God's sake. No one would do that.'

'Don't you believe it,' snorted Mary Jane. 'If the money was right, I'm quite sure any chauffeur would murder his employer. Why not? He'd probably meant to jump out before the car hit the tree.'

'Well, I'm sorry he didn't make it then,' said Stuart, standing up. As he crossed the room, he felt his cheeks burn and his legs buckle beneath him. 'Anyway, thanks for having us all over, Mary Jane. Next time, you must come to Ardnessaig.'

It was over breakfast on Sunday morning that Abigail announced her wonderful news. 'I just have to tell you guys. I've been holding out on you. I'm – we're – going to have a baby.'

'No! Oh, Abby, that's so lovely.' Mary hugged her friend. Only her slight anxiety that something might once again go wrong made her hold back. 'When's it due?'

'March. I'm four-and-a-half months gone already. My doctor says it's OK to start telling people, I'm through the danger phase.' Abigail had tears in her eyes. 'You've all got to keep your fingers crossed for me, but it really does look good this time. I can hardly believe it myself, it's like a miracle.'

Mary hugged her again and kissed Jamie. Clara, guessing something was up, hugged her godfather who hugged her back. Stuart, announcing they had to celebrate, fetched a bottle of champagne from the fridge and made a large jug of Buck's Fizz. Jean, declaring that Abigail had to have a proper breakfast, since she was eating for two, immediately added extra rashers of bacon and sausages to her pan, and bread into the toaster. Understanding how much her friend had longed for this baby, Mary said a quiet prayer to herself. She worried Abby wouldn't survive another disappointment.

Jamie sat across the table, saying nothing, spreading a croissant with marmalade.

'You are a dark horse,' Stuart told him. 'How long have you known about all this?'

'Couple of months. I'm gradually getting used to the idea. The biggest shock was when Abby told me, because we didn't think we could.'

'You mean it wasn't by IVF?' Mary asked, amazed.

'Totally natural. Conceived on Marcus's yacht. A quickie in the cabin before lunch.'

'Jamie! Honestly, you shouldn't say that.' Abigail was bright red, but laughing. 'It's indecent. Especially in front of Stuart's mother.'

'Wham-bam-thank you, ma'm,' Jamie went on. 'Hit the bull's-eye first time. The golden shot. A lot more fun than beating the bishop in that fertility place, I promise you.' In fact, Jamie felt slightly shifty about the circumstances of conception, since he remembered he'd been fantasising about Saffron in her bikini at the moment of ejaculation. 'You know what I think?' he declared, all puffed up with triumph at siring a child. 'Half these sperm doctors are just con artists. All that buggering about with thermometers and test tubes. I'm telling you, if you want to get a bird up the duff, a decent rogering at sea does the trick every time, no problem.'

48: March, 1994

Poppy Harriet Margaret Temple was born in the Lindo Wing of St Mary's Hospital, Paddington, weighing a healthy eight pounds, seven ounces.

Having missed the birth by fifteen minutes, because he was busy testing cocktails with Bender Barraclough in the new Chatsworth bar at 60 Montpelier Gardens, Jamie spent much of the rest of the week shuttling between the maternity floor and Victoria Wine across the road, buying vast quantities of champagne with which to toast his daughter's arrival.

While Abigail sat up against pillows nursing her beautiful baby, and exclaiming over the dozens of bunches of flowers that arrived at five-minute intervals, Jamie stalked the corridors in search of glasses and ice buckets, or surreptitiously watched cartoons on the television at the foot of his wife's bed. Knowing he was already in trouble for skipping the birth, he felt unable to leave the hospital, yet couldn't work out what he was meant to be doing there. As he decanted an overpowering arrangement of lilies, roses and stephanotis, sent by Marcus, into a too-small cut-crystal vase, he lustfully eyed up the younger nurses and even a pretty mother in an adjacent room.

Abigail was besotted with Poppy. She had no doubt that her longed-for baby was the most beautiful and intelligent child the world had ever seen. Even when Mary, Clara and Stuart came to visit, she could hardly lift her eyes from the baby to say hello. It was left to Jamie to invite Mary and Stuart to become Poppy's godparents, along with Camilla Silcox and Nipples Ayrton-Phillips. And when Charlie dropped by wearing a dinner jacket, en route to a charity ball at the Dorchester, Abigail could scarcely bring herself to ask about Miranda's new baby, Marina, who had been born ten weeks earlier at the Portland.

494

'Miranda was already pregnant on *Marketmaker* actually,' Charlie said, 'though we weren't aware of it at the time. She felt bloody awful the entire cruise. Thought it was seasickness.'

He eyed the flower arrangements around the room. 'Are those from Marcus? He sent Miranda exactly the same sort.' Examining the tag, he said, 'At least it's only signed from Marcus. If Flora's name was on the card too, then we should worry.'

A happy consequence of Poppy's birth was a rapprochement with Zubin and Harriet, who flew to London on the first available Concorde, weighed down by Bon Point smocked sleep suits, elaborately crocheted bonnets and cashmere swaddling blankets for their granddaughter. Zubin appeared utterly unembarrassed that he hadn't set eyes on his daughter for almost eight years, or even met his son-in-law before, whose hand he wrung for so long, and with such vigour, that Jamie thought it might be broken. Later that evening, declaring Harriet and Abigail needed to spend time alone together to discuss women's subjects, Zubin insisted on Jamie joining him for cocktails in the American Bar of the Savoy, where he assured him how satisfied he and his wife were with Abigail's choice of husband, even though it was a terrible thing for a Jewish father when a daughter married out, and how he was planning on settling a large sum of money on Poppy, just as soon as his attorneys could draw up the necessary papers. Jamie, who would have preferred any surplus cash to have come in his own direction, nevertheless thanked his father-in-law profusely and, by the time he'd finished his seventh tequila, implied he was seriously considering converting to Judaism himself one day, in the hope it might do him some good.

Harriet, meanwhile, was busy terrorising the staff and nurses of the Lindo Wing, which had shocked her with its spartan conditions and lack of en-suite bathrooms. She told the Irish sister she couldn't believe Princess Diana had really had the royal princes there, or how she'd ever put up with it.

Abigail implored her mother to shut up and stop

embarrassing her, but she was in such a state of rapture that nothing could spoil her contentment. Poppy was adorable and perfect, and her parents were pleased with her at last. Jamie had had a successful evening bonding with her father, judging by their colossal mutual hangovers; Zubin even told her how much he liked Jamie, and how she must be sure to look after him properly.

Even when Margaret Temple arrived at the hospital far too early, and had to be introduced to Zubin, it had all gone far better than it might have done. Margaret presented her granddaughter with a Victorian napkin ring – the only one, as it happened, that Jamie had somehow overlooked during his druggy phase – which, to Harriet's eyes, looked rather scratched and tarnished, and didn't even come in a smart box.

When Zubin mentioned how delighted he was that Jamie would shortly be embarking on a course of instruction in Hebrew, prior to his conversion to Judaism, Margaret was fortunately too occupied explaining the history of the English napkin ring to his wife to pay attention.

49: September, 1994

His stomach full to bursting with *bratwurst*, roast venison with black cherries and black forest gâteau, Stuart staggered on to the evening flight from Frankfurt to London City airport and fell gratefully into his seat. The only drawback to working for the Germans was the vast meals they expected their executives to consume; in the six months he'd been working for Darmstadt Commerzhaus, he'd put on eleven pounds, and his suit trousers were straining at the waistband.

In all other respects, he was more than satisfied with his decision to leave McKinsey and join Europe's sixth largest bank. Originally founded more than a hundred years earlier in the medieval town of Darmstadt, it had long ago shifted its headquarters north to Frankfurt and grown and diversified until it employed more than 55,000 people around the world, with a major corporate finance arm, asset management, an equities and bond area, and expertise in retail banking. After his transmigrant existence at McKinsey, Stuart relished the commitment to one mighty organisation, particularly one with offices and opportunities across so many continents. Under his new arrangement, he spent six working days a fortnight in London and four at Head Office in Frankfurt. Although the culture of Darmstadt Commerzhaus was defiantly Teutonic, with its aversion to risk-taking and emphasis on strong internal controls, he nevertheless enjoyed the hybrid backgrounds of his co-workers that he'd first encountered at college in the States. Working cheek-by-jowl with Germans, Austrians, Greeks and South Americans, in a driven atmosphere in which class counted for little and ability and hard work for everything, Stuart felt he was building his career on a level playing field, on which the ingrained prejudices of the British financial establishment held no sway. In any case, as he often asserted, ten years out there wouldn't be a British-owned merchant bank or firm of stockbrokers left in the City, the whole lot would be bought up by Americans, Japanese and Europeans. Better to accept that reality now than hang about waiting to get picked off. When he'd shared the theory with Charlie Crieff on Marcus's yacht, Charlie had dismissed it with a sneer. 'I daresay a few of the smaller players might agree to prostitute themselves to the Yanks or the Krauts but, believe me, it won't happen at Cruickshank & Willis. I can't see Wanker or Iain selling out to some New York corporate bean counter who drinks milk at dinner.'

Stuart's increased salary and bonuses at the bank had enabled him to complete the work at Ardnessaig, and he now spent as many weekends up there as possible. Bit by bit, he made friends among his neighbours, and most Saturdays was asked over for lunch or dinner at one monstrous pile or other. Far from avoiding the self-made lad from Birmingham, the local gentry, bored rigid with their own company, were only too delighted to secure a new face for their parties, particularly as the new owner of Ardnessaig was so unpretentious, single and evidently rich. Stuart's latest project, which he was planning with characteristic thoroughness, was the conversion of the old coach house into an indoor swimming pool for the benefit of his goddaughters, Clara Gore and Poppy Temple. Having no children of his own, he was keen to do as much for his godchildren as possible.

Shortly before the London flight backed away from the stand, the seat next to Stuart was taken by a tall, imperious, middle-aged businessman in a taupe-coloured coat with a brown velvet collar. He was carrying a black leather briefcase with an Executive Club leather luggage tag, and a copy of that morning's *Financial Times*. 'Bloody hell,' he exclaimed, as the plane became airborne. 'Do I deserve a whisky! Celebrate getting out of the Fatherland in one piece. Always half think one's going to get dragged off by the ruddy Gestapo, and never seen again.'

In no mood for conversation, Stuart smiled grimly.

'Name's David Fitzbiggin. Cruickshank & Willis.' The man stuck out his hand.

'Er, Stuart Bolton. I'm with the Gestapo, sort of. Darmstadt Commerzhaus.'

'Oh, I *see*,' his fellow passenger replied reproachfully. 'Consorting with the enemy. Too bad.'

'I know someone at Cruickshank's actually: Charlie Crieff.'

'Charlie! His Lordship. Good man, Charlie. How on earth do you two know each other?'

'We share a godfather, so our paths cross from time to time.'

'Charlie's a good bloke. Bit of a jerk sometimes, but then who isn't? Actually, I feel a bit sorry for him. You know he had to sell his family seat up in Scotland?'

Before Stuart could reply, David Fitzbiggin went on, 'It was bought by some fearfully naff self-made chap from the Midlands and he's totally ruined the place, according to Charlie. You can just imagine: gold swan taps in the bathrooms, Jacuzzis everywhere. Terrible shame, isn't it, when the old estates fall into the wrong hands? As Charlie said, "You can take the boy out of Birmingham, but you can't take Birmingham out of the boy."'

50: December, 1996

Of the many exclusive and fashionable private nursery schools in Holland Park, none was quite so exclusive or fashionable as Busy Lizzie's in Campden Hill Road. No less an authority than the London Life section of the *Evening Standard*, in a light-hearted survey of the capital's pre-school education, described Busy Lizzie's as 'a net-worker's paradise, where parents include two senior controllers of the BBC, an Oscar-winning independent film-maker, three national newspaper editors, two Tory cabinet ministers, a multi-millionaire socialist peer and last year's winner of the Turner Prize'. Even to secure a place on the waiting list for the kindergarten was proof of massive social prominence in the city; every year, the list of disappointed parents grew longer and more distinguished. It was reported that Madonna had been informed there was no way her daughter could be added to the waiting list at only a year's notice, and an American senior partner of Goldman Sachs, relocating to London, was rumoured to have promised Busy Lizzie's Headmistress, Lizzie Frobisher, fifty thousand dollars in cash if his two-year-old son, Mitchell, could jump the queue; an offer she immediately and sharply rejected.

Charlie Crieff had rung from Miranda's bedside at the Portland hospital, within six hours of Pelham and Marina's births, to reserve places at Busy Lizzie's, and even then the Crieffs had twice been called in for lengthy interviews with Lizzie Frobisher before their places were confirmed. Charlie was fond of observing that, 'The waiting list for Busy Lizzie's is longer than the waiting list for White's – and a lot more expensive once you're in.' It therefore greatly annoyed him when Jamie and Abigail managed to secure a last-minute place for Poppy, after a famous rock star couple pulled their daughter out at the eleventh hour, having been advised to live overseas for a year for tax reasons.

Had Abigail not run into her godfather Marcus, entirely by chance, in the lobby of 60 Montpelier Gardens, she never would have invited him to come and watch Poppy perform in Busy Lizzie's end-of-term Christmas nativity play, which was taking place a few days later in an upstairs classroom at the nursery school. Afterwards, she couldn't think what had come over her. Possibly she had been feeling guilty, she told Jamie, having done nothing for Marcus since the Black Sea cruise three years ago. In any case, she found close proximity to him always had the effect of sending her into a blind panic, and blurting whatever came into her head. He had enquired after her baby, and Abby had replied, 'Poppy's quite a big girl now. She goes to Montessori and she's being an angel in their little play. It's so sweet. You should come see her.' Marcus had replied he'd be delighted to come if he was free, and maybe Abigail could let Barbara Miles know the date and time of the performance. To Abigail's horror, Barbara rang that very afternoon for the details and, having consulted Marcus's diary, confirmed the great tycoon's attendance at his goddaughter's daughter's matinée.

Abigail told Miranda on the school steps what she'd done ('I must have been crazy') and Miranda reported the conversation that evening to Charlie, who was furious. 'Isn't that just typical of the Temples?' he stormed. 'Is there nothing they won't stoop to?'

'What do you mean?' Miranda asked, only half paying attention. She was briefing Maha on Pelham and Marina's costumes for the play, instructing her to make angel wings out of wire and netting, and a gold-paper crown for Pelham who was to be one of the Three Kings.

'You're not listening, Miranda,' Charlie said. 'This is serious. They're being totally opportunistic. Don't you understand, their whole plan is to suck up to Marcus? It's so obvious and cynical. Imagine using your children in that way.'

'Abigail said she met Marcus by accident in Jamie's hotel.'

'Oh, yes? Believe that, you'll believe anything. Anyway, it's not going to work, because we'll be there as well.'

'*You're* coming to the nativity play? That's a first. You usually say it's too far to come from the City.'

'It is ruddy inconvenient. I'll have to cancel two important meetings. But I'm not giving the Temples a clear run at Marcus. If he's going, I'm going.'

The day of the great performance arrived and, as he journeyed home on a half-empty lunchtime tube, Charlie was in a stinking mood. He had jacked out of rather a key board meeting with Iain and Wanker, and knew exactly who to blame: Jamie. First he provided Marcus with short-time hotel rooms in which to get his rocks off in the afternoon; now he was parading his child to win Brownie points. Between Jamie, Abigail and Suzy Wong, Charlie felt there was a conspiracy to cut him out of the picture altogether.

By the time he arrived at Busy Lizzie's, there were already more than a hundred people crammed into the tiny class-room: mothers with babies sitting on their knees, doting grandmothers, big sisters with braces on their teeth, Filipino housekeepers and Croatian au pairs, a few fathers here and there who obviously didn't have anything more important to do. Charlie was full of contempt for these idle, under-stressed househusbands, whose jobs were of such little significance they could afford to take the afternoon off to watch a Christmas play. Pushing to the front in his long black overcoat, he searched for a place to sit down.

Miranda was desperately signalling to him from the front row: 'I've kept you a place.' Charlie saw a vacant orange moulded plastic seat – a child's chair big enough only for a midget. And there, astonishingly, already perched on the very next chair, was Marcus in a beaver-lapelled overcoat, legs stretched out in front of him, drawing on a large and highly pungent cigar. Miranda gave Charlie a look that meant, Have I done well or have I done well? She said, 'Unfortunately Abigail arrived too late to reserve any seats. She and Jamie are standing at the back. So I asked Marcus to sit with us.'

Lizzie Frobisher made a breathless speech about how hard everyone had worked, particularly the children, and how official videos of the performance could be ordered afterwards at a cost of £25 each and, for those who had been asking, fresh supplies of Busy Lizzie sweatshirts and baseball caps would shortly be in stock and advance orders were being accepted in the school office. Charlie surreptitiously glanced at his watch and wished they'd hurry up and start, or rather finish, since he wanted to collar Marcus about some interesting investment opportunities.

Several pretty young teachers shepherded the children on to the shallow stage. Charlie scanned their faces until he found his own offspring, who looked annoyingly shy and whey-faced compared to others in their class. Pelham at four and a half years old struck Charlie as soft. With his curly blond hair, claret-coloured velvet knickerbockers that he'd recently worn as a pageboy, frilly white shirt and long cashmere cloak made from one of Miranda's old evening wraps, he looked like Little Lord Fauntleroy staring vacantly into space. Charlie felt sure that, at the same age, he'd had far more get-up-and-go than his son; he tried to catch Pelham's eye, to ginger him up in front of Marcus, but the boy was miles away, picking his nose in a dream. Marina, in Charlie's opinion, was hardly much better. Impeccably turned out in a long white nightie and the perfectly symmetrical gauze wings that Maha had worked on late into the night, she was easily the most angelic of the three angels; her fine, very blonde hair was cut into a perfect bob, with a little sprig pulled up on top and tied with a bow in Crieff tartan. Her tiny buckled shoes shone with Maha's polish. And yet, standing next to the extrovert and untidy Poppy Temple, Charlie felt his daughter looked slightly anaemic, even cowed, as she refused to look up and sucked her thumb. Not that he wanted Marina to emulate Poppy, of course. Miranda was fierce on the subject of Poppy: how Abigail allowed her to dress for school in whatever she chose – lime green leggings, pink ra-ra skirts, even Barbie trainers if she felt like it. With her luxuriant black hair which seldom saw a comb, and big brown eyes, Poppy looked like a gypsy child to Charlie. But he couldn't deny she'd inherited Jamie's charm and sense of mischief. She was perched on her tiptoes, bright as a button, blowing kisses to her parents at the back of the hall.

'I like that little girl throwing kisses, look,' Marcus said. 'She's cute. Is she one of yours, Charlie?'

'Er, no, I'm not sure who that is,' he replied. 'The girl in the dirty gym shoes, you mean?'

The nativity play made no sense to him. In order to fit in as many cameo roles as possible, so that every child in the school had something to do or say, the Christmas story had been stretched to its limits. As well as Mary and Joseph, the shepherds, angels and Three Kings, there were astronauts, dinosaurs, Ninja turtles, robin redbreasts and a Mr and Mrs Santa Claus. A pair of twin brothers appeared as Batman and Spiderman, having refused point blank to take part as anything else. The little oriental girl playing the part of the Virgin Mary was the daughter of the Chinese Ambassador to London, Charlie whispered to Marcus, rolling his eyes.

The afternoon dragged on interminably, as each pupil sang a little song, or uttered some wooden line of dialogue. Charlie felt desperate with boredom and was relieved that it had been Abigail who had invited Marcus along, and not them. To make matters worse, numerous parents insisted on clambering to the front for their child's moment of glory, causing maximum disruption, in order to capture it all on brushed-steel video cameras with flip-out screens. The Three Kings, with detestable political correctness, were bringing gifts of fruit and organic vegetables to the infant Jesus, but Pelham, suddenly overcome by shyness, burst into tears before he reached the crib and ran to Maha, burying his face in her bosom and howling.

'Now that one *is* yours, isn't he?' Marcus said.

'God knows what's wrong with him today,' Charlie replied. 'Must be ill. Normally he's very tough. Football mad.'

The three small angels, led by Poppy, shuffled to the front of the stage, and a teacher struck a chord on the piano. Poppy, her wild hair crowned by a halo of tinsel, began singing in a magical, haunting voice:

> *'O, Christmas tree,*
> *O, Christmas tree,*
> *How lovely are your branches . . .'*

The audience fell into a rapt silence. Her reedy voice, so sweet and pure, soared around the classroom. Several parents quietly activated their camcorders, even though it wasn't their own child. The second angel, meanwhile, chimed in loudly on the chorus ('O, Christmas tree,' she shouted, having no volume control), while Marina, contorted with self-consciousness, mouth clamped tight shut, stared miserably down at her shoes.

Picking up on the audience's approval, Poppy became ever more demonstrative, performing hand jives in time to the music and a little jig. Twice she waved to Jamie across the classroom, and several people craned their necks to identify the parents of this enchanting natural star. Miranda, lips pressed into a fixed smile, felt waves of hot fury, and jealousy began to squirt its poison around her system.

At the end of the carol, the crowd erupted into thunderous applause and Lizzie Frobisher, with an eye to her video sales, hoped that it had all been recorded properly and clearly, because they'd be in hot demand.

'What a star.' Marcus turned to Miranda, 'She looks exactly like Jamie too, she has to be his daughter.'

'They are awfully alike,' Miranda replied cattily. 'Slightly disorganised, but really very sweet in their lovely scruffy way.'

Marcus looked as though something was troubling him, then spoke quite sharply. 'I do hope you're not being patronising about the Temples, Miranda. I wouldn't like it one bit if you were. Abigail and Jamie are two of my favourite godchildren. Nor am I impressed when my godchildren or their wives try and score cheap points off each other.'

Spurred on by Marcus's rebuke, the Crieffs decided it would be politic to invite the Temples to share their summer holiday in Tuscany. It had become their tradition to rent, for the first three weeks of August, a large and conspicuously comfortable farmhouse on a hillside between Lucca and Siena. The property of an Italian jet-set couple, Manfredi and Paola Ruccola, who had become friends with Miranda during her marriage to Boobie van Haagen, Il Oliveto had several times been the subject of decorating features in glossy magazines such as Italian *Architectural Digest* and American *Town & Country*. With its numerous shady terraces, swimming pool bordered by cypress trees and giant terracotta pots, tennis court and deep loggia for outdoor dining, the villa had been filled for several summers in succession with the Crieffs' smartest Eurotrash friends. As Miranda liked to say, Il Oliveto was 'rather a special place'.

'I really think it would be a good move to ask Jamie and Abigail this year,' Charlie had said. 'If Marcus wants us all to be bosom buddies, we'd better go for it.'

'But who can we have them with?' Miranda had complained. 'They're not going to fit in with the rest of our crowd. And that daughter of theirs – Poppy – is out of control, she never goes to bed. She'll still be running about when we're trying to have grown-up dinner.'

'We could invite them on their own, I suppose. Jamie, Abigail and, er, Poppy, plus the four of us and a nanny – that makes eight – and whoever we get to cook.'

'Seems a bit of a waste,' said Miranda doubtfully. 'The house sleeps sixteen. If we're paying eight thousand pounds a week, it's a lot just to entertain the Temples.'

'Can't see we have much option. We must be able to tell Marcus we were all on holiday together. Look on it as an investment.'

Despite serious misgivings, the Temples quickly accepted the Crieffs' invitation. Having never been invited to either Upper Phillimore Gardens or Old Testbury Hall, they were slightly surprised by it, and Abigail, who'd sensed Miranda's antipathy towards her on the school steps, was inclined to refuse. But Jamie, seeing a free holiday, and realising they were far too broke to pay for their own, was disposed to go along with it. 'Charlie is my oldest friend,' he reminded Abby. 'He was best man at our wedding. I'm sure it'll be a laugh. Poppy will love the pool, and she likes Marina Crieff.'

'Actually they loathe each other. She didn't even want Marina at her last birthday party.'

'Well, I still think we should go. We can't spend the whole summer in London. And we can probably get charter seats to Pisa if you move fast.'

Jamie Temple was delighted by Italy, he was having the best holiday. Arriving at Il Oliveto with a green inflatable crocodile as a house present, and six bottles of supermarket plonk he'd picked up for a pound a throw in the village, he felt his obligations as guest were more than discharged. He occupied his days drifting back and forth across the pool on a lilo, occasionally projecting himself off the side with his toes, or squirting the children with one of the many plastic Supersoakers he'd discovered in the changing hut. Not since their last holiday with Marcus had Jamie stayed anywhere so completely comfortable and relaxing. With an Italian housekeeper to take care of the copious washing and ironing, a cook who arrived each morning by Vespa from the village, and the Crieffs' New Zealand nanny, Sherelle, to keep an eye on the children, the most arduous fixture in Jamie's programme was his nightly table tennis championship with Charlie, and their expeditions to play table football in a bar in the local hamlet.

'Christ, Charlie, this is an amazing set-up,' he said on the first evening when the two friends were driving back together from the Bar Jolly. 'You must be coining it in at that stockbrokers.'

'I wish,' Charlie said. 'I'm actually seriously underpaid. I've told Iain Cruickshank that unless they come back with a realistic package, I'm going to walk.'

'Really?' Jamie was astounded. 'I thought you earned half a million or something.'

'A bit more than that, thank you very much.' Charlie sounded aggrieved, as though his friend had insulted him. 'A lot more actually.'

'Well, then, what's the problem? You're rolling.'

'You don't get it, do you, Jamie? It's all right for you, you and Abigail haven't got our responsibilities, two big houses to run and everything. It costs an arm and a leg. Let me ask you a question: what do you think our outgoings are per week, and this is just staff wages I'm talking about?'

Jamie shrugged. He hadn't the faintest idea. Abigail looked after Poppy herself, and the woman who came over from the council flats once a week to clean was paid twenty quid for four hours. 'A hundred and fifty?'

'Eleven hundred. That's a week. Do you realise how much I have to make before tax to cover that? The best part of a hundred K a year. That's for Maha and the nanny and the couple down at Testbury and the old guy who looks after the garden. And now Miranda's set her heart on buying a couple of hunters, so there'll be a girl groom on the payroll next.'

'Girl groom? Oy, oy. Well, you know what they say about women who ride a lot.'

Charlie smiled thinly. He didn't think Jamie was taking his predicament seriously. Increasingly, Charlie saw himself as a martyr, taken advantage of at work – 'ripped off' he was inclined to say – by senior partners who took for granted his contribution. After all, if it weren't for him, they'd never have Marcus as a client. And, at home, Miranda's reckless ambition for larger and better houses, parties, clothes and holidays alternately exhilarated and scared him. He hardly dared open the bank statements which arrived, or so it seemed to him, almost every day; instead he thrust them, unread, beneath the large pile of Christie's saleroom catalogues and begging letters from charities on the hall table.

Although their careers had long ago diverged to the point where Charlie, on being asked whether he still saw anything of Jamie, would report patronisingly on his old friend's progress ('He works behind reception at one of these poncey knocking shops in Knightsbridge'), he had never lost the habit of being slightly jealous of him. Objectively, he could write Jamie off as a hopeless failure who had drifted from job to job, never really getting stuck into anything. And yet . . . he envied Jamie, whose life, as he imagined it, was wonderfully free from pressure and obligations. Jamie wasn't expected to buy £5,000 tables at gala balls in aid of who knew what good cause. Jamie didn't have to hand over £350 a week *in cash* to Maha, even when they were abroad on a holiday for which Maha couldn't even come along and help because her status was illegal and she'd never be allowed back into the country. When they went out to eat in London, Jamie and Abigail could walk round the corner to the neighbourhood Greek taverna named Costa's, but Miranda expected always to be taken to expensive and fashionable places. No wonder Jamie managed to look so carefree. Charlie suspected too, but didn't know, that his old friend still had a high old time on the side with other women. He hardly imagined he'd be satisfied with Abigail who hadn't, thus far, recovered her figure after the birth of Poppy, and was fatter than ever.

'Are you really considering leaving Cruickshank's?' Jamie asked.

'Thinking about it. It's a tricky one. As you know, I look after Marcus's investments and don't want to leave him in the lurch. But I've got to do something. Unless I can somehow jack up my income, we might have to get rid of Old Testbury Hall and Miranda would murder me. Don't mention anything about any of this to her, by the way. She's not particularly sympathetic when it comes to money.'

Awakened by the sound of Maria the housekeeper laying the table for breakfast in the loggia beneath their bedroom,

Miranda slipped through the mosquito net of the huge white four-poster and pulled on her white silk dressing gown over her white silk nightdress. It was essential she caught Maria before she left to go home. The house was in the throes of a *towel crisis*. Every morning, when Maria arrived at Il Oliveto at six o'clock to tidy around the drawing room and keep a sharp eye out for breakages to report to the Ruccolas, she would remove the dirty towels from the various bathrooms, and the damp swimming towels that had been left out overnight on the sunbeds by the pool, but *never replaced them with fresh ones*. Four days into the holiday, there were almost no towels left at all. Miranda knew where they were kept, of course: they were inside a vast, eighteenth-century armoire in the linen room. But the armoire was locked and the big key jealously kept by Maria.

Miranda crept downstairs, the marble floors cold against her bare feet. She noticed with approval that Maria had plonked up the cushions in the drawing room and forced corks back into several opened bottles of wine. To her irritation, she saw Poppy Temple's little pots of glittery nail varnish littered all over the window-seat; it was typical of Abigail not to have tidied them away at the end of the day. Already she was finding it quite a trial having the Temples in the house. Abigail wasn't her kind of person, being interested neither in serious shopping nor the social gossip of Miranda's set. Nor did she know who anybody was, so Miranda's hilarious story about the occasion that Philippe Fontainebleu was meant to be meeting Stephanie of Monaco for lunch in St Tropez at Le Club 55 and they totally got their wires crossed, and Stephanie was stood up with all the paparazzi milling about, was completely lost on her, never having heard of Philippe and barely knowing who Stephanie was either. Miranda was wondering how she'd get through the next ten days. She keenly felt the injustice of it all, since last summer they'd been such a great group.

She went outside into the loggia and saw the breakfast table already set with an array of *contrada* plates from Siena, painted with heraldic giraffes, porcupines and caterpillars. She groaned. Pelham claimed he was scared of some of the creatures, and yesterday had left the table in tears when Charlie had insisted he stop fussing and eat up properly from the caterpillar plate. Little bowls of apricot jam and honeycomb had been left out for them under a muslin cloche, already circled by a swarm of angry-looking wasps, as well as a turret of *biscotti*, the dry Italian rusks Maria insisted on providing in place of the croissants Miranda had clearly and repeatedly requested.

'Maria, *come sta*?' Miranda poked her head gingerly around the kitchen door. The fact was, the Ruccolas' housekeeper was one of the few people in the world Miranda found intimidating. Small, wiry, thin-lipped and suspicious-looking, it was obvious that Maria relayed their every move straight back to her employers, and if you didn't keep on the right side of her she could block your return in future years. Miranda had already instructed Charlie to bung Maria an enormous tip, both at the beginning and the end of the holiday.

Outside in the back driveway she heard the sound of a car engine turning over. It couldn't be, it just couldn't. She sprinted across the short coarse grass in the direction of the bamboo-thatched car port. 'Maria! *Maria*, stop!'

She reached the rutted drive in time to see the tail end of a white Fiat disappearing around the corner in a cloud of dust and exhaust fumes.

The Temples will just have to use bathmats as towels, she thought bitterly, as she stumped upstairs to wake Charlie.

Under a blazing Tuscan sky, Abigail tried to get Poppy to stand still long enough to baste her from head to foot in factor 50. Poppy wriggled and squirmed as her mother rubbed it into her shoulders and under her arm-bands.

'Poppy, darling, it's no use trying to escape. You can't swim until Mummy's finished. It's very dangerous to go into bright sunshine without sunscreen.'

At that moment an arc of water blasted into the air from Jamie's pump-action Supersoaker before falling, like the vapour line behind a jet aeroplane, across Abigail's back.

'Jamie, how dare you? I've told you before: *don't ever do that*. OK?'

'Sorry, Abby, I was aiming at Poppy, not you. She likes it, don't you, Pops?'

'Do it again, Daddy! Squirt me again!' Tugging herself away from her mother's clutches, she leapt off the side of the pool on to her father's lilo and nuzzled into his chest.

'Come back here, Poppy,' Abby was shouting. 'I haven't finished. Send her back right now, Jamie.'

'Oh, let up, Abby,' he replied. 'Stop fussing, she'll be fine. I never wear sun cream and nothing's ever happened to me.'

Abigail wondered how she'd survive the remainder of the holiday. She would like to have driven into Florence to see the paintings in the Uffizi, but she couldn't trust Jamie to be responsible about sun protection and their daughter would be burnt toast. If she went at all, she'd have to take Poppy with her.

Miranda was thinking this was no holiday for her. Everybody else was poolside having a lovely time, and here she was sorting out domestic crises as usual, all on her own. The cook, Giancarla, who had come so highly recommended by the Ruccolas, had turned out to be a dreadful disappointment. Miranda had discovered she wasn't really a cook at all, she was a sculpture student at Padua University. And since she had no car, only a Vespa, she couldn't even do the shopping because there was no way of transporting all the bags of food and boxes of booze up to Il Oliveto. The only solution was for Miranda or Charlie to spend most of every morning in the Co-op eight miles away, filling up trolleys, which enraged Charlie who didn't see why he should when he was paying a housekeeper, a cook and a nanny.

Distantly, from the direction of the pool, she could hear the sound of a child crying. Pelham, she imagined, it generally was. What on earth had happened to that New Zealand nanny? Already she was regretting the absence of old Nanny Arbroath, whom she had sacked for burning a Bon Point smocked dress with a flat iron. Ever since they'd arrived, Sherelle had been sullen and supercilious. The first thing Miranda would do on getting back to London was fire her, but she couldn't afford to lose her before the end of the holiday. Yesterday, Sherelle had disappeared for three hours until Miranda found her down in the olive grove. She had dragged a sunbed all the way from the pool, a distance of two hundred yards, and was lying there, bold as brass, reading a Stephen King novel with her Walkman on. She appeared to think she was on holiday herself, which she most certainly was not.

Jamie was wearing his shades in the swimming pool so he could surreptitiously eye up Sherelle. He was trying to work out whether or not he remotely fancied her. With her frizzy mop of hennaed hair, fat legs protruding from a black Lycra swimsuit and pale skin burnt tomato red by the sun, she certainly wasn't a candidate for Miss World. On the other hand, she was twenty years old and he knew where her bedroom was. He had spotted her emerging from a poky room on the ground floor, next to the larder where they kept the drinks fridge.

Jamie sighed. Sometimes he thought he was getting too old for all this. But too old for what exactly? Too old to pull birds like Sherelle, who would once have crawled into the Tunnel of Love on five minutes' acquaintance, or too old for everything else? The responsibilities of being a husband and father were awfully onerous, he felt, when he stopped to think about it.

Miranda wished Jamie wouldn't fill her children up with fizzy drinks all day long. She had asked him several times not to, but Poppy drank Coca-Colas and Limcas every five minutes, so it was impossible to stop Pelham and Marina. She thought half the problems on this holiday could be explained by the chemicals swirling around her children's systems. No wonder they couldn't rest properly during their siestas, they were juddering with sugar-highs and artificial colouring. She would get Sherelle to put the children to bed at six o'clock tonight, and stay outside their doors until they went to sleep. And that included Poppy. Last night, she had appeared during dinner six times, after she'd been said goodnight to, and it had spoiled the whole evening. Jamie and Abigail had encouraged her, by allowing her to sit on their knee at the table. Was there to be no grown-up time on this holiday at all?

She collected together several Pepsi cans that had been left by the pool and placed them on a tray. Most of the cans were still half-full, she noticed; it was absolutely typical of Jamie to allow the children to open new ones when they hadn't even finished their old ones. She hated, in any case, the whole idea of drinking straight from cans. It wasn't as though they were short of tumblers.

Carrying the tray up to the loggia, she left it on the table for Giancarla to find when she came up to start preparing dinner. Jamie would be the most hopeless, exasperating husband, she decided, but he was rather dishy in his bathing trunks. He had kept his figure much better than Charlie had. For the briefest of moments, lustful thoughts entered Miranda's mind. Jamie slightly reminded her of Boobie when they'd first got together.

Charlie was in a seriously stroppy mood. He needed to speak urgently to his office in London but his mobile phone wouldn't work out by the pool. He walked fifty yards to the edge of the tennis court: still nothing. There didn't seem to be any coverage at all on this side of the house. God, these ruddy useless phones irritated him sometimes. He had actually rung his mobile phone provider before leaving England and asked them – point blank – 'Will my Nokia work in Tuscany?' 'Oh, yes', he'd been assured, 'you have full coverage for the whole world these days with the exception of North America, Fiji and the Comoros.' Well, here he was in the middle of Europe, with half the newly elected Labour Government just up the road in their vast Palladian villas, and he couldn't get a line to Cruickshank & Willis. It was pathetic. He hoped Tony Blair wasn't having the same trouble, or rather, he hoped he was.

Charlie decided he hated hot holidays. It was Miranda

who made him go on them. No sooner had they got through one holiday than she was thumbing through brochures planning the next. The weather in Italy was so humid he couldn't breathe, he'd been sweating like a pig ever since they'd arrived. His stomach and forehead were running with sweat. His skin was bright red and blotchy, he felt like a sausage under the grill. As soon as he'd touched base with London he'd crack open another beer. None of this would be necessary, he reflected, if he hadn't been tricked into selling Ardnessaig to Stuart Bolton. Visions of his childhood home, with its bracing walks across moss-coloured hills, came into his mind, filling him with resentment and self-pity. If he hadn't sold Ardnessaig for a pittance, they could have gone up there every August and saved a fortune.

He climbed up to a terrace above the villa, to an area of tilled ground where the Ruccolas had planted vines. The higher he climbed, the hotter it became. The land beneath him was brown and arid, with not a blade of grass to be seen. The vines had shrivelled into dry sticks. Manfredi Ruccola was inordinately proud of his local wine and had suggested to Charlie he should buy all his supplies from the family *fattoria*, an offer Charlie was doing his best to avoid.

He switched on the phone and – glory be – the panel lit up with the letters of some unidentifiable Eyetie frequency. He began punching digits when his eye was caught by a large pink and red shape, which he first imagined was a dead animal of some kind, a calf perhaps, or a giant sow. Picking his way across the broken ground, he saw it was a female, stark naked, sunbathing on her stomach on an inflatable lilo, listening to a Sony Walkman.

'Sherelle?'

He had to say her name several times before she heard him, and then she squealed and reached for a towel to cover herself.

'Oh, it's you, Lord Crieff. You made me jump.' Her strong Kiwi accent, which had been annoying Charlie all holiday, converted u's into i's: 'You made me jimp'.

'Shouldn't you be down at the house helping with the children?'

'Not on a Wednesday. It's my afternoon off. I am entitled to time off, you know.'

Uncertain whether Sherelle was or wasn't entitled to time off, but feeling he should say something else before carrying on with his phone call, Charlie said, 'Well, I hope you're having a good holiday. It's very hot, isn't it? You probably don't have weather like this on the North Island or the South Island, whichever it is you come from. Anyway, don't stay up here too long. Lady Crieff will be needing a hand soon, I'm sure.'

At that moment a terrible scream sounded from the villa below, followed by a child's wails that echoed around the valley. Charlie heard his wife's voice: 'Charlie! Sherelle! Quickly, everybody. Marina's hurt.'

Charlie panted back down the terraces, past the swimming pool, up to the house and found his daughter lying on the stone floor of the loggia.

'She's been stung on her tongue by a wasp,' Miranda snapped. 'She took a swig from one of those damned Pepsi cans, which nobody ever finishes up. A wasp was inside. Her tongue has swelled up, she can't swallow. We must get her straight to hospital, wherever that is. Quickly, Charlie, bring the car round. And that's the last fizzy drink we're having on this damned holiday! I'm pouring the whole lot down the sink.'

Sherelle Grogan felt she'd been sold a pup. She hadn't travelled all the way from Auckland to end up stuck at the end of this dirt track in the middle of nowhere, with nothing to do and nowhere to go. She'd been told by Giancarla there was a discotheque in Poggibonsi but she didn't see how she could get there without transport, and anyway she couldn't drive. Not that Miranda would be likely to give her the time off, she was expected to babysit – *for free* – every night, while the Crieffs and their guests got pissed over a four-course meal, from which she was pointedly excluded.

Sherelle didn't know which she detested most: the food, Lord and Lady Crieff or their children. Apart from plain pasta with grated cheese, she hadn't been able to eat a thing all holiday. Everything was covered in oil, which made her skin break out, and she couldn't think how anyone could stomach roasted peppers, mozzarella cheese or those purple salads. Last night, she'd tried one mouthful of stuffed zucchini flowers and almost chucked. Later, when she'd fused all the lights by turning on the shower while the dishwasher was still going, Miranda had bitten her head off as though it had been her fault.

The Crieffs she couldn't make out at all. Miranda wore the trousers in that marriage, she reckoned, and didn't lift a finger to help. In London, she was out all the time, and hadn't been home at bath-time once in four months. When Sherelle spoke to Charlie, he always asked her exactly the same question: did she come from the North or South Island? Jeez, was that the only thing he knew about New Zealand? She thought the Crieffs' marriage must be fairly rocky, judging by all the shouting and slamming of cupboard doors. Once she'd overheard them having a real set-to about someone called Marcus, who Charlie wanted to ask to stay at their country place while Miranda said she couldn't face the thought of all the cooking – not that she'd be doing it anyway.

As for the kids, Pelham and Marina were the pits, Marina especially. She was such a little sneak, that one. One evening, when she was supposed to be babysitting and the Crieffs were late back as usual from some function, Sherelle had bunked off to the Hippodrome to meet some friends, leaving the kids on their own in the house. Marina must have heard her slip out, and was waiting on the stairs when her parents got back. Miranda had nearly sacked the nanny the next morning, and would have done so if she hadn't had a hectic month in view. Not that Sherelle would have cared. She'd be sacking herself first thing when she got home.

As far as Sherelle was concerned, Marina could have bitten off her tongue when the wasp stung it, it would have served her right.

'You'll never guess who I met in Perugia,' Abigail said, returning from her one and only cultural expedition with Poppy.

'Peter Mandelson?' suggested Charlie. Abby shook her head. 'President Blair and his fragrant wife Cherry?'

'Someone we all know.'

'Tony Lambton? God, I don't know, tell us.'

'Stuart. Stuart Bolton.'

'Really? What the fuck's he doing in Tuscany?'

'Working. He's here for his bank, privatising Perugia Telecom, I think he said. Hope you don't mind, I've asked him over for supper tonight. He's Poppy's godfather and she wants to show him her swimming.'

Charlie minded very much, but didn't feel he could make a fuss, especially as Stuart was another of Marcus's godsons. He would post Marcus a card tomorrow, telling him they were all together in Tuscany, getting on like a house on fire. Privately, he thought that having wangled Ardnessaig from him, the very least Stuart could do was make proper use of it in August, rather than butting into their villa holiday uninvited.

Charlie had heard from a variety of reliable sources how well Stuart was doing at Darmstadt Commerzhaus, and how he'd used part of his obscenely large salary to install an Olympic-sized swimming pool into the old Ardnessaig coach house. He could just imagine it, reeking of chlorine like a public baths. How his sister Mary Jane could bring herself to swim there several times a week, he couldn't understand. It struck him as an act of disloyalty.

The information that Stuart was raking it in hand over fist at Commerzhaus only increased Charlie's anxiety about his own finances, which had now reached obsessional proportions. How Iain and Wanker expected him to live on £800,000 a year with all his commitments was beyond him. By the time he'd paid tax, he was left with a little over five hundred K in his pocket, less various pension and school fees schemes which skimmed another fifty off the top. The mortgages on two large houses – he was still borrowing around *three million quid* – were costing him almost two hundred and forty thousand a year, and that was just for the interest, never mind repaying the capital. Staff wages, Miranda and the children's clothes, his own hand-made suits, the odd day's shooting, their clubs and restaurant bills, together these came to another hundred and fifty. And then there were the holidays – three already this year, skiing in Meribel, a long weekend in Rome and now . . . *this* . . . there would be no change from twenty-eight thousand pounds by the time you took in the Business Class flights, the food, the tips . . . Twenty-eight thousand quid for nineteen days in the sun. Was that really what it cost? How much should he be enjoying it, to justify twenty-eight K? More than this surely. But then Charlie seldom felt that his pleasure in anything these days matched the exorbitant outlay. Whatever they did *cost*. If they had ten friends to supper at home, in their own house, it cost . . . what? . . . he no longer knew, no longer dared work it out. Here he was, swimming up and down the pool at Il Oliveto and it was costing him . . . his mind whirred . . . twenty or thirty pounds *per length*. And now Stuart was coming for dinner to enjoy the Crieffs' hospitality for free.

On the other hand, a visit from him might galvanise the party which was in danger of lapsing into moroseness. Since the episode with the wasp, Miranda had hardly bothered to disguise her irritation with the Temples, and was counting the days until she could go home. Furthermore, Pelham claimed he had spotted a viper in the long grass behind the swimming pool, and almost trodden on it in bare feet, so the children had been banned from playing in the garden without supervision, which meant Sherelle had been unable to sunbathe for four days in succession and was more sullen than ever. Marina had decided she was frightened of the inflatable crocodile in the pool and refused to swim if it was in there; Poppy refused to swim if it was not. Unable to leave the villa, and so having seen almost nothing the entire holiday – hardly a painting, hardly a fresco – Abigail was barn stale, and quite perked up at the prospect of Stuart's visit. Apart from the hours she'd spent in the pool teaching Poppy to swim, which had been some of the happiest she could ever remember, she had felt permanently uncomfortable staying with the Crieffs and wished she hadn't come.

Stuart arrived from Perugia in a rented Saab with two

bottles of Brunello di Montalcino that he handed to Charlie together with a pile of English newspapers. He carried a beer down to the pool to watch Poppy, who was desperate for him to see her do a whole width with her face in the water and no arm-bands. When he returned to the house, Charlie was holding up the *International Herald Tribune* looking stricken.

'Did you read this?'

'About Flora Huang? That's why I brought it, in case you hadn't seen it.'

'I can't believe Marcus has done that. Why make her a Vice President? For Christ's sake, it's one thing to bonk her, another to give her management responsibility.'

'This is in his Hong Kong satellite outfit. Well, I guess Flora's Chinese, so that's one credential. People say she's pretty smart. And she's got good contacts inside China. If Marcus wants to beam Planet Brand across the whole continent, he needs access to government.'

Jamie and Abigail appeared on the terrace for dinner, followed by Miranda who had decided to use the excuse of Stuart's visit to wear her new Jemima Khan *shalwar kameez*.

'Who are we all talking about here – Miss Saigon?' asked Jamie, pouring himself a large vodka. 'Marcus brought her round to the hotel. She's looking great. Can't think what she sees in him though.'

'Then you must be very naive,' Charlie snorted. 'If Marcus has appointed her a VP of Planet Brand, she must have him by the short and curlies. This whole satellite thing is a big enough risk without putting your strumpet on the board. I'm telling you, if he gets this one wrong, the whole company could be in deep shit.'

'All the same,' Jamie said, 'if it was my company, I'd definitely want Flora on the board. I couldn't take my eyes off her, she's a cracker. Whoops, sorry, Abby, present company excluded of course.'

'Actually, I've been asking around about Flora,' Charlie said. 'She isn't quite as innocent as she likes to make out, Miss Flora Huang. From what I hear, she's been married once already, to her tutor at Peking University – the Beijing

Foreign Studies University as they call it. And her father wasn't a farmer, he was the governor or deputy governor of some big province. He started out as one of the official translators to Zhou En-Lai.'

'How did you discover all that?' Stuart asked. 'That's detailed stuff.'

'Oh, I have my sources,' Charlie replied grandly. 'Actually I got the research department at Cruickshank's to pull a run on her.'

'I wonder why she invented all that stuff about growing up in a rice paddy?' Abigail asked Charlie. 'When we talked about it in Turkey, she was really convincing.'

'I'd have thought it was pretty obvious. Part of her cover. It's fairly predictable if you think about it. Someone like Marcus starts to do business with China, the first thing the commies do is put someone on the inside to keep tabs on him.'

'You're suggesting Flora's a plant?' asked Stuart.

'Happens a lot. They select these girls – just like Flora – very early on while they're still in their teens, the daughters of high-up party officials. Brainwash them, put them through the top foreign language universities, send them overseas to study. Circumstantially, it's a cert.'

'So she's a Chinese Mata Hari?' said Jamie. 'Well, lucky old Marcus. She's bound to be amazing in bed. Like that Chink I had at the Ritz in Paris – she was sensational. If they're using Flora as an agent, she'll have been trained. She probably worked in a whorehouse in Peking for a couple of years, to pick up special tricks. You know, like Mrs Simpson did, the one who made King Whatshisname abdicate.'

'If that's true about Flora, it's really scary,' Abigail said. 'If the Chinese have got their claws into Marcus, shouldn't we tell someone?'

'I considered taking him out to lunch and having a quiet word,' Charlie said. 'But maybe it's better to let the thing run its course. I don't know how well it would play if I had to break it to him.'

They carried their drinks through to the candle-lit loggia,

and Charlie opened Stuart's Brunello to go with the rabbit risotto.

'You sounded sceptical before dinner about Marcus's satellite venture, Charlie,' Stuart said when they'd sat down. 'Is that based on anything in particular?'

'He's taking a hell of a punt. Murdoch's Star-TV is in its fifth year and still hasn't made a cent. I'm wondering whether Marcus hasn't left it a bit late. Some of his people came in the other day to present to our analysts. No doubt he'll get it right – he always has before.'

'I'll ask our lot what they think. We have a big position in Brand stock at DC. As you say, everything he's touched so far has come good. The interims were impressive.'

'The thing about Marcus is he plays it by intuition. End of the fingertips stuff. With his private client investments, we send him all the C & W reports but I don't believe he opens them. Same with his businesses. He gets a feeling about a company and goes for it.'

'He can't always be right though, can he?' Abigail asked. 'He must get it wrong sometimes.'

'Not so far,' said Charlie. 'Remember when we were on *Marketmaker* and he said he was going into Russia in a big way, and nobody believed the Soviet economy would come through? Well, he got in early and the market's doubled in six months. Apparently he's made half a billion over there since February.'

'God, I admire men who make real money,' Miranda said pointedly. 'Don't you just hate not having any?'

Charlie looked furious and, addressing his remark to nobody in particular, replied, 'Some of us round here are doing our best. But if anyone else wants to get off their backside and go out to work every day, the management will gladly accept their contribution.'

An uneasy silence settled on the table, broken by Jamie who said, 'Talking of Marcus and *Marketmaker*, I've never told you about a really weird incident on that cruise. Something Dick Mathias told me one night before dinner . . .'

He recounted to an increasingly rapt audience his extraordinary conversation with Marcus's lawyer, and how Dick had as good as told him it was Marcus who had had Jamie arrested and thrown into the Indian jail all those years before, when he'd wanted a clear run at Saffron. When he'd finished the story, nobody spoke.

'Christ,' said Charlie at last. 'You never told me that before. Do you think Dick made it up?'

'I'm sure he'd forgotten I was the person in question. He was quite pissed, he'd had seven martinis. And it must have been me he was referring to: you wouldn't have two different episodes involving an Indian jail and Marcus and the seduction scene and everything.'

'If true, it's unbelievable,' said Stuart, 'a really immoral thing to do to anyone, let alone your godson. Do you believe it, Jamie?'

'I didn't know what to think. I thought Dick must have been pulling my leg at first. But the more I've thought about it, the more possible it seems. I'd always wondered how I got out of prison so quickly after he came to see the police. And Marcus definitely moved in on Saffron that night. That's when it all started.'

'I believe it,' said Abigail. 'I've never trusted Marcus. He shafted my dad over a deal. There are plenty of stories.'

Charlie made a mental note of Abigail's disloyalty and wondered how best to exploit it.

'You haven't told that story to anyone else, have you?' he asked.

Jamie shook his head.

'I wouldn't if I were you. If it got out, it might be misunderstood. And I particularly wouldn't want Marcus to hear we were sitting around this table in Tuscany trading gossip about him. Because that's all it is: unsubstantiated gossip.'

'So you're advising Jamie to hush it up then, Charlie?' said Stuart. 'In case it reflects badly on you?'

'In case it reflects badly on all of us, actually,' he replied. 'I don't know about anyone else, but I feel a lot of loyalty towards Marcus. He's a great man. And as with all great men, he has his detractors. People love spreading rubbish about tycoons. It happens with Jimmy, it happens with Tiny, it happened with Bob Maxwell. All I'm saying is that if his own godchildren start spreading gossip, then where will it end? I just think Jamie should keep his trap shut. It wouldn't be clever to cross Marcus.'

Part Five

52: September, 1997

Too cowardly to curb Miranda's spending, Charlie recognised that he needed a dramatic initiative to escape the spiral of poverty which threatened to engulf him. The solution, he saw, lay in the booming new economy of Russia, where the Nijny Novgorod had been on a two-year bull run and was showing no signs of slowing down. Compared to the turgid, mature equities markets of London and Frankfurt, there were compelling arguments for punting every available dollar into Russia. The old Soviet industries and utilities, for so long starved of investment, were poised to grow exponentially. The opportunities were, quite literally, mind-boggling. The great oil and gas reserves of Novasobersk and Surgut City were scarcely tapped, and you didn't need to be a genius to imagine the colossal returns of modern extraction methods. Similarly, the emergent Russian telecoms were surely a licence to print money in a country where half a billion people were expected to purchase a mobile phone, or sign up for internet access, within five years.

Inspired by Marcus's record of success in Russia, and confident that his own reputation in the markets would assure sufficient investor support, Charlie decided to set up a fund – the Crieff Emerging Markets Russia Fund – to invest in listed Russian equities and ride the boom.

When he announced his intention of leaving Cruickshank & Willis, Iain Cruickshank was pleasingly panicked by his defection, fearing the loss of Marcus as a client, and instantly offered Charlie an increase in his compensation to a million pounds a year, including a performance-related bonus which could henceforth be regarded as guaranteed. But Charlie was not persuadable. He took the view that this was an opportunity to make serious, meaningful money. Were he to pass it up, he'd never forgive himself. He had done his sums and, if the fund performed, and he was able to attract the level of investment he anticipated, in two or three years' time he could make . . . what? . . . fifteen, thirty million? Frankly, the sky was the limit in an economy going gang-busters.

The fuss surrounding his resignation only confirmed Charlie's conviction that he'd been disgracefully underpaid for years, and when Iain and Wanker took him out – together – for lunch at the City Club, an unprecedented accolade, to make one last attempt to get him to reconsider, Charlie felt a wonderful sense of vindication. Consequently, when Iain and Wanker made a surprising offer to invest fifteen million in his fund on behalf of Cruickshank & Willis, and to back his new management company by taking a thirty per cent stake in it, Charlie almost rejected the overture out of hand, believing that other, better offers, from more prestigious outfits than Cruickshank & Willis, would be sure to follow. Before he had attracted a penny of investment, or bought a single Russian stock, he knew that his new venture was on a roll, and at least, with C & W as backers, it was a case of the devil you know.

His original idea that his wife and the children should relocate with him to Moscow, and Upper Phillimore Gardens and Old Testbury Hall each be rented out to some American investment banker for several thousand pounds a week to subsidise their finances until the fund started producing income, was firmly rejected by Miranda. They spent a weekend together in Moscow, in a suite at the Kempinski, looking at possible flats and getting a feel for the city. At the end of two cold days of filthy restaurant meals and gloomy apartment buildings, in which Miranda could no sooner imagine herself living than going to the moon, Charlie conceded that his wife and children would stay in England while the head of the family, in time-honoured fashion, ventured overseas, alone, to make his pile and send home the bacon. 'In any case,' as Miranda pointed out, 'you won't want to spend every weekend in this depressing dump. You'd go mad. Much nicer to come back to Testbury every so often and see your friends.' And when she announced she was pregnant for the third time, with a baby conceived during their summer holiday at Il Oliveto, any idea of her coming to Moscow at all was put out of the question.

With an increasingly heavy heart, and paying much the same monthly rental as for a large house in Holland Park, Charlie took a three-bedroomed apartment in Dom Na Naberezhnaya – the House on the Embankment – erected by Stalin in monumental style to billet his apparatchiks, and now colonised to the exclusion of all others by Western bankers, heads of multinationals, sundry consultants, corporate strategists and carpet baggers who had swarmed into town on the back of the great Soviet bull market. The flat on one side was occupied by the local President of Nestlé, on the other by a VP at Credit Suisse First Boston. From his narrow balcony at the front of the building, Charlie had a view across the wide grey floes of the Moskva, with the walls and towers of the Kremlin beyond. Having rented the place furnished for hard currency, from a Chechnyan gun runner who preferred to direct operations from his luxury apartment on the Corniche in Cannes, Charlie spent much of his first week overseeing the removal of monumental dark-wood wardrobes, Soviet crystal chandeliers and glass-fronted cabinets with their decorative samovars and gold-rimmed china, and the desperate oils of winter scenes by Georgian artists, substituting a container load of furniture and household items that arrived overland from England. Unwrapping mixed parcels of old pictures that had lain in store at Testbury, he found a Victorian mezzotint of Ardnessaig that had once hung in his first flat in Ennismore Mews; positioning it above his bed, he later took it down in annoyance and thrust it in the back of a cupboard. By some sleight of logic that was wholly irrational, Charlie was disposed to link the sale of his ancestral estate, and its purchase by Stuart Bolton, with his gloomy mission to rebuild the family fortunes in Moscow.

He rented office space in a modern block on Tverskaya, in a building occupied by other Western companies, and set about recruiting a local team: a Russian General Manager, Valeri Fedorov, who was said to have good relations with the local Mafias without himself being directly or excessively corrupt; two young Russian analysts who came respectively from the Moscow Oil and Gas Institute and the Orex-Moscow Business School; a chauffeur, Oleg, who doubled as bodyguard, had a degree in engineering, drove the Saab like a policeman and was presumed to be ex-KGB; plus two secretaries and the office cook Valeri insisted was mandatory, there being nowhere to eat lunch in Tverskaya, and anyway, every Russian office had its cook, it was normal. With Valeri's special connections, the Crieff Emerging Markets Russia Fund was able to secure computers and screens and – more remarkable still – their rapid installation, so that within barely a month of Charlie's arrival in Moscow, the company was up on its feet and ready to start trading.

Compared with the businesses he was accustomed to investing in at home, the Russian equities market was shambolic. Ownership structure, long- and short-term strategies, dividend history, even the names of the principal executives, all were hard to pin down. In his first seven weeks, Charlie and an interpreter visited eleven companies all over the country, many of them around the Siberian oilfields of Surgut City, but seldom returned from these trips with greater insight than before they went. He would arrange to meet investor relations managers of factories occupying small parts of once great state enterprises, in razor-wired compounds of long-abandoned sheds and rusting plants; and if these meetings took place at all (they were regularly postponed with no reason given) they were seldom very enlightening, as though the management had not yet shaken off the habitual secrecy of pre-*perestroika* communism, and could not understand by whose authority a fund manager felt he had the right to cross-question them on matters of business they considered confidential.

Overcoming his misgivings, Charlie bought heavily. And everything he touched . . . *rocketed*. Assets were unbelievably cheap. He bought Lukoil, Rostelcom and UES – Unified Energy Systems – and doubled his investment. In the first two months, the Crieff Emerging Markets Russia Fund went up by 153 per cent. The fund grew to thirty million, then sixty, then a hundred and forty. Institutional investors in Zurich and New York, who had told Charlie they would wait and see before taking a position in Russia, now pumped money into the fund on an unprecedented scale, almost begging him to take it off their hands. It seemed to him there was no Russian company too dubious or unpromising not to attract investor support. When Dick Mathias rang him one afternoon on Marcus's behalf, and indicated the tycoon was considering putting ten million into Russian equities, Charlie replied, 'Well, he'd better get a move on or he'll miss the boat. Tell Marcus if he'd placed ten million with me at the beginning, it'd be worth twenty-six now.'

Charlie read in *Time* that there were 50,000 ex-pats living in Moscow, but he found it hard to make friends. There were few English, and those that there were weren't Charlie's kind of Englishmen. He accepted invitations to parties given by Swedes, Germans and Americans, but their terms of reference were too far removed from his own; they did not automatically recognise him as their social superior. Once, he would have alluded to the Ardnessaig Estate as a kind of shorthand, the existence of which – vast and baronial – would have done the trick, but thanks to Stuart this was denied him. He found it less easy to impress upon strangers the magnificence of Old Testbury Hall. He joined the Moscow Country Club, with its high-security gates and chalet-style club house set in a pine forest fifty minutes' drive from the city, but the round of ex-pat diversions – the golf and hockey fixtures – were intolerably naff.

Over time, he gave up on the whole idea of a social life in Moscow. Instead, after work, he preferred to head home, fill up a wire basket with overpriced imported food at the Finnish Stockman supermarket situated in the basement of the block, and watch CNN and BBC World until it was time to go to bed. Moscow struck him as parochial and depressing. He came to detest the restaurants, with their Georgian goulash soups and balalaika music. He hated the dirty slush that lay in brown mounds on the pavements and the corners of streets, and the way that he was pulled over in the car, several times a day, by traffic police who saw the foreign number plates and demanded spot fines without bothering to invent a pretext.

Desperately lonely and bored, he dialled Miranda in London more than once a day, but replaced the receiver if it was answered by Maha or the new nanny. Once, when he had left several messages for his wife on one evening, she accused him of being pathetic. 'For heaven's sake, Charlie, don't hound me. What are you, the KGB? I hear you asked Maha where I was. I do have things to go to in London, you know.' Little by little, he came to resent the round of cocktail and dinner parties that constituted his wife's social programme. When they did manage to speak, Charlie found himself listening – at four dollars fifty cents a minute – to reports almost ludicrously irrelevant to his present predicament. Only the thought of the money he was accumulating as his fund grew, and the certain prospect of more to come, kept Charlie sane.

Once a month, he returned to England for a long weekend, and it became the Crieffs' custom to spend these in Hampshire, with a large houseparty of their friends, so that, as Miranda said with a little laugh, 'Charlie can have a break from social Siberia.' The contrast between the comforts of Old Testbury Hall, with all the stops pulled out, and Charlie's increasingly bleak existence in Moscow, never failed to reassure him, reminding him what it was he was working for. Miranda's organisational skills, and talent for arranging weekend houseparties, meant that every fire was blazing for Charlie's homecoming and the central heating turned up so high that his first act, on stepping through the front door, was always to heave open a sash window. In the kitchen, he could see their new couple, Mr and Mrs Farley, hard at work preparing the succession of elaborate lunches and dinners that were a hallmark of the Crieffs' hospitality.

'Evening, Mr and Mrs Farley. All well with you both?' Then, picking up a little pastry tart filled with smoked salmon mousse and popping it into his mouth, he'd ask,

'Not sure how many we are this weekend? Any idea who's coming?'

'Nice to see you home again, Lord Crieff,' said Reg Farley, who had been headhunted by Miranda along with his wife from a neighbouring banking family, the Pooles of Hungerford, and had previously butled at Woburn. 'It's quite a houseful this weekend. Sir Iain and Lady Cruickshank are in the yellow trellis bedroom. The Princess is in the toile de jouy room. Mr van Haagen's in the hibiscus suite. Mr and Mrs Deloitte are up at the top in the chintz room, and Lady Crieff has put Mr and Mrs Temple above the coach house.'

Charlie considered the weekend's social mix. Zara Deloitte, who had recently married a crass but unquestionably loaded Chicagoan reinsurance broker, Bud Deloitte, was his old neighbour in Angus, Zara Fane, with whom he had enjoyed a prolonged snog one birthday party. The prospect of seeing Zara again, when he had barely set eyes on her in the interim, filled him with vague sexual expectation; having been there once, he felt a repeat performance was surely his for the asking. He knew Zara's marriage to Bud – who was an investor in Charlie's fund – was a relatively new initiative; according to Jamie, her history over the past two decades contained several shady episodes, including marriage to a Lebanese businessman with interests in the port of Dubai. It was Charlie's intention, over the weekend, to persuade Bud to ramp up his exposure in Russia by several times. He reckoned his adolescent episode with Zara at Ardnessaig could only help.

He was pleased Jamie and Abigail had accepted his invitation; he wasn't convinced they would. But Marcus was coming over for dinner on Saturday night and the Crieffs had decided it would send the right signals to have them there too.

At the mention of Boobie van Haagen, Charlie looked perplexed. Recently, Boobie had been spending a lot of time with Miranda; rather more, he guessed, than she'd let on. 'Oh, Boobie's gay,' Miranda always said. 'That's why I left him, he's as bent as a corkscrew.' But Charlie felt there was something inappropriate about his wife consorting so publicly with her ex-husband.

The Crieffs liked to entertain at Testbury on a scale, and with a level of formality, which to other members of their set seemed entirely normal, but to outsiders appeared almost wilfully anachronistic. Before lunch, a giant pitcher of tomato or Clamato juice was brought into the drawing room by Mr Farley, to be ritually laced by Charlie with three-quarters of a bottle of Smirnoff, the juice of six lemons, twelve generous sloshes of Worcester Sauce, twelve staccato stabs of Tabasco, a tablespoon of horseradish, a tumbler-full of dry Fino sherry, half a teaspoon of celery salt, a pinch of rock salt, fresh ground pepper and whatever other embellishments came to hand as the Master of Testbury prepared his knock-out snifter. At lunch, which they ate in the spectacular new conservatory Miranda had built adjoining the kitchen, where Mr and Mrs Farley, Maha and a lady from the village were already well advanced with preparations for dinner, Charlie prided himself on his choice of wine. At dinner, eschewing black tie as too stuffy, the Crieffs directed their male guests to wear 'Hampshire code': informal dress of such precision that it practically constituted a uniform, namely a velvet smoking jacket with satin lapels and frogging in one of two colours – dark blue or claret – an open-necked white dress shirt and velvet slippers embroidered in gold thread with initials or some humorously appropriate motif. Sir Iain Cruickshank, fervent Eurosceptic, had the dreaded Euro symbol on his slippers with crossed bones beneath; Bud Deloitte, having made his fortune in the insurance racket, which he likened to gambling, had one-armed bandits on his Trickers pumps. At the end of dinner, after the women had left the dining room, and the men discoursed on the utter ghastliness of the gnome-like Foreign Secretary, Robin Cook, and Blair's lesbian so-called 'babes', whom none of them would touch with a barge-pole, Charlie padded around his long mahogany table offering cigars from a Regency humidor and making a great business of circumcising their ends with the Asprey's sterling-silver cutter that had been their wedding present from Marcus.

As he approached his forty-first birthday, Charlie had developed a range of patrician mannerisms that were not uncommon among his set. For instance, crossing his Colefax-upholstered drawing room to lift a log from the wicker log basket and toss it on to the fire, he walked with a slight limp, as if his left leg was afflicted by rheumatoid stiffness or an old sports injury was playing up. Picking up the *Financial Times*, he would frown, screw up his eyes, then hold the newspaper at various distances from his face, as though he was finding the small type of the share prices difficult to read and was seeking the perfect calibration. First thing in the morning, and over breakfast, he groaned and sighed, and noisily cleared his throat; the burden of leadership, he seemed to imply, lay heavily upon his shoulders, and he was only delaying the moment when he must reluctantly relinquish the leisure of his breakfast table to sort out the problems of the world.

The only bugger about having people to stay for the weekend, Charlie thought, was how to entertain them between meals. For several weeks, he had been seriously considering buying a shoot. A country house without a shoot increasingly struck him as a fairly futile exercise, like a holiday villa without a swimming pool. It was all very well inviting players like Iain and Bud down to Testbury, but you had to provide something for them to do. To this end, Charlie had contacted the sporting department of Savills, where a very helpful girl named Sarah Whitley was sending out to Moscow details of available shoots. Already, he was interested in a couple of hundred acres over towards Basingstoke. A decent shoot, he reasoned, could legitimately be regarded as an investment; he would rent out the days he didn't need to some cash-rich time-poor London syndicate, and keep the best for himself. Marcus, he knew, was an excellent shot.

In honour of Marcus, they were to be sixteen sitting down to dinner on Saturday night. Mr Farley had retrieved the extra leaf for the table from the cellar, and spent much of the day buffing its surface and polishing silver in his special apron. Miranda had particularly requested the home team to be bathed and ready downstairs in good time, since a number of rather smart neighbours were coming, and it was vital they were all on parade to welcome them. Jamie, who had been looking forward to watching *Blind Date* on the telly, made a face behind her back.

'It should actually be quite a fun evening,' Charlie told everyone, as he poured them drinks to take up to their baths. 'We've wheeled in some local big shots to amuse you. My godfather Marcus, of course, who most of you know; he's in flying form at the moment having pulled off some big coup with the Russian government, cornering the Siberian salt market. Now, who else have we got? Michael and Serena Waitrose. I've told Michael, I don't care how good he thinks his ruddy supermarket plonk is, don't bring any. Not necessary.' He laughed. 'Then there's the McVities, Torquil and Janey, who everyone round here calls the Digestives. And Lavinia Gilborne, who used to be married to Honkie, still looking pretty fantastic for sixty and lives down in the village with a much younger restaurateur – who we haven't actually invited this evening.'

'What about Flora?' Abigail asked. 'Is Marcus bringing her?'

'Happily not. I felt I had to ask her, but she's abroad. Barbara Miles was uncharacteristically vague. I took that as a positive sign.'

Wallowing in a hot tub in his blissfully comfortable bathroom, with several drops of Miranda's rose geranium Floris scenting the water and a large whisky resting on the deep marble shelf, Charlie felt his life was back on track. All things being equal, he would shortly be gratifyingly rich in his own right, notwithstanding whatever else might eventually flow from Marcus. The mortgages on Phillimore Gardens and Testbury should be paid off in full within eighteen months; suddenly their purchase no longer seemed reckless, but a shrewd and timely investment in a rising property market. Marcus was coming to dinner – alone – and would recognise, from the calibre of the other guests, how seriously Charlie was rated these days. The presence of Jamie and Abigail would prove he was also a team player. As for Stuart Bolton, Charlie thought he could make the point to Marcus, very subtly, that he'd heard poor Stuart had come unstuck as a management consultant, and it had been a case of jump or be pushed, which explained his present job with the Krauts.

As he turned the tap with his big toe to add more hot water, Charlie could see Miranda next door in their bedroom, doing her face at the dressing table. Perched on a wicker stool in her bra and knickers, her face reflected three times in the triptych mirror, she presented an alarming sight: glossy, still pin-thin despite her pregnancy, her mouth, as she applied lipstick, pursed into a slightly dissatisfied frown. He wondered whether she really had been unfaithful with Boobie. On balance, he felt not, though Boobie had been oddly solicitous all day, over-praising the wine at lunch and congratulating him on the Russia Fund, which could be interpreted as signs of a guilty conscience. Charlie's own sex life with Miranda had recently tailed off sharply, partly because of her pregnancy, partly geographical separation. There was a time when they'd always shared a bath together and discussed the events of the day, until Pelham had wandered into their bathroom one evening and innocently pointed out the discrepancy between Miranda's heavily highlighted blonde hair and her mousy-coloured pubes; since when she had chosen to bathe alone with the door firmly locked.

Charlie's feelings about his children were ambivalent. He had been elated at producing a son and heir, and one of his proudest moments had been ringing Beetle Trumper, son of the great Archie Trumper, at Broadley Court from Miranda's room at the Portland and putting Pelham down for his old preparatory school. Continuity was important to him. When he sold Ardnessaig, he had felt genuine guilt at being unable to pass it on to Pelham, though when he'd tried to explain this to Miranda she'd mocked his sentimentality. Conversely, in buying Old Testbury Hall – and even in accumulating a lot of money – he always envisaged leaving it eventually to his children. Shortly after moving to Hampshire, while giving Pelham a ride on the jump seat of the new John Deere lawnmower, Charlie had said, 'I hope you like our new house, Pelham. One day, you know, after Mummy and I are dead, it will be yours.'

But although he kept framed photographs of Pelham and Marina on top of his chest of drawers in Moscow, Charlie was capable of going for days on end without giving them much thought. In his more desolate moments, he felt he missed them terribly, but within a few minutes of seeing them he was wishing they were less underfoot, and was directing them to the television or computer. When Marina appeared in their bedroom in her tutu, desperate to demonstrate her latest ballet steps learned at Busy Lizzie's, Charlie watched her with glazed eyes, his mind on his fund price or the Surgut oilfields.

Meanwhile, in their bedroom above the coach house, Jamie was rummaging through the wicker basket of toiletries Miranda provided in all the bathrooms for her guests' comfort. There were spare toothbrushes, toothpaste, disposable razors, shower caps, waxed dental floss, aspirin and a dozen miniature bottles of herbal shampoos, conditioners and bath gels. Slipping two unopened toothbrushes and a packet of Nurofen into his spongebag, he called out to his wife, 'Hey, Abby, need any Tampax? There's a whole big box of them through here.'

'Actually, Jamie, I don't – as you should remember from this morning.'

'Right, sure, I'd forgotten that. Anyway, you may as well take some if they're going. You'll need them before long.'

Visiting Old Testbury Hall for the first time, the Temples had been first amazed, then wildly jealous and eventually mocking of their friends' country estate. Unable to cope with the sheer perfection, their only defence lay in identifying its apparent pretensions. 'Did you clock the Bennison drapes in the living room?' Abigail asked with a sneer. 'There's so much fabric in the pelmets, I don't know how they stay up.'

'And what about the hats in the cloakroom? They must have fifty, all on numbered hooks. It's like some nightmare out of *House & Garden*.'

'Funny you should say that. Miranda told everyone they've been down to photograph the house for the magazine. She pretended she'd been talked into it, but you can tell she's delighted.'

'And where've the paintings appeared from all of a sudden? They must buy them in bulk. They're so over-cleaned, they look like tarted-up tea trays hanging on the wall.'

'It makes our house look very dingy. Poppy's scribbled in crayon over every wall. We should get a painter round to fix the place up.'

'Let's not do anything,' Jamie said quickly. 'I tried to get two hundred quid out of a cash machine yesterday, and it wouldn't pay out. We must be overdrawn.'

'Tell me about it,' said Abigail. 'They won't accept Poppy back at her school after half-term unless we pay the fees.'

Feeling the chill winds of penury whipping at their ankles, Jamie lifted half a dozen teabags and a jar of Nescafe from the tin tray on the dressing table, and thrust them into his suitcase. 'If your father wasn't being such a bloody Jew about forking out some cash,' he complained to his wife, 'we wouldn't be in this hole at all.'

Surveying his dinner party from the head of his long mahogany dining table, Charlie had the gratifying sensation that it was all going brilliantly. Sir Michael Waitrose, considered a dry stick locally and short on small talk, had discussed skiing in Telluride with Marcus before dinner, and was now chatting away amiably with Abigail. Jamie appeared to be getting on like a house on fire with Lavinia Gilborne, as though they'd known each other for years. Marcus, seated between Miranda and Princess Marie-Christine Schoenmann-Ausberg-Konwitz, didn't look noticeably bored. Charlie hoped his wife was saying all the right things. Effortlessly conducting a conversation on automatic pilot with both Serena Waitrose and Camilla Silcox, he surreptitiously appraised Zara. Her voluptuous breasts, bursting out of a red strapless dress, filled him with nostalgia; Miranda's obsessional dieting, for which she consulted several different nutritionists, had shrunk her tits to wrinkled satsumas. Zara's eyes were framed by a web of crow's feet, and her skin was rough close-up, but she exuded a casual sexiness that excited him. He couldn't help believing that, given the choice, Zara would still choose himself over Bud every time. On the other hand, Bud was far richer, and this wasn't the moment to upset the apple cart. Dressing for dinner, Miranda had already irritated him by commenting on the size of Zara's pink diamond engagement ring, which glinted like a lithium camera battery on her fourth finger. It rather irked Charlie that Zara, always a borderline neighbour who had been lucky to get invitations to Ardnessaig, had some-how snared this fat, rich Yank.

Charlie caught Miranda's eye at the end of the table, and made a coffee-pouring gesture which was their signal that she should take the women through to the drawing room, leaving the men to talk money and politics over brandy and port. They reconfigured at one end of the table – Marcus, Bud, Jamie, Iain Cruickshank, Michael Waitrose, Torquil McVitie and the egregious Boobie van Haagen – where Charlie produced some especially good Cuban cigars from his elegant walnut humidor.

'These are excellent cigars, Charlie. Glad to know the fund's doing so well,' said Iain Cruickshank who, as the largest investor, was keen to talk it up.

'I'm kind of kicking myself now I didn't go in bigger at the beginning,' said Bud Deloitte.

'Oh, still plenty of upside to come, Bud,' said Charlie. 'We were at two-thirty-six close of play Friday. We're telling investors it can go all the way to four hundred.'

'So you're not anticipating any kind of market correc-tion?' asked Marcus, drawing on a mammoth Montecristo. 'Haven't picked up any disturbing signals?'

Charlie gulped and glanced at Bud. The last thing he needed was Marcus sowing any doubts in the minds of his investors. Even a note of caution from someone like Marcus Brand was enough to make people windy.

'No, not the slightest sign,' he replied firmly. 'Quite the reverse actually, there's colossal investor support. I've never seen anything like it. Our challenge is obtaining sufficient stock at justifiable prices.'

'The person to watch,' Marcus said, 'is Putin. I find him tremendously able, a quite different calibre of individual from either Yeltsin or Gorbachov. Tony Blair asked me to bring them together: they hit it off straight away. Make no mistake, whatever does or doesn't happen in Russia in the next few years will be entirely down to Putin.'

'How well have you got to know him? Putin, I mean,' Charlie asked.

'How well does anyone really know somebody like Vladimir? They tell you what they think you want to hear, nine times out of ten. Put it this way, I've called on him half a dozen times at the Kremlin, and a couple out at his *dacha*. He spent a weekend with me at Sandy Cove in Nassau, but that's strictly off the record. Socially, we get on like a house on fire. I find him reasonably realistic, he isn't under any illusions about his country's problems. There again, his background's KGB. Last time I saw the Man Himself I put it to him: "Vladimir, mind if I ask you a direct question? You know as well as I do you can't afford a full-service military capability. Those days are over. Your troops haven't been paid for six months, half of 'em. Sixty per cent of your tanks couldn't drive a mile down the road. As for your subs, I wouldn't go down in one if you paid me. So why bother? Sell the whole lot off, lock, stock and barrel. Sell 'em for scrap." Told him I'd take 'em off his hands myself, if he'd like me to, whole bloody lot. Invest the proceeds in putting new infrastructure in place, I told him. Build some decent roads. "Have you driven more than fifty miles outside Moscow lately?" I asked him. "Have you seen the condition of your horrible potholed highways?" Know what he replied? "No, Mr Brand," says Putin. "Since joining the Politburo I never travel anywhere by road. I prefer to fly in a Russian air force jet. Just as you, I am informed, prefer your Gulfstream." That's what he said: "I prefer to fly in a Russian air force jet." "I'll bet you do too, Mr Next President," I told him. "And when you come and stay with me in Wyoming, you can land it on my airstrip." That'd

541

give the local air traffic control boys in Jackson Hole something to think about, tell 'em Vladimir Putin is arriving in their airspace by Soviet Mig.'

As Marcus finished his story, the men who had been listening to the great tycoon with rapt attention broke into appreciative guffaws. Even Sir Michael Waitrose, who considered himself an Establishment insider, nodded his head respectfully at Marcus's remarkable proximity to power. There wasn't a man in the dining room who didn't feel that his own status had been vicariously enhanced by listening to Marcus. Watching this distinguished group in their smoking jackets, all puffing on his cigars, all except Jamie at the very top of their respective trees, Charlie felt privileged to preside over them at the head of his table. He doubted any of his fellow godchildren could deliver the goods by assembling a group as genuinely influential as the one here tonight.

'So your message is – stick with Russia?' asked Sir Michael Waitrose, who was considering the acquisition of a Russian grocery chain.

'At the right price – which should reflect the remote possibility of the whole place going up the spout – certainly. Any corporation not looking seriously at Russia at the moment deserves a kick up the pants. As far as my own company's concerned, we've got the place on watch, while remaining cautiously positive. Brand Muzik, our satellite music channel, which has already taken nineteen per cent of the Beijing and Canton markets, is starting up in Moscow next month. Our splendid VP for New Markets, Flora Huang, is over there now, signing the contract with the government for bandwidth.'

53: November, 1997

If there was one thing Charlie couldn't stand, it was travelling anywhere by car with his children, particularly in his own car, his new S-class Mercedes. Normally, Pelham and Marina were banned from the Mercedes; the Crieffs kept a Toyota Land Cruiser for the regular journeys up and down the M3 between London and Hampshire. As far as Charlie was concerned, the brats could smear their sticky fingers over the Land Cruiser to their hearts' content, cover the floor with crisp packets, Walkman batteries, plastic toys and old tapes, he really didn't care; it was Miranda's car. But in the Mercedes, he minded acutely. Already, in the fifteen minutes since they'd left Old Testbury Hall, Pelham had managed to spill a packet of Smarties over the leather seats in the back, and Marina had done something idiotic to jam her seatbelt.

If they hadn't all been invited to West Candover Park to lunch with Marcus, he'd never have allowed them near his car. As it was, he hadn't much choice.

'Can you please *stop* that moronic singing back there?' he barked over his shoulder. 'Pelham, stop it right now, or you'll get out of this car. And you too, Marina. I can't drive with this racket going on.'

Miranda, who decided she preferred the children's singing to the alternative, which was listening to her husband telling her how rich he would soon be, said, 'Oh, don't make such a fuss. They're only singing. They're children!' Then, turning to the back, she said, 'But keep the volume down, please. Papa's got a hangover from drinking too much red wine last night, and we don't want him to get any grumpier, do we?'

Charlie drove on in furious silence, accelerating past lorries on blind corners and slamming on the brakes seconds before ramming slow traffic. He hated to be late for anything, let alone for Marcus. Why, he wondered, did it take children twenty-five minutes to put on their shoes and get into the car? And why was Hampshire full of caravans in November? Grockles with caravans shouldn't be allowed on the roads. If Charlie were Prime Minister, the first thing he'd do was ban caravans altogether, or at the very least restrict them to driving at night.

He gripped the steering wheel more tightly. He always felt tense before seeing Marcus. He wondered which of the other godchildren would be at lunch today; he only knew Jamie and Abigail were coming for sure, and that they were bringing Poppy, which was a good thing because she'd be bound to behave badly. He hoped he could count on his own offspring to be a credit to him.

In the back, Pelham was tunelessly intoning some moronic song, over and over again, setting Charlie's teeth on edge.

'Twinkle, twinkle, chocolate bar,
My dad drives a rusty car . . .'

Where did they learn this rubbish? Charlie wondered. School, he supposed, though he doubted there were many rusty cars parked outside Busy Lizzie's in Holland Park.

'Pelham, this is unbearable, don't you know any other songs? Can't you recite us a poem or something instead? You must learn poetry at that overpriced school of yours.'

'I do know one poem,' Pelham replied. 'We say this one to Sammy Chou in our class:

Me Chinese,
Me Japan,
Me no like you,
Bing – bong – bam.'

Charlie roared with laughter. Chortling with paternal pride at his son's casual racism, he felt better all of a sudden. 'And you chant that poem to Sammy Chou at school? What does poor Chou say about it, then?'

'He likes it,' Pelham declared. 'He's my best friend. At Chou's house they've got an Olympic-sized swimming pool in the basement, and he's going to ask me over to swim.'

Sensing he'd scored a hit with his rhyme, and had pleased his father for once, Pelham was determined to milk it to the max.

> 'Me Chinese,
> Me Japan,
> Me no like you,
> Bing – bong – bam . . .'

'No, that's not it,' Marina was interrupting. 'That's not how it goes. The real one is:

> Me Chinese,
> Me Scooby-Doo,
> Me no like you,
> Do a big poo.'

'No,' moaned Pelham, 'that's not right. It goes:

> Me Scooby-Doo,
> Me Chinese,
> You got very
> Hairy knees.

'And you *have* too, Marina. You have got very hairy knees. They're really hairy. And you've got a hairy face.'

Marina began to sob and pummelled Pelham with her fists. Then Pelham thumped her back, much harder.

'All right, *that's it*,' said Charlie, jerking the car to a halt and yanking up the handbrake. 'Out of the car this minute, both of you. You can walk home. Go on, out of the car.'

But, even as he said it, he knew he didn't mean it. They were expected at Marcus's at half-past twelve and it was twenty-five to one already.

Revisiting West Candover Park for the first time since the great dance twenty years earlier, Charlie was struck by how little it had altered, at least on the outside. Even in winter, the parkland was impeccably manicured; a flock of black-and-white-spotted Jacob's sheep grazed between the ruins of a small Roman temple, which Marcus had somehow acquired and transported from Libya. Swans glided across an ornamental lake. As they turned the final bend in the long drive, and the great mansion with its Doric portico came into view, Charlie slowed down to allow his wife and children to drink it in. 'A lot of people think this is the most beautiful house in England,' he declared, full of godfilial pride. 'This is where your father had his twenty-first birthday party, Pelham and Marina. The owner is my godfather, and he's very important, so I need you to be very, very well behaved today. Understood?'

A security guard at a gatehouse waved them to slow down and checked their names on a typed list. Reading the list upside down, Charlie saw that the Temples had arrived before them, as had Mary Gore with that disabled daughter of hers, and Stuart. Saffron's name was noticeably absent, he didn't know why. The thought of her in the context of West Candover Park made him wonder what might have happened between them that night at the dance, if Stuart hadn't waded in and sabotaged the whole thing. As Charlie saw it, it had been in the bag. Stuart had a lot to answer for.

Marcus, Flora and the other godchildren were congregated around the fireplace in the drawing room, drinks in hand. Bartholomew the butler was circling with a bottle of champagne wrapped in a linen napkin.

'Good God,' Charlie said, as he greeted Marcus. 'What happened to the pictures in here? You've changed them all.'

'That's uncharacteristically observant of you, Charlie. Well done. We have indeed changed the paintings. Flora told me all those horses and grooms wouldn't do any more – too boring, wrong zeitgeist. Hope you approve.'

Charlie blinked dumbly at the Jackson Pollocks, Schnabels and de Koonings, which reminded him of the scribbles Marina brought home from school, and which Maha stuck on the fridge door with magnets.

'Yah, they're wonderfully . . . modern,' he replied. 'But what happened to all the Constables and the Stubbs?' He had secretly hoped to be left at least some of these in Marcus's will.

'Sold 'em. Hand it to Christie's, they did a halfway competent job for once. Went for twice their estimates.'

Then, turning to Abigail, he said, 'Afraid Charlie doesn't approve of my new pictures, Abby. Think he might be a bit of an old fogey, hasn't signed up to Cool Britannia like the rest of us.'

'Oh, don't get me wrong, Marcus,' Charlie said quickly. 'I actually like modern art very much. We're planning on getting some for Testbury, as a matter of fact.'

'Ask Abigail to help you,' Marcus advised. 'She's the great expert. Helped Flora a lot. Well, I look forward to seeing your collection, Charlie. I'm delighted you are finally developing an appreciation for modern art. Full marks. Had you marked down as a traditionalist, can't think why.'

Across the drawing room, Miranda was attempting to make small talk with Flora, but was finding the going tough. She was struck by how much more confident Flora was these days. With her manicured pale pink nails, perfect Asian skin and sugar pink Chanel suit, she was every inch the chatelaine, Miranda thought irritably; anyone would imagine she was Marcus's *wife*, not just his mistress, or 'god-daughter' as the euphemism went. As someone who rated small talk as one of life's essential accomplishments, Miranda was antagonised by Flora's stiffness. She felt that, as Marcus's . . . partner, Flora had a duty to keep the conversation flowing. When she complimented her on her Chanel outfit, Flora waved her hand dismissively, implying clothes were of no consequence to her, and said, 'Thank you. I've bought it for the World Economic Forum in Davos. There are some dinners we have to attend.'

From the corner of her eye, Miranda watched Pelham and Marina perched shyly on the edge of a sofa, being talked to by the obnoxious Stuart Bolton. Well, at least they were behaving, which was more than could be said for Poppy Temple who was doing handstands against the wall. If her feet went any higher, they'd go through a canvas. Miranda thought how much nicer her own children looked – Marina in her best tartan dress, Pelham in his little checked shirt, dark green corduroys and lace-up shoes – than Poppy in red and white stripy tights, a bubblegum-pink tutu and all those frightful pink plastic clips in her hair and sparkly playnail varnish. It really was extraordinary that the Temples allowed her to go out to lunch dressed like that.

Mary was wondering why she'd accepted Marcus's invitation, and was hoping it wouldn't all be too much for Clara. At the age of fourteen, she had recently started at a weekly boarding school outside Bristol for children with special needs. She seemed to be loving the school, but still needed so much supervision over every little thing, and Mary worried about taking her to a smart lunch party. Strangers found it difficult to understand what Clara was trying to say, which frustrated and embarrassed her. As usual, Mary found herself scrutinising her daughter for any resemblance to Marcus, and winced. As Clara had grown older, she had also become heavier, and her build probably owed something to him, she thought with a shudder.

Mary knew she never should have come. She'd told Stuart she didn't want to and wasn't going to, but then Barbara Miles had love-bombed her with telephone messages, and she'd felt the emotional blackmail. And she felt, too, a hardly explicable compulsion to bring Clara to her father's house, just once, and show her West Candover Park, even though she would never disclose to Clara or Marcus their biological tie. All she could think of when she looked at her daughter was how extraordinary she was and how much unfairness life had dealt her. She could never know the identity of her real father, and the wonderful man who should have been her father – Crispin – was dead. Clara was a happy child, Mary thought, but her neediness was overwhelming. At home in Billing Road she would follow her mother all over the house, everywhere she went, even into the bathroom. Sometimes, waking at night, Mary would sit up in bed with the lights off, staring into the dark, worrying what would happen to Clara after she'd gone, supposing Clara outlived her.

'Before we all go through to lunch,' Marcus said, clapping his hands for silence, 'I would like to show you a new painting Flora and I bought together at auction a couple of weeks ago in New York. And since I know several of my godchildren are in to modern art in a big way – Abigail, Charlie – you might find it amusing.'

He led them across a flagstoned hall into a library which was evidently used as his study. A pair of computer consoles stood on an enormous desk, and an array of telephones and satcom technology. To her surprise, Mary saw several framed photographs of herself and her fellow godchildren arranged along a bookshelf, taken in Wyoming and aboard *Marketmaker*.

'See what you think,' Marcus said. He pulled a cord and a pair of velvet curtains opened, revealing a post-Impressionist painting of a field of sunflowers.

'Ohmigod, is that what I think it is?' Abigail asked in amazement.

'Van Gogh. Or Van Go as you Americans insist on mispronouncing him. Glorious, isn't it? Moment we saw it, we knew we had to have it, didn't we, Flora?'

She nodded. 'It's awesome, Marcus.'

Jamie hissed to Abigail, 'What do you think it cost?'

She shrugged and whispered, 'Fifty? Sixty?'

'Is that in thousands or millions?'

'Millions, for Christ's sake.' Then, louder, to Marcus: 'It's the most beautiful Van Go – Van Gogh – I've ever seen. I read about it coming up, but they never said who'd bought it.'

'I cut a deal with the auction house the day before the sale, and they withdrew it. And please, all of you, I do want to keep this one private. Jamie? Not a word. Can I trust you all on this?'

The godchildren nodded. Charlie, while not actually particularly liking the painting, nevertheless found himself wondering what would become of it eventually. He hoped Marcus wouldn't leave something so valuable to a museum or, worse, to Flora. Far more sensible to flog it and divide the proceeds between the lot of them.

They entered a long dining room with French doors and six sash windows looking on to a terrace. Whatever influence Flora had had on the choice of art in the drawing room had not yet extended into the dining room, in which hung several enormous Claude Lorrains of mythological figures pursuing stags through classical ruins. At opposite ends of the room two tables were laid for lunch: a long one for the adults and a smaller, round table for the children. Mary, Abigail and Miranda felt their hearts sink, wondering how their young would cope through the meal unsupervised.

'I've put all your offspring together down there, so we can hear ourselves speak and have some decent conversation,' Marcus announced. 'And, Abigail, I hope your high-spirited daughter won't be continuing her circus act all through lunch, otherwise it's going to be rather tiresome for the rest of us.'

'I'm sorry, Marcus. Once we get some food inside her I'm sure she'll settle down.' Then, grabbing Poppy who was cartwheeling across an Aubusson rug, she hissed, 'Don't you *dare* misbehave. Stop messing about, sit down at your place and don't move.'

'But I was showing Clara my gym,' protested Poppy.

'Well, don't. Poppy, you've simply got to co-operate today. I'm asking you. Just for one hour. If you do, I'll buy you sweets on the way back.'

'Can we stop at that service station with the pick-and-mix?'

'Anything. Just park your butt on that seat and stay put, OK?'

At that moment, Bartholomew and two waitresses entered the dining room with the first course, which was tiny individual partridges on a bed of red cabbage.

'Yuk, what's this?' asked Pelham, prodding the bird with his fork and seeing blood spurt on to the plate.

Miranda, standing over him, said, 'Partridge. It tastes like chicken. Eat it up and don't make a fuss.'

'But it's all covered with blood. It's revolting.'

'Pelham, I told you, don't make a fuss. What did we agree earlier? If we don't like anything, we leave it quietly on the side of the plate.' Then, firmly, into his ear: 'Papa's told you it's best behaviour today. Don't you dare start crying or it's no television for a week.'

Bartholomew appeared at the children's table with a tray of soft drinks. 'What would they all like to drink with their lunch?'

Before Miranda and Mary could answer 'water', Poppy had reached out for a can of Coke and cracked open the tab, which meant everybody else had to have Coke too. Mary, who was cutting up Clara's bird for her, whispered, 'Just eat what you can, darling. And be very careful about not spilling anything on this lovely polished table.' As she headed for the grown-up table, Mary watched her daughter anxiously, wishing she could sit with the children for lunch.

'Thing that beats me,' Marcus was proclaiming, 'is how you people don't have proper keepers for your children these days. When I told Flora none of you was bringing a nanny, she was amazed. Says it would never happen in Hong Kong at a Sunday lunch party.'

Miranda began to explain that their new Serbian au pair, Kosova, didn't work weekends, but Marcus interrupted. 'Don't let's talk about children. Whole point of parking them on a separate table. I'm more interested in asking Stuart and Charlie how they think this new government's shaping up. Come on, Stuart, how does it look from Germany? What are Chancellor Kohl and his well-fed Eurodictats saying about Tony and his cronies?'

'That they've made a reasonably good start, I think. They certainly approved of giving the Bank of England its independence, like the Bundesbank's had for years. They're impatient for us to join the Euro, of course, and hope Blair won't drag his feet.'

Charlie felt irritation rising inside him. 'Well, I hope you've told them, Stuart, what a total balls-up Tony's made of everything he's touched so far. First he raids the pension funds, which is tantamount to theft, pure and simple, then he allows that stunted dwarf Robin Cook to bang on about an ethical foreign policy, which upsets half our best allies like the Indonesians and Chile. Personally I find it hilarious that we've managed to land the most tactless man in Britain with the job of running our diplomats. He's a walking ruddy disaster. As for Gordon Brown and his pathetic moral stand about not wearing white tie at the Mansion House . . .'

At that moment a cry went up from the children's table and Clara leapt to her feet, her dress spattered in Coca-Cola.

'Oh, Lord, Clara, what have you done?' Mary sprinted across the dining room, dabbing at Clara, the table and the Aubusson rug with a napkin, while Bartholomew went to fetch wet cloths from the kitchen. 'I'm so sorry, Marcus, poor Clara's spilt her drink everywhere. I just hope it doesn't mark the table.'

'It wasn't her fault,' Pelham announced. 'It was Poppy's. She was tipping some of Clara's drink into her own glass, and it toppled over.'

Now Abigail and Miranda were at the small table too, scolding and comforting their children and begging them between gritted teeth to behave.

'If they hadn't had Coca-Cola to start with, this never would have happened,' Miranda said flintily, glaring at Abigail. 'And it's ridiculous Clara hasn't brought a special mug with a lid, if she isn't capable of drinking properly.'

Mary, who felt like slapping Miranda, replied, 'Actually, Clara's been doing very well. It isn't easy for her, all on her own over here.'

A rib of beef and half a dozen dishes of vegetables were laid out on the sideboard, and the three mothers, juddering with suppressed tension, lined up to serve their children. But after the excitement of the spilt Coke, the children were bored and mutinous and showing no inclination to sit down. Poppy was demonstrating backwards somersaults behind her chair, and Clara and Marina had clambered on to a window-seat and were drawing pictures in their breath on a pane. Mary saw Flora glare crossly at Clara, while discussing with Bartholomew the best means of removing Coke stains from mahogany.

'My God, this is *intolerable*!' Marcus's voice boomed across the dining room. 'Please get those *damned brats off that bloody window-seat* and out of this room this instant. I'm sorry, but I can't stand it. If you can't keep them properly under control, they must get out, simple as that. Out into the garden. Go on, *scram*!' He scraped back his chair and bore down on the terrified children. 'Yes, I do mean you, Pelham – and you, Poppy, all of you, Clara, Marina – out you go. Go on, into the garden.' He turned the key in the

French doors and shooed them on to the frost-covered terrace. Mary was horrified at them going outside without coats, but Marcus was ordering his godchildren to stay seated. 'Please, can we have half an hour of undisrupted conversation today? Is that too much to ask? I will *not* have children bobbing up and down at the table like yo-yos, and their mothers pandering to them in this ludicrous fashion. Sit down and let's try to be civilised for five minutes. Now, Jamie, how has the change of government affected the hotel business . . . ?'

Mary was hating today even more than she'd expected. Impervious to Marcus's overpowering magnetism, she regarded him only as a bully and a show-off, and failed to understand why Stuart continued to turn up on command. She had tried discussing Marcus with him, but he wouldn't be drawn, quickly changing the subject. With Charlie and Miranda, their motivation was all too obvious, they were shameless. Across the table, she could hear Charlie chatting up Flora, praising Marcus to her and, with an incredible lack of subtlety, advising her not to have children. ('They're a hell of a tie, they'd cramp your lifestyle bigtime.')

Mary longed to go outside and take Clara her coat, but the waitresses were approaching with a lemon soufflé, and Marcus would erupt if she left the table. Jamie, sitting on her right, whispered, 'Any idea what's happened to Saffron today?'

'No.'

'Apparently she refused to come. Marcus is furious. She told him she hates Flora, for obvious reasons.'

'Poor Saffron.'

'Yes, it is poor Saffron. She asked Marcus for a reference and he refused to give her one. Flora told him not to, apparently.'

'How very petty of her.'

'Oh, she's a complete bitch,' Jamie said softly. 'Charlie thinks she'll get us all cut out of Marcus's will.'

Mary shrugged. 'It won't bother me, I assure you.'

'Well, it bothers me. Abby and I are flat broke, we're

relying on it. Look at Flora talking to Charlie now. You can't tell what she's thinking, her face is inscrutable. Charlie says she's completely scheming, he doesn't trust her an inch. She's bloody attractive though, isn't she? I wouldn't say no to a quickie.'

'Jamie! I'm shocked. I hope that was a joke.'

He grinned. 'Sure. But you've got to admit, her nipples look fantastic under that camisole thing.'

There was a rapping at the French window and, to her dismay, Mary saw Clara trying to come inside. Sensing Marcus's irritation, she shook her head and pointed in the direction of the back door. She mouthed, 'Go round to the side, if you want to come in.'

But Clara persisted, thumping at the glass and rattling the handle, trying to open it.

Mary saw Charlie exchange glances with Miranda, relieved it wasn't one of their own children making the racket.

'I think she's trying to tell us something,' Mary said. 'She wants us to come.'

'Oh, for goodness' sake,' Charlie said. 'Ignore her. She probably just wants someone to push her on the swing.'

'She's looking very distressed. I'd better find out. Sorry, Marcus.'

Mary unlocked the door and Clara stumbled into the room. Her skirt, shoes and socks were sopping wet, and she was struggling to get words out. 'Poppy go swim. Poppy pool.' Her diction, always difficult to understand, was almost incomprehensible as she tugged at her mother, dragging her out into the garden.

'I think she's saying Poppy's in the swimming pool. Is that possible, Marcus?'

'The pool? Well, it's shut down for the winter and the gate into the walled garden should be locked . . .'

Abigail was already on her feet, followed by Stuart. Mary and Clara were twenty yards ahead of them, racing across the lawn past the wellingtonia in the direction of the greenhouses and walled garden.

'Ohmigod, how did they get near the pool?' Abby was gibbering. 'It can't have been left unlocked.'

In the dining room, Charlie allowed Bartholomew to pour another glass of claret for him. Miranda, Jamie, Flora and Marcus stayed put too. Charlie felt it was important that at least some of the party remained behind with their host, they couldn't all go haring off in the middle of lunch.

Stuart and Mary arrived together at the flint-and-brick garden wall. An ornamental iron gate, framed by the tangled grey branches of a wisteria, stood open and inside they could see a thatched summer house surrounded by garden furniture, draped with tarpaulins for the winter. Their first reaction was one of relief. Pelham and Miranda were standing by the edge of the pool, which had a quilted plastic cover over its entire surface. But: 'Where's Poppy? Where's Poppy?' Abigail desperately shouted.

'Underneath the cover,' Pelham said. 'We told her not to go swimming, but she wanted to.'

'Jesus Christ!' said Stuart, grabbing at the edge of the cover. Down near the bottom, close to the sump, he could see a small pink figure floating amidst autumn leaves. A pink plastic hair band was bobbing on the surface against the filter. Kicking off his shoes, he dived into the icy water, swam down and carried her to the surface. Her tiny body, in the weightlessness of the pool, seemed impossibly light.

'Quickly, take her, Abby, she's not breathing.'

Stuart heaved himself out of the pool and showed Abigail how to tip Poppy's head back to open the airways. Then he attempted mouth-to-mouth resuscitation, pressing his lips over hers, holding her nose and praying her little chest would respond.

'Somebody call an ambulance,' he gasped between breaths. 'There's no time to lose. And, Mary, see if there are any towels or rugs in the hut.' Mary ran back with three stripy towels which she pulled clumsily round Poppy's body.

Abigail was sitting on the ground, rubbing Poppy's tiny hand which had turned blue with hypothermia. Her shrivelled fingers still glistened with glittery nail polish. 'But she knows how to swim,' Abby kept repeating over and over. 'She learned to swim in Italy. You saw her swimming, Stuart.'

555

Alerted by shouts from the pool, Marcus, Flora, Jamie, Charlie and Miranda joined the others in the walled garden, still holding their wine glasses. Abigail was wailing inconsolably, and Jamie stood uncomfortably by, trying to comfort her. 'How could anyone have left that bloody gate open?' she was screaming. 'How could they be so dumb?' She glared at Marcus, as though holding him personally responsible.

'Come on, calm down, Abigail,' Charlie said. 'Blaming people won't help. It was a bloody stupid idea anyway, to swim without adults around.'

'The gate was *unlocked*. Of course kids will go in, if it's left unlocked.'

'We're all upset, Abby. It's a ghastly situation. I'm just saying it's not Marcus's fault, that's all, if Poppy's disobedient enough to go swimming.'

Realising the other children needed to be shielded from the unfolding tragedy, Mary began shepherding Clara and the younger Crieffs away from the pool. Stuart was still kneeling over Poppy, trying to breathe life back into her cold, unresponsive body. She looked like a rag-doll stretched out on the paving stones, her pink tutu stuck to her legs and her hair plastered across her face. Flora in her pink Chanel suit was jabbing keys on her mobile to find out why the ambulance hadn't arrived.

'Her chest moved, I definitely saw it move.' Abigail was transfixed as Stuart exhaled into his goddaughter's lungs. He had been blowing and pumping for fifteen minutes and, just as he had started to lose hope, he'd felt a faint response. Her tiny diaphragm seemed to reflate of its own accord, like a car with a flat battery responding to jump leads. Hardly daring to believe it, he gave Abby a half thumbs-up, indicating he couldn't be sure.

Marcus and the godchildren were all gathered around Stuart now, watching Poppy for signs of a sustained rally. If he could somehow keep her alive until the ambulance arrived, maybe it might be all right. Mary was still keeping Clara, Pelham and Marina as far away from the action as possible; inside the summer house was a pile of tartan picnic rugs, and she draped them around the children's shivering shoulders. Pelham, entirely oblivious to the drama, had found a snorkel and flippers and was pestering Mary to put them on him.

'Where the hell is this damned ambulance?' Marcus was barking orders to Bartholomew on Flora's mobile, telling him to have a helicopter on standby in case Poppy needed to be flown to London. Instinctively wanting to regain the initiative from Stuart, who had hitherto assumed command, Marcus began issuing instructions to everyone at once, insisting on speaking to Barbara Miles, Makepiece and Dick Mathias, and arranging for world-famous paediatricians to be located and put on alert.

Stuart was in despair. Even as he knelt over Poppy and pushed down on her ribcage, he could feel her slipping away. In desperation he blew harder and harder, willing her to hang on to life, but each time the response became fainter, until he realised there was no spark left inside her at all. Still he continued, hope against hope, while Abigail stood by in silent despair clutching her tiny hand.

He continued to administer the kiss of life right up until the arrival of the ambulance from Basingstoke, when the paramedics, having done their tests, pronounced her dead.

Mary was desperately worried about Abigail, wondering how she'd ever make it through the funeral and even how she'd get her to the church. Abby was sitting on Poppy's bed in the little bedroom at the top of the house, neither speaking nor moving, lost in a trance of desolation. In the nine days since the tragedy she had barely slept or eaten, just sat on Poppy's bed in her untidy bedroom surrounded by Barbies, teddies and picture books, staring at the wall. The tablets supplied by the Temples' GP were having no effect at all.

'Abigail, Abby darling, you've simply got to get moving. I'm so sorry to nag you, but the funeral begins in half an hour.' Mary ran a bath in Poppy's bathroom, and found and carried upstairs appropriate clothes from Abby's cupboard for her to wear to the service. Now she had to get her into the bathroom, cleaned up, dressed and round to St George's, Campden Hill Square, as quickly as possible.

It had been Jamie, assisted by half the front-office staff of 60 Montpelier Gardens, who had organised the funeral, as well as contacting Poppy's grandparents in New Jersey and Fulham, putting the death announcement in *The Times*, and attending to the numerous gruesome formalities, including the coroner's office, which followed the accident in remorseless succession. He had barely had time for the shock to settle in, so occupied had he been with doctors, vicars, firms of undertakers, Abby's mother who rang six or more times a day from Franklin Lakes, and his own who kept offering to come round and help, but then cancelled having failed to find a dog-sitter for her Jack Russell. Whenever he arrived home, he found Abby perched on the edge of Poppy's bed, still as a waxwork, refusing to speak or even look at him, or else lying prostrate beneath her eiderdown, weeping and wailing. In her despair, she directed her bitterness principally against Marcus, whom she blamed for banishing the children outside to the unlocked garden. But she also blamed Jamie for remaining behind in the dining room with Marcus, rather than coming outside with her to find Poppy. When he tried to tell her the arrangements he'd made for the funeral, Abby shook her head and waved him away.

With Abigail leaning on one arm, and Clara on the other, Mary somehow supported them both for the short walk to the church. Jamie was waiting outside on the steps, watching out for them, surrounded by a crowd of mourners. Mary thought how haggard and neglected he looked, his eyes ringed with dark circles, his hair greasy and uncombed. As she kissed him a sombre hello, she thought she smelt whisky on his breath.

Leading Abby into the nave, and then down the aisle to her reserved pew at the front, Mary saw that the church was already three-quarters full. The whole of Poppy's class at Busy Lizzie's had come, along with many of their parents, and all the teachers from the school. As they neared the altar, several members of the congregation smiled compassionately in Abigail's direction, but so absorbed was she in her own despair, she could not see them. In front of the altar rail, on a wooden trestle, stood a pitifully small black coffin, on top of which lay a masterfully understated arrangement of white peonies, chosen by Jamie's boss, Bender Barraclough. Mourners in the first pews could see that the tag read: 'We will love you for ever, Mummy and Daddy'.

The congregation was still filing into the church. Surreptitiously glancing around her, Mary saw that the verger was unlocking the wooden door up to the organ loft, to accommodate the overflow of mourners. Several little girls from Poppy's class were already crying, and Mary wondered whether it really was a good idea to bring such young children to a funeral; others, oblivious to the significance of the occasion, were messing about in the pews and trying to stamp on each other's feet. Mary saw Miranda Crieff arrive on her own, dressed head to foot in black Valentino, and slip into a pew between Camilla Silcox and Nipples Ayrton-Phillips. Bender Barraclough, wearing an immaculate Ascot morning coat with an ink-black chrysanthemum in the buttonhole, occupied a front-row pew. Having several times collected her goddaughter from Busy Lizzie's after school and taken her to her once-a-week gym club, Mary recognised Poppy's Nigerian gym teacher sitting in a side pew, and the delightful old newsagent from Holland Park Avenue where Poppy loved to stop on her way home and buy Pokemons and sweets. He had always had such a soft spot for Poppy. But then everyone had a soft spot for Poppy. Mary wondered how Abigail and Jamie would ever recover.

Lizzie Frobisher and several Montessori teachers were handing out Orders of Service. Printed on the front of the stiff off-white card was a black and white photograph of Poppy in a t-shirt, taken three months earlier in Tuscany. Underneath was printed: POPPY HARRIET MARGARET TEMPLE (2 March 1994 – 11 November 1997). On the back of the card was a second, larger picture of Poppy as an angel in the Christmas nativity play.

Poppy's American grandparents, Zubin and Harriet Schwartzman, had now arrived and were ushered into a pew between Margaret and Michael Temple and Abigail. Mary, who hadn't set eyes on Harriet since Abigail and Jamie's wedding eleven years earlier, thought she resembled a little plastic doll, the skin on her forehead and cheeks practically rigid with Botox, making it impossible for her to register emotion. Zubin looked aged and bent, and walked with the aid of a stick. Mary had been told by Jamie that Zubin's first reaction, on being told the circumstances of Poppy's death, was to sue Marcus to kingdom come, and it had required all Jamie's best efforts to dissuade him.

As Charlie approached St George's from the direction of Holland Park tube, he saw his godfather step out of a Bentley and forge inside. Later, standing at the back of the church in his long dark overcoat, he spotted Marcus sitting close to the front, like a big black immovable rock in a sea of weeping mothers. Several people in the congregation were turning round and craning their necks to get a proper look at him, and a whisper went round the church: 'That's Marcus Brand over there. Poppy drowned in his pool.'

Abigail had also seen Marcus arrive and she shook with fury. She couldn't believe he had the effrontery to turn up. Earlier in the week he'd even had the nerve to have Barbara Miles call to ask if he might give a speech at the funeral. What's more, Jamie had almost agreed. Abby had sent back the message that she couldn't stop Marcus coming, but if he so much as spoke to her, she would not be answerable for her actions.

Suddenly there was a hush, as the vicar, an ancient man in a long rusty cassock, proceeded slowly down the aisle. ' "I am the resurrection and the life, Saith the Lord: he that believeth in me, though he were dead, yet shall he live: and whosoever liveth and believeth in me shall never die." '

Abigail felt she had iron bands around her chest. She could scarcely breathe. She was exhausted and broken, she had cried for ten days and hadn't slept. The intensity of her longing for Poppy was indescribable. Nothing in the world mattered any longer.

' "We brought nothing into this world, and it is certain we can carry nothing out. The Lord gave, and the Lord hath taken away; blessed be the Name of the Lord." '

The vicar was inviting the children and teachers in Poppy's class to come up to the altar, where they were to sing a special song in her memory. Even before they began, half the congregation was crying.

'We always called this "Poppy's Song",' announced Lizzie Frobisher, 'because it was her very favourite. She often used to sing it in morning assembly, in that beautiful voice of hers that none of us will ever, ever forget. So, children: "Poppy's Song" . . .'

A teacher gave a note on a piano, and the class began singing: ' "You are my sun-shine, my only sunshine. You make me hap-py, when skies are grey . . ." '

Abby knew she would break down any moment. Watching Poppy's classmates, so many of whom had come over to their house for tea, she felt the terrible injustice that all these beautiful children were still alive, but little Poppy was dead.

Why did it have to be her? And of course she knew the answer. Because none of these other children's parents were cursed with Marcus Brand as their godfather.

Looking at the poignant little coffin on its trestle, Mary remembered the last funeral she'd been to – Crispin's – and wished desperately that he was there with her now, standing by her side. If he hadn't been killed, he would have been forty-four. She wondered what their life would have been like, how many children they would have had and where they would have ended up living. She tried to picture herself raising four children in an old rectory in some Norfolk village near Fakenham. She never would have started her business, which now seemed such a defining part of her life. There was no way of telling whether or not she'd have been happier.

'"Please don't take my sun-shine away,"' sang the children. '"Please don't take my sunshine a-way."'

Just then, a terrible eerie lowing sound filled the church, reminding Jamie of a cow that has fallen over a cliff at night and is in dreadful pain. Seconds later, he realised it was Clara trying to join in the singing, but her voice, suffused with emotion, was coming out even stronger than usual. Mary tried to shush her without hurting her feelings. It scarcely sounded human: animal noises emitting from a fourteen-year-old girl.

Invited by Jamie to give a short funeral address, Stuart had spent all of the flight from Frankfurt wondering what to say. He always felt self-conscious speaking in public, believing that his by now almost imperceptible Birmingham accent made him difficult to understand. In the event, he handled it perfectly. Looking painfully grave and solid in a grey pinstripe suit, he began: 'This is the hardest job I've had to do in my life. What a lot of joy Poppy brought to her parents, her godparents and everyone else who was lucky enough to know her. All those handstands and cartwheels, she was a ball of energy . . .' By the time he'd finished, there wasn't a dry eye in the church, and all the parents were clutching their own children.

Watching from the back, Charlie wondered why on earth

the Temples had asked Stuart to give the address. He hadn't realised they'd all become such good buddies. Not that he wanted the trouble of making a speech himself, but he did feel slightly miffed. He wouldn't have minded making a really good one in front of Marcus; he would have emphasised that Poppy's death was a total accident, and nobody's fault, especially not Marcus's. He had been shocked by the way Abby had let rip at their godfather by the pool. In fact, it was very decent of him to turn up today, considering how she'd behaved.

Charlie could see Jamie in the front pew, unshaved and totally out of it. He had to admit, things had gone awfully badly for his best friend lately, and felt genuinely sorry for him. He hardly made a bean, he was married to an American nutter and now, after all that palaver at the wank bank conceiving Poppy, it had been a total waste of effort. He thought he should probably invite the Temples down to Old Testbury Hall for another weekend soon, but doubted Miranda would be prepared to have them. Last time, a rather expensive Braun hairdryer had disappeared from their bedroom.

The congregation was finishing the final hymn and Abigail was clenching and unclenching her fists. Picking up on her friend's rising hysteria, Mary looped her arm around the back of her coat, preparing to guide her up the aisle the minute the service ended; the quicker she got back to her bed the better. Abby kept glaring over her shoulder at Marcus, who was sitting in his pew with a slightly sardonic, detached, well-fed air about him, as though he was watching an opera. Mary noticed that the mourners on both sides had instinctively left him a bit of extra space, either out of respect for his money or contempt for his person, it was hard to say which.

'How *dare* that fucking man show his face at Poppy's funeral?' Abby was muttering. 'I loathe him, I loathe him . . .'

' "Whosoever believeth shall live, though he die," ' intoned the vicar, ' "and whosoever liveth, and believeth in him, shall not die eternally . . ." '

The service was ended. Mary steered Abigail into the aisle and, pausing only for Clara to catch up, began frog-marching her in the direction of the door. Behind her, she could hear Bender Barraclough telling Harriet, 'Mrs Schwartzman, I insist you admire the flowers on the casket. I selected them myself, you know. Nobody does peonies like Paula Pryke.'

They were passing the end of Marcus's pew when, to Mary's horror, he stepped out into the aisle in front of them, blocking Abigail's way, kissed her and declared, 'Do let Barbara know if there's anything at all I can do to help.'

For a moment Abby just stood there, shaking. Then, speaking very clearly and very loudly, she replied, 'Why don't you just fuck off, you sick bastard? The most helpful thing you can do is leave us alone.'

Marcus stood his ground, raised one eyebrow in an expression which acknowledged that she was obviously under tremendous pressure, bowed, and stepped out of her path. Then, addressing himself to Mary, he said, 'I under-stand her grief.' His voice was silky and soft. 'My own wife died in the most tragic of circumstances. I thought I would never get over her.'

Mary threw him a look of absolute contempt. 'Yes, Marcus, you told me that once before. Shortly after my husband died. I'm sure you remember what happened next.'

55: November, 1997

The little cottage in Hillgate Place was a shrine to Poppy. A month after her death, Abigail could not bring herself to touch any of her things or tidy anything away. Poppy's school bag remained in the narrow hall, stuffed with her old reading books and pencil case. Her toys were scattered all over the house. Her clothes lay, unwashed, at the bottom of the dirty clothes basket. The place was a tip. Utterly absorbed by her misery, Abigail drifted around all day in her nightdress, wouldn't take a bath, wouldn't get dressed.

Realising his wife was succumbing to a serious break-down, Jamie took compassionate leave from the hotel to look after her, which only made matters worse. Cooped up together in the cottage, their days were filled with recrimin-ations. Abigail's bitterness towards Marcus seemed to increase over time, and her rages became violent and irrational. 'And where was that stupid bitch Flora at the funeral?' she demanded. 'She didn't even bother to come. Not that I wanted her to.' She berated Jamie for hours on end, for having remained behind with Marcus and the others in the dining room at West Candover Park, 'drinking more fucking claret when your daughter was drowning in the swimming pool'.

Already devastated by Poppy's death, Jamie came to resent the way that Abby was hijacking the grieving process for herself, as though she had been Poppy's only parent. In fact, he missed Poppy intensely. He remembered how she used to creep downstairs in the middle of the night, and climb into bed between her parents, curling up in 'the warm place' as she called it. And how she would toss and turn, and change her position, so that when he woke up her little pink foot would be pressed into his side, or even his face, and she would be fast asleep, horizontal, across the eiderdown. Each morning, he still half expected to find Poppy there, before the awful reality of her death hit him anew.

The house was a minefield of undetonated memories. It contained dozens – hundreds – of reminders of Poppy, waiting to spring out and take him by surprise. Jamie would open the bathroom cabinet and there was Poppy's toothbrush and banana-flavoured toothpaste; the larder was full of her cereals, Cheerios and Coco Pops. When he opened a drawer searching for light bulbs, he found a single pink Barbie shoe and stirrups from a My Little Pony.

Desperate to escape the house and Abigail, he started to visit his old girlfriends in the afternoon, Camilla Silcox and Nipples Ayrton-Phillips. Nipples had recently reverted to her maiden name, following the acrimonious break up of her marriage to Hugo Gilborne. Both women were only too eager to comfort Jamie, his grief making him madly attractive to them. On being told about Abigail's current behaviour and attitude, Camilla Silcox, who had never particularly taken to Miss Schwartzman in the first place, gave Jamie a long lecture on how he must stick up for himself, and how he should certainly feel no guilt over Poppy's death, parenthood being a series of false alarms. He couldn't have been expected to know about the swimming pool. 'If it all becomes too unbearable,' she told him, 'come and spend a couple of weeks with us in Barbados. Iain's coming out for part of the time, otherwise we'll be very quiet. It'd do you good to have a break.'

Letters of condolence arrived by every post, but Abigail neither read them nor replied. Instead, she wrote three mad letters to Marcus – each ten or twelve pages long – blaming him for Poppy's death, telling him she'd never forgive him, never wanted to set eyes on him again, and only just stopping short of accusing him of leaving the pool unlocked on purpose. 'You've destroyed the only thing I've ever loved,' she wrote. 'Your whole life is a hollow sham, perfect on the outside, rotten on the inside.' She did not tell Jamie about the letters, and slipped outdoors with her coat over her nightdress to post them at the end of the street.

When she received no response to her crazy missives, she

took to leaving abusive messages on Marcus's answerphone at St James's Place. She would ring the number ten or fifteen times a day, slamming down the receiver if it was picked up by Bartholomew, and waiting until she got the machine. Then she would tell him exactly what she thought of him – 'Murderer!' – until the tape ran out.

Entirely unaware of his wife's campaign of harassment, the first Jamie knew about it was when Barbara Miles rang the house. He picked up the phone in the kitchen while Abby was trying to rest on a sofa next door.

'Oh, Jamie – good – you're just the person,' said Barbara. 'This is a slightly sensitive matter, and I'm very pleased to have got you.' She explained to him about the nuisance calls. 'Mr Brand has told me to ask you to stop your wife leaving messages on his machine. I'm afraid he's quite annoyed about it.'

Overcome with embarrassment, Jamie said, 'Yes, of course, I'm very sorry indeed. Please apologise to Marcus. I'll do my best to stop them.'

As he walked back into the sitting room, Abigail pulled herself up on the sofa and yelled at him, 'Thank you for taking Marcus's side, Jamie. That's absolutely fucking predictable. "Please apologise to Marcus." Why doesn't *he* apologise to *me* for murdering my daughter? You know what I think, Jamie? I don't think you even care that much about Poppy. All you care about is keeping in with him.'

56: December, 1997

As compensation for spending so much time away in
Moscow, Charlie promised to take Miranda to the Amanpulo before Christmas. Recently the word Aman had joined
Chanel, Michaeljohn, Ferragamo, Colefax and Cartier right
at the top of Miranda's lexicon of favourite vocabulary, and
she had struggled to decide which of the dozen luxury Aman
resort hotels she most hankered after. In the end, she had
chosen Amanpulo in the Philippines for her treat, as offering
the most alluring combination of white sandy beaches,
deeply private *casitas*, masseurs, beauty treatments and
blissful peace. If she and Charlie had to spend a week alone
together (and the prospect did rather fill her with dread)
then it might as well be somewhere lovely, where she could
really unwind and not lift a finger.

From Charlie's point of view, he was anxious to put
the maximum distance between his wife and Boobie van
Haagen. Although at five-and-a-half months pregnant, he
hardly imagined Miranda was up to anything, he had grown
resentful of her ex-husband's constant presence at her side.
On the flight from Moscow to London, idly opening up a
glossy magazine, the first thing Charlie had seen was a
photograph of Lady Crieff and Mr Boobie van Haagen
together at the opening of some shop. Boobie was as brown
as a nut, and looked suspiciously like he was wearing
eyeliner. If Charlie had his way, Miranda would have
nothing more to do with him.

Aside from these nagging misgivings, Charlie was in high
spirits. The Crieff Emerging Markets Russia Fund was on a
seemingly unstoppable roll. After an awkward few months in
the middle of the year, when the Russian stockmarket
wobbled and he had had his work cut out to hold his
investors in place, the economy had rebounded strongly.
An article in the *Investors Chronicle* had named the Crieff

fund as one of the ten most impressive launch funds, mentioning in passing that the great tycoon Marcus Brand had been in from the beginning. Reflecting on his first five months in business, Charlie couldn't help feeling he'd done a bloody amazing job. He hadn't put a foot wrong. The stocks he'd personally picked had shot through the roof. When he thought of his old colleagues at Cruickshank & Willis, stuck in a rut behind their desks, and contrasted their levels of initiative with his own in Moscow . . . well, he deserved every rouble – every single million – that was headed his way.

He had other reasons for feeling happy too. Marcus still hadn't married Flora Huang, and was showing no signs of doing so either. With every month that passed it became less likely he ever would, and without a ring on her finger, Flora's status was at best ambivalent. Marcus described her as his goddaughter, but there had been no christening, or not that Charlie had ever heard about. He doubted she was even a Christian. He was pretty sure now that, in due course, Flora would go exactly the same way as Clemence, Christina and Saffron . . . yesterday's news.

The third reason for his good spirits was almost too sensitive to acknowledge. But, privately, it filled him with glee. Abigail Temple had evidently gone round the twist and, according to Jamie who had rung him in a panic for advice, was bombarding Marcus with libellous phone calls and letters. Marcus had gone ballistic. Charlie guessed Abby had as good as written herself out of Marcus's will. He'd hardly be likely to leave several hundred million quid to someone accusing him of murder. Frankly, it placed Jamie's share somewhat in jeopardy too. Which all boded nicely for Charlie.

A private plane met them at the Ninoy Aquino International airport for the short hop to Pamalican Island. As the small propeller aircraft skimmed across the Sulu Sea, Charlie was relieved to see the weather down below was perfect. He hoped this would help to lift Miranda's mood. Ever since Heathrow she'd been in a major strop, furious at having to fly Business Class. Charlie, who had been assured their Club tickets would be instantly upgraded to First at the desk, on production of his British Airways Premium Card, had barely got a word out of her for twenty hours.

Fortunately Miranda was enchanted by the Amanpulo, which was everything she'd been yearning for. As she settled into her air-conditioned beach *casita*, with its private terrace, yards of closet space and enormous teak and marble bathroom, she felt all the pressures of her existence melt away. As she said to Charlie, 'We must ring the children, but apart from that I'm on strike. I'm not thinking about a single thing. I've had it up to here with nannies, housekeepers, all of them, asking me things all day long: "Lady Crieff, should Marina take her medication after breakfast?" They'll just have to think for themselves for a change.'

Charlie, who wondered how well their latest Serbian au pair, Kosova, would cope on her own, merely replied, 'We'll ring home after dinner. But not for too long please, Miranda, it's about twenty quid a second to England from here.'

Their days passed in gorgeous indolence. It was Miranda's aim to do the absolute minimum on this holiday and in this she was wholly successful. They got up late, ordered breakfast of coffee and papaya in their *casita*, then spent much of the morning wallowing in the teak and marble bathroom. At midday, wrapped in matching white bathrobes, they staggered the twenty yards to their white sunbeds on the beach, where Miranda perused *Tatler* and Charlie read John Grisham. Before lunch at the club house, Miranda had a fruit cocktail and Charlie two cold beers. After lunch they rested back at the *casita* until four o'clock when Miranda's masseur arrived. At five they checked out the dive centre and considered whether or not to go snorkelling over the coral wall one afternoon. At 7.30 they began dressing for dinner. Miranda wondered whether she had made the right decision to bring only her 'travelling' jewellery, the Kiki McDonough topaz and tourmaline ring ('which wouldn't matter if it got lost') and the Theo Fennell diamond cross. At dinner by the floodlit swimming pool, feeling wonderfully brown and mellow from all the sun,

Miranda ordered her favourite Thai prawns with ginger and coriander, most of which she left on her plate.

Once they rang the children at Old Testbury Hall, but the call, in Charlie's opinion, was a total waste of effort. Still painfully shy, Pelham refused to come to the telephone, and Marina, Charlie thought, was almost impossible to understand, having picked up an impenetrable Filipino-Serb accent from Maha and Kosova. Having established their offspring were still alive, they quickly rang off, resolving not to repeat the exercise.

Revitalised by the warmth and expense of it all, Charlie and Miranda's sex life perked up, once he got over his squeamishness about clambering on top of his wife's increasingly swollen belly. The fact she let him do it at all made him think his suspicions about Boobie must be unfounded, and he felt ashamed he'd ever doubted his beautiful, efficient wife, and longed to make it up to her. When she mentioned over dinner that she thought they should buy a holiday house – 'somewhere lovely in the sun that isn't too difficult to get to, like the South of France' – Charlie put up only token resistance. 'It would be so much cheaper, apart from anything else,' Miranda argued. 'We can't keep renting these expensive villas, year after year. Much better to have our own. The flight to Nice is only an hour, we could nip down for weekends.'

Once, for a change, they chartered a hotel boat, just the two of them and the six or seven crew, to explore the neighbouring Cuyo archipelago. A lavish Amanpulo picnic was heaved into the bow, with iceboxes, silver cutlery, champagne and a giant tropical umbrella. As the bare-chested Filipino hands, in their white shorts and baseball caps, manoeuvred the boat out of the shallows, Miranda complained that the motion and her pregnancy were making her feel nauseous. Irritated by the fuss, Charlie took a cold San Mig up to the prow.

After an hour's sailing, they arrived at a cove on a neighbouring island with a harbour and native village. A dozen small children were having a tremendous game, hurling themselves from the wooden jetty into the sea and diving through car tyres. There was a little tin shack with wooden tables and Coca-Cola crates piled up outside and a ghetto blaster playing 'Bridge Over Troubled Water'.

'You would like to disembark and explore?' asked the Captain of the hotel boat.

'Definitely not,' snapped Miranda, before Charlie could reply. 'I wouldn't dream of stopping here, it looks totally unhygienic. Take us somewhere quiet.'

Eventually they found a sandbar where the crew waded through the turquoise shallows to erect the tropical umbrella, the bamboo table and chairs, and unpack the hamper and wine cooler. Having positioned everything to their satisfaction, the boat together with the majority of its crew moved away to a discreet distance, leaving only a butler to draw the corks and unfurl the linen napkins. Soon, the only sound on the sandbar was the gentle lapping of the waves against the shore, and the scurrying of sand bugs into their burrows.

'You have to admit, Miranda, this is bloody cushy,' Charlie said, as the butler poured them both a glass of champagne.

'Apart from the glare,' she replied. 'I don't know why they brought us here, with not a single scrap of shade. I can feel the back of my heels burning.'

'Jolly nice, though,' Charlie went on. 'I mean, it's pure Robinson Crusoe from start to finish. One day, when Marcus's money kicks in, I'm going to live like this all the time. I might even buy an island like Pamalican. Apparently you can still pick up islands in the Philippines for a couple of hundred thousand dollars.'

'There's no point depending on Marcus, he might not leave us anything at all. He hasn't promised anything. And he'll probably live to be a hundred.'

'I wouldn't count on that,' Charlie replied. 'I thought he was looking zonked last time he came to dinner. He's got to be sixty-five, he might actually be older, he doesn't give his date of birth in *Who's Who*. And the pace he works, he could keel over any time. Seriously, he could have a massive heart attack in his plane over the middle of the Atlantic and that'd be it. Finito.'

'I do like Marcus,' Miranda said, 'but there's something peculiar about him. I can't work him out. I mean, where was he born? His accent is upper-class English, but he sounds slightly foreign when he's excited or annoyed.'

Charlie shrugged. 'Oh, God, there are so many theories about Marcus. My mother used to say he was Estonian or Latvian or something. One of those Baltic states. His family came over to England to escape the Nazis, apparently. But I've never heard that from Marcus. Mama probably made it up because she was so anti-Semitic.'

'What was he like when you first met him? He was married to a Scottish neighbour of yours, wasn't he?'

'Lucy Macpherson. It only lasted a short time. He was exactly the same as now, actually. He hasn't changed in all the time I've known him, just become richer.'

'And his family? What are they like?'

'Haven't an earthly. He never talks about them. I've always assumed they were dead. The thing about Marcus is, he doesn't exactly encourage personal questions. Not his style.'

'So what you're saying is, you don't really know anything about him?'

'Actually,' replied Charlie, affronted, 'I do know a great deal about Marcus, thank you very much. I probably know him as well, if not better, than just about anyone else, other than Dick Mathias and Barbara Miles. The only thing I don't know much about is his origins. Well, so what? I don't know all that much about your family either, Miranda, come to that.'

57: December, 1997

Realising he had to get his wife out of London to have any
hope of breaking her cycle of despair and recrimination,
Jamie purchased two tourist-class flights to Athens. Having
visited Greece in high summer twenty years earlier, he
carried vivid memories of whitewashed houses against a
backdrop of the blue Aegean, and the remarkable cheapness
of the food and accommodation. When he spotted a bucket
shop in Notting Hill Gate offering return tickets for £64
each, he snapped them up. He envisaged himself and Abby
drifting from island to island, as the whim took them,
repairing their hearts and marriage under blazing Cycladean
skies.

It surprised him, when the plane touched down in
Athens, that it was raining and bitterly cold; he had
imagined that, even in winter, Greece would be warm,
being so near to Turkey. Having booked nowhere in
advance to stay, Jamie asked a taxi to drop them at a cheap
hotel close to the port of Piraeus, from where they would
catch a ferry next morning.

'Don't worry, Abby,' he reassured her as they drove
through deserted, rain-washed streets. 'This weather's a
freak. By tomorrow, it'll be sweltering, I promise you.'

Abigail, who had brought only summer clothes, nodded
grimly between chattering teeth, and hoped he was right.

They spent the night in a fleapit, in a room with two
single beds and no heating or hot water. When they turned
on the bathroom taps, the system coughed, the taps
shuddered and ice-cold rusty water jerked into the tub.

There was no breakfast, the kitchens being shut for the
winter. Instead, they were directed to a taverna along the
quay, reeking of meatballs and dead fish, where they were
the only customers but managed to obtain a pot of instant
coffee and a basket of rolls. The sea in the harbour outside

was grey like gunmetal, and an icy wind whipped around their faces.

'Cheer up, Abby,' Jamie said. 'I tell you, the minute we reach the islands it's all going to be totally different. You'll be praying for rain then! Did I ever tell you about coming here with Nipples Ayrton-Phillips? We were both completely out of it the entire holiday. Nipples only had a t-shirt and bikini bottoms and we dossed on the beach. You don't want to know what we got up to on Andros.'

It was a blow to discover the ferry timetables were so truncated in winter. The ticket agencies on the port were closed or unattended. Eventually, in the corner of a vast customs shed, they found a notice detailing the low-season schedule, indicating that the next sailings to Paros, Mykonos, Naxos, Ios and Santorini would commence at 18.50 hours.

'I want to go back home,' said Abigail. 'I hate this place, please take me home.'

'Tell you what,' Jamie said, 'let's check out of that dump from last night, collect our stuff and we'll get a cab to some decent hotel. There must be one somewhere around here. We'll hole up for the day, have some drinks, then come back again this evening to buy our tickets.'

Abigail, gently crying, trailed him back to the fleapit. Somewhere en route they passed a toy shop, its windows full of plastic dolls in Greek national costume. This sudden reminder of Poppy made her dizzy with grief, and she collapsed on a bollard, unable to go on.

'Keep going, Abby, don't stop now, you're almost there,' said Jamie, becoming exasperated. He was beginning to doubt that the weather would be so very different on the islands, and was wondering what the hell to do next. Their air tickets, being so cheap, were unalterable.

'I wish I was dead,' his wife said. 'There's no reason to be alive any more.'

'I know, Abby, I know. We're both devastated. But we've got to keep going.'

'You say that now. But if you hadn't been so keen on cosying up to Marcus, Poppy would still be alive. She never

575

should have been outside unsupervised. A three-year-old with an unattended swimming pool? It's unreal.'

'Let's find somewhere to get a drink, OK? I said OK? If I don't have a whisky, I'll go crazy.'

'That's always your solution, isn't it? A large Scotch and everything will be all right. Well, it may surprise you to know, Jamie, that no number of drinks is going to bring Poppy back. Thanks to you and Marcus, she's dead, my poor darling Poppy.'

The doorway to a bar beckoned across the street from the hotel. Inside, a concrete floor, some wooden tables, a shelf displaying bottles of Ouzo, brandy and Greek wine.

'I'm going in here. Coming?'

Abigail shook her head. 'I'd throw up if I drank a thing. I'm going to pack.'

'See you then,' said Jamie, not bothering to turn around.

He drank three Ouzos and then, tiring of the cloudy aniseed, ordered a bottle of Metaxa. With each new drink a tiny saucer of olives, feta and pickled octopus arrived. The more he drank, the more desperately unhappy he became; his whole life, he now saw, had been singularly pointless. He had had some fun, or thought he had at the time, but he had achieved nothing, owned nothing, done nothing of which he was proud. The only thing of value in his life had been Poppy, and Poppy was dead. Abigail was right, he did bear some responsibility for that, he couldn't deny it. He was forty-one years old, and for the first time ever felt his age. Although there was a Peter Pan quality to Jamie's metabolism, which caused him never to lose a single hair from his head, or to gain a kilo in weight, his eyes had recently lost much of their sparkle and were rimmed with red from booze, grief and exhaustion.

Metaxa on top of Ouzo on a thinly lined stomach did its business. His mood switched from one of moroseness to depression to furious rage against Abigail. At that moment, he hated his wife with a passion. He felt that he had always hated her. He couldn't remember why he had even married her in the first place, unless it was for her money which had never materialised. He found it inexplicable how, after so many beautiful girlfriends – the sexiest women in Chelsea – he had wound up marrying a fat, barren American. She had brought him nothing but disappointment. The prospect of spending two more weeks with her in Greece, let alone the rest of their lives together, filled him with a terrible panic, which could only be obliterated by more brandy. Marcus, he felt, had a great deal to answer for too, where Abigail was concerned. If it wasn't for Marcus, Jamie never would have met her, let alone married her. It was Marcus who had kept pushing her at him, on all those holidays. He had even paid for their honeymoon, for Christ's sake! And if Marcus hadn't stolen Saffron off him in India, Abigail wouldn't even have got a look in.

Eventually, unsteadily, he staggered across the road to the fleapit. It was two o'clock in the afternoon, he had been in the bar for four and a half hours.

Their bedroom on the third floor was unlocked, his clothes and suitcase piled on top of his unmade bed. Of Abigail and her luggage there was not a trace.

He saw the envelope on the top of the chest of drawers, addressed to him in Abby's familiar scrawl.

Dear Jamie,

I'm sorry but I can't go on any longer, not after everything that's happened. I need some time out. I'm flying home from here to the States to visit with my parents, and plan on staying several months at least. I don't know what our future can be, or whether we even have one. I need space to think.

Please don't ring or try to contact me. I'll get in touch when I'm ready.

Or maybe I won't. Without Poppy there is no point in being alive. Abby.

58: January, 1998

Jamie passed a dismal Christmas with his mother in Fulham. Having heard nothing from Abigail since her flight from Athens, he dialled the Schwartzman mansion to wish her a Happy Christmas, but was informed by Zubin, who picked up the phone, that Abigail was resting and did not wish to speak to anybody, least of all her husband. He said that, after the holidays, Jamie would be receiving a letter from his daughter's attorneys.

Finding it too painful to move back into the rented cottage in Hillgate Place, and too dangerous to reinhabit his old bedroom in Clancarty Road, which was threatening to collapse into the garden from subsidence, Jamie lived at 60 Montpelier Gardens, shifting his belongings from suite to suite as they became available. Aside from Bender Barraclough, and the staff and guests of the hotel, he saw almost nobody. When Mary left a message inviting him round to supper with Stuart at Billing Road, he couldn't even bring himself to return her call. Riven with delayed shock and grief at losing both his daughter and his wife in such quick succession, he declined dinner with Camilla Silcox and remedial sex with Nipples Ayrton-Phillips, explaining he was up for neither at the moment.

As the weeks passed, and the pain showed no signs of abating, he began to feel that only by changing everything did he have any prospect of rebuilding his life. He had received a letter from a firm of New York lawyers petitioning for divorce on the grounds of his unreasonable behaviour towards Mrs Abigail Schwartzman Temple, and citing a litany of his ostensible crimes throughout their marriage, including addiction to strong liquor. He replied on a sheet of hotel writing paper, contesting nothing, promising nothing, and pointing out that he was flat broke, which happened to be true. The following day he gave notice on

578

the Hillgate Place cottage and chucked in his job at 60 Montpelier Gardens. He had, in any case, become fed up with being a hotelier, with its long, unsocial hours and culture of institutionalised subservience. Charlie had been right, he didn't want to be handing out umbrellas in the lobby aged fifty.

Casting around for something new to do, he had the idea of becoming a dealer in contemporary photography. He had read in a magazine that limited edition and original prints by famous photographers were going to be the next big thing, and that already, in Manhattan, they regularly changed hands at twenty to thirty thousand dollars a throw for Mapplethorpe, Horst and Lartigue. Despite knowing nothing whatever about the subject, Jamie was convinced there was easy money to be made, if he could only find a backer for the enterprise.

His immediate thought was Marcus. He, with his modern art thing and limitless capital, was surely the man to back his godson's gallery. Jamie's initial overture via Barbara Miles was promising. Mr Brand, the message came back, confirmed his interest in the project, and would like to see a detailed investment plan as soon as possible. For the first time in months, Jamie felt a sense of purpose, and a resurgence of some of his old fun and mischief. As he said to Charlie, 'This photography lark is a total scam, you realise. What you do is, you get your hands on the original negatives from some famous photographer, run off a set of so-called limited prints, and then just keep on printing more, as many as you need. Who's to know? I bet that's what all the galleries do.'

'And Marcus has definitely agreed to be your backer?' Charlie asked.

'As good as. Thanks for reminding me, I need to finish the business plan and get it over to him. I'm sure he'll go for it. Flora's right behind me too. She's nuts about photography.'

'So you've been seeing Flora Huang?' Charlie found the information surprising and vaguely disquieting.

'She's been great. She's been teaching me about photographers like Herb Ritts and Yando. I'd never even heard of them before, but they're really famous. Some of their pictures are practically porn. I tell you, I get quite horny looking at them with Flora standing over me.'

'Jamie, don't even think about it. Believe me, Marcus wouldn't be remotely amused.'

'Come off it, Charlie, you think I'd be daft enough to try and get a leg over Flora? I agree, it's a ruddy nice thought, and I bet she goes like a train, but you'd need your head examined.'

'Just so long as you remember that,' cautioned Charlie.

In retrospect, Jamie never could quite remember the exact sequence of events that led him into bed with Flora Huang. One minute they were examining an Erwin Blumenfeld gelatin silver print of a nude, stamped and dated Paris 1938, the next they were locked in a passionate clinch on one of Marcus's symmetrically placed sofas in the St James's Place flat. It being Bartholomew's afternoon off, they soon progressed next door to Marcus's vast suede-covered bed and were rutting away in a heartbeat. There Jamie learned, to his considerable pleasure, that all his speculations about Flora being an oriental love goddess were more than justified. Having been almost completely faithful to Abigail throughout their twelve-year marriage, as her weight oscillated between plump and gross, he found sex with his godfather's lithe, flat-chested and virtually hairless girl-friend refreshing and invigorating. Unlike Abby, who had never drawn breath during sex, telling him about her shopping trips to the Europa Stores, and how they'd stopped selling live yoghurt at Cullen's on Holland Park Avenue, Flora made love in complete silence, occasionally sighing deeply and clenching her pussy muscles as she reached her own release.

Afterwards, she padded wordlessly into the bathroom, showered, and emerged five minutes later redressed and with her make-up immaculate.

'Get up at once, Jamie, and straighten the covers,' she commanded. 'Now you must study the work of Henri Cartier-Bresson.'

*

The letter from Marcus, dictated but not signed, typed by one of his four personal assistants under the supervision of Barbara Miles, and hand-delivered to the front desk of 60 Montpelier Gardens by Makepiece the chauffeur, from whence it was collected later that same day by Jamie, was terse and to the point. 'Mr Brand thanks you for the opportunity of investing in your proposed venture in contemporary photography. He has reviewed the financials you sent him, but regrets that it no longer fits into his present investment strategy. He hopes you are successful in finding alternative funding.'

'I don't ruddy believe this,' Jamie complained to Charlie on the telephone. 'I thought it was sewn up. Now what am I meant to do? I'm really pissed off with Marcus, the money wouldn't have meant a fart in the wind to him.'

Charlie, who was secretly relieved Jamie had been rebuffed, on the grounds that the business would almost certainly fail and the lost investment be money which would otherwise pass to himself, said, 'I'm really surprised. I thought it was right up Marcus's street. You haven't offended him, have you?'

Jamie considered the question. It was inconceivable Marcus could know about him and Flora. She was hardly likely to have told him herself, and they'd been alone in the flat all afternoon.

'Not that I'm aware of.'

'Not been rogering Miss Suzy Wong or anything?' Charlie sniggered. 'Not been a-messin' with sweet and sour Miss Piggy?'

Jamie felt a cold chill. 'Ha, ha. So bloody likely.' But he thought: was it possible that, somehow, Marcus had dis-covered?

He had rented, on a short-term basis, a furnished ground-floor studio in Nevern Square, in a building adjacent to the one in which Mary had shared a flat, so many years earlier, with Sarah Whitley and Nipples Ayrton-Phillips. He made no effort to make the place comfortable, living out of the two suitcases into which he had thrust whatever came to hand when he packed up Hillgate Place. With no job to go to, and without the discipline or the momentum to commence the search for another backer, he spent much of the day in bed. His excursions outdoors were confined to food shopping in the Earl's Court Road and sporadic visits to a launderette in Trebovir Road. Unable to sleep, he watched television late into the night, drinking vodka and beer until he achieved oblivion.

Late one evening, about a week after Marcus's letter, he was returning to Nevern Square from an off-licence where he had been stocking up on Carlsberg Special Brew. Arriving at the doorstep, he put the shopping bags down while he hunted in his jeans pockets for the key.

The two thugs appeared out of nowhere. He felt the grip of a strong hand on his upper arm, and a sharp object was rammed into his ribs. He looked down quickly and saw a small, very sharp knife like a Kitchen Devil.

'Right, mister, we're coming inside your house. Move it or we'll fuckin' kill you.'

He considered yelling, but people were always yelling in Nevern Square, nobody would react. Anyway, the streets were deserted that January night.

So he did as he was told: slowly unlocked the door to the common parts, then fumbled for the other key to his studio. He had a clear view of his assailants now: one white, the other black, almost identically togged out in black baseball caps, black jeans, black Puffa jackets and heavy black boots. As he played for time with the key, they became restive and shoved him roughly through the door. He stumbled and was taken unawares by a violent blow with what felt like a heavy object.

Lying stunned with a large boot resting heavily on his chest, pinning him to the studio floor, Jamie could see the bigger of the two men moving about the room, drawing the curtains and chaining the front door.

'Right, you bastard. We're here to teach you a lesson. You've been a very stupid boy. I'm sure you get my meaning, you little prick.'

The word 'lesson' had a chilling ring to it. Jamie felt he had been propelled into a depraved scene from a Tarantino movie. Just then the knife was plunged into his left thigh and he felt a wave of nausea. The pain was excruciating.

'Look – take what you like but just leave me alone,' he pleaded. Even as he spoke, he recognised the ludicrousness of the remark. Apart from his Walkman and a mobile phone, what was there of any value to take?

'I told you to shut the fuck up,' said the tormentor with the knife.

After that, the beating intensified. His hands were tied behind his back and his feet bound together so tightly with electric flex that he rapidly lost all feeling in them. Heavy industrial tape was wrapped around his eyes and face. Then he was punched repeatedly in the face, kidneys and stomach.

'Get up to any of your little tricks again, we'll fucking slay you. You really cocked up big time, and somebody's very unhappy with you.'

Unable to reply, Jamie braced himself for the next blow. Dimly, it entered his mind that these men could have been sent by Marcus, to administer reprisals. The idea was appalling. Surely his godfather would never sanction anything like this?

He lay curled up on the floor, eyes taped shut, plunged in darkness, awaiting each new kick and punch. Once, following a particularly violent blow to his face, he felt his cheekbone crack and thought he would faint with pain.

Eventually the tape was ripped off his mouth and one of the men demanded his credit card and pin number, which Jamie willingly gave to him, praying the beating was at an end. Having tried to withdraw fifty pounds from a hole in the wall earlier that day, and been refused, he knew it would do them not the slightest good. His mouth was then retaped and some kind of white mask pulled over his head and down over his eyes; he heard the studio door slam behind them as the men left, followed by the main door out to the street and then the sound of footsteps retreating along the pavement outside.

For the next fifteen minutes he could do nothing but lie there on the carpet, unable to move. Before the men had gone, a sharp object – probably the knife – had been forced through the tape into his left nostril, clearing the passage for air and giving him a lifeline of sorts. Breathing through one bleeding nostril required practice and timing. He began to blow out blood, take a breath and then, as the blood began to congeal again, repeat the procedure.

Slowly, painfully, hands tied behind his back, he edged across the room into the galley kitchen where the telephone was resting on a breakfast bar, and pulled it down on to the floor. Feeling behind his back for the number nine button, he pressed it three times with his bruised fingers.

By the time the police and paramedics found him, he had passed out. Stretched across his face was a pair of ladies' white cotton knickers, with a 'Made in China' label stitched inside.

59: January, 1998

Mary, already late, was stopped on her way out of Billing Road by the telephone.

'Mary? It's Stuart. I know you're rushing but I've just had a call from Casualty at St Mary's. Apparently Jamie's been beaten up.'

Even before the Nevern Square incident, Stuart and Mary had been in regular touch over the deteriorating Jamie and Abigail situation. As the only friend from England whose calls Abby would still take, Mary was under no illusions about her state of mind or the almost pathological hostility she had developed towards her husband. 'I'm really worried about her, Stuart,' she would tell him after the latest long, recriminatory phone conversation. 'And I don't think her parents are helping much. They want to take Jamie to the cleaners.'

'They should take his overcoat along too while they're at it,' said Stuart, making a rare joke. 'I dragged him out for a drink last week. He looks like he's been sleeping in his clothes.'

It had been Mary's hope that, given sufficient time and space, Jamie and Abigail would get back together and give the marriage a second go, but even her gentle optimism was undermined by Abby's vituperation. Soon she was conceding that, 'Maybe they should just call it a day. It's going to take Abby years to get over Poppy, and she's still blaming Jamie. I've tried to tell her how unfair she's being, but she won't listen. You only have to mention his name to set her off. I'm beginning to think there's no point their even trying.'

'It's Jamie I'm worried about,' Stuart said. 'I rang him six times last week, but he doesn't pick up the phone. In the end I went round and forced him out to the pub. He's in a bad way.'

'What about Charlie? He's Jamie's best friend. Is he doing anything to help?'

Stuart shrugged and made a face. 'You know my opinion of Charlie. Jamie said they'd spoken on the phone, but I don't exactly see Charlie rallying round in a crisis.'

The news of Jamie's ghastly mugging, dragging him further down at what seemed already his life's lowest ebb, struck Mary and Stuart as unbearably cruel. The first time they visited him in hospital, they were shocked by his injuries, which were far worse than they could possibly have imagined. His face was so badly bruised that they hardly recognised him, and the left cheekbone criss-crossed with plaster and gauze. He lay immobile in bed in a corner of a public ward, scarcely able to raise a bandaged hand in greeting. Afterwards, a nurse told them that when he'd first been brought in, they'd seriously doubted he would make it. The beating had been one of the most vicious they'd seen.

'What's so incomprehensible is why anybody would want to do something like that,' Stuart said. 'It's so totally pointless. It wasn't even as though there was much to steal. According to the police, they nicked his credit card and tried to use it at a hole in the wall, but the machine wouldn't cough up.'

'I suppose it *was* a random thing, Jamie being attacked?' Mary said. 'I mean, they didn't set out to get him?'

'I wondered about that too. I doubt it. I just don't see who'd have any reason, unless it was to do with drugs. It's possible he was using again, given all the stress.'

'God, I hope not. Seeing him like that just now really scared me. I had this awful feeling he wasn't going to last much longer. It's just so tragic when you remember what he used to be like, so good-looking and everything. And what's he going to do when he comes out? He can't go back to that flat.'

'I've talked to his mother about that already, and suggested he goes up to Ardnessaig to recuperate, if he'd like to. The place is empty most of the time apart from Mum, and she'd love to look after him. She's always saying she hasn't got enough to do.'

'Stuart, you're so kind and thoughtful. Honestly, you're the busiest person I know but you always make time.'

He stared at her meaningfully. 'You'd be surprised,' he said. 'My schedule's crammed, sure. I can tell you what meetings I'm going to be at eight months from now, at which conference hotel in which city. But sometimes I think my life is emptier than anyone's I know. Apart from you and Clara and my old mum, I hardly see anybody. Not that I'm complaining, of course.'

With Clara away at her special needs boarding school during the week, for the first time in fifteen years Mary found herself with time on her hands. She continued to put in long days at work – she was, in fact, inclined to linger slightly later in the office, to the dismay of her assistants who were anxious to be off – but, once home, she found her evenings unusually empty. Without Clara to cook supper for, and bath and read to, she found herself reflecting on her own life, and what, if anything, she intended to do with herself for the next twenty years. In six weeks' time, she would be forty. Needless to say, she had made no plans for this landmark birthday; it would never have occurred to her to give a party for herself and besides, other than her loyal staff at the agency, and Clara and Stuart, there was nobody she especially wanted to invite. Increasingly, after work, she went to the cinema on her own, which she actually rather enjoyed, feeling totally without responsibility. If the movie failed to engage her, she crept out and left.

When her father experienced a massive heart attack on the fourteenth hole of the Frimley Forest Golf Club and died three hours later on a trolley in a hospital corridor, while the local National Health Trust tried to locate an available bed, Mary inherited a new obligation in her elderly mother. Derek's meagre pension from the Brand Corporation would diminish still further upon his death, and Mary doubted whether Belinda could afford to continue living at Fircones which, it emerged, was remortgaged to the hilt. The only feasible solution was for her mother to come and live with them in Billing Road, though the prospect privately filled Mary with gloom. Was she destined, she wondered, in a rare moment of selfish introspection, never to have any life of her own?

Unexpectedly catching sight of herself in the mirrored-glass window of a shop, she felt she had lost her bloom. In this she was, in fact, mistaken, but she felt it. Her thick black hair was showing traces of grey around the temples, and her wonderful skin had creases around the eyes. Having spent the last fifteen years caring for Clara, the future seemed to hold another fifteen spent caring for her mother.

She doubted she would ever remarry now; she had left it too late. Reading an article in the *Daily Mail* about normal-looking housewives who had apparently had more than three hundred lovers apiece, Mary reflected that she had only been to bed with three men in her life: first with Charlie, who had come over her bush in that cottage on Lantau; then with Crispin, of course, and finally and most confusingly with Marcus. Since then, men had sometimes invited her out to dinner, and one or two had even taken soundings about a future together, but none had come close to matching Crispin and, what with Clara and the business and one thing and another, she had never given them much encouragement. Her mother had taken to asking her whether 'she ever met anyone nice', and Abby Temple had kept urging her to get out more, but until the perfect person came along she couldn't see the point. Now, she wondered whether she'd missed the boat.

Of course Mary was not blind to the attractions of Stuart. There were certainly moments when the prospect of marrying lovely, dependable, kindly Stuart entered her mind and lingered there. Clara, she knew, would adore it. In fact, more than once, she had made the suggestion herself: 'You and Godfarva Stew should get married.' When Clara said her prayers at night, she always included her godfather, and she had made a collage of holiday snaps of Stuart and Mary at Ardnessaig which hung in her bed-room. Although no one had ever described Stuart Bolton as good-looking, there was a certain solid manliness about him that was decidedly attractive. He was one of those people who had grown into his looks. He dressed much better these days too and, in his Aquascutum and Gieves & Hawkes grey flannel suits, appeared almost if not quite distinguished.

But the problem with Stuart, as Mary was all too aware, was that she wasn't his first choice. There was always Saffron. There had always been Saffron, and there always would be. He still only had to hear her name for his ears to prick up. When she hadn't shown up at Marcus's lunch party at West Candover Park, Mary had sensed Stuart's disappointment, though he'd tried his hardest to disguise it.

Fretting about her mother, and what to do about the house in Dorking, Mary consulted him after the next Merrett & Associates board meeting. 'I'm worried sick. Mummy can always move in with us at Billing Road, but where would she even sleep? The house is so small. I could move Clara downstairs on to a sofa bed in the sitting room, I suppose,' she said doubtfully.

'Easier to buy a bigger house, surely?'

'How? You know what I pay myself. I won't get much of a mortgage on that.'

'Then take a pay rise. The business can stand it. You made a profit of over a hundred and twenty grand last year, and what will you make this year? Double that at least. The updated forecast is two hundred and seventy.'

'But it could easily drop again next year. You keep telling me yourself how cyclical recruitment is. And the executive search side is even more vulnerable. I don't want to borrow a lot of money and find I can't manage the repayments.'

Stuart looked thoughtful. 'You know one thing you could consider? Sell the business. I'm serious, make a trade sale to one of the big boys. On a multiple of ten to twelve times profit, you'd raise two and a half to three million. They won't want to pay you that in one go, of course, there'd have to be an earn-out, but it's worth thinking about. We're probably pretty near the top of the cycle already.'

Mary was stunned. 'You're telling me my little company might be worth three million quid? You're pulling my leg.'

'I assure you I'm not. It might actually fetch more than that. Why not? There's a lot of goodwill. Your clients are very loyal. When was the last time you lost an important one?'

Mary considered the question. 'Five, six years. But that was only because the account merged with somebody else.'

'You see? It's a solid proposition. And opening the executive search office in the City was a smart move, it's given you a much higher profile. Anyway, think about it. It's a big step for any founder to sell their company, like selling your baby. Not to be rushed into. Meanwhile, how about we celebrate your new-found wealth with a glass of champagne at that new wine bar on Berkeley Square? It's not every day I get a chance to buy a drink for a millionairess.'

Following the company's diversification into headhunting two years earlier, Mary now divided her week between two different offices. On Mondays, Tuesdays and Fridays, she based herself at her old head office in Dover Street, over-seeing the core activity of the provision of high-class temps; Wednesdays and Thursdays she spent at her new venture in the City, where she had taken premises in Fenchurch Street, close to the side entrance of Leadenhall Market.

As the executive search company approached its third year in business, Mary began to lose some of her anxiety, and was almost prepared to concede it was a roaring success. Only her innate caution made her hold back. She had learned from bitter experience that it was always when everything seemed to be going so well that disaster struck.

For now, however, she felt almost relaxed. She had assembled an excellent small team, and Merrett Executive Search was winning new business at a gratifying rate. In the fourth quarter of 1997, they had placed eleven senior executives in significant positions, as well as fifteen experi-enced analysts and information technology managers. For some reason, they had been particularly successful in placing executives in Dutch and German-owned financial houses such as WestLB and ING Baring's. Stuart had also told her who the right people were to contact at Darmstadt Com-merzhaus, though obviously he couldn't intercede person-ally.

For Mary, the most interesting part of the job was the assessment of candidates, which she still got directly involved with herself. Her two days in Fenchurch Street were filled with face-to-face interviews, generally with men in their late-forties or early-fifties who, for one reason or another, felt they needed a change of air. Often, they were so well paid already, and so highly geared in terms of their financial commitments, that they felt trapped: stale in their roles, but incapable of quitting. Or else they were terrified by the waves of mergers and takeovers sweeping the City, worried they would be swept away by their new European or American masters. Increasingly, Mary felt more like a priest or psychiatrist than a headhunter. The candidates stepped into her little office and . . . confessed. She heard about their frustrations, their bosses, their bonuses, wives, children and mortgages. Some even told her about their mistresses. They asked for her advice and her approval, not only about their next job but their lives. It all poured out. She had always been a good listener and her gift for identifying the soundest of six candidates for any position readily trans-ferred itself to the financial markets. As Stuart put it, 'Your nose for bullshit is even more useful up here than in Bond Street.'

All of her 'gentlemen callers', as she liked to describe them, came in confidence, arriving at her door with coat collars turned up, as though they were entering a brothel. 'It is essential nobody from Baring's – or Morgan's, or Chase – gets to hear I came here,' was generally their opening line. Part of Mary's role was to put them at their ease. One of her favourite gambits was to invite a candidate to tell her the three worst things and the three best things about their job. An hour later, they were usually still going strong on the worst.

One surprising aspect was the number of executives seeking to escape from the Brand Corporation, or who had had bad experiences there in the past. Whenever Brand was mentioned, Mary heard the same pattern: the executive had joined the group with high expectations, but quickly became disillusioned. Careers there had a habit of ending badly and precipitately. Turnover of senior management was high, and there appeared to be an institutionalised culture of blame in which scapegoats were arbitrarily rounded up and fired. More than one candidate hinted, too, at fundamental business problems within the group. Marcus – while still revered as a charismatic leader – spent too much time away from the office, and had become more autocratic than ever. Some recent decisions, particularly the group's enormous exposure to the old Soviet Union, were questioned by his people.

'What does Mr Brand say when you ask him about it?' Mary enquired. She was always careful never to give the slightest indication that she knew Marcus, let alone that he was her godfather.

'Oh, you can't get near Marcus,' they replied. 'He's protected by rooms full of assistants. It's like the holy of holies up there.' One executive mentioned that, in twelve years with the group, much of it managing the metals dealing division, he had never once visited the seventh floor of Brand House, which was Marcus's corporate lair.

'That's one of the reasons I want to move on,' he told Mary. 'The whole organisation's run like the Gestapo, and nobody outside the inner circle has a clue what's going on. I couldn't tell you how the other divisions are performing. Not very well, a lot of them, if you believe the rumours. Not that you'd guess that from reading our Annual Report. Colleague of mine suggested they should enter it for a fiction-writing competition. If they did, it'd win first prize, no trouble.'

Abigail's first task each morning, having collected a tray of coffee in Styrofoam cups for the department, was to study the death sheets. Between forty and sixty pages long, this daily collection of photostated clips, garnered from local newspapers across the country, comprised obituaries and announcements of prominent Americans who had recently passed away. It also gave approximate valuations of their estates and noted the legal firms appointed by their executors. Abigail's job, as part of Sotheby's New York business development team, was to comb these lists for anybody she knew, or whose family she knew, or had met or heard of, or, failing even that, whose friends of the family she might once have chanced upon, somewhere along the way. Having identified a possible lead, her next task was to fire off a letter of condolence, while offering, with just the right degree of subtlety, the services of Sotheby's local representative in any future disposal of their furniture and paintings.

Within a month of joining the department, Abigail was able to gut and fillet the death sheets in less than an hour, expertly sifting the stiffs with potential from the also-rans. The newly dead rich of Miami, Palm Beach, New York and Texas, she learned, were far more liable to have assembled collections worth selling than the rich of the Midwest. And certain states were more likely to offer up particular treasures: Delaware, for example, was stuffed with American high-style furniture, and Philadelphia was disproportionately rich in European antiques. Among the nine junior department members and interns who shared the squalid little office on the second floor of Sotheby's York Avenue headquarters, there was intense social competition to score the highest number of corpses every morning, particularly when members of prominent old families were listed. Abigail understood that her own sphere of expertise – and very likely the reason she'd been employed by Sotheby's at all – was the new-money Jewish community of New Jersey and similar wealthy suburbs which, as the daughter of Zubin and Harriet Schwartzman, she was presumed to know intimately.

She had sought a position at the auction house because, after a month of living back home with her parents, she could endure it no longer, and a job in the city seemed the only viable means of escape. She was also anxious to work again in the art world. She hoped that, if she immersed herself in something that interested her, she might be able, even for a few hours a day, to push her desolation over Poppy to the back of her mind. She knew she could never find happiness again, and that the most she could strive for was a marginal lessening of her anguish. If she got through the day without breaking down, she considered she was making progress. On her first morning in the office, she pinned a photograph of Poppy above her desk but later removed it because it devastated her just to see it. Once, walking home after work across the park, she passed a family of children in bright yellow sou'westers and Ralph Lauren bobble hats, and finding herself in floods of tears, had to be helped into a cab by a passing jogger.

After a good deal of arm twisting, she persuaded Zubin to help her buy an apartment on the Upper West Side, on the twenty-second floor of a new high-rise on 80th and Riverside Drive. As the realtor noted, it comprised 1,100 square feet of living space, with two bedrooms, a sitting room with panoramic views of the Hudson, a bathroom and walk-in kitchen. The second bedroom she utilised as a study, installing a personal computer and her collection of art reference books, which were almost the only possessions she had shipped from Hillgate Place. Her evenings she spent at the gym, exercising aerobically to regain her figure, or studying at her desk, occasionally staring, catatonically, at the lights of freighters ploughing their course up the river, and at the yellow, phosphorescent haze of New Jersey beyond.

Although it irked her that her success at work was largely

measured by who she knew, rather than what she knew, she nevertheless found the job therapeutic. She worked hard and conscientiously, while doing her best to avoid the relentless social one-upmanship and territorial turf fights of the rest of the development team. On Monday afternoons, when her boss liked to initiate departmental brainstorming sessions, extracting from each of his team any ins to this or that billionaire, Abby kept her head down. She left it to the interns, many of whom seemed to be the children of friends of Sotheby's Chairman Alfred Taubman, to squabble over who was closest to Henry Kravis, Walter Annenberg or Ron Perelman. Only once, when they were asked whether anybody had connections with the tycoon Marcus Brand, and the group for once sat dumb in defeat, did Abigail intervene.

'Er, I actually know Marcus a little,' she said quietly.

The Director of Business Development regarded her disbelievingly. He had formed the opinion that Abigail Schwartzman was a bit of a dork, with little meaningful access. '*You* do? How's that exactly?'

'Well, he's my godfather.' Afterwards she could hardly explain what had made her volunteer this information, unless it was some psychological flaw which impelled her to show off in front of the group.

Realising he had underestimated her, the Director's voice softened. 'Is that right? Well, do you happen to know whether your godfather plans to attend the Duchess of Windsor sale next week?'

Abigail shook her head. 'I . . . haven't spoken with him for several months.'

'Then may I suggest that you do speak with him? It would be very helpful to have Mr Brand at the sale. Fedex him a catalogue, please, and keep me in the loop on his reaction. He's a remarkable man, has accumulated the most impressive collection in a very short space of time. But you know that already, Abigail, being his goddaughter. Oh – and if he would care to have a private preview of the sale, please tell him I'd be more than delighted to arrange it, and to give him lunch afterwards, if he could find the time. You can join us, if you think that would help.'

Abigail said nothing, but knew she had no intention of renewing contact with Marcus, not if her life depended on it.

There were two aspects of her job that Abby particularly enjoyed. The first was her daily proximity to wonderful paintings, the contemporary sales especially. Frequently, she would sneak out from the department to view the pictures on display in the main auction rooms. She loved the ease with which, having seen something she liked, she could revisit it several times a day, always finding some new aspect to admire, while en route to a coffee run or to collect a catalogue from the library. In her first four weeks at Sotheby's, she reckoned she'd spent more face-time with first-rate works of art than she had done in the last six years of her marriage to Jamie. And, having dropped twenty pounds in weight, she found her self-respect coming back along with her waist.

Her other pleasure was taking bids on the phone, for which the services of the business development team were sometimes required at particularly busy and fashionable sales. During these great gala occasions, when the audience rolled up in cocktail dresses and black tie, and the auction was conducted under a blaze of television lights, as many as forty telephone lines were manned on both sides of the rostrum. As each new lot was announced, Abby was hooked up to a different client to relay their bids to the auctioneer. The majority of these telephone bidders, she knew, were calling in from right across the country. Others, simply preferring anonymity, were patched through from the darkened skyboxes above the main auction rooms or, for the biggest players, from the second-floor boardroom from which they viewed the proceedings by live video link.

The sale of the goods and chattels of the Duke and Duchess of Windsor was Sotheby's largest American auction since the record-breaking disposal of Jacqueline Kennedy Onassis's effects two years previously. Three thousand lots were to be sold over nine days, and the media hype had created a climate of hysteria in which hundreds of Americans, who had never previously bid at auction, and had only dimly heard of the Windsors, clamoured to secure one of their personal possessions: a cushion emblazoned with the crest of the English King, or a monogrammed toothmug or engraved cufflinks. For the business development team, all leave had been cancelled and telephone duty was mandatory.

The bids were coming in so thick and fast Abby could hardly keep up. One minute she was speaking to Pensacola, Florida, about a pair of Wallis Simpson's velvet-bowed evening shoes; the next she was semaphoring wild bids from Kansas City, Missouri, to secure a wicker dog basket, once the bed of a royal pug.

Two hundred lots into the second day, the Duchess's handbags began to go under the hammer. A Christian Dior evening bag made six times the estimate, followed by a Chanel purse. Dede Brooks, Sotheby's CEO, vaguely intimidating at the rostrum in red satin with a pearl choker, knocked it down for an astonishing one hundred and thirty thousand dollars, and a gasp went up from the audience.

A voice on the switchboard alerted Abby that Client Relations were putting a new client on to her line.

'Abigail?' She recognised the voice at once. 'Is that you?'

'Hello, Marcus.' She couldn't believe it was him. She felt cold inside and suddenly tongue-tied. Even hearing his voice brought memories of Poppy rushing back. Her mouth went dry and her knees started to shake beneath her.

'Er, where are you calling from, Marcus?'

'Upstairs in the boardroom where I'm enjoying an extremely agreeable glass of Krug with Al Taubman. I'm watching you now on the monitor. Hope you don't mind my saying so, but you've lost a bit of weight, unless it's this screen.'

She wanted to scream or, better still, slam down the phone. But a security camera in the ceiling was pointing straight at her, and she couldn't allow him the satisfaction.

'Now,' he said, 'look lively, Abigail, I'm here to bid, and you know how I hate to lose anything. I'm relying on you to catch that auctioneer's eye. Think you can manage it all right? Lot 207 – that's the one I'm after. Big shiny black handbag, made by Ferragamo. Found the right one? Good, knew you would. Reason I asked for you.'

Glancing down at her open catalogue, Abby saw that the Ferragamo handbag, which had been carried by the Duchess of Windsor at her wedding in exile at the Château de Candé, bore one of the highest estimates of anything in the sale.

'Lot 207.' Dede Brooks consulted her book of absentee bids. 'Shall we open the bidding at sixty thousand dollars? Sixty thousand. Who'll give me sixty thousand? Anybody? Thank you, sir. Sixty-five, seventy, seventy-five. I have seventy-five thousand dollars. Eighty . . . ninety . . . one hundred . . .'

'Would you like to make a bid, Marcus?' Abby murmured into the mouthpiece.

'Lord, no, not this early. No point showing our hand. I'll tell you when to bid.'

'One hundred and sixty . . . one hundred and eighty . . .' The audience was becoming excited as the price continued its climb. 'I have one hundred and eighty thousand dollars. All done? Thank you, madam. I have two hundred thousand dollars . . .'

Abby was watching the price on the electronic board, displayed in dollars, pounds, francs, lira and yen. What the hell did Marcus want a yukky old handbag for anyway? She felt sure that it smelt. She assumed it must be meant as a gift for Flora. Well, she was welcome to it. Out of the blue, she remembered Jamie's remark in Italy, when they were all staying with the Crieffs that summer, that Flora must be like the Duchess of Windsor and know special sexual tricks. Despite herself, Abby smiled.

'How are we doing down there?' Marcus asked her. 'Still going strong?'

'It's reached two hundred and sixty thousand dollars.'

'Tell me the moment the bidding begins to peter out.'

But the bidding was still powering ahead, as a blue-rinsed matron in the front row sparred with the African-American owner of a celebrity burger chain for possession of the historic accessory. It reached two hundred and ninety thousand dollars . . . and stalled. The matron, fired up with adrenalin, had realised the enormity of her folly. Suddenly panicked, she stopped dead in her tracks.

'Against you, madam,' said Dede Brooks. 'I have two hundred and ninety thousand dollars.'

'Three hundred,' breathed Marcus into Abigail's ear. She signalled his bid to the auctioneer.

'Three hundred on the telephone. Sir?'

'Three hundred and ten,' nodded the burger mogul, who was intending to display the handbag in his new restaurant in Harlem, alongside a pair of Elton John's diamante spectacles.

'Three hundred and twenty,' confirmed Abby for Marcus.

The burger mogul hesitated, closed his eyes, and shook his head. He would go no further.

'Three hundred and twenty thousand dollars. All done?' Dede Brooks surveyed the room one last time, then brought down her gavel with a thud. The handbag was Marcus's for three hundred and sixty-eight thousand dollars, including buyer's commission.

'Congratulations, Marcus,' Abby said uncertainly. 'It's yours.'

'Actually, it's yours,' he said. 'Present for you. You need a decent handbag, living in the city.'

Abigail was aghast. There was nothing she wanted less than this ridiculous, absurdly overpriced, vintage curiosity.

'I couldn't possibly.' She still half thought it was a joke. The security camera was aiming directly at her, and she was desperately conscious of her godfather watching her from upstairs. 'You've bought it for Flora, I'm sure.'

'Nonsense,' declared Marcus down the phone. 'Last thing Flora needs is another bag. Got cupboards full of the things. I bought it for you. Came here 'specially to get it for you. Took the hint when you sent me the catalogue. In any case, I'm not giving Flora anything at the moment – banished her to Wyoming in disgrace. Still feel bad about that business with your daughter in my pool. Least I can do is buy you a decent present.'

Then, before she could refuse, he replaced the receiver.

Strolling down West 44th Street on the balmiest day of spring, Jamie began to feel life wasn't so bad after all. It was a quarter to one, he had just rolled out of bed, and he was meeting Leah and Calypso Blackwater at the bar of the Royalton for lunch. Since arriving in New York five weeks earlier, when he'd met the sisters on his second night in the city, he had been living at their apartment in the West Village. Much of the time they were out of town in any case, on modelling assignments, so he had the place to himself. It was a really cool pad, belonging to the girls' old man, Nick Blackwater of the supergroup Blacktongue. In an on-off kind of way, Jamie was having a fling with Calypso, who appeared in the Gap Jeans advertisements and was famous for her amazing legs and trademark truculence, but both recognised the affair was only short-term. According to Calypso, what first really attracted her to Jamie was his scarred face: 'Kind of like a duelling scar, which is *so* sexy.'

After nearly three months in Scotland, being nursed back to health by Stuart's kindly but deadly dull mother, Jamie felt supercharged with repressed energy, finally released. The last couple of months at Arnessaig had been a form of torture. There had been nothing whatever to do, except sit around watching television and wait for Jean to bring him meals on trays. He had been driven round the bend by the classical music she insisted on playing all over the house. And there had, quite literally, been nobody to see. It was an indication of how bored and frustrated he'd become that he'd seriously considered getting his leg over Mary Jane Crieff, Charlie's sister, until he saw her in her bathing costume in Stuart's indoor swimming pool.

His convalescence had, at least, given him plenty of opportunity to think, though whether he was any clearer about anything by the end of it was a moot point. He was certain now that he didn't want to get back with Abigail, not that it was exactly an option. Abby's attorneys, no doubt urged on by her father, continued to send him threatening letters, demanding the moon. In reply to their latest demand, Jamie had simply forwarded them his bank statement, showing that he was nineteen thousand pounds overdrawn. 'That's my lot, I'm afraid,' he scrawled across the bottom of the sheet. 'If Zubin would care to take half of it, he's welcome.'

He brooded, too, about Marcus's role in his mugging. Sometimes, he still found it too far-fetched to be possible. Surely Marcus wouldn't stoop to having his godson beaten up, even assuming he'd found out about Flora. But how else to interpret the remarks of those thugs? *'Somebody's very unhappy with you,'* they had said. And, *'You've been a very stupid boy.'* That all pointed to Marcus. Unless it was Zubin Schwartzman, which was hard to credit, though you did hear certain rumours about his underworld connections. And what about the panties left across his face, with the 'Made in China' label inside? Was that a coincidence? Millions of pairs of knickers like those must exist, it didn't necessarily mean anything. Still, as a coincidence, it was a helluva pointed one.

He had been shown the underwear by the police when they had taken a statement in which Jamie had insisted he'd no idea who or what might have lain behind the attack. Barring further evidence, the case officer was content to record it as a random act of violence, of the sort regrettably common in inner cities, especially in areas like Earl's Court with serious drugs problems. Jamie wasn't convinced. The knickers themselves didn't look like they belonged to Flora: too cheap. He struggled to recall what her underwear had actually been like, that afternoon in Marcus's flat. He remembered yanking it off, but couldn't call it to mind. His attention had been elsewhere.

Liberated from Abigail and exhilarated by New York, Jamie felt twenty again. All his old irresponsibility came rushing back. With nobody to please but himself, and living rent-free at the Blackwater apartment, he devoted himself to having fun. He began to frequent nightclubs that were popular with teenage girls, and was gratified to discover all his old chat-up lines worked as reliably as ever. When Leah and Calypso were safely off the scene, and he thought the coast was clear, he invited girls back to their place, blithely implying it belonged to him. Having mostly steered off the booze for ten lousy years, under Abby's watchful eye, his rediscovery of cocktails was joyful and intense. By keeping himself in a state of permanent semi-inebriation, through a constant stream of one-nighters with as many gorgeous birds as possible, he discovered he could obliterate his numbing despair about Poppy for hours at a time.

Knocking back margaritas with Calypso and Leah, Jamie couldn't believe he'd wasted so much of his life working at that poncey hotel. Already, the world of Bender Barraclough and 60 Montpelier Gardens seemed light years away. Had he really spent a whole decade tooling about in the lobby wearing a tailcoat? It was unreal.

'Hey, Calypso, your bum looks fanfuckingtastic in those jeans. How about we spend the whole afternoon in bed?'

She looked at her watch. 'Fat chance. I've got to take my book into an agency for a casting.'

'Oh, come on, be reasonable. You can't have a body like yours and not let me near it. It's cruelty to mankind.'

'Oh, all right then,' replied Calypso with a shrug. 'I hate schlepping across town for look-sees, in any case.'

'Tell you what,' said Jamie, grinning, 'let's do it to your dad's old record, *Next Best Thing*. It was one of the first albums I bought at school.'

'Don't ever tell him. He gets really paranoid about things like that. When he was going out with this much younger girl called Saffron, she hadn't even heard of his records, and it freaked him out.'

Jamie had been in the city for ten weeks when he reckoned he'd better try and find a job. His strategy of living scot-free with the Blackwater babes, and never even paying for drinks, was working up to a point, but he still had to buy breakfast sometimes, and shell out for cab fares, and he was nearing the end of his cash.

Having entered the country on a ninety-day tourist visa, and lacking a green card, he soon realised it wasn't going to be easy. Confronted by requests for resumés from prospective employers, he was forced to recognise that his curriculum vitae could be considered patchy: advertising commission-rep, gigolo, failed landscape gardener and hotel greeter. When the Palace Hotel and Dunkin' Donuts both turned him down in the same afternoon, he became dispirited. If he didn't score some funding soon, he'd be forced to take desperate measures, such as flogging part of Nick Blackwater's CD collection to a thrift store.

Casting about for other possible sources of cash, he cursed the fate that had saddled him with a family so unforthcoming. Michael Temple was living in a cottage outside Beaconsfield these days with wife number three, attempting to sell water coolers to his neighbours. Last time Jamie had spoken to him, he'd claimed to be virtually skint. His mother, meanwhile, was working three mornings a week for a property relocation company, which specialised in helping American ex-pats find expensive London homes and schools for their kids. She had made it perfectly clear that Jamie could expect nothing further. He considered touching his sister Lucinda for a loan. She and her husband Rupert inhabited an enormous Victorian pile overlooking Wandsworth Common, full of small children and nannies, but Lucinda always claimed they were strapped. It even crossed his mind to call Abby at Sotheby's, where he'd heard she had a job. But, somehow, he didn't feel she'd dole out the greenbacks just yet.

One afternoon, trudging through the Upper East Side, he decided to chance his luck at some of the art galleries along 73rd Street. At the fourth gallery he entered, he found himself in conversation with an elderly and well-manicured dealer named Hershel Gluckstein.

'So you're looking for a job?' It so happened that Hershel's latest receptionist had walked out that morning, as they all eventually did, complaining about their meagre salaries.

'That's right,' replied Jamie.

'Know anything about pictures?' asked Hershel. He looked the applicant up and down. He recoiled at his jeans and trainers, but the boy was cute enough and the British accent no impediment.

'A bit,' Jamie lied. 'My ex-wife was an expert. And, er, one of my godfathers is a big collector.'

'Do I know him?'

'I couldn't tell you. He's called Marcus Brand. He's English.'

'I know Marcus, he's a client. Was a client, I should say. Recently he's started buying contemporary. Terrible investment, I've told him that several times. The bubble will burst.' Then, an idea floating suddenly into his head, Hershel asked, 'You ever met this Chinese lady he goes around with? Flora Cheong or Hong, whatever?'

'Flora Huang. Sure I know Flora. We often discuss art together.'

'Is that right? Now, listen, James, I think I might just be able to help you out here with a position. Nothing permanent mind, but for a month or two. See that small Miró over there, hanging in the alcove? I want to sell that to Marcus. He's seen it and he wants it, no question. He told me that. Only thing is, the girlfriend doesn't. Now I'm prepared to take you on at the gallery, but your number one assignment is to convince Marcus to come through on the Miró. If he's your godfather, that should be a shoe-in. And if you're friendly with Flora too, so much the better.'

Part Six

62: May, 1998

When the Russian economy spectacularly collapsed on 27 May 1998, nobody was more surprised than Charlie Crieff. He hadn't seen it coming. In fact, he wasn't even in Moscow at the time the Central Bank tripled its interest rate to 150 per cent and the stockmarket went into freefall; he was accompanying Miranda on a villa-hunting jaunt in the South of France, staying at the Hotel Bel Air Cap Ferrat. The first he knew about it was the front page of the *International Herald Tribune*, which had been delivered on the breakfast tray to their suite.

'Bloody hell!' Charlie erupted, leaping out of bed and spilling Miranda's demitasse of black coffee on to the Provencal eiderdown. Fumbling for the bedside phone, he began punching numbers for the office in Moscow, but all lines into the country were permanently engaged.

'Jesus, this is unbelievable.' He tore around the suite, searching for his attaché case which he had concealed somewhere behind the minibar, Miranda having a phobia about briefcases being on display when they were meant to be on holiday. Switching on his mobile, he managed to get hold of Valeri Fedorov.

'Valeri? Charlie here. What the fuck's going on over there? And why didn't you ring me?'

He listened while his General Manager explained that Charlie's mobile had been turned off, and the Crieffs had instructed the hotel switchboard to block all calls. Fifteen messages had been left on his voice mail.

'Yes, well, all the same,' spluttered Charlie. 'You might have tried a bit harder, this is a bloody catastrophe.'

He flicked on CNN and watched their reports on the deepening economic crisis while Valeri described the impact on the fund. Its value had been halved overnight and, furthermore, there was little possibility of selling anything because there was nobody to buy it. Most of the oil and telecoms stocks had dropped by 70 or 80 per cent. President Yeltsin was due to make a statement at four o'clock that afternoon, assuming he wasn't pissed by then. To make matters worse, a dramatic slump in world oil prices had left Russia facing a trade deficit. Foreign investors, mostly German institutions, were in an equal state of outraged fury and blind panic. A statement by Sergei Kiriyenko, the newly appointed thirty-five-year-old Prime Minister, that the rouble was sacred and would not be devalued, only increased speculation that it shortly would be.

Meanwhile, there were panicked queues outside all of the clearing banks of people trying to withdraw their life savings. Several of the banks along Tverskaya had already run out of money and put up their shutters. 'The secretaries and the cook have been standing in line since five o'clock,' Valeri reported. 'And they are asking to be paid in dollars this month, not roubles.'

'Tell them not to hold their breath,' Charlie said irritably. 'What about our investors? Have we taken any calls?'

'Everybody is calling. From Switzerland, from United States. All want to speak to you urgently. They are very nervous. And Sir Iain Cruickshank called from England. He wants you to call him back in the countryside, he left a number.'

'You didn't tell him where I am?'

'I said only that you are in the South of France, looking for a house to buy. I didn't tell him the name of the hotel.'

Charlie exhaled grimly. 'Thanks, Valeri, you great communist plonker! Listen, I'll be back in Moscow as soon as possible. Tonight, I hope, flight permitting. I should be able to get one direct from Nice, or failing that Paris. Until then, try and stop everyone freaking out and don't let them out of the fund. Got that? And if Iain Cruickshank rings again, tell him you were mistaken and I've been calling on oil companies in Surgut.'

Shaken and white-faced, he fell back into a sofa upholstered and piped in a coral and white Manuel Canovas diamond print. 'Now,' he told Miranda, 'we really are up shit creek. From what I'm hearing, Russia's about to re-enter the Stone Age. I'd better start finding a flight.'

'Not today you're not,' she replied from her bed. 'Not before we see that house in St Paul de Vence. Boobie's organised the whole thing, we're having lunch with the owners and playing tennis. Sometimes, Charlie, you're so inconsiderate. With you it's just work, work, work. That's all you think about. Now, how about fetching a towel from the bathroom and mopping up the coffee you spilled every-where on this bed?'

Charlie flew back into Moscow with mounting trepidation and a sense of dread. He had picked up all the newspapers at CDG and events were evidently heading from bad to worse. The stockmarket had dropped by another 8 per cent over-night. President Yeltsin had demonstrated his willingness to take tough action by dismissing the head of the state tax service, Aleksandr Pochinok, for his failure to collect billions of dollars in overdue revenues from big corpora-tions. The highly publicised raids by Russian tax police, carried out in flak jackets with AK47 automatic rifles, had been focused, it had emerged, only on small businesses without influence. In the last four days, foreign investors had withdrawn more than $700 million from Russia, and the flotation of the giant state-owned oil company, Rosneft, had been a failure, with not a single bid being tendered for stock. Russian coalminers, claiming not to have been paid any wages since August of last year, had taken to cutting the Trans-Siberian railway to draw attention to their plight. 'We have no crisis in Russia,' President Yeltsin was quoted as saying, before disappearing to his *dacha* to concentrate on writing a speech.

Charlie's first thought was how the deteriorating situation would impact on his own bonus and fees. Whichever way he looked at it, the news struck him as dire. The way things were going, the combined capitalisation of the entire Nijny Novgorod would soon be less than an average European clearing bank. He doubted any new investors would come within a million miles of Russia for the foreseeable future, and guessed it wouldn't be easy to convince his existing lot to hang on in there either. His expectation of paying off the mortgages on Upper Phillimore Gardens and Old Testbury Hall suddenly seemed ludicrously unrealistic. He wasn't even sure how he'd cover the payroll this month, with the banks shut down and the system fucked. According to a CNN evening newscast, President Yeltsin had today telephoned the German Chancellor Helmut Kohl, President Chirac of France and Tony Blair, to seek support for his attempt to persuade the International Monetary Fund to shore up the rouble with a $15 billion loan. Charlie wondered whether, while they were about it, they might consider a $5 million loan for himself, if he agreed to a similar programme of retrenchment.

During his first forty days back in Moscow, he saw the value of his fund plunge from £160 million to £20 million. He couldn't believe the lack of loyalty from cretinous Swiss lawyers and crass German institutional investors, who only a month earlier had been toasting him in schnapps and Jägermeister in their ghastly, overpriced ratskellers. The Americans were hardly better, two of them already threatening him with legal action for soliciting their investment without adequately warning them of the risks. When he managed to get through to Miranda in London, she told him about another villa in the South of France she wanted to check out, in the hills behind Grimaud, which was being put on the market by the rock star Nick Blackwater. With the new baby, Leonora, less than a month old, and Marina's fifth birthday party looming, Miranda said she was feeling under a lot of pressure. 'It doesn't help that you're never here to support me,' she told Charlie.

'I'm sorry, darling, but it's not a lot of fun for me either at the moment, with all the problems we've got out here.'

'You are coming back for Marina's party, aren't you? I need you there to supervise the drinks.'

'The drinks? I thought this was a children's party. They'll be having Ribena, surely, not cocktails. When is it, anyway?'

'Thursday, for heaven's sake. I've told you that already. There are forty children coming plus mothers and nannies.

It would be nice if you could offer the grown-ups a glass of Pimm's. Boobie's going to help, but he can't manage all on his own.'

Wearily, Charlie agreed. 'OK, darling, I'll be there. Promise.'

'Good. And I'll tell you what would be helpful, too – if you could bring several large tins of Russian caviar with you. The proper stuff, not the paste. Then Maha can make some little eats for when people come to collect.'

By the time Charlie arrived home at Upper Phillimore Gardens, direct from the airport after an infuriatingly delayed flight, Marina's fifth birthday party was drawing to its close. Uncle Archie, the fashionable children's entertainer, had produced a real white rabbit from his magic sack, and a queue of little girls in party dresses were awaiting their turn to stroke it. The drawing-room floor, cleared of most of its furniture, was now strewn with scraps of coloured tissue paper, left over from pass the parcel, which Maha and Kosova were gathering up into black binliners. A monthly nurse was jiggling Leonora. Several of Maha's Filipino friends, including Conceptia and Mercy, were circling the room with plates of smoked salmon squares and mini-blinis spread with caviar.

'Thank you for getting back so late, Charlie,' snapped Miranda, glaring at him. 'Poor Maha had to rush out and buy the caviar in Holland Park Avenue.'

'The ruddy plane sat on the runway for three hours.'

'Never mind that now, just open the champagne. Marie-Christine Schoenmann is about to die of thirst. And so is everybody else.'

Venturing into his drinks cupboard behind the wall of dummy books, Charlie noticed that eight bottles of Veuve Clicquot had been finished already, and that Boobie had considerately placed another half dozen in the fridge to cool. Panic attacks about money had recently become so central a part of his life that his head and stomach were in a semi-permanent spasm of anxiety. He couldn't bring himself to speculate on how much Marina's birthday party was costing, when you factored in the champagne, caviar, Uncle Archie and double-time for Maha, Conceptia, Mercy and the rest of the Manila mafia.

Weaving, ghoul-like, between the throng of mothers and au pairs milling about in the hall, he saw the forty gold going-home bags lined up on the table, filled with tissue-wrapped presents and sweets. Knowing Miranda, each bag had cost a minimum of fifteen pounds to assemble. Fifteen times forty was . . . he was unequal to it.

He spotted his daughter tearing between the legs of grown-ups, pursued by half a dozen giggling school friends, none of whom Charlie had ever set eyes on before. Marina was wearing a new velvet dress with a tartan sash and lace collar, and a plastic silver tiara.

'Hello, Marina,' he called to her as she shot past. 'Come and say hello to Papa.'

She ignored him, continuing to race about and shriek with her friends.

'Marina, come here. I want to say happy birthday to you.'

This time he felt sure she'd heard him, and her disobedience enraged him. Here he was, spending a small fortune to give her this party, and she wouldn't even say a proper hello to her father, whom she hadn't seen for weeks.

'*Marina!* I'm talking to you. Come here this minute, goddamn you!' He realised he was shouting, and several mothers turned round and stared. Well, let them. What did he care about these ghastly, spoiled, prinked-up society women and what they thought of him? At that moment, he felt they were parasites, eating his caviar and drinking his champagne – the champagne he could no longer afford. All that mattered was that Marina receive a sorely needed lesson in respecting her elders.

Lunging at her velvet dress, he yanked her towards him by the scruff of her neck. '*Marina!*'

He felt the lace collar rip free in his hand, and suddenly his daughter was staring up at him, frozen in shock, her eyes brimming with tears.

'Sorry, sweetheart. Truly I am. I shouldn't have blown my stack like that.'

Marina was still gazing up at him, open-mouthed, accusatory – moronically, Charlie felt – as though he were some sort of criminal child abuser. Talk about over-reaction! Already, he regretted apologising to her. It should have been Marina apologising to him, not the other way round.

He felt the eyes of Miranda's friends boring into him as he carefully laid the lace collar on a window seat. From the corner of his eye, he saw Camilla Silcox and Zara Deloitte watching him from the sofa.

'Come on, cheer up. It's not the end of the ruddy world. Kosova or Maha can sew it back on, for God's sake.'

Marina was crying now in great self-indulgent howls, and wiping her nose on her sleeve. A snail-trail of mucus shimmered against the royal blue velvet.

'Jesus, will you stop snivelling? Just stop it, right now, this minute.'

With a final ghastly howl of self-pity, Marina turned and bolted upstairs, where a bathroom door was heard to slam. Of Miranda and Boobie there was no sign.

At that moment Maha appeared in the hall from the kitchen. 'Lord Crieff, telephone call for you.'

'Not now, Maha. Tell whoever it is I'll ring them back later, please.'

'It's Sir Cruickshank,' persisted Maha. 'He says very important. Please come to the phone.'

Belgravia Limousines, the car company that Charlie used on his trips home to London, was going through a phase of employing mostly Iranian drivers. Normally, he was prepared to forgive their total cluelessness about London's geography as the quid pro quo for their smart and deferential appearance. He liked to tell people that the drivers were all former members of Savak, the Shah's secret police.

Tonight, however, as they circled the Barbican for the third time searching for the entrance, Charlie became exasperated. He didn't want to be late, even though he didn't see why the hell he should arrive on time. The whole idea of this meeting sickened him. He was furious with Iain, who he believed had stitched him up. And he was furious

613

with Stuart Bolton, who must be relishing every minute of it, and had no doubt approached Cruickshank & Willis with the specific intention of humiliating him.

Charlie still couldn't believe that Iain, a friend, would do this to him. Whenever Iain and Camilla came to stay at Old Testbury Hall they were put in the yellow trellis bedroom, second in comfort only to their own. Camilla was one of Pelham's godmothers, for heaven's sake. He, Charlie, had introduced Iain to Marcus Brand, not just socially but as a client, making the company millions in the process. For Iain to turn round and stab him in the back was outrageous.

Eventually, Charlie located the tower block where Stuart apparently chose to live, when he wasn't lording it at Ardnessaig. Ascending to the eleventh floor in the chi-chi yellow plastic and mirrored lift, Charlie thought it was all precisely what he'd expect of Stuart: soulless and naff. The entire development reminded him of a hospital. He'd always wondered what kind of saddoes chose to inhabit the Barbican. Now he knew: saddoes like Stuart Bolton.

Stuart opened the door in chinos and an open-necked denim shirt. 'Charlie, good to see you. Drink?' He led him into a large, under-furnished living room with ash floorboards and spectacular views across the City of London through floor-to-ceiling plate-glass windows. Two vast, beige four-seater sofas flanked a fireplace without a mantelpiece. Aside from a glass dining table and several modern lamps, the sole feature was a state-of-the-art Bang and Olufsen music centre and two towers of CDs. While Stuart fixed him a whisky, Charlie inspected the boxes: Mozart, Brahms, Chopin. To Charlie, who played country music or James Bond themes in the car, it seemed absurdly pretentious for someone like Stuart to pretend to appreciate classical music.

'There you go,' Stuart said, handing him a tumbler. 'Scotch and soda. If I've made it too strong, and you need more water in that, just shout.' He pointed to a sofa. 'Make yourself comfortable. I'm afraid I've never done much to this flat. I use it mostly as a place to sleep and work. I think of Ardnessaig as home.'

Charlie nodded bleakly. He didn't feel in the mood for small talk, especially with Stuart.

'Family well?' Stuart asked. 'Miranda and the kids? She's recently popped another one, hasn't she?'

'Yes,' replied Charlie, coolly. 'Another girl, Leonora. My wife and the children are all perfectly well.'

'So, you've spoken to Iain Cruickshank. You know what all this is about?'

Charlie nodded. 'Iain and I had a conversation. I won't pretend to be over the moon.'

'I understand. You've put a lot into that business, and done an impressive job too, under the circumstances. That's the reason Darmstadt Commerzhaus is interested in buying into it, for the quality of the management team – you, in fact.'

Charlie felt the anger rising inside him. He didn't need to be patronised by Stuart.

'The fact is,' Stuart said, 'the present problems in Russia are outside your control. The place is in meltdown, and it looks set to stay that way for at least another two, three years. Some of my colleagues think it could take five to come back, if it ever does.'

Charlie regarded him non-committally. Who did Stuart think he was to give Charlie a lecture on the Russian free market economy? Far as he remembered, Stuart's last lecture on Russia was in Nassau twenty years ago, when he'd expounded on his pet enthusiasm for Marxist-Leninism.

'I don't know how much you know about Darmstadt Commerzhaus,' Stuart went on, 'but it's an impressive organisation. German-owned, of course, and consequently very much in it for the long haul. At DC, we tend to think in ten- or fifteen-year timeframes. And we continue to regard Russia as a market with tremendous potential, whatever the short-term turbulence. Put simply, we need to be there. We want an important position in the equities market, and we're prepared to give it time. My own boss, Manfred Friemel, who heads up New Markets, is personally committed to building up our Russian and Eastern bloc operation. It's a

615

bit of a pet project of his. And, as Iain has explained, we want to buy your company and use it as a base for further expansion. Manfred asked me to sound you out. Obviously, if the idea doesn't appeal, we'll look elsewhere.'

'I understand you've already made a deal with Cruickshank & Willis behind my back to take over their share,' Charlie said bitterly.

'A deal in principle only. C & W wants out, as you know, and are seeking buyers for their thirty per cent. In the present climate, they'll be lucky to find one. Not many financial institutions are looking to gear up in Moscow – apart from Darmstadt Commerzhaus, for the reasons I've explained. But without your personal commitment, we won't proceed. We've explained that to Iain. It's you and your team we're interested in. Without you guys, there isn't a business.'

Charlie closed his eyes. Objectively, he knew this was a golden opportunity, a lifeline. His investors were peeling off like bikini tops on a French beach. The way things were going, the fund would be bust in a month or two, maybe sooner. Already, its value had plunged by 87 per cent. He hardly dared pick up the phone for fear of hearing another disgruntled investor. To be bought out by an outfit like Darmstadt Commerzhaus, with its deep Kraut pockets, and to continue running the fund as before, was almost a dream come true.

Watching him, Stuart hoped he was pitching things persuasively enough to win Charlie round. He was determined their decades-old personal antipathy should not be an issue; this was a serious business proposition and he must play it professionally. As he'd said to Mary, 'Charlie and I are chalk and cheese, and we're never going to be bosom buddies, but if we do end up working together, I'll give it one hundred per cent.'

Stuart took away Charlie's empty glass and returned with a refill. 'I'll tell you something else that's outstanding at DC, and that's the quality of our research. We have more analysts, and of a higher calibre, than I've encountered anywhere. We could hook you up with our Russia desk and you'll reap the benefits immediately. There's a bloke I've brought in who used to teach me at college back in Birmingham – Professor Barry Tomkins. Got fed up with academia – and the rotten pay – so I pounced on him. Knows more about Soviet economic planning than anyone else alive. Incredible.'

Charlie shuddered. 'What would the reporting structure be?' he asked Stuart.

'Yes, I need to talk you through that,' Stuart replied. 'If this went ahead, your management company would become a subsidiary of DC's New Markets division which is headed up, as I mentioned, by Manfred Friemel, President of New Markets, Europe and Asia. I am Manfred's VP of Operations, and effectively work as his number two, overseeing Eastern Europe and the Pacific Rim day-to-day. Under the proposed structure, I would become your line manager and fly into Moscow about six times a year, more often at the beginning, to review the business with you. Manfred chairs the half-yearly strategic conferences, generally in Frankfurt. We would stay in regular contact by fax, e-mail, phone etcetera. I would see my role as providing support and advice while very much leaving you to run your own show as Chief Executive.'

Charlie stared at him in disbelief. If Stuart thought he was going to start reporting to a little shit like him – the chauffeur's son – he must be stark raving mad.

'What else can I tell you?' Stuart asked. 'As far as remuneration is concerned, DC has a reputation for being generous. I think you'll find, if you ask around, that we compensate our senior executives at the top of the scale. Obviously we would also put a significant personal incentive plan in place for you, which we would work on together.'

Charlie was seething. He was not, repeat not, about to start discussing his salary with Stuart Bolton.

'So, what do you reckon, Charlie? I hope you'll at least agree to meet Manfred. I promise you, you'll find him impressive. Ask Marcus for his opinion, if you want to, he's met Manfred several times. And I'll tell you who else has met him – Mary Gore. The three of us had dinner together last time he was over. She could give you the low down.'

For close on half a minute, Charlie regarded the fellow godson he despised without replying. Fat, crimson-faced and belligerent, the sweat running down inside his too-heavy Hunstman suit, it seemed truly appalling that suddenly his only options were financial ruin or the abject humiliation of working for Stuart Bolton. Then, slowly, deliberately, still grasping his tumbler, he stood up and crossed the floor to where Stuart was sitting. Positioning the glass directly above Stuart's flies, he tipped the remaining whisky and fast-melting ice all over his chinos.

' *"The morning sun, when it's in your face, really shows ya' age,"* ' warbled Jamie in the shower, ' *"but that don't worry me nuffin, coz I just blah-di-blah . . ."* '

Next door, in the bedroom, he heard Amaryllis groan, turn over and groan again. 'Jamie, put a sock in it, won't you? It's too early. Anyway, what is the fucking time?'

'Half-past eleven,' he shouted, stepping out of the shower.

'Jesus Christ, then. What are you doing up at this hour?'

Outside, across the Hoxton street where they lived, Jamie could see the Paki shop where he would shortly buy milk and orange juice for breakfast. Later, if he felt up to it, he would walk the two blocks to the studio space he shared with two other conceptual artists.

It had been Amaryllis's idea that he should turn his hand to conceptual art, and Jamie wished he'd thought of it years earlier. As far as he could see, the whole business was another total scam. People actually paid money – and quite a lot of money at that – for the jokey installations he knocked out in a matter of days. A gallery named White Cube had already offered to represent him, and a magazine called *Art Review*, which Jamie had never heard of, had sent round a weird girl with black lipstick to do an article.

Catching sight of himself in the bathroom mirror, he grimaced. He looked wrecked. Why they'd started on the third bottle of Smirnoff at two o'clock in the morning, he couldn't imagine. Dropping three effervescent Solpadene into the coffee mug that served as a toothglass, he rummaged about for a towel and, finding none, dried himself on a shirt from the dirty clothes basket.

The thing that was so great about Amaryllis, he reflected – and in this it was a clear case of like mother, like daughter – was that she was completely non-judgemental. She neither expected anything of him, nor asked him to do anything, other than run across the road to buy fags. Some days they didn't even bother getting dressed, just drifted about the flat in the buff, smoking the weed, boozing and occasionally screwing. She must be pushing sixty, but she was a knock-out, kind of Marianne Faithfull but without the turtleneck. From behind, with her blonde hair worn so long that she could still sit on it, she looked eighteen. And he adored her laugh, throaty from all the nicotine.

Following the unpleasantness in New York over the summer, when he'd been fired by Hershel Gluckstein for failing to offload the Miró on to Marcus, and then ejected from the Blackwater apartment when the sisters discovered he'd slept with both of them, it was a relief to be back in London. The first time he'd seen Amaryllis, in a pub on the Fulham Road called the Goat in Boots, he'd actually thought it was Saffron sitting there in the gloom, and had made a beeline only to realise it was her mum. 'Why go with the repro when you can have the original?' Amaryllis had asked that first evening when she'd taken him home. With her long-term boyfriend Paul the reflexologist out of the picture, having collapsed and died one day on his portable treatment table, Amaryllis had come into a bit of money for the first time in her life, and bought the place in Hoxton. 'I do still miss Paul in some ways,' she told Jamie. 'He used to press a special place on my instep with a piece of pumice stone, and it connected straight to the G-spot.'

'Don't worry, baby,' Jamie had replied. 'I've got something here much harder that'll do the trick just as well.'

Frequently, when he and Amaryllis were on the job, and he was nearing his climax, Jamie liked to mentally switch horses, imagining it was Saffron he was making love to rather than her mother. With their almost identical physiques, it was a simple enough illusion to sustain. He imagined himself and Saffron back at the Hotel Vishnu in Jaipur, and wondered what might have happened to their relationship had Marcus not waded in and sabotaged it. Lately, he had come to see that his godfather had brought nothing but trouble. Unlike Abby, he didn't believe Marcus was actually responsible for Poppy's death, but she had died in his pool and it had been Marcus who had bullied them all into sending the children outside. Right down the line, it had been Marcus: having Jamie thrown in the slammer in India, stealing Saffron off him, introducing him to the dreaded Abigail, pulling his backing from the vintage photography business and, in all likelihood, having him done over in Nevern Square. Right now, Jamie didn't give a toss if he never saw Marcus Brand again.

The whole conceptual art scene amazed and amused him. It truly was money for old rope. If he'd really pulled his finger out, he knew he could have churned out pieces at a rate of two or three a week. As it was, he still completed one a fortnight with minimum effort. The concepts themselves were a cinch. All his pieces were based on infantile puns: 'Hot Cross Bunnies' recreated a rabbit warren in papier mâché, with a chrome kettle suspended above the installation on a tensile wire pulley. According to the gallery, Charles Saatchi had shown interest in purchasing it as an investment. Another of Jamie's pieces involved a stuffed kangaroo that he had found in a skip, and dressed up in an old cardigan. He entitled the work 'Woolly Jumper'. A third piece, inspired by the episode years earlier at his preparatory school, called for half a dozen alarm clocks to be concealed inside an upright piano, and primed to go off randomly. When the Dutch investment banker and collector, Boobie van Haagen, travelled all the way to Hoxton with Charlie's nightmare wife to look at Jamie's work, and made an offer on the kangaroo, Jamie said, 'Sorry, mate, you can't talk to me about money, you need to talk to my dealer. And that is my art dealer I'm referring to here, in case you're wondering.'

Seldom really alive, as she put it, much before tea time, Amaryllis compensated for her surfeit of daylight sleep by staying up half the night. Generally their evenings began in a pub-restaurant round the corner, where they lingered until closing time, followed by several hours of serious boozing back at the flat. With a couple of bottles of white inside her, Amaryllis could become one of the earthiest and most indiscreet women alive. But the characteristic which most distinguished her from her daughter was her sense of humour, Jamie noticed, something which had never really filtered down to Saffron. Amaryllis had a tendency, in her cups, to reminisce about her rackety love life, and the sexual shortcomings of her numerous lovers.

'I hope you won't talk about me one day like this,' Jamie said to her, sternly.

'No need, love. It's only the old buggers who can't get it up. You've got to laugh, haven't you? It's the only way. Did I ever tell you about Major Bing? What an old so-and-so he turned out to be. Victor Bing. "Victor" my arse! He certainly didn't win any prizes in the sack.'

Sometimes on these evening jaunts they were joined by one or other of Amaryllis's children, Lorcan and Saffron. Already nineteen years old, Lorcan was a tall, stringy redhead who increasingly resembled his father, Niall McMeakin. Like his dad, he had ambitions of becoming a chef, and had already done shifts in a Moroccan couscous restaurant behind Regent Street. As for Saffron, currently between boyfriends, she announced one evening that she was considering starting a shop near the Portobello Road, selling scented candles and antique birdcages, with Marcus's backing.

'Sure that's a good idea?' Jamie asked. 'Having him bankroll you, I mean.'

Saffron shrugged. 'I don't have a lot of choice, do I? I asked Nick Blackwater but he turned me down, for now anyway. He's got to sell his place in France first.'

'Yeah, well, it's just that Marcus isn't all that reliable. He said he'd back a business of mine once, then pulled out at the last minute.'

Amaryllis, who was preoccupied drawing a cork, began to cackle, and said, 'Must have been the one and only time he has, then. Marcus, pulling out at the last minute? If I had a quid for every bird he promised he'd do that over the years.'

Considerably less pissed than her mother, Saffron tensed. She had told barely a soul, and certainly not Amaryllis, about the baby Marcus had made her abort years earlier at that terrible clinic in Switzerland. It was her deepest, darkest secret, and almost the only incident in her chequered life which she genuinely regretted. Even today, she often thought about the baby. He would be coming up to his tenth birthday. She thought of it as a he; Saffron had never had any doubt that she'd been carrying a male child.

'What do you mean, Amaryllis?'

Her mother, suddenly sobering up, was evasive. 'Nothing, love, nothing at all. Nothing you need know about anyway.'

'Amaryllis, tell me.' Saffron persisted, seized by the conviction that her mother was concealing something important.

'Forget it, love. I told you, it doesn't matter. It all happened so long ago.'

'Tell me.'

Amaryllis looked at her daughter and then had another gulp of vodka. 'Well, I don't think this is wise, but if you insist . . .'

Amaryllis talked and Saffron listened, and when her mother had finished her tale, Saffron went into the bathroom and threw up into the lavatory bowl, and then, without addressing one word to anyone, she closed the front door behind her and walked away across Hoxton Square.

64: September, 1998

'You know who I think we should get to be one of Leonora's godparents?'

'Who's that then?'

'Marcus.'

'Marcus Brand?'

'Do we know any other Marcuses?' Since the collapse of the Crieff Emerging Markets Russia Fund, Charlie was in a permanently stroppy mood and, as Miranda frequently reported to Boobie, becoming impossible to live with.

'That's a perfectly ridiculous suggestion,' she replied. She was examining a glossy brochure sent to her by a company that specialised in constructing manèges, or all-weather dressage rings, with a view to installing one at Old Testbury Hall. 'He's already your own godfather. You can't choose the same person again for one of your children.'

'Says who?'

'It's just not done. Anyway, it's much too late. The christening's next Sunday. It would look funny asking him now.'

'I've been thinking, it could be rather perfect timing.'

Signalling her lack of interest in pursuing the conversation further, Miranda returned to her brochure. It was a terrible imposition, she felt, having an out-of-work, non-salary-generating husband hanging about at home, day in, day out, particularly when you were trying to conduct a love affair with his predecessor.

'Listen, hear me out,' Charlie said. 'This could be important and, God knows, we need a break.'

Without raising her eyes from the coated glossy pages, Miranda said, 'Go on, I'm listening.'

'It's all to do with highlighting our special relationship with Marcus. It's pretty good already, I won't deny that, but when you think about it, we're actually only on a par with five or maybe six other people. I'm talking about my fellow godchildren: the kleptomaniac artist and part-time junkie Jamie, his ex-wife the Jewish princess, the dreaded Bolshevik-turned-laird Stuart, the ever-lovely Mary from the Job Centre, sexy Saffron and, subject to status, Suzy Wong. At the risk of sounding revoltingly mercenary here, that adds up to seven of us as viable beneficiaries of the whole Brand estate. And we are not talking millions here, we are talking billions. Five billion for certain, maybe ten, depends who you listen to. Now this is where Leonora comes in . . .'

Charlie waited while Maha, who had entered the dining room with a fresh pot of coffee, refilled his cup. He thanked her without catching her eye. Lately, Charlie had done his best to blank Maha and Kosova, as well as Mr and Mrs Farley and the girl grooms in the country. He couldn't bring himself to work out how much they were all costing him each week. Barring some rapid and drastic turn-around in his finances, he knew they would have to be let go, but the thought of having that conversation with Miranda filled him with terror.

'This is about competitive advantage,' he resumed, when Maha had left the room. 'Look at it from Marcus's point of view. Presumably he's made his will already but, knowing him, he revises it pretty frequently, depending on who's in and out of favour. Dick Mathias would be the man in the frame here, not that he's ever given the slightest indication, even after five martinis, and I've tried to draw him on the subject more than once. What we need to do is find some means of demonstrating to Marcus that we're his closest and most deserving dependants. First-division godchildren. And the way to do this is via Leonora.'

'Doubling the ties, you mean?'

'Precisely. Got it in one. In fact, if you think it through logically, we ought to get more kudos for signing him up as Leo's godfather than for him being my own. In my case, it wasn't of course me personally who appointed him, it was my parents. It was they who chose him. But with Leo, it's us doing the inviting. It's a brilliant way of showing how much we like and respect him. What we'd essentially be saying is,

"Look, Marcus, you've been a superb godfather to me, the absolute tops, so much so that we're requesting a repeat performance for our daughter Leonora."'

'You don't think it's an imposition? Being a godparent always seems like one-way traffic. You keep buying all those birthday and Christmas presents and get nothing back.'

'That's not how people think. It's like being invited to loads of parties. Proves how popular you are. Everybody likes to be able to say, "I've got twenty godchildren" or whatever. More the merrier. I once asked Stuart how many godchildren he's got and he only has two. Speaks volumes, doesn't it? I told him I've got six. That shut him up.'

'Well, I wish you'd buy them all their Christmas presents yourself,' snapped Miranda, 'instead of always leaving it to me to do. I'm sick to death of traipsing round Harrods toy department for your damn' godchildren.'

'Yah, well. I mostly send them money these days, in any case.' But as he said it, he flinched, wondering for how much longer there would be any left to send.

'Another consideration,' Miranda said, 'is that we've chosen six godparents already for Leonora. Seven would look ridiculous. The vicar was quite surprised when I mentioned we had six.'

'We have six? You sure?'

'Well, there's Bud Deloitte and the Princess. That's two. And Janey McVitie, three. Michael Waitrose and Boobie. And Camilla Silcox. Six.'

'We can jack Camilla for starters. I'm not having any Cruickshanks at the font. Marcus can take her slot.'

'But we've already invited her. You rang her from the Portland, remember.'

'Then uninvite her. Send her a postcard. Tell her we're bringing Leo up as a Moslem.'

'Talking of which, is Marcus even eligible to be a godparent? I thought you said he's Jewish. The vicar at St Mary Abbots was quite definite about that: all the godparents have to be practising Christians.'

'Oh, honestly. What the hell's it got to do with him anyway? God, I hate it when priests start trying to muscle in on christenings. Remember when I became a godfather to Fudge Fitzroy's daughter Eleanor – Helena, whichever – and there was all that mumbo-jumbo shaking hands with total strangers in the middle of the service and making signs of peace? So naff. Anyway, we don't know what faith Marcus is. Probably a Taoist or Maoist by now with little Miss Slanty Slit around, all that Tantric sex.'

'Won't he be offended if we invite him this late? It's going to seem awfully odd.'

'Not if we pretend the letter went astray. Probably the best thing is for you to ring Barbara first thing tomorrow, saying it's all tremendously embarrassing but we haven't heard anything back yet, don't mean to hassle him, etcetera, etcetera. Barbara will get into a flap, she hates things like letters going missing, takes it all personally, and we repeat the invitation by phone. I very much doubt Marcus will actually make it to the church, not at such short notice, but that's not the point. The point is to invite him. Get him signed up.'

'Charlie,' said Miranda, 'I think you must be the most cynical, manipulative person I've ever met.' But, in saying so, she knew that he was not. That particular honour belonged to herself. Surreptitiously, she glanced at her watch. If she left soon, she could be round at Boobie's maisonette in Chester Square by eleven o'clock, by which time his French-Algerian bumboy, Moulais, should be safely off the premises. 'So long as I never have to meet him,' she'd told Boobie.

'In actual fact I rather take exception to that last remark,' said her husband, peevishly. 'I am neither cynical nor manipulative. I just think that, with something as important as this, it's worth going the extra mile. I mean, when you consider what's at stake. Marcus could be dead and buried in less than a year – he could keel over tomorrow actually – and we're either in line for the biggest jackpot of all time, or we're not. And I'll tell you something else. If you think there's a cat in hell's chance of a hand-out from any of my other godparents, you've another think coming. The only thing old Jock Kerr-Innes ever forked out was a pair of gold

627

cufflinks and a leather-bound prayer book, of all things, for my Confirmation. My godmother is my sister Mary Jane, another dud.'

'And you really think it'll make a difference, having Marcus for Leonora?'

Charlie shrugged. 'Put it this way, it certainly can't do any harm. Where Marcus is concerned, we need to cover all bases.'

65: January, 1999

'Jesus Christ, I do not believe what I am reading here.'

Charlie was staring, aghast, at the front page of that morning's *Daily Telegraph*. Staring back out at him was a large colour photograph of Marcus Brand wearing an academic gown, with a mortar board perched on his big head, flanked by the Vice Chancellor of Cambridge University and the blind Secretary of State for Education.

The story underneath announced a £70 million endowment by the billionaire entrepreneur, to establish a new Department of Business and Management Studies at the university, to be known as the Brand Institute for Wealth Creation.

Charlie could hardly have been more affronted if he'd been asked to write the cheque personally. 'This really is outrageous,' he told Jamie, when he eventually tracked him down by phone at his studio. 'Seventy million quid! You know what that means? We've effectively handed over ten million each to Cambridge-ruddy-University. And that's not even the end of it. It says here Marcus is going to fund a whole load of scholarships and bursaries, so students from Eastern Bloc countries can come and freeload over here and be taught how to become good capitalists.'

Jamie snorted down the line. 'Your trouble, Charlie, is you get so hung up about everything. If Marcus leaves us a whacking great mound of cash, well, that's great, I'm all in favour. But if he doesn't, fuck him, he's always been a jumped-up vulgarian sod, throwing his weight around, and always will be.'

'Jamie, I'm surprised to hear you talking like that. Marcus is one of your patrons, isn't he? Miranda told me he bought some ridiculous rubbish you made out of condoms.'

' "Ride a cock horse". Good piece that, one of my faves. You've hit on rather a sore point there, actually. He bought it at the exhibition but never paid for it. We sent about six invoices and reminders but no joy. In the end I gave up and flogged it to Boobie van Haagen.'

'Probably it just slipped his mind. That office is chaotic sometimes.'

'Maybe. But he's done it before, apparently. Announces he's giving money to something or other, some good cause, then doesn't. Same thing with buying art. He's got quite a reputation. Probably he won't even cough up the money to Cambridge, so you'll get to keep it after all, Charlie. Bear that in mind, it should cheer you up.'

In an eighth-floor chrome-and-smoked-glass meeting pod in the Darmstadt Commerzhaus building on Wilhelm-Epstein Strasse, Stuart, his immediate boss Manfred Friemel, two VPs of the bank's North European equities division – one French, the other Swedish – together with several research and analysis managers and their departmental head, Professor Barry Tomkins, had assembled to review, in what was a regular monthly fixture, part of their 73 billion DM portfolio of quoted investments. Stuart had recently been drafted into the investment conferences on account of his special knowledge of the Brand Corporation, in which Darmstadt Commerzhaus held such a large position.

In a long and sometimes tendentious morning session, the group had already resolved, as a matter of bank policy, to increase by four percentage points their exposure to telecoms and new technology stocks, to the detriment of bricks-and-mortar retailers, brewers and the insurance sector. Now, for the remainder of the afternoon, their agenda determined a company by company briefing on the dozen or so global conglomerates which straddled so many different sectors, and were of such a size, that they defied easy categorisation.

'There is one company that is most important today to consider,' said Manfred Friemel. 'We are speaking, of course, of the Brand Corporation.' At the age of forty-five, Manfred only five years senior to Stuart, already looked like an old man. Having spent most of the past sixteen years sitting in front-row left-hand seats of First Class aircraft cabins, which he considered his 'lucky seat' when shuttling between financial conferences, one half of Manfred's face was permanently mottled with ultraviolet rays, while the other retained an unhealthy pallor. His life, as he proudly admitted, was consumed exclusively by work: 'No wives, no kiddies, no sports, no sailboats.'

'I have asked Herr Doktor Tomkins to prepare some detailed analysis of the Brand Corporation's short- and medium-term prospects, in the light of recent unfortunate economic corrections in Russia.' Manfred gave a tiny bow of the head towards Barry Tomkins, indicating that the floor was now his.

'Well, this is an interesting one,' said Barry. 'I would even go so far as to describe it as a bit of a conundrum.' Each time Stuart watched his old tutor in action, he was struck by the degree to which he had changed since joining the bank, beginning with his appearance (the grey ratstails had long gone), then the clothes (today a grey flannel suit worn with a navy Ralph Lauren polo shirt), the voice (recently, the Black Country accent had been superseded by an almost Germanic intonation) and finally even his politics, which had swerved furiously to the right, though he could never resist the odd anti-capitalist crack for old time's sake, especially when Stuart was around.

'I should preface my remarks by pointing out that Marcus Brand and I have something of a history,' Barry began. 'More than twenty years ago, he was the subject of a monograph in my seminal publication *The New Slavemasters*. In the course of mapping the expansion of the Brand Group, I made several derogatory observations about global piracy by international conglomerates, and their propensity for domiciling themselves in territories outside the jurisdiction of recognised tax authorities, which did not play well with friend Marcus or his legal representatives. Injunctions were served not only on myself, but on the publishers, the printers and typesetters, booksellers and distributors. The whole intention was to tie us in legal knots. Marcus's chief corporate lawyer, a shyster by the name of Mathias, claimed to have identified more than one hundred and forty errors of fact in the twelve pages about the company. Total baloney, of course, but that's what he said, and the lawyer's letters were designed to put the fear of God up everyone. Anyway, they worked. The book trade, needless to say, caved in immediately, pulling *Slavemasters* from the shelves and giving written undertakings not to stock it in future. Almost the entire print-run was withdrawn and pulped. The few remaining copies were bought up by Marcus's people and, I was informed, incinerated.

'So you will have to make allowances,' Barry continued, 'if I foster a somewhat jaundiced view of Mr Marcus Brand and his nefarious business ventures, though I shall do my best to keep my natural scepticism, not to say cynicism, in check. After all, gentlemen, we must try to keep this impartial.'

For the next forty-five minutes, Professor Tomkins did his best to deconstruct the web of interlinked holding companies, semi-detached subsidiaries, offshore trusts and registered headquarters on Caribbean sandbars and in Liechtenstein backstreets that constituted the corporate structure of the Brand Corporation. When he attempted to encapsulate it graphically via a PowerPoint presentation, with scrolling bubble charts illustrating Marcus's privately owned and publicly quoted ventures, the result resembled one of those abstruse gossip features in Sunday newspapers, far too baffling to understand, showing the tangled love-histories and who's-had-whos of Hollywood filmstars. Even Stuart, with his years of experience, was hard put to follow the practically circular ownership structure through which Marcus maintained total control of the twenty-billion-dollar public company through half a dozen box numbers and trusts, of which next to nothing was known and no consolidated results were ever published.

'What troubles me about the whole set-up,' Barry concluded, 'is that fundamentally we know nothing at all. From the outside, Brand Corp maintains the impression of a first-rate blue-chip proposition. Makes all the right noises, the numbers look good – the ones you get to see anyway, they don't exactly trip over themselves to break them down for you – and they've undeniably got some good businesses in there. The only catch is that it all has to be taken on trust. Ask me for hard data, and I can't give you much. It's not even clear where the dividing line lies between the publicly traded stock and Brand's private ventures. He seems to shift assets around. Take the cargo aviation business in China, Ming Airways. I'm buggered if I can tell you who owns that one. It used to be a joint venture between BPTC and the Shenjo Corporation, a Taipei-registered trading company, which, it so happens, is 70 per cent owned by Brand through a Grand Cayman trust, not that that particular item of information has ever passed into the public domain. Whether Ming Airways still belongs to Brand Corp share-holders, or to Marcus Brand personally, or to the Queen of England for that matter, I haven't the slightest idea. No more does anyone else.'

'And you believe we might be exposed to some risks here?' asked Manfred. 'You are implying the Brand Corporation is not reliable?'

'I'm not implying anything, I'm saying we just don't know. I've never come across a company with less transparency. With a structure that complex, you've got to assume they made it that way on purpose, to muddy the waters. Last time I counted, there were more than twenty-seven hundred subsidiaries, two hundred in Russia alone.'

'Stuart,' said Manfred, 'you know Marcus Brand. Do you find the man trustworthy? Or can't you say? I believe you mentioned he was formerly your guardian or something of that kind, did you not?'

Stuart coloured as all eyes in the meeting pod focused on him. Barry, he saw, looked astonished. His jaw was practically resting on his laptop. For one reason or another, Stuart had never found the right moment to declare his compromising relationship with Marcus Brand.

'Not my guardian, Manfred, my godfather. As to how trustworthy he is or isn't, I couldn't tell you. But I do think we need to keep our position in Brand Corp under serious review. As of this morning, Darmstadt Commerzhaus is the second largest single shareholder after Marcus himself. I'm not necessarily saying that's a bad thing, but it would be a big position to offload if Barry's misgivings did prove to be well founded.'

'How long did your love affair with Marcus go on for, incidentally?'

'My love affair? Oh, Jamie darling, what a lovely old-fashioned gentleman you can be sometimes. Our "love affair" as you grandly call it, which unkinder people than yourself might describe less generously – comprising, as it did, a couple or three mid-afternoon quickies in the old Rembrandt Hotel in South Ken – lasted two weeks. No, wishful thinking, not quite so long. One week. With a weekend in the middle when he returned to his wife. That was the full extent of our "love affair". And all I can say is, like the song, nobody does it better. Present company excluded, of course.'

'It's weird to think of Marcus being married. I can't imagine it. All the times we've been to stay with him, there've always been girlfriends, but none you'd exactly call wife material.'

'Probably he never got over the first one dying like that. He never treated her very nicely, not once he'd got her, and I suppose there was a lot of guilt wrapped up in it. That's what we said at the time at least. We never saw much of him afterwards. It seemed to change him, he withdrew into his work.'

'What was she like?'

'Lucy was a lovely little thing. Sweet, innocent and trusting, as pretty and fresh as a flower. Much too good for Marcus, of course, a whole different class, but she fell for him hook, line and sinker. They met in a club called the Stork Rooms where a crowd of us used to hang out back then. Down behind Liberty's department store, it could still be going for all I know, torches outside and red banquette seating. That's where they first met, Marcus and Lucy. She'd been brought along by some lah-di-dah deb's delight, but Marcus soon saw him off. Did I mention how good-looking Marcus was then? Marvellous heavy-lidded eyes and that pistachio-coloured skin. He can't have been much older than twenty-five, twenty-six. Always wore a beautifully cut dinner-jacket and looked quite the part. Anyway, the minute he saw Lucy, that was it. You know how it is with Marcus, always impatient, especially where women are concerned. She didn't stand a chance, poor lamb. He moved in on her so fast, it was practically cradle-snatching. She was barely seventeen. Next thing we heard, he's asked her to marry him and we were heading up to Scotland for the nuptials.'

'You went to Marcus's wedding? I never knew that.'

'Before you were born. You stick with me and you never know what else you might discover.'

'And what was it like? The wedding, I mean.'

Amaryllis pulled a face. 'Not sure I can remember much about it. We were pissed as farts, I do know that; we all were, Marcus's London contingent. God knows what the Macphersons' Scottish neighbours made of us – not a lot probably. The whole place was crawling with dukes and grandees in their tartans and tailcoats. And the house was a socking great monstrosity, looked more like a church with stained glass windows and whatnot. Gave me the creeps. I've never been so pleased to get back on a train.'

'And what was Marcus like, back then? Was he always so sure of himself?'

'I'll say this for Marcus, he does know how to fill the role. We always knew he wasn't quite out of the top drawer, darling, but you could almost believe he was that day. He made a very gracious speech, thanking his parents-in-law and the bridesmaids and all that. Faultless, I'd say. He always did pick things up fast. If you hadn't known better, you'd have said he was to the manner born.'

'The funny thing is, even though he's my godfather, I hardly know the first thing about him. I don't even know what his parents were like.'

'Well, they weren't at the wedding. None of his family was. I'm sure about that, because I asked. There were so many different stories going round about where Marcus came from, I was interested.'

'I've never heard any stories. This may sound strange but I've never thought of Marcus as coming from anywhere. He just is. I sort of imagined he was born fully formed.'

'It was only ever rumours. No one asked him directly, not that I'm aware of, they wouldn't have dared. We were all slightly in awe of him, even then. But you did hear things. Someone told me his people lived down by the seaside, down Southend way, and that his old man was a vicar. Couldn't tell you whether there's anything to it. And then there was this big theory that his mother had it off with an Egyptian, who got her pregnant, which would explain the swarthy skin.'

'Why an Egyptian?'

'That story went that Marcus's dad was a soldier not a vicar, stationed out in Alexandria. And his mother got the hots for some local boy, a teacher or a student, I think it was. But it was only ever rumours. Nothing you could call definite.'

'A mystery then. The funny thing is, Charlie always insists Marcus is Jewish.'

'Now that I can help you on. He isn't. On that one, I've got eye-witness proof.' She laughed throatily. 'He was such a naughty boy in those days. I told him, "Marcus, you're wicked. Rotten to the core."'

'And how did he react to that?'

'He agreed. He could hardly deny it, could he? He'd only been married a few months, and already back to his old tricks. But he was generous, I'll say that for him. First rumpy-pumpy, then shopping. There was always a nice little bit of jewellery to take home afterwards.'

'But you didn't keep up with him?'

'Well, it was difficult. I was still married to Billy at the time, you see, and it never really felt right. I'm not naturally devious; one bloke at a time, with sometimes a little overlap if it happens that way. And when Lucy died in that awful accident, it did rather put the kibosh on things. Then Saffron came along, and Billy pushed off to Ireland, and what with one thing and another . . . Anyway, we all knew Marcus would go on to bigger and better things. That was obvious from the beginning. He always knew exactly what he wanted, that one. Couldn't wait to drop us, minute he made a few bob.'

'Charlie's sister Mary Jane said he got left all Lucy's money.'

'That was only the start of it. Blokes like Marcus, who really understand money, it comes so easy to them. From what I heard, he made another pot gambling at the Clermont Club. Blackjack became his obsession. You know he's got a photographic memory? He recalculates all the odds in his head, depending on which cards have come up before.'

'I remember my father saying he first became friendly with Marcus at the Clermont. They moved in the same set for a bit.'

'Marcus worshipped that place. It's where he got to know all those other big tycoons. From then on, there was no holding him.'

67: September, 1999

Ten days after Charlie finally put Old Testbury Hall back
on the market, following a painful showdown with his bank
manager who presented no alternative course of action,
Miranda announced her decision to leave him and the
children and move back in with her ex, Boobie van Haagen,
the Dutch investment banker and art collector. As she
explained to Charlie, while they were snarled up in a four-
mile tail back on the M3 leading to the Hogarth Roundabout, she had already put up with a very great deal, and
nobody could have put more into a marriage than she had,
but, quite simply, enough was enough. She had been
thinking about this a lot, and it would be better for everybody if they now went their separate ways. She could hardly
be expected to do everything. Anyway, Charlie had undergone a total personality change, and was no longer the
person she'd married. All their friends agreed with her about
this. The fact was, it had probably been a mistake their
getting married in the first place. She had always had much
more in common with Boobie, they were so much more in
tune and had much more to say to each other. Sometimes
she really wondered which planet Charlie was living on. And
the idea of selling Old Testbury Hall was perfectly ridiculous, and wouldn't even be necessary if he had pulled his
finger out and got himself another job as any sensible person
would have done in his situation.

And so Miranda instructed Maha to pack up all her
clothes, and these were duly transported in a convoy of
hired Mercedes space wagons to Boobie's maisonette in
Chester Square. Watching the Iranian drivers from Belgravia Limousines struggling downstairs and across the flagstoned hall with his wife's outsized Louis Vuitton luggage,
Charlie experienced a terrible sensation of emotional and
financial failure. For the whole of his life he had been

surrounded by a procession of strong women – first his mother and Nanny Arbroath, later Miranda – all of whom had provided stability while imposing their draconian expectations upon him. Never once had it occurred to him that he had any genuine freedom of action in the direction of his life, in his choice of employment and houses, in his received opinions or in his selection of friends. Even when he had married Miranda, which had at the time so enraged the former Lady Crieff, he had simply substituted one social strait-jacket for another. His wife and mother now occupied an almost identical place in his psyche: beings whose expectations must never be disappointed.

For Verena Crieff, all her suppositions about the world order were based on whether or not a neighbouring family possessed land in long ownership, and good shooting, and some kinsmanship, however convoluted, with her stately cousins the Arbroaths. For her daughter-in-law, the criteria was ownership of property in specific Chelsea or Holland Park streets, and the ability to secure tables and accommodation at short notice in sought-after restaurants and resorts.

In Charlie's conventional, chivalrous and frequently cowardly code, the ancient concept of man the provider had morphed into an unspoken requirement to furnish Miranda with designer clothes upon demand, Aman *cabãnas*, swimming pools with electronic jelly covers, thoroughbred hunters, couples and girl grooms, corner tables at Santini, Tuscan villas, Hermès 'Kelly' bags and anything else that suddenly seemed so essential, or else that other, richer friends already possessed. Never in their eight-year marriage had Charlie considered that he might deny his wife anything; her insistence upon certain standards made such a notion impossible. His ambition was only to supply what everybody else had, while, of course, enjoying every minute of it once he'd capitulated. He lived for the transitory female approval that invariably followed when he did the right thing. His very first reaction, on being informed by Miranda that she was leaving him, was relief that his mother was no longer still alive to hear about it.

Miranda made it clear that, while she would continue to see a good deal of their children, there was no possibility of their moving in with her in Chester Square on account of Boobie's furniture. 'Sticky little fingers and Biedermeier cabinets do not go together,' she declared. Instead, it was agreed that Maha would transfer with her mistress directly on to Boobie's payroll, while Kosova would remain with Charlie and the children, at least for the time being, until the house in Upper Phillimore Gardens had been successfully disposed of and the family had found a new, smaller home, probably south of the river in Wandsworth or Tooting. Miranda told everyone she was sure this was the most sensible and civilised way of resolving things: 'Especially as Charlie's only hanging about the house all day, with nothing to do.'

The only occasion on which she had the slightest misgivings about leaving him was when, skimming through a profile of Marcus and Flora in *Tatler* while having her hair coloured at Michaeljohn, it was suddenly brought home to her, by the photographs of Marcus's many houses and new yacht, *Marketmaker II*, exactly how amazingly rich he actually was. She wondered how she would feel if Marcus did suddenly snuff it, and left hundreds of millions to Charlie, and whether she would have forfeited her right to sue for her rightful share.

Charlie, meanwhile, did his inadequate best to keep the show on the road, for his children's sake. Never having had much aptitude for this side of life, he felt hopelessly put upon whenever Kosova nipped out to the shops or, worse, had an afternoon off, and he was left in sole charge of an eighteen-month-old baby, an increasingly recalcitrant Marina and the worryingly introverted Pelham. Charlie thanked his lucky stars that he'd put a school-fee savings scheme in place for Pelham at the time of his birth, which meant he'd still be able to manage Broadley Court, which would no doubt do the boy a power of good. In the meantime, it was only too apparent how much the children were missing Maha, if not their mother, and numerous were the occasions on which Charlie wished that old Nanny Arbroath could be drafted back to sort things out, had she not recently popped her clogs in Perth.

One Sunday afternoon, close to the end of his tether with no Kosova to help him all weekend and a houseful of whining and squabbling children, Charlie in desperation took them out for tea at Tootsies on Holland Park Avenue. As ever, in such places, he felt instantly claustrophobic at the closeness of the wooden tables to one another, the ghastly naff high-chairs the waitress insisted on bringing, the stench of char-broiled hamburgers and relish tray, the ketchup-smeared plastic menus, the paper cartoon table mats that 'kids' were encouraged to colour in with stunted, blunted crayons; he felt a terrible despair welling up inside him at the unfairness of life and the rotten hand it had dealt him, when all he had ever wanted was the best for himself and his family. The prospect of living south of the river filled him with shame and remorse. If only he had hung on to Ardnessaig, they could have moved back up to Scotland and existed, perfectly contentedly, on the income from the estate cottages. Instead, all that money – his family money – was being systematically siphoned off by Stuart, month after month, to be wasted on ghastly, vulgar indoor swimming pools and gold-plated Jacuzzis, which must surely be making him the laughing stock of Angus. People like Stuart – and suddenly there were so many of them in New Britain – with all the brass but none of the class, always imagined they could buy their way into anything, but it wouldn't work up in Scotland, Charlie could tell him that for nothing.

Charlie's sole remaining key to salvation, as he understood it, lay in Marcus's grasp. Marcus's money could still change everything, instantly and irrevocably. As he shuffled along the cherry-lined streets of Kensington – streets to which he scarcely felt he still belonged, or had any business to walk – Charlie found that most of his waking hours were taken up with thinking about Marcus. His former so-called friends, who had lately dropped him with a giant thud – all the Camilla Silcoxes and Janie McVities and the rest of them – they'd be scurrying back soon enough with their tails between their legs when Marcus's billions came flooding through. And as senior godchild, it was scarcely a question of if but when.

When Charlie read the clothes list that arrived from Broadley Court, he had to sit down for fifteen minutes until he'd stopped shaking. He had never seen anything like it. For a start, it ran to five closely typed pages featuring football kit, gym kit, everyday uniform, half changes, church parade and Sunday exeat home clothes. Pelham was going to require a green herringbone tweed jacket, a grey flannel suit, a blue blazer, a hooded Barbour, four guernseys – *four*? Who on earth needed four? Even Charlie himself didn't have four guernseys – a tweed overcoat, a grey belted raincoat and a navy blue towelling swimming-robe. As for shoes, it was evident the school bursar was some distant cousin to Imelda Marcos; the list called for black lace-up chapel shoes, brown sandals (two pairs), indoor trainers, outdoor trainers, slippers, gumboots and rugby boots (metal studs only, please). All of the above, Charlie read in despair, constituted the Broadley Court wardrobe for the Michaelmas term only. Further lists would be issued nearer the time for Lent and Summer.

It had become obvious to Charlie, from the moment he re-entered the gates for Pelham's three-hour entrance examination, that there had been a number of questionable changes at his old private school in the intervening years. For one thing, plonked right in the centre of the First XI cricket square, now stood a large, multi-coloured, inflatable bouncy castle, on which dozens of small boys were leaping and tumbling and shrieking their heads off, with no sign of an Assistant Master anywhere on duty. Charlie's second shock came on seeing some of the other parents. Having given considerable thought to the issue of what he and Pelham should appropriately wear for the examination (or 'assessment' as the school insisted on calling it), and having ordered a reluctant Kosova to polish Pelham's shoes to within an inch of their life, Charlie was amazed to find himself the only father on parade in a proper jacket and tie. The other fathers struck him as a distinctly mediocre crew, drifting about the premises in blue jeans and open-necked shirts and extraordinary suede jerkins with zips up the front. A few of them even wore beards. Charlie dreaded to think what old Archie Trumper would have made of it all, had he still been around as headmaster.

The children and their parents were congregated in the old panelled Assembly Room, which now seemed to have been converted into a serve-yourself dining hall, with a steel shelf around the walls for plastic trays, and a blackboard listing today's specials, including vegetarian and nut-free options. Clipping on a school name-badge which billed him, rather over-familiarly, Charlie felt, as 'Charles Crieff (Dad of Pelham)', he half tuned in while a succession of matrons, house-mistresses, a chaplain and, finally, the new head-master himself, reassured potential punters about the super-lative standards of pastoral care and facilities. Regarding 'Beetle' Trumper, who had taken junior chapel choir in Charlie's day and been written off as an almost total nonentity by the boys, the kindest thing to be said was that he was still no chip off the old block. Where his father Archie had been an awe-inspiring and frankly terrifying figure, who rampaged around the school like an African dictator, issuing barbaric and contradictory ultimatums as the mood took him, Beetle was almost pitifully ingratiating as he struggled to coax another generation of fee-payers through the school gates. To Charlie, Beetle seemed less like a private school headmaster than the marketing man-ager of a hotel.

While Pelham was whisked away for his assessment ('At Broadley Court, it really isn't a question of pass or fail, we simply want to find out whether we and your son are right for each other'), Charlie tagged on to a group of parents being given the tour by a South African junior matron. As an Old Broadlean himself, he couldn't really see much point, since he obviously knew the whole place backwards already, but he had to fill in the time. He certainly made it clear to the other parents, at the earliest opportunity, that he and Broadley Court went back a long way.

As they traipsed this way and that, up and down staircases

and in and out of Portakabin classrooms that had never even existed in Charlie's time, he saw that the place had been transformed out of all recognition. Apart from the school chapel, he barely recognised a single landmark. The dormitories, once spartan barracks with rows of iron bed-steads and scratchy grey blankets, boasted wooden bunks with individual reading lamps and Dennis the Menace and Arsenal Football Club duvet covers.

'I think I remember this dorm anyway,' Charlie announced at one point. 'It's called Basutoland. My friend Jamie Temple was in the next bed.'

But, to his dismay, Basutoland was now renamed Panda. 'All the dormitories are called after endangered animals and trees,' explained the matron.

Charlie could certainly understand why the fees were such an arm and a leg these days. In a huge new block devoted to information technology, they found forty boys e-mailing their parents on the latest computers. In an adjoining classroom, a study group was researching Hindu festivals on the Internet. Charlie's old French classroom had been converted into a multi-tracked language laboratory, where a class of eleven-year-olds were being taught to speak Mandarin Chinese. According to the over-earnest beak in charge, Chinese had recently superseded Italian and German at Broadley as the most popular optional subject for Common Entrance.

'And what about Latin?' Charlie asked. 'Still much call for the old *mensa*, *mensa*, *mensam*, is there?'

The Head of Languages chuckled. 'Ha, ha, that does rather date you I'm afraid, sir. That one fell off the syllabus long ago, along with Ancient Greek and Scripture.'

Eventually, they emerged in a sports hall and swimming pool complex of such a size and glamour that it reminded Charlie of an Olympic stadium.

'Blooming heck, this is all pretty amazing, I must say. When did all this go up? In my day we used to bathe in a pond at the bottom of the playing fields.'

'Oh, this is four or five years old, I believe. It's named the Marcus Brand Sports Hall, after the businessman who gave some of the money on condition that it was named after him.'

Eighteen months before she died, as if guessing what was coming and preferring to spend her final days in her own bed, Jean Bolton told Stuart she had decided to take a short break from Ardnessaig and would be moving back home to Smethwick. Aware that his mother was rapidly being eaten away by cancer, though she made a point of never mentioning the illness unless absolutely necessary, Stuart rearranged his schedule so as to spend as much time with her as possible. By flying on Friday afternoons direct from Frankfurt to Birmingham City Airport, and picking up a cab at the terminal, he found he could do the journey in under four hours door-to-door, and be home for a cooked tea before Jean turned in immediately after the nine o'clock news.

It must have been fifteen years since he was last in Smethwick, Stuart calculated, to his slight shame. He never returned to the city of his childhood without a sense of unease. In certain company, when people asked him where he had grown up, he would defiantly reply 'Birmingham, in the Black Country' to make it plain that his Midlands roots were a source of pride to him. In fact, he hardly gave the place a second thought. He was grateful for the first-class education he'd received there, and for what he sometimes described as the local 'values', but he knew the West Midlands were somewhere to get out of while you still could. Recently, having been contacted by his old school, St Edward's, which had somehow got hold of his address in Germany for their Millennium appeal, Stuart had bunged a cheque for a thousand quid into an envelope and sent it off, but when they invited him back to the school to give a talk about being a high-flying businessman, he'd made his excuses.

Driving through Birmingham city centre, with its latest cat's cradle of newly built ring-roads, flyovers and underpasses, none of which had been standing on his last visit, Stuart found it almost impossible to connect with the place. The old loading yard and assembly line of the Smethwick

Chassis Works, finally shut down by Marcus in the late eighties, had been flattened and turned into a car auction centre. Shiplake & Clegg, having gone under in the deep manufacturing recession of 1991, had seen its premises reborn as an aerobics and tanning studio. Occasionally, Stuart would recognise a landmark from his youth – a municipal public building now dwarfed by the long finger of a minaret – or some of the old *balti* houses where he'd courted, and almost become engaged to, Lauren Webb. According to Jean, who always knew these things, Lauren had become a remedial sports physiotherapist and lived somewhere down in the West Country with her husband and three children.

The sight of his mother shocked him. Even though she told him she was feeling so much better, and had made a tremendous effort to be up and about, with her hair tidy and a meal waiting on the table, it was evident she was very weak. Stuart felt she had shrunk by a couple of inches since Christmas; she suddenly seemed a much smaller, dryer version of her previous self, her bones frail and her skin papery. As ever, the flat was flooded by classical music. They ate their tea to Chopin's 'Nocturnes'.

That night, for the first time in two decades, Stuart slept in his old bedroom, under his old blue bedcover, with his posters still up on the wall, and his swimming trophies and badges ranged along the shelf. His framed degree certificate from Birmingham University hung above the washbasin. The bookshelf was full of his old economics text books and course notes. Having turned in for the night at the same time as his mother, and still revved up from his week in Germany, he had difficulty getting off to sleep, and lay awake thinking about his life and how surprised he would have been when he left college had he known then that he would get this far. And yet, as time moved on, he felt dissatisfied by his material success. Notwithstanding his immense salary and bonuses, which had given him a level of security he could never have imagined, and a level of insecurity that stopped him sleeping, he sensed the lacuna at the centre of his life. Even up at Ardnessaig, his delight at the solitude and space quickly turned into loneliness. The last few times he'd spoken to his mother, she had asked him, rather pointedly, whether he had any plans ever to get married, but the truth was, he seldom met anybody. At an IMF conference in Kuala Lumpur he had had a one-night stand with a pretty American delegate, but by the next morning both parties had thought better of the idea, and avoided one another for the remainder of the session. Afterwards, he wondered whether the reason he'd gone to bed with her was due to her faint physical resemblance to Mary Gore, which set him thinking about his feelings about his oldest friend. Mary wasn't beautiful like Saffron, but she was pretty, no question. He definitely found it easy to think about her in that way. But he knew, too, that he would never broach that subject. After Crispin, Mary would not consider someone like Stuart, and he didn't want to risk their friendship by making a move which might embarrass them both.

His week at Darmstadt Commerzhaus had not been particularly easy, and Stuart felt anxious about that too. Twelve out of the fourteen equities markets in which they held big positions had been showing consistent large gains, quarter after quarter, and he was beginning to think that stocks were overheating. Even Moscow, where DC had established its own fund after Charlie's refusal to sell, was on the up. And Bombay and Seoul were unbelievable, powered by the prevailing mania for new technology stocks. He was concerned, too, about the Brand Corporation, which had recently announced a raft of Internet-related businesses, including a global ISP, Brand.com, which had provoked a 25 per cent leap in the stock price. At the most recent review conference, Barry Tomkins had been full of dark prognostications about the company and Marcus's shenanigans in manipulating the share price, but nothing could be substantiated, and Barry anyway found it impossible to be impartial on the subject of Brand. For the time being at least, Manfred was content to continue holding stock. 'Just don't say I didn't warn you,' Barry had said, hating it when his research unit went unheeded.

On his fourth visit home to Smethwick, Stuart noticed the further deterioration in his mother at once. She seemed much shakier and was having some difficulty in walking, and he had to be firm about refusing to allow her to cook. The local Social Services, it transpired, shared his concern, and had proposed moving her into a residential home, a suggestion which Jean had declined even to consider. Only with great difficulty did Stuart persuade her to agree to a home help, who would pop in twice a day, check she was all right and do the grocery shopping. He pretended that this service cost much less than it actually did and arranged to settle the bills himself.

For as long as Stuart could remember, Jean had kept a photograph of her late husband on the mantelpiece. It stood in a wooden frame, an old black-and-white studio portrait, backlit like a thirties starlet, and in all the dozens of times he had looked at it, Stuart had never been able to form the slightest impression of what Ron Bolton, with his fish eyes and neat moustache, had actually been like as a person. The photograph was one of those possessions, along with Jean's old wicker sewing basket and a dull metal carriage clock, that formed the topography of his childhood.

Tonight, realising that he might not have a million other opportunities, he asked his mother, 'What was Dad actually like?'

'Your father? He was a wonderful man. A marvellous husband to me, and would have been a wonderful father to you.' Jean was drinking a cup of tea and listening to the new CD player Stuart had bought for her in duty-free. For some reason, he sensed a reluctance in her reply, as if she didn't wish to be questioned further.

But, this time, he wouldn't allow the moment to pass.

'I have to ask you, Mum. I've tried to talk about this with you before, but you've always evaded the subject. What exactly did happen when he died?'

'No, pet. It was all so long ago, it's best left alone.'

'That's what you said last time, but I'm afraid it won't do. I'm forty-one years old and I need to know. Please tell me.'

Jean looked at him, as if making up her mind, and

eventually said, 'All right then, I will tell you. But I'm breaking a confidence, and I'm only telling you now because I won't be around for much longer. I gave my word, and I hate to break it.'

'Gave your word to who exactly?' But he knew the answer already.

'To Mr Brand. And to his lawyer person, Mr Mathias. They made me sign some papers, swearing me to secrecy, so I could get in terrible trouble . . .'

'What happened, Mum?'

Slowly, hesitantly, she began her story. 'Well, your father had been working for Mr Brand for five years by the time you were born, and he worshipped the man. He had to work terrible long hours, up before dawn, out until I don't know what hour, restaurants, casinos . . . he never went to bed, Mr Brand, and expected Ron to be outside waiting for him, no matter how late it got. But he was a generous employer and, as I said, your father enjoyed driving him and considered it a privilege too.'

'And he sometimes drove Lucy Brand?' Stuart prompted his mother to get on with it, and tell him what had happened that night of the accident.

'On occasions, yes, though Mrs Brand wasn't always down south. She stayed put up in Scotland quite a lot of the time – they had a house near her parents' place on the Macphersons' estate. Ron used to tell me sometimes, in confidence of course, that Mr Brand didn't always behave very well when his wife was out of town. He had an eye for the ladies, you see.'

'But Dad did drive her that night in Scotland?'

'Yes, your father was driving that night – not that he had any business to be. He shouldn't have been on the road in his condition.'

'So he *was* drunk?'

'He had been drinking, yes. What you have to take into account is that he'd already driven Mr Brand all the way from London up to Scotland. There were no motorways in those days so it was quite a journey, between twelve and fourteen hours it generally took him. And Mr Brand hated to stop, he was all for pushing on, so it was a dreadful strain on poor Ron, stuck behind the wheel for that length of time. He was worn out when they got there, and he did pour himself a large whisky, several in fact, to help him relax. He always had a few drams after the drive north. He never expected to be going back out again that evening, never expected it at all. We used to stay in a little bothy close to the Brands' house, and I was already up there myself with you, giving you your first experience of the country.'

'But why did Dad have to go out again that evening?'

'We were going upstairs to bed when the telephone rang at eleven o'clock. We couldn't imagine who it could be. But it was Mr Brand calling, saying your father must drive Mrs Brand straight to Edinburgh to see a doctor.'

'Couldn't he have said no, if he'd been drinking whisky?'

'He did try to. He explained the situation very clearly, but Mr Brand wasn't interested. He became quite agitated. I could hear him from where I was sitting. And he told Ron that, if he refused to bring the car straight round to the front, he could consider himself dismissed.'

'So Dad did?'

'He didn't have any choice. He wasn't happy about it, but what could he do? So he fetched the car from out of the garage and drove down to the Brands'. I was very worried, because he wasn't in a fit state to drive anywhere. He was all over the place. I told him to drive with the window down, for the air.'

'And he picked up Mrs Brand and, not surprisingly, they crashed into a tree. Is that what happened?'

'They had hardly driven ten miles and, according to the policeman, it was a wonder they'd got so far.'

'What the hell can Marcus have been thinking of? It's insane. He knew Dad wasn't sober. Why allow his wife to get into the car? It was a death trap. It's almost as if he wanted her to be killed.'

'I couldn't explain it either,' Jean said. 'He must have realised when he saw her into the car that Ron wasn't safe. He could barely walk in a straight line.'

'And they were both killed instantly?'

'According to the doctors, your father was killed on impact. Mrs Brand died in the ambulance on the way to Dundee Infirmary.'

'Tragic – and pointless,' Stuart said. 'Why were they even going to Edinburgh in the middle of the night? What was so important?'

'They said at the time Mrs Brand had thought she was expecting, and her husband had insisted she see a doctor in Edinburgh, but it turned out to be a false alarm. She wasn't pregnant after all.'

'It doesn't make any sense. The whole thing's ridiculous. Even if she had been pregnant, why check it out in the middle of the night and drive two hours to Edinburgh? And shouldn't Marcus have gone with her?'

Jean shrugged. 'There were many things I never understood. There was a lot of talk in the village, though I never listened to it. It was an uncomfortable position to be in, in any case. Mrs Brand was a popular lady locally, and it was my husband who had caused her death. Some of the people on the estate refused to have anything to do with me.'

'But couldn't you have explained what happened? That Marcus had forced Dad to drive?'

'I suppose I might have done, but then Mr Brand and Mr Mathias called on me at the cottage, and I was in a terrible state, not knowing what I was going to do, and what would become of us. You were only six weeks old at the time, Stuart, a tiny wee thing, and I was dreadfully worried we soon wouldn't have a roof over our heads and wondering how I was going to look after you. And that's when Mr Brand made his generous offer.'

'What offer?' Already, Stuart was gripped by a terrible dread of what his mother was about to say.

'He said how sorry he was about everything, and how he never should have asked your father to drive the car that night. He admitted it was his own fault, and he wanted to make things right for us, but he said he didn't want any bad publicity or anybody mentioning the telephone conversation with Ron. He said he was so upset about his wife and everything – and Ron too – he couldn't take any more criticism. Then his lawyer, Mr Mathias, produced a piece of paper, very official-looking it was, and said if I signed it I'd be paid an allowance every month until you reached the age of twenty-one. When I saw the amount of money, I could hardly believe my eyes. Nearly half what your father had been paid as his wages. And then he gave me another big cheque too, five thousand pounds, which I never spent. I put it aside for you. It was the money we used for your university in America.'

'Oh, my God,' was all Stuart could say. 'I should have guessed. Christ, he paid you hush-money to cover up the deaths of two innocent people! How could you take it from that bastard?'

'Now, there's no need to use bad language, Stuart. I knew I never should have told you. Mr Brand was only trying to make amends. And it wasn't just a question of money. He wanted to do his best for you. That's why he insisted on becoming your godfather.'

68: November, 1999

Abigail Schwartzman Rosedale returned from a lunchtime
dash to Bergdorf's to be told that her presence was
immediately required by the President and Chief Financial
Officer of Sotheby's. In her twenty months with the company, she had never exchanged one word with either of these
luminaries, and her first thought was that she must be in
some trouble. Her mind raced with possible misdemean-
ours. She couldn't think of anything, but her innate guilt
made her flush with anxiety. Even the security of a rich new
husband had done nothing to reduce Abigail's sense of
inferiority.

'I appreciate your making the time to see us, Mrs Rosedale,' said the President of Sotheby's, North America. Close
up, he came across as more like an investment banker or
accountant rather than an art lover; Abby knew he served as
a non-executive director on the boards of several American
corporations. 'I don't know whether you've met my associate before, our CFO, and I would also like for you to meet
our new Vice President of Corporate Client Relations.'
Abigail shook hands with another silver-haired suit, who
faintly reminded her of her new husband, Forrest Rosedale,
and a crisp, beady, Armani-clad woman in her mid-fifties.
'Before we embark on the subject of our meeting this
afternoon,' continued the President, 'I must tell you that
everything you hear is in the strictest confidence. Not one
word of our discussion may be repeated outside of this
room, not in your department, not to your family. That is
the understanding on which we proceed. I trust it doesn't
present a problem for you?'

Abby shook her head, but felt wary. She couldn't imagine
what she was doing there, or what it was they were about to
tell her. And it worried her that she was being asked to keep
a secret from Forrest. In the four months they'd been

married, they had made a point of sharing everything. If there was a problem between Abby and one of Forrest's children by his earlier marriages, they confronted it. If Forrest had a rough day at Paul, Weiss, Rifkind, Wharton & Garrison, where he was a partner in corporate law, they talked it through. This policy of total honesty and transparency, coming after her years with the slippery Jamie, was one of the many things she appreciated about being married to Forrest.

'Let me begin by confirming something with you,' said the President. 'Marcus Brand. We are correct in believing he's your godfather and a longstanding family friend?'

Abby looked at him in surprise. 'Er, I guess you could say that, yes. Marcus has been my godfather since I was born, obviously. I'm not sure you could exactly call him a family friend. He and my father don't see so much of each other these days.'

'But you continue to enjoy warm relations? We understand you regularly vacation on the Brand yacht and at several of his homes.'

Abby nodded her assent. Everything he said was undeniable. She had visited virtually all of Marcus's houses; the only ones she hadn't seen were the apartments in Manhattan and Paris.

'He has a country place in Hampshire, England? A house named . . . West Candover Park?' The President and his associates consulted file notes on the table in front of them.

'That's right. It's an amazing place, enormous. I've only been there twice in my life, and once was more than twenty years ago.'

'Mrs Rosedale, would you mind taking a look at this photograph and telling us if you recognise the painting?'

He passed over a black and white print which Abigail instantly identified as Marcus's van Gogh.

'It's a van Gogh,' she said. 'One of the sunflowers series.'

The President exchanged a meaningful look with his CFO. 'It is indeed by Vincent van Gogh. *Sunflowers at Arles*. Now I must ask you, have you ever seen the original of this painting?'

Abigail nodded. She remembered precisely where and when she'd seen it: on the same day Poppy drowned in Marcus's pool, shortly before lunch on the worst day of her life.

'At West Candover Park. Marcus keeps it in his library – his den, I guess you could say.'

'And when exactly was this, do you remember? Don't worry if you can't recollect the precise date. You may be able to figure it out at a later time.'

'No, I can remember. It was about two years ago. Saturday the eleventh of November 1997.' It was a date forever etched into her soul.

'Thank you, Mrs Rosedale. That was remarkable. So the painting was definitely still in Marcus Brand's possession in November '97, and hung at his mansion outside of London.' He made some notes on a legal pad. 'You are no doubt wondering why we are asking you these questions. I will tell you but, once again, I must emphasise its extreme sensitivity. However, we have resolved to take you into our confidence because we believe there may be a way you can assist us, given that Mr Brand is your godfather.'

At this point the CFO took up the story, explaining to Abigail about Sotheby's Credit, a discretionary facility the auction house provided to help very rich clients pay for works of art by instalments. 'Obviously this facility is restricted only to the highest-ticket artworks, and only to individuals whose credit rating is triple-A. In the case of Marcus Brand, we were happy to extend the facility to assist him in the purchase of the van Gogh.'

'You mean, Marcus didn't pay for it? I didn't realise that was even possible.'

'As I explained, only in exceptional circumstances. You have to appreciate that Mr Brand paid almost eighty million dollars to secure the painting, which was close to a world record at the time. Not many people, even those as wealthy as Marcus Brand, have assets of that magnitude sitting around in cash. It's good business sense to make things as easy as possible for them to commit to the transaction. In the case of *Sunflowers at Arles*, there were probably only six or eight individuals or institutions in the world that could be regarded as serious prospects, including the Getty Museum and two or three Japanese insurance companies.'

'Do you mind if I ask you something?' Abigail said. 'Why are you telling me all this?'

'We were getting to that,' said the President of Sotheby's, North America. 'We have been placed in a position of some awkwardness. In short, Marcus Brand defaulted on his most recent quarterly repayments. He has in fact missed the last two dates, and we don't know what's going on. Up until then, the money always arrived on the nail, but suddenly, nothing. Our people have been in communication with his offices, but they're being given the run-around. Calls are passed from office to office. Nobody can tell us where he is, or how we can reach him.'

'And . . . you want me to help?'

'All we need at this point is a contact number and a steer on where he actually is. The Brand Corporation office on Park Avenue is saying he's in Moscow, his people in London say Manila or Wyoming. We can't find anybody who'll give a straight answer.'

'Well, I'll try,' Abby said doubtfully. 'I suppose I could call his personal secretary, Barbara Miles. She's usually quite helpful.'

'Anything you can discover would be much appreciated. You've told us one thing already that is slightly reassuring, concerning the location of the van Gogh. At least we know the painting entered the United Kingdom. Not that it necessarily means it's still there. There's a story he's transferred it across to Russia, which is a worrisome development if we are eventually forced to repossess it.'

Charlie was resting on his bed in the new house in Balham, half watching the early-evening news. Outside, through uncurtained windows, he could see an Alldays 24-hour convenience store, a bus stop and a block of sheltered housing for old people. Recently, he had taken to spending much of the day upstairs in his bedroom, pretending to work and avoiding the children. For a short time following

Miranda's departure, he had striven to eat with his offspring every day, and even to try and help Pelham and Marina with their homework; but the task had been too hard for him, and increasingly he chose to skulk upstairs.

He was also avoiding Kosova, to whom he owed five weeks in back wages plus £300 housekeeping money. Where this was going to come from, he really had no idea; his overdraft was wretched. Hidden underneath the bed were the children's christening presents, in the big cardboard grocery box into which he had dumped them after retrieving them from the safe in Upper Phillimore Gardens. It occurred to him that, if the worst came to the worst, he could always flog them, or anyway pawn them for a few months, if pawnbrokers still existed, which they probably did in a benighted area like the one in which he was now forced to live. Heaving the box up on to the bed, he removed the gifts one by one from their original carrier bags. First he examined Pelham's haul: a silver tankard engraved with his initials in an extravagant copperplate script – that one had come from his godfather Iain Silcox; a pair of gold Asprey cufflinks in a satin-lined box engraved with the Crieff crest, and another pair in silver from Mappin & Webb, a gold Cartier propelling pencil, a sterling silver Swiss Army knife in a Tiffany box, and a silver-plated hip flask. At the very least, Charlie reckoned, he should be able to get six to seven hundred quid upfront for this lot. Marina's presents were slightly less substantial than Pelham's: a Boodle & Dunthorne child's gold bangle, a coral and pearl necklace from Annabel Jones and a gold charm bracelet. For Leonora, the booty was lighter still – a silver Tiffany rattle from the dreaded Boobie. Not for the first time, Charlie was enraged that Marcus had turned down their invitation to be Leo's godfather. If he had divvied up a decent present, there would at least have been something worth selling. Surveying the array of expensive, but oddly pointless, trinkets spread across the bedcover, Charlie felt real regret that he had lost touch with all his children's godparents, whom he could never invite to his present, low abode. The engraved cufflinks and hip flask seemed almost a reproach, because his circumstances had altered so utterly.

The news item about Marcus came third in the running order, following some fresh scandal about New Labour spindoctor Peter Mandelson. Marcus and Flora were shown walking arm in arm through an unidentified airport, trailed by Dick Mathias, Barbara Miles and Bartholomew, who was wheeling a trolley piled high with luggage. Charlie reached for the remote and turned up the volume.

'The tycoon Marcus Brand has today married long-term girlfriend Flora Huang in a civil ceremony in Nevada,' the newscaster was saying. 'The billionaire, whose manufacturing-to-media business empire is capitalised at more than twenty-five billion pounds, tied the knot at the Mirage gambling resort in Las Vegas. He told reporters his decision to wed thirty-year-old Huang, who is a senior executive of his Brand Corporation, was a spur-of-the-moment one. Asked whether he and his wife had signed a prenuptial agreement, Mr Brand said that he "didn't believe in them. In my personal dealings, as in my business dealings, everything is undertaken on a basis of trust".'

Charlie, frozen, stared at the screen. He couldn't believe what he'd seen. Why now, for God's sake? Marcus had been with Flora since 1993, which was *six years*. Seven years was when you canned your mistress, not married her. He must have been manipulated into it by Flora, it was the only explanation. Charlie could hardly bring himself to look at her, smirking at the cameras like a Siamese cat digesting the canary. She was draped all over Marcus like the First Lady at a Presidential jamboree. The whole thing was totally sickening; he couldn't bear to think what it might spell for him personally. The fact the godchildren hadn't even been invited to the wedding was a chilling portent.

'Mr Brand! Over here, Marcus! This way, Marcus!' A posse of television reporters was pressing in on the tycoon as he and Flora approached the barrier. 'Where are you taking your wife on honeymoon, Mr Brand?' 'Oy, Marcus, is it true Mrs Brand is going to run the company after you?' Marcus in his overcoat with the beaver lapels was shielding Flora from the flashbulbs as he marched, impassively, towards a waiting limousine.

Then, apparently changing his mind, he stopped and faced the cameras. 'I have three things only to say to you gentlemen today,' he declared. 'The first is that I consider myself extremely fortunate that Flora has consented to become my wife . . .' I'll bet she has too, thought Charlie bitterly, the scheming Chinese bitch! 'We will not be taking a honeymoon,' Marcus continued, 'owing to pressing work obligations elsewhere, but we hope to take time off together later in the year. Our immediate destination is Beijing, where my company is in advanced negotiations with President Jiang Zemin. At the Brand Corporation we presently have three priorities, which are "China, China and China".'

Charlie, devastated, killed the picture with the remote. He considered ringing Jamie, or even Saffron, to double check that none of his rival godchildren had known about the wedding in advance.

It crossed his mind, too, that he probably ought to send Marcus and Flora a wedding gift, but he wondered whether there was any longer much point. It might simply be throwing good money after bad.

Stuart caught up with the wedding announcement on a BBC in-flight newscast between Heathrow and JFK.

His purpose in travelling to New York was to confer with colleagues in Darmstadt Commerzhaus's Wall Street office about disturbing market rumours concerning the Brand Corporation. These rumours, as yet unconfirmed, suggested that Marcus would shortly face an investigation by the Securities and Exchange Commission for insider dealing.

'*At the Brand Corporation we presently have three priorities,*' Marcus was proclaiming. '*China, China and China.*'

Stuart rolled his eyes. You had to hand it to the old rogue, he had chutzpah. He had enjoyed the bit, too, about the prenuptial agreement and everything in Marcus's life being done on a basis of trust. Stuart wondered if there was anything he wouldn't believe of his godfather these days, considering what he now knew about the death of his own father.

For almost a month, ever since Jean's revelation, he had been brooding. And the more he thought about it, the more furious he became. There was no question, Marcus was at least guilty of manslaughter, if not murder. His insistence that Ron should drive the car that night had led directly to his death, and then he and Dick Mathias had systematically used Marcus's money to hush the whole thing up. It was outrageous, and Marcus shouldn't be allowed to get away with it. Slowly and deliberately Stuart pulled out his mobile and started dialling.

Stuart convened the council of war – as the great summit meeting of the godchildren was for ever-afterwards known – within a week of the arrival of Marcus's invitations for them all to spend the Millennium in Bali.

One by one, Stuart rang all the other godchildren (with the sole exception of Flora, for obvious reasons) and invited them for the weekend at Ardnessaig. 'I can't say too much over the phone,' he told each of them, 'but it's very important and it concerns Marcus. If you can possibly make it, you must.'

Mary and Saffron agreed to come at once, as did Jamie, though there were an awkward few days when Amaryllis was insisting on tagging along too, which Stuart was determined not to allow: 'This weekend is strictly godchildren only.' Amaryllis took offence and tried to stop Jamie from going, but in the end he'd headed off regardless. Abigail was initially worried about abandoning Forrest at such short notice, but the prospect of an intrigue involving Marcus was too tantalising, knowing what she now did about the van Gogh. Telling herself she might learn something crucial to her job, she left the refrigerator in their apartment full-to-bursting with every possible delicacy to keep her new husband happy, and caught the redeye from JFK to Heathrow followed by the shuttle up to Edinburgh.

The only godchild strongly resistant to the thought of a weekend at Ardnessaig was Charlie. He found the experience of being telephoned at home by Stuart an intrusion; he didn't even like Stuart knowing where he lived, particularly not now, and demanded to know how he'd got hold of his number. When Stuart said he'd got it from Jamie, Charlie rang his old friend and gave him what-for.

Charlie insisted he didn't have the slightest inclination to spend a weekend with Stuart Bolton, especially not at

Ardnessaig. Nor, if truth be told, did he really have the spare cash for the flight.

But having returned an emphatic no, and been thoroughly obnoxious to Stuart in the process, he later had second thoughts. It crossed his mind that the weekend might involve a challenge to Marcus's will, were he to leave the whole lot to Flora. In which case, it made sense to find out exactly what was going on. He certainly didn't want to be left out, if the other godchildren were planning a carve-up; it would be typical of Stuart to try and cut him out of the deal.

He also reckoned that, if the others were planning on going behind their godfather's back, it could be a shrewd move to get the low-down and then report straight back to Marcus. For loyalty like that, there would surely be a handsome reward.

And so, with considerable ill-grace, he rang Stuart back and said that, after all, he might as well come along, though it really was highly inconvenient, and he hoped it wouldn't be a complete waste of his valuable time.

The others were immediately conscious of a change in Stuart's demeanour. Possibly it was just seeing him in his own environment, but he seemed more authoritative and assured. Collecting them from the airport in a Land Rover, he drove mostly in silence, and refused to be drawn on the real purpose of the gathering. 'I'll tell you at dinner,' was all he would say.

Mary, Jamie and Abigail, who had stayed at Ardnessaig before on Stuart's watch, noticed further improvements to the estate. The new trees he had planted along the drive were growing strongly, and the pink of the castle walls had mellowed by time and rain. As they rolled up the long drive, Saffron, squashed into the back between Jamie and Charlie, said, 'Didn't you once invite me to stay here, Charlie? When we were in Lyford Cay? I should have come: I love that pink.' Predisposed to sneer, Charlie was privately conceding that Stuart's repairs weren't nearly as ghastly as he'd hoped and expected; the kennels and outbuildings, partially roof-less throughout his childhood, had been faithfully restored, and the once-potholed drive was seamless. The price Stuart had paid for the estate now struck Charlie as almost scandalous, and he hated him for it.

In the afternoon, Charlie left the others to swim in the over-chlorinated indoor pool while he skulked around the grounds, observing every change, longing to disparage them but thinking they were pretty much what he would have done himself, had he ever been as loaded as Stuart evidently was. Inside, the house was all typically tasteless and vulgar, of course, but outside he hadn't done a bad job, considering.

In the pool complex, Jamie was eyeing up Abby. He had to admit his ex-wife looked a whole lot better than the last time he'd seen her, which was on that disastrous holiday to Greece. She'd lost at least thirty pounds, had finally got her wardrobe together and done something about her hair. She looked less loopy too, though he couldn't be certain about that, because she was wearing shades and you couldn't see her eyes. All in all, she reminded him of one of those sleek, driven American female executives you saw in movies: perfectly groomed, but mad as snakes underneath.

As soon as they'd helped themselves to supper in the kitchen, Stuart called for silence.

'You're probably wondering why I invited you up here,' he began, 'especially at such short notice. And I appreciate the efforts you've all made to get here, Abby especially. Sorry if it sounded a bit mysterious. I won't keep you in suspense for much longer, I promise. I've been thinking about this a lot, about what is the right thing to do, and that's where you guys come in. We're all godchildren of Marcus's. I don't know about the rest of you, but I've got pretty mixed feelings about him. He's taken us on some very fancy vacations and given us some great experiences, I won't deny that. We all owe him something – some more than others, perhaps. But often I've felt uneasy about him. I don't mind admitting I used to be terrified of him, he scared the life out of me as a kid. In France and the Bahamas, it made me quake just to look at him. I don't know if any of the rest of you ever felt the same way?'

He looked at the five adults sitting round the pine table.

Mary was nodding in agreement and so was Abigail. Jamie, serious for once, looked down at his knife. Charlie stared at Stuart expressionless, wondering where all this was leading. He certainly wasn't going to admit how much Marcus had freaked him out. Saffron, meanwhile, seemed to have withdrawn into a world of her own.

'Quite a few of us have worked for Marcus in one capacity or another, and we've all got more involved with him than most godchildren do with their godparents.' Stuart purposely avoided catching anybody's eye, particularly Saffron's and Abby's. 'We all know him in different ways and with different degrees of intimacy.' Now he could look nowhere. 'I am not going to betray any confidences' – Saffron – 'but I do know how much unhappiness he has been responsible for over the years. Only recently, I became aware of a new episode which this time concerned myself . . .'

He related to his fellow godchildren, as dispassionately as he was able, what he had been told about the circumstances surrounding his father's death, and Marcus's complicity in the cover-up.

'Up until then,' he said, 'I had always thought of Marcus as an opportunist, a lovable rogue if you like. Someone who, for all his faults, makes the world a more exciting place. I've never agreed with his politics but, all right, I admired him despite myself. He's a big man. If people like Marcus didn't exist, we'd all have a duller time. Rightly or wrongly, that's what I reckoned. But now, knowing what I do, I'm no longer so sure. Morally, I find him difficult to stomach. Evil may be putting it too strongly, but the more I learn about him, the less far-fetched it seems. That's the conclusion I've been coming to. And – through my job at Darmstadt Commerzhaus – I find myself placed in an awkward position. There's a lot of negative stuff going round about the Brand Corporation. You might have picked up on some of it.' Again, Stuart looked round the table.

'Yeah, I've been hearing certain things in New York,' Abby said quietly. 'I'm not allowed to say much, but there do appear to be cash-flow problems. I'm sorry, I can't go further than that.'

'I've heard stories too,' murmured Mary, 'through my agency. I don't know how reliable they are. They mostly come from ex-employees.'

'Exactly,' intervened Charlie. 'You want to be highly sceptical of sources like that, it's probably just sour grapes and they have their own agendas. Marcus's business is capitalised at about twenty-five billion, isn't it?'

'Twenty-six,' replied Stuart. 'The markets are certainly maintaining their faith in him. But for how much longer?'

'I hardly think he'd be inviting us all to Bali after Christmas if he was on the skids,' Charlie said. 'We're being flown out by private jet. Don't you think this is all rather pathetic? You haven't dragged us all the way up here just to discuss whether Marcus's business is going down the tubes, which it obviously isn't.'

'No,' Stuart replied. 'This isn't a financial question so much as a moral and ethical one. My questions for us are actually very simple. Is Marcus an evil influence? Is he truly a bad person? And if so, should we be doing anything about it?'

'Crikey,' said Jamie. 'This is like one of those philosophical debates they made us have at school. Do you remember old Talbot-Jones? He got totally over-excited about all that moral and ethical bilge: "My country, right or wrong".'

'Can it, Jamie,' Abby said. 'This is serious. And I think Stuart's right, there is a principle at stake here. If you know someone's a terrible person and you don't do anything about it, it's like you're condoning them. The group here – his godchildren – probably know more about Marcus, and what he's really like, than anyone. If we don't step up to the plate, who will?'

'Well, what *do* we all think about him, then?' Charlie asked. 'I always understood that at least some of us had rather a soft spot for him,' he added, looking lubriciously at Saffron.

She flinched and looked away.

'I don't mind starting,' Abby said. 'I'm not telling you anything I haven't told my shrink a hundred times already. I used to be totally obsessed with Marcus. At one time, I would have done anything for him, I was infatuated, desperate for his approval and affection. Mary knows all about it and so does Stuart, I 'fessed up to them enough times. But think how I feel now! The man who was responsible for Poppy's death? I despise him. I despise him so deeply, I don't even know where to begin. He's manipulative, he's a bully, he's self-satisfied, insincere . . . a child killer, a monster. Is that enough to be getting along with? I could go on.'

Stuart turned to Mary, who was at first reluctant to speak. 'I . . . I can't really talk about this. There are things that happened I've never told anybody, that I just can't talk about. Can we leave it at that?' Then, her eyes blazing, she said, 'I *hate* Marcus. I loathe him more than you could possibly imagine. There, now I've said it. I've never said that out loud before. I've hated him for years. All those holidays he's made us go on – they've been torture from start to finish. And he gave us that bloody car as a wedding present that killed Crispin. And then he did something else to me that I can never, ever forgive or forget.'

Charlie was thinking, If only I had a tape recorder. How the hell will I remember all this? Marcus is going to be riveted.

'How about you, Jamie?' Stuart asked.

'Well, he's a complete tosser, isn't he? If I told you half the things I know, you'd be amazed. Hair-raising stuff. I don't trust him further than I could throw him, which is no distance at all, he's a big bloke. But, seriously, I'd say he's a total sod and dangerous with it.'

'Saffron, is there anything you want to add?'

'I'm like Mary,' she began hesitantly. 'There are things I don't want to talk about, they're too painful. Something I heard recently . . . I'm trying not to think too deeply about it, but it's hard. Marcus has fucked up my whole life. He very nearly destroyed it. He's a vicious bastard. That's all I have to say really. I'll shut up now.'

The intensity of Saffron's outburst, following on from Mary's and Jamie's, silenced the room. For a moment there was complete quiet in the kitchen.

Then Stuart asked, 'Charlie? You heard the others. What's your take on Marcus? You traded his stocks for long enough, and you worked for him in the Far East.'

Charlie hardly knew how to reply. His feelings about Marcus were at this point so confused he wasn't sure what he felt. His sentiments towards his godfather vacillated with his own prospects at any particular moment. With Marcus hitched to Flora, who could say?

So he shrugged and hedged his bets. 'He's an amazing character. A legend really.'

'And you trust him?'

'Well, in as much as you can trust any of those big tycoons. They all cut a few corners on the way up. One can't be naive.'

'So I return to my original questions,' Stuart said. 'Is Marcus evil, and should we be doing anything about it? Perhaps I should go round the table, and you can give me your verdicts – yes or no. Abigail? Mind if I start with you?'

Abby thought for a moment before replying. Then she said, 'Yes – and yes. Yes to both parts.'

'Mary?'

'Yes and yes.'

'Jamie?'

'As I said, he's a plonker. Two definite yeses.'

'Saffron?'

She nodded. 'Sure. Same here.'

'That's four straight yeses to both questions. I'm a double yes too. Which only leaves you, Charlie.'

'Do I really have to give an opinion? This is all getting pretty juvenile.'

'Come on, Charlie, off the fence,' Jamie said. 'Are you a yes or a no?'

'To the "Is Marcus evil?" bit – I haven't got a clue, and nor has anybody else. It's a really meaningless question. Should we do anything about it? Depends what you have in mind. If you're suggesting we shove him into the swimming pool with all his clothes on, no way, I'm not getting involved. What *are* you thinking of, as a matter of fact?'

'To confront him, for a start,' Stuart replied. 'While we're all together in Bali. We'd need to plan the timing very carefully, and really work it out, exactly what to say and when to say it. Then get him to face up to the misery he's deliberately caused. He's used us for his own sick games. We can't just sit there, as if we're all eight years old still, and say nothing. Mary and Saffron can't even bring themselves to discuss what happened to them, it's that bad. He's done terrible things to nearly all of us. We can't ignore it.'

'So we're proposing to challenge him over dinner one night in Bali? Puh-leeze! And what is Marcus supposed to do then, for heaven's sake: apologise?' Charlie was incredulous. 'It would be like another of those ghastly phoney apologies this politically correct socialist government keep making: We're so sorry to the niggers about slavery, we're so sorry about the Irish potato famine, we're so sorry about burning all those Catholics at the stake. They'll be apologising to the dinosaurs next for making them extinct! And you expect Marcus to stand up and say, "Sorry, everyone, for being such a god-awful godfather. Sorry for killing your dad, Stuart, it won't happen again. Sorry for getting my leg over you, Saffron, I shouldn't have done that, it was uncalled for. Sorry, Abigail, for leaving the gate open to the swimming pool. Big mistake. Sorry, sorry, sorry . . ." The whole thing's risible, frankly. And tell me something else, what if he refuses to apologise? What then? Or haven't you thought that far?'

'Actually,' said Stuart carefully, 'that's exactly why I've called us all together. There is plenty we can do. I want to tell you about my predicament at Darmstadt Commerzhaus, and a decision I have to take . . .'

'There may be something else where I come in too,' added Abigail.

'Christ . . . happy holidays,' muttered Charlie.

70: 28 December, 1999

The new Gulfstream V which flew the godchildren and their families from RAF Northolt to Bali was upholstered in the maroon and light blue livery of the Brand Corporation. Two pilots and three stewardesses sported the Brand insignia, a tasteful BC discreetly woven into the epaulettes of their uniforms. A pair of digital screens mounted on the cabin walls showed the exact position of the jet at every moment during its sixteen-hour flight, constantly updated by the on-board GPS as it powered over Northern Europe and across Iran and the Bay of Bengal, down over southern Thailand to Indonesia and Marcus's latest stronghold where he and Flora were expecting them for the Millennium holiday.

Charlie, already well stuck into his seventh whisky, was beginning to take the view that things couldn't be nearly so serious as the scaremongers were making out. It was absolutely bloody typical of the newspaper johnnies to be taking potshots at someone like Marcus, just because he was so much richer and more successful than they were themselves. God, Charlie despised journalists. If they did their ruddy homework for once, and realised Marcus had bought this amazing new plane, they wouldn't be going round casting aspersions on the credit rating of the Brand Corporation.

'Another large Glenfiddich-no-ice and another plate of those canapés,' he told the stewardess. There were no two ways about it, if you were flying long haul, this was the way to do it. He had made sure, when they were dishing out the seats, that Kosova and the children were put as far away as possible, so they couldn't bug him on the journey. He could just see Pelham in the back, hunched over his Gameboy, seated next to the ghastly Stuart who was working on a naff-looking lap-top.

He wondered what it was Stuart was busy with: probably

the latest draft of his dreaded showdown speech against Marcus. He could hardly believe Stuart and the rest of the godchildren were really intending to go through with it, though they'd talked of little else since the weekend at Ardnessaig. The others had hardly been off the telephone, plotting and planning. The big encounter, Charlie knew, was set for the penultimate dinner of the holiday. *J'accuse!* Charlie had made it perfectly clear he wouldn't do any of the talking. Stuart could do that – and face the consequences. Charlie knew where his loyalties lay.

Too pissed to focus on his Dick Francis, he borrowed a *Hello!* from a selection at the front of the cabin. Already, the parties and galas photographed in the magazine belonged to a different world, in which Charlie realised he was no longer remotely a player. It had been more than a year since he'd worn a black tie or eaten dinner in the Great Room of the Grosvenor House or made up the numbers at a charity ball. How he would like to take back all the thousands of pounds he'd spent – *frittered* – on buying tables at parties he could barely now remember! Blearily turning the pages, he spotted Iain Silcox and Michael Waitrose at a clay-pigeon shooting competition, and then his ex-wife and Boobie at the Red Cross Ball in Monte Carlo. Miranda was dressed in a strapless satin ballgown and a huge pearl necklace, smiling thinly. Boobie had one arm draped across her shoulders and the other wrapped around the waist of a dodgy-looking young Arab boy with perfect white teeth.

Saffron, Mary and Clara were seated together next to the bulkhead. It would be hard to say which of the goddaughters was dreading the holiday the most. Saffron would never have dreamt of coming, had Marcus not put up the money for her shop. She would far rather have remained at the boutique, right through the post-Christmas sale, but Marcus had insisted, so she'd left the place in the hands of her business partner, Calypso Blackwater. They had been up-and-running for five months now, and so far the reaction had been incredible. That whole area of Ledbury Road was really coming up, and they'd had two great mentions – one in *Vogue* and one in the *Evening Standard* magazine. In the last two weeks, Madonna had come to the shop twice, as well as Meg Mathews and, of course, Calypso's dad Nick. The beaded evening bags, suede gloves and chunky handknits were flying off the shelves, as were the aromatherapy oils and sandalwood foot-massage rolling pins. At this rate, they'd soon be breaking even.

The prospect of seeing Marcus filled Saffron with dread, especially as her mother would be there too, now that she and Jamie were an item. The thought of Marcus made her flesh crawl. She couldn't believe he ever could have done that, it was obscene. And it made her feel differently about herself, as though she was a changed person. Never normally introspective, recently she had found herself thinking and thinking about it all, tying herself in knots as she considered the implications. Probably she should see a shrink, but she'd had her fill of those at the clinics in which Marcus had incarcerated her. And when she thought about the baby – probably her last chance of a child – her eyes filled with tears. She realised now that her godfather had ruined her whole life. It was unforgivable. She was half terrified at the prospect of the impending showdown, half longing for it. It would just be so great, watching him whipped by the lash of their combined contempt. She wanted to see him squirm.

Mary was helping Clara with her lunch. Apart from while eating and getting dressed, Clara had lately become much more self-reliant. Her school had done wonders for her. Now that she was sixteen, however, Mary worried about her in other ways, particularly over boys. Clara was so trusting, she would be easy to take advantage of. Sometimes she still acted like a small child, happily watching the *Lion King* video three times through, over and over; she didn't enjoy, and couldn't follow, grown-up movies. And she painted beautifully, like a talented ten-year-old, presenting her mother with pictures of sunsets and sunrises in lurid oranges and yellows. Lately she had become quite religious, saying 'Let's pray for poorly Granny' or 'Let's pray for Godfarva Stew'. Once, she'd said, 'Mummy, let's both pray for your godfarva – Marcus,' which made Mary shiver.

Clara made her anxious in other ways too. She could be over-affectionate with strangers, pressing herself on visitors who came to the house. Her blossoming sexuality, out of kilter with her mental development, made her a danger to herself. At the only teenage dance Mary had allowed her to go to, she had snogged half the boys in the room. As she had grown up, her Down's Syndrome had become physically more obvious, but in the stygian gloom of a discotheque she appeared almost normal.

Why, Mary wondered, had she ever agreed to come to Bali? Because Stuart had insisted she be there. 'The only way this is going to work is if we're all there, every single godchild. If anyone's missing, the showdown won't be nearly so powerful. We have to confront him as a united group.'

Already she was beginning to regret her decision. The whole business of planning for Bali, of buying swimsuits and holiday clothes for Clara, of packing and liaising with Barbara Miles over the flights, had reawakened memories she thought she had buried long ago. The last time she had seen Marcus, face to face, had been at Poppy's funeral when she had referred to his seduction of her, all those years earlier. Now she wished she'd never mentioned it, as it had probably gratified him that she still minded. Stuart was right, they did have to confront him. But the thought of doing so made her almost sick with apprehension. On the flight back down to London after the Ardnessaig weekend, she had broken her vow of silence and confided in Stuart about being coerced into sleeping with Marcus, and how she suspected Clara was his child. Stuart had gone almost mad with fury, she'd never seen him so angry before. Now she regretted telling him, and had made him promise not to include that particular outrage in his speech.

Glancing behind her to where Abigail and Forrest were sitting, hand in hand, Mary was delighted her friend had at last found happiness. It was plain they were besotted with one another. So far, Mary didn't feel she knew Forrest Rosedale well enough to form an opinion of his character. She knew he'd been married twice before, to 'total airheads' as Abby described her predecessors, and that he was a successful corporate lawyer who also did valuable *pro bono* work for victims of the Holocaust, negotiating the return of looted Jewish assets from Swiss banks. There was no question, he was very good-looking for a sixty-year-old, tall and fit with crisp, curly grey hair. According to Abby, Zubin was delighted by the marriage, since the Schwartzmans and the Rosedales had been attending the same temple for years. She said they hadn't yet decided whether or not to try for a baby.

It had initially been Forrest's idea that he and Abigail take up Marcus's invitation. Abby was amazed they'd been asked at all, considering her stream of poisonous letters and phone calls, but there it was: 'Flora and I would be so happy if you could join us for the New Year holiday. It would give us enormous pleasure to host you over the Millennium at our new beach house in Nusa Dua, which none of you has yet seen. Barbara Miles will take care of the travel arrangements.'

'I wouldn't go if you gave me a million dollars,' Abby had said vehemently.

'I have already given you a million dollars,' Forrest replied. 'Far more in fact. And we really should be there, you know. I'd be interested to meet Marcus Brand, he sounds an impressive guy. I read the story in *Vanity Fair*.'

'Believe me, Forrest, you do not want to know Marcus.'

'Come on, Abby, it's a big thing to have him as your godfather. He's a clever, prominent guy. Anyway, we've been trying to rope him in as a client at Paul, Weiss for years. If his business is in trouble, he might need representation.'

Abigail knew she would still never have agreed to come if it weren't for Stuart's master scheme. Now, at thirty-five thousand feet, she was having serious second thoughts. As the miniature icon of Marcus's Gulfstream inched and jerked its way across the digital world map, she felt physically sick at the prospect of the impending confrontation. Ten days in Bali, ten excruciating days. Ten full-on lunches, ten prolonged dinners. How would she ever get through them all, when even the sight of Marcus wrenched her heart with thoughts of Poppy? And all the time, hanging over them, the promise of conflict and, perhaps, terrible recriminations.

She knew that, somewhere inside the Vuitton hand-luggage at her feet, was her laptop on which she would send her instruction, one way or the other. Before she'd left New York, her bosses at Sotheby's had made her promise she'd e-mail them on the agreed day. It was all in her hands now. 'Review the situation and give us your best assessment. Is he going under or isn't he?'

But at least nothing was going to happen, either way, until after the New Year. Her ultimate decision would finally depend on Marcus's level of remorse at the showdown.

Jamie was pretty sure Amaryllis was asleep in the window seat next to him, which gave him an opportunity to chat up the highly fanciable red-headed stewardess. Quietly slipping along to the tiny galley at the rear of the cabin, he was soon mixing her double rum and Pepsis and proposing some imaginative new applications for her hot towels.

'No way am I going in there with you, you dirty beast,' protested the stewardess, as Jamie tried to coax her towards the cubicle. 'A passenger might need to use it.'

'Tell you what then,' he said. 'I'll give you my phone number in Bali, and if you're up for a drink or anything one evening, give me a bell.'

Jamie's feelings about the holiday were, at best, ambivalent. A year ago, wild horses wouldn't have dragged him to Indonesia to visit Marcus. All his worst suspicions remained. In fact, knowing what he now did about Amaryllis, his low assessment of his godfather played out in spades. Stuart's idea of telling Marcus a few home truths struck Jamie as potentially rather a good wheeze, if foolhardy. God only knew how Marcus would react, probably go ballistic. Stuart had gone way up in his estimation for agreeing to be the main spokesman. Rather you than me, Jamie thought. The holiday was going to be awfully tense, he could tell, and there was no way of predicting how it would all pan out when they blew the fuses.

Now that he was actually airborne, however, Jamie was coming round to the idea. He could do with some sun and free booze. Recently, to his considerable amazement, he had actually started making a few bob; his recent show at White Cube² had sold out and he'd pocketed eighty-something thousand quid after the gallery took its cut. He hadn't actually divulged the full amount to Amaryllis, in case she started touching him for rent.

It felt good having a bit of ready cash again. Already he'd bought a motorbike and two Paul Smith suits and several cases of really good wine, which he'd had delivered to the studio so thirsty Amaryllis couldn't get her mitts on it, otherwise the whole lot would be polished off in a couple of days. He still got on fine with her, but increasingly he felt the need for variety. It crossed his mind Saffron might be back in the running, now Marcus had finally married Flora.

On the subject of Flora – 'Little Miss Slanty Slit' as Charlie insisted on calling her – Jamie was sure he no longer felt the slightest attraction towards Mrs Marcus Brand. He'd considered the proposition from every possible angle, and every stage of undress, but that horrendous beating up in Nevern Square had forever killed his lust for her. He still had a long scar right down his thigh, highly conspicuous in bathing trunks. He was curious to see how his godfather reacted to it.

Across the aisle, he could see Abigail and her new man sitting together, trying to look like the perfect couple. Forrest was reading a fat biography of Alan Greenspan, while Abby nuzzled into his shoulder. Jamie hadn't yet taken a measured view of his successor, but thought he looked like a total tosser. At Northolt, when Jamie had introduced himself in the tiny terminal building, Forrest had glared accusingly at him and cut short the conversation. No doubt Abigail had been filling him up with a load of crap about their marriage. Jamie was already referring to Forrest as Forrest Gump.

In as much as he'd thought about it, Jamie's policy on this holiday was to stay chilled, to steer well clear of Marcus, to steer clear of Abby and of Forrest Gump, to cool it slightly between himself and Amaryllis, sound out Saffron, have some beers with Charlie and maybe check out the talent on the beach. Bali was meant to be crawling with gorgeous Australian backpackers.

Two rows behind him, Stuart shut down his computer, closed his notes away in his briefcase and tried to strike up a conversation with Pelham, who was bent almost double over his Gameboy, tilting the screen away from the glare of the window.

'How's the game going?'

Pelham shrugged. 'OK.'

'You winning?'

He nodded. 'I'm on level five. Except every time I get close to the windfish, one of the monsters gets me.'

'Will it disturb you if I ask how old you are?'

'Eight-and-three-quarters.'

'And you enjoy school?'

'It's fine. I'm at Broadley Court. You were there too, weren't you?'

Stuart shook his head. 'No, I went to school in Birmingham.'

Pelham looked up from his Gameboy. 'Birmingham? Golly, isn't that really dangerous? It's full of muggers and football louts, isn't it?'

Stuart laughed. 'About the same number as in London, I think. It's probably Jamie Temple you're thinking of. He went to Broadley Court with your father.'

Pelham nodded. 'Probably. Papa said there was going to be another man on the holiday who went there. He told me that at home.'

'And where do you live these days?'

The small boy coloured. 'Well, we actually live in Balham at the moment. It isn't a very nice house. But before that we lived in Kensington and Papa used to own a castle in Scotland.'

Stuart nodded awkwardly.

'Are you looking forward to the holiday?' he asked at last.

'I am *quite*. The only thing is, I might have to share a bedroom with my sister Marina, and she gets really silly sometimes and keeps annoying me when I'm trying to get to sleep. And Papa says we have to be really good all the time, and be on best manners, because Godfather Marcus is really rich, and Papa hopes he might leave us all his money when he dies.'

'Did you know I went on holiday with your dad when we were both about your age? In fact, quite a lot of the grown-ups on this aeroplane went on the same holiday. We all stayed in France with Marcus, who is my godfather too.'

'Oh, yes, Papa told us about that holiday. He said there were these tyres like tractor tyres, and what you did was you tied them behind a speedboat and got towed along, and it was really brilliant. He's going to ask Mr Brand if we can do it again on this holiday, though he said they maybe don't have tractors in the place we're going, so there might not be any tyres.'

'What's your swimming like?' Stuart asked. 'Are you good at it?'

'I can do twenty lengths with no armbands. At school, we have this Olympic-sized pool in the Marcus Brand Sports Hall, and I passed all my tests first time. Kosova's sewed the badges on my trunks.'

'It's really important to be able to swim well. When I was at college, I swam almost every day.'

'Papa said that in France, when they were doing that tyre thing behind the speedboat, there was this one boy who couldn't even swim and he nearly drowned. He was working-class, you see, so he didn't learn swimming at school, and he was really spastic and nobody liked him, and when they chucked his shirt out of the window as a joke, he started blubbing and went and sneaked to Mr Brand.'

Bartholomew slowed down in front of formidable wooden gates and his big arm stretched out to stab an intercom button. An electronic buzz and a loud click, and the gates slowly opened on to Marcus's newest magic kingdom. From a jump-seat in the second jeep, Jamie noticed several armed security guards lurking in the undergrowth, covering them as the convoy of vehicles moved inside the compound, and two more on an observation platform overlooking the approach road and strip of private beach.

As they drove up an asphalt road to the main house, Mary saw that the entire compound, steeply terraced, was enclosed by a high wall. Ten Balinese guest cottages were dotted throughout the property, as well as pavilions for dining and playing table tennis. A vast stone statue of a reclining Buddha was positioned on a terrace above an infinity swimming pool whose blue water seemed to meld into the sea beyond.

It was beside the pool that the godchildren caught their first glimpse of Marcus and Flora. They were both upside down, doing headstands with their legs crossed in the lotus position, in an open-sided *casita* carpeted with tatami mats.

'What the hell's going on over there?' Jamie asked. 'Looks like he's shagging her.'

'Don't be puerile, Jamie,' said Abby. 'You know perfectly well it's yoga.'

Over lunch, several of his godchildren scrutinised Marcus for any signs of tension and stress. Nobody could read so much negative press about themselves and their businesses, and be subjected to such a level of derogatory comment, without it taking its toll. For more than a fortnight the newspapers had turned on the great tycoon, questioning every aspect of his strategy and performance. 'Which divisions actually produce profits these days?' demanded the *Economist* in a cover story which predicted that, once the Securities and Exchange Commission had published its much-leaked report, Marcus would be indicted for, *inter alia*, insider dealing and tax evasion.

Either Marcus was playing a mean hand of poker, Charlie thought, or the whole thing really was a storm in a teacup. He had never seen his godfather looking more relaxed, or more in control of his own destiny. He must be nearly seventy, but certainly didn't look it. Sitting at the head of the table in his bathing trunks and a polo shirt, you could see he didn't have an ounce of surplus fat on his body. In fact, he looked fitter and sleeker than he had seven years earlier, during the Turkish holiday on board his yacht. Charlie wished the same could be said of himself. Ever since they'd landed in Bali, he'd been sweating like a pig. Far from losing weight since giving up work, he'd actually piled it on. Increasingly, he lived on junk food and the white bread and cheese sandwiches Kosova fed to the children.

He wondered to what extent Flora was responsible for Marcus's infuriating good health, and whether, as had been suggested in one of the newspapers, she had encouraged him to have a facelift. He certainly looked suspiciously unlined. All this struck Charlie as bad news. If Marcus really had lost his golden touch at work, it might actually be preferable for his godfather to die now, and leave them all he could, rather than linger on, making duff decisions and destroying shareholder value. At least with Flora around there was always a hope of him sustaining a fatal heart attack in bed, while they were on the job.

'Haven't seen you, Charlie, since that wife of yours ran off with a poof,' Marcus declared at lunch from the head of the table.

'It was very unfortunate,' he mumbled.

'Obviously not for her, though, else she wouldn't have done it. Terrible thing when women bugger off like that. In her case the motive was money, I suppose. Wouldn't stick with you once you lost all yours. Women! You'd never do that, would you, Abigail? Walk out on a husband just because he's short of a few bob?'

Abby, colouring, replied, 'I like to think I'd never quit any relationship solely for financial reasons.'

'So it was the sex then? Always is, of course. Sex or money. One or the other, every time.' He stared pointedly down the table at Jamie who, pretending not to hear, was thinking how juicy Saffron looked in her lime-coloured string-bikini.

'How about you, Mary? What motivates you most in your relationships? Sex or money? Sex, money or power, I should say. A lot of women love to go to bed with powerful men, never mind how old or ugly they are. Drawn to them like flies. Oldest cliché in the book that power's an aphrodisiac, but like a lot of old clichés, it also happens to be true. Isn't that right, Mary?'

'I wouldn't know, Marcus. I've never been out with anyone powerful.'

'Haven't you now?' His eyes rested on her playfully. 'Saffron? You ever slept with a powerful, older man? And I don't, incidentally, regard that geriatric pop star you used to hang around with as powerful. Not sure I even regard him as all that rich these days, from what I hear.'

Saffron bit her tongue. She longed now for the showdown, when they'd all tell him exactly where to get off. She wouldn't hold back then.

'Abigail, then? Let's consult the newlywed. What first drew you to your clever senior citizen, Abigail? The power, the money or was it the sex? Maybe all three, of course. They do say these New York corporate lawyers have become terrifyingly powerful. Isn't that right, Dick? American attorneys? They wield all the power nowadays. Not an original thought between the lot of them, but taking over the world nonetheless.'

Dick Mathias, nursing a formidable martini, nodded and slurred, 'They know how to charge, Marcus, I know that.'

'Essential to know how to charge,' Marcus declared. 'Stuart knows how to charge at Darmstadt Commerzhaus. Experts at it, like all German enterprises. And Mary down there, she knows how to charge. Always very quick posting off her little invoices. And Saffron. My God, that shop of yours knows how to charge! Went in the other day to pick out something for Flora, came out needing a float from the World Bank. Daylight robbery. Marvellous. Kudos.'

Stuart had taken to jogging each morning before breakfast. Every night before turning in, he would reopen the teak shutters that the maids had closed while tidying his room during dinner, so he'd be awakened by the first light, shortly before six o'clock. Then he'd quickly shower, pull on a pair of shorts, t-shirt and trainers, and slip out of the *casita* into the still-chilly dawn. The security guards at the gate were accustomed to him now, and lowered their weapons at his approach. They would then unbolt a postern door and he'd run five or six miles, down through the deserted native village at the foot of the hill, along the coast road past the luxury hotels and down to the public beach where, at that hour, the fishermen were still hauling in their nets. It had become part of his routine to order a cup of coffee and *pisang goreng* – banana fritters – at a beach café, where the owner slept on a mat underneath the counter but woke up with a start when Stuart trotted in.

He believed that, without these two hours on his own, he would surely go insane. He was finding the atmosphere this holiday more claustrophobic than ever. Maybe it was just the climactic encounter that hung over them all, but he felt the beach house was full of suppressed tension. Mary felt the same way too, because they'd talked about it, *sotto voce*, at dinner. He had the impression that Marcus, behind the outward assurance, was actually less relaxed than he wanted to make out, watching and measuring everything. Stuart found the way Marcus was baiting several of the godchildren completely unacceptable, and suspected he was mostly doing it to divert attention from his own precarious position. They hardly saw him between meals as he was constantly cloistered in the communications room with Dick Mathias. Stuart didn't need to ask what they were conferring over.

Up at the house, he had the feeling of being watched all the time. During dinner last night, he had twice felt Marcus staring at him, as though sizing him up. Obviously Marcus and Dick were both aware of Darmstadt Commerzhaus's pivotal holding in Brand Corp stock, somewhere above 16 per cent. Only Marcus himself held more.

When Stuart had rung his mother in Smethwick from the *casita*, to say he'd arrived safely and check she was OK, he'd been conscious of strange clicks on the line, and suspected his calls were being monitored. When he communicated with Frankfurt, he'd do so by e-mail.

So much about this holiday struck him as bogus. Different, somehow, from its predecessors – although, God knows, on every one of those lavishly choreographed get-togethers, they had all had to dance to Marcus's tune. Each trip felt like a continuation of the one before, in which they were all expected to resume their same parts. If you strung together all the holidays they'd spent with Marcus in the South of France, in Lyford Cay, in Wyoming, in Turkey and now here in Bali – they would hardly add up to ten weeks, and yet Stuart realised they had distilled an intensity of emotion and anxiety he had experienced nowhere else. Objectively, he found Marcus despicable. He represented everything Stuart found unacceptable about the world. And yet . . . how colourless life would have been without him.

Marcus's effect on his fellow godchildren was plain to see. Charlie had become a pitiful figure, Stuart felt, evidently seeing Marcus as his only lifeline out of the hole he was in. At lunch, it was actually painful to watch the ludicrous way Charlie hovered around him, laughing at all his jokes, accepting any humiliation with a propitiatory grin, shoving others out of the way to get a seat next to him. Stuart no longer felt anything for Charlie beyond pity. And he realised Marcus must accept the blame for a lot of it. Without him, Charlie might have buckled down to something and done a halfway decent job.

The fishermen were dragging the nets on to the beach now, and Stuart could see several of Marcus's cooks and houseboys bartering with them for parrot fish and lobster for the lunchtime buffet.

Stuart hoped Saffron would lighten up a bit on this holiday. She had been morose and withdrawn ever since they'd arrived, hardly bothering to speak to anybody and sunbathing on her own. At first he'd guessed it was all to do with Jamie and Amaryllis; it must be strange having your mother living with your ex. Or maybe she was just nervous about the impending showdown? It would be understandable if she was. As Stuart knew better than anyone, Saffron had every cause to feel injured, with Marcus having forced her to have that abortion. The strange thing was that he knew he didn't love her any more. Once he'd been consumed by a passion for the beautiful, unattainable Saffron. Now he could think of her with affection, warmth and even pity, but not with love.

All the godchildren seemed on edge, in fact: Abby, Mary,

even Jamie. The tension was stifling. Something had to break.

Perhaps it was just the weather, Stuart thought. Perhaps they were due for a storm.

There were only two days left to go now until the great confrontation, and then there'd be a storm all right, one god-almighty storm. The thought of it filled him with trepidation.

Stuart reckoned he'd better keep his running shoes to hand, he might need them.

Jamie was having an early breakfast in the dining pavilion, where coffee, juices and platters of tropical fruit were laid out on a buffet table, and a Balinese chef was presiding over a burner with a frying pan, waiting to take individual orders for eggs. A dozen small glass bowls were filled with diced pineapple and papaya and grated coconut for special Nusa Dua pancakes.

Pelham Crieff was the only other guest up so early, tucking into a plate of fried eggs, bacon and hash browns.

'How's school going?' Jamie asked his godson.

'Fine.'

''Fraid I forgot to send you a Christmas present this year.'

Pelham nodded. 'None of my other godparents remembered either, except for Godfather Boobie. He's only an honorary godfather, but *he* gave me fifty pounds.'

'Wow! Well, when we get back to England, I *am* going to give you a present. It's to take back to school.'

'What is it?'

'A mobile phone.'

Pelham's eyes lit up. 'But they're not allowed. They're banned at Broadley.'

'That's exactly why you need one. You have to sneak it in and hide it somewhere. I've thought of a really good trick you can play. Do you still have a really wet teacher at the school called Beetle Trumper?'

'He's our headmaster.'

'Thought he might be. He's the person the trick's going

684

to be on. Now, what you do is this. In the village at the end of the school drive there used to be a Chinese restaurant – I bet it's still there. You ring it up on the mobile pretending to be Beetle Trumper. Can you do his voice? Good, all squeaky, that's it. Then you order this huge take-away Chinese meal, everything on the menu, sweet and sour pork, chicken with cashew nuts, special fried rice, prawn crackers, the lot. Tell them to deliver it to the school for Mr Trumper. Then you watch out of the window while the Chinkies turn up with the food, and Beetle blows his fuse. He'll never know who did it. And the Chinkies will probably make him pay up too, which makes it even funnier.'

'You're not really supposed to call them "Chinkies", you know,' Pelham said primly. 'Papa said we should never use that word on this holiday, because of Mrs Brand being one.'

Abby waited until Forrest was in the bathroom before retrieving her laptop from the overnight bag. She freed it from its red leather Hermès travel case, then plugged it into the international telephone adaptor she'd been issued with by the office, and switched it on.

After a few seconds' delay, the monitor lit up and she heard the familiar beeps and shirrs as the computer began to boot up.

Quickly, she switched it off again and thrust it back inside her luggage. She didn't yet want anybody to know she'd come equipped to communicate directly with the outside world.

Tomorrow she would send her message to New York. If her decision went the way she figured it might, the consequences could be hideous. There was no way of guessing how Marcus would react when he discovered what she'd done.

The thought made her retch with apprehension. She didn't mind admitting it, she was sick with terror.

The Millennium came and went, marked by a lavish dinner and spectacular firework display, with rockets launched from rafts moored in the bay. But for the godchildren the change of century passed in a blur, so distracted were they by anticipation of the momentous showdown ahead.

The climactic dinner of 3 January, which afterwards came to be known as the Last Supper with Marcus, began slowly that evening, as though the godchildren were subconsciously dragging their feet in order to postpone the moment of confrontation.

Mary and Clara arrived late on the terrace, having stopped their golf cart en route to watch Jamie and Charlie on the tennis court lose in three straight sets to Abby and Forrest. Stuart was playing table football with Pelham and Marina in the games pavilion. Kosova was watching a cable music channel with Saffron up at the main house, while trying to pat Leonora to sleep on the sofa next to her. Amaryllis, who had drunk far too much at lunchtime, was still flat out on her bed in her *casita*.

By the time Mary and Clara reached the terrace, changed and ready for drinks, only Marcus and Flora were there before them. Marcus, already noticeably tense, flew into a rage, demanding to know where the bloody hell everybody was, and threatening that if they didn't show up *in the next three minutes*, as far as he was concerned they could damn' well miss dinner altogether.

'I'm sure they won't be very long,' Mary said appeasingly. 'The tennis ran a bit late. It was quite an exciting game.'

'I don't give a toss how exciting it was or it wasn't. We have a well-established rule in this house that we are down here for drinks by half-past eight. It is now twenty minutes before nine. So where are they? Bartholomew, will you please go and inform my guests that if they don't pitch up here quick and sharp, they will earn my extreme displeasure. Thank you, Bartholomew.'

The godchildren surfaced one by one, hurriedly making their apologies, and Marcus's mood deteriorated. He snapped at Saffron and Abigail, and told Charlie that if any of his brats weren't in bed and asleep in five minutes' time, he would 'personally fire that bloody useless Serbian keeper of yours'. Charlie bustled off to find Kosova and give her a hard time. Dick Mathias and Flora both looked wary of Marcus, and were giving him a wide berth this evening.

As they sat down to eat, the atmosphere became increasingly unbearable. While the houseboys circulated with plates of giant Thai prawns, the godchildren glanced surreptitiously towards Stuart. It had been decided that, as soon as the first course had been served, and Bartholomew and the other staff had withdrawn from the terrace, Stuart would seize the moment and launch into his broadside. He had practised it so many times it was now word perfect: a fifteen-minute diatribe that would leave Marcus chastened and, they hoped, penitent. When he realised that they had joined forces in their search for retribution, he'd be flattened.

Everyone had been served their prawns now, and the houseboys were retreating to the kitchen. Stuart swallowed. There was no turning back. He was shaking, but he had to go through with it. He could feel the eyes of the others on him, waiting for him to begin.

'Come on, Stuart, get on with it. Shouldn't you be telling me what a prize shit I am or something?' Marcus was staring at him tauntingly from the head of the table. 'That *is* the plan for tonight, isn't it? Tear a strip off your godfather for conduct unbecoming? Or have I mistaken the day? Perhaps it's tomorrow evening you're all going to have a go at me, tell me I've been a travesty of a godfather?'

For a moment, Stuart was stupefied. He felt the rug jerked from underneath him. How on earth had Marcus guessed? Of course . . . Suddenly the godchildren were all looking at Charlie, whose face had turned a deep crimson.

'You are, of course, quite right in suspecting young Lord Crieff,' Marcus said. 'As my senior godchild, he rightly saw it as his duty to tip me off on the palace revolution. Jolly good thing he did too: I detest surprises. If there's a coup d'état in the offing, much sooner know about it beforehand.'

'Actually, Marcus, there are a few things we want to say to you,' Stuart began.

'So I understand. Can't wait to hear what they are. Riveted, frankly. You've all agreed to rough me up as the

687

special dinner-time entertainment. Sounds fair enough. Fly out here on my private plane, stay in my house, eat my food, drink my drink, all expenses paid and then – why not? – lay into your host as well. Serve me right for inviting you in the first place.'

'It's not the holiday we have a problem with . . .' Stuart continued.

'Thank God for that! Thought maybe it was. Worried you found the guest cottages uncomfortable or something. Beds too hard, showers not powerful enough . . .'

He paused for a moment and regarded his godchildren sitting uneasily around the table.

'Tell you what,' he said, 'before you reel off your litany of complaints, let's see if I can guess any of them first, shall we? See how well your godfather really knows you, see whether he's been paying proper attention all these years. After all, I have known you for – what? – the best part of four decades. Had you to stay all over the world, at all my houses virtually. Ought to have a fairly good grasp of your various characters by now. We shall see.'

Stuart felt helpless. Somehow he had let slip the initiative and Marcus had taken over, powering ahead, unstoppable. He was regarding the godchildren one by one, his eyes moving over them, deciding where to begin.

'Abigail, I think. Why not? Good a place to start as any. What do I really think of Mrs Forrest Rosedale, formerly Temple, née Schwartzman?' He beamed at Abby with ruminative malice and she felt a shiver down her spine.

'Well, on the credit side, she is certainly one of my more intelligent godchildren, not that that's saying a great deal. Knows a certain amount about modern painting. Reasonably, if not outstandingly, hard-working. Has inherited some of the work ethic of her father, but fortunately little of his crassness or her mother's social-climbing skills. As far as looks go, regrettably the picture is less favourable. As a lover? Barely average, I would assume. I have no first-hand experience, Jewish princesses have never been my bag. You are, Abigail, as it happens, the only one of my four god-daughters I have never slept with, which I appreciate was a source of considerable regret to you at one time. Your various husbands, past and present, would know more about you than I do in that respect.'

Marcus surveyed the table to see how his little character sketch was playing with the audience. Abigail and Mary were ashen. The other godchildren seemed frozen in their seats.

'Psychologically, of course, you're in terrible shape, Abigail, and always have been. A complete mess. I believe it was during that holiday at Lyford Cay, or anyway soon afterwards, that you first formed your obsession with me. Lasted about five years, far as I remember. You were forever having your calls put through to my hotel room in New York, and then putting down the receiver when I answered. Infuriating! Dread to think what you spent on shrinks and so forth. Can't entirely blame you for that, being American, but you picked up a ghastly line in psychobabble in the process even before the accident with your daughter which tipped you further over the edge. Which is the reason you hate me, of course. Part of the reason anyway. For killing your daughter. But also, I suggest, for declining to respond to your obsession. Am I not right? No, don't answer, you don't need to.'

He paused and took a sip from his wine glass. Abby was hyperventilating. For a moment it looked as though Forrest was going to stand up and say something, but Marcus shot him a look which stopped him dead in his tracks.

'Now, who's next?' Marcus said. 'Mary! Ah, yes, Mary. Miss Mary Merrett, briefly Gore. Brave, kind, selfless Mary. Example to us all. Diligent, good-natured, a paragon, really. Not, perhaps, my most scintillating goddaughter in terms of a lively dinner companion, but certainly the most hard-working, and done particularly well considering her family's track record and a father devoid of all initiative. Done it all off her own bat. Well done, Mary. But does this near-perfect example of womanhood have no character blemishes at all, I hear you ask? Could she, perhaps, be considered a little overpious, a little lacking in character? Insipid, even? Don't be misled: she certainly despises me, by all accounts. Detests me! Holds me responsible for her husband's death and for sacking her bloody useless father, but that's only half of it. The real reason, of course, is that she believes I'm the father of her disabled child.' He surveyed the table triumphantly. 'Thought that would surprise you, that the spastic is my daughter. Ask Mary if you don't believe me, see if she denies it. But even that isn't the real reason for her hatred. She detests me because I was the best fuck she'd ever had. And she hates herself for betraying her dead husband within a few weeks of his funeral . . .

'Which leads us rather neatly to Saffron . . . poor, beautiful, lost, unfulfilled Saffron. Wonderful-looking girl. As a sixteen-year-old, nobody came close. Saffron was the first of my goddaughters to become my lover. But then we've all been slightly in love with Saffron, have we not, Jamie, Charlie, Stuart? She's had that effect on all of us, at one time or another. "Arm candy": that's the modern term for it, I believe. Never felt more proud of you, Saffron, than taking you into a restaurant and half the faces in the place were gawping at you, and thinking what a lucky bugger Marcus Brand was having a girl like that to take home to bed. Not that you were actually ever that great in the sack; too beautiful, really, to put in the graft. Does tend to happen, that, with attractive women. It's the ugly ones who screw for Britain.

'And finally, with Saffron, as with most passive women, it was never quite enough. You remind me of your mother, the apple fell too close to the tree. Isn't that right, Amaryllis? You and Saffron are too much alike? Drifting from man to man, sugar daddy to sugar daddy? Or maybe that should be toy boy to toy boy with the tides of time.' His glance flicked over Jamie. 'That and a fatal weakness for booze or, in Saffron's case, drugs and pills. I did sincerely try to help her over all that, though I know she doesn't see it that way. You doubt my sincerity as well as my ethics, Saffron. And there lies the real reason for your hostility, of course. Because you have discovered that I am your biological father. Why Amaryllis felt she had to betray that particular confidence, I have no idea. All I can say in my own defence is that all the time you were occupying the position of my mistress, I never for one minute thought of you as my daughter. Lover, yes; goddaughter, sometimes; daughter – never. It never impinged. Except for that one incident when you carelessly allowed yourself to get pregnant, and I had to get you sorted out in a hurry. You can understand now, I'm sure, why that was so necessary. Apart from that one occasion, far as I was concerned, you were always my mistress, never my daughter. Simple as that.'

Around the table, the atmosphere was electric. Too shocked to intervene, or even to move a muscle, the godchildren sat rooted to their chairs, none of them daring to look at Saffron. The Thai prawns lay untouched, small pink corpses on the plates. Night-lights flickered inside their glass domes and threw long shadows across the terrace. Mary nervously tore into tiny shreds the frangipani blossoms that had been sprinkled on the tablecloth. Only Dick Mathias, now on his fourth martini, seemed capable of lifting a glass to his lips.

'That concludes my report on my goddaughters, with the sole exception of Flora who now fills a dual role in my life and to whom I will turn in due course. For the moment I intend to move on to my assessment of my three godsons. I don't know whether any of them will remember this, but many years ago, when I took them to Paris for dinner and afterwards treated each of them to an exquisite French callgirl for their eighteenth birthday present, I made a prediction about their future. Your characters, I told them, are already set in stone. Drive and determination, either you've got them by now or else you never will. I said at the time that I could already tell which of you would be successful in life, and which would not. I recall Stuart asking me to elaborate, and I refused. Now, of course, we all know the results perfectly well, and I am glad to see that I had it spot on.

'Jamie, one realised even then, was destined to be a drifter, and wouldn't ever amount to much. I can't see this art business lasting, any more than the gardening, public relations or hotel work did. You've never been a sticker, Jamie, any more than your father was. You're certainly my best-looking godson, no question about that, and the most amusing in a slow field. I would also describe you as seriously amoral and congenitally idle. When you worked for me, you made very little impact on anyone or anything beyond the girls in the office. We have two things in common, you and I, and two things only. Saffron and Flora. You have the unusual distinction of having screwed three out of my four goddaughters, though not the same three as I've had myself. That, I regret to say, is the extent of our similarity. Just like the others, you appear to have developed a healthy dislike of me, though I doubt it runs very deep. It's not in your nature. You suspect me of having you arrested and imprisoned in India, when it was important for me to have you out of the way for a few hours, and later of instigating that little comeuppance in London after you had behaved so injudiciously with my then girlfriend, now wife. You are, of course, perfectly correct in both instances. I did initiate those events. But the real reason you dislike me, Jamie, is because you are competitive in matters of screwing. And you appreciate that, in the end, I have been much more successful than you as a ladies' man. Aren't I right? Of course I'm right!'

Charlie was quaking. He still half hoped Marcus would spare him the humiliation of a character report, as a reward for spilling the beans about Stuart's treacherous plot, but now his godfather was looking directly at him, screwing up his eyes in judgement.

'From Jamie we move logically to Charlie,' he was saying. 'It always pleased me when you two became such friends as schoolboys – it is gratifying when my godchildren develop ties between them. That's how it should be: we root for each other whenever we can. As my godchildren, you have an obligation of loyalty not only to me but to the whole group, which lasts for ever, even when I'm long dead and gone. Kindly remember that, please.

'Whether Charlie will remember it, I am not so sure. One of his chief defects, I fear, is an almost complete absence of loyalty.'

'Oh, that's not fair,' Charlie interrupted. 'Seriously, that's out of order, Marcus. I'm an incredibly loyal person, particularly to you.' Charlie thought the put-down totally unjust. He had tipped Marcus the wink about tonight, hadn't he? What greater proof of loyalty could there be than that?

'To me personally you may well display loyalty,' Marcus responded. 'No doubt you have your reasons, which we will examine presently. But towards the rest of my godchildren, no, I wouldn't describe you as remotely loyal. I have noticed the way you undermine them, Stuart in particular, even your old friend Jamie on occasions. Nor am I especially amused that you have consistently disparaged my various lady friends, as well as my Chinese wife; don't bother denying it, it is well documented. You have always been my most arrogant godchild. Arrogant, selfish, insular and, I'm sorry to say, lacking in intelligence. Your attitude has been consistent with that of numerous other young Englishmen who have received a first-class education, and interpreted their advantages as an excuse to belittle those less fortunate. I refer specifically to your attitude towards Stuart who has always demonstrated many of the character strengths which you are so conspicuously lacking in yourself.

'Please don't think I'm unmindful of the disadvantages of your background, Charlie. I am well aware of the genetic difficulties you have had to confront – an overpowering mother; inbred, exhausted, aristocratic genes; an imbecile for a father with neither drive nor ability. I have already factored in these considerations. Your real trouble, of course, is rooted in your attitude to money. You've worked reasonably hard, I'll give you that, despite having no aptitude for business. Even when you were ostensibly advising me on my equities portfolio, you will remember I seldom, if ever, acted upon your tips. To have done so would have resulted in penury. No, you have no feel for business or finance, as your experience with your Russia fund has proved. Your greatest misjudgement, however, has been your assumption that you can run your entire life on my backing. I am well aware that you imagine I'm going to leave you an obscene amount of money one day. God only knows why, I've never promised you anything. In fact, I have never subscribed to the idea that inherited wealth is a good thing *per se*, it takes away the motivation and ambition. Let me make one thing crystal clear so you can plan your affairs accordingly – I shan't be leaving you a penny, Charlie. Not one penny.'

Charlie was stunned. He felt a numbness stealing over his whole body. The consequence of what Marcus was saying was too much to cope with, and he felt his brain shutting down. It was outrageous! Marcus couldn't do that to him. Not only did he need the inheritance – need it desperately – but he *deserved* it. After all, if it wasn't for Marcus, he'd have conducted his life entirely differently. Most of the decisions he'd made had been taken with half an eye to his godfather. The two impressive houses in London and Hampshire had been bought for the express purpose of entertaining him. If it weren't for Marcus, he'd probably still be living up at Ardnessaig in his family home, perfectly content. Marcus couldn't back out now, it was impossible.

'Look, Marcus,' he pleaded. 'Obviously it's your money and you can do what you like with it. I certainly don't expect to be left anything at all. You've been generous enough already. All I ask is that you remain flexible on the subject and remember how loyal I've been over the years, inviting you to dinner at home etcetera, and maybe you could somehow reflect this in your will. Not that you're likely to snuff it for many years to come, of course, which is terrific news, absolutely terrific.'

Marcus regarded him contemptuously. 'Quite finished, Charlie? Good. In which case, let me leave you with one final thought. You're pathetic, completely and utterly pathetic. If we hadn't known it before, we certainly know it now, after that demeaning performance. You should be ashamed, though I rather doubt you fully understand the concept of shame.'

Without missing a beat, he turned to face Stuart. 'Stuart Bolton. Here, of course, the story is rather different. Stuart is my most successful godchild. He has come a very long way. He is the only one of you who has made some real money and who holds a significant corporate position within a global organisation. Not bad for the son of my dead chauffeur. He is also the ringleader of this putative uprising. If it weren't for Stuart, we wouldn't be having this little pow-wow at all. In any case, none of my other godchildren would ever have the balls to confront me. Wouldn't say boo to a goose, most of you, whatever you may believe to the contrary. But Stuart is made of sterner stuff, which is why he is the only godson for whom I have any genuine respect. Reasonably intelligent, diligent to a fault and with a good head for numbers.

'His treachery is founded, as you are doubtless all aware, on his conviction that I killed his father by obliging him to drive when under the influence of alcohol. We will suspend for the time being the awkward fact that Ron Bolton was a professional driver and had no business to be drunk, either on or off duty. It is nevertheless true that I bear a measure of responsibility for the tragic accident, which also killed my wife, and for which I have subsequently tried to make reparations. It was as a direct consequence of Ron Bolton's death that I took Stuart on as a godchild. Under normal circumstances, it would have been wholly inappropriate and yet I did so gladly, and invited him on numerous holidays on an equal footing to the rest of you. For the same reason, I supported him financially throughout his childhood and university years.

'Why then, you ask, has Stuart made himself the chief architect of this uprising? Because of Ron's death, certainly. Nobody likes to learn that their father died as the innocent casualty of a domestic dispute, particularly when that death was caused by their father's obscenely rich employer and the son in question is a conviction socialist. That, beyond question, is the principal cause of his rancour. But it is not, I think, the only reason he feels such hostility towards me. There is also the question of Mary, the woman Stuart has adored from afar, never quite daring to close on the deal, just as he never dared chance his arm with Saffron, when he had the hots for her. When he learned I'd had Mary, which was something he'd longed to do himself but never had the guts to get on with, he was furious. Furious with me, furious with himself.

'And that, in the end, is your great defect, is it not, Stuart? You're timid. Timid in love, timid in business. Why else would you consent to serve as a wage slave for an outfit like Darmstadt Commerzhaus, rather than take the plunge and strike out on your own – as I have done? I'm sure they look after you very nicely, your German bosses in Frankfurt, reward you with regular pay increases and hefty, guaranteed bonuses. But you know and I know that you're never going to be a principal in any business, never an owner. You'll never be properly rich because you lack the killer instinct.

'You're not a risk-taker. Even tonight, you have conceded the competitive advantage to me. Too slow! I struck first! There you go, you see, another life lesson for you from your godfather. That's if you're still capable of learning lessons at this point in the game.'

Marcus stood triumphant at the head of the table, eyes gleaming in the reflection of the flickering night-lights. During the course of his long address, darkness had fallen on the terrace, and a milky moon hovered above the ink-black surface of the Indian Ocean.

'That concludes the analysis of my original six godchildren,' he said. 'Perhaps, in the interests of balance, I should refer to my most recent addition, Flora Huang, now of course Mrs Marcus Brand. Flora is my most sophisticated godchild. She is the only one of you with whom I can have a decent, intelligent conversation, and who helps me with my business. There are those, I know – Charlie among them – who regard her as an ambitious Chinese popsy on the make. They may well be right! I am not so naive as to think that Flora would stay with me for five minutes were I not immensely rich and part of a world populated by other immensely rich and powerful individuals. Flora is nothing if not a networker. Could one fairly describe her as a gold-digger? Most certainly. Or a prostitute, which is, I think, a term my godson Charlie has employed on more than one occasion? Depends how you define the word. But I can tell you this about Flora: her sexual skills are certainly worthy of a professional, no question about that at all.'

He stood in the half light, towering over them, magnificent in his self-assurance.

'So there you have it: the godfather's end-of-term report. I hope you don't feel I have been over-severe in my judgements. If you do, then all I can say is, "Tough titty": I'm not really that interested in what you think, frankly. On balance, I'm disappointed in all of you. I had hoped you'd go further than you have. I tried to present you with some opportunities, expose you to some interesting situations. But, by and large, you never seized the moment. Looking at you now, I cannot pretend that, as a group, you are in any sense exceptional. Some of you may be asking yourselves why, if this is the case, I ever bothered with you at all, and persisted in inviting you to my various homes. It's a reasonable question, particularly as you are evidently so ungrateful. Perhaps my interest is best explained as a social experiment: to see how you'd all perform in life's great test. As we have seen, the majority of you have failed that test.

'Probably the moment has now arrived to bring the experiment to an end. This will be the final gathering of my godchildren. There will be no more holidays. You will not see me again after Bali.

'On which note, I shall bid you all goodnight. Breakfast will be served in the dining pavilion as usual from eight o'clock. Flora – come along now, bedtime. And the rest of you: you can all bugger off to your own cottages as well, if you don't mind. I'm sure I've left you with plenty to think about.'

Then, without another word, Marcus appraised his godchildren one last time before crossing the terrace in the direction of the house.

Abigail tilted her laptop away from the sun's glare. The e-mail she had been awaiting in reply to her own had pinged on to the screen. For a moment she let it sit there, unopened, half dreading and half exhilarated by what it would say . . .

Alongside her, by the infinity pool, Stuart was tapping away at his own computer. For the last four hours they had

697

scarcely exchanged a word as he had sent and received a stream of communications between Bali, Frankfurt, London and New York. Ever since Marcus's chilling performance at dinner last night, there had been a grim determination about Stuart. He was furious with himself for losing the initiative at dinner, felt he had totally failed his fellow godchildren. Despite all their meticulous planning, Marcus had once again stolen the show. Far from their chastening him, he had brilliantly turned the tables and humiliated them all.

Abby gazed out across the ocean, feeling treacherous. Half a mile out, she could see the speedboat with the inflatable banana towed behind, and Pelham and Marina Crieff shrieking with pleasure and holding on for dear life as it bounced along the tops of the waves. Jamie and Charlie were accelerating across the bay on jetskis. Jamie, as usual, was acting the ass, trying to ram his machine into the back of Charlie's like a dodgem car. Watching him from this distance, Jamie looked so young still. It struck Abby as strange that she'd left this overgrown yet disarming adolescent for a man like Forrest, who was so much older and, at times, pedantic. For all his faults, she found herself missing Jamie's spontaneity.

Soundlessly, a Balinese houseboy approached Abigail and Stuart, handing them fruit cocktails and cold towels. 'May I bring you something else?' he asked. 'Coca-Cola? A cold beer?'

Regarding the perfect swimming pool and turquoise ocean beyond, the billowing hibiscus and bougainvillaea and the statue of the reclining Buddha, Abby wondered what would become of this slice of paradise if everything fell apart.

Slowly, and with grave misgivings, she placed her cursor on the unopened e-mail and clicked.

'Stuart, I think you ought to see this,' she said, scrolling through the press statement.

The strain was telling upon Saffron.

If she'd had any money she'd have left the villa last night, immediately after Marcus's dramatic diatribe, and checked in to one of the tourist hotels around the point. She knew there was a Hilton and a Sheraton close by. But without funds, she couldn't even afford a flophouse, and she was stranded here, until it was time to fly home.

The prospect of facing Marcus again appalled her after last night. His caustic character analysis reverberated in her head: 'You were always my mistress, never my daughter.' She wondered whether she would ever learn to live with this final rejection. Even now she sensed Marcus's proximity in the yoga pavilion, on the terrace above the sundeck. How could they possibly all sit through dinner at the same table tonight, after everything that had been said? Marcus's capacity for mental cruelty terrified her.

A quarter of a mile out from the shore, she could see Jamie and Charlie zig-zagging across the bay. She was surprised Charlie's machine could even stay afloat, with him on it; he must weigh two hundred and fifty pounds. His belly flopped over the top of his bum-bags like a roll of carpet. She wondered how he was coping with Marcus's character assassination at dinner, particularly after he'd betrayed them all. She guessed he must be feeling pretty desolate.

Inside the cocoon of her Walkman, she avoided eye-contact with Amaryllis. Recently, their relationship had been even more problematic than normal. Saffron found it hard enough to accept her mother's affair with Jamie; the disclosure about Marcus had been unendurable.

Large salty tears began to roll down her face as she thought of her baby, the grandson Marcus had forced her to abort. She wondered then – and recently her thoughts had been nowhere else – whether, despite everything, she should have fought to keep the child, and whether this would have made her happy.

Stuart knew that, as soon as he'd completed placing the Sell Orders, he must go and find Mary. He was desperately worried for her. Last night he had sat up almost until dawn, comforting and reassuring her. Following the terrible public revelation of Clara's parentage she had completely fallen apart, as though the pressure of so much secrecy over such a long period had been suddenly lifted in one mighty release of emotion that left her tremulous and exhausted.

Stuart had found himself enfolding her in his arms for the first time, kissing her hair and hugging her close, as though he could never let her go, and when Clara, awakened by the conversation in the sitting room, padded in and joined them, it seemed the most natural thing in the world to bring her into the circle and hold and hug her too.

In the grey light of dawn, he no longer had any doubt about what he should do. As soon as the financial markets opened, he'd dump the stock at any price.

Dick Mathias and his martini sat in the communications room watching the screens. The stockprice was in freefall, with more than a billion shares changing hands in the past two hours alone.

The public announcement that Sotheby's was intending to repossess the famous van Gogh, *Sunflowers at Arles*, for which Marcus Brand had paid – or, as it turned out, not paid – a record-breaking eighty million dollars had provoked panic in the market as the remaining financial institutions scrambled to get out of Brand Corporation stock.

It was Darmstadt Commerzhaus that had started the stampede by disposing of its entire position in a firesale that sent the price into tailspin.

Dick lifted a house telephone and dialled the yoga *casita* to update Marcus on developments.

As usual, the first person to arrive on the terrace before dinner was Flora. She checked that the champagne was the marque her husband preferred, and that the canapés prepared by the French chef were properly presented. Night-lights were flickering prettily on the table.

At least one good thing had come out of last night, she thought: this was the last time Marcus's godchildren would ever set foot in any of his houses. Their visit had not amused her. She blamed them entirely for Marcus's unfortunate outburst. They had provoked him to it through their treachery.

Socially, she found none of the godchildren either decorative, amusing or useful, and wondered why her husband had ever bothered with them. The group she was putting together for a networking weekend in Wyoming in February was far more promising. She was sure that Sumner Redstone, Steve Jobs and Laurence Stroll would contribute to a really stimulating few days.

The godchildren were arriving on the terrace now, looking variously shifty, mutinous or wrung out after last night. Mary and Clara both appeared exhausted. Then Abigail and Forrest arrived together, arm in arm, followed by Charlie, Jamie, Amaryllis, Saffron, Stuart and Dick.

Flora couldn't think where Marcus was, it wasn't like him to arrive late unless he was making a point. She had hardly seen him all day. Walking over to the pergola, she pressed a number on the house telephone. Receiving no reply, she instructed Bartholomew to delay dinner for a further fifteen minutes. If he wasn't here by then, they would have to start without him.

The plates were being cleared for a Thai green curry when they became aware of a commotion down below on the beach. The security guards who patrolled the compound were shouting to each other in high, excitable voices, and there was a sound of heavy boots running in the direction of the house. Then two of the guards appeared on the terrace, followed by Bartholomew apologising for the intrusion.

One of the jetskis, they reported, had disappeared from the beach. There were tracks in the sand, indicating it had been dragged into the sea.

Stuart said, 'Probably a thief came in round the point. Maybe some of us should take a look around.'

'Someone should tell Marcus too,' said Mary.

Epilogue

Afterwards, the hundreds of thousands of words that were written about Marcus Brand made him, for a month or two, the most notorious man alive. And in those first weeks following his abrupt disappearance from the beach house in Nusa Dua, the world was in no doubt that Marcus was alive.

His picture was published everywhere. It looked out from the covers of news magazines in a dozen different countries. It appeared on posters inside police stations, on Interpol's intranet and on the scores of internet sites that proliferated with conspiracy theories. And, above all, the last photograph of Marcus – taken with the camera belonging to his beautiful goddaughter Saffron Weaver at lunchtime on the day before his vanishing act – was syndicated around the globe.

The photograph added, in its way, to the mystery. Because the man sitting in a rattan armchair with the turquoise Balinese sea behind him appeared so self-assured, so conspicuously unrattled, that it was impossible to believe he would condescend to cut and run.

It was reported that Saffron Weaver earned more than half a million dollars from the syndication of that one photograph, which was some small compensation for everything else that had happened to her.

Over time, it had become the defining image of the whole Marcus Brand scandal. Even at the age of sixty-eight, he remained strikingly handsome. Nobody looking at the photograph could doubt how devastating he must have been in his prime. His eyes stared out at the camera lens with an expression that suggested, at the very least, supreme confidence. His hair remained thick and straight and dark, with just the right amount of grey at the temples. His pink polo shirt was embroidered – but discreetly – with the initials MHdeVB, which stood for Marcus Henry de Vere Brand.

If you looked carefully, you could just make out, upon one wrist, the platinum strap of a Patek Philippe tank watch; on his other lay the steadying hand of his wife, so many years his junior. According to the numerous accounts of the Brands' last days at the beach house, they had spent their afternoons meditating and practising yoga together on tatami mats, in a *casita* specially erected for the purpose. It amused many people that Marcus, who had never stayed put for more than ten minutes in his life, so restless and impetuous was he, should have devoted his final days on earth to meditation. They would more easily have credited it if he'd spent them para-skiing or shark fishing or bawling out a subordinate on the telephone in his global communications centre.

On the Sunday after the balloon went up, it was no exaggeration to say that Marcus's disappearance featured in virtually every newspaper around the world. As a story, the Marcus Brand affair crossed national boundaries, and every editor, every section editor, every television newscast, wanted a slice of it. For the business sections, of course, the ramifications were endless. In the immediate aftermath of his disappearance, Brand Corporation stock nose-dived from $78.40 to under $3 on the New York Stock Exchange, and the prospect of so many significant businesses coming into play at once commanded every millimetre of space. The news pages were filled with three-dimensional maps marking the exact location of Marcus's villa at Nusa Dua, its private beach and the surrounding islands, and explaining the directions of the ocean currents that might have dragged his body out from the seashore. Two weeks after his disappearance, the missing jetski had still not been found.

There were hour-by-hour reconstructions of his final days, including his supposed conversations with his principal offices in London and Hong Kong, and thumbnail biographies of the godchildren who had been his guests over the fateful Millennium holiday. There were hastily written accounts of Marcus Brand's life and times and, it had been supposed, unimaginable wealth. The comment pages, depending upon which newspaper you read, were regretful or censorious. The *Wall Street Journal*, which had always held a candle for Marcus, the enlightened capitalist, wrote of 'an Icarus who flew too close to the sun'. There was sadness at the passing of an inspired risk-taker who had successfully opened up so many markets, particularly among the old communist nations.

Other voices, in London above all, were ungenerous, and his obituarists did not hesitate to portray Marcus as a stain on the reputation of big business. Several commentators insisted that it had been 'an open secret in financial circles that the Brand Corporation was in serious trouble', and these pundits – who had never previously mentioned these suspicions in their columns – now called for a public enquiry, and castigated the regulatory authorities for their failure to take action.

The features pages were given over in their entirety to 'Marcus and his Women': three decades of photogenic girlfriends, culminating in the wedding-day pictures of the tycoon with his immaculate young Chinese bride posing on board his yacht, *Marketmaker II*. Saffron became thoroughly sick of seeing fifteen-year-old pictures of herself, hanging on her hated father's arm. Jamie particularly enjoyed the publication of several forgotten photographs of Marcus with Clemence in the South of France, taken thirty-five years earlier. He still thought she looked highly fanciable, and wondered what had become of her.

In the arts sections, questions were raised over the ownership of the famous van Gogh, and whether Sotheby's had behaved reprehensibly over the business of its original funding. Their spokesperson said that the policy on credit had since been changed, following adverse comment from dealers.

Even the property sections got in on the act, speculating on what would be the future of Marcus's houses in Cap Ferrat, in Lyford Cay and in Hampshire, the ranch in Wyoming, the beach property in Bali and the apartments on Park Avenue and St James's Place.

As for the godchildren, the news that Marcus had died bankrupt, a minus millionaire several hundred times over, caused them little grief, except Charlie who could barely bring himself to read the pages of analysis in the papers, explaining how the Brand Corporation had been trading insolvently for many months, its share price supported by an illegal network of offshore trusts, secretly dealing in its own stock. Had Marcus survived, he would have faced charges for securities fraud in half a dozen territories.

For several months following his disappearance, and well beyond the inconclusive inquest, the godchildren were seldom out of the newspapers, much to the mortification of Stuart and Mary, who hated every minute of it. Nor did Jamie help matters when he sold his version of events, as well as his holiday snaps, to *OK!* magazine, revealing all of them sitting around the lunch table on the terrace, and Charlie looking like Humpty Dumpty on a jetski. That picture was captioned 'City financier Lord Crieff was among the celebrity godchildren on the paradise island', which made Jamie roar with laughter.

Shortly after publication, he announced his intention of leaving Amaryllis and England, and moving to the West Coast of America to work as a movie actor. Later, as he admitted to Charlie, the sector of the movie business he was chiefly occupied with was pornographic. He assured his old friend that he was having 'the best time – you have to get over here'. The job consisted of unlimited sex with blondes – generally several at a time – with huge silicone breasts. His pseudonym, Jamie said, was Ricky Thrust.

It made the majority of their fellow godchildren deliriously happy when Mary and Stuart quietly announced their engagement. Abigail, who was the first person they told after their respective mothers, exclaimed that it was the only genuinely good thing to have come out of all those years of Marcus, and insisted on flying over for the wedding.

They married on a bitterly cold Saturday morning in June, in a tiny white kirk outside Bridge of Esk, followed by a lunch for twenty-five friends at Ardnessaig. Clara was a bridesmaid and Stuart's boss, Manfred Friemel, was chief usher. Stuart's mother, who nobody really thought would be well enough to make it up to Scotland for the service, was pushed in her wheelchair by Abby to a front pew where she sat between Belinda Merrett and Mary Jane Crieff. Despite the atrocious weather, everyone said that it was one of the happiest weddings ever, and that Mary and Stuart made a perfect couple, and how wonderful the marriage would be for Clara who was plainly devoted to her new stepfather. It made Mary's day when, to her utter amazement, both of Crispin's brothers, Guy and Rupert, made the long journey from Norfolk to Angus for the wedding. At first it made her slightly awkward, having them both there, in case they felt that she was betraying their brother's memory by remarrying, but they seemed so genuinely happy for her, and sent so many good wishes from the entire Gore family, that she soon felt quite relaxed about it. 'My parents very much hope you and Stuart will bring Clara to stay soon,' said Guy Gore. 'We haven't seen nearly enough of you recently. My mother is missing her granddaughter.' If there was a mild reproach implicit in the message, he delivered it with such good humour that Mary could not possibly take offence.

Two months after the wedding, a small brown parcel turned up one morning at the Boltons' new London house near Hurlingham, postmarked Los Angeles. Tucked into the wrapping was a scribbled note from Jamie: 'Sorry I never replied to your invitation. I've had my hands full out here, in more ways than one! Anyway, here's a late wedding present. Not in great taste, I know, but it might make you laugh. If you can't guess what it is, ask Charlie, he knows.' Inside, enfolded in a length of bubble-wrap, was a cheap-looking paperweight with two pieces of hair floating in a clear plastic orb.

Mary examined it without enthusiasm and passed it to Stuart. 'I do love Jamie, but why do you suppose he sent us this?'

'God knows. I'm not sure about those hairs either. They look highly suspect. You don't think they're his?'

In the end, they couldn't resist ringing Charlie, who remembered exactly: 'Bloody hell, was that Jamie's wedding present? How really gross. They're Marcus and Saffron's pubes.'

706

It wasn't until he was travelling into work by tube that Stuart had his brainwave. Gingerly, over supper that evening, he broached the idea with Mary. If she hated it, or thought it was better not to know, then she should say so, and of course he'd respect her judgement. But, having carefully considered it overnight, Mary decided they may as well go for it. The worst that could happen, anyway, was that it would confirm her suspicions.

When the results of the DNA test arrived, she scarcely dared open the envelope. But the report was unambiguous: the unidentified white male, whose pubic hair had been sent for analysis could not possibly be the biological father of Miss C. Gore. Marcus wasn't Clara's father! She had been Crispin's child all along! Mary truly believed nothing in the world could make her happier than she felt at that moment. But in this, at least, she was mistaken; shortly before Christmas she learned she was pregnant with her second child, and this time round there was not the slightest doubt who the father was.

It was agonising having to break the news of her pregnancy to Abigail, because she knew how Abby was yearning for a baby herself, and how her doctors in Manhattan were becoming daily more pessimistic about her prospects. Abby was terrified of imparting this news to Forrest, even though he had made it abundantly clear he didn't want more kids. Five, he had told her, was already plenty to ensure the Rosedale line for posterity. But, as Abby confessed to her shrink, as well as to Mary, she would never feel completely secure with Forrest until she'd fettered him to her with a child of their own. Already, after barely a year of marriage, she suspected him of conducting an affair with a much younger lawyer at work. The suffering this caused reminded her of Jamie all over again.

Saffron, while understanding that it would take a lifetime to come to terms with the knowledge that Marcus had been her father, nevertheless did her best to keep her demons at bay. Through heroic self-discipline, and daily attendance at NA and AA meetings, she succeeded in overcoming a temporary relapse with drugs and alcohol and threw herself into the success of the boutique, seldom working fewer than six days a week and building up a client base that was the envy of Westbourne Grove. When Marcus's investment in the business was seized by the Brand Corporation's liquidators, Saffron and Calypso had waltzed Nick Black-water out for a boozy lunch and twisted his arm to come through with the necessary. 'I do like a lady who enjoys a good Burgundy,' he had told Saffron, unaware she was on cranberry juice.

In its second year of trading, the boutique, which they had named NBF – New Best Friend – made a sizeable profit, and there was talk of a second NBF in South Molton Street, in the former premises of Sole of Discretion, the shoe shop at which Saffron had once worked as a sales assistant. Increasingly, she discovered a real aptitude for the commercial side of the business, which she attributed to Marcus's genes. It was ironic that all she had finally inherited from him was a head for figures.

Although the six godchildren never saw quite as much of each other in the future as they had intended, they did keep in touch, and there was generally a gathering of some sort whenever either Jamie or Abigail hit town. When Mary and Stuart's baby daughter, Constance, was born, they decided not to appoint any godparents at all. But they told their friends, 'If you like her, come and see her, that would be more than enough.' Abigail, in particular, turned out to be wonderfully attentive, especially after her marriage to Forrest fell apart and she decided to move back to England to be close to Poppy's grave. Whenever she remembered Constance's birthdays, Saffron stuffed some ethnic mittens or a Rasta hat from the shop into a jiffy bag, which never entirely went with any of Constance's other clothes.

For some reason, Jamie was always best at keeping them briefed on the whereabouts of Marcus's old entourage. Flora, he had discovered, having reverted to her maiden name of Huang, had gravitated to Shanghai and was now shacked up with a senior party cadre in the Chinese government. 'This bloke she's going with, some people are tipping him as the next President of China but one. Good for Flora, I say. She was one horny chick. I taught her everything she knows, of course.'

It was Jamie, too, who claimed to have run into Dick Mathias, still wanted by Interpol, in the bar of the Beverly Wilshire Hotel. He had grown a moustache but was still drinking martinis. He had pretended to be someone else when Jamie approached him. 'Pity, really, we need a bent accountant at the film studio. He'd have done perfectly.'

But it was Stuart who learned what had become of Bartholomew, Marcus's loyal butler, who the godchildren had always rather liked. He had secured a position as Assistant Head Waiter at the Savoy Grill, where he had become a great favourite with the tycoons and captains of industry who ate there, many of whom already knew him from his previous incarnation.

As for Charlie, after a further desperate eighteen months in the wilderness, when it became evident he would never again secure employment in financial services, his luck finally turned. Entirely by chance, he knocked into his old flame Zara Deloitte, who told him she and Bud had just embarked on an acrimonious divorce. She would be citing his infidelity with a notorious scrubber named Nipples Ayrton-Phillips, whom they'd met on holiday in St Bart's, and Zara had been assured by her solicitor she was in line for a divorce settlement of between four and six million pounds, no trouble.

Two days after the decree absolute and the big cheque came through, Charlie and Zara tied the knot at Chelsea Register Office. Jamie once again did the honours as best man and afterwards treated the new Lord and Lady Crieff and their three young attendants to lunch at 60 Montpelier Gardens, in the newly installed Indonesian brasserie. 'Thought it would remind us of Nusa Dua,' he said, surveying the menu. 'I do strongly recommend the shark soup, by the way. It's probably the one that ate Marcus.'

Realising he needed a steady income, Charlie persuaded Zara to invest part of her settlement in a twenty-seven-bedroomed Edwardian shooting lodge near Perth, which he turned into an exclusive hotel and shoot aimed at rich

Americans who wished to stay with genuine aristocracy. The bedrooms and suites were soon named after castles with associations with the Crieff family, such as Arbroath and Ardnessaig. After dinner, in the Great Hall, at which Charlie presided at the head of the table in his claret-coloured smoking jacket, he delighted in regaling his paying guests with heroic anecdotes from his family history, especially how James IV of Scotland had invaded Northumberland with thirty of his most gallant barons, including all of Charlie's forebears. His natural arrogance was a priceless asset in his new life.

The public fascination with Marcus persisted, in one form or another, and shows little sign of abating even now. There have been positive sightings by credible witnesses in locations as far apart as Santa Cruz in Bolivia and Lake Van in Eastern Turkey, and to this day there are people who swear that they encountered the fugitive billionaire, disguised yet identifiable, in the early years of the new Millennium.

It is, however, now generally accepted that Marcus is dead. Enough time has elapsed and, although no body was ever found, it would be surprising if one turned up at this stage. There are still those who believe he is around somewhere, existing on some remote *estancia* with his face refigured by cosmetic surgery, but then people will always suggest that when some notorious figure disappears in mysterious circumstances.

The movie version of his story, which for a time seemed a done deal, will probably never now see the light. But in one other respect his reputation lives on in the public consciousness. Nobody today who invites a friend to be a godfather to their child can do so without calling to mind, just for a moment, the saga of Marcus Brand. His extraordinary role as godfather to Saffron, Jamie, Stuart, Charlie, Abigail and Mary was so widely discussed that the very concept of a 'godfather' (with all its Mafia connotations too) has come to evoke something faintly sinister and unwholesome.

When you ring your best schoolfriend, your most loyal, most long-standing crony, and announce, 'We've just had a baby daughter, and we'd love it so much if you would agree to be one of Alice's godfathers,' you can be sure that your old friend will reply, 'I'd be honoured. But I'll try not to model myself too closely on Marcus Brand.'

And then you will both laugh at the very absurdity of such a thing.